PLAGUE

A GONE Novel

PRAISE FOR THE GONE SERIES

Gone

"This intense, marvelously plotted, paced, and characterized story will immediately garner comparisons to *Lord of the Flies* or even the long-playing world shifts of Stephen King, with just a dash of *X-Men* for good measure. A potent mix of action and thoughtfulness—centered around good and evil, courage and cowardice—renders this a tour de force that will leave readers dazed, disturbed, and utterly breathless."

—ALA *Booklist* (starred review)

Hunger

"Readers will be unable to avoid involuntarily gasping, shuddering, or flinching while reading this suspense-filled story. The tension starts in the first chapter and does not let up until the end. The story is progressing with smart plot twists, both in actions and emotions."

—*VOYA* (starred review)

PLA

KATHERINE TEGEN BOOKS
An Imprint of HarperCollins Publishers

GUE

A GONE Novel

MICHAEL GRANT

OTHER *GONE* BOOKS BY MICHAEL GRANT:

Gone

Hunger

Lies

Katherine Tegen Books is an imprint of HarperCollins Publishers.

Plague

Library of Congress Cataloging-in-Publication Data
Grant, Michael.
 Plague: a Gone novel / Michael Grant. — 1st ed.
  p. cm. — (Gone)
 Summary: A deadly, flulike epidemic and plague of flesh-eating creatured threaten the lives of the children at Perdido Beach while Sam, Astrid, Caine, and Diana each struggle with doubts and uncertainties.
 ISBN 978-0-06-144912-3 (trade bdg.) — ISBN 978-0-06-144913-0 (lib. bdg.)
 [1. Supernatural—Fiction. 2. Good and evil—Fiction. 3. Survival—Fiction. 4. Sick—Fiction. 5. Plague—Fiction.] I. Title.
PZ7.G7671P1 2011   2010021834
[Fic]—dc22   CIP
                                                                    AC

Typography by Joel Tippie
11 12 13 14 15   LP/RRDH   10 9 8 7 6 5 4 3 2 1
❖
First Edition

For Katherine, Jake, and Julia

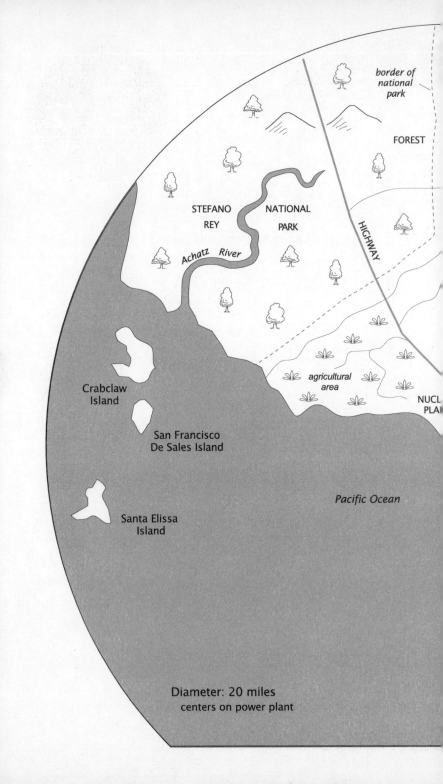

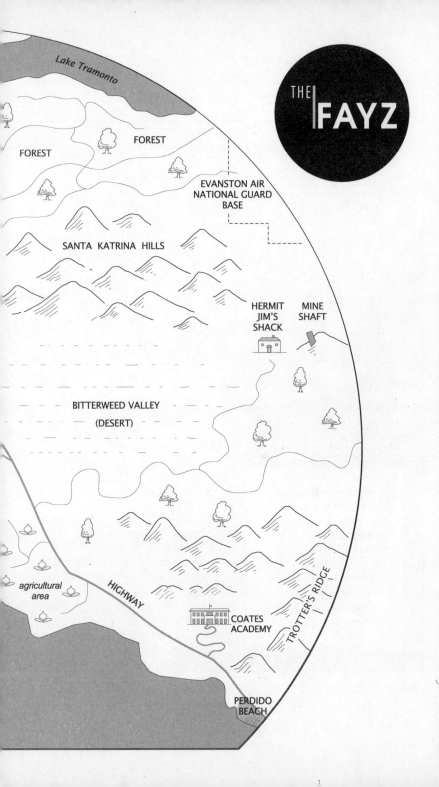

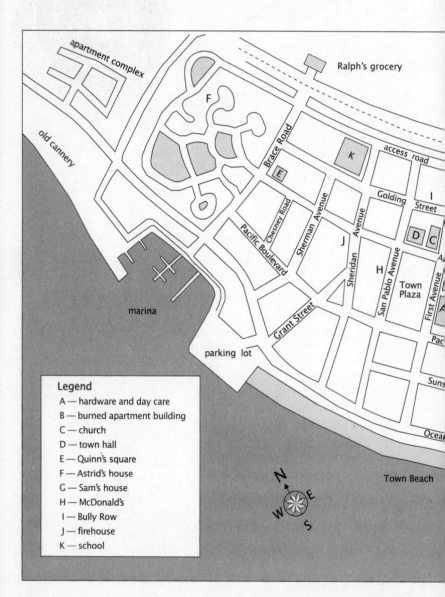

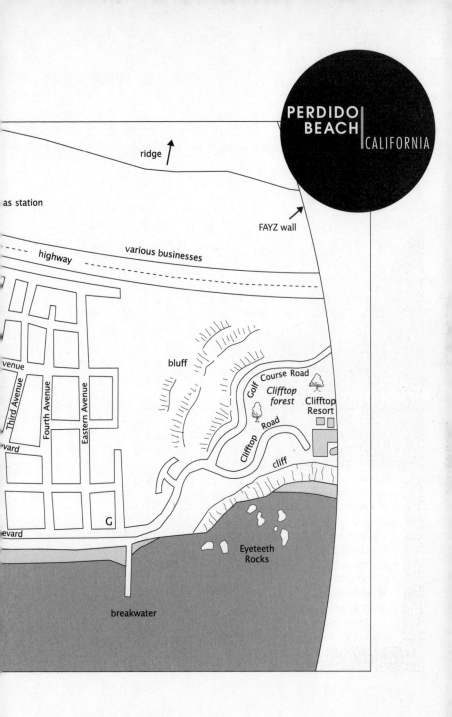

PLAGUE

A GONE Novel

PETE

HE STOOD POISED on the edge of a sheet of glass. Barefoot. Perfectly balanced. One foot in front of the other. Arms at his side. That was the game now.

The sheet of glass went down and down and down forever. Like a shimmering, translucent curtain.

The top edge of the glass was thin, so thin it might cut him if he slipped or fell or took a too-hasty step. That top edge was a thin ribbon of rainbow reflecting bright reds and greens and yellows.

On one side of the glass, darkness. On the other, jarring, disturbing colors.

He could see things down there on the right side, down below his right hand, beyond the reach of his fingers. Down there were his mom and his dad and his sister. Down there were jagged edges and harsh noises that made him want to clap his hands over his ears. When he looked at those things, those people, the wobbly, insubstantial houses, the sharp-edged furniture, the claw hands and hooked noses and staring, staring, staring eyes and yelling mouths, he wanted to close his eyes.

But it didn't work. Even through his closed eyes he saw them. And he heard them. But he did not understand their wild, pulsating colors. Sometimes their words weren't words at all but brilliant parrot-colored spears shooting from their mouths.

Mother father sister teacher other. Lately only sister and others. Saying things. Some words he got. Pete. Petey. Little Pete. He knew those words. And sometimes there were soft words, soft like kittens or pillows and they would float from his sister and he would feel peace for a while until the next jangling, shrieking noise, the next assault of stabbing color.

On his left, down, down below the endless sheet of glass, a very different world. Quiet, ghostly things drifted silently, shades of gray. No hard edges, no loud sounds. No horrible colors to make him start screaming. It was dark and so very, very quiet.

Down there was a softly glowing orb, like a faint green sun. It would reach out to him sometimes. A tendril. A mist. It would touch him as he stood balanced, one foot in front of the other, hands at his side.

Peace. Quiet. Nothingness. It would whisper these thoughts to him.

Sometimes it would play. A game.

Pete liked games. Only the left side would play his games

his way; games had to be his way, the same way, always and unchanging. But the last game Pete had played with the Darkness had turned harsh and overbright. It had suddenly stabbed Pete with arrows in his brain. It had broken the game.

The sheet of glass had shattered. But now it was whole again, and he balanced on top and as if it was sorry the soft green sun said, *Come down here and play,* in its whispery voice.

On the other side—the agitated, jangly, hard side—his sister, her face a stretched mask beneath yellow hair, a mouth of pink and glittery white, loud, was pushing at him with hands like hammers.

"Roll over. I have to get this sheet out from under you. It's soaked."

Pete understood some of the words. He felt the hardness of them.

But Pete felt something else even more. A strangeness. An alienness. Something wrong, a deep, throbbing musical note, a bow drawn over strings, that pulled his focus away from the left and the right, away even from the sheet of glass on which he balanced.

It came from the place he never looked: inside him.

Now Pete looked down at himself, like he was floating outside himself. He looked down at his body, puzzled by it. Yes: that was the new voice, the insistent note, the demanding voice more compelling even than the soft murmur of the Darkness or the jangly words of his sister. His body was demanding his attention, distracting him from his game of balancing on the sheet of glass.

"You're sweating," his sister said. "You're burning up. I'm going to take your temperature."

ONE

SAM TEMPLE WAS drunk.

It was a new experience for him. He was fifteen and had once or twice snuck a sip of his mother's wine. He'd drunk half a beer when he was thirteen. Just to see. He hadn't liked it much, it was bitter.

He'd taken a single hit off a joint back before the FAYZ. He'd practically hacked up a lung and then spent an hour feeling bleary and strange and finally sleepy.

It had never been his thing. He'd never been part of the partying crowd.

But this night he'd gone to check on the caged monster that was both Brittney and Drake and had heard Drake's vile, obscene threats and howling, murderous rage. And then, far worse, he'd heard Brittney's pleas for death.

"Sam, I know you're listening," she'd said through the barricaded door. "I know you're out there, I heard your voice. I can't take it, Sam. Sam, end it. Please, I'm begging you, let me go, let me go to Heaven."

Sam had been to see Astrid earlier in the evening. That hadn't gone too well. Astrid had tried, and he had tried, but there was too much wrong between them. Too much history now.

He had kissed her. For a while she had kissed him back. And then he'd pushed it. His hands went where he wanted them to go. And she'd shoved him away.

"You know I'm going to say no, Sam," she said.

"Yeah, I've kind of gotten that message," he said, angry and frustrated but trying to maintain some semblance of cool.

"If we start, how long do you think it will take before everyone knows?"

"That's not why you won't sleep with me," Sam said. "You won't do it because you think it would mean giving up control. And you are all about control, Astrid."

It was the truth. Sam believed it, anyway.

But if he were being honest instead of just angry, he'd have admitted that Astrid had her own problems. That she was filled with guilt and didn't need one more thing to feel guilty about.

Little Pete was in a coma. Astrid blamed herself, although it was stupid to do so and she was the furthest thing from stupid.

But Little Pete was her brother. Her responsibility.

Her burden.

After that rebuff Sam had stood awkwardly while Astrid spooned artichoke and fish soup into Little Pete's nerveless lips. Little Pete could swallow. He could walk if she guided him. He could use the slit trench in the backyard but Astrid had to wipe him.

That was Astrid's life now. She was a nurse to an autistic boy with all the power in their world locked inside him. Beyond autistic now: Little Pete was gone. No way to know where he was in his strange, strange mind.

Astrid hadn't hugged Sam when he said he was leaving. Hadn't touched him.

So that had been Sam's evening. Astrid and Little Pete. And the twinned undead creature Orc and Howard kept watch over.

If Drake somehow escaped, there were probably only two people who could take him on: Sam himself, and Orc. Sam needed Orc to act as Drake's jailer. So he had ignored the bottles beside Orc's couch and "confiscated" only the one in plain view on a kitchen counter.

"I'll dump this," Sam had told Howard. "You know it's illegal."

Howard shrugged and smirked a little. Like he'd known. Like he'd seen some gleam of greed and need in Sam's eye. But Sam himself hadn't known. He had intended to smash the bottle or dump it out on the street.

Instead he had carried it with him. Through the dark streets. Past burned-out houses and their ghosts.

Past the graveyard.

Down to the beach. He'd cracked the seal, ready to pour it

out on the sand. Instead he'd taken a sip.

It burned like fire.

He took another sip. It burned less this time.

He headed up the beach. He knew in his heart where he was going now. He knew his feet were taking him to the cliff.

Now, many sips later, he stood swaying at the top of the cliff. The effect of the booze was undeniable. He knew he was drunk.

He looked down at the small arc of beach at the base of the cliff. The slight surge painted luminescent curves on the dark sand.

Right here, right where he was standing, Mary had led the preschoolers in a suicide leap. All that kept those kids alive was Dekka's heroic effort.

Now Mary was gone.

"Here's to you, Mary," Sam said. He upended the bottle and drank deep.

He had failed Mary. From the start she'd taken charge of the littles and run the day care. She'd carried that load almost alone.

Sam had seen the effects of her anorexia and bulimia. But he hadn't realized what was happening to her, or hadn't wanted to.

He'd heard nervous gossip that Mary was grabbing whatever meds she could find, anything she thought would ease her depression.

He hadn't wanted to know about that, either.

Most of all he should have seen what Nerezza was up to,

should have questioned, should have pushed.

Should have.

Should have.

Should have . . .

Another deep swallow of liquid fire. The burning made him laugh. He laughed down at the beach where Orsay, the false prophet, had died.

"Good-bye, Mary." He slurred, raising his bottle in a mock toast. "Least you got outta here."

For a split second on the day that Mary poofed, the barrier had been clear. They had seen the world outside: the observation platform, the TV satellite truck, the construction underway on fast food places and cheap hotels.

It had seemed very, very real.

But had it been? Astrid said no: just another illusion. But Astrid was not exactly addicted to the truth.

Sam swayed at the edge of the cliff. He ached for Astrid, the booze had not dulled that. He ached for the sound of her voice, the warmth of her breath on his neck, her lips. She was all that had kept him from going crazy. But now she was the source of the crazy because his body was demanding what she wouldn't give. Now being with her was just pain and hollowness and need.

The barrier was there, just a few feet away. Impenetrable. Opaque. Painful to touch. The faintly shimmering gray dome that enclosed twenty miles of Southern California coastline in a giant terrarium. Or zoo. Or universe.

Or prison.

Sam tried to focus on it, but his eyes weren't working very well.

With the exaggerated care of a drunk he set his bottle down.

He straightened up. He looked at the palms of his hands. Then he stretched out his arms, palms facing the barrier.

"I really hate you," he said to the barrier.

Twin beams of searing green light shot from his palms. A torrent of focused light.

"Aaaaahhhh!" Sam shouted as he aimed and fired.

He shouted a loud curse. And again, as he fired again and still fired.

The light hit the barrier and did nothing. Nothing burned. Nothing smoked or charred.

"Burn!" Sam howled. "Burn!"

He played the beams upward, tracing the curve of the barrier. He raged and howled and blazed.

To no effect.

Sam sat down suddenly. The bright fire went out. He fumbled clumsily for the bottle.

"I have it," a voice said.

Sam twisted sideways, looking for the source. He couldn't find her. It was a her, he was pretty sure of that, a female voice.

She stepped around to where he could see her. Taylor.

Taylor was a pretty Asian girl who had never made a secret of her attraction to Sam. She was also a freak, a three bar with the power of teleportation. She could instantly go any place she'd ever seen or been before. She called it "bouncing."

She wore a T-shirt and shorts. Sneakers. Unlaced, no socks. No one dressed well, not anymore. People wore whatever was halfway clean.

And no one traveled unarmed. Taylor had a large knife in a nice leather sheath.

She was not beautiful like Astrid. But not cold and remote and looking at him with defensive, accusing eyes, either. Looking at Taylor did not fill his brain to overflowing with memories of love and rage.

She was not the girl who had been the center of his life for all these months. Not the girl who had left him frustrated, humiliated, feeling like a fool. Feeling more alone than ever.

"Hey, Taylor. Bouncy bouncy Taylor. T'sup?"

"I saw the light," Taylor said.

"Yeah. I am all about light," Sam slurred.

She held out the bottle tentatively, not sure what she should do with it.

"Nah." He waved it off. "I think I've had quite enough. Don't you?" He spoke with extreme care, trying not to slur. Failing.

"Come sit with me, Taylor, Taylor, bouncy Taylor."

She hesitated.

"Come on. I won't bite. Good to talk with someone . . . normal."

Taylor rewarded him with a brief smile. "I don't know how normal I am."

"More normal than some. I was just checking on Brittney," Sam said. "You have a monster inside of you, Taylor? Do you have to be locked in a basement because inside you is some psycho with a whip arm? No? See? You are so normal, Taylor."

He glared at the barrier, the untouched, unfazed barrier. "Do you ever beg to be burned into ashes so you can be free to go to Jesus, Taylor? Nah. See, that's what Brittney does. No, you're pretty normal, bouncy Taylor."

Taylor sat beside him. Not too close. Friend close, conversation close.

Sam said nothing. Two different urges were battling in his head.

His body was saying go for it. And his mind. . . well, it was confused and not exactly in control.

He reached over and took Taylor's hand. She did not pull her hand away.

He moved his hand up her arm. She stiffened a little and glanced around, making sure they weren't seen. Or, maybe, hoping they were.

His hand reached her neck. He leaned toward her and pulled her to him.

He kissed her.

She kissed him back.

He kissed her harder. And she slid her hand under his shirt, fingers stroking his bare flesh.

Then he pulled away, fast.

"Sorry, I . . ." He hesitated, his wallowing brain arguing against a body that was suddenly aflame.

Sam stood up very suddenly and walked away.

Taylor laughed gaily at his back. "Come see me when you

get tired of mooning over the ice princess, Sam."

He walked into a sudden, stiff breeze. And any other time, in any other condition, he might have noticed that the wind never blew in the FAYZ.

TWO

IT WAS AMAZING what decent food could do for a starving girl's looks.

Diana looked at herself in the big mirror. She was wearing clean panties and a clean bra. Skinny, very skinny. Her legs were knobby, with knees and feet looking weirdly big. She could count every rib. Her belly was concave. Her periods had stopped and her breasts were smaller than they'd been since she was twelve. Her collarbones looked like clothes hangers. Her face was almost unrecognizable. She looked like a heroin addict.

But her hair was starting to look better, darker. The rusty color and the brittleness that came from starvation, they were disappearing.

Her eyes were no longer dead, empty shadows sunk into her skull.

Now her eyes sparkled in the soft lamplight. She looked alive.

Her gums weren't bleeding as much. They were pink, not red, not so swollen. Maybe her teeth wouldn't fall out after all.

Starvation. It had driven her to eat human flesh. She was a cannibal.

Starvation had deprived her of her humanity.

"Not quite," Diana said to her reflection. "Not quite."

When she had seen that Caine would destroy the helicopter with Sanjit and his brothers and sisters she had sacrificed her own life. She had toppled from the cliff to force Caine to make the choice: save Diana or kill the children.

Surely that act of self-sacrifice balanced out the fact that she had bitten and chewed and swallowed a cooked chunk of Panda's chest.

Surely she was redeemed? At least a little?

Please? Please, if there is a God watching, please see that I have redeemed myself.

But it wasn't enough. It would never be enough. She had to do more. For as long as she lived she would have to do more.

Starting with Caine.

He had shown just a glimmer of humanity, saving her and letting his intended victims go free. It wasn't much. But it was something. And if she could find a way to change him . . .

A sound. Very slight. Just a scrape of foot on rug.

"I know you're there, Bug," Diana said calmly, not looking back. Not giving the little creep the satisfaction. "What do you think Caine would do to you if I told him you were spying on me in my underwear?"

No answer from Bug.

"Aren't you a little young to be a pervert?"

"Caine won't kill me," a disembodied voice said. "He needs me."

Diana crossed to the California king–sized bed. She slipped on the robe she'd chosen from among the many in the closet. They belonged to the woman whose bedroom this had been. A famous actress with very expensive taste who was only one size bigger than Diana.

And her shoes fit almost perfectly. Close to seventy pairs of designer shoes. Diana slipped her feet into a pair of fleece-lined slippers.

"All I have to do to get rid of you, Bug, is to tell Caine your powers are increasing. I'll tell him you're becoming a four bar. How do you think he'll react to having a four bar sharing this island with him?"

Bug faded slowly into view. He was a snotty little brat of a kid. He'd just turned ten.

For a moment Diana felt something like compassion for him: Bug was a damaged, messed-up little creep. Like all of them, he was scared and lonely and maybe even haunted by some of the things he'd done.

Or not. Bug had never shown any evidence of a conscience.

"If you want to see naked girls, Bug, why don't you creep up on Penny?"

"She's not pretty," Bug said. "Her legs are all . . ." He twisted his fingers around to demonstrate. "And she smells bad."

Penny was eating better, like Diana. But she was getting worse. She had fallen from one hundred feet onto water and rocks. Caine had levitated her back up the cliff. But her legs were broken in a dozen places.

Diana had done what she could to set the breaks, made splints out of duct tape and boards, but Penny was in constant agony. She would never walk again. Her legs would never heal.

She lived now in one of the bathrooms so that she could drag herself to the toilet when she needed to. Diana brought her food twice a day. Books. A TV with a DVD player.

There was still electricity in the house on San Francisco de Sales Island. The generator supplied a weak and faltering current. When Sanjit had lived here, he'd been worried that fuel for the generator was running out. But Caine could do things Sanjit couldn't. Like levitate barrels of fuel from the wrecked yacht rusting at the bottom of the cliff.

Life here was very good for Diana and Caine and Bug. But life would never be good for Penny. Her power—the ability to make others see terrifying visions of monsters and flesh-eating insects and death—was of no help to her now.

"She scares you, doesn't she, Bug?" Diana asked. She laughed. "You tried, didn't you? You snuck in on her and she caught you."

She saw the answer on Bug's face. The shadow of a terrifying memory.

"Best not to make Penny mad," she said. She pulled on slacks. Then she patted Bug on his freckled cheek. "Best not to make me mad, either, Bug. I can't make you see monsters. But if I catch you spying on me again, I'll tell Caine it's either me or you. And you know who he'll choose."

Diana left the room.

She'd resolved to be a better person. And she would be. Unless Bug kept bothering her.

The three Jennifers. That's what they called themselves. Jennifer B was a redhead, Jennifer H was blond, and Jennifer L had her hair in black dreadlocks. They hadn't even known one another before the FAYZ.

Jennifer B had been a Coates kid. Jennifer H was home-schooled. Jennifer L was the only one who'd attended the regular school.

They were twelve, twelve, and thirteen, respectively. And for the last couple of months they had shared a house on a cul-de-sac away from the center of town.

It was a good choice: the big fire had come nowhere near the development.

Now, though, it seemed like a bad choice. The so-called hospital was blocks away and the three of them could all have used a Tylenol or something because they all had the same head-ache, the same sore muscles, and the same hacking cough.

It had started twenty-four hours ago, and they had just figured it was the flu coming back around. There'd been a mini-epidemic of flu that had left a lot of kids feeling bad. But it hadn't been very dangerous except that it kept some kids immobilized who could have been working.

Jennifer B—Jennifer Boyles—had been asleep for no more than an hour when she was awakened by a loud, percussive sound close by, not from outside, from the room next to hers.

She sat up in bed and fought down the woozy, head-swimming feeling. She felt her forehead. Yeah, still hot. Definitely hot.

Whatever the noise was, forget it, she told herself. Too sick to get up. If something was breaking into the house to kill her, so much the better: she felt rotten.

Kkkrrraaafff!

This time the walls seemed to shake. Jennifer B was up and out of her bed before she could think about it. She coughed, paused, then veered toward the door, eyes not quite focused, head pounding.

In the hallway she found Jennifer L. Jennifer L was coughing, too, and looking as scared as Jennifer B. They were both in sweatpants and T-shirts, both miserable.

"It's in Jennifer's room," Jennifer L said. She had her weapon, a lead pipe with a grip bound with black electrical tape.

Jennifer B was annoyed with herself for having forgotten her own weapon. You didn't jump out of bed at night in the FAYZ without going armed. She staggered back to her bed and fished out the machete. It was stuck into a canvas scabbard between her mattress and box spring, handle protruding.

It wasn't all that sharp, but it looked crazy dangerous and it was. A two-foot-long blade with a cracked wooden grip.

"Jennifer?" Jennifer B called at Jennifer H's room.

Kkkrrraaafff!

The door rattled on its hinges. Jennifer B opened the door and stood with her machete at the ready. Jennifer L was right behind her, pipe clenched in nervous hand.

Jennifer H had always had a fear of the dark so she had a very small Sammy sun in one corner of the room, hovering beneath what had once been a hanging light fixture. The light was green and eerie, more creepy than illuminating. It showed Jennifer H. She wore a flower-print nightgown.

She was standing up in her bed. She clutched her throat with one hand and held her stomach with the other.

She looked like she'd seen death.

"Jen, you okay?" Jennifer L asked.

Jennifer H's eyes bulged. She stared at her two roommates.

Her stomach convulsed. Her chest heaved. She squeezed her own throat like she was trying to choke herself. Her long, blond hair was wet, sweat-matted, plastered to her face and neck.

The cough was shockingly loud.

Kkkrrraaafff!

Jennifer B felt the explosion of air. And something wet slapped her face.

She reached her free hand and peeled a small shred of something wet from her cheek. She looked at it, unable to make sense of it. It looked like a piece of raw meat. It felt like chicken skin.

Kkkrrraaafff!

The power of the cough threw Jennifer back against the wall.

"Oh, God!" she moaned. "Oh . . ."

Kkkrrraaafff!

And this time Jennifer B saw it. Pieces of something wet and raw had flown from Jennifer H's mouth. She was coughing up parts of her insides.

KKKRRRAAAAFFF!

Jennifer H's entire body convulsed, twisted backward into a crazy C. She crashed into the windowpane. It shattered.

KKKRRRAAAAFFF!

The next spasm threw Jennifer H into the wall headfirst. There was a sickening crunch.

The other two stared at her in horror. She wasn't moving.

"Jen?" Jennifer B called timidly.

"Jen? Jen? Are you okay?" Jennifer L asked.

They crept closer, now holding hands, weapons still at the ready.

Jennifer H did not answer. Her neck was twisted at a comic angle. Her eyes were open and staring. Seeing nothing. Liquid, black in the eerie light, ran from her mouth and ears.

The two Jennifers fell back. Jennifer B sank to her knees. Her strength was gone. She let the machete fall from her hand.

"I . . . ," she said, but had no second word. She tried to stand but couldn't.

"We have to get help," Jennifer L said. But she too had sunk to her knees.

Jennifer L tried to stand but sat down again. Jennifer B crawled back to her room. She wanted to help Jennifer L, she did. But she couldn't even help herself.

Jennifer B struggled to push herself up and into her bed. Need help, she thought. Hospital. Lana.

Some still-functioning part of her delirious mind understood that the best she could hope to accomplish for now was to reach the sanctuary of her bed.

But finally even that was too much. She lay on the cold wood floor staring up at her bed, at the motionless ceiling fan. With the last of her strength she pulled the mess of dirty sheets and blankets down on top of herself.

She coughed into the once-soft quilt she'd taken from her mother's room long ago.

The thing on Hunter's shoulder didn't hurt. But it did distract him. And he couldn't be distracted when he was hunting Old Lion.

The mountain lion never bothered Hunter. The mountain lion didn't want to eat Hunter. Or maybe it did, but it had never tried.

But Hunter had to kill the mountain lion because Old Lion had stolen too many of Hunter's own kills. Old Lion crept around behind Hunter after he had taken a deer. Hunter was off chasing other prey and Old Lion had snuck around and dragged off Hunter's deer.

Old Lion was just doing what he had to do. It wasn't personal. Hunter didn't hate Old Lion. But just the same he couldn't have the mountain lion running off with the food for the kids.

Hunter hunted for the kids. That's what he did. That's who he was. He was Hunter the hunter. For the kids.

Old Lion was out of the woods now, over the hill, over where the dry lands started and the rocks grew big. Old Lion was heading home for the night. He had eaten well. Now he was heading back to his lair. He would spend the day lying out on the sun-baked rocks and toasting his bones.

Hunter walked carefully, weight balanced, light on his feet, quick but not rushing. Dangerous to rush about with nothing but moonlight to show the way.

He had learned a lot about hunting. The killing power from his hands didn't reach very far. He had to get close to make it work. That meant he had to really concentrate, which was hard ever since his brain had gotten hurt. He couldn't concentrate enough to read or remember lots of words. And words still came out of his mouth all messed up. But he could concentrate on this: on swift and quiet walking, on weaving through the red rocks while keeping his eyes peeled for the cat's faint star-silvered tracks in the little deposits of sand.

And he had to look out for Old Lion changing his mind and deciding he would like him a tasty boy after all. Old Lion didn't just steal food, he killed it, too. Hunter had seen him once, his tail flicking, his whiskered jaw juddering, quivering with anticipation as Old Lion watched a stray dog.

Old Lion had exploded out of cover and crossed one hundred feet in about one second. Like a bullet out of a gun. His big paws had caught the dog before the dog could even flinch. Long, curved claws, fur, blood, a desperate whine from the dog and then, almost leisurely, taking his time, Old Lion had delivered the killing bite to the back of the dog's neck.

Old Lion was already a hunter back when Hunter was just a regular kid sitting in class, raising his hand to answer questions and reading and understanding and being smart.

Old Lion knew all about hunting. But he didn't know that Hunter was coming after him.

Hunter smelled the cat. He was close. He smelled of dead meat. Dried blood.

Hunter was below a tall boulder. He froze, realizing suddenly that Old Lion was right above him. He wanted to run, but he knew that if he backed up, the cat would drop on him. He was safer closer to the rock. Old Lion couldn't drop straight down.

Hunter pressed his back against the rock. He stilled his own breathing and heard the big cat's instead. But Old Lion wasn't fooled. Old Lion could probably hear the heart pounding in Hunter's chest.

The thing on Hunter's shoulder squirmed. It was growing. Moving. Hunter glanced and could see it move beneath the fabric of his shirt. It seemed almost to be trying to chew a hole through Hunter's shirt.

Hunter had no word for the thing. It had grown over the last day. It had started out as a bump, a swelling. But then the skin had split apart and gnashing insect mouthparts had been revealed. Like a spider. Or a bug. Like the bugs that crawled on Hunter as he slept.

But this thing on his shoulder wasn't a regular bug. It was too big for that. And it had grown right where the flying snake, the greenie, had dropped its goo on him.

Hunter strained to think of the word for the thing. It was a word he used to know. Like worms on a dead animal. What was the word? He leaned forward, hands to his head, so mad at himself for not being able to find the word.

He had lost focus for just a few seconds but it was enough for Old Lion.

The cat dropped like mercury, liquid.

Hunter was knocked to the ground. His head banged against the rock. Old Lion had missed his grip, though, and he had to scramble in the narrow space. The cat spun, bared his yellow teeth and leaped, claws outstretched.

Hunter dodged, but not fast enough. One big paw hit him in the chest and knocked him back against the rock, knocked the wind from him.

Old Lion was on him, claws on his shoulders, snarling face just inches from Hunter's vulnerable neck.

Then, suddenly, the mountain lion hissed and leaped back, like it had landed on a hot stove.

The lion shook its paw and flung droplets of blood. One claw toe had been badly bitten. It hung by a thread.

The thing on Hunter's shoulder had bitten Old Lion.

Hunter didn't hesitate. He raised his hands and aimed.

There was no light. The heat that came from Hunter's hands was invisible. But instantly the temperature in Old

Lion's head doubled, tripled, and Old Lion, his brain cooked in his skull, fell dead.

Hunter pulled his shirt back from the shoulder. The insect mouthparts gnashed, chewing on a bloody chunk of the lion.

THREE

ASTRID HAD FED Little Pete.

She read a little, perched beside the window, book held at an uncomfortable angle to try and take advantage of the faint moonlight.

It was slow going.

It wasn't a book she'd ever have read back in the old days. She wouldn't have been caught dead reading some silly teen romance. Back then she'd have read a classic, or some work of great literary merit. Or history.

Now she needed escape. Now she needed not to be in this world, this terrible world of the FAYZ. Books were the only way out.

After just a few minutes Astrid set the book aside. Her hands were trembling. Attempt to escape into the book: failed. Attempt to forget her fear: failed. It was all right there, still, right there in front of every other thought.

Outside, a breeze caused tree branches to scrape the side of the house. A corner of Astrid's mind noticed, and wondered, but set it aside for more pressing concerns.

She wondered where Sam was. What he was doing. Whether he was longing for her as she longed for him.

Yes, yes, she wanted him. She wanted to be in his arms. She wanted to kiss him. And maybe more. Maybe a lot more.

All of it, all the things he wanted she wanted, too.

Stupid jerk, didn't he get that? Was he so clueless he didn't know that she wanted it all, too?

But she wasn't Sam. Astrid didn't act on impulse. Astrid thought things through. Astrid the Genius, always so irritatingly in control. That was the word he'd thrown at her: control.

How could Sam not realize that if they crossed that line it would be one more sin? One more abandonment of her faith. One more surrender to weakness.

There had been too many of those. It was like little pieces of Astrid's soul were flaking off, falling away. Some pieces not so small.

Her self-control had crumbled so swiftly it was almost comic. After all the temptations and provocations, the calm, civilized, rational girl had evaporated like a bead of water on a hot skillet, sizzle, sizzle, all gone. And what had emerged then had been pure violence.

She had tried to kill Nerezza. In screaming, out-of-control rage. The memory of it made her sick.

And that wasn't all of it. She had wanted Sam to burn Drake to ashes even if it meant murdering Brittney as well.

Astrid couldn't be that person. She had to put herself back together. She had to take time to rebuild herself. She was afraid she would shatter. Like a glass sculpture, chip chip chip away and all at once it would shatter into a thousand pieces.

And yet, a cool, calculating part of her knew she could not alienate Sam too much. Because it was only a matter of time before everyone else figured out that there was a way out of the FAYZ.

The exit door was right in front of them. Lying just a few feet from Astrid.

A simple act of murder . . .

Others had seen what Astrid had seen on that cliff, when Little Pete's mind had blanked out, overwhelmed by the loss of his stupid toy game.

A simple act of murder . . .

She sat beside her motionless brother. She ought to brush his teeth. Ought to change his pajamas. Ought to . . .

His forehead was damp.

Astrid put her hand to his head. He'd been hot all night, but this was worse. She pushed the button on the thermometer by the bed, waited for it to zero out, and stuck it under Little Pete's tongue.

She felt a cool breeze in the room. Her eyes went instantly to the window. It was open wide. Pushed all the way up.

There was no question: it had been closed. She'd been sitting beside it. It had been locked. And now it was open.

And for the first time since the coming of the FAYZ, a

cool breeze blew into the room and wafted over the damp forehead of the most powerful person in this little universe.

Drake felt the Darkness touch his mind. He shivered with pleasure.

It was still out there, Drake was sure of it. Still calling to him, to Drake, the faithful one, the one who would never turn against the Darkness.

Drake cracked his whip hand just to hear the sonic-boom snap of it. And to let Orc hear it, too.

"Hey, Orc! Come down here so I can whip that little patch of skin off you!" Drake demanded.

Drake Merwin could see a little by the light of the tiny, dim Sammy sun. He hated that light—he knew where it had come from, and what it represented: Sam's power, that dangerous light of his.

Drake remembered the pain of that light. He'd been on his back, helpless. And Sam, his face a mask of rage, glorying in his moment of revenge, had burned off Drake's legs and was working his way methodically up Drake's torso.

Then that stupid little pig Brittney had emerged.

Drake didn't know what happened next, he couldn't see or hear when Brittney was in control. All he knew was that Sam hadn't vaporized him. And here he was, trapped. Locked in this basement listening to Orc's heavy tread upstairs.

Drake didn't know what had happened to make him this way, to cause him to share a body with Brittney. Much of recent life was a mystery. He remembered Caine turning on him. He remembered the massive uranium rod flying straight toward him.

And the next thing he knew, he was in a nightmare that went on and on and on forever. There was a girl in the nightmare, the little piggy, the stupid little metal-mouth moron, Brittney.

Hadn't they killed her? Long ago? He remembered a crumpled, bleeding form on a polished floor.

Brittney had died. Drake had died. And then, neither of them was dead, and both somehow were connected in a nightmare world where dirt filled their mouths and ears and held them pinned.

Digging like worms. That was the nightmare reality. Drake and the piggy digging in a nightmare, digging dirt, pushing it aside, compressing it to buy half an inch of clearance.

Dark, that dream. Utterly dark. No Sammy sun. No light.

He remembered thinking in the nightmare, thinking, "There's no air."

Buried alive, there couldn't be any air. No light and no air, no water, no food, forever and forever.

It had taken a long time before his mind had cleared enough for him to realize the wonderful truth: he was dead . . . but alive.

Unkillable. Buried in the damp earth and yet somehow alive.

And then, hard-won freedom of a sort. The nightmare was no longer one of being buried in the earth but of walking the earth. He would be in one place, and then quite suddenly, in another. It took him a while to realize what had happened. The piggy was a part of him. They were joined, connected. Melded into one creature with two minds and two bodies.

Sometimes Drake and sometimes Brittney Pig.

Sometimes himself, and other times that little idiot with her lunatic visions of her dead brother.

Then the fight with Sam, the burning, and yet he had survived.

Unkillable.

"You're a monster, Orc! You know that, right?" Drake shouted the taunt. "People look at you and they throw up. You make them all sick."

Trapped. For now. In this dank, gloomy basement. Nothing down here but a wooden work table. They had cleaned the place out, Sam and Edilio and the rest. Barely a nail left behind on the concrete floor.

A roomier grave than the one he'd shared with Brittney Pig before. Here there was air. But Drake no longer needed air.

They shoved food in, and Drake ate it but he didn't need it.

Unkillable.

What could not be killed could not be imprisoned forever. Just a matter of time. Orc was a stupid drunk. Howard was a clown. Drake would have already dug his way out—he had loosened a section of cinderblock wall, working at the mortar with a piece of broken glass.

But he had to be careful not to leave any clues for Brittney to find when she emerged.

That meant working slowly. Putting the piece of glass back in the sweepings right where she would expect to see it.

In the meantime as he worked and waited he howled threats up at Orc. There were two ways out of this trap: working on the wall, and working on Orc's mind.

"Hey!" Drake shouted. "Orc! If I whip that last bit of skin off you, what do you think will happen? Might as well get rid of it and be all gravel. Why pretend you're still human?"

Orc stomped the floor, which was Drake's ceiling. But he did not come down to do battle.

Not yet. But he would eventually. Orc would snap. Then Drake would have his chance.

Through the wall or through Orc: one way or the other, Drake would escape.

He would go then to the Darkness. The gaiaphage would know how to kill the Brittney Pig and let Drake live free.

"I'm going to kill you!" Drake screamed.

He whipped at the walls, whipped at the ceiling, screamed and kicked and whipped in a lunatic frenzy.

Until at last, exhausted, his whip hand bleeding, he fell to his knees and became Brittney.

"Brittney Pig," Drake slurred as his cruel mouth melted and twisted and became the braces-toothed mouth of his most intimate enemy.

Lana, too, felt the dark distant mind of the gaiaphage reach out for her.

She woke, eyes open quite suddenly. Patrick was beside the

bed, panting, worried, wagging his tail uncertainly. He could tell, somehow.

"It's okay, boy, go back to sleep," Lana said.

Patrick whimpered, but then went back to his bed, turning around a couple of times before settling himself in.

The gaiaphage could no longer trick her into believing it had a voice. Those days were gone. But it could still touch her with a tendril of consciousness. It could still remind her of its presence, and of her connection to it.

This must be what it was like to be a victim of some awful crime, and to know that the person who did it to you was still alive, still looking for a way to do it again.

The gaiaphage lusted after Lana's power. Using her power it could do miraculous things. Like replace an amputated arm with a snakelike whip.

But she was no longer quite so weak.

"Anxious, are you?" she asked the cool night air. "Down under the ground nibbling on your uranium snack?"

The Darkness did not answer. But Lana felt her instinct was right: the creature was anxious.

But not afraid.

Lana frowned, thinking about the distinction. Anxious but not afraid. Anticipating? Waiting for something?

She was torn between getting up and smoking a cigarette—she was hooked, she accepted that now—and lying there with her eyes closed and failing to fall asleep. Sleep, even if it came, would now be invaded by nightmares.

So she sat up, fumbled for and found the pack of Lucky

Strikes and her lighter. The lighter sparked, the cigarette glowed, and the smell of smoke filled her nostrils.

"What are you up to?" she asked. "What do you want?"

But of course there was no answer. And she could sense the Darkness turning its attention away.

Lana got up and padded over to her balcony. The moon was high overhead. It was either very late or very early.

The barrier was so close, she felt as if she could almost touch it.

Was it true that the world was just on the other side of that barrier? Was it really so close that she'd have been able to smell the french fries at the Carl's Jr. they built for gawkers who came to see the dome?

Or was that just another lie in this small universe of deceptions?

What if it came down? Right now, just pop: no more barrier? Or what if it cracked, like a gigantic egg?

Her mom and dad . . .

She closed her eyes and bit her lip. The pain of memory had snuck up on her, hit her when she wasn't ready.

Tears filled her eyes. She wiped them away impatiently.

Suddenly, just down on the cliff above the beach, an eruption of blazing green-white light. Sam stood silhouetted by his own light show. She heard him yelling, roaring in frustration.

He was trying to burn his way out of the FAYZ.

It went on for a while and then stopped. Darkness returned. Sam was invisible to her now.

Lana turned away.

So, she was not the only one fantasizing about cracking the shell and emerging like a newborn chick.

Strange, Lana thought as she stubbed out the end of her cigarette, I've never thought of it as an egg before.

A gust of breeze blew her smoke before her.

FOUR
63 HOURS, 41 MINUTES

SAM WOKE UP in the last place he'd have expected: his bedroom.

He hadn't been to his former house in ages.

He'd hated it when he lived here with his mother. Connie Temple. Nurse Temple.

He barely remembered her. She was from another world.

He sat up on the bed and smelled the sick. He'd thrown up on the bed. "Nice," he said with thick tongue.

His head exploded in supernovas of pain.

He wiped his mouth on the blanket. This was one house no one had raided or vandalized or moved into. It was still his, he supposed. There might still be drugs in the bathroom.

He staggered there. Leaned against the sink and threw up again. Not much came up.

In the medicine cabinet nothing but a small bottle of generic ibuprofen.

"Oh," Sam moaned. "Why do people drink?"

Then he remembered. Taylor.

"Oh, no. Oh, no."

No, no, he hadn't made a grab for Taylor, had he? He hadn't kissed her, surely? The memory was so hazy it could almost have been a dream. But pieces of it were too immediate and real. Especially the memory of her fingertips on his chest.

"Oh, no," he moaned.

He swallowed two ibuprofen dry. They didn't go down easily.

Holding his head, he went to the kitchen. Sat down at the little table. He'd had meals here with his mom. Not a lot of days, because she'd be up at Coates, working.

And keeping a worried eye on her other son.

Caine.

Caine Soren, not Temple. She had given him up for adoption. They had been born just a few minutes apart, fraternal twins, him and Caine. And their mother had given Caine away and kept Sam.

No explanation. She'd never told either of them. That truth hadn't come out until after the coming of the FAYZ.

And no real explanation for what had become of their father. He was out of the picture before Sam and Caine were born.

Had it just been too much for their mother? Had she decided she could handle one fatherless boy but not two? Eeny meeny miny moe?

He had a new family now. Astrid and Little Pete. Only now he didn't have them, either. And now he had to ask himself what he had done to deserve it, his father's disappearance, his mother's lies, Astrid's rejection.

"Yeah," he muttered. "Time for self-pity. Poor me. Poor Sam."

He meant it to sound ironic, but it came out bitter.

Caine probably had a pretty good case of resentment, too. He'd been rejected by both birth parents: two for two.

And yet, Caine still had Diana, didn't he?

How was it fair? Caine was a liar, a manipulator, a murderer. And Caine was probably lying in satin sheets with Diana eating actual food and watching a DVD. Clean sheets, candy bars, and a beautiful, willing girl.

Caine who had never done a single good or decent thing was living in luxury.

Sam, who had tried and tried and done everything he could, was sitting in his house with a raging headache, smelling vomit with a pair of ibuprofen burning a hole in his stomach lining.

Alone.

Hunter brought his kills to the gas station any day he had some. Today, bright and early, with the sun just warming the hills behind him, he had walked down from his hillside camp carrying four birds and a badger and two raccoons and a bag of squirrels. He forgot how many squirrels. The bag felt heavy, though.

It was a lot to carry. If you added it up it was probably about as heavy as carrying a kid. Not as heavy as a deer though—those he had to butcher and carry down in pieces.

No deer today. And he had not yet butchered Old Lion. That was a big job. He wanted to keep the skin in one piece, so he had to take his time.

He would wear the lion's skin over him when he had dried it out. It would be warm and remind him of Old Lion.

Hunter carried the squirrel bag slung over one shoulder. He roped the other animals together and draped the rope over his other shoulder. He had to be careful about that, though, because of the thing on his shoulder.

That kid named Roscoe was coming. He was pushing a wheelbarrow. He didn't look very happy. Every day Hunter came it was either Roscoe or this girl named Marcie. Marcie was nice. But Hunter knew she was scared of him. Probably because he couldn't talk well.

"Hey, Hunter," Roscoe said. "Dude, are you okay?"

"Yes."

"You're all clawed up, man. I mean, jeez, that has to hurt."

Hunter followed the direction of Roscoe's gaze. His shirt was ripped exposing his stomach. Two claw marks, deep, bloody, just beginning to scab a little, were plowed right across his stomach.

He touched the wound gingerly. But it didn't hurt. In fact he couldn't feel it at all.

"You're a tough dude, Hunter," Roscoe said. "Anyway, looks like you have a good haul today."

"I do, Roscoe," Hunter said. He spoke as carefully as he could. But still the words didn't sound like how he made words back before. He sounded as if his tongue was covered with glue.

Hunter carefully lifted the rope off his shoulder. He was careful not to scrape the thing on his shoulder. He set the animals in the wheelbarrow. Then he upended the squirrel bag and dumped the squirrels on top. They all looked the same. Gray and bushy-tailed. Each cooked inside a little. Enough. Sometimes he cooked their heads and sometimes their body. It wasn't that easy to aim the invisible stuff that radiated out of his hands.

He forgot what it was called. Astrid had some name for it. But it was a long word.

"You doing okay, Hunter?" Roscoe asked again.

"Yes. I have food. And my sleeping bag is dry after I cleaned it in a stream."

"You got fresh water to wash in, huh?" Roscoe asked. "I'm jealous. Feel this shirt." He invited Hunter to feel the stiff saltwater-washed cotton.

"It feels okay," Hunter said warily.

Roscoe made a rude noise. "Yeah, right. Salt water. Feel your shirt." And Roscoe reached out to touch Hunter's shirt. He touched the shoulder of Hunter's shirt.

The wrong shoulder.

"Aaahh!" Roscoe cried in shock and pain. "What the—"

"I didn't mean to!" Hunter yelled.

"Something bit me!" He held out his finger for Hunter to examine. There were teeth marks. Blood.

Roscoe stared hard at him. And at his shoulder. "What's

on your shoulder, man? What is that? What's under there? Is that some kind of animal?"

Hunter swallowed. No one had seen his shoulder. He didn't know what would happen if anyone did.

"Yes, Roscoe, it's an animal," Hunter said, seizing gratefully on the explanation.

"Well, it bit me!"

"Sorry," Hunter said.

Roscoe grabbed the wheelbarrow handles and hefted it. "I'm not doing this job anymore. Marcie can do it every day, I'm not dealing with this."

"Okay," Hunter said. "Bye."

Jennifer B set out sometime around dawn.

If she stayed in the house she was sure she would die. She'd slept for an unknown period of time—hours? days?—on the floor, with her blankets gathered around her.

The chills came in waves. She would be too hot and would kick off her blankets. Then the fever would start to spike again and she would feel cold, cold all the way down to her bones.

Jennifer H was dead. Jennifer L didn't answer when Jennifer B moaned to her to join her.

"Jen . . . I'm going to . . . hospital."

No answer.

"Are you alive?"

Jennifer L coughed, she wasn't dead, and she coughed

normally, not the crazy spasms that had killed Jennifer H. But she didn't answer.

So Jennifer Boyles set off, on her own. She slid on her butt down the stairs, blankets gathered around her. Shivering, teeth chattering.

She managed to stand long enough to reach the front door and open it. But she sat down again very unexpectedly on the porch. Hard on her butt. She sat there shaking until the chills passed.

She tripped walking down the porch stairs. The fall bruised her left knee badly. This destroyed the last of her will to stand up. But not the last of her will to live.

Jennifer began to crawl. Hands and knees. Down the sidewalk. Impeded by her blankets. Delayed by coughing fits. Pausing whenever the chills rattled her so hard she could only moan and hack and roll onto her side.

"Keep going," she muttered. "Gotta keep going."

It took her two hours to crawl as far as Brace Road.

She lay there, facedown. Coughing wracked her chest. But it was not yet the superhuman coughs that had killed Jennifer H.

Not yet.

FIVE

"LESLIE-ANN, TRY TO do a little better on cleaning my night pot, okay?" Albert told the cleaning girl. "I know it's not a fun job, but I like it clean."

Leslie-Ann nodded and kept her eyes down. She was a little afraid of him, Albert knew. But at least she didn't seem to hate him.

"There's not much water," Leslie-Ann mumbled.

"Use sand," Albert said patiently—he'd already told her this. "Use sand to scrub it clean."

She nodded and fled the room.

Not everyone liked Albert. Not everyone was happy that he had become the most important person around. Lots of people were jealous that Albert had a girl to clean his house and the porcelain basin where he did his business at night when he didn't want to go outside to the only actual outhouse in Perdido Beach. And that he could afford to send his clothes to be washed in the fresh water of the ironically named Lake Evian.

And there were definitely people who didn't like working for Albert, having to do what he said or go hungry.

Albert traveled with a bodyguard now. The bodyguard's name was Jamal. Jamal carried an automatic rifle over his shoulder. He had a massive hunting knife in his belt. And a club that was an oak chair leg with spikes driven through it to make a sort of mace.

Unlike everyone else Albert carried no weapon himself. Jamal was weapon enough.

"Let's go, Jamal."

Albert led the way toward the beach. Jamal as usual kept a few paces back, head swiveling left and right, glowering, ready for trouble.

Albert bypassed the plaza—there were always kids there and they always wanted something from Albert: a job, a different job, credit, something.

It didn't work. Two littles, Harley and Janice, moved right in front of him as he walked briskly.

"Mr. Albert? Mr. Albert?" Harley said.

"Just Albert's fine," Albert said tersely.

"Me and Janice are thirsty."

"I'm sorry, but I don't have any water on me." He managed a tight smile and moved on. But now Janice was crying and Harley was pleading.

"We used to live with Mary and she gave us water. But now we have to live with Summer and BeeBee and they said we have to have money."

"Then I guess you'd better earn some money," Albert said.

He tried to soften it, tried not to sound harsh, but he had a lot on his mind and it came out sounding mean. Now Harley started to cry, too.

"If you're thirsty, stop crying," Albert snapped. "What do you think tears are made of?"

Reaching the beach Albert scanned the work site. It looked like a salvage yard. A five-hundred-gallon oval propane tank lay abandoned on the sand. A scorched hole in one side.

A second, slightly smaller tank should have been resting on steel legs right at the water's edge. Instead it was tipped over. A copper pipe stuck out of the top. This pipe was crimped tightly over a slightly smaller pipe that bent back toward the ground. A third, still narrower pipe was duct-taped heavily in place and this pipe reached the wet sand.

In theory at least, this crude, jury-rigged contraption was a still. The principle was simple enough: boil salt water, let the steam rise into a pipe, then cool the steam. What dribbled out of the end would be drinkable water.

Easy in theory. Almost impossible to do practically. Especially now that some fool had knocked it over.

Albert's heart sank. Soon Harley and Janice wouldn't be the only ones begging for water. The gasoline supply was down to a few hundred gallons at the station. No gas: no water truck. No water truck: no water.

Even worse, the tiny Lake Evian in the hills was drying up. There had been no rain since the coming of the FAYZ. Kids knew there was a plan to relocate everyone to Lake Evian when the last of the gas was gone; what they didn't realize was that things were far worse than that.

The first tank, the burned one, had been an earlier effort to create a still. Albert had tried to get Sam to boil the water using his powers. Unfortunately Sam couldn't dial it down enough to heat without destroying.

This new effort would require a fire beneath the tank. Which would mean crews of kids to rip lumber from unused houses. Which might make the whole thing more trouble than it was worth.

The crew was lounging. Tossing pebbles at the surf, trying to get them to skip.

Albert marched over to them, his loafers filling with sand. "Hey," he snapped. "What happened here?"

The four kids—none older than eleven—looked guilty.

"It was like this when we got here. I think the wind knocked it over."

"There is no wind in the FAYZ, you . . ." He stopped himself from saying, "moron." Albert had a certain reputation for being in control of himself. He was the closest thing they had to an adult.

"I hired you to dig a hole, not play around," Albert said.

"It's hard," one said. "It keeps filling up."

"I know it's hard. It won't get any easier. And if you want to eat, you work."

"We were just taking a break."

"Break's over. Get on those shovels."

Albert turned and walked away with Jamal in his wake.

"Those kids are flipping you off, boss," Jamal reported.

"Are they digging?"

Jamal glanced back and reported that they were.

"As long as they do their work they can flip me off all they like," Albert said.

It was then that Roscoe came up to report his haul from Hunter. And to tell Albert a crazy story about Hunter's shoulder biting him.

"Look," Roscoe said and held out his hand for Albert's inspection.

Albert sighed. "Save the crazy stories, Roscoe," he said.

"It's like, like, green, kind of," Roscoe said.

"I'm not the Healer or Dahra," Albert said.

But as he walked away something nagged at the edges of Albert's thoughts: the wound really had looked a bit green.

Someone else's problem. He had plenty of his own.

It was then that he spotted someone lying on the sand, just lying there like he might be dead. Far down the beach.

He felt in his pocket for the map.

Was it time? He glanced back at the still. The hopeless still.

His insides squirmed a little at what he was about to do. Panic would not be good. Everyone was on edge, weird, freaked since Mary's dramatic suicide and attempted mass murder.

The people could not take another disaster. But disaster was coming. And when it hit, if there was panic, then Sam would be needed here in town.

But there was no one else Albert could trust with the

mission he had in mind. Sam would have to go. And Albert would have to hope that no new disaster arose while he was gone.

Sam felt a shadow.

He squinted one eye open. Someone was standing over him, face blanked by the sun behind him.

"Is that you, Albert?" Sam asked.

"It's me."

"I recognize the shoes. I don't feel good," Sam said.

"Would you mind sitting up? I have something important to talk to you about."

"If it's important, go talk to Edilio. He's in charge."

Albert waited, refusing to speak. Finally, with a sigh that became a groan, Sam rolled over and sat up.

"This is just between us, Sam," Albert said.

"Yeah, that always works out so well when I keep secrets from the council," Sam said sarcastically. He rubbed his hair vigorously to knock some of the sand out.

"You're not on the council anymore," Albert said reasonably. "And this is about a job. I want to hire you."

Sam rolled his eyes. "Everyone already works for you, Albert. What's the problem? Does it bother you that I don't?"

"You liked it better when no one was working and everyone was starving?"

Sam stared up at him. Then he made an ironic two-finger salute. "Sorry. I'm in a lousy mood. Bad night followed by bad morning. What's up, Albert?"

"There's a big problem with the water supply."

Sam nodded. "I know. As soon as the gas runs out we're going to have to relocate the whole town up to Evian."

Albert tugged at his pants, then sat down carefully on the sand. "No. First of all, the water level in Lake Evian is dropping faster than ever. There's no rain here. And it's a small lake. You can see where it's dropped from, like, ten feet deep to half that."

Albert pulled a folded map from his pocket and opened it. Sam scooted closer to see.

"This isn't a very good map. It's too big to show much detail. But see this?" He pointed. "Lake Tramonto. It's like a hundred times bigger than Evian."

"Is it inside the FAYZ?"

"I drew this circle with a compass. I think at least part of Lake Tramonto is inside the barrier."

Sam nodded thoughtfully. "Dude, it's, like, what, ten miles from here?"

"More like fifteen."

"Even if it's there and even if the water is drinkable, how are we going to bring it down to Perdido Beach? I mean, look." Sam traced lines with his finger. "Going or coming back it's right through coyote country. And that would take a lot more gas, that drive. I mean, a lot more."

"I don't think my saltwater still is going to work," Albert admitted. He gazed moodily down the beach toward his work crew. "Even if it does, it may not produce enough."

Sam took the map from him and studied it intently. "You know, it's weird. I kind of forgot there were such things as paper maps. I always used to use Google maps. Maps dot Google dot com. Remember those days? What's this?"

Albert peered over the edge of the map. "Oh, that's the air force base. But look, it's pretty much all on the other side. The runway, the buildings and all. Why? Were you hoping to find a jet fighter?"

Sam smiled. "That might be useful if it came with a pilot. It's one thing for Sanjit to crash-land a helicopter. It's a whole different thing flying a Mach two jet around inside a twenty-mile-wide fishbowl. No. I don't know what I was hoping for. Maybe a magic ray gun that could blow holes through the barrier."

"You know," Albert said, trying to sound casual, but sounding instead like he was delivering a well-rehearsed speech. "I read in a book where in the old days—I mean, really old days—businessmen would hire explorers to go search out new territory. You know, to find gold or oil or spices. Of course these explorers would have to be tough and be able to deal with all kinds of problems."

Sam had no trouble grasping Albert's meaning. "You want to hire me to explore this lake."

"Yes."

Sam looked around at the sand. "Well, as you can see, I'm very busy."

Albert said nothing. Just waited and watched Sam like a lizard watching a fly.

"You don't want the council to know about this. Why?"

Albert shrugged. "Anything the council hears about, the whole town knows ten seconds later. You want panic? Anyway, it's not about them. It's me doing it. Me and you. And a couple of other kids to back you up."

"Why not just send Brianna? She'd get there fast."

"I don't trust her. Not for something like this. I mean, Sam, we could be in trouble on water really soon. I mean, soon. I've got a truck going later, after that, maybe half a dozen more runs."

Sam fell silent. He drew little abstract shapes in the sand, thinking.

"I'll do it," Sam said. "I'm not happy about keeping it secret from Edilio."

Albert pressed his lips into a line. Like he was thinking. But Sam could see Albert had an answer ready. "Look, secrets don't last long in this place. For example, Taylor's been telling an interesting story all over town."

Sam groaned. Had to be Taylor, he reproached himself. What was he going to tell Astrid? Not that it was really her business. They'd never said he couldn't see anyone else, make out with anyone else. In fact once, in a flash of anger, Astrid had told him to do just that. Only she hadn't said "make out." She'd used a phrase he'd been a little shocked to hear coming from Astrid.

"Sam, Edilio's a good guy," Albert said, breaking in on Sam's gloomy thoughts. "But like I said, he'll tell the rest of them. Once the council knows, everyone knows. If everyone knows how desperate things are, what do you think will happen?"

Sam smiled without humor. "About half the people will be great. The other half will freak."

"And people will end up getting killed," Albert said. He cocked his head sideways, trying his best to look like the idea had just occurred to him. "And who is going to end up kicking butts? Who will end up playing Daddy and then be resented and blamed and finally told to go away?"

"You've gained new skills," Sam said bitterly. "You used to just be about working harder than anyone else and being ambitious. You're learning how to manipulate people."

Albert's mouth twitched and his eyes flashed angrily. "You're not the only one walking around with a big load of responsibility on your shoulders, Sam. You play the big mean daddy who won't let anyone have any fun, and I play the greedy businessman who is just looking out for himself. But don't be stupid: maybe I am greedy, but without me no one eats. Or drinks. We need water. You see anyone else in this town that's going to make that happen?"

Sam laughed softly. "Yeah, you've gotten good at using people, Albert. I mean you offer me a chance to go off and save everyone's butt, right? Be important and necessary again. You have me all figured out."

"We need water, Sam," Albert said simply. "If you find water up at this Lake Tramonto and come back and tell people they have to move up there, they'll do it. You tell them it's going to be okay and they'll believe you."

"Because I'm so widely loved and admired," Sam said sarcastically.

"It's not a popularity contest, Sam. People love you when they need you, and then ten minutes later they're tired of you. In a very short while they're going to realize we're very close to all dying of thirst. And there you'll be with the solution."

"And they'll love me. For ten minutes, until they've had enough to drink."

"Exactly," Albert said. He stood up. "We have a deal?" He extended his hand down for Sam to shake.

Sam stood up. "And the lake? I mean, if it's there?"

"If it's there, it's my lake," Albert said coolly. "I'll sell the water and control access. Maybe then we won't end up in the same bind all over again."

Sam shook his hand and laughed out loud. "You are less full of crap than anyone around, Albert. If it's there, I'll find it. I'll leave tonight."

He took the map.

"You want someone to go with you?"

"Dekka." Sam thought a moment longer. "And Jack."

"You want Computer Jack? Why?"

"It's a good idea to have someone around who's smarter than you are."

"I suppose so," Albert said. "You need someone to communicate, too. Take Taylor."

"Not Taylor. I'll take Brianna."

Albert shook his head. "You kissed her, get past it. We need someone in this town who can fight if necessary. I mean at the freak level, no diss on Edilio. Taylor's useless in a battle of any kind, while Brianna can take on just about anyone."

Sam nodded. It made sense. If he wanted Dekka along he'd have to leave Brianna behind. But Taylor?

Suddenly the trip, which he had started to anticipate just a little, seemed much less like fun.

Lana disliked going into town. In town people asked her for things. But she needed a gallon of water to take back up to Clifftop anyway, so she figured she might as well stop by the so-called hospital and clear up the usual backlog of kids with broken arms, burned hands, and a rumored cut wrist.

She wasn't that sure she should be fixing anyone dumb enough to try and slit his wrist. After all, the FAYZ would kill you soon enough, why be in a hurry? And if you wanted a quick trip out of the FAYZ there was always Mary's way: the cliff.

Dahra Baidoo was reading her medical book and telling some kid with a sore tooth to be quiet. "It's just loose, it will come out when it wants to come out," she said irritably.

She looked up with a weary smile when she noticed Lana. "Hey, Lana."

"Hey, DB," Lana said. "How's medical school?"

It was an old joke between them. They had worked together closely in times of crisis. The flu that had gone around a couple of weeks ago, the various battles and fires and fights and poisonings and accidents.

Dahra would hold the injured kids' hands and feed them

Tylenol while waiting for Lana to come around. The fire had been the worst. The two of them had been down here together for days, barely seeing the sun.

Bad, bad days.

Dahra laughed and tapped the book. "I'm ready to perform heart transplants."

"What do we have?" Lana asked. "I heard you had an uncommitted suicide."

"No suicides. Broken ribs. And a burn. Not too bad, and I should probably let her suffer since she got it from trying to light a bag of poop and throw it."

Lana heard a hacking cough from a very sick-looking girl. "What's that?"

Dahra gave her a significant look. "I think our flu is back. Or never went away." She pulled Lana off to the side, to where the patients couldn't hear. "I think this may be worse, though. This girl is hallucinating. Her name is Jennifer. She came crawling in here this morning. She keeps talking about some other girl named Jennifer who coughed so hard there were pieces of her lungs coming up. And then she supposedly coughed so hard she broke her own neck."

"Fever brings on the crazy sometimes," Lana said.

"Yeah. Still, I wish I had someone to go check on her house. See if there's anything going on."

"Where's Elwood?"

Dahra sighed. "That's over."

Lana had never liked Elwood much and she kind of wanted to know what had happened—Dahra and Elwood had been going out for a long time. But Dahra didn't look like she was interested in spilling her guts.

Lana healed the broken ribs, then checked out the girl with burned fingers. "Don't do stupid things like this," Lana snapped at the girl. "I don't want to be wasting my time on stupidity. Next time I'll let you suffer."

But she healed the burn as well and did a quick touch-and-go with the coughing girl.

"Can I fill a jug before I head out?" Lana asked.

Dahra winced. She had an old water cooler in one corner with a clear glass five-gallon jug on top. But there was nowhere near five gallons in there.

"How about half a gallon?" Dahra said.

"Deal," Lana said. "Albert needs to keep you better supplied. Me, too, while we're at it. He's supposed to send one of his people up with a gallon a day. It's been two days. It's not smart for a hypochondriac like Albert to grind my nerves."

Then, with a nod to Dahra, Lana headed off again, back toward her lonely eyrie.

She took a shortcut that took her up the hill to Clifftop. It was a bare trail through the brush, a place where a hungry coyote might be. But Patrick would warn her long before she walked into a coyote. And in any case Lana carried an automatic pistol she had no compunction about using.

Suddenly Patrick growled and Lana had the automatic out and aimed with both hands in a split second.

"Step out where I can see you," she said.

There was no coyote. Instead there was Hunter. Lurking.

Looking ashamed to be here. He had been banished from town, although he was allowed to come see her anytime. Still he preferred to stay out of sight.

Lana liked Hunter. First because he often saved her some tasty morsel, a rabbit or a couple of plump frogs. And he brought stomachs and intestines for Patrick to eat.

Second because even though he was brain damaged he at least had the sense not to waste her time. If he was looking for her there was a reason.

"T'sup, Hunter?" she asked. She stuck the gun back in her waistband. "Whoa. I see: bad scratches there."

"No," he said. "It's something else."

He pulled on his T-shirt neck.

Lana didn't breathe for a few seconds. "Yeah," she said. "That is something else."

SIX

NO ONE KNEW quite how to deal with Hunter. He wasn't supposed to come into town. So the council had to go to him.

They met on the highway.

No one had ever cleaned up the crashed and abandoned cars on the highway. They were all just where they'd been since the coming of the FAYZ.

The big FedEx truck was still on its side. Kids had long since broken into the back and rifled through the packages. The wrapping, torn paper, plastic packing peanuts, curls of tape, and packing slips had mostly drifted into a section of construction barrier on the side of the road.

Funny, Lana noticed: it looked almost cleaned up today. As if someone had come along with a leaf blower and scooted all the garbage off the road.

The town council was now Dekka, Howard, Albert, Ellen, and Edilio. Sam was entitled to attend but he usually didn't. Astrid had made it clear she wanted no part of it anymore, but Lana had sent Brianna to tell her to be there. She wanted Astrid's eyes on this.

So Astrid was there. Sort of. Lana had seen Astrid in a lot of different situations and moods, but this was a new Astrid: withdrawn, preoccupied. Like she was somewhere else entirely. She was biting her lip, twisting her fingers together, then catching herself and wiping her hands on her jeans.

Lana was sure she saw Astrid start guiltily when she noticed the trash blown against the barrier. But maybe she was just feeling touchy because of the story going around about Sam and Taylor.

Edilio was in charge. Which was fine with Lana. Almost everyone else had shown some weakness, some bit of crazy. Very much including herself, she acknowledged wryly.

Edilio seemed like the last sane, decent person left in the FAYZ. The undocumented kid from Honduras was the single most trusted person around. And yet, if the barrier ever came down, Edilio and his family—if they were still alive out there—would be kicked out of the country.

Of course, Lana thought, if the barrier ever came down, half the kids would be shipped off to juvie and the rest would be sent to mental institutions or rehab. So maybe getting kicked out wasn't so bad.

Hunter looked like he was meeting the president. He stood tall and tried to smooth his hair down—a hopeless effort. Lana hid a smile as he picked a tick off his arm and flicked it away.

"Hi, Hunter," Edilio said. "First up, man, thanks for all the good work you do, right? You're helping to keep everyone fed and healthy, so thanks."

Hunter searched for something to say, eyes shifting left, right, and finally down. "I am the hunter."

"Well, you're a good hunter," Edilio said. "Lana says you have a little medical problem."

Hunter nodded. "Mouths."

"Yeah. Well, do you mind letting us look? We don't want to embarrass you or anything."

"Just take off your shirt," Albert said a bit abruptly. He considered Hunter an employee. But then Albert considered almost everyone an employee.

"He can take it off or not, it's up to him," Dekka said in her low growl.

Hunter was confused by the back-and-forth. So Lana said, "Would you mind taking your shirt off, Hunter, so we can see? Might as well take off your jeans, too."

Hunter pulled his T-shirt over his head. He dropped his jeans to his ankles.

There was a collective gasp.

Lana stepped up beside Hunter. She pointed to the protruding mouthparts on Hunter's shoulder. It looked exactly like a very large ant's head, or maybe a wasp's head, but with oversized, gnashing mouthparts. "This was the first one. I tried to cure it. You'll notice it didn't work."

She pointed to a smaller silvery, almost metallic, mouth on his calf. "Do us a favor and raise your arms up, Hunter."

He did. Albert looked away.

There was a third mouth gnashing its teeth in Hunter's armpit.

Lana watched Astrid watching Hunter. Her ice blue eyes flickered.

"You have a question, Astrid?" Lana asked.

Astrid pursed her lips like she didn't, but her curiosity got the better of her. "Hunter, has anything bitten you?"

"Yes. Fleas bite me. And ticks."

"How about a wasp?" Astrid asked.

"No," Hunter said.

"Why a wasp?" Edilio asked Astrid.

Astrid shrugged. "I'm just trying to get information." She was lying, Lana thought. That scary smart brain of hers was already onto something. Something she didn't want to talk about in front of Hunter.

"Anything else strange happen?" Edilio asked.

"Just the greenie," Hunter said.

"The what?" Edilio asked.

"They're no good for hunting. I caught one and cooked it but it shriveled all up and there wasn't any meat on it."

"What's a greenie?" Albert demanded.

Hunter frowned, looking for a way to describe it. "It flies. It's like a snake that flies."

Howard said, "Oh, good, I was worried we didn't have enough weirdness to deal with. Flying snakes. That's excellent."

"They squirt," Hunter said helpfully. Then his eyes widened. "It squirted me once. Right here." He pointed to his shoulder. To the slowly gnashing insect mouth.

"Does anyone have anything sharp?" Astrid asked.

Three knives flashed out.

"I was kind of thinking of a pin," Astrid said. But she took a knife from Howard. "Don't worry, Hunter," she said. She poked very gently with the point of the knife just beside the largest mouth. "Did you feel that?"

Hunter shook his head.

Astrid poked again, farther from the first spot. And again on Hunter's upper arm.

"I guess I don't feel stuff much." Hunter seemed baffled.

"Something's anesthetizing him," Astrid said. A spasm, a look of nausea, quickly suppressed, twisted her lips.

"It doesn't hurt," Hunter said.

"You can get dressed," Edilio said kindly. "Thanks for showing us."

Hunter obediently pulled his clothes back on.

"Back to work, huh, Hunter?" Edilio said with a wretched, forced smile.

Hunter nodded. "Yes. I have to get Albert some meat or he gets mad."

"No I don't," Albert protested weakly.

Hunter started to walk away. Albert called after him. "Where did you see this flying snake of yours?"

Hunter, eager to answer Albert's question, smiled because he knew the answer. "They're all over on the morning side."

"The what?"

"That's what I call it. On the other side of the hills. There's a cave. By the road."

"The road to Lake Evian . . . the lake where we get water?" Albert asked in a quiet voice.

Hunter nodded. "Yes. By the dirt road that goes there."

"Thanks," Edilio said, dismissing Hunter, who looked relieved and walked quickly away without looking back. Edilio turned to Astrid. "Okay, Astrid. What are you thinking?"

"I think the reason Lana couldn't heal him is that it's not a disease."

"It sure looks like a disease," Howard said. "Like a disease I don't want to get."

"It's a parasite," Astrid said.

"Like when a dog gets worms?" Edilio asked.

"Yes."

"But they're coming out through his skin," Edilio said.

Astrid nodded. "He should be in excruciating pain. They're probably secreting something that deadens the pain."

"What's going to happen to him?" Dekka asked.

"There's a type of wasp," Astrid said. "That's why I asked him about wasps. It lays its eggs inside a caterpillar. The eggs hatch. The larvae then eat the living caterpillar from the inside out."

Lana felt sick herself. She had long since learned to protect herself by affecting a certain indifference to the pains and wounds she healed. But this was awful beyond anything she had ever seen. And she had been powerless to help.

"Everyone keep this quiet till we figure out what it is," Edilio said. "No one talk to Taylor, that girl can't keep quiet for . . ." He trailed off, noticing a stony glare from Astrid.

"Council meeting tonight," he finished lamely.

Lana called to Patrick, who was sniffing around in the weeds beside the road, and headed toward home.

Astrid caught up to her.

"Lana."

"Yeah?" Lana had never been Astrid's biggest fan. She admired Astrid's smarts and looks. But they were very different people.

"It's Little Pete. He . . ."

"He what?" Lana demanded impatiently.

"He has a fever. I think he has flu or something."

Lana shrugged. "Yeah, one of the Jennifers has it, too. I don't think it's any big deal. Take him to see Dahra, I'll stop by there later."

Lana expected Astrid to nod her head and take off. But Astrid glanced down the road to make sure no one was coming toward them. This got Lana's attention.

"I need you to come to my house," Astrid said firmly.

"Look, I get that you're more important than, you know, normal people," Lana snarked. "But I'll take care of him later. Okay? Bye."

Astrid grabbed her shoulder. Lana turned back, angry now. She didn't like being touched, let alone grabbed.

"It's not about me," Astrid said. "Lana . . . I have to ask you. The gaiaphage . . ."

Lana's face darkened.

"Can it see what you see?" Astrid asked quietly. "Can it know what you know?"

Lana felt a chill. "What is going on, Astrid?"

"Maybe nothing. But come with me. Come see Petey. Help me out, and I will owe you one."

Lana laughed derisively. She was the Healer: everyone owed her one. But she followed Astrid just the same.

CAINE HAD FOUND a telescope in the house. He carried it out to the cliff on the eastern edge of the island. It was afternoon. The light was pretty good, low, slanting rays that lit up the far shore. Sunlight glinted off windows and car windshields in Perdido Beach. Bright red tile roofs and tall palm trees made it seem so normal. As if it really was just another California beach town.

The nuclear power plant was closer. It, too, looked normal. The hole in the containment tower was on the far side, not visible from here. The hole he'd made.

He was startled by the sound behind him but didn't show it. Much.

"What are you looking at, Napoleon?" Diana asked.

"Napoleon?"

"You know, because he was exiled to an island after he almost took over the world," Diana said. "Although he was short. You're much taller."

Caine wasn't sure he minded Diana tweaking him. It was better than the way she'd been lately, all depressed and giving up on life. Hating herself.

He didn't mind if she hated him. They were never going to be a cute romantic couple like Sam and Astrid. Clean-cut, righteous, all that. The perfect couple. He and Diana were the imperfect couple.

"How did it work out for Napoleon?" he asked her.

He caught the slight hesitation as she searched for a glib answer.

"He lived happily ever after on his island," Diana said. "He had a beautiful girlfriend who was far better than he deserved."

"Stop worrying," he said harshly. "I'm not planning on leaving the island. How could I, even if I wanted to?"

"You would find a way," Diana said bleakly.

"Yeah. But here I am anyway," Caine said. He aimed the telescope back at the town. He could see the blackened hulks of burned-out homes just to the west of downtown.

"Don't do it," Diana said.

Caine didn't ask what she meant. He knew.

"Just let it go," Diana said. She put her hand on his shoulder. She caressed the side of his neck, his cheek.

He lowered the telescope and tossed it onto the overgrown sea grass. He turned, took her in his arms, and kissed her.

It had been a long time since he'd done that.

She felt different in his arms. Thinner. Smaller. More frail. But his body responded to her as it always had.

She did not pull away.

His own response surprised him. It had been a long time for that, too. A long time since he'd felt desire. Starving boys lusted after food, not after girls.

And now that it was happening, it was overwhelming. Like a roar in his ears. A pounding in his chest. He ached all the way through.

At the last second, the second when he would have lost the last of his self-control, Diana gently but firmly pushed him away.

"Not here," she said.

"Where?" he gasped. He hated the neediness in his voice. He hated needing anyone or anything that badly. Need was weakness.

She detached his hands from her body. She took one step back. She was wearing an actual dress. A dress, with her legs showing and her shoulders bare and it was like she was a visitor from another planet.

He blinked, thinking maybe it was all a dream. She was clean and wearing a yellow summer dress. Her teeth had been brushed. Her hair was brushed, too, still a mess from cutting it all off and having it grow back while too hungry, but a shadow at least of its former dark, tumbling sensuality.

She bent down demurely and picked up the telescope. She handed it to him.

"Your choice, Caine. You can have me. Or you can try to take over the world. Not both. Because I'm not going to be part of that anymore. I can't. So it's up to you."

His jaw dropped. Literally.

"You witch," he said.

Diana laughed.

"You know I have the power . . . ," he threatened.

"Of course. I would be helpless. But that's not what you want."

Caine spotted a boulder, not far away. Impressively big. He raised one hand, palm out, and with a scraping sound the boulder lifted into the air.

"Sometimes I hate you!" he yelled and with a flick of his wrist sent the boulder flying off the cliff and falling toward the water below.

"Just sometimes?" Diana raised one skeptical brow. "I hate you almost all the time."

They glared at each other with a look that was hate but also something else, something so much more helpless than hatred.

"We're damaged people," Diana said, suddenly sad and serious. "Horrible, messed-up, evil people. But I want to change. I want us both to change."

"Change? To what?" Caine asked, mystified.

"To people who no longer have dreams of being Napoleon."

She was her usual smirking self again as she looked him slowly up and down. Slowly enough that he actually felt embarrassed and had to overcome a modest urge to cover himself. "Don't decide right now," she said. "You're in no condition to think clearly."

And she turned and walked back toward the house.

Caine threw many more large boulders into the sea.

It didn't help.

Sam stood on the street corner watching Lana and Astrid enter the house he had shared with Astrid. Lana was carrying a water jug. Patrick stopped and stared in Sam's direction, but the girls didn't notice him and Patrick quickly lost interest.

He had come to tell Astrid he was going out of town. Astrid would keep the secret. And he wanted at least one person other than Albert to know where he was and what he was doing.

Anyway, that was what he told himself. Because admitting that he still, even now, even after everything that had happened, and everything that hadn't happened, couldn't just walk away from Astrid . . . that would be too big an admission of weakness.

He couldn't not tell her he was leaving. She had to know that he was still . . . whatever he was. He kicked at a crumpled soda can and sent it skittering down the trash-strewn street.

Why was Lana going over to see Astrid? Little Pete must not be feeling well. But how could anyone tell what Little Pete was feeling?

Sam frowned. He didn't want to have some scene with Astrid in front of Lana.

The sky was getting dark. He would be leaving soon. Dekka, Taylor, and Jack would be meeting him across the highway. Each was supposed to keep the whole thing secret.

In reality, of course, Jack would tell Brianna. Taylor would keep it quiet only because she didn't know what was going on, and by the time she did they'd be out of town. Dekka would tell no one. And Sam? He would tell Astrid.

Sam knocked at Astrid's door.

No answer.

Feeling strange and wrong he opened the door to what had until very recently been his own home and went inside.

Astrid and Lana were upstairs; he could hear the murmur of voices.

He took the stairs two at a time and called out, "Astrid, it's me."

They were in Little Pete's room. Astrid and Lana stood a few feet apart with their backs to Sam.

A woman—a grown, adult woman—was sitting on the bed with Little Pete's head in her lap.

"Mom?" Astrid said.

The woman was in her late thirties. She had streaked blond hair and Astrid's translucent pale skin, somewhat aged by sun. Her eyes were brown. She smiled sadly and cradled Little Pete's head. She stroked his hair.

"Mom?" Astrid said again, and this time her voice broke.

The woman did not speak. She did not look up at Astrid. She kept all her attention focused on Little Pete.

"She's not real," Astrid said, and took a step back.

Lana glared at Astrid. Then she noticed Sam, standing there.

Lana's eyes narrowed. "You knew about this, didn't you?" she accused.

"She's not real," Astrid said again. "That's not my mother. That's . . . it's an illusion. He's sick. I was out so . . . so he made her appear. To comfort him."

"He made her appear." Lana practically spit the words. "He made her appear. Because that's something just anyone can do, any of us can just make a three-dimensional real-life mommy appear to cuddle us when we feel bad."

"Stop it, Petey," Astrid said.

The woman—the illusion of a woman—did not react but kept stroking Little Pete's head.

"Cure him, Lana. Cure him and it will stop." Astrid was pleading. "He has a fever. He's coughing."

As if demonstrating, Little Pete coughed several times.

It was weird. He didn't cover his mouth or change his expression. He just coughed.

"Give it a try, Lana," Sam urged. "Please."

Lana rounded on him. "Interesting power for an autistic to have, isn't it?" she demanded. "Especially when you think about all the stories going around about how the dome went clear for a few seconds when Little Pete blacked out."

"There are a lot of mutants," Sam said as blandly as he could.

"Wasn't he at the power plant when the FAYZ came?" Lana asked.

Astrid and Sam exchanged a glance. Neither spoke.

"He was at the plant," Lana said. "The plant is the center of the FAYZ. The very center."

"Please try to heal him," Astrid urged.

"He's got a fever and a cough, big deal," Lana said. "Why is it so urgent that he be healed?"

Again, Sam had no answer.

Lana moved closer. The woman's hand was still on Pete's forehead. But she didn't react when Lana laid her own hand on Little Pete's chest.

"So, that's your mother," Lana said more calmly.

"No," Astrid said.

"Weird seeing an adult, isn't it?"

"It's an illusion," Astrid said weakly. "Little Pete has the power to . . . to make his visions seem real."

"Yeah," Lana said dryly. "That's all it is. The blink, when everyone saw the outside, that was just an illusion. And your mom, here, that's an illusion."

The woman disappeared suddenly. Little Pete's head fell back against his pillow.

"You're helping him," Sam said. "He's getting better."

"You know what's interesting?" Lana said in a mockery of casual chitchat. "The sun and the moon and the stars here are all illusions, too. So many illusions. So many coincidences. So many secrets."

Sam didn't look at Astrid. He wished he hadn't come. More, he wished Astrid hadn't brought Lana here, although he understood it.

After a while Lana stepped back from Little Pete. "I don't know if that fixed him or not."

"Thanks," Astrid said.

"I can feel it, you know," Lana said softly.

"The healing?"

Lana shook her head. "No. It. I can feel it. It touches him. It watches him. I can feel it. It reaches him." Her brow creased and she seemed almost to be wincing in pain. "Just like it reaches me."

Without looking at either of them, Lana rushed from the room.

They stood silent, neither knowing what to say.

"I'm going to be away for a couple of days," Sam said finally. "The water situation . . . I'm going to search out another lake."

A tear spilled down Astrid's cheek.

"That must have been hard," Sam said. "Even knowing it wasn't real."

Astrid used one finger to brush away the tear. "Lana's smart. She'll put it all together." She sighed. "If things get bad they'll come after him. The kids will come after Petey."

"Before I go I'll ask Breeze to keep an eye on you," Sam said.

Astrid stared gloomily at her brother. He coughed twice and then lay quiet. "The thing is, I don't know what would happen."

"If he got sick?"

"If he died. I don't know. I do not know."

PETE

THE DARKNESS WAS watching him, touching him with its wispy tendril, listening for him to speak.

He would not speak. The Darkness could not help him. The Darkness only wanted to play, and it was so jealous when Pete played with anyone else.

Come to me, it said over and over again.

Pete's legs were weak. He stood poised atop the glass but his legs hurt and his feet, too, like the glass sheet was slicing into him.

He had felt better when his mother was there. She was quiet, the way he liked. She had not tried to touch him except to let him lie there against her breast and feel the soft rise and fall of her breathing.

But then the breathing had begun to wear on him, making him distracted. If it didn't stop . . .

But then it did stop when he made her go away. He could remember the good part, before the sound of breathing got to be too much, and not have to hear it anymore.

Loud sister was talking and then another. The other touched him with her hand. He looked at her and was puzzled. A faint green tendril spiraled up to touch her. She seemed to be on both sides of the glass at once.

He felt her touch and it made him tense. He endured it, but inside he was feeling worse and worse.

Hot. Like fire was inside him.

He didn't want to hear any more from his body.

The other left. She took her hand away and left. But he could feel an echo of her inside him. She had touched the Darkness, but she refused its pleas to come and play.

He wondered . . . but now his body was drawing his attention again. Hot and cold, hungry and thirsty.

It bothered him.

EIGHT

54 HOURS, 21 MINUTES

"**KILL IT!** KILL me!"

It was muffled, but you could still hear it. They'd closed the air-conditioning vents—wasn't like there was air-conditioning anymore—but still the desperate wail came up from the basement.

Howard was out at some kind of stupid meeting. Some big deal. Howard always had big deals.

Charles Merriman, who everyone called Orc, rummaged in the mess beside his couch. There had to be something left in one of these bottles. He didn't want to have to go into the back room closet and get another bottle.

"It's the only way. Sam! Sam! Tell Sam to do it!"

Orc wasn't drunk. Not drunk enough to ignore the sound of that stupid girl's voice. That took a pretty good drunk and right now he was only drunk enough that he didn't want to get up off the couch.

His stony fingers lifted a bottle. Wild Turkey. Only about

half an inch of brown liquid left in the bottom. He twisted the cork. The glass neck of the bottle shattered in his grip. That happened fairly often. Orc had a hard time gauging his strength when he was a little drunk.

He blew slivers of glass away. He raised the bottle high, careful to keep the sharp points away from his still-human mouth.

The one part of him that could be cut: his mouth.

Well, his mouth and his eyes.

He drained the fiery liquid into his mouth and swallowed. Oh, yeah. Yeah. But not enough.

Orc levered himself up. He was heavy, like you'd expect of a boy made of wet gravel. Like a walking creature of wet cement. He couldn't fit on a scale although Howard had tried once to weigh him.

He had crushed the scales.

He stomped toward the booze closet where Howard kept his stash. With the exaggerated care of a person not in control of his body, Orc opened the closet door.

A few bottles of clear booze. A few bottles of brown booze. A couple bottles of Cabka, the liquor Howard made by distilling cabbage and rotten oranges. It was nasty stuff. Orc preferred the brown booze.

He snagged a bottle and after a few seconds of clumsy fumbling he gave up and twisted the glass neck off.

"Is that you up there, Orc? I hear you stomping around." Drake. The girl Brittney was gone now, replaced by Drake.

"You still alive, you stupid, alcoholic pile of rock?" Drake taunted. "Still following Sam's orders? Doing what you're told, Orc?"

Orc stomped angrily on the floor. "Shut up or I'll come down there and smash you like a bug!" Orc roared.

Drake laughed. "Sure you will, Orc. You don't have the stones. Wait, that was a funny! The stone monster who doesn't have any stones."

Orc stomped again. The entire house shook when he did it.

Drake called him various names, but now Orc had about a quarter of the bottle inside him. The warmth spread throughout his body.

He yelled something equally rude back at Drake. Then he staggered back to his couch and sagged heavily into it.

He didn't mind Drake so much. Drake was a creep.

It was the girl who made Orc want to cry.

She was a monster. Like Orc. Begging for death. Begging for someone to let her go to her Jesus.

Kill me, kill me, kill me, she begged every day and every night.

Orc took a deep swig.

Tears seeped from his human eyes and fell into the rocky crevices of his face.

Someone was knocking at the front door. Normally Howard would answer. But then Orc heard Jamal's voice yelling, "Hey, Orc! Open up, man."

Jamal was one of the very few people besides Howard who ever came to see Orc. Of course it was just so he could get a drink. But still, any company was better than listening to Drake or Brittney.

"Want a drink, Jamal?"

"You know it," Jamal said. "Albert's busting on me all day."

"Yeah," Orc said. He didn't care. He snagged a bottle and handed it to Jamal, who took a deep swig.

Orc flopped onto his mattresses, the floor groaning beneath him. Jamal took a chair and kept the bottle.

"Who is that up there?" Drake's voice floated up. "Is that Jamal or Turk? Too heavy to be Howard."

"It's Jamal," Jamal yelled.

"Don't talk to him," Orc said, but without much conviction.

"Hey, Jamal, how about letting me out of here?" Drake asked, almost playful.

Orc yelled something obscene back at him.

"Only if you kill Albert first," Jamal shouted, then laughed and took another drink.

"How come you work for Albert if you hate him?" Orc asked.

Jamal shrugged. "I'm tough, he needs someone tough."

"Yeah," Orc said.

"But he treats me like crap."

"Yeah?"

"Should see how he's living, man. You think he's living like the rest of us? Get this: at night he doesn't even go out to take a leak. He's got, like, a jar he pees in."

"I got a jar I pee in."

"Yeah, well, he's got a maid to take it out and dump it for him."

Orc's head was buzzing, not really paying attention, but Jamal was getting fired up, listing complaints about Albert, starting with the fact that Albert had meat every day and kids to clean up after him.

"See, man, he loves it like this, right?" Jamal said, already slurring his words. "Back in the world Albert was just some shrimpy little nothing. In here he's a big man and I'm, like, his, you know . . ."

"Servant," Orc supplied.

Jamal's eyes flared angrily. "Yeah. Yeah. Like you, Orc, you're Sam's servant."

"I ain't anyone's servant."

"You're babysitting Drake all day and night, man, what is it you think you are? You're doing what the Sam Boss tells you."

Orc didn't have a ready answer. He wished Howard was home because Howard was smarter at talking.

Jamal pushed it. "Guys like you and me and Turk and Drake, right? We used to be in charge. Because we were tough and we weren't afraid and didn't take anyone's crap, right?"

Orc shrugged. He was feeling very uncomfortable. "Where's Howard?" he muttered.

Jamal made a rude noise. "Howard's not the one stuck being a jailer, you are, Orc. Sam's prison guard. Keeps you busy, right, and trapped here all the time. So it's like Turk said."

"What'd Turk say?"

"Said Sam got you and Drake locked up at the same time."

"It's not like that."

Jamal laughed derisively. "Man, all you have to do is see who is top dog and who is bottom dog. See, that's where Zil was wrong: it's not about moofs and normals, freaks and non-freaks, it's about top dog, bottom dog. You and me, Orc, we're bottom dogs. Should be top dogs."

Just then Brittney's voice came up from below. "Is Sam there? Get Sam! You have to call Sam!"

Orc levered himself up off his bed and yelled, "Hey shut up. I already gotta listen to Drake all day and night."

He swayed, tried to catch himself and couldn't. He slipped and fell back on his rear. Jamal exploded in derisive laughter.

This time Orc leaped to his feet. "Stop laughing!"

"Orc, get Sam!"

"It was funny, man," Jamal said through his own braying laughter.

"Orc, Drake is trying—"

Orc cursed loudly. He stomped on the floor. "Shut up, shut up!"

And suddenly, with a rending, ripping sound, the floor beneath Orc gave way.

He fell through wood and plaster. He landed hard and lay flat on his back, winded. Splinters and dust settled on him.

He blinked, too stunned to make sense of what had just happened. His first thought was that Howard would be pissed. His second thought was that Sam would be even more pissed.

Brittney was standing over him, looking down at him.

Flat on his back. Drunk and foolish. A monster. And from above came Jamal's donkey laughter.

Orc reached to touch the skin that still stretched over a part of his face. He was bleeding. Not bad, not a lot, but bleeding.

In blind rage Orc got to his feet. He punched Brittney with all his strength. The girl went flying into the wall. Her head snapped against cinderblock, a hit that would have killed any real, living girl.

But Brittney couldn't die.

Which was the final straw. Something in Orc's brain snapped. He leaped, trying to grab the floor above and pull himself through, but he slipped and fell again and Jamal was pointing and laughing and Orc ran for the door, the barricaded door that had kept the Drake/Brittney thing locked up. He body-slammed the door. It held, but barely. He reared back and kicked and kicked and splinters flew.

"No! No!" Brittney screamed. "He'll escape!"

Orc stepped back, raised both his gravel-skinned arms and ran straight at the door.

It didn't fly open, it simply came apart. The frame shattered and splintered. The door itself split. And Orc tore through.

"Want to laugh at me?" he roared as he pounded up the stairs and emerged in the kitchen.

Jamal was still standing next to the hole, laughing.

"You wanna laugh?" Orc roared.

Jamal spun around, realizing too late the danger he was in. Orc was over six feet tall and almost as wide as he was tall.

His legs were like tree trunks, his arms like bridge cable.

Jamal fumbled for his gun, but Orc wasn't having any of that. He grabbed Jamal by the neck, lifted him off the floor, and threw him down the hole.

Jamal hit hard. The gun flew, scraping across the floor.

Orc was panting, sweating, heart pounding in his chest. Now reality was starting to penetrate the alcohol-fueled rage and he saw what he had done.

Howard. He should . . . Or Sam . . . Someone, he should tell someone, get someone . . .

It was all over now for Charles Merriman. He had redeemed himself, he had been given something important to do. But now all that was gone. And he was just Orc again.

He wanted to cry. He couldn't face it. He couldn't face Howard's disappointment and pity. Sam's cold anger.

Down in the dark basement a long, reddish tentacle reached for the gun.

Orc turned and ran.

Sanjit Brattle-Chance had not enjoyed his first week in Perdido Beach. Virtue Brattle-Chance had enjoyed it even less.

"It's like a giant lunatic asylum," Virtue said.

"Yeah. It is, kind of," Sanjit said. They had spent the afternoon inspecting the helicopter. Edilio had assigned them the job of reporting back on whether it was totally broken or just mostly broken.

So far it was looking totally broken. Both skids—the ski-like things it landed on—were crumpled. Part of the glass bubble canopy was shattered, just gone, and the rest of it was starred and cracked.

Night had fallen and that was the end of inspecting anything. Virtue had wanted to go straight home. Sanjit had stalled.

"Let's just hang out and talk, Choo," Sanjit said. "I mean, look, we've had all this stress, right? But now Bowie's getting well—"

Virtue made a rude noise. "If you believe that so-called Healer."

"I believe her completely," Sanjit said.

The girl named Lana had come and laid her hand on Bowie. She'd barely spoken, had replied to polite inquiries with single-syllable answers or grunts. Or annoyed silence.

But Sanjit had been fascinated. He'd thought about little else ever since. After all, how could he not be attracted to a girl who could heal with a touch and yet walked around with a massive automatic pistol stuck in her belt?

His kind of girl.

He had learned that she lived up here at Clifftop. In fact Edilio had carefully and repeatedly warned Sanjit not to irritate her while he was checking out the helicopter.

His exact words had been, "For God's sake, don't get in Lana's way."

To which Sanjit had said, "Is she dangerous?"

Edilio had given him a strange look. "Well, she shot me once. But it was under the influence of the Darkness. Which she had tried to kill all by herself with a truckload of gas. And

then she healed me. So I don't know if that makes her dangerous. But if it was me, I would definitely not make her mad."

So Sanjit and Virtue sat on the grass and watched the sun
go down and the stars appear. And Sanjit secretly watched
the hotel.

"Did you hear about the talking coyotes?" Virtue
demanded. Like if there were such a thing, it was Sanjit's
fault.

"Yeah. Creepy, huh?"

"And the thing they call the Darkness?" Virtue shook his
head dolefully. He'd always been gloomy. The cloud to Sanjit's sunshine, the pessimist to Sanjit's optimist. They were
adopted brothers, from Congo and Thailand, respectively.
From a desperate refugee camp, and from the tough streets
of Bangkok.

"Yeah. I wonder what it is?"

"The gaiaphage. That's the other word they use. 'Gaia,' as
in world. 'Phage,' as in a worm or something that eats something up. I'm going to go way out on a limb here and say I
don't think something that calls itself a 'world eater' is a good
thing."

"No?" Sanjit made an innocent face, deliberately provok-
ing his brother.

"Fine." Virtue pouted. "But have you seen the graveyard
they put in the plaza? There's, like, two dozen graves there."

Sanjit twisted around to look back at the helicopter. It had
saved them. It seemed a shame just to let it lie there dead. "I'd
need some big wrenches. A ladder. Hammer. And then, you

know, someone who actually knew what to do with all of it."

"Fine, you don't really want to talk."

They had landed the helicopter—well, crashed it, anyway—behind Clifftop hotel. In some scruffy trees and bushes just past the parking area.

The barrier was close at hand. So even if the helicopter could ever be flown—and Sanjit couldn't imagine what the point would be—it would take a lot of luck not just to fly it straight into the barrier.

The barrier was a trickster. At ground level it was opaque, while suggesting translucence.

Higher up it was sky. But when you were up there it wasn't like you could see beyond the barrier. If you tried, the barrier was just opaque again.

Tricky tricky. Like a street magician's sleight of hand, Sanjit thought.

He realized Virtue was talking again.

" . . . once Bowie's completely better. Maybe Caine isn't totally unreasonable. I mean, he was starving before and that would make anyone unreasonable."

"Choo," Sanjit said. "Caine is pure, distilled essence of evil. What are you even talking about?"

"Okay, even if he's evil, maybe we can work out some kind of deal."

"You don't even believe that," Sanjit said.

Virtue slumped back, deflated. "Yeah."

"We are not going back to the island, my brother. We've been voted off. This is our home now."

Virtue nodded. He looked like a kid who had just gotten the news that he would be shot at dawn.

"Cheer up, Choo," Sanjit said. "There are a lot of good things about this place."

"You heard about the zombie, right? The one they've got locked in a basement? Half the time it's this nice Christian girl. And the rest of the time it's a psychopath with a whip for an arm?"

Sanjit made a thoughtful face. "I do believe I heard something about that. But really, Choo, it's not like a basement-dwelling Dr. Jekyll and Mr. Hyde zombie is all that unusual."

Despite himself Virtue very nearly smiled. "Fine. Be that way, Wisdom."

"Don't use my slave name." It was an old joke between them. Sanjit had been born Sanjit, a homeless Hindu street kid in Buddhist Bangkok. When the actors Jennifer Brattle and Todd Chance had adopted him, they'd given him an aspirational name: Wisdom.

It never had fit. Wisdom meant . . . well, wisdom.

"You're not looking at the bright side, Choo," Sanjit said. He had in fact just spotted the bright side.

"Bright side? There's no bright side. What bright side?"

"Girls, Choo," Sanjit said, smiling hugely. "You'll understand in a few years."

Lana had come around the back of the hotel and was throwing a tennis ball to her dog. They were outlined against the faint glow of western horizon, and illuminated by the light of the moon just coming from behind the hills.

"I'm going to refuse to do puberty," Virtue grumbled. "It makes you stupid."

Sanjit barely heard him. He was walking toward Lana.

"Hi."

"What are you doing here?" Lana snapped. "No one comes to Clifftop without me saying so."

Sanjit said, "You missed a beautiful sunset."

"It's an illusion," Lana said. "It's not the real sun. None of it's real. The moon, the stars, all of it."

"Still beautiful, though."

"Fake."

"But beautiful."

Lana glared at him. And Sanjit had to admit: the girl could glare. The pistol in her waistband definitely added to the tough-girl look. But more it was that hurt-but-defiant expression.

"So asking you to take a moonlit walk with me, that would totally not work?"

"What?" Again that glare. "Go away. Stop being an idiot. I don't even know you."

"You're healing my little brother Bowie."

"Yeah, that doesn't make us friends, kid."

"So no moonlight."

"Are you retarded?"

"Sunrise? I could get up early."

"Go away."

"Sunset tomorrow?"

"Just what is your problem, kid? Do you know who I am? No one messes with me."

"Do you know my name?"

"Which part of 'go away' do you not get? I could shoot you and no one would even say anything."

"It's Sanjit. It's a Hindu name."

"One word to Orc and he'd play basketball with your head."

"It means 'invincible.'"

"That's great," Lana said.

"Invincible. I can't be vinced."

"That's not even a word," Lana said. Then she ground her teeth, obviously annoyed with herself for having been baited.

"Go ahead: try to vince me," Sanjit said.

Just then Patrick came rushing over. He dropped the ball at Sanjit's feet, grinned his delirious dog grin, and waited.

"Don't play with my dog," Lana said.

Sanjit snatched up the ball and threw it. Patrick went tearing after it.

"You don't scare me," Sanjit said. He held up a hand, cutting Lana off before she could answer. "I'm not saying I shouldn't be scared. I've heard some of the stories about you. About what happened. You went up against this gaiaphage thing all by yourself. Which means you are the second bravest girl I ever met. So I probably should be scared. I'm just not."

He watched her struggle to resist asking. She lost. "Second bravest?"

"I'll tell you the story when we go for that walk," Sanjit said. He jerked a thumb toward the helicopter. "I better get back to town. Edilio wants a report from me."

He turned and walked away.

NINE

SAM FOUND HIS little crew where they were supposed to be.

Dekka was almost smiling. Almost smiling was giddy for Dekka.

Taylor was checking her fingernails, being elaborately bored. Sam wondered if he should say something about the kiss. Something like, "I'm really sorry I groped you."

Yeah: that would be really helpful.

Better to pretend it all never happened. Unfortunately Taylor was not known for letting things just drop.

Furthermore, she irritated Dekka. Dekka was Sam's friend and his ally. The three people Sam knew he could always count on were Edilio, Brianna, and Dekka. Strange, because it wasn't like they hung out together. Sam spent his time alone or with Astrid. He barely saw Edilio lately. He had nothing at all in common with Brianna—she was too young, too crazy, too . . . too Brianna to be someone Sam would hang with.

Quinn had been his best friend back before. But Quinn had a big job, a job he loved. Quinn's friends were all his fishing crews. They were as tight as a very close family, the fishermen.

The fourth member of the expedition was Jack. Formerly Computer Jack—there were no longer any functioning computers around. Jack was wasting his days reading comic books and pouting.

Jack's superhuman strength might come in handy, but Jack had never been much use. Although, Sam noted thoughtfully, Jack had stepped up during the big fire. Maybe he was growing up a bit. Maybe getting his head out of a computer was actually a good thing.

"You guys up for this?" Sam asked.

"Do I have to go?" Jack whined.

Sam shrugged. "Albert's paying you, right? It's better than playing strong man for him all day, isn't it?"

Jack's eyes flashed. Albert had started using Jack's physical strength—to carry loads to the market, to move furniture—and Jack resented it. In Jack's mind he was still the tech genius, the supergeek, not the freak strong man.

"Why do we have to do this in the middle of the night?" Taylor asked.

"Because we don't want the whole town knowing why we're going and where we're going."

"How can I tell anyone if I don't even know myself?" Taylor stuck out her lower lip.

"Water. We're going to look for water," Sam said.

He could almost hear the wheels in Taylor's head spinning. Then, "OMG, we're out of water?" She bit her lip, took a couple of dramatic breaths, and wailed, "Do you mean we're all going to die?"

"That would be a pretty good example of why we're keeping this secret," Sam said dryly.

"I just need to go—"

"Uh-uh!" Sam said. "No you don't, Taylor. You don't bounce anywhere or talk to anyone without me agreeing. Are we clear?"

"You know, Sam, you're nice. And so very, very hot," Taylor said. "But you're not really much fun."

"Let's get out of here while we can," Dekka said. "I brought a gun, by the way."

"Are we going to be in danger?" Taylor cried.

"The gun's in case you get on my nerves, Taylor," Dekka warned.

"Oh, so funny," Taylor said.

Sam grinned. For the first time in a while he was actually looking forward to something. A mission. And at least a temporary escape from Perdido Beach.

"Dekka's right. Let's get out of here before something happens I have to deal with," Sam said.

Just at that moment he heard a sound like something large breaking. It was some distance away. A noise like twigs snapping. Probably some drunk idiot.

Sam chose to ignore it. Edilio's worry, not his.

He headed toward the dark hills above town.

After a while Dekka took Sam's arm and slowed him down. She let Jack and Taylor move out in front.

"Did Edilio or Astrid tell you?"

"I haven't talked to Edilio. I steered clear. He's going to be mightily annoyed with me when he realizes I skipped town and didn't even tell him."

Dekka waited.

"Okay," Sam said with a sigh. "Tell me what?"

"It's Hunter. He's got some kind of . . . Well, it's like these bugs all inside him. Astrid says they're parasites."

"Astrid says?" Sam snapped.

"So I guess you did see her before you left. And she didn't tell you?"

"We had other things going on."

"Oh?"

"No," Sam said. "Not like that. Unfortunately. Tell me about Hunter."

Dekka told him.

Sam's face grew darker as he listened. So much for getting out of town before anything went wrong. This had "wrong" written all over it.

It sounded as if Hunter wasn't going to be hunting much longer. Which meant the town would be running out of meat as well as water. They could probably survive without Hunter's kills, but it sure would increase the sense of panic.

This mission had just gotten more important, not less.

"He said the greenies are on the morning side? Off the lake road? That's what he said?"

Dekka nodded.

Sam called up to the other two who were arguing over something stupid. "Taylor! Jack! Veer right up there. We're stopping off to see Hunter."

Hunter woke suddenly. A noise.

It was a noise unlike anything he'd ever heard before. Close! Very close.

Like it was on him. Like it was . . .

Just in one ear.

He twisted his head. It was full night. Black as black in the woods far from the starlight.

He couldn't see anything.

But with his hands he could feel. The thing on his shoulder.

His ear . . . gone!

A terrible fear wrung a cry of horror from Hunter.

He couldn't feel it, his ear, or his shoulder, couldn't feel with anything but his fingers and he felt, reached beneath his shirt, felt the flesh of his belly pulse and heave.

Like something inside him.

No, no, no, it wasn't fair. It wasn't fair!

He was Hunter. The hunter. He was doing his best.

He cried. Tears rolled down his cheeks.

Who would bring meat for all the kids?

It wasn't fair.

The sound of munching, crunching started again. Just in one ear.

Hunter had only one weapon: the heat-causing power in

his hands. He had used it many, many times to take the life of prey.

He had fed the kids with that power. And in a moment of fear and rage he had accidentally taken the life of his friend, Harry.

Maybe he could kill the thing that was eating his ear.

But it was too late for that to help.

Could he kill himself?

He saw Old Lion's head, eyes closed, hanging where he'd hung him for skinning. If Old Lion could die, so could Hunter.

Maybe they would meet again, up in the sky.

Hunter pressed both palms against his head.

Drake was free! Before him the shattered door. Above him a collapsed ceiling. His jail cell had been torn apart by his own jailer.

Now Drake was worried. At any minute the Brittney Pig might emerge. She could call for help, run to Sam, something, anything.

Drake had Jamal's gun. He ran his whip hand over it, loving the feel of it, loving the weight of it in his hand. With this gun and his whip he was unstoppable.

Except that he wasn't just himself, he was Brittney, too.

His mind raced feverishly. What could he do?

Jamal groaned. He started to get up but leaned on an arm that gave way with a sickening crunch.

Jamal shrieked in pain. His left arm hung limp, the shoulder dislocated. There was blood running freely from his nose.

Blood seeping out of his ears. Oh yeah, Drake thought, the boy had taken a hard fall.

Drake straddled Jamal. He wrapped his whip arm around Jamal's throat, cutting off his cries of pain. He pressed the gun barrel against Jamal's forehead.

"You have three seconds to make a decision," Drake said, his voice silky. "Are you with me or against me?"

It didn't take Jamal three seconds. "I'll help you, I'll help you!" he blurted as soon as Drake relaxed the pressure on his throat.

"Yeah? Well, listen good, jerkwad, because I don't give second chances. Mess with me, disobey me, even hesitate, and I won't kill you."

Jamal's brow creased in confusion.

"No, see, death, that's the end of pain," Drake said. "No, no killing. But I will whip you."

With sudden gleeful ferocity Drake reared back and struck with his whip hand. It cut through Jamal's pants and cut a stripe on his thigh.

Jamal bellowed.

Drake struck again, twice more while Jamal writhed and tried to cover himself with his one good arm.

"I wanted you to know what it will feel like," Drake said. "Hurts, doesn't it?"

Jamal was crying now, crying and too terrified to answer.

"I said: it hurts, doesn't it?"

"Yes! Yes!" Jamal sobbed.

"No matter what you do, Jamal, no matter how smart or

how tough you think you are, if you betray me, if you even look like you might betray me, I'll whip you. And I'll make it last. For hours. And I'll leave you where the Healer can't find you. Do you believe I'll do that, Jamal?"

Jamal nodded frantically. "Yes! I believe it!"

"I can't be killed, Jamal," Drake said.

"I know!"

Drake handed him the gun. He watched closely to see whether Jamal truly did understand. He could see the moment when Jamal thought, "I can shoot him and run away."

But he also saw the wheels spin in Jamal's head as the boy worked it through to the inevitable conclusion.

He saw Jamal's resistance evaporate.

"Smart boy," Drake said. "Now, here's what you do."

TEN

"**WHY DID WE** have to sneak out of town in the nighttime?" Jack grumbled. "I'm tripping over everything."

Jack, Sam, Dekka, and Taylor were across the highway, past the gas station, and climbing uphill. Moonlight touched the tall, dry grass with silver. But it didn't reveal the smaller rocks that poked up through the dust-dry ground and stubbed toes or tripped you so you landed on your hands and knees and looked like an idiot.

Jack was not interested in going on some long, dangerous walk. Especially at night. Or in the daytime, for that matter. What he wanted to do was just lie in his bed. Just lie in his bed and read.

He had a pile of books. They were the only thing to do. No internet. No computers. Not even electricity.

Of course that was his fault. His fault for being tricked by Caine and especially that witch, Diana.

He had a hard time saying no to girls. Especially Brianna,

who seemed to be able to get him to do anything she wanted.

Brianna kind of lived with him. They were kind of going together, he guessed. Although they didn't actually do anything. Like make out or anything. That didn't happen.

Jack had thought seriously about asking Brianna if she would make out with him. She was cute. He liked her. He guessed she liked him. They had taken care of each other when the flu was going around.

But . . . It occurred to Jack that Sam had not answered.

"Why are we sneaking out in the night?" Jack repeated.

"I already explained," Sam snapped. "If you don't listen—"

Taylor jumped in to say, "Because otherwise Astrid would find some way to stop him." She mimicked Astrid's voice, injecting it with steel and a tense, condescending tone. "Sam. I am the smartest, hottest girl in the world. So do what I tell you. Good boy. Down, boy. Down!"

Sam remained silent, walking steadily just a few feet ahead.

Taylor continued, "Oh, Sam, if only you could be as smart plus as totally goody-goody as I am. If only you could realize that you will never be good enough to have me, me, wonderful me, Astrid the Blond Genius."

"Sam, can I shoot her now?" Dekka asked. "Or is it too soon?"

"Wait until we're over the ridge," Sam said. "It'll muffle the sound."

"Sorry, Dekka," Taylor said. "I know you don't like talking about boy-girl things."

"Taylor," Sam warned.

"Yes, Sam?"

"You might want to think about how hard it would be to walk if someone were to turn off gravity under your feet every now and then."

"I wonder who would do that?" Dekka said.

Suddenly Taylor fell flat on her face.

"You tripped me!" Taylor said, more shocked than angry.

"Me?" Dekka spread her hands in a completely unconvincing gesture of innocence. "Hey, I'm all the way over here."

"I'm just saying: you can see where that could make a long walk just a lot longer," Sam said.

"You guys are so not fun," Taylor grumped. She bounced instantaneously to just behind Sam. She grabbed his butt, he yelled, "Hey!" and she bounced away innocently.

"To answer your question, Jack," Sam said, "we are sneaking out at night so that everyone doesn't know we're gone and why. They'll figure it out soon enough, but Edilio will have to have more of his guys on the streets if I'm not there playing the big, bad wolf. More stress for everyone."

"Oh," Jack said.

"The big, bad wolf," Taylor said. She laughed. "So, when you play that fantasy in your head is Astrid Little Red Riding Hood or one of the Three Little Pigs?"

"Dekka," Sam said.

"Hah! Too slow!" Taylor said. She was suddenly twenty feet away and behind Dekka.

They had reached the ridge. The trees started in the valley beyond and spread up the next hill. The small valley tended to capture damp breezes off the ocean—back when there were breezes. And a small stream—now almost dry since it was cut off from the high, snow-capped peaks beyond the barrier—ran along the floor of the valley.

"Try not to make too much noise, huh, guys? Hunter may be out hunting. We don't want to stomp around and scare off his prey."

"So no more falling on your face, Jack," Taylor teased.

A sound, a wail, rose from the trees downhill.

"What was that?" Jack asked.

It came again. A cry of utter despair.

Jack expected Sam to take off running. Instead he took a deep breath and in a low voice said, "I don't think you guys need to see this."

"See what?" Taylor asked.

Sam set off downhill. He didn't ask them to come with him. But he didn't order them not to. So they followed.

Once in the pitch-blackness under the trees Sam used his powers to turn one hand into a sort of dull, glowing green light. It made it easier to see the trees, but it turned everything into a nightmare scene.

"Hunter?" Sam called out.

"Don't come here!" Hunter's voice, wracked with sadness, was closer than Jack expected.

They followed the sound of his voice. Closer, and now they could hear him crying. It wasn't a big kid's cry, it was like a toddler's. Big, heaving sobs.

Again Sam said, "Guys, stay back. You don't have to see this."

But again they ignored him. Not Jack at first but Dekka, who went because she was brave and wanted to help, even though she guessed what she would find; Taylor because she was curious and wanted to see; Jack because he didn't want to be left behind alone in total darkness.

Hunter was sitting up. He was in the middle of a neat camp: glowing embers from a dying fire, a small tent, a makeshift shelf of sticks and vines where Hunter had a pan and a pot and a plate. A mountain lion hung from a rope looped over a high branch.

Hunter's entire body writhed and squirmed.

The side of his head was partly gone. A creature, like some monstrous melding of insect and eel, protruded from Hunter's shoulder and as they stood there rooted in horror it took a vicious bite of Hunter's flesh.

Taylor was suddenly gone.

Dekka's face was grim, her eyes wet.

"I tried . . . ," Hunter said. He held up his hands, mimicked pressing them against his head. "It didn't work."

"I can do it," Sam said softly.

"I'm scared," Hunter said.

"I know."

"It's 'cause I killed Harry. God has to punish me. I tried to be good but I'm bad."

"No, Hunter," Sam said gently. "You paid your dues. You

fed the kids. You're a good guy."

"I'm a good hunter."

"The best."

"I don't know what's happening. What's happening, Sam?"

"It's just the FAYZ, Hunter," Sam said.

"Can the angels find me here so I can go to heaven?"

Sam didn't answer. It was Dekka who spoke. "Do you still remember any prayers, Hunter?"

The insectlike creature was almost completely emerged from Hunter's shoulder. Legs were becoming visible. It had wings folded against its body. It looked like a gigantic ant, or wasp, but silver and brass and covered with a sheen of slime.

It was emerging like a chicken breaking out of an egg. Being born. And as the creature was born, it fed on Hunter's numbed body.

Jerky movements beneath Hunter's shirt testified to more of the larvae emerging.

"Do you remember 'now I lay me down to sleep'?" Dekka asked.

"Now I lay me down to sleep," Hunter said. "I pray the Lord my soul to keep."

Sam raised his hands, palms out.

"If I should die—"

Twin beams of light hit Hunter's chest and face. His shirt caught fire. Flesh melted. He was dead before he could feel anything.

Sam played the light up and down Hunter's body. The

smell was sickening. Jack wanted to look away, but how could he?

Sudden darkness as Sam terminated the light.

Sam lowered his hands to his side.

They stood there in the darkness. Jack breathed through his mouth, trying not to smell the burned flesh.

Then they heard a sound. Many sounds.

Sam raised his hands and pale light glowed.

Hunter was all but gone.

The things that had been inside him were still there.

His knock at her door was soft. Diana almost didn't hear it.

She took a shaky breath. He had come. She'd figured he would.

"Who is it?" Diana asked.

"Sam," Caine said.

Diana opened the door. He was leaning against the frame. His body language and expression were not those of someone who was happy.

"Funny," Diana said.

Caine pushed past her into the room. "Close the door and lock it," Caine ordered. "Bug: if you're in here and I catch you I will kill you. You have till I count to ten to get out."

Caine and Diana both waited and watched the door. It did not open.

"I don't think he's here," Diana said. "I can usually smell him."

They stood awkwardly apart. Like strangers. Diana noticed

that Caine had bathed and combed his hair. He was usually as well put-together as circumstances would allow. But this was a special effort.

Diana had decided against any special outfit. It wasn't about lingerie or whatever. She was dressed in jeans and a blouse. Barefoot. She had avoided makeup.

"You want me to be Sam," Caine said. "I'm not Sam. I'm me."

"I don't want you to be Sam," Diana said.

"You don't want me to be me," Caine said.

Diana considered him. Handsome, no question. Cruel. Intelligent.

"There's more than one you, Caine," Diana said.

He blinked. "What's that mean?"

"You're not Drake."

Caine waved off the suggestion and his face registered disgust. "Drake's a sick creep. I just do what I have to do. I don't get off on it. He's a psycho. I'm . . ." He searched for the right word. ". . . ambitious."

Diana laughed. Not a derisive laugh, a genuine laugh of astonishment.

"What? I *am* ambitious," Caine said.

"That's one word for it," Diana said. "Power hungry. Domineering. A bully."

"I'm not good at taking orders," Caine said.

Diana grinned. "No. You're not."

They both fell silent. Diana looked at him. He looked down at the floor.

"But you did take orders. From the Darkness, Caine."

Caine flushed angrily. He turned away. He walked quickly back to the door. But he stopped before touching the handle.

"The lights are off in Perdido Beach because you took orders," Diana said.

"Who was it that buried that thing in its mine shaft?" Caine demanded, his voice ragged.

"You."

"Yeah," Caine said. "And saved Sam in the process."

"Yes. And soon after that we became cannibals."

"We have food now," Caine said. "Lots of food."

He walked back to Diana, reached to touch her, but this time she walked away. She stood at the window. The false moon was setting. It dabbed the distant hilltops with silver.

"It was too much," Diana said, almost to herself. "Everything else I could kind of accept. The violence. The battles. What we did to Andrew and what you did to Chunk. And all the rest. I mean, it all sort of left a bruise on me, you know?"

Caine did not answer.

"Inside. In my heart. In my soul." She laughed at herself. "Diana Ladris's soul. Right."

"It was a low point," Caine admitted.

"You think?" Diana snapped, looking over her shoulder at him with a trace of her usual mockery. "Eating human flesh, that was a low point?"

"We had no—"

"Oh, shut up," Diana said. She turned away from the window. There were tears in her eyes and she hadn't wanted him to see. The last thing she wanted was to seem weak.

But he did see now. The shock on his face almost made her laugh again.

"All my life I've been a tough girl," Diana said. "I was cool with that. People would say, *Diana's a bitch. Diana's a slut. Diana's mean.* All that I could deal with because I guess it was basically true. Now they're going to look at me and say, *Diana's a cannibal?* How do I live with that?" She was shouting suddenly.

"Who are these people you're worried about? Penny? Bug?"

"What if we get out? People! People!" She hesitated. "And God." She lowered her voice to a whisper. "And my kids. Someday."

"Kids?" Caine's look of confusion and consternation finally did force a laugh from Diana.

"Yes. Someday. Could happen. That's right: the day may come when I have a baby. Maybe even more than one."

Caine said, "Um . . ." He made a vague gesture with his hands. He made several attempts to say something. None were successful.

"Do you love me?" Diana asked.

Caine's eyes widened. She could actually see him twitch. Like a startled animal. Like a rabbit who had just heard a fox.

"It's a yes or no question," Diana said acidly. "But I'll accept a nod or a shake of the head or an incoherent grunt."

"I . . . I don't know what you mean by that," Caine said lamely.

"When I jumped off the cliff, you saved me even though it meant letting Sanjit and the others escape."

"You didn't give me much choice," Caine said peevishly.

"You had a choice. You wanted to destroy them."

"Okay."

"Why did you make that choice?"

Caine swallowed and seemed to find his palms sweaty since he rubbed them on his sides.

Diana walked to the door. She unlocked it and held it open. "Go away," she said. "Come back when you figure out your answer."

"But . . ."

"Yeah: not happening. Not tonight."

Caine escaped into the hallway.

Diana undressed and crawled under the sheets. Then she beat the pillows with her fists until feathers flew.

ELEVEN

"EDILIO. WAKE UP!"

Edilio blinked. Rubbed his eyes. Saw Brianna standing there next to his bed.

"What?" he mumbled.

"Albert told me to get you," Brianna said.

Brianna always looked determined, pugnacious, and tough. Just sitting around, she looked all of those things. But now she was armed for battle.

She had a small runner's backpack converted to a sort of holster. She'd cut a hole in the bottom so the barrel of a sawed-off shotgun could stick through. The stock was just where she could reach over her shoulder and grab it.

She had a long knife, a bowie knife, in a scabbard hanging from a camouflage belt. The scabbard was tied to her leg so it wouldn't flap when she ran. A dozen red plastic shotgun shells rode snugly in slots on the belt.

A summons in the middle of the night was bad. A

summons in the middle of the night from a heavily armed Brianna was worse.

Much worse.

"What happened?"

"Drake," Brianna said. Then she grinned. Because that was Brianna.

Edilio sat up. "Okay. You got Sam?"

"Can't find Sam," Brianna said.

Edilio felt an overpowering desire to go back to sleep. Drake on the loose? And no Sam? "Where's Albert?"

"He said he'd meet you at town hall," Brianna said. "He's rounding up the others. The council." She said that last word with a sneer.

Edilio stabbed a finger at her. "You do not go after Drake on your own."

"Yeah? Who else you got?" Brianna said.

Edilio didn't have a good answer to that. "Get Dekka. And get Astrid. I don't care if you have to drag her by her hair, you get Astrid to town hall."

Brianna was way too happy at that prospect. She spun, blurred, and was gone.

Edilio dressed quickly, grabbed his weapons, and ran the few blocks to town hall, hoping he could make it that far without running into Drake. He would fight if he had to, but it was hard to win a fight against someone who couldn't be killed.

He was the first to arrive at town hall. Albert was next, dressed in spotless business casual as always. Howard came in, looking shell-shocked.

"I can't find him. I can't find him." Howard was weeping. "I think he fell through the floor, I mean, you know how big Orc is. Then Drake, he busted out and . . . Orc's most likely drunk."

"Most likely," Edilio snapped. "Since you make sure he stays that way, Howard."

"We didn't ask to be running some prison for zombies," Howard shot back.

"Where were you when this went down?" Edilio accused.

"I was . . . I had to see a dude."

Delivering bottles of booze, Edilio knew. When would the alcohol supply run out? Everything else had run out. "Have either of you seen Sam? Brianna can't find him."

Albert sighed. "He's out of town."

Edilio felt the blood drain out of his face. "He's what?"

Astrid arrived, coldly furious. "I'm not on the council anymore. You have no right—"

"Shut up, Astrid," Edilio said.

Astrid, Albert, and Howard all stared. Edilio was as amazed as any of them. He considered apologizing—he had never spoken to Astrid that way. He'd never spoken to anyone that way.

The truth was he was scared. Sam was out of town? With Drake running loose?

"What makes you think Sam is out of town?" Edilio asked Albert.

"I sent him," Albert said. "Him and Dekka. Taylor and

Jack, too. They're looking for water."

"They're what?"

"Looking for water."

Edilio shot a glance at Astrid. She looked down. So: she knew it, too.

Edilio swallowed hard. He was finding it hard to breathe. And at the same time he was finding it hard not to scream at Albert and Astrid both. Both of them so smart, so superior. Dumping this on him now.

Howard said, "Orc must have gone after Drake. Oh, man, I don't know if he can beat Drake, not like Drake is now. Oh, man."

Edilio hoped Howard was right that Orc was chasing Drake. He hoped it mightily because the alternative was that he had not one but two monsters running around town. Mostly when Orc was drunk he just sat. But sometimes he got himself worked into an angry drunk, and then things got crazy.

Edilio glanced at the door. One or both could come busting in here at any second.

His gun was at his side. For all the good it would do.

"Brianna's looking for Drake," Edilio said, thinking out loud.

"You sent her out against Drake?" Albert demanded.

"Sent her? Who sends Brianna out to get into a fight? She goes on her own. Anyway, it's not like you've left us with anyone else."

Albert had the decency not to say anything to that.

"You know, you guys put me in charge. I didn't ask to be in charge. I didn't want to be in charge. Sam was in charge and all you guys ever did was give him grief," Edilio said. "You two, especially." He pointed at Albert and Astrid. "So, okay, Astrid takes over. And then Astrid finds out it's not so much fun being in charge. So it's like, okay, let's get the dumb wetback to do the job."

"No one ever—," Astrid protested.

"And me, like a fool, I'm thinking, okay, that must mean people trust me. They asked me to be in charge, be the mayor. Come to find out, I'm not making decisions; Albert's making decisions. Albert's deciding we need to find more water and sending our two best fighters off into the countryside. Now I'm supposed to fix everything? It's like you go, 'Fight a war,' but you sent my army off on a wild goose chase."

"The water situation's worse than you realize," Albert said.

"Listen to yourself, man!" Edilio exploded. "Why don't I know what the water situation is? Because you run all that and you don't tell me. You don't tell me what's going on and then you send Sam off on a nice walk. You know, Albert, you want so bad to be the big man, the Donald Trump of Perdido Beach, why don't you go deal with Drake? Why are you coming to me?"

He was starting to fantasize about using his gun on Albert when Taylor suddenly appeared in the room. Everyone jumped about six inches.

"Jeez, would you stop that?" Howard yelled. "Give me a heart attack."

"Hunter's dead," Taylor said without preamble. "It was these . . . these things. They came crawling up out of him and were eating him, oh God, I mean, it was like . . . I mean he was crying and Dekka prayed with him and he tried to fry his own brain just like he did with Harry only I guess it didn't work, I guess he couldn't do it, so Sam . . ." She swallowed. "Anyone have some water?"

"What about Sam?" Astrid demanded.

"He did it for him. Sam. I mean, he . . . Hunter was, you know . . . so Sam." She pantomimed raising her hands, like Sam, like he would do when using his power.

Astrid closed her eyes and crossed herself.

"Rest in peace," Edilio said and crossed himself as well.

"Sam burned the boy?" Howard asked. Then, bitterly sarcastic said, "Yeah, you all pray to Jesus. Because Jesus is really providing a lot of help here. Sounds to me like Sam was the one doing what had to be done."

"Look, I need a glass of water or something," Taylor pleaded. She sat down on the floor, leaned back against the wall, and started crying.

Edilio pulled open a drawer in the big desk. He had a water bottle, but just an inch was left in it. Reluctantly he handed it to Astrid, who passed it to Taylor.

Taylor drained the water. "That's not all. Sam sent me to give you a message, Edilio. He said, 'Tell Edilio I couldn't kill the bugs.'"

"The things that came out of Hunter?" Howard asked.

Taylor closed her eyes. Tears squeezed out and rolled down

her cheeks. "Yes. The things that came out of Hunter. Sam shot them, you know, with his light. But they're like, reflective or whatever. Anyway, it didn't kill them."

"Sam can burn through a brick wall," Howard said. "What kind of thing is it he can't kill?" Then he answered his own question. "Something very nasty."

"Taylor, bounce back and tell Sam to come back to town," Albert said.

"I'm not going back there!" Taylor cried.

"Whoa," Edilio said, holding up both hands. "Hey, you don't decide this, Albert. You don't give orders. I'm the mayor, and there are four council members here. You, me, Ellen, and Howard."

Albert looked like he might argue, but Astrid stepped in. "Taylor, what did Sam say he was going to do next?"

"He said something about going to take out the cave where the greenies live. Where Hunter told them they are. That's why I'm not going back. You didn't see those things crawling out of Hunter, eating him alive."

Suddenly Albert jerked. Like someone had stuck a pin in him. "I forgot. I was busy . . . I was . . ." His eyes were fearful. "Roscoe. Roscoe was bitten by one of those things in Hunter. He told me, I didn't think that . . ." He looked at Astrid. "When Hunter was delivering his kills. Roscoe said something under Hunter's shirt bit him. I just forgot."

From outside there came the sound of a bellowing, anguished roar. Then the sound of smashing glass.

"Orc," Howard said.

"See if you can find him, talk to him," Edilio said. But Howard was already on his way out the door.

No one spoke for a few minutes. They heard another smash, more like metal this time.

Edilio used the silence to think. Orc drunk and on a rampage. Well, it wasn't the first time, but it was bad. Orc had become an asset lately. If he was back to being a danger again then that was very bad news. More likely it was just temporary and Howard would get him under control.

The Roscoe thing was bad. Very bad. Edilio knew what he should do. And he didn't like it.

As for Drake, well, that was the real problem, that and the water.

Edilio had some help, some soldiers, some pretty good, some pretty useless. He had Brianna.

Could Brianna take on Drake?

"What will Drake do?" Edilio asked.

"He's not just Drake," Astrid said. "Remember, he's Brittney, too. That makes it hard for him. If he makes some plan, she can unmake it when she takes over. If he tries to sneak up on anyone, he has to worry that she'll emerge and screw it up."

"Yeah," Albert said, brightening. "Yeah, that's right. It's not Drake, it's Drake slash Brittney."

"If we get a chance at Brittney, we could tie her up, lock her up," Edilio said. "Yeah. If Brianna finds him we have her follow him, watch, and let us know when Brittney comes out."

"That's a plan," Albert said, obviously relieved. "So we let Sam keep going."

Edilio nodded. "For now. But Taylor, we may still need—"

Taylor was no longer in the room.

TWELVE

SO VERY, VERY sweet to be out of that basement. To be breathing fresh air.

Drake stuck close to the shadows of burned-out houses so the fresh air smelled of ash and charcoal and melted plastic. But it was better than the mildew and dust in the basement.

Drake had a list in his head. Sam. Caine. Dekka. Brianna. They would die first. As quickly as Drake could kill them.

That had been his big mistake with Sam at the power plant. He had taken his time to enjoy whipping him. Even now the memory of it sent a shudder of sheer pleasure through Drake's body.

But he had taken too long killing Sam and then Brianna had showed up.

Not this time. This time he would start by killing Sam. Then, if he could find him, Caine.

That was the thing with the powerful freaks, you had to kill them quick. You had to strike with speed and surprise.

Sam. Caine. Dekka. Brianna. Orc and Taylor, too.

And then, with them gone, he could take his sweet time with Astrid. And even longer with Diana.

Drake laughed out loud.

Jamal said, "What's so funny?"

"I'm Santa Claus, Jamal. Making a list, checking it twice."

Jamal stayed a few steps behind him. Toting his big automatic rifle in his one good arm. The other arm in a makeshift sling. Scared out of his mind, no doubt. Still feeling the burn of Drake's whip. Oh, yes, he would feel that for quite some time.

"Where is Sam staying?" Drake asked Jamal.

"Albert sent him off to look for something out in the woods or whatever. Out there." Jamal gestured vaguely. "I wasn't supposed to know, but I heard."

Drake turned on Jamal. "What? Sam's not here?" He'd missed out on a lot, being trapped like an animal.

"He'll be back in a couple days, I guess."

Drake cursed. "Where's Caine, then?"

"He's on some island, like, where these rich dudes lived in the old days."

Worse and worse.

No. No . . . Better and better.

Drake grinned. Neither of the big powers was around to stop him. Change of plans.

"Dekka?"

Jamal shrugged. "I don't know, man, I don't follow that scary dyke around town."

"Now, now," Drake chided mockingly. "We mustn't diss people because of what they are." He took Jamal's face in his hand and squeezed. "I'm going to kill her but not because of what she is, right? I'm going to murder her because she has to be murdered. You good with that, Jamal?"

Jamal was as tense and stiff as a board. He made an affirmative grunt.

"You down with murder?" Drake pressed, sticking his face right in Jamal's. "I want to hear it from you."

He watched as a curtain dropped behind Jamal's eyes. Jamal said, "Yeah. Yeah, Drake."

"Then let's go murder some people," Drake said cheerfully and released Jamal's face.

Drake walked half a block and stopped.

"Not now," he groaned. He cursed extravagantly, but already he was changing. Metal braces formed on his teeth. His lean body grew flabbier.

"Brittney's coming," Drake snarled. "But I'll be back, Jamal. Don't for—"

Sam, Dekka, and Jack had stopped for a meal a half mile from Hunter's camp. Some cooked fish that smelled none too fresh, boiled artichokes, and some pigeon jerky.

They'd thought about just going to sleep, but no one had wanted to. The horror was far too fresh. Sleep would only mean nightmares. And Sam did not want to see Hunter again.

In the dark they could only make slow progress, but everyone wanted some distance and to get the expedition done.

The high spirits were gone. Fear and loathing tracked them in the dark.

Jack was trailing well behind when Sam and Dekka had started talking, killing time as they walked slowly, cautiously, through waist-high brush. Talking, talking about anything but Hunter's sad cries.

It had started with Sam admitting that yes, he had made a play for Taylor but noting that he had been very, very drunk. From there it had gone to his relationship with Astrid, which he did not want to talk about. Any thought of Astrid was laced with pain and loneliness. What he had done to Hunter, what he had seen happening to Hunter, filled him with a powerful longing to be with Astrid. They had been through so much already. How many times had he held her and reassured her everything would be all right? How many times had she kissed him and put her arms around him when she knew he was spiraling down into depression?

From the start, from the first day, they had been each other's strength.

Not that they'd never fought. They were both strong willed and they had fought many times over things large and small. But the fights had always gone somewhere, they'd been worked through and resolved.

But now this cold distance between them. Something inside Astrid had broken after Mary's death. That day had killed some part of Astrid and now it was like she didn't even care enough to fight.

Sam said some of that to Dekka, talking out of sheer

loneliness and need. But it made him uncomfortable, like he was betraying Astrid even talking about her.

And the truth was, so much of the problem between him and Astrid wasn't about anything earth-shattering, it was just about sex. And Sam couldn't really talk about that without sounding more like a jerk than he could stand.

So he diverted the conversation to Dekka. Which led to talking about Brianna. And Sam found himself quickly trapped in a conversation that was every bit as uncomfortable as talking about Astrid.

"I know you mean well, Sam," Dekka was saying.

"The worst that happens is Brianna says, 'No way, I'm not gay.'" He glanced back at Jack to make sure he was out of earshot.

Dekka sighed. "You don't understand, Sam. You think that's all there is to it, just be honest. But see, right now I have this little, tiny like, like flower of hope, right? It's not much, but it's what I am holding on to. I just . . . I can't have her look at me and laugh. Or make a face and be grossed out. Because then I have nothing."

It was the longest speech Sam had ever heard Dekka deliver.

"Yeah," he said. "I get that." He fervently wished he'd never opened his mouth.

There was a noise in the bushes off to one side. "Is that you, Jack?" Sam called in a loud voice.

"I'm over here," Jack said, from the completely opposite direction. "I'm . . . I'm peeing."

Sam stopped. He made a gesture to Dekka, indicating she should shield her eyes. Then he launched a fireball into the air, a Sammy sun. The bushes immediately became a green-tinged ghost space.

Just off the trail a coyote flinched at the light but did not run away. It snarled, bared its teeth, and crouched for a leap.

Dekka was faster than Sam. The coyote found itself floating a few feet off the ground, unable to kick, unable to leap.

It was a bizarre sight, the mangy, dirt-yellow coyote squirming and yowling in midair. But at last it let itself go limp.

"Why are you attacking us?" Sam asked. "Does Pack Leader know you're trying to kill humans?"

"I Pack Leader," the coyote said in its strangled, weird voice.

Sam stepped closer. Humans were not the only creatures to have evolved in the lawless universe of the FAYZ. One of the earliest had been the coyotes who served the gaiaphage. Some had mutated to develop the shorter tongues and flattened muzzles that allowed them a mangled sort of speech.

"Look," Jack said. He was coming closer, pointing. "He has them, too."

Sam walked cautiously around Pack Leader to see the other side. There were the insect jaws protruding from the matted fur. Two, maybe three of them.

"I came for hunter kill me," Pack Leader said.

Sam knew this was not the original Pack Leader. Lana had killed that Pack Leader. But whether this was the second coyote to hold the title or some other coyote, he didn't know. This one had slightly better powers of speech than the first.

"Hunter's dead," Sam said.

"You kill."

"Yes."

"Kill me, Bright Hands."

Sam had no sympathy for the coyote. The coyotes had participated in the town plaza massacre. There were bodies buried in the cemetery that had been so badly ripped by coyote teeth that they were unrecognizable.

"The flying snakes cause this?" Sam asked, pointing at the awful parasites.

"Yes."

"Where are they?"

Pack Leader made a purely coyote growl deep in his throat. "No words."

"Then show us," Sam said. "Take us to them."

"Then you burn me?"

"Then I'll burn you."

At first Brittney was confused. She wondered if she was dreaming. Dreaming of fresh, cool air and a sky overhead.

But no, she was not in the basement.

Drake had escaped!

She had to do something. Had to warn someone. Even if it meant being returned to the basement. If Drake was loose in the world, he would do evil.

But to be locked away again . . . Surely she could take just a moment to be free. Just a moment . . .

She realized she was not alone.

"Who are you?"

"Jamal. I . . . I work for Albert, kind of. A bodyguard, like."

The boy stood stiff, rigid, hand gripping the stock of his rifle too tightly. His other arm had been hurt.

"Why are you here, Jamal? Are you here to catch Drake?" She noticed a few feet of rope coiled and hung from Jamal's belt. "I don't think you can tie him up. He's very dangerous."

"I know that," Jamal said. He was tugging the rope free.

Brittney suddenly understood why Jamal was there. She bolted.

Jamal ran after her.

"Don't run or I have to shoot you," Jamal cried.

He was faster than she was. Everyone was faster than Brittney. But he was fumbling one-handed with the rope and had to sling the gun over his shoulder. All Brittney had to do was run.

She burst into the town plaza. Not knowing what she was looking for, not consciously. But she found herself running up the stone steps toward the ruined church.

Jamal caught her on the steps, grabbed her hair, and yanked back. Her legs went out from under her and she fell hard on her back, slamming onto sharp-edged granite.

But Brittney no longer felt real pain. She had long since gone beyond pain.

Jamal tried to straddle her, but he tripped on the rope and she pushed away from him.

"Stop it!" Jamal yelled.

Brittney rolled down a couple of steps, climbed to her feet, and plowed straight back into Jamal. She knocked him aside and dashed past him.

The church roof had collapsed long ago. But a path had been cleared to the inside. The cross had been propped back upright, leaning a bit but still there, silver in the moonlight.

Brittney ran toward the cross, tripped on debris, and slammed into a pew.

Jamal was on her in a flash, cursing, fumbling, trying to grab her, swat away her punching hands, trying to get the rope around her.

"No! No! No!" Brittney shouted.

Jamal punched her in the side of the head.

Brittney blinked and punched back. She kicked and flailed and punched as well as she could from her position half beneath a pew. And Jamal kicked her back viciously.

But Jamal could still feel pain. He backed away suddenly, eyes wild and dripping sweat. He leveled the rifle at her.

"I don't want to shoot you," Jamal pleaded.

"You can't kill me," Brittney said and got heavily to her feet.

"I know. Drake told me you'd say that. But I can blow up your face and then you won't be better right away. That's what he said. He told me to shoot you right in the face and tie you up."

"I wish you could kill me," Brittney said. And then, in a loud voice, trying to shout at heaven, she cried, "Jesus, I am in your house. I am in the house of the Lord begging you for death!"

"Just let me tie you up," Jamal pleaded. "He'll whip me if I don't." There were tears running down his face and Brittney felt sorry for him. They were both bound to Drake, unable to get away from him.

Jamal aimed the gun at her face.

"Don't," Brittney said. "We have to fight Drake, we have to get help. Sam. He has to burn Drake to ashes and scatter the ashes in the ocean."

"Please don't make me do this," Jamal pleaded.

Brittney yelled, "Help! Some—"

Orc had run until he was tired. That didn't take long. He was drunk and dehydrated. Weaker than he should have been. More easily tired.

But despair drove him on, staggering and weeping and bellowing in rage through the night.

"Never wanted to be no guard," he yelled at the closed and darkened houses. "Everybody hear that? I didn't ask to be no prison guard!"

He stood swaying back and forth, big stone-fingered fists clenched.

"No one wants to talk to me, huh?"

He smashed one arm down on the roof of a car. The driver's-side window had long since been beaten in so the door could be opened and the car could be searched. The trunk was open, too, and the recoil from Orc's blow made it bounce.

"Need another bottle," he muttered. Then louder, yelling at the darkened windows and locked doors, "I want a bottle. Someone give me a bottle so I won't hurt anyone."

No answer. The streets were silent.

He started crying again and brushed angrily at the tears. He started running once more, ran for a block and stopped, wheezing and threatening to topple over.

Then he spotted the boy. A kid. Maybe eight, maybe nine or ten, hard to say. The boy was walking bent over, holding his stomach. Every few feet he would stop and cough and then groan from the pain of coughing.

"Hey-ey!" Orc yelled. "You! Go get me a bottle." The word "bottle" came out "bah-hull."

The sick boy blinked and seemed only then to notice the monster in the street ahead of him. He clutched a stop sign to keep himself from collapsing.

"Hey. You, kid. I'm talking to you!"

The boy started to answer, then started coughing. He coughed and groaned and sat down.

Orc stomped over to him. "You ig, um, ig . . . ignoring me?"

The boy shook his head weakly. He made a gesture toward his throat, tried to speak, couldn't.

"I don't want to . . . ," Orc began, but lost the thread of his speech. "Just go get me a bah-hull."

The boy coughed in Orc's face.

Orc swatted him with the back of his hand.

The boy hit the signpost so hard it rang. Then fell onto his back on the sidewalk.

Orc stared stupidly, expecting the boy to start crying. But the kid wasn't moving. Wasn't coughing.

Orc felt ice water flood his veins.

"I didn't . . . ," Orc started to say.

He looked around, feeling sudden, overwhelming shame. No one had seen him.

He tried to lean down and prod the boy with his finger, but the blood rushed to his head and he almost passed out.

"Whatever," Orc said sullenly, and headed off again into the night.

But quieter now.

THIRTEEN

BRIANNA TOOK A deep breath of chilly night air. Was that a breeze? Excellent: a breeze for the Breeze.

"Here, Drake-y, Drake-y," she said.

She was in the middle of the street. As long as Drake hadn't found a gun, she would be safe. Drake was quick with that whip hand of his, but not Breeze quick. No one was Breeze quick.

"Oh, Dra-ake," she sang in a loud voice. "Oh, Dra-ake. Come out, come out wherever you are."

She ran down Pacific Boulevard, turned onto Brace, and shot back up Golding.

She heard Orc bellowing drunkenly in the distance. It would be easy to locate him. But Orc wasn't the problem.

No sign of Drake. She paused at the corner. Either she could just zoom randomly around or she could go methodically, street by street.

Methodical was not Brianna's thing.

Better to taunt him, tease him into showing himself. "Here, Drake-y, Drake-y."

She zoomed to Astrid's house. No sign of him there.

She zoomed to the firehouse. To the school. To Clifftop and down the beach, kicking a tail of sand behind her as she ran.

Where would he go? What would he do?

It dawned on her then: Brittney. What was Drake going to do about Brittney?

As far as Brianna knew, Drake had no power to stop Brittney from emerging.

Where would Brittney go if she were free?

Brianna turned her gaze to the ruined church. And just then, she heard the sound of voices from within.

She zoomed up the stairs and into the church as . . .

BLAM!

The explosion, a stab of yellow, blinded her. She stopped as fast as she could, but not fast enough. She slammed into a pew and flew headfirst through the air, unable to see.

Anyone else would have smashed face-first into the marble altar, but Brianna was not anyone else. As she was flying she tucked, spun, and landed on her feet on the altar. Like a cat.

The wave of pain from the impact with the pew made her gasp. But she fought down the urge to scream.

Then she saw.

And then she did scream.

The rifle blast had hit Brittney in the face and neck. The entire left side of her face was gone. Her neck was torn open. She should be spouting blood. But although the shattered flesh was red and raw as uncooked hamburger, no arteries sprayed.

And Brittney was still standing.

Jamal made a sound like a tortured animal, a howl of fear.

He leveled the gun at Brittney's chest but in the half second it took him to find the trigger with his finger Brianna was on him.

She hit the barrel and knocked it away just as *BLAM!*

She grabbed Jamal by the neck, yanked him forward so fast his head snapped back. She punched him six times in less than a second and Jamal crumpled, blood gushing from his nose and lips.

"Don't hurt me, it's not my fault!" Jamal wailed as he dropped and curled into a ball protecting both the gun and his face.

Brianna did not want to look at Brittney, really really didn't.

"Are you okay?" she asked over her shoulder. No answer from Brittney. Not surprising since her mouth was smeared all around the back of her head.

Brianna steeled herself and shot a glance at Brittney, but the whip hand was already reaching, yanking Jamal's rifle away.

Brianna pulled her knife free and leaped at Drake.

She buried the knife in Drake's chest. It was a huge blade, a bowie knife, as big as a chef's knife and a lot thicker. The blade was in all the way, up to the hilt.

Drake grinned. "This should be fun."

Brianna expected him to try to turn the gun toward her but instead he tossed it aside. Then, with his real hand, he drew the knife out of his chest, slowly, as if relishing every inch of steel.

Brianna stared, mesmerized. And almost missed the sudden flick of Drake's tentacle arm as it swept behind her.

Almost missed.

Not quite.

Brianna dropped and the whip went over her head. Drake threw Brianna's own knife at her, but it wasn't even close. The knife stuck into the back of a pew.

Brianna pulled her sawed-off shotgun from her runner's pack, leveled, aimed, and fired.

The blast caught Drake in the mouth. It turned his thin-lipped smirk into a gaping hole, like a sinkhole.

Drake reached with his tentacle to feel the hole. He stuck the end of his whip hand into his own destroyed mouth. The pink-red tip came out through the back of his head and waved at Brianna.

Drake made a grunting sound that might have been a laugh if he'd had tongue and teeth and lips.

Brianna dropped back a few feet.

Drake's face seemed to melt and re-form. She could see individual teeth, white pearls in the starlight, moving like insects, crawling out of the shredded flesh to find places in newly reshaped gums.

Brianna felt for the wire she hung from her belt. It was an E string from a cello she'd found. She'd wrapped the ends around short pieces of wood to form a four-foot-long garrote.

"This is what you were going to do to me at the power plant, remember, Drake?" Brianna winced as Drake's tongue grew inside the still-gaping hole of his mouth.

"Oh, sorry, you can't really chitchat, can you?" Brianna taunted. "Well, the thing is, whether it's me running into a wire at two hundred miles an hour, or the wire running into you at two hundred miles an hour, it works just the same."

She grabbed the garrote and was behind Drake before he could blink. The wire went around Drake's neck as she was still running. The wire bit and sliced, and she felt a powerful jerk in her hands that tore one handle from her grip as the wire sliced through neck bone.

Drake's head fell. It hit the stone floor hard, and rolled onto its side, rocked a few times, and lay still.

Not enough, Brianna thought, turned, raced back, threw the loose end of the wire around Drake's waist, caught the handle, and gripped with all her strength as she backpedaled at super speed.

The wire cut through Drake's still-standing torso just below his ribs. It stopped at the spine.

Brianna yanked, but the wire would not cut the spine. She yanked and yanked and the meat of Drake's body twisted sideways so she could see the insides, see the organs, the sliced raw flesh like steak, the pale intestine, and all of it clinical, like a drawing, like some hideous display.

And suddenly her frenzied yanking, legs pummeling the slippery marble for purchase, succeeded, and with a grinding, grisly sound the spine parted and Drake fell in two pieces to the floor.

Brianna was aware of screaming. Jamal, hand over his face but eyes staring in horror. Screaming and screaming like he would never stop.

Brianna wanted to scream, too. But not in horror. In sheer, vicious triumph. She wanted to dance and smear herself with the blood of her beaten enemy. She wanted to leap atop the body chunks and kick them in contempt.

Brianna threw back her head and howled at the broken rafters and the sky beyond. "Yaaaaah! Yaaaaah! The Breeze!"

Jamal stopped screaming. He was gibbering, making word-like sounds, like a crazy street person. He was crawling away across the floor.

Brianna laughed. "What's the matter, tough guy? Did you figure out you picked the wrong side?"

The tentacle was around her legs before she knew what had happened.

She looked down and stared, unable to believe what she was seeing. Drake's whip hand was coiled twice around her ankles, squeezing hard, crushing the bones together.

Brianna tried to kick but couldn't even budge.

Drake's head was four feet away from his upper torso, but now the cruel mouth was back, and grinning. The cold eyes were watching.

Alive!

The upper torso used its good hand to shove itself toward the head while the tentacle held her tight with a python's strength. The lower torso—stomach, hips, legs—was kicking and flailing, trying to move toward the upper torso.

Drake was putting himself back together.

Brianna fell on her butt. She reached reflexively for her knife, but it was too far away.

Her sawed-off shotgun. She had re-holstered it. Her hand found it, yanked it free. She took aim at the tentacle that held her fast, aimed at the part just beyond her feet, pulled the trigger.

BLAM!

The blast came from Jamal's gun. He had found it. She saw smoke curling from the muzzle.

Brianna fumbled with her shotgun, but her fingers wouldn't work right and her ears were ringing and somehow there was blood all over her chest.

Drake's head made a silent laugh.

Brianna lay helpless, watching as the legs, the lower third of the creature began to change. Not Drake's legs. A girl's chubby limbs.

Drake's head cried out without sound.

The tentacle was already sliding away.

Jamal walking as if in a dream, his smoking rifle held at his side.

Brianna could see Drake's lips form the words, "Kill her. Kill her."

But without lungs, no sound came out.

The body parts moved together. The arms of a girl fumbled for and found what was now Brittney's head and dragged it to its perch on her shoulders.

The legs kicked and scrabbled until the lower third melded back. Brianna watched it all, unable to move, unable to think clearly.

The last thing she saw was Jamal using Brianna's wire to wrap Brittney's hands tightly behind her. He tore a sleeve from his own shirt and made a gag of it and stuffed it in Brittney's mouth.

Then he stepped back to Brianna. She could barely hear his words through the ringing sound and could barely understand what she did hear.

"I could kill you," Jamal said. He pointed the automatic rifle down at her, the barrel an inch from her face. "Most likely Drake comes out on top. But if not, you remember that I coulda killed you." He shouldered the gun. "But I didn't."

It was only a few minutes before Edilio, accompanied by Ellen, both armed with automatic rifles of their own, came rushing in. Jamal and Brittney were long gone.

Edilio knelt beside Brianna. She saw worry and compassion in his dark eyes and in her delirium really liked him for that.

"Ellen, get Lana. Now!" Edilio ordered.

To Brianna, he said, "Is he gone?"

Brianna found it hard to get her voice to do what she wanted. But she managed after a few tries to say, "Have to . . . get Sam. Sam. I . . . I can't beat Drake."

Edilio looked grim. "Yeah, that's a good idea," he said as

he examined the bloody wounds in her shoulder. "Unfortunately Taylor took off. And no one exactly knows how to find Sam."

"Jamal . . . ," Brianna whispered. But before she could complete the thought, the marble floor seemed to open wide and drag her swirling down into darkness.

Lance came bursting in the door.

"Drake is out!" he yelled.

Turk—formerly Zil's number one guy, at least he thought so, and boss of what was left of Human Crew—said, "Yeah, whatever."

Human Crew had been a group formed to defend the rights of normals against freaks. At least that was the Human Crew line. Most people now saw Human Crew as a straight-up hate group.

Lance grabbed Turk's shoulder and practically yanked him up off the stinking couch where he lay. "Turk, listen, man, listen to me: don't you see what this means?"

Turk did not see what it meant, or at least not whatever Lance thought he should see. Turk mostly disliked Lance. They were friends, kind of, but only because they'd both been with Zil and riding high. And now they were reduced to doing the worst work Albert could find for them: digging slit trenches for kids to go in, and then covering them up when they were full.

Cesspool diggers. The Crap Crew, kids called them.

And they had to kiss Albert's butt because otherwise they didn't eat. They'd been lucky they weren't exiled. Turk had talked the council out of sending them off to live in the wild. He'd begged, that was the truth of it. He'd convinced them that it was better to find a place for him and the others from Human Crew.

He'd put all the blame for the fire on anyone but themselves. Kept saying, "It's not our fault, guys, not me and Lance and all, we were forced by Zil and Hank. Hank was scary, man, you know that. You know he was a creep and he would have shot us or messed us up."

Turk had whined like a baby. And wept. And in the end convinced that smug wetback Edilio, and especially Albert, that they wouldn't make trouble anymore, ever again, lessons learned, their lives all turned around now.

The Human Crew became the Crap Crew. And harsher names as well. A laughingstock.

Turk hated Albert with a burning, undying passion. Albert had everything and tossed the worst crumbs to Turk and Lance and the former Human Crew.

Lance wasn't going away. His handsome face was lit up with excitement. "Dude, don't you get it? If we hit Albert now, everyone will blame Drake."

That got Turk's attention. "We tried to pin the fire on Caine and no one believed us."

"This is different. Look, do you like living like this?" He looked wildly around the room, stabbing his hand finally toward the reeking stew pot they used as an inside toilet. "Eating the worst food, doing the worst job, and being in this dump?"

"Yeah, I love it," Turk said with savage sarcasm. "I just love being the biggest loser in town."

"Then listen to me." Lance rested his hands on Turk's shoulders. Turk shrugged them off. "Because I'm telling you: Drake can't be killed or stopped. So everyone's scared. Maybe we find a way to hook up with Drake, right? Or maybe we just wait until everyone's freaking out over him, and we make our move."

Turk didn't dismiss it out of hand. Maybe Lance was right. Everyone knew Albert had tons of gold and 'Bertos and all kinds of food—even cans of stuff from before, good food.

"I don't know, man," Turk said. "Human Crew is supposed to stand for something. I mean, we're the defenders of humans against freaks, right? We stand up for normal people. We don't just steal stuff. We're not, like, a gang."

Lance laughed derisively. "Man, sometimes you are clueless. You don't even see what's happening." He perched himself on the arm of the couch so he could look down at Turk. "It's not just about freaks. I mean, you're the guy who thinks of ideas and all, but you're missing it. You don't even notice that the whole council is either black or Mexican. See, that's what's happening: it's all these minorities hooked up with freaks."

The wheels in Turk's mind began to turn slowly. But they

were picking up speed. "Jamal's with us and he's black."

"So? We use Jamal. He gets us into Albert's. You do what you gotta do. All I'm saying is, you and me, we're normal people. We're not black or queer or Mexican. And we're the ones digging toilets. How come?"

Turk knew the answer: because they had failed in their attempt to take over. But he'd never thought about this new angle.

"Astrid's a normal white person," Turk argued halfheartedly. "So's Sam."

"Sam's a freak, and I think he might even be a Jew," Lance said. His eyes were glittering. He was showing his teeth, grinning as he talked. It wasn't a good look for him. "And Astrid? She's not even on the council anymore."

Turk was buying it. He felt the new ideas settle into the dark places in his aggrieved mind. "Drake's white. So is Orc, you know, underneath it all. But they're kind of like freaks. Only . . . only not really. Because they didn't like, turn into freaks, they had accidents or whatever that made them what they are now."

"Exactly," Lance said.

Yes, Turk thought. This could be good. This could be very good. Taking out Albert would cause more problems than burning a bunch of houses. Albert was the one who was really in charge. He had the money and the food. That made him even more important than Sam.

Lisa came in then with cabbages she'd picked from the

fields, and a fat rat she'd bought. Turk's mouth watered: dinner was late.

"Let's eat," he said. "Then we think about what comes next."

FOURTEEN

EDILIO WAITED UNTIL the sun was up to go for Roscoe.

It was all very peaceful. Roscoe wasn't the kind of guy to make much trouble.

"We just have to put you somewhere safe," Edilio explained.

"So I don't give it to anyone else," Roscoe said.

"Yeah. While we figure out how to cure you."

"I want to say good-bye to Sinder," Roscoe said softly. He jerked his head indicating that she was in the house.

"Of course, man. But listen. Don't let her touch you, okay? Just in case."

Roscoe struggled a little then, not against Edilio but against himself. He fought to stop a quiver in his lip. Fought to keep the tears from filling his eyes.

Edilio took him to town hall. There was an unused office with a cot. Edilio had made sure there were books for Roscoe to read. And a covered pot for Roscoe to do his business. A jug of water was on the shelf next to the window. A cabbage and a cooked rabbit were there, too.

The rabbit was a delicacy.

Roscoe thanked Edilio for being decent.

Edilio closed the door. Then he turned the key in the deadbolt.

Quinn's fishermen had had a good day. The boats were reasonably full of fish, squid, octopi, and the weird things they called blue bats. Those they fed to the zekes—the worms in the fields—to buy safe passage for the vegetable pickers.

The prize of the morning's work was a five-foot-long shark. Quinn's boat was actually cramped because of the thing. He was sitting on the tail as he rowed, which was awkward and would give him a backache later. But no one in the boat was complaining. A shark was a twofer: not only was it great eating, it was a competitor for the limited supply of fish.

"Here's what we ought to do," Cigar was saying as he pulled at his oar. "We ought to sell the teeth at the mall. I mean, did you see all those teeth? Kids would pay a 'Berto for, like, a necklace of teeth."

"Or they might, like, glue them onto a stick and make a gnarly weapon," Elise suggested.

"What do you think it weighs?" Ben wondered.

"Ah, not much," Quinn said.

That got a laugh. It had taken eight kids just to haul the fish over the side into Quinn's boat, and then they'd practically swamped the boat.

"Weighs more than Cigar," Ben said.

Cigar plucked at his ragged T-shirt and revealed a hard, almost concave, stomach. "Everything weighs more than me nowadays. When this all ends and we get out, I'm writing a diet book. The FAYZ diet. First, you eat all the junk food you can. Then you starve. Then you eat artichokes. Then you starve a little more. Then you eat someone's hamster. Then you go on the all-fish diet."

"You left out the part where you fry up some ants," Elise said.

"Ants? I ate beetles," Ben bragged.

They went on like this for a while, rowing their heavy-laden boat and bragging about the awful things they had eaten.

Quinn noticed something he hadn't seen in a long time.

"Hold up," he said.

"Aw, is Captain Ahab tired of rowing?"

"You've got good eyes, Elise, look over there." Quinn pointed toward the barrier across a half mile of water.

"What? It's still there."

"Not the barrier. The water. Look at the water."

The four of them shielded their eyes from the sun and stared. "Huh," Quinn said at last. "Does that or does that not look like there's a breeze blowing over there? It's a little choppy."

"Yeah," Cigar agreed. "Weird, huh?"

Quinn nodded thoughtfully. It was something new. Something very strange. He would tell Albert about it when they got into town.

"Okay, enough with that. Let's get back on those oars." The other boats were catching up to them. Quinn could see each of them in turn stop and stare at the clear evidence of wind.

"What's it mean?" Ben asked.

Quinn shrugged. "That's above my pay grade, as my dad used to say. I'll let Albert and Astrid figure that out. Me, I'm just a dumb fisherman," he said.

"Oh, look," Elise teased. "I see an oar with no one pulling it."

Quinn laughed. He seated himself properly, braced his feet, and grabbed the available oar. His back, like those of all the fishing fleet, was thick with muscle.

He was happy. This life made him happy. The sun, the salt water, the smell of fish. The backbreaking work. It all made him happy.

It was simple. It was important.

Quinn thought about the breeze blowing across the water. There was nothing sinister about a nice breeze. And yet he had the feeling it spelled trouble.

Dahra Baidoo had seven new cases of flu. That made thirteen in all. The so-called hospital rang with the percussion of coughing.

No one had died in the night.

But no one had gotten well yet, either. Lana's touch did not heal this illness. Which meant Dahra was no longer in the business of keeping kids comfortable until Lana came around and made everything better: she was now in the business of trying to understand this sickness.

She took temperatures. She kept more-or-less careful charts showing the progression of the sickness.

She tried not to think about Jennifer's story. Jennifer wasn't backing off her tale: she had seen the other Jennifer cough herself to death.

Dahra also tried not to think about what it meant if illness could develop an immunity to Lana.

A kid named Pookie was her worst case right at the moment. She stared at the thermometer in her hand, not quite believing it—106 degrees. She had never seen a number that high.

Pookie was shaking like he was freezing. He was no longer able to answer questions sensibly. He had started talking to someone who was not exactly there, talking about how he didn't want to go to school because he hadn't finished his report.

And his cough was getting louder and more violent.

The flu had laughed at the Tylenol she gave Pookie. His fever had burned right through it. Whether or not he developed some kind of killing cough, he would die of fever if it rose much higher. She had to bring it down.

The book suggested an ice bath. The odds of that were precisely zero. No water, let alone ice. If Albert didn't arrange a water delivery soon, kids would be falling out from thirst, not even waiting to die of fever or cough.

Dahra made a decision. Ellen was there helping out, along with one of the new kids from the island, Virtue. She wished she had time to talk to Virtue: Dahra's parents were from Africa. And so was Virtue himself.

"We have to cool him down," Dahra said. "Virtue? Hold down the fort here, okay? We're going to the beach."

Ellen and Dahra maneuvered Pookie into a wheelbarrow. The three of them made an odd procession down San Pablo Avenue to the beach.

Crossing the sand was the hard part. But finally they made it to the lacy surf and set the sick kid down. Water surged around him.

Not an ice bath, maybe, but close enough. She figured the cold salt water should drain away some of the heat inside Pookie's body.

"There," Ellen said. "Hopefully he can walk back on his own."

Dahra flopped onto the sand beside Ellen. Ellen said, "You heard about Drake, right?"

"Him escaping? Yeah. Don't worry, Sam will get him."

Ellen shook her head. "Sam's out of town. Albert got him to go off for water. Or something like that."

"Sam's gone?" Dahra looked nervously over her shoulder. No reason Drake would come after her. But Drake didn't need a reason. "It'll be okay. Dekka and Brianna and—"

Pookie coughed, coughed, doubled over, choked on seawater, and then coughed so powerfully that it made a clear indent in the water.

"Whoa," Ellen said.

Pookie sat up. His head lolled back and forth like a

marionette with a loose string.

He coughed and the force of it threw him backward into the water with a splash.

Dahra ran to pull him up, but he'd done it on his own. He got to his feet, staggering.

He coughed and it was like an explosion. He flew backward. Like he'd been hit by a car.

"Oh, my God," Dahra cried.

Pookie rolled over, on hands and knees, and coughed again so powerfully that sand flew. Something pink and raw was sprayed across the sand crater.

"No, no, no," Dahra moaned and backed away.

Pookie coughed again and the force of it lifted him up onto his toes, bent him back in a C. Blood sprayed from his mouth and drained out of his ears.

With blank, uncomprehending eyes he stared at Dahra.

And fell dead, facedown in the surf.

No one spoke.

Dahra barely breathed.

For several very long seconds Dahra stood paralyzed.

She blinked. "Ellen, quick, into the water. Get wet all over. Scrub off with your hands!" Dahra followed her own advice. She plunged in and submerged.

When she came up, she yelled, "Now stay away from Pookie's body. Stay in the sun for a while. Until you're dry. Sunlight is supposed to kill flu virus on your skin."

"Oh, my God," Ellen said and her face went pale. "He coughed his insides out."

"Just do what I tell you! Face up to the sun, I have to go!"

She ran back across the beach, her insides churning, panic eating at her.

She spotted Quinn and the fishing fleet pulling wearily up to the dock down at the marina. She ran as fast as she could, waving her hands over her head to attract attention.

Quinn and some of the others saw her, they just didn't understand why she was yelling. Dahra was sweating hard by the time she reached the dock.

"No! No! Don't come any closer!" she yelled to Quinn.

"What the—"

"Pookie just died," Dahra panted. "Flu. Maybe. But, oh, God. Just don't come any closer. In fact, don't get off the boats."

"I already had the flu," Cigar said.

"So did Pookie," Dahra said. "Listen to me: it's catching and it's way bad."

Quinn motioned for his people to stay in their boats. "What are we supposed to do, Dahra? We can't just float around forever."

Dahra sighed. "Let me think."

"I have to go check on my—," one of the fishermen said.

"Shut up, I'm thinking!" Dahra yelled. She had acquired a fair amount of medical knowledge since stupidly volunteering to run the so-called hospital. But that didn't make her a doctor.

She remembered reading about flu, though. Nothing spread faster. Nothing mutated and adapted faster. Hand washing removed it, alcohol killed it, sunlight killed it a little, anyway. But once it was in your nose and lungs it could go crazy and kill you. Especially some new strain.

"Stay in your boats," Dahra said. "We're still going to need food. Throw your fish onto the dock. I'll get Albert to send someone here to collect it. Then go back out, row up the coast a little ways, and camp out."

"Camp out?" Quinn echoed.

"Yes!"

"You're serious."

"No, it's my idea of a joke, Quinn," Dahra snapped. "Pookie just coughed up a lung and fell over dead. You understand what I'm saying? I mean he coughed his actual lungs out of his mouth. Hah hah hah, it's so funny."

Quinn took a step back.

Dahra waited for him to make up his mind. She had no right to give orders. Except that she knew what was happening and no one else did.

"Okay," Quinn said. "There's a spot just up the shore. Tell Albert to send someone right away for the fish. We have a nice big catch here. We got a shark."

"Yeah, whatever." Dahra's thoughts were already turning to her next move. The virus was the enemy: she was the general in this battle. But only two thoughts were really clear in her mind: One, Jennifer B had been telling the truth. And two, how could Dahra hope to avoid catching it?

FIFTEEN

"NEAR," PACK LEADER said.

"Where?" Sam asked wearily. It had been a long night, followed by a long morning of tired feet and bruised shins.

They were over the hills, coming down the long slope toward the road and Lake Evian. It would have been easier to come up the road, this was definitely the long way around, but Sam had needed to see Hunter first.

To kill Hunter.

And now, if he could, he meant to find the nest of greenies and take them out.

Once more he saw the dark, troubled looks of the judges he feared would someday weigh his every action. He heard their questions. *What right did you have to take Hunter's life, Mr. Temple? Yes, we understand that he did not wish to be eaten alive, but still, Mr. Temple, don't you understand that every life is sacred?*

The road was below them, cut off from view by a large,

rocky outcropping. He'd been down that road a few times, back during the early water runs. Enough times to picture the spot in his head.

"The rock is all busted up down there, boulders and crevices," Sam said. "It's like a shallow cave, only it doesn't go in very far, I don't think."

"The snakes that fly are there," Pack Leader confirmed. "Now kill me, Bright Hands."

"How do I know you're not lying?"

"Why lie?" Pack Leader snarled.

"Because you're a murderous creepy animal who obeys the Darkness," Sam said. He was too tired and sleepy to be diplomatic.

"The Darkness is dead," Jack said.

"No," Pack Leader said.

"No," Sam agreed with a significant look at Jack. This was the first outside confirmation that the gaiaphage still lived. If you could call it living.

A new bug mouth erupted from Pack Leader's flank. The canine looked at it, snapped at it, and bit it. Black liquid gushed from the insect head.

"Is this his doing?" Sam asked. "Are these things creatures of the Darkness?"

"Pack Leader not know."

Sam nodded. "How do we kill it? The Darkness, I mean? How do we kill the gaiaphage?"

"Pack Leader not know."

Sam sighed. "Yeah, well that makes two of us."

Sam could see the creatures writhing within Pack Leader's skin. Like he was a baggie full of worms.

"Ready?"

"I am Pack Leader," the coyote said. He tilted back his head and howled at the sky.

Sam aimed both his palms at the beast just as his hide split open.

The killing light burned and burned. Pack Leader was dead instantly. His fur stank as it burned. His flesh crisped like bacon.

The creatures, the insects, whatever they were, crawled out of the flames and popping fat. Unfazed. Unharmed. Bright-lit and yet seemingly invulnerable.

Sam had used his power to burn through concrete and solid rock and steel. It was impossible that he couldn't kill these things. It was like they had some magical power to shrug off his deadly light. Like they had developed an immunity to him.

"Jack," Sam said. "Get a rock. A big one."

Jack was frozen until Dekka smacked him on the back of the head. Then he leaped to a rock the size of a Smart Car. It was half-buried in the ground. Jack grunted with the effort, but the rock tore free of the dirt with a little gravity-canceling help from Dekka.

Jack lifted the rock high over his head. He smashed it down with all his strength on two of the squirming, escaping bugs.

The rock hit so hard it shook the ground, literally making Sam bounce.

"Now push it back off," Sam ordered.

Jack did. The rock rolled easily from Jack's shove.

Beneath it were two very crushed bugs. Their carapaces were dully reflective, like smoky mirrors. They had short, crushed wings held tight against their bodies. Their wicked, curved mandibles had not been broken. Their slashing mouthparts still glittered like tiny knives.

"Like cockroaches," Sam said. "Hard to kill. Not impossible."

"Yeah. Roaches. A couple more over there," Dekka said, and pointed. As she pointed she suspended gravity and the two bugs lifted into the air. They motored helplessly on their legs.

"Your turn, Jack," Sam said.

Dekka let gravity flow, the boulder rose and fell and scored two more dead bugs.

Others, though, were skittering down the hill.

Sam, Dekka, and Jack pelted after them, high on the discovery that the nasty creatures could in fact be killed.

Half a dozen of the monsters raced over rock and through scrub grass.

Jack snatched up a smaller boulder and threw it one-handed. It hit one of the bugs and missed the others.

"Dekka!"

"Yeah," she said, and raised her hands. Dirt and litter and gravel floated into the air ahead. Another one of the insects floated with it. Jack grabbed a rock but it wouldn't come free, it was an outcropping of something too big even for Jack's strength.

He scrabbled and found a head-sized rock. He threw it hard and missed the floating bug.

"The others are getting away!" Sam yelled.

"What's that noise?" Dekka cried, and made a shushing gesture.

The three of them froze and listened. A sound like a mountain stream rushing over stones.

No, a beating of wings.

"Greenies!"

The flying snakes came in a cloud, rushing up from their lair below like swarming bats emerging from a cave at sundown.

Like tiny dragons, most just a few inches long, some as much as a foot long. They had leathery wings and whipped their tails back and forth to sustain a very shaky aerodynamic ability.

Sam yelled a curse and fired. Too late to catch them by surprise. A mistake that might prove fatal.

Bright beams of light sliced through the attacking cloud. Greenies burned and fell flaming.

Not enough. Not nearly enough and the greenies were not backing off.

Dekka canceled gravity beneath the leading edge of the swarm, but it only had the effect of disorienting some of the snakes, who responded by flying upside down or in wild circles.

They began to squirt greenish-black fluid.

Sam remembered Hunter telling him about being hit by

some secretion from a greenie.

"Don't let them hit you!" Sam yelled. "Run!"

Running uphill would be too slow on the steep slope. They ran at right angles to the swarm, ran all-out, panic speed, tripping and jumping back up, oblivious to bruises and scrapes.

The swarm was slow to react, but react they did, and wheeled after them.

Sam hit the road, staggered, caught himself, and spun around. The swarm was still emerging from its lair in the rock face above. Sam aimed hastily and fired.

Brush on the hillside instantly caught fire. Rocks heated and cracked. He played his light on the cave itself, lighting it up, making it a bright, blazing green mouth.

The swarm was lost now, unsure. It swirled in the air, dropping green-black droplets like an evil rain, but not over Sam and the others, not yet.

Confident he had burned out the cave, Sam swept his light upward into the swarm itself.

A mistake. Attacking their lair confused the greenies, but a direct attack on the swarm gave them a target.

Sam aimed again at the rock wall, hoping to distract them. Too late: the swarm was coming.

"Run! Run!"

Dekka ran backward, canceling gravity behind her. A cloud of gravel and dirt rose into the swarm. This slowed them.

Dekka turned and ran full speed after Sam and Jack.

The swarm seemed to be losing interest in following them.

But a few of the more persistent greenies were still after them as they ran.

Dekka fell hard. Sam could see she was winded. He ran back to her but the greenies were faster than he was.

Dekka rolled over and looked up just as one of the greenies fired its fluid. The dark drop hit her bare shoulder. A second drop hit her jeans. Other drops fell around her.

Sam fired. The hovering greenies flamed.

Dekka jumped to her feet. "It got me, it got me!"

"Get your jeans off," Sam ordered.

She complied. Jack grabbed the garment and carefully inspected the fabric. "It didn't get through."

"My shoulder," Dekka moaned. "Oh, my God, it got me. It got me. Oh, God."

"Hold out your arm, Dekka," Sam ordered. "This is going to hurt."

"Do it," Dekka agreed. "Do it, do it!"

Sam formed a narrow beam of light. Carefully, carefully he moved it closer and closer to the dark splotch on Dekka's shoulder.

Dekka gritted her teeth.

The beam of light burned and she cried out in pain but then yelled, "Don't stop, don't stop!"

But Sam did stop. He quickly grabbed Dekka as she came close to fainting. "Let me see the arm," he said.

There was a burned scoop mark in Dekka's skin. Maybe half an inch deep. Twice as wide. The flesh was cauterized, so there was no blood.

"Got it," Sam said.

"You don't know that," Dekka said through gritted teeth.

"I got it. It didn't get anywhere else. I burned it off."

Dekka grabbed the neck of Sam's shirt. "Don't let it happen, Sam."

"It's not going to, Dekka."

"Listen to me: don't let it happen. You understand? You see it happen, you take care of me. Like Hunter."

"Dekka . . ."

"Swear to me, Sam. Swear it to me by God or by your own soul or whatever you believe, swear to me, Sam."

Sam gently pried her fingers loose.

"I won't let it happen, Dekka. I swear it."

"Stay inside unless absolutely necessary," Edilio shouted into the megaphone. Using up precious batteries. Albert had not wanted to give up the batteries. But he really didn't care what Albert wanted or didn't want.

He walked down San Pablo, shouting through the megaphone. "We have flu going around and it's dangerous. Stay inside unless absolutely necessary! Work is canceled today. Mall is closed."

Flu. Yeah. A flu that makes you cough up your insides.

It was unreal, Edilio thought as he walked halfway down the street and repeated the loudspeaker warning.

Epidemic. The so-called hospital was full. All through the morning, feverish, coughing kids had dragged themselves to the hospital. The disease was spreading like fire and Lana was useless.

No way to know how many it would kill.

Maybe everyone who got it.

Maybe everyone, period.

"Quarantine," Dahra had said, pounding her fist into her palm. "You have to shut everything down."

"Kids have almost no food or water in their homes," Edilio had protested.

"You think I don't know that?" Dahra had cried in a shrill voice tinged with panic. "If we don't stop this epidemic, no one will be thirsty, they'll be dead. Like Pookie. Like that Jennifer girl."

Kids poked their heads out of windows or stepped out onto the darkening streets. Which was kind of the opposite of what he was going for.

"I already had the flu," kids would yell.

"Yeah, well, no one is immune," Edilio would shout back.

"How am I supposed to eat?"

"I guess you'll be hungry for a day. Give us time to work things out."

"Is this the thing with bugs coming out of your body?"

How had that news spread so fast? Everyone knew about Roscoe being locked up. No phones, no texts, no email, nothing, and still kids heard things almost instantly.

"No, no, this is just flu," Edilio said, stretching the truth almost to the breaking point. "Coughing and fever. One kid's already died, so just do what I'm asking, okay?"

In fact, three kids had died. Pookie and a girl named Melissa and Jennifer H. Three, not one. And maybe more than that, no way to know what was happening in every house in this ghost town. No point in spreading more panic than was necessary.

One death should be enough to get their attention. Three deaths, on top of the bugs some kids were nicknaming maggots and others were calling gut-roaches, that was enough to create panic.

Edilio had no idea if a quarantine would work. He would get his guys to try and enforce it: the sheriffs at least would still be on the street. But what were they supposed to do if kids decided to ignore it? Shoot them to save them?

He couldn't tell people to wash their hands: no one had washing water in their home. He couldn't tell them to use hand sanitizer: not enough to go around and what they had was just for the so-called hospital.

Nothing they could do but ask kids to stay home.

Probably too late.

Three dead. So far.

Edilio thought of Roscoe locked in his prison. Were the bugs eating him from the inside yet?

He thought of Brianna—Lana's healing touch had fixed her, but the Breeze was shaken up. Scared.

He thought of the monstrous thing that was both Drake and Brittney.

He thought of Orc. No one had seen him. Plenty had heard

him, and there were a few smashed cars testifying to his previous presence.

He thought of Howard, out walking the streets looking for Orc, refusing to stop, even when Edilio ordered him to get to some shelter and stay inside.

And he thought of the two people who had held his job before him: Sam and Astrid. Both beaten into despair by trying to hold this group of kids together in the face of one disaster after another. Both of them now happy to let Edilio handle it.

"No wonder," Edilio muttered.

"Stay inside unless absolutely necessary," Edilio shouted, and not for the first or last time wished he was still just Sam's faithful sidekick.

SIXTEEN

BLAZING SUNLIGHT, DIRECTLY overhead, woke Orc.

It took him quite a while to sort out where he was. There were desks. The kind they had in school. He was on the floor, a cold linoleum-tile floor, and the desks were tossed and piled around him. Like someone had tossed them all around in a rage.

Someone had.

There was a chalkboard. Something was written on it, but Orc's eyes wouldn't focus well enough to read it.

The really confusing thing was the hole in the ceiling and part of the wall that allowed sunlight to pour so directly on his face, on his blinking eyes. The wall had been partly torn down, and without support a part of the ceiling had collapsed.

He felt something in his right hand. A hunk of wallboard.

He had done it. He had attacked the desks and the windows and the walls.

The memories were flashes of desaturated color and

wild, jerky motion. He saw, as if standing outside himself, a drunken rock-bodied monster storming and rampaging and finally beating at the walls with great stone fists.

Orc groaned. His head was pounding like someone was using a sledgehammer on it. He was thirsty. His stomach felt as if it had been filled with coals.

Other memories were coming back. Drake. He had let that psycho creep get loose.

Howard would . . . well, actually, Howard wouldn't say much. Howard knew better than to ever really attack Orc.

But what about Sam? And Astrid?

Sudden fear. Astrid. Drake would go after her. Drake hated Astrid.

He should do something. Go and . . . and find Drake. Or guard Astrid. Or something. Astrid had always been good to him. She'd always treated him nice, like he wasn't a monster. Even back in school.

Suddenly Orc recognized the room. It was the room they used for after-school detention. Astrid would sometimes come tutor him there.

Truth was, he had always liked it better in detention than at home.

Orc squeezed his eyes shut. He needed a bottle. Too many things coming into his head. Too many pictures and feelings.

He noticed an awful smell and knew right away what had caused it. When he had passed out his muscles had all gone slack. He'd wet himself and worse.

He was lying in a puddle of urine and feces.

With a sob he rolled over onto hands and knees. The fat-guy sweatpants he wore were stained and reeking.

Now he would have to walk down to the beach to clean off. He'd have to walk down there like this, like this depraved, disgusting, drunken, stinking monster.

Which was what he was. What he'd always been.

And then, one more memory. A sick little boy. A stop sign.

God, no. God . . . no.

Orc stumbled from the room, sick and weeping and hating himself so much more than anyone else could ever hate him.

Drake became conscious and was likewise confused about where he was and why.

His hands were tied behind his back and the wire cut uncomfortably into the pulpy flesh of his whip hand.

"Untie me," he snapped at Jamal, who was dozing with his back against a palm tree, rifle cuddled to his chest like a stuffed animal. Jamal looked about six years old when he was asleep.

Drake noticed a rope tied from his ankle to Jamal's ankle. He yanked on it and Jamal snapped awake.

"Untie me," Drake repeated.

Jamal crawled over and fiddled with the knot until Drake was free.

"Where are we?" Drake asked.

"Down the highway. You know, up past Ralph's?"

"What are we doing here?"

"I had to get Brittney out of town," Jamal said. "I barely got you out of the church before Edilio came."

Drake remembered the fight with Brianna. It brought a savage grin. "Did you finish that skinny little witch?"

Jamal shrugged. "I shot her."

"Did you finish her?"

"No, man, I don't think so."

Drake stared hard at him. "I told you to do her."

"Did you?" Jamal licked his lips. "I saw you saying something, but you were, you know, changing and all. It was hard to understand."

Drake knew he was lying. Jamal had disobeyed him. But did he really want a Jamal tough enough to shoot a helpless person in the face?

No, he needed Jamal to be a little weak. Just a little. Still . . .

Drake snapped his whip and caught Jamal across the back.

Jamal cried out and backpedaled away.

"Don't disobey me," Drake said. Then he smiled in what he hoped was a friendly way. "I didn't cut too deep. Just a little reminder for you."

"It burns like fire!"

"Yeah, well, man up, Jamal. And get me some water. I'm thirsty."

"Don't have any water."

"Well get some!"

"Where?"

Drake jumped up and looked around. They were near where the road came down from Coates and met the highway. He tried to think if there was anything left at the old school. Had to be some kind of water up there.

Or he could head back into town. Of course they'd be ready for him now. And by the time he got there he might be Brittney Pig again.

Drake felt a surge of frustration. If it was just him, he'd go straight into town and take out anyone who got in his way. He might not be able to take Orc down, but he could wear the stupid, fat drunk out. And Brianna? Bring it on.

With Sam and Caine both away there was no one who could take him on in a fight. But if Brianna was backed by a few of Edilio's guys with rifles, well, they might be able to get Jamal, and if they got Jamal, they could grab him when the Brittney Pig emerged. Lock him up again. And this time when Sam came back Sam would finish the job.

It had been supernaturally cool putting himself back together after being sliced in three pieces. But he wasn't sure that would happen if Sam incinerated him, burned him to ashes.

Threw the ashes in the ocean.

That image made Drake very nervous.

He had to find a way to rid himself of the Brittney Pig. Otherwise he'd be dependent on Jamal. But how was he supposed to do that? It was hopeless. For a moment Drake felt despair. He would be trapped like this forever.

But then, faint hope. Maybe there was someone who could help. He felt its touch on his mind. It had never forgotten him.

"Get up. We're going," Drake said.

"Where to?" Jamal asked.

"Going to see . . ." He'd been about to say, "a friend." But friend wasn't the right term. Not a friend. Much more.

"My master," Drake said, self-conscious about the word. But when Jamal didn't laugh, Drake repeated it, more confidently. It felt good. "Going to see my master."

Sanjit found flowers easily enough. A lot had been picked for eating, but there were still untended gardens behind abandoned houses where it was possible to pick a small rose or a marigold or whatever. He didn't really know what flowers they were. Some were probably just weeds.

When he had a half dozen he stopped to check in on Bowie, who was being watched by Virtue. Bowie was better today. Maybe a permanent improvement, maybe not. Sanjit never counted his chickens before they'd hatched.

Virtue stared at him and at his flowers. He stared like Sanjit had lost his mind.

"What are those?"

"These?" Sanjit looked in mock surprise at the bouquet. "I think these may be flowers."

"I know they're flowers," Virtue said. "Why are you carrying flowers?"

"I'm bringing them to someone."

"That girl?"

"Yes, Choo. They are for that girl."

"You should stay away from her. She's a very scary girl."

"Hot, though, don't you think?"

Virtue stared at him. "Don't you know there's a quarantine?

Where have you been? No one is supposed to go out."

"A what?"

"A quarantine. That flu going around. Everyone is supposed to stay inside."

"I've had flu before, big deal," Sanjit said dismissively.

"Look, if they put on a quarantine they have good reasons. You don't know these people, I think most of them are crazy. You don't know what they might do if they catch you out."

"I'll be back," Sanjit said with a jaunty wink. "Unless I get really lucky."

"Or she shoots you with that big gun of hers."

"That's also a possibility," Sanjit said cheerfully.

He patted Bowie on the head and checked on the others. Then he headed out into the sunlight.

The streets of Perdido Beach had never exactly been busy. It wasn't New York or Bangkok. But they were particularly quiet now. Not a soul in sight.

Maybe Virtue was telling the truth about a quarantine after all. But hey, who better to be with than Lana, the Healer?

He reached Clifftop without seeing anyone.

He pushed through the lobby doors. He knew that Lana had the best room on the highest floor, a room with a balcony that looked down at the cliff and the beach and out at the ocean.

He was confronted with a confusing hallway full of doors, some closed, many showing signs of having been kicked open or battered down so kids could raid the minibars.

He found what he thought was the right door. He

straightened his clothes and his flowers and knocked. From inside Patrick erupted in loud barking.

He saw the peephole go dark as someone looked out.

He smiled and waved.

Soft cursing from inside. Then, "It's okay, Patrick, it's just some idiot."

The door opened. Lana had a cigarette hanging from the corner of her mouth. She had her pistol in her hand.

"What?" she snapped at Sanjit.

"Flowers," Sanjit said, and held them out to her.

Lana stared at the flowers. "Are you kidding me?"

"I would have brought candy, but I couldn't find any."

"Are you retarded? There's a quarantine on. No one is supposed to be outside."

He had hoped for a little smile. He detected no smile. Instead he smelled alcohol on her breath. Although she didn't seem drunk, her words weren't slurred, and her eyes focused the full intensity of her incredulity quite effectively.

"May I come in?" Sanjit asked.

"In?" Lana echoed. "Here?"

"Yes. May I come in?"

Lana blinked.

"Okay," she said, and her eyebrows shot up like she was amazed the word had come out of her mouth. She stepped back and Sanjit stepped through.

The room had once been a sterile, anonymous hotel room.

It still was. Lana had hung no pictures, collected no precious possessions. No stuffed animals lay on the bed. The room was filthy, of course, but so was just about every room in Perdido Beach.

It smelled of cigarette butts, whiskey, and dog. A huge shotgun leaned against one wall. Patrick seemed almost as agitated as his owner. Neither Lana nor Patrick was used to receiving guests.

There was a small Sammy sun in the closet so that when the closet door was left open there would be light, and when closed less light.

Sanjit crossed to the glass door. "Great view."

"What do you want?"

"I want to get to know you," Sanjit said.

"Why?"

"You're interesting."

"Yeah," Lana said. "But not in any way you're going to like."

Sanjit sat down on the desk chair. He laid the flowers on the hutch next to the TV set. He noticed a scratch from a thorn. It was bleeding a little, no big deal.

"No," Lana said, "I'm not going to heal your scratch."

"Good," Sanjit said.

"Good? Why good?"

"Because when you hold my hand, I don't want it to be work for you."

"Hand holding?" Lana barked out a laugh. "That's what you want? Hand holding?"

"Well, we would work up to that. If we like each other."

"We don't."

Sanjit smiled. "You seem awfully sure of that."

"I know me, and I've met you," Lana said. She sighed. "Okay, look, I get it. You're one of those people who thinks they have to help screwed-up people. Or maybe you're attracted to dangerous, unbalanced people. But listen up: I'm not Edward and you're not Bella."

"I don't understand what that means," Sanjit said.

"You're not going to get some kind of contact cool off me, okay? You're a normal kid, I'm a crazy freak, it's not really the basis for true love."

"Oh. You think I'm normal."

"Your mom and dad are movie stars."

"My mom was a teenage prostitute who died of pneumonia after a bout of hepatitis. My father was any one of maybe a thousand guys. If you know what I'm saying." Sanjit made a fake perky smile. "Up until I was adopted half of everything I ever ate was stolen, and the other half came from some charity." He let this sink in for a moment. "Oh, and see this?" He opened his mouth and pointed to a gap where two molars should have been. "Got beaten up really bad by a pimp who wanted to sell me to some old dude from Germany."

Lana glared at him. Sanjit met her gaze and refused to look away.

Finally, she said, "Okay. You want to talk, okay. I'll talk, then you get it through your head and you leave." Lana lit a new cigarette, puffed it, and looked at him through the smoke. "I went up there to kill it. The gaiaphage. I drove a tank of propane up there, let it flow into the mine shaft, and all I had to do was light a match. The coyotes came after me. I shot them. I still could have set off the explosion, but I didn't. Is that the story you want?"

"Is that the story you want to tell?"

"It was inside my head. I couldn't kill it. Instead it made me crawl to it. Hands and knees. Like a worm. I gave myself to it. I became part of it."

Sanjit nodded because he felt like he should.

"It made me shoot Edilio. Bang." She pantomimed it.

"He survived."

"Sam and Caine knocked the gaiaphage pretty hard. I was freed."

"And you saved Edilio. But you don't want to talk about that, right?"

"You know, it's not a big wonderful thing when you save someone you just shot."

"You didn't shoot him, this monster did. You cured him. That was you."

Lana's eyes were so penetrating he almost couldn't meet her gaze. But he held steady. She was looking for weakness in him. Or maybe she expected disgust.

"You went up there on your own to kill it," Sanjit said.

"And failed."

"But tried. If you were a guy, I'd say you had a big brass pair."

Lana laughed, caught herself, laughed again. Then she kept laughing, stopping, trying not to laugh again, and failing.

"I don't know why I'm laughing," she said, almost apologizing and definitely puzzled.

Sanjit smiled.

"I don't know why I'm laughing," Lana said again.

"You're probably a little stressed," Sanjit said dryly.

"You think?"

Lana laughed again and Sanjit realized he was really enjoying her laugh. It wasn't silly or hysterical. It was, like everything about this strange girl, wise, sardonic. Profound. Mesmerizing.

"Oh, dude," she said, sobering. "Is that what you're here for? Laughter is the best medicine? Is that it? Am I your act of charity or whatever? Heal the Healer with the power of laughter?"

The full force of her cynicism was back on display.

"I don't think I want to heal you," Sanjit said.

"Why not?" she snapped. "I mean, let's not lie, huh? I'm about as screwed up as a girl can be. I am a monument to screwed up. Why don't you want to heal me? I'm a freaking mess!"

Sanjit shrugged. "I don't know."

"You think I'm so messed up, it will be easy to get into my pants, is that it? I'm an easy target?"

"Lana," Sanjit said, "you carry a pistol and look like you'll use it. You have a dog. You tried to kill a monster all on your own. Trust me when I say, no one. No. One. No one looks at you and thinks, 'She'll be easy.'"

Lana sighed wearily, but Sanjit didn't believe the sigh or the weariness. No. She wasn't tired of him.

He said, "I saw you. I heard your voice. I connected. It's not very complicated. I just had a feeling. . . ."

"Feeling?"

Sanjit shrugged. "Yeah. A feeling. Like the whole point of my life, from the alleys in Bangkok, to the yachts and private island, to coming here like a crazy person trying to fly a helicopter, like all of it, from birth to here, point A to point Z, was all some big cosmic trick to get me to meet you."

"Whatever," she said dismissively.

He waited.

"The other day you said I was the second bravest girl you ever met. Who was number one?"

Sanjit's smile disappeared. In the space of a heartbeat he was back there, in that filthy alley smelling of rotten fish, curry, and urine.

"The pimp who knocked my teeth out? He was going to finish me off," Sanjit said. "You know? To send the message that you couldn't refuse him. He had a knife. And man, I was already half dead. I couldn't even move. And this girl was there. No idea where she came from. I never saw her before. She, uh . . ."

Suddenly, to his own amazement, he couldn't talk. Lana waited until he found his voice again. "She came up to the guy and just said, 'Don't hurt him anymore.'"

"So he let you go? Just like that?"

"Not quite. Not quite. She was a pretty girl, maybe eleven, twelve years old. So, you know, a nice-looking young boy is worth some cash to a pimp. But a pretty young girl, well, she was worth more."

"He took her?"

Sanjit nodded. "I was sick for about a week, I guess. Thought I was going to die. Crawled as far as a pile of garbage and just . . . Anyway, when I was able to move again I looked for her. But I didn't find her."

The two of them sat there looking at each other. It seemed to go on for quite a while.

"I have to go to town," Lana said finally. "I can't seem to cure the flu thing. So much for being the Healer. But I can at least deal with the usual broken bones and burns and so on."

"Of course," Sanjit said and stood up. "I'll let you go."

"I didn't say you couldn't come with me," Lana practically snarled.

Sanjit suppressed the smile that wanted badly to break out across his face. "Whenever you're ready."

SEVENTEEN

"**DEKKA. WAKE UP.**"

Her eyes opened. She blinked up at Sam. It was full daylight. Not even early morning, later. She had slept a long time.

A sharp intake of breath. She jumped up and began patting her body, probing, pushing, feeling for anything that shouldn't be there.

The divot in her shoulder burned like fire.

Her stomach growled. Her feet ached. Her scraped shins hurt. So did her back from sleeping on a rock.

"I hurt all over," Dekka said.

Sam looked concerned.

"I mean, that's good. Hunter couldn't feel much of anything, right?"

Sam nodded. "Yeah. Yeah, that's good. So I guess burning a hole in you was actually a good thing?"

"Not quite ready to find that funny, Sam. Where's Jack?"

Sam pointed toward the top of a hill. They were in a very

dry and empty place. The hill wasn't much more than two hundred feet high and was more of a dirt mound than a mountain.

Jack was at the top, shading his eyes and looking to the northeast.

"What do you see?" Sam yelled to him.

"There's a place over that way that looks like it's all burned."

Sam nodded. "Yeah. The hermit's shack. What else?"

"Bunch of rugged-looking hills, all rocky and stuff," Jack yelled. He started to climb down but the dirt was loose, so he slid and slipped and fell. Then he stood up again and jumped.

He jumped thirty feet and landed very near Sam.

"Dude," Sam said.

"Huh," Jack said. "I never realized I could do that."

"There might be other ways you can use that strength, too," Sam said.

"I wish I could use it to find some water."

"Dekka, what do you think? We climb those mountains or go through the burned zone?"

"I kind of hate climbing."

"The mine shaft isn't too far from the shack," Sam pointed out.

"Yeah. I remember where it is," Dekka said. "We just don't go there."

It wasn't far to the shack. Or more accurately the few charred sticks that marked Hermit Jim's shack. Sam pulled out the map again. He measured with his fingers. "It looks like six or seven miles to the lake. I guess we'll all get a drink when we get there."

The Santa Katrina Hills were on their left now. They were bare stone and dirt, and some of the rock formations looked as if they'd been shoved right up out of the earth, like the dirt was still sliding off them. Off to the right there was the taller mountain, and the cleft in that mountain, which hid the ghost town and the mine shaft.

None of them spoke of that place.

It was an hour's thirsty walk across very barren land before they reached a tall chain-link fence. The dirt was the same on either side of the fence. As far as they could see there was nothing that needed fencing.

There was a dusty, rusty metal sign.

"'Warning, restricted area,'" Jack read aloud.

"Yep," Sam said. "We are subject to search."

"How great would it be if someone did come and arrest us?" Dekka said wistfully.

"Jack. Rip down the fence."

"Really?"

"The barrier's that way." Sam pointed. "We should hit the barrier and follow it to the lake. And like Dekka says: if there was anyone around here to arrest us, it would be great. They'd have to feed us and give us something to drink."

Sam wasn't sure quite what he expected to find at the Evanston Air National Guard base. He wasn't sure quite what he'd been hoping for. Maybe a barracks full of soldiers. That would have been excellent. But failing that, maybe a giant tank of water. That would have been nice, too.

What they found instead were a series of underground bunkers. They were identical on the outside: sloping concrete ramps leading down to a steel door. Jack kicked the first one open.

Sam provided illumination. Inside was a long, low room. Completely empty.

"Probably kept bombs here or something."

"Nothing here now," Jack said.

They opened four more of the bunkers before admitting that there was nothing to be found.

Wandering through the bunker field they came upon a truck with the keys in the ignition. The battery was dead. But there was a liter bottle of Arrowhead water, half full.

The three of them rested in the shade of the truck and shared the water.

"Well, that was disappointing," Sam acknowledged.

"You wanted to find bombs?" Dekka asked.

"A giant supply of those meals soldiers eat, what are they called?"

"MREs," Jack said. "Meals ready to eat."

"Yeah. Some of those. Like, maybe a million of those."

"Or at least the truck could have worked so we could drive and not walk," Dekka grumbled.

They started walking again. Already the half liter of water seemed like a distant memory. They began to notice the blankness of the barrier looming ahead. It rose sheer from the sand and scrub.

"Okay, so we hang a left. Let's go find this lake and get back to town," Sam said.

They kept the barrier on their right. The terrain was getting more difficult, with deep gullies, like dry riverbeds, cracks in the desert smoothness.

Ahead, shimmering like a mirage, was a low building that reminded Sam of the kind of "temporary" building schools sometimes resorted to. There were few windows and these showed the horizontal slats of ancient blinds. Air-conditioning units poked out of the walls in several places.

In a parking area there were more sand-colored camouflaged trucks. A couple of civilian cars. All neatly squared away between white lines.

A tall antenna stabbed at the sky. And beyond the building a tumbled mess of huge rust- and ochre- and dust-colored blocks.

"Hey, that's a train!" Jack said.

Sam checked the map. Only now did he notice the crosshatched line indicating a railroad track. He hadn't known what it was before.

Sam wished he'd thought to bring binoculars. There was something off about the building. It was too isolated. Although, Sam reminded himself, there might be a whole bunch of buildings just beyond the FAYZ wall. So maybe this one building was just at the edge of a big compound.

But it didn't feel that way. It felt like this place was deliberately far from anything else. He doubted it would even be noticeable from a satellite photo. Everything except the few cars were painted the same ochre color as the surrounding emptiness.

"Let's check the building first."

The door was unlocked. Sam opened it cautiously. Dirt and dust had filtered onto the polished linoleum floor. A main room, two hallways leading away, and two private offices behind glass partitions. There were half a dozen gray-painted metal desks in the main room and old-style rolling office chairs, some with mismatched cushions. The computers on the desks were blank. Lights off. Air-conditioning obviously off, too; the room was stifling.

Sam glanced at framed photos on a desk: someone's family, two kids, a wife, and either a mother or a grandmother. He spotted a stress ball on another desk. There were official-looking binders and racks of ancient floppy disks.

Everything was dusty. Flowers in a tiny vase were just sticks. Papers had flowed from desks onto the floor.

It was eerie. But they had all seen plenty of eerie: abandoned cars, empty homes, empty businesses.

One thing they had not seen in a very long time: a jar of Nutella was open on one desk, lid nowhere to be seen, and a spoon standing inside.

The three of them leaped as one.

"There's some left!" Jack cried with the kind of pure joy that should have signaled the discovery of something far more important.

Sam and Dekka both grinned. It was a large jar, and it was at least half full.

Jack lifted the spoon. The Nutella dripped languidly.

Jack closed his eyes and stuck the spoon in his mouth. Without a word he handed the spoon to Dekka.

It was like a religious ritual, like communion. The three of them taking spoonfuls, one after the other, each silent, each awed by the wonder of intense flavor, of sweetness after so much fish and cabbage.

"It's been, like, how long?" Dekka asked. "It's sweet."

"Sweet and creamy and chocolaty," Jack said dreamily.

"Why is it still creamy?" Sam asked.

Jack had the spoon. He froze. "Why is it still creamy?" he echoed.

"This jar had to have been opened months ago, back before FAYZ fall," Sam said. "It would be all dried out. All crusty and stiff."

"I'd still eat it," Dekka said defiantly.

"This wasn't opened months ago. This hasn't been open for even a few days," Sam said. He put the jar down. "There's someone here."

Jack had started reading some of the papers strewn carelessly about. "This was a research station."

Dekka was tense, looking around for intruders, enemies. "Research on what? Weapons? Aliens?"

"'Project Cassandra,'" Jack read. "That's the header on most of the memos and stuff. I wish I could get into these computers."

"Someone is here," Sam said, sticking to the most important fact. "Someone who can unscrew a jar of Nutella and eat it with a spoon. Which makes it not a coyote. There's a person here."

"Someone from Perdido Beach?" Dekka wondered. "Maybe someone left town and found this place and never came back. It's not like we would notice everyone who ever left."

"Or someone from Coates." Sam made a motion with his hand, indicating silently that he would go down the hallway to the left and Jack and Dekka should be ready to back him up.

It wasn't a long hallway. Just four doors on each side. Milky light came through a reinforced glass window in the door at the far end of the hallway.

Sam opened doors, one at a time. The first two opened onto empty private offices. The next opened to a dingy room with a metal table and chairs, facing each other. A screen was on one wall. A clipboard was on the floor.

Sam picked it up. "'Project Cassandra,'" he read aloud. "'Subject 1-01. Test number GV-788.'"

He placed the clipboard on the table and went to the next room.

He opened this room and instantly knew someone was inside. Even before he saw anyone.

This room had a window of regular glass and sunshine poured in. There was a bed, a desk, a large blank TV mounted on one wall. Game players lay dusty beneath the screen.

Books were piled high on a side table.

And one book was in the hands of a boy who sat in a reclining chair with his feet up on the desk. He was maybe twelve. His black hair hung down his back almost to his waist. He would probably be tall when he stood up. Thin. Dressed in jeans, sneakers, and a black-and-white Hollywood Undead T-shirt.

"Hi," Sam said. He frowned.

The boy barely reacted.

"Don't I know you?" Sam pressed.

The boy looked at him with eyes narrowed to slits. He smiled a little. He seemed to want to go back to his book.

"Dude," Sam said. "Aren't you Toto?"

The boy's eyebrows went up. His lip quivered. He said, "Is he real?"

He was speaking to a life-sized Styrofoam head of Spider-Man, complete with blue and red cowl, that rested on a shelf.

"I'm real," Sam said. Then he yelled, "Dekka! Jack!"

"Why is he yelling?" Toto asked Spidey. "He could be a Decepticon."

"I'm not a Decepticon," Sam said, feeling a bit ridiculous.

"It's the truth," Toto told Spidey. "He's not a Decepticon. But maybe he works for the Dementors, for Sauron, for the demon."

"What are you talking about, Toto?" Sam asked.

Jack and Dekka came rushing up. "Whoa," Dekka said.

"He knows what I'm talking about," Toto told Spider-Man. "He guesses, he's testing. 'What are you talking about, Toto?'

he says. Right. He knows. He knows the demon."

"I don't work for anyone," Sam said.

"Liar, liar, pants on fire. Someone sent you."

"Albert, but—"

"They always try to lie, but it never works, does it?" Toto said.

Sam turned to Dekka. "I think our boy here has been alone for a long time."

"He means I'm crazy." Toto addressed Dekka directly, not Spider-Man, though he glanced back at the Spidey head and seemed torn between Dekka and the web slinger. "The truth teller, truth teller Toto."

"Are you test subject 1-01?" Jack asked.

Toto didn't seem to hear. But now tears were welling in his eyes. "One zero one. Yes. One zero two, what happened to her, do you want to hear?"

"Yes," Sam answered.

"Should we say, Spidey?" Toto bared his teeth and snarled, "She used to live across the hall. Darla. She was eight. All her stuff was Hello Kitty. She could walk through walls. She didn't want to stay, she wanted to go home, so she tried to just walk right through the wall to the outside and the guards tased her as she was going through and you know what happened?"

"Tell us."

"He doesn't want to know, not really, does he?" Toto asked Spidey. "He's seen too many bad things, hasn't he? But I'll tell him anyway, which is that the Taser froze her halfway through the wall. She died. They had to bust out the whole wall to get her out of there."

"Albert's cat," Jack said.

Sam nodded. They'd all heard the story of the teleporting cat that misjudged and solidified with a book inside it.

"They aren't surprised," Toto said. He tilted his head and shook it back and forth, vastly amused by some secret joke. "They know, don't they?" he asked Spidey.

"Yeah, we know," Sam said. He raised his hand, palm out, and fired a brilliant green beam at Spider-Man's head. The fabric of the cowl caught fire and the Styrofoam within melted.

Toto's pale face went paler. He swallowed hard and looked directly at Sam for the first time.

"Sorry, man," Sam said. "But honestly we have all the crazy we can stand. And we don't have all day."

"Yes, he's telling the truth, he's in a hurry."

"He's still talking to Spider-Man," Dekka pointed out. "He's nuts."

"Yeah, well, we're all a little nuts, Dekka," Sam said.

"No, he's not nuts, the Sam boy," Toto said and he shook his head back and forth. Then, slyly, he added, "Anyway, he doesn't think he is."

"We're looking for a big lake. Lake Tramonto. You know how to get there?"

"We don't know how to get anywhere," Toto said. Suddenly

he looked as if he might cry. "Where's Spidey?"

"How long have you been here?" Sam asked impatiently.

It was Jack who answered. "A little more than a year. The start date for subject 1-01 was several months before the FAYZ."

Sam thought it over for a few seconds. Wondering what to do. He couldn't just dump the kid and walk away. Could he? Especially after he'd impatiently burned Spidey.

On the other hand, the very last thing he needed was another person to keep track of. And it didn't look like this kid was going anywhere. Sam could always pick him up later. And in any case, if they found the lake then the whole town would probably be moving, and they'd pass this way again.

"Listen, Toto, I'm going to pretend you're not completely crazy. I'm going to leave it up to you. So you either come with us and start acting at least a little bit normal, or you stay here. Your choice."

Toto kept glancing back at the brown and black magma that had been the Styrofoam head. But in between he looked at Sam and Dekka and even Jack.

"What do you have to eat?" Toto asked.

"Dried fish. Cabbage. Artichokes."

To Sam's amazement Toto literally licked his lips. "You have some other things, too, but you don't want to share. That's okay. I've only had Nutella. Ever since."

"You must have a whole lot of Nutella," Dekka said, unable to conceal her greedy hope.

"Yes."

"Show us," Sam said. "Show us what you've got. Then we'll go find this lake."

Sam led the way outside. Jack and Dekka fell in beside him. "They knew, didn't they?" he asked Jack.

Jack still had a fistful of papers scooped up from one of the desks.

"Yes," Jack said, still fascinated, reading through printed sheets of data as he walked. "I don't think they knew what, or knew what was causing it. But they knew."

"What did they know?" Dekka asked.

"Whoever was running this place," Sam said angrily. "They knew something was going on with kids in Perdido Beach."

Jack caught up to him, grabbed his shoulder, and handed him a piece of paper. "A list of names."

Sam's eyes went directly to his own name, third on a list of five names. "Toto, Darla, me, Caine, and Taylor." He shoved the paper angrily back at Jack. "Not all of the freaks, but some of us, anyway."

He didn't know what to say or think. It made him angry, but he didn't even know why it should. Of course they would want to learn about kids who suddenly developed supernatural powers.

And of course they would want to keep it secret.

But still it made him angry and uneasy. "This means they know. People on the outside, they've been able to guess some of what happened."

"The real data are on those computers," Jack said. "This printout is just a small file. If the power was back on . . ."

Sam glared at the barrier near at hand. And wondered, not for the first time, what kind of welcome they would get if that barrier ever came down.

EIGHTEEN

TOTO LED THEM from the facility to the train.

It was farther than Sam had thought. It had been a trick of perspective in the desert emptiness that had made the train seem to be right beside the building. In fact, they were a ten-minute walk away.

There were two yellow and black Union Pacific diesel engines. Both still stood upright on the track.

Behind the engines was a rust-colored boxcar, also still on the track.

Behind these came a jumbled mess. There were seven derailed flatbed railcars. Each had spilled two containers—massive steel rectangles—onto the dirt and stunted bushes.

At the far end, the barrier had sliced a boxcar in half. The barrier had snapped into place, bisecting the burnt-orange boxcar, and the sudden shift must have derailed the other cars.

But Sam, Dekka, and Jack were not very interested in such

speculation. Dozens of plastic-wrapped pallets had been flung across the tracks and the ground, spilled from the sliced-open boxcar.

Each of the pallets was piled high with flats of Nutella.

"That's, like, hundreds and hundreds of jars," Sam said.

"Thousands," Jack said. "Thousands. We're . . . we're rich."

If each jar had been a giant diamond, Sam would still have preferred the Nutella.

"This is the greatest discovery in the history of the FAYZ," Dekka said, sounding like she was witnessing a miracle.

"What is á phase? What do they mean by phase?" Toto asked.

"FAYZ. Fallout Alley Youth Zone," Sam said distractedly. "It's supposed to be funny. Dude: what's in the rest of these containers?"

Toto looked uncomfortable. He squirmed so much he looked like he was dancing. "I don't know."

"What do you mean, you don't know? Are you lying?" Dekka demanded sharply.

"No lies," Toto said, eyes flashing. "I'm Toto the truth teller, subject 1-01. Not Toto the liar."

"Then what are you saying? You never looked in any of these containers? There's fourteen containers. Plus that first boxcar. What do you mean you don't know?" Dekka found it outrageous.

Toto did his squirmy dance again. "I couldn't get them open. They're locked. And they're steel. I hit them with chairs, but they wouldn't open."

Sam, Dekka, and Jack all stared at the strange boy.

Then they stared at the containers.

Then they stared at one another.

"Well," Sam said, "I do believe we can get them open."

Approximately eight seconds later Sam had burned the lock from the nearest container. Jack then pushed the door open.

The contents of the container were wrapped in plastic but still unmistakable.

"Toilets?" Dekka said.

Many of the porcelain fixtures were cracked from derailing, the shards held in place by the shrink-wrap.

A second container revealed more toilets.

The third container held what had to be thousands of medium-sized cartons. The cartons contained baseball caps. Dodgers caps.

"One size fits all," Dekka said, disgustedly. "But I'm an Angels fan."

"This is going to take us a while to go through everything," Sam said. "But I think it's probably worth it."

The fourth held wicker lawn furniture.

"Or not," Sam said, disgusted.

The fifth container was wicker flowerpots and cracked terra-cotta pots as well as two pallets of plaster yard pretties: cherubs, gnomes, and the Virgin Mary.

The sixth was house paint and deck stain.

The seventh was better, a mixed load, pallets of shrimp-flavored Cup-a-Noodles, chicken-flavored ramen, coffee filters and coffee makers, and boxes of mixed teas.

"I wish I'd had some of those noodles," Toto said wistfully. "It would have been nice to have noodles."

"Noodles are fine," Sam agreed.

"I wouldn't say no to some noodles," Jack said.

"True, true statement! He would not say no to noodles," Toto babbled.

The eighth container was empty. Nothing.

The ninth was two big pieces of industrial machinery. "Whatchamacallits," Jack said. He searched for the words. "You know. Like industrial lathes or whatever."

"Yeah, great," Dekka said. "All we need is two hundred and twenty volts and we can set up a machine shop."

Sam was starting to feel anxious. Nutella and noodles were fine. Great, in fact. Miraculous. But he'd been hoping for more food, more water, more medicine, something. It was absurdly like Christmas morning when he was little: hoping for something he couldn't even put a name to. A game-changer. Something . . . amazing.

When Jack opened the tenth container he just stood, staring.

Sam said, "Okay, what is it?"

No answer.

Sam leaned over Jack's shoulders to look. Pallet after pallet of heavy cartons. Each carton was emblazoned with the Apple logo.

"Computers?" Sam wondered. "Or iPods?" Neither would be of any use.

At last Jack moved. He rushed to the nearest pallet, then hesitated. He carefully wiped his hands on his pants. Then he tore away the shrink-wrap and gently, cautiously, opened the first carton.

It was with trembling fingers that he lifted out a white box. On the box was a photo of a laptop.

"That would be great if we had internet," Sam said. "Or electricity."

"They ship them fully charged," Jack snapped, angry at Sam's interruption. Like Sam had started talking in church. "It's been so long but . . . but they may still have some charge."

"Okay," Sam said. "So you can play some games. Let's move on to the next—"

"No!" Jack cried, his voice somewhere between anguish and rapture. "No. I have to . . . I have to see."

He spent five full minutes carefully opening the box, lifting out Styrofoam packing pieces like they were fragile works of art.

It was like watching some unfamiliar but profound religious ritual. Sam found it almost moving. He'd never seen Jack so emotional.

He picked patiently at the small piece of tape that held the laptop's thin foam sheath in place.

And finally he held up the silver laptop as if holding a baby in his trembling hands.

He turned it over. By now the suspense was even getting to Sam.

Jack closed his eyes, took a steadying breath, turned the

laptop over, and pressed the battery indicator light. Two tiny green lights blazed.

"Two!" Jack exulted. "Two! I was afraid it'd be one blinking light." Then, in a whisper. "Two. That's maybe an hour and a half. Maybe two hours even."

"Dude. Are you crying?"

Jack wiped his eyes. "No. Jeez."

"He's lying, he's crying," Toto called out unhelpfully.

"You need some time?" Sam asked. He doubted any power on earth could convince Jack to move on yet.

Jack nodded.

"Okay. Dekka and I will get the next one."

The eleventh container was more lawn furniture.

The twelfth container was filled from bottom to top with the greatest sight Sam and Dekka had ever seen in their lives.

This time it was they who stood, awestruck. Overcome by emotion.

There was no mistaking that logo.

"Can you put Pepsi in Cup-a-Noodles?" Dekka wondered.

They leaped at the shrink-wrapped pallets and ripped cans free.

Crack psst!

Crack psst!

Crack psst!

The sound that had not been heard in the FAYZ for months was heard once again. Pop-tops were popped, and Sam, Dekka, and Toto drank deep.

"Oh," Dekka said.

"So good," Toto said.

"It's . . . It's like life is all right again. Like the universe has finally decided to smile at us," Sam said with a huge smile.

Burp.

"Oh, yeah," Dekka said. "Soda burp."

The three of them were grinning. "Jack!" Sam yelled.

"I'm busy!" he called back.

"Get over here. Now!"

Jack came running like he was expecting trouble. A grinning Sam held a can out for him.

"Is that . . . ?"

"It is," Sam assured him.

Crack psst!

Burp.

Jack started crying then, sobbing and drinking and burping and laughing.

"You going crazy on us, Jack?" Dekka asked.

"It's just . . ." He couldn't seem to find the words.

Sam put his arm around Jack's shoulders. "Yeah, dude. It's too much, isn't it? I mean too much like the world before."

"I eat rats," Jack said through his tears.

"We all eat rats," Dekka said. "And glad to get a good juicy one, too."

"True," Toto muttered with some concern. "They eat rats. They didn't mention rats before, Spidey."

The sun was well past noon. Sam said, "We need to check the last containers. Then get moving. Just because we're living large doesn't mean people at home are."

"We don't need to find water, we have Pepsi!" Jack said.

"Which is great," Sam said. "Might last a few days. If we could get it back to town."

That sobered Jack. He nodded briskly and said, "Yes, you're right. Sorry. I was just . . . I don't know. For a few minutes there it was like maybe it was all over."

Just to do something different they went to the boxcar. The instant they rolled back the door they were assailed by a sickly sweet smell.

The boxcar had been full of oranges. But this was only obvious because of the perky labels on the flats. The oranges themselves had long since rotted in the heat. A sticky liquid covered the floor of the car. Some of the crates sprouted fantastic growths of furry mold.

"A little late on this one," Sam said regretfully.

"Oranges would have been good," Toto said.

The very last container was a mixed load: Stanley brand screwdrivers and saws and assorted hand tools, and exercise equipment of various types.

But by then no one cared, because it was the next-to-last container that weighed on their minds.

The thirteenth container had been loaded with shoulder-fired missiles.

The so-called hospital had sounded even worse after the fire. Because then kids had been screaming. Screaming Lana's name.

No screams this time, Lana noted. Coughs. Lots of deep,

rasping coughs. Like kids were trying to cough their lungs right out.

Dahra was standing over one of the cots, laying a wet cloth on a kid's head. She hadn't noticed Lana walk in with Sanjit.

Lana did a quick count. Twenty? Twenty-one? Some of them were on cots, some were on mattresses covered in piled-high blankets from a dozen homes, a dozen beds. Some were lying with very little clothing on the cool tile floor.

And most were coughing, coughing, coughing.

Dahra looked up at the sound of their voices. "Lana. Thank God. You want to try again?"

Lana spread her hands helplessly. "I'll do whatever. But the magic isn't working on this thing."

Dahra wiped sweat from her brow. She looked like she hadn't slept. Maybe ever. "Look, secondary infections, they're called. Someone gets a virus and then something else moves in, too. A lot of times that's what kills people."

"You're the boss," Lana said. She meant it, and she meant it only for Dahra.

"Her." Dahra pointed. "Start with her. One hundred and six fever. That's what Pookie was before . . ."

Lana went to the girl. She looked familiar; Lana thought her name might be Judith, but it was hard to recognize someone whose face was red from coughing, drenched in sweat, hair plastered down, eyes scared, bleary, and defeated.

Lana laid her hand on the girl's head and almost yanked it away. She was hot to the touch. Like touching a plate fresh from the dishwasher.

Lana had no particular ritual for healing. She just touched the person and tried to focus.

"Who are you?" Dahra snapped at Sanjit.

"Lana's boyfriend," Sanjit said.

"No, he's not," Lana said.

"You shouldn't be here," Dahra said to Sanjit. "We've got three known dead already. Go wash yourself off in the ocean and go home."

"Thanks, but I'll stay. I want to help."

Dahra stared, eyes narrowed, trying to figure out if he was crazy. "You really want to help? Because I need someone to empty out the bucket. If you really want to help."

"I do. What bucket?"

Dahra pointed to a plastic trash can with a lid. Around it was a reeking pile of Tupperware containers that Dahra used as bedpans.

Sanjit scooped up the bedpans and balanced them on top of the bucket of urine and feces. The stench filled the room.

"There's a trench in the square. Then, if you're motivated, you could rinse everything out in the surf."

"I'll be right back," Sanjit said.

When he was gone, Dahra said, "I like your boyfriend. Not many guys volunteer to carry ten gallons of diarrhea and vomit."

Lana laughed. "He's not my boyfriend."

"Yeah, well, he can be mine if he wants to be. He's cute. And he carries crap."

Lana felt the girl under her hand shudder and shake.

Dahra was moving automatically from bed to bed, cot to cot, pile of blankets on the floor to pile of blankets on the floor. She sighed as she wrote down another temperature. She was keeping records. Probably not as good as a doctor would do, but better than the average fourteen-year-old girl with twenty-one hacking, shivering patients could be expected to do.

"Why can't I do this?" Lana wondered aloud. "The first round of flu it worked, mostly."

"Immunity, right?" Dahra said. "The virus gets into you, and then your body fights back. The virus learns, comes back ready for a new fight. So instead of reprogramming to beat antibodies it reprogrammed to beat you."

"I'm not an antibody," Lana said.

"Yeah, and this isn't the old world, is it? This is some freak show where nothing works exactly the way it should."

His freak show, Lana thought. A single match and she could have burned it out, killed it. Maybe. How many deaths had come because Lana had failed?

A boy Lana knew, a first grader named Dorian, suddenly stood up and started running for the door. It was a weaving, unsteady run.

Dahra cursed and made a snatch for him.

The kid was out the door in a flash.

A moment later Sanjit reappeared with Dorian under one arm and the now semi-clean toilet bucket and containers in the other.

"Come on, little man," he said. "Back to bed."

But Dorian wasn't having it. He started screaming and flailing around.

Pandemonium erupted. Two kids started crying loudly, a third rolled off his bed onto the floor, and a fourth was shouting, "I want my mommy, I want my mommy."

Then, a cough that was so loud it drew every eye. The little boy, Dorian.

He was standing up. He seemed startled by what had just come from his mouth.

He reared back and coughed again.

"No," Dahra gasped.

Lana leaped to the little boy's side and pressed her hand against the side of his head.

He coughed with such force it knocked him down, flat on his back.

Sanjit straddled him, holding him down, while Lana lay her hands on him, one on his heaving chest, the other on the side of his throat.

Dorian coughed, a spasm so powerful Sanjit fell backward and Dorian's head smacked against the floor with a sickening crack. Lana kept her hold on him.

"He's so hot I can barely keep my—," Lana said as Dorian convulsed, bent into a C, and erupted in a cough that sprayed bloody chunks over Sanjit's face.

Lana did not waver, did not pull back, but Dorian coughed again, and now blood seeped from his ears and pulsed from his lips.

Lana stood up suddenly and backed away.

"Don't stop," Dahra begged.

"I can't cure death," Lana whispered.

Just then two kids appeared in the doorway carrying a third. Lana could see from clear across the room that the girl they were struggling to carry was already gone.

Dahra saw it, too. "Set her down," she said to them. "Just set her down and get out of here, wash yourselves in the surf, and then go home."

"Will she be okay? She lives with us."

"We'll do everything we can," Dahra said flatly. And when they beat a hasty retreat, she added under her breath, "Which is not a damn thing."

Lana closed her eyes and could sense the Darkness reaching out for her, questing, a faint tentacle reaching to touch her mind.

So this is how you destroy us, Lana thought. This is how you kill us off. The old-fashioned way: plague.

NINETEEN

ORC TOOK A small detour on his way to the beach to tear his old home apart looking for a bottle. He found two.

With one bottle in each hand he headed toward the water. He was drinking from both bottles, a swig from the left, a swig from the right, and very soon he was finding the weight of feces in his pants almost funny.

"Orc. Man, where you been?"

Howard. Right there in front of him.

"Go away," Orc said. Not angry, too happy now to be angry.

"Orc, man, what is going on with you? I been looking everywhere for you."

Orc stared dully at Howard. He drank deeply, tilting the bottle back so far he almost lost his balance.

"Okay, that's enough," Howard said. He stepped forward and reached for the bottle and got his fingers around it.

Orc's backhand sent him flying. He had a sudden savage urge to kick Howard. Howard was looking at him as if he had already been kicked and not just swatted away. A look of betrayal. Of hurt.

Orc closed his eyes and turned his head away. Not up for this. He had turds in his pants, his head hurt, bad memories were bubbling up inside his brain, and he didn't need this.

"Dude, come on, man, this isn't right. I'll take care of you, man." Howard stood up and made a show of being fine. His voice was soothing, like he was talking to a baby. Or to some stupid animal or something.

"I got what I need," Orc said. He held the two bottles out like trophies.

Howard stood cautious, ready to jump back. There was blood running from his nose. "I know you're feeling bad about Drake. I know that, because you and I are best friends, right? So I know how you're feeling. But that's done. Anyway, it was just a matter of time, sooner or later it was going to happen."

Orc liked this line of reasoning. But he felt like maybe there was a diss hidden in there, too. "'Cause no one could trust me, right?"

"No, man, that's not it," Howard said. "It's just, no jail was ever going to hold Drake forever. This is all Sam's fault, if had just done what he should have done—"

"I think I hurt some little kid," Orc said.

Just like that. Out it came. Not planned. More like it had to escape. Like Drake: it was going to get out sooner or later.

The comparison made Orc laugh. He laughed loud and long and took another drink and was feeling almost cheerful until his bleary eyes settled on Howard's face once more. Howard was grave. Worried.

"Orc, man, what's that mean? What do you mean you hurt some kid?"

"I just want to go wash off," Orc said.

"This kid you hurt. Where did it happen?"

"I don't know," Orc growled. He looked around like he might be in the right place. No, this wasn't it. It was . . . He spotted a stop sign at the far end of the block.

There was a pile of rags at the bottom of the sign.

Orc felt an icy cold fill his body. Howard was still talking, but his voice was just a distant buzzing sound.

Orc stood staring, unable to speak, unable to move, unable to look away, unable to breathe. Stared at the little pile of rags that was so clearly, so terribly clearly, a body.

Memory. Orc was back in his old body, the one before, the one made of flesh and not rock. He was raising his baseball bat, intending to teach Bette a lesson. Just a tap. Just a smack to show her he was in charge.

He had never meant to kill her, either.

"I'll get rid of it," Howard was saying from far away. "I'll hide it. Or something."

It. Like the pile of rags wasn't a little kid.

Orc walked away, numb, indifferent to Howard's pleas.

It was a small, sandy area, not quite a cove, not really large enough to be much of a beach. It was just a sandy space between jumbled rocks on one side and a stand of scruffy-looking palm trees and grass on the other.

The five fishing boats—the fleet—were beached, pulled up onto the sand. It was like one of those picture postcards from quaint European fishing villages, Quinn thought. Not that the boats were very pretty, really, they were actually rather scruffy, and lord knew they smelled.

Still, kind of perfect.

Quinn and his fishermen had set up a reasonably pleasant campsite. There was never any rain so the fact that they had no tents or other cover didn't matter.

"We'll camp out old-school," Quinn had announced as though it was all a fun diversion.

There were nineteen of them all together and they soon discovered that the beach was alive with fleas, tiny sand crabs, and assorted other animals that made sleep really unpleasant.

It was going to be a long night.

Then someone had the bright idea of burning a patch of grass on the theory that the cleared area would be relatively bug- and crab-free.

This of course gave way naturally to a bonfire of driftwood. It smoked way too much and was hard to keep burning, but it improved everyone's mood and soon they were cooking an early dinner of fish, including some excellent steaks from the shark.

The dinner talk was all about what was happening back in town. Quinn hoped someone would think to update them.

Not just forget about them. He made a point of reassuring his crews that Sam and Edilio would be taking care of their siblings and friends.

"This is just so we don't get sick and can keep working," Quinn explained.

"Oh, goody: work," Cigar said, and everyone laughed.

None of the fishermen seemed sick. No one had complained. Maybe the fact that they were a sort of self-contained group who mostly hung out together and spent most of their time out on the ocean had kept them safe. Maybe they would be okay.

Quinn watched the sun plunge toward the horizon. He walked out alone onto a spit of rock and sand that stretched a few dozen feet from the shore. Weird how much he had come to love his job and being out on the water. He'd always loved surfing, and now that was gone, but the water was still there. Too calm, too peaceful, too much like a lake, but it was still a remnant of the actual ocean, and he loved being near it and on it and in it.

If the barrier ever came down, what would he do? Wait until he was old enough and move to Alaska or Maine and become a professional fisherman? He laughed. That was not a career path that would ever have occurred to him in the old days.

But now he just could not even pretend to care about college or being a lawyer or a businessman or whatever it was his folks thought he should be.

He had crossed a line. He knew it and it made him a little sad. None of them would ever be normal children again. Especially those who had found ways to be happy in the FAYZ.

A light. Down in the direction of the islands. It would never have been noticed back in the days when Perdido Beach itself was lit up.

Quinn had heard the story about Caine and Diana occupying one of the islands. It was weird to think that the light might be coming from Caine's bedroom. And that Caine might be gazing out at the dark night.

Life would never be totally peaceful as long as that guy was alive.

Quinn turned his gaze south. The Sammy suns in people's homes weren't bright enough to light up the town. But the red glow of the setting sun painted the bare outline of Clifftop, snug up against the nearest arc of the barrier.

Lana. Quinn had liked her. Had even thought maybe she liked him. But something had changed in Lana. She was, in some sense, too large and powerful a person for Quinn.

Like Sam, who had once been Quinn's closest friend. They were both part of some different class of person.

Sam, a hero. A leader.

Lana? She was grand and tragic. Like someone out of a play or a book.

And Quinn was a fisherman.

Unlike them, though, he was happy. He turned back to look at his crews, his fishermen. They were cleaning their nets, tending to their reels, cutting grass to make beds, complaining, joking, telling stories everyone had already heard, laughing.

Quinn missed his parents. He missed Sam and Lana. But this was his family now.

Roscoe had fallen asleep from sheer exhaustion. He awoke to find persistent itching on his stomach. He scratched it through his T-shirt.

He went back to sleep. But dreams kept him from sleeping soundly. That and the itching.

He woke again and felt the itchy spot. There was a lump there. Like a swelling. And when he held still and pressed his fingers against the spot he could feel something moving under the skin.

The small room was suddenly very cold. Roscoe shivered.

He went to the window hoping for light. There was a moon but the light was faint. Roscoe pulled his shirt over his head. He looked down at the spot on his stomach.

It was moving. The flesh itself. He could feel it under his fingertips. Like something poking back at him. But he couldn't feel it from the inside, couldn't feel it in his stomach. And he realized that his entire body was numb. He could feel with his fingertips but not the skin of his stomach—

The skin split!

"Ahhhh!"

He was touching it as it split, and he shrieked in terror and something pushed its way out through a bloodless hole.

"Oh, God, oh, God, oh, no no no no!"

Roscoe screamed and leaped for the door. His hand clawed at the knob as he babbled and wept and the door was locked, locked, oh, God, no, they had locked him in.

He banged at the door, but it was the middle of the night. Who would hear him in the empty town hall?

"Hey! Hey! Is anyone there? Help me. Help me. Please, please, someone help me!"

He banged and the thing in his belly stuck out half an inch. He was scared to look at it. But he did and he screamed again because it was a mouth now, a gnashing insect mouth full of parts like no normal mouth. Hooked, wicked mandibles clicked. It was inside him, chewing its way out.

Hatching from him.

"Help me, help me, don't leave me here like this!"

But who would hear him? Sinder? No. Not anymore. That was over. All over. And he was alone and friendless. No one even to hear as he screamed and begged.

The window. He grabbed the pillow from his bed and pushed it against the glass and then punched it hard. The pane shattered. He took off his shoe and smashed at the starred glass until most of it fell tinkling to the street below.

Then he screamed for help. Screamed into the Perdido Beach night air.

No answer.

"Help me! Please, please, oh, God, please help me! You can't just leave me locked up!"

But still, no answer.

Fear took hold of him, deep crazy-making fear.

No. No. No no no no, this couldn't be happening. He hadn't done anything to hurt anyone, he hadn't done anything awful. Why? Why was this happening to him?

Roscoe fell to his knees and begged God. God, please, no, no, no, I didn't do anything wrong. I wasn't brave or strong but I wasn't bad, either. Not like this, please, God, no no no, not like this.

Roscoe felt an itching in the middle of his back.

He sat down and cried.

DIANA FED PENNY a little late. But Penny didn't complain. She was off in some dream that had her smiling to herself, smiling at her own illusions.

The bathroom reeked of human waste. Penny was sitting on the tile floor, legs twisted in front of her, just sitting on a plastic exercise mat.

"Hey, you want to take a shower?" Diana asked.

Penny didn't respond, just giggled at something Diana couldn't see.

Diana bent down and tapped her shoulder. She had to do it several times before Penny's faraway eyes focused on Diana.

Penny laughed. "Oh, that's the real you, isn't it?"

"As real as I get," Diana answered.

"You come to feed the zoo animal?"

"Here's your food. But I thought you might want to take a shower or bath. I could help you."

"Is it because I smell like a sewer? Is that it?"

"Yes," Diana said bluntly. Without waiting for an answer, she went to the tub, a huge oval affair, all pink marble.

How long the water would last, Diana didn't know. But for right now there was water and it was even hot. There was an assortment of Bulgari bath beads, salts, and shampoos. She popped a couple of the bath cubes into the water.

Penny wasn't wearing much, just a dirty yellow tank top and a pair of stained pink shorts. She had two pairs of socks on over her broken ankles.

"How's the pain?" Diana asked.

"Painful. Feels kind of like someone broke my legs and my ankles and my feet. I'll show you what it feels like."

Suddenly a pack of rabid, vicious dogs were there in the room. Their eyes were red, their breath steamed, they snapped at Diana, ready to launch themselves and rip her apart.

Then they were gone.

"Like that," Penny said, taking malicious pleasure from the way Diana had leaped back, batting wildly at the illusion.

Diana calmed herself. Getting upset would just give Penny more of a sense of power.

"Sorry," Diana said for lack of anything else to say. "Eat something while the tub fills."

"You don't have to stay here. I can haul myself up into the tub." She scooped some of the spaghetti and meat sauce into her mouth with her hand.

"You could drown."

"Yeah, that would be terrible, wouldn't it?"

Diana didn't answer. There was nothing but pain in

Penny's future. There was no way to fix her legs, not without Lana, and nothing to treat the pain but Tylenol and Motrin. It was like trying to put out a forest fire with a squirt gun.

"It's good you have your power," Diana said.

"Yeah. It's great. Really great. It's like having my own kind of sucky movie theater. You want to know what I was seeing when you came in?"

Diana was pretty sure she did not.

"I was creating monsters with needle teeth. Like vampires, I guess, but more like wolves, like rabid bats, like every scary thing you see pictures of living down at the bottom of the ocean. And you know what they were doing?"

"Let me help get your shorts off."

Diana knelt and worked Penny's shorts down her thighs. Carefully, as gently as she could. But still Penny made a rising, shuddering cry of pain.

"They were ripping you apart, Diana," Penny gasped through gritted teeth. "They were all over you, Diana, doing every horrible thing I could think of."

"Lift your arms."

Diana pulled the shirt, none too gently, over Penny's head.

"Watching you scream in my head helps keep me from screaming," Penny said.

"Whatever works," Diana said.

She put her arm under Penny's, bent low, and lifted her. The girl wasn't heavy. Food had not cured Penny's runway-model thinness.

"Oh, oh, ohhhhhh," Penny sobbed as Diana lifted her.

Diana rested Penny on the edge of the tub, reached awkwardly to turn off the water.

"Caine could do this easier," Penny said. "But he won't, will he? He doesn't want to come in here and see his handiwork. Not the mighty Caine."

Diana maneuvered to bear most of Penny's weight and lower her bottom first into the hot water. Her twisted pipecleaner legs dragged, then followed their owner into the tub.

Penny screamed.

"Sorry," Diana said.

"Oh, God, it hurts, it hurts, it hurts!"

Diana stood back. Penny was sweating, even paler than before. But she stopped screaming. She lay back against the tub, up to her chest in water and bubbles.

"There's a sprayer. I'll wash your hair." Diana turned on the nozzle, tested the water temperature, and played it over Penny's lank hair.

She worked in shampoo until it foamed.

"Just like the hair salon," Penny said.

"Yeah. Probably where I'll end up working someday," Diana said.

"Nah, not you, you're too smart," Penny said. She had closed her eyes. Diana rinsed shampoo down Penny's face and neck. "Beautiful and smart and you have Caine all to yourself now, don't you?"

Diana sighed. "I'm a loser, Penny. Same as you."

Caine burst in. He looked startled. "I heard screaming."

"Oh, sorry about that," Penny snarled. "I hope I didn't

wake you up, you piece of—"

"You okay?" Caine asked Diana.

"She's perfect," Penny said. "Perfect hair, perfect teeth, perfect skin. Plus she has legs that work, which is really cool."

"I'm out of here," Caine said.

"No," Diana said, "Help me lift her back out."

"Yeah, Caine, don't you want to see me naked? I'm still kind of hot. If you don't mind my legs. Just don't look at them. Because they'll kind of make you sick."

To Diana's surprise Caine said, "Whenever you're ready."

Diana popped the drain.

"Why don't you just kill me?" Penny demanded. "You know you will sooner or later, Caine. You know you can't take care of me forever. You want to do it, don't you?"

Diana tried to read the answer in Caine's eyes. Nothing. There were times she was sure she saw human decency there. And other times when his dark eyes were as pitiless as a shark's.

"Okay, raise her up," Diana said.

Caine stepped closer and lifted up his hands. Penny rose from the water like some awful parody of a surfacing dolphin. She rose and the water fell and bubbles slid off her.

Diana took the nozzle and sprayed Penny off as she floated a few feet in the air. Even the touch of the water on her legs made Penny wince and grit her teeth.

Diana spread a clean towel over the mat and Caine set Penny down slowly. Gently.

"I could fill your head with living nightmares," Penny said

to Caine. "I could make you scream like I scream."

"But then I would kill you, Penny," Caine said coldly. "And I don't think you're quite ready to die."

Albert stared at the ledger book like it could answer his worries. But it was the source of his worries. The columns where he normally entered the amount of produce coming in from the fields, the number of pigeons or gulls caught by Brianna, the number of rats sold to him, the quantity of birds, raccoons, opossums, squirrels, or deer brought in by Hunter, were all empty for this day.

Albert reminded himself to get someone down to the dock to bring up the catch. He should have done it earlier, but it had been a hectic day. Maybe he could send Jamal. Speaking of which, where was Jamal? He was supposed to be back by sunset and it was well after that.

Albert made a mental note to himself: give Dahra something nice as a reward for her quick thinking. If Quinn and his people had been brought down by this flu, the situation would be even more desperate.

Albert had a page for water. Bottled water found in homes or cars: nothing in days. Water trucked in: nothing in a day.

Just like that, in the blink of an eye, Perdido Beach had gone from self-sufficient at a very, very basic level to disaster.

Albert glanced around the room. His natural caution had become something closer to paranoia lately. The house was empty—even the maid was away. But what he was about to do would have been troublesome if observed: he opened his desk and pulled out a bottle of water.

It made a snapping sound as he broke the seal on the bottle of Arrowhead water. He drank deep, then carefully sealed the bottle and hid it away again.

He closed the ledger. Nothing to add to the incoming columns.

Then an unmistakable noise: shattering glass.

Albert froze. The sound was from close by. The kitchen?

He hesitated only a moment, running through his options. Then he reached under the desk, fumbled for and found the pistol taped to the underside.

A door opened. He heard the sound of it and felt the air pressure change and pushed back his chair and tried to rip the tape free so he could hold the gun properly as he'd been shown by Edilio, but he was too slow, too late, they were in the room and on him.

Turk, Lance, Watcher, and Raul. All armed.

It was Watcher—a quiet eleven-year-old who had been caught stealing—who whacked his knee with a crowbar.

"Aaahh!" It hadn't been that hard a swing but the pain shot up his leg and for a second he could think of nothing else. He'd never felt pain like that. His ankle and foot were tingling like he'd stepped on a downed power line.

"Get him!"

"Yeah!"

"Hit him again!"

"No!" Albert yelled, but the next blow came from Turk, who smashed the butt of his rifle into Albert's face. His nose gushed blood. This was more numbing than painful. His thoughts were scattered, ripped into fragments.

"Wha . . . ?" he said.

His pistol, gone. Where? He squeezed his hand, stupid for a few seconds, not able to figure out—

Turk grabbed him from the back of his neck and slammed him facedown on the ledger. A distant part of Albert's mind worried that his blood would seep onto the pages and make them hard to read.

He groaned as someone punched him in the back and in the side and ground his face savagely against the ledger.

Turk yanked him back and shoved him against the wall. Albert's legs gave way and he fell on his rear end.

The four of them loomed over him. Albert knew he was crying as well as bleeding. And he knew that both his tears and his blood would make the creeps happy.

"What do you want?" he said, slurring his words, realizing a broken tooth was stuck into his tongue.

"What do we want?" Turk mocked. "Everything, Albert. We want everything."

After cleaning Penny, Diana felt the need for a shower herself.

She shampooed. She conditioned. She shaved her legs and armpits. So normal. So like being home. Except that here her mother's creepy boyfriends didn't sneak in to get a look at her and pretend they'd come looking for aspirin or whatever.

She turned off the shower with great reluctance. She could stand there under the spray forever. But in the back of her mind was the knowledge that they had all wasted food until they were starving. She had learned a deep lesson about waste.

She wrapped one of the soft bath sheets around herself and brushed her teeth.

She went toward her bed and found Caine waiting there for her. He was standing awkwardly, chewing his thumbnail.

"Napoleon?" she asked him.

"No," he said, and looked down at the floor.

"Uh-huh."

"I helped with Penny."

"Yes, you did. And you only threatened to kill her once."

A flicker of a smile. "Even Sam would have threatened her."

Diana went to him. They did not touch. But they stood just inches away. Close enough for Diana to feel his breath on her face.

"Why did you save me?" Diana asked.

Caine sucked in a deep, steadying breath, like he was getting ready to dive into a pool. "Because I . . ." He paused, blinked, seeming surprised at the words coming out of his own mouth. "Because what would I do without you? How would I live without you? Because."

"Because?"

"Because you are the only human being I need."

Diana looked at him skeptically. Was he changed? Even a little? Or was it all just manipulation?

She might never know. But at that moment she also knew this was all she would get from him. And she knew that it was enough. Because she was not going to turn him away.

She grabbed his head in both hands and drew him to her. She kissed him hard. It was a hungry, needy, wild kiss. No time to breathe, no time to be gentle, no time for any more stupid questions or doubts.

Diana took a step back, unwound the towel, and let it drop.

Caine made a sound like a strangling animal.

She pushed him hard. He landed on his back on the bed.

He began to fumble with his shirt, trying to get it off.

"No, I'll do that," Diana said. "I'll do everything."

PETE

SOMETHING WAS NOT right. He could no longer balance atop the sheet of glass. He had fallen. He was falling still.

There was a ringing in his ears. A fire burned inside his body and that body was almost all he saw now. The sister was a faint echo. The Darkness was far away. He was inside himself, burning, twisting, and falling forever and forever.

He tried to make his mother appear, but she wavered and slipped away.

The cool breeze could not reach inside him, it sliced his skin but did not put out the fire.

He felt his body empty out. Wrong. Wrong even to see himself, wrong to have his body be so big a part of his mind, pushing everything else aside.

Pain. An explosion, one of many, erupted from him and shot white-hot spears into him again and again.

His sister was upset, her distraught, too-bright, too-blue eyes swam around like fish in an aquarium.

The pale tentacle reached, quested, but could not find him because he was no longer high atop it all, perched and balanced, he was falling, spinning downward into thirst and burning and pain.

He had to make it stop.

But how?

TWENTY-ONE

LITTLE PETE LICKED his lips. They were dry and cracked.

Astrid was thirsty, too. She'd gone out a couple of times, defying the quarantine, to look for water.

Her plan now was to wait for dawn when the dew would settle on the leaves of the trees, on the siding of the house.

She had a squeegee and a bucket and some fairly clean rags. She had to get water. She had to get Pete something to drink.

No one to call on for help. Sam was gone. She had looked for Edilio but not found him. Who could get her anything? Who could help her?

Little Pete coughed hoarsely and licked his lips as he hung in midair, twisting slowly, like a chicken on a rotisserie, hovering in the breeze that blew strong through the window.

Afterward Diana lay alone in her bed. She'd kicked Caine out and Caine was relieved to go.

Diana would not have minded him staying. But she sensed

he needed to go off and think, wonder what he'd gotten himself into, and regret any implication that he had cleaned up his act and accepted her terms.

It was all a fantasy, of course, the idea that he would change. Maybe someday. Maybe when he was older. Maybe when he got a career and a house and a wife and all the other things that cause wild boys to turn into men.

Not that men were always better behaved than boys.

Diana stayed on her side of the bed, just as if Caine was still there. That had become his side of the bed. It belonged to him.

Of course if that was true she was going to have to find some condoms. From just the two times the risk of pregnancy wasn't great, especially given the fact that her body was half wrecked. But still. The last thing anyone wanted was a baby.

What chance would any kid have with Caine as father and Diana as mother? Diana laughed softly. And could not later recall the exact moment or the exact reason that her laughter turned into bitter tears.

Edilio stood completely still in the hallway outside of Roscoe's room.

He could barely breathe.

What could he say? What could you say to a boy who was going to die? The terrible truth was that he could do nothing for Roscoe. It was good that Roscoe was calling to God because only God could save him. Edilio could not.

And what Edilio had to do next would destroy Roscoe's last hope.

Edilio looked at the plywood. Three half sheets, each four by four feet. A hammer and nails. Two-by-fours.

It had to be done. It had to be. Roscoe—the things inside him—could not be allowed to escape.

Edilio dragged the first sheet across the dark hallway and propped it against the door.

"I hear someone out there!" Roscoe yelled.

"It's me, Roscoe. It's Edilio," he said.

"Edilio! Please, can you help me?"

Edilio opened the box of nails, grabbed the hammer, lined the nail up so it would go through the plywood into the door molding.

"Roscoe, there's nothing I can do, brother. I have to . . . You're going to hear some hammering."

"What?"

Edilio slammed the hammer into the nail. He had to be careful; it was dark, and operating by feel alone was a bad way to hammer nails.

This was going to take a long time.

"Roscoe, I have to do this, man," Edilio said.

"You're going to lock me in here and let me die?"

Edilio hesitated. "Yes."

"No way. No way. No!"

"And I have to do the same thing to the window, man."

"Edilio, no. No, man. You don't want to do this."

"No, I don't want to do this," Edilio said.

Roscoe fell silent as Edilio nailed the remaining plywood in place. Edilio propped the two-by-four against the plywood and nailed it into place. The other end he nailed into the floor with massive long nails that took forever to hammer in.

Outside in the fresh air, Edilio steeled himself for what came next. He leaned the ladder against the building and with some difficulty wrestled a sheet of plywood up the ladder. He was going to fall and kill himself, he thought, and it would be justice, wouldn't it?

Roscoe was there at the window. His face was ghostly in the pale moonlight. "Isn't there anything . . . ?" Roscoe pleaded.

"Sam can't even kill the things," Edilio said. "He tried but he couldn't. I can't let them hurt more people."

"Yeah," Roscoe said. He nodded, jaw so stiff his teeth were cracking audibly.

"Sorry, man," Edilio said. He slapped the wood into place against the window, resting it precariously on the narrow sill.

"Tell everyone I was ever mean to that I'm sorry," Roscoe said, his voice muffled now.

"You were never mean to anyone, man. You were a good guy." Edilio winced, realizing too late that he was using the past tense. He quickly drove in the first nail. He hit his thumb with the hammer. The pain was stunning.

He welcomed it.

Orc woke to a headache and shivers.

He was facedown. On the sand. The surf was lapping at his legs, covering his feet, gently surging to wash over his calves.

His head was a single giant ball of pain.

There was sand in his mouth. Sand in the cracks between the pebbles that formed his skin.

He could see the bottles. Just a few inches from his head, empty. Not even a tiny little drop left.

He was still drunk, he had not slept long enough to sober up. But he was no longer blacked-out, brain-dead drunk.

He was naked. That surprised him a little. But he had vague memories of ripping his stained, filthy clothes off and rampaging like a wild animal through the water. Bellowing.

There was no one to see him anyway. No one around. No one was going to hang around when Orc went crazy.

Scared of me, Orc thought. Surprise, surprise. Orc the monster, all covered in his own crap and staggering and lurching through waist-high water trying to get clean, scared people.

He decided to go look for another bottle, quick, before it all came rushing back into his head but it was too late because it was all coming back now.

He got to his knees. He might be a filthy, disgusting drunk, but he was still strong.

He'd have to walk naked through the dark streets. What did it matter? He wasn't a boy, he was a monster. A naked Orc was just a curiosity for people to laugh at. One more thing for people to find disgusting.

He tried to stand up but somehow ended up rolling onto his back. He vomited. It dribbled over the side of his face, over the last patch of human skin.

There were stars in the sky. They kind of swam around and sometimes doubled and blurred.

Here he was: Charles Merriman.

He hated himself. Hated himself so much. He had what he deserved: cold sand and colder water and pain.

Why couldn't he just die? He deserved to die. He needed to die. If there was some kind of God up there looking down at him, then God was wanting to throw up.

Of course God probably liked doing stuff like this. Charles Merriman was probably, like, his favorite person to beat on. Yeah, it was, like, *I'm going to give this kid a violent drunk for a daddy, and a dumb dishrag for a mother, and I'm going to make it hard for him to even learn to read, and then, just when he's starting to finally get some respect, I'll turn him into a monster.*

No one ever treated Charles Merriman like he might be a kid. Like he might not be totally worthless. Except Howard, and that was just so Howard could use him.

The only other person who had been nice to him was Astrid. Not like she liked him, but she didn't think he was scum. Like he wasn't just some nothing.

He had saved her life once. But even before that she'd been nice to him. One person. Ever.

With a supreme effort, Orc got to his feet.

In the end Sam decided to camp for the night by the train. They had crates to burn and a reassuring fire roared high into the night sky.

They made a camp out of lawn furniture. They ate Nutella

and drank Pepsi, nowhere near tired of the sweetness.

They stared into the flames and up at the sparks.

"If we bring kids here, they're going to find out about the missiles," Dekka said.

"Yeah," Sam agreed. He made a *keep it down* gesture and added a significant glance at Toto, who was dozing fitfully on a wicker chaise lounge.

"We can't get all this to town. They have to come here."

"Yep," Sam said.

"What we need right now is a bunch of . . . what were they called?"

"M3-MAAWS," Jack said. "Multi-role Anti-Armor Anti-Personnel Weapons System." He was reading the instruction manual by the light of the fire.

Sam rolled his eyes. "M3s. Yeah, this would be, like, the last thing I would want to see getting into a kid's hands."

"Can we hide them?" Dekka suggested.

"I won't tell anyone," Jack said distractedly. "I don't want kids coming here and stealing my 'puters, anyway."

"We have a new member of our little band," Sam said. "Toto the truth teller. I don't think he's great at keeping secrets."

He got up to throw another wooden crate on the fire. The fire would most likely keep the coyotes away. He yawned and flopped into the wicker rocking chair and hefted his sore feet onto the little table.

"You know what?" Sam said. "I keep forgetting: I am not the guy in charge." He laughed contentedly. "I'll tell Albert.

I'll hand Toto off to Edilio. Then? Not my problem."

"Yeah, that's totally going to work, Sam," Dekka said.

Sam noticed her feeling her stomach, pressing in on it, frowning.

"Anything the matter?" he asked.

Dekka shook her head. "I think I'll get some sleep."

Sam nodded off. At some time in the night he woke to see the fire had burned down to glowing coals. He saw Dekka some distance away, just outside the circle of firelight. She had her back to him, her shirt lifted up to expose her stomach, which she prodded and poked.

Sam went back to sleep and came fully awake what felt like mere seconds later, though the fire was almost entirely out and Dekka was on her own chair, snoring.

Something. Something out there in the dark.

Coyotes? He didn't want a fight with coyotes—if he or one of the others was badly hurt, there was no easy way to get back to Lana.

He raised his hand and tossed a Sammy sun into the air. It hovered ten feet up, casting a sickly light over the camp. Jack and Toto asleep. Dekka, no longer.

"What is it?" Dekka hissed.

"Don't know." He pointed to the direction he thought the sound had come from. Then, in a voice pitched loud enough to be heard but not loud enough to wake his sleeping companions, he said, "If anyone's out there, I am Bright Hands. I will burn you if you bother us."

No answer.

A faint but definite rustling sound. Maybe a clicking. Maybe not. Then silence.

"So much for sleep," Sam said.

"I'll sit watch," Dekka said.

"Dekka: you have anything you need to tell me?"

He heard her sigh. "Just being paranoid, Sam. Just, you know, making sure. My stomach was just rumbling and I thought maybe . . . You know."

"Dekka, the last time you had anything even a little bit sweet was months ago. It's not a surprise your stomach would be a little off."

"Yeah. I know. Is yours?"

"Sure. A little," Sam lied.

Jack woke with a loud snort and a crash as he smashed his arm down, crushing a table.

"What?" he yelled. He sat up. Rubbed his face. Found his glasses. "Why are we awake? It's still night."

"It's true: it is nighttime," Toto said.

"Well, if we're all up, we might as well push on. Sooner the better," Sam said with a sigh. "Let's go find this lake."

Sanjit was slight in build. But he was strong. So when Lana collapsed he was able to catch her and hold her.

Dahra saw it happen. "She needs sleep," she said to Sanjit. "Get her out of here."

"What about you?" Sanjit asked.

"I've gotten really good at grabbing power naps," Dahra

said. "Besides, Virtue is almost as much use around here as you are."

"Almost?" Virtue grumbled.

He had come to the so-called hospital with word that Bowie was doing much better. He had tucked the rest of his brothers and sisters into bed with too little water and too little food. And now he was helping Dahra.

Dahra put a hand on his shoulder and said, "You're a lifesaver, Virtue. My little African brother, here."

That brought one of Virtue's rare smiles. Dahra's folks came from Ghana and Virtue's from Congo, so they weren't exactly from the same neighborhood, but it gave them something in common, Sanjit realized. That, plus the fact that they were both incredibly decent people.

"I can't carry Lana to Clifftop," Sanjit said. "But I can get her a place to lie down."

Lana woke up long enough to say, "Urrhh. Wha?" And then her eyes rolled back in her head and Sanjit lifted her in his arms. Virtue brought him a couple of blankets and draped them over his shoulders.

He carried her up out of the basement, up through the hallway crowded with hacking, miserable kids, and out to the plaza.

Five unburied bodies lay there side by side. Mismatched blankets covered each one, corners tucked underneath, faces covered by chenille or satin or tartan wool.

They'd given the plague a name, a callous nickname. The SDC they called it: Supernatural Death Cough.

But at some point during the day they'd begun to notice that some kids were getting better, too. The flu was awful. But it wasn't a death sentence to everyone who caught it.

They'd been unable to keep complete records, but according to Dahra's hasty notes and frazzled memory about one in ten progressed to full-blown SDC.

Sanjit was struggling a bit to carry Lana, but he was unwilling to lay her down near the dead or within sound of the hacking coughs.

She wasn't just going without sleep. She was going without love and hope. She was living with guilt for having failed to be Superwoman, having failed to kill the evil in the mine shaft, having failed to see what was happening to Mary.

He took her to the beach and laid her down on one of the blankets, which he spread on the soft, dry sand. She was lying on top of the gun in her belt, so he slid it out and lay it on her stomach. Then he covered her with the other blanket.

Her faithful dog had followed them the whole way and now Patrick snuggled beside her. He looked up at Sanjit, questioning.

She would almost certainly be safe here alone. No one wanted to hurt the Healer. And Patrick would bark if anyone came close.

But Sanjit couldn't just leave her here all alone. So he settled into a sort of yoga sitting posture, sighed, and decided to await sunrise.

•   •   •

Albert did not resist. Maybe, he thought, a braver kid would have. But he wasn't that kid. When Turk demanded to know where Albert's secret stash was, Albert told him.

Simple as that.

Albert had wet himself. He had cried. Still was crying.

He was going to die. He knew that. They would figure out pretty soon that there was no safe way to release Albert.

They would know that. He knew it, so how could they not know it?

But he could negotiate, maybe. Maybe now that they had all his stuff, his stash of canned food and bottled water.

It didn't look like much. It wasn't, although it was untold wealth in the FAYZ. They had filled two small boxes with his things and filled their hoodie pockets as well.

"You got what you wanted," Albert said, trying desperately but failing to keep the sobby quaver out of his voice. "Just go away. I won't tell anyone."

"Man, you were hiding cans of Beef-a-Roni," Raul said. He was disbelieving. "You had three cans!"

"Take it," Albert pleaded. "Take it all."

Turk glanced at Lance. Even in his despairing, shattered state, Albert knew they weren't quite sure just yet. Hope rose like a tiny flame inside him. Maybe. Maybe they wouldn't.

"Look, you want food and water, right?" Albert pleaded.

"You have more?" Lance demanded angrily.

"Not-not-not here."

"Not-not-not," Lance mimicked.

"N-n-n-n-not h-h-h-here," Watcher said, and laughed.

"So where is this other stuff?" Turk asked, and kicked him almost tentatively. It was enough, though, to send a breathtaking spike of pain up Albert's leg from his broken knee. The knee was already swelling to twice its normal size. It was the worst of many agonies in his body.

"I don't have anything else here," Albert said. "But listen, I make more, right? I buy more. I control what gets made and picked and all."

"Yes," Turk said, mock-serious. "You're a big man, Albert. Too bad you peed yourself."

That set off another round of laughter.

"You think we're stupid?" Lance demanded. "You think we're just some stupid white boys who don't know you can snap your fingers and have Sam or Brianna or one of those freaks come after us?"

"I wouldn't do that," Albert said. His jaw was quivering so bad he almost couldn't speak. "I wouldn't. Because if I did that, you'd, you'd, you'd tell people I cried."

"And wet your pants." Watcher seemed the most likely to let him go, but Albert knew the decisions were being made by Turk and Lance.

There was no pity in either face. Lance was aglow with hatred. Turk was less emotional.

"You know what we ought to do?" Turk suggested, laughing in anticipation of his punch line. "We ought to throw him in one of the slit trenches we dug for him."

"No, no, don't do that," Albert begged. A dunking in

excrement was infinitely better than being killed. "No, don't, I'm begging you."

Lance squatted down, brought his handsome, chiseled face right down to Albert's level. "You just think you've got it all, don't you? Yeah, it would be fun to see you wallow around in the crap like you made us do. But then you'd just climb out and next time one of us turned around, there'd be Sam Temple. Flash of light and *zap*, we'd be dead."

"I'm not . . . That's not . . . ," Albert said. "Please. Please don't kill me."

Turk looked offended. "Did we say we were going to kill you?" He turned to Lance. "Where did he get that idea?"

Lance played along. "I have no idea, Turk."

"Maybe because of this," Turk said. He leveled his rifle at Albert's face.

Something exploded.

Albert heard no sound.

He was on his side.

Blood covered his right eye, blinding him. Or maybe his eye wasn't there anymore, he didn't know.

He tried to breathe and heard gurgling in his lungs. Heard his heart slow . . .

Turk looked at once alarmed and ecstatic. Lance's face became sullen. The two younger kids backed away, tripping over each other, and ran.

Lance punched Turk's shoulder in rough congratulations.

Albert's one good eye went dark.

TWENTY-TWO

"THAT IS A lake," Sam said. "That is definitely a lake."

"I can't believe we didn't even know this was here," Dekka said.

The sun was still not up, but a pearly gray light showed a long slope heading down to a vast body of water. Bigger than anything Sam had seen outside of the ocean.

Dry grass grew in tufts. Amazingly scraggly, stunted pine trees showed here and there, but the shore itself was formed by a line of large jumbled rocks broken up by narrow, half-hearted sand beaches.

At the limits of their vision was a small marina with perhaps two dozen boats at the dock.

The barrier sliced right across the lake, but the part on the inside was more water than the kids of Perdido Beach could ever need or want.

"You think it's drinkable?" Dekka wondered.

"Let's find out," Sam said. He jogged downhill toward

the shore, careful not to trip, but anxious to see and taste. It would be too cruel to get here and find that it was salt water. That would be one more dirty trick, one more disappointment. Not to mention the fact that it might doom them all.

He reached the lakeshore with the others close behind. The pale rock was shifting and unsteady, so he felt his way gingerly.

He pulled off his shoes and then impulsively dived in a flat arc into the water.

It was shallow near the shore and he scraped his chest on submerged rocks, but with two strokes he was out in water over his head.

Sam gulped a mouthful. Treading water he looked back to see Jack, Dekka, and Toto standing uncertainly on the rocks. "Ladies and gentlemen," Sam said, his face split by a huge grin, "we have fresh water."

In something less than five seconds, the three of them splashed in after him.

"It's water!" Jack cried.

"It is so totally water!" Dekka agreed.

"She's telling the truth, Spidey!" Toto said.

Sam turned a joyful somersault. The lake was cold but not bone-chilling. The surfer part of his brain calculated he'd have been warm and toasty enough with a 3/2 wetsuit.

He gulped some more water and swam over to his friends.

"Fresh water," Dekka said. "Cold fresh water. Brrr."

Sam scanned the shore. "This isn't a great place to set up a new town, really. We'd need something flatter. And then we'd have to be careful about not having everyone's sewage end up flowing into our drinking water. I guess we . . ." He stopped himself. Albert and Edilio could figure out the details. He had done what he needed to do.

"I saw boats," Jack remarked. "I wonder if there are fish."

Toto said, "Fish, yes, fish."

"You know something?" Sam asked him.

"My dad used to take me fishing." Then, as if puzzled by his own words, he looked for the Spidey head that wasn't there and said, "This isn't that lake, is it? No, that was Lake Isabella."

"Okay," Dekka said patiently. "Were there fish in that lake?"

"Trout," Toto said. "Bass. Also crappie. Fish."

"If we find fishing poles and stuff on the boats, it means there are fish," Jack pointed out.

"It's only, like, half a mile. We could swim," Sam said.

"You could swim half a mile," Dekka said. "Me, I'll walk."

They climbed out, Sam with great reluctance. It was invigorating, this new and unexplored body of water. Who knew what might be found on or around the lake?

But he understood that Dekka and the others might not be thrilled by a long, cold swim.

The shore was a series of curves, like the edge of a lace doily made with sketchy sand beaches and rocky promontories. They soon came upon a trail and were laughing and chatting lightheartedly.

Sam knew logically that without gas—and a lot of it—they'd never get enough water down to—

He stopped dead. "Marinas," he said. He felt a chill that had nothing to do with temperature. "Marinas. You know what they have?"

"Boats?" Jack suggested, like he was afraid it was the wrong answer.

"Boats." Sam grinned. "Sailboats, maybe. But you know what else? Motorboats. Jet skis."

"You want to jet ski?"

"What do jet skis run on, my friend?"

"I want to say water," Dekka said.

"Gas!" Jack cried.

Sam slapped him on the shoulder. "Yes! A marina isn't a marina if they don't have fuel."

He grinned and started to run toward the marina. A nagging voice in his head warned him not to hope, not to expect a good answer. *It's the FAYZ,* the voice said.

It's still the FAYZ.

But after so much pain, so many disappointments, and so many horrors, surely they were due for some good news?

Surely.

Lana opened her eyes.

Patrick licked her face. Which was probably why she opened her eyes.

Something heavy lay on her chest. A head. Long, dark hair.

She pushed it away and it groaned, and said, "I'm awake."

Sanjit sat up, looked at her, and wiped drool from the corner of his mouth.

Lana was on the beach. The sun was up but had not yet cleared the mountains. How she had come there she did not know. Instinctively she felt for her gun. It was not in her waistband. It had become tangled in the blanket.

"How did I get here?"

"I brought you here."

Lana absorbed that. "Why?" she demanded suspiciously.

"You passed out."

Lana ran her hands through her tangled hair. She wiped her mouth and made a face, tasting the inside of her mouth. "You have any water?"

"Sadly, no," Sanjit said.

She sighed and looked at him with tired eyes. "What is it with you? You don't even have a blanket," Lana said.

"I wasn't going to sleep."

"Tell me you weren't watching me sleep, because then I'd have to throw up."

Sanjit grinned. "I did. I watched you sleep. And heard you sleep, too."

"What does that mean?"

"Well, you farted once. But mostly you talk in your sleep. Groan in your sleep."

"What did I say?"

Sanjit made a show of trying to recall. "Well, mostly it was, urrgh, mmmm, unh, unh, don't try to . . . urggh. And the fart was very, um, genteel. Like: *poot-poot!* Almost musical."

Lana stared at him.

He shivered.

"Are you cold?" she asked.

"Just a little chilly. You know, from just waking up." He shivered again and wrapped his arms around his drawn-up legs.

She pulled her top blanket off, balled it up, sand flying, and shoved it at him. He draped it over his shoulders.

"How many more dead?" she asked.

"It was five total when we left."

Lana hung her head down for a moment and Sanjit remained silent. Then she stood up. She walked down to the water's edge. She stripped off her outer clothing, leaving only her underthings.

Then, gritting her teeth, she ran into the surf, and as soon as the water was up to her knees, she dove headfirst. It was freezing. But it was clean. It washed away the blood and the grime.

She rinsed her mouth with salt water.

Then, shivering, she came back out of the water and ran back to Sanjit.

"You're staring," she said.

"Yes. I am. I'm a teenage boy. Beautiful girls in wet underwear have a tendency to cause staring in teenage boys."

She bent down, picked up the blanket, shook the sand out of it, and wrapped it around her. Sanjit stood up.

She kissed him on the mouth.

A real kiss.

He cupped her wet head in both hands and kissed her back.

"That wasn't as bad as I thought it would be," Lana said.

For once, she noted with satisfaction, Sanjit did not seem to have a glib comeback. In fact he looked just a little sick, and very much as if he meant to kiss her again.

"Back to the hospital," she said.

Brittney rose to consciousness on a narrow dirt path. Seven-foot-high dirt and stone walls hemmed her in, towered over her. And perched atop those walls, coyotes leered down, their mouths open, tongues lolling out.

Jamal was behind her, checking the wire that held her arms pinned together at wrist and elbow.

Her ankles, too, were tied, but with a loose rope so that she could take short steps, but not run.

"Where are we?" Brittney asked.

Jamal shrugged with his one good shoulder. "Somewhere Drake wants us to go." He yawned, glanced up nervously at the coyotes, and yawned again.

"You should get some rest," Brittney said. "You're in pain and tired."

"Here?" He laughed bitterly. "This feel like the place for a nap?"

No, Brittney acknowledged silently. There was something dark about this place, even though the sun was up in the sky. Something about the air. Something about the look in the

eyes of the coyotes. A darkness that reached inside to her un-
beating heart.

"I want to go back," Brittney said.

"Yeah? Me, too," Jamal said. "But if I do, old Drake will
whip the skin off me."

He shoved her forward. She stumbled when the rope
snapped at her ankles and almost fell. But she caught herself and shuffled on, not knowing what else she could or
should do.

What must I do, Lord, to earn my true death and my place
in your heaven?

"This is a bad place, Jamal," Brittney said. "I can feel it."

"Yeah," he said. "Drake is a bad boy, and he goes to bad
places. But better off with him than against him, I figure."

They emerged from the cut-through in view of a half-
ruined hole in the side of a sheer rock face. There was just
enough pale pink light to see that the mine shaft was blocked
by tons of fallen rock. The massive timbers that framed the
hole were splintered and looked as if they might snap.

Whatever evil Brittney felt, it came from there, from that
hole, that pile of rocks.

"Where are we?"

"The mine shaft," Jamal said. "Haven't you heard all about
that? In there? That's the thing that gave Drake his whip."

"In where?" Brittney said. "It's all collapsed. It's sealed up."

"That's probably good, huh? 'Cause if that thing feels this
bad from out here, I don't want to know what it feels like up
close." He bit his lip and in a low voice said, "Like a big claw

holding your heart. Like icicles in your brain."

"Jamal, if you ran away . . ."

He shook his head. "Drake would come after me. Look, you can't be killed, right? And he can't be killed, right? Which means, I betray him, sooner or later he gets me."

"Maybe fire," Brittney said softly. "Maybe God's holy fire can destroy us both."

"Yeah, well, I don't happen to have any of that."

"Only Sam can end this."

Jamal put up his hands in a *who, me?* gesture and said, "I am cool with that. If big Sam wants to take Drake out, I'm not going to say anything to stop him. But listen: all you're trying to do is slow Drake down, girl. Him and Sam, they're going to get into it eventually, right? So maybe you should be trying to speed him up, you see what I'm saying?"

Brittney stared at Jamal. Was it a trick?

Is this the devil tempting me?

"What did the demon Drake ask you to do?"

Jamal nodded at the cave. "He just said be here. He's got in his head that he can talk to that thing in there. Or at least hear what it says."

Brittney could believe that. How could she not believe in things that seemed supernatural? Her brother sometimes spoke to her as an angel. And God was with her always. Wasn't He?

And she herself, this gruesome remnant of the girl she once was, she herself was something outside of nature.

Was Sam the Lord's servant? The very tool God had chosen

to liberate Brittney? She'd begged Sam often for liberation. But God's ways were not knowable to her. His time was not her time. His will be done.

"What does Drake want of me?" Brittney asked.

"Just, you know, don't always be trying to run away so I have to tie your legs and slow us down and all."

"Is he going after Sam? Is that his plan, to go after Sam?"

She thought she caught just the slightest falseness in Jamal's eyes as he said, "That's exactly his plan. Straight for Sam, as soon as he checks in with . . . you know."

"You can sleep, Jamal," Brittney said. "Sleep until Drake comes back. I won't run away."

"How am I going to trust you?"

"Because I swear it. On the blood of the Lamb, I swear it."

Jamal woke to the pain of Drake kicking him.

"What?"

Drake was actually smiling. It wasn't a good look for him.

"You were asleep," he said. "And I'm still here."

Jamal jumped up and quickly untied Drake. "Yeah, I did just what you said, Drake. Just like you said. I told her that you would go after Sam first thing. Then Sam would burn you both up and . . ."

He gulped, suddenly realizing that this might be taking it too far.

But Drake was in a charitable, expansive mood. He patted Jamal lightly on the cheek with the tip of his whip. "You did good. And I will get Sam Temple. Sooner or later."

Drake gazed at the mine shaft. What he felt toward the Darkness within was something very much like love. Fear, yes, but the Darkness deserved his fear. His fear and his devotion.

If he had to pull the rocks out of there one by one, and if it took weeks, he would reach the Darkness and free him.

"My old body's down there," Drake said, realizing it for the first time. "My old body is down there with him."

Drake felt a sudden pang of longing. He wanted to press his body against the rocks in the mine's mouth. It would bring him closer. Maybe the Darkness would reach out to him, touch his mind, tell him what to do next.

But he couldn't do that in front of Jamal.

"Start hauling rock," Drake said. "You have to pile it, like, back over there." He pointed a relatively flat space. "I don't know how far the rock fall goes. It may take us a while. Put Brittney Pig to work when she comes back."

For two hours or more they lifted and carried. It would have helped if they had a wheelbarrow. It would have helped if Jamal's arm weren't broken. They had to lift each chunk of stone, each shattered timber. Some were big enough that they had to each take an end. Some were so big they couldn't even budge them and had to just go around them.

At the end of two hours they'd moved no more than a foot and a half deeper into the shaft.

Brittney had reappeared once during that time and she had bought into the idea of helping with the digging. But Drake couldn't kid himself: they weren't getting anywhere. It could take months. Years. Forever.

The coyotes came and went, watching, no doubt thinking about eating Jamal. So when Drake heard the sound of movement coming from around the bend in the road, he assumed it was coyotes.

Only it wasn't the usual stealthy *pad-pad-pad* of coyotes. This was a sound with clicks and sudden rushes.

Drake wiped his brow and turned warily toward the sound.

It looked like something from a science fiction movie. Like an alien or a robot or something, because it was way too big to be just an insect.

It was silver and bronze, dully reflective. It had an insect's head with prominent, gnashing mouthparts that made Drake think of a Benihana chef flashing knives ceremonially. Its wickedly curved mandibles of black horn or bone protruded from the side of its mouth.

It smelled like curry and ammonia. Bitter but with a tinge of curdled sweetness.

More came now, scurrying up beside the first. They had eyes and antennae. The eyes were arresting: royal blue irises that could almost pass as human. But with nothing of human awareness, nothing of human vulnerability or emotion. Like ice chips.

They ran in a rush on six legs, stopping, starting, then skittering forward again at alarming speed. Their tarnished silver wings folded back against bronze carapaces, like beetles or cockroaches. The wings sometimes flared slightly as they ran.

Bugs. Maybe. But each at least five feet long and three feet tall, with antennae adding another foot.

Drake stared into the soulless blue eyes of the first bug.

He was ready with his whip hand, and Jamal was ready with his rifle, but Drake didn't like his chances much if they were looking for a fight. There were a dozen of the creatures, jostling around one another, like ants pouring from a mound or wasps storming angrily from a disturbed hive.

Drake felt a stab of fear: could he survive being eaten? Chopped into chunks by those gnashing mouths and swallowed?

A coyote, keeping a cautious distance, loped to the top of the rise and spoke in the strangled speech his species had achieved.

"See the Darkness," the coyote said.

"Them?" Drake asked. The coyotes and these monstrosities could communicate? "They want to see the Darkness? Fine," Drake said. He jerked his thumb over his shoulder toward the mine. "Go for it."

"They hungry," the coyote said.

Drake didn't have to ask what he was supposed to do about that. Because now the same foul, insinuating voice that was speaking through the coyote reached him directly, touched his willing, submissive mind and flooded it with a deep and awful joy.

Drake closed his eyes and rocked slowly back and forth, feeling the touch of his master.

Soon Drake would be with the Darkness. The Darkness would give him all he needed. And Jamal had served his purpose.

"So tell them to eat something," Drake said. "Sorry, Jamal."

"What?" Jamal waited for Drake to laugh, like it was a joke. But Drake just smiled and winked and said, "Dude, sooner or later I was going to kill you anyway."

"No, no!" Jamal gasped. He backed away. He turned and ran.

The nearest bug, icy blue eyes focused with terrible intensity, flashed out something that might have been a tongue. It was black, and as thick as a rope with a barbed tip like a cluster of fishhooks. The tongue caught Jamal's leg and Jamal fell facedown.

"Drake! Drake!" Jamal yelled. "Please!"

Drake laughed. He gave a little wave as the rope tongue yanked Jamal toward his doom.

Jamal fired. *BLAM BLAM BLAM.* At close range, then closer range, then inches from the bug's hideous face.

The tongue released and snapped back. Then scimitar mandibles cut Jamal in half and there was no more firing, just a hopeless wail of despair.

The massive bugs surged, and within seconds nothing was left of Jamal.

Then, without a pause, the blue-eyed monsters went to work moving rocks at dazzling speed, pushing with their mandibles, rising on their hind four legs and gripping with their front two.

Drake felt Brittney returning. But that was okay, because now his Lord and Master, the Darkness, Drake's one true God was with him, filling his heart and soul.

And It would not be thwarted.

TWENTY-THREE

9 HOURS, 14 MINUTES

ASTRID WAS IN the backyard using the slit trench when it happened. She had sat by Little Pete's bed for two days, waiting, fearing.

But even dehydrated, she still had to go eventually. She'd hoped it would be safe. She'd hoped to see that Albert's people were delivering water and food and the epidemic was past.

But the streets were abandoned. She heard no distant sounds of truck engines, nor even the squeaky wheels of hand-drawn wagons.

So she did what she had to do at the slit trench in the yard and continued to pray as she had almost constantly.

Whooosh-craaack!

The entire upper floor of the house blew apart.

There was no fire. No flame.

The top floor—the tile roof, the siding, the walls, wood, and drywall, all of it—blew apart almost quietly. A big chunk of roof spun over her head, throwing off red tiles as it spun and dropped with a massive crash against the wall of the house next door.

She saw a window, the glass still somehow in place, go whirling straight up like a rocket. She followed it with her eyes, waiting for it to come spiraling down at her. It crashed into the branches of a tree and finally then the glass shattered.

The bed from her own bedroom was on a roof two houses down. Sheets and clothing fluttered to the ground like confetti. It was almost festive, like someone had set off a Fourth of July rocket and now she could oooh and aahh as the sparkles came down.

But no fire. No loud explosion. One second it had been a two-story house and now it was a one-story house.

One of Astrid's kneesocks from her dresser landed on the grass, draped over the lip of the trench.

Astrid remembered she could move. She ran for the house yelling, "Petey! Petey!"

The back door was partly blocked by a small piece of siding. She threw it aside and ran through the kitchen and up the debris-strewn stairs.

The full weirdness struck her then. The handrail of the stairs stopped as it reached the level of the upper floor. The steps themselves ended on a splintered half riser.

Astrid stepped out onto what was now a platform, no longer the second floor of a house. Everything was gone. Everything. It was as if a giant had come along with a knife and simply sliced off the top, cutting through walls and plumbing pipe and electrical conduit.

All that was left was Little Pete's bed. And Little Pete himself.

He coughed twice. He licked his lips. His eyes stared blankly up at open sky.

Astrid followed the direction of his gaze. And there, in the blue morning sky, a puff of gray cotton. Directly above the house.

Brianna was seething. She seethed a fair amount at the best of times, but she was still doing a long, slow burn over the fight with Drake and the fact that Jack had left town without even telling her so she had to hear it from Taylor.

She didn't much like Taylor. She had once suggested that Taylor should adopt a cool name, like Brianna had with "the Breeze." "The Teleporter," maybe. Taylor had laughed at her.

Brianna wasn't supposed to be on the street. The quarantine was still in effect. But she was thirsty, hungry, humiliated, and furious, and she was looking for trouble.

Or at least a sip of water.

She was giving this whole waiting-around thing a few more minutes and then she was going to run up to Lake Evian herself for a drink. Taylor said the road was dangerous, that the greenies were there. But Brianna didn't fear flying snakes. Not even flying snakes that peed green bug eggs, or whatever that was all about. She was too fast for some stupid snake, flying or crawling.

Someone had nailed plywood up over a window in town hall.

"What's that about?" she wondered aloud.

She shrugged and was getting ready to zoom when she heard a sound like chewing. Like a lot of chewing getting rapidly louder. And coming from the window with the—

Splinters pushed out through the bottom of the plywood. They were pushed by something silvery that moved with respectable speed.

Brianna stared up at it for a few seconds and then, quite suddenly, metallic-looking insects, each the size of a small dog, began to force their way through the plywood.

The first to emerge spread beetlelike wings and floated to the ground.

Brianna had plenty of time to observe its gnashing mouth and its antennae, and to be utterly creeped out by eyes the color of rubies.

She could guess what they were. These were the things that Taylor had gotten all freaked out by. The things that had supposedly come out of Hunter's guts. Only now they were right here and pouring down the wall from the second floor of town hall.

The instant the first bug landed it launched itself at Brianna. She sidestepped it like a matador with a bull.

"You're quick, I'll give you that," Brianna said. "But you're not the Breeze."

As one the swarm raced toward her, scythe mandibles slashing and mouthparts gnashing and red eyes blazing.

This was more like it. She could just zoom far away, of course, but she was enjoying this game.

Until Edilio came at a run, unlimbering his automatic rifle and yelling at the top of his lungs.

"Oh, well," Brianna said. "Time to end this, I guess."

She unsheathed her big knife and sliced the antennae from the nearest bug. Then, just for show, just because it was a cool move, she somersaulted and landed almost astride another bug. She stabbed it, aiming for the space between its hard-looking wings. Her blade bit the wing instead and did not penetrate.

The bug twirled, fast, very fast. Not fast enough. Brianna stabbed straight for the bloodred eyes and the blade sank deep into one.

The bug stopped moving.

"That's why you don't bug the Breeze," Brianna said.

Edilio had almost arrived and Brianna was pretty sure he would spoil her fun. So she awaited the charge of another bug, dropped low, swept her knife, and sliced through its two front legs. It crashed forward onto its horror-movie face.

BLAM! BLAM!

Edilio fired at one of the bugs that had evidently had enough and was running from the Breeze.

Brianna saw the bullets hit. And she saw them ricochet off the hard wings.

"Head shots!" she yelled to Edilio. "You have to get 'em in the head!"

She had meant to point to the one she killed as an example.

But the dead bug was moving.

So was the bug from whom she had subtracted the front legs.

With a frown she pulled out her shotgun. She caught up to the wounded bug, placed the muzzle right in its eerie eyes, and pulled the trigger.

The bug head blew most of the way off. Greenish-black brain goo sprayed.

The bug shook itself like a wet dog. Then kept moving.

"No, no, no," Brianna said. "I may lose to Drake, but I do not lose to a bunch of bloodshot roaches."

BLAM! BLAM!

Edilio shot his bug twice more. Then, seeing Brianna hesitate, he yelled, "Try to crush them!"

"With what?"

Edilio looked around helplessly. "I don't know."

"They're getting away!"

The bugs, half a dozen of them, were ignoring Brianna and Edilio now and racing off down the street, away from town.

"They're too fast for you," Brianna said.

Edilio looked like he was going to have a stroke. He glanced at the window above, the bugs racing away, and Brianna could have sworn his next move would be to throw up his hands and say, "Forget it, I'm outta here!"

But he gritted his teeth, took a deep breath, and visibly steeled himself for a decision he knew might be wrong. Might even be fatally wrong.

"Breeze," he said grimly. "Listen to me before you go tearing off. I want you to follow them, see where they go. But this leaves us with, like, no one playing defense. Orc's off on a drunk, Sam and Dekka and Jack are out of town, kids are falling out sick all over the place, and Drake may still be lurking . . ." He stuck his finger at her. "Don't take risks, don't be your usual reckless, stupid self: come back as soon as you can, as soon as you see where they're going."

Brianna executed a mock salute—she didn't mind being called stupid so long as he was acknowledging her bravery—and loped off at an easy sixty miles an hour to catch up with the swarm.

"Don't sweat it, Edilio," she called over her shoulder. "The Breeze is all over these bugs."

Orc was running dry. He stared balefully at the bottle in his hand. Shouldn't he be dead by now? How much booze did it take before you just died already?

His mind labored to work out solutions to the problem. Probably still a couple bottles back at the house, if kids hadn't looted them. If not, he had another option, but it was a long walk and he wasn't really in the mood for a long walk. A long walk would sober him up.

He was on his way to the house and drowning his brain in booze again when he thoughtlessly walked past the stop sign.

No body lay crumpled there.

For a moment he thought he might be in the wrong place.

Or that maybe he was mistaken about the body. But then he vaguely recalled running into Howard and Howard promising to fix things.

So now the little boy's body would be rotting in an unused house. Probably not the only body lying around. Probably.

Orc took a drink. He was shaky in body and mind. He was used to booze, but even by his standards he had punished his body in the last day. His stomach burned. His head hammered. Now he had to fight down an urge to run and run and run until . . .

Until what?

Run where?

They would figure it out, sooner or later. That he had slammed that little boy, that little boy who never hurt Orc or probably anyone else. Just some sick kid.

Someone would have seen it happen, or one of the smart ones—Astrid or Albert or Edilio—would figure it out. And he wouldn't even be given a chance to explain. They would make him leave, go live outside town, like they had Hunter.

But he wasn't Hunter. He couldn't live out there. Out there was where the coyotes were.

Orc remembered the coyotes. He remembered the way they had sunk their muzzles into his living guts and ripped and torn his insides out.

That's when it had started. That's when the ripped-up flesh had turned into gravel and the rocky, pebbly, monster skin had grown to take over his whole body.

No. They couldn't make him live out there.

Astrid had rules, though; she had made them up and that's what they would do, push him out, *Go away, Orc, go away and die, you freak.*

Yeah, well, Charles Merriman was inside this monster. He was not an orc. He was Charles Merriman.

He had to talk to Astrid. She'd always been nice to him. The only one who'd been nice to him. They were her stupid rules, so she would be able to figure out something. She was smart, after all. And nice.

With that vague thought sloshing around in his brain, Orc stomped off toward Astrid's home.

Two blocks away he noticed something very strange. So strange he thought he might be imagining it. Because it wasn't right, that was for sure.

There was a cloud. Up in the sky. As he gaped up at it the sun started to slide behind it.

Cloud. A dark, gray cloud.

He kept moving. Kept drinking. Kept looking at that crazy cloud up in the sky.

He stepped onto Astrid's street. From half a block away he saw the wreckage strewn out over trees and yards and draped over fences.

Then the house. That stopped him dead in his tracks. The top of the house was gone.

And there stood Astrid, right up on top, right out in the open because the walls were all gone, and there was her 'tard brother, only he was kind of, like, floating in the air above a bed.

Orc gaped up at Astrid, but she didn't notice him. She was looking up at the sky, up at the cloud. Her hands were at her side. In one hand she held a huge-looking pistol.

A brilliant flash lit everything up.

A tree not ten feet away blew apart.

CRRR-ACK!

BOOOOM!

Lightning. Thunder.

Splinters and leaves from the tree came down in a shower all around Orc.

And suddenly the cloud seemed to drop from the sky, only it wasn't the cloud itself, it was rain. Gray streamers of water, pouring down.

It was like stepping into a cold shower. The rain fell on Orc's marveling, upturned face. It pooled in his eyes, it ran in streams through his quarry of a body.

Astrid cried out, words irrelevant. Orc heard the despair, the fear. She was soaked through, standing there with her big gun, screaming at her brother, sobbing.

Orc opened his mouth and water flowed in. Clean, fresh, as cold as ice water.

TWENTY-FOUR

BRITTNEY SAW THE huge, blue-eyed bugs. She saw the cave. And she understood none of it.

Then she saw Jamal's gun. Shreds of his clothing. The blood that soaked them.

Nothing left but his clothing, his shoes, and his gun.

The bugs skittered madly past her carrying rocks eight, nine, ten times their own size. Like busy ants. But ants the size of wolves or Shetland ponies.

Coyotes watched. They were anxious, skittish, scared of the massive insects.

She wished she could ask Jamal what was happening. But Jamal would not be answering any more questions.

She wondered if she could flee. She wondered if she should flee. But what difference would it make?

The bugs had piled up a small mountain of rocks. Bigger and bigger stones were being hauled out.

She stepped in front of one of the insects. It was carrying a rock that could easily crush her. It would be nothing for these bugs to attack her, tear her apart as they'd apparently done to poor scared Jamal.

But the bug just scuttled around her.

Why? Why would they eat Jamal and not her? Because they ate only truly living flesh? Or because they knew that she was Drake and Drake was she and they could not harm Drake?

What was stopping them?

Who was stopping them?

But Brittney already knew the answer. She knew that something, someone, some mind was touching hers. It was as if she'd always known it. As if that cold consciousness had always been there in the background watching her even as she averted her eyes and looked to heaven.

When she was still in her grave, clawing at the dirt, she had felt it.

When she looked deep into the eyes of her brother, Tanner, she could sometimes catch glimpses of it, in layers down beneath his disguise as an angel.

She had known but had not wanted to know that Drake was its creature, the creature of this devil, just as she was God's creature.

She looked at the mine shaft, stood there as the insects cleared the rocks. Like a rock herself in the midst of rushing waters.

They were freeing the evil one. She could do nothing to stop them. She would do nothing to stop Drake from going to be with it. The devil would win this battle.

The dark mind teased at the edges of her own muddled thoughts. In faint, wordless whispers it made promises.

"What do you want with me?" she asked.

To give you what you want.

"I want to die," Brittney said. "To go to heaven."

When she closed her eyes she felt, rather than saw, something very like a glowing smile from a deep pool of darkness.

She had begged God to free her. Maybe this was His way. Maybe it wasn't Sam who would free her, but this devil inside the mountain.

Brittney walked into the mine shaft, lifted a small rock, and carried it away.

"Can you make any sense out of that?" Sam asked Jack.

They were in the marina's office. Two dozen boats sat placidly in the water. Several dozen more were raised out of the water in a long boathouse. There were papers on a desk, books in gray steel shelves, two broken-down rolling office chairs. The out-of-date calendars were reminders that no one had been here in a very long time.

The computers were useless, of course, without electricity. But Jack had insisted on carrying three of the half-exhausted laptops from the train. And a search had turned up a flash drive.

"It's some kind of proprietary software. I had to open it in Preview and it's hard to make sense of."

Toto was rummaging through cupboards, finding nothing

much. Dekka was sitting in one of the chairs with her feet up, gazing gloomily out at the lake. From time to time she surreptitiously ran her hands over her stomach, shoulders, thighs, checking for any sign of infestation.

And from time to time she would pull her shirt back to check the cauterized wound from Sam's fire.

"Hah!" Jack said. "I think I've got it. They had a truck deliver marine gas just a week before the FAYZ. A thousand gallons in round numbers. That should have brought them up to about twelve hundred gallons total. And they have diesel, too. I just can't find those. . . ."

He trailed off, lost in the numbers again.

This, thought Sam, is why I brought Jack.

Sam was feeling amazingly contented. He'd had a sudden flood of good news. They had found food. They had found soda. They would undoubtedly find beer and more soda and maybe a few bags of ancient chips once they searched the boats, the kind of stuff people took for a day on the lake.

Best of all, the lake was huge and filled with fresh water. More fresh water than they could ever use in a thousand years.

They'd also found a clipboard with scrawled figures indicating that the lake had recently been restocked with trout and bass.

It was like stumbling into the Garden of Eden. They could move the whole population up here. Use the boats as housing. Fish the lake. Drink the water. Use the gas to haul the crops from the fields up here.

It wasn't perfect. But for the FAYZ it was heaven.

If only Astrid were here.

He tried to push that thought aside. He was mad at Astrid. He was sick of Astrid. And yet, all he could think of was her face when he handed her a jar of Nutella and a can of Pepsi.

"Why didn't they do something?" Dekka wondered aloud.

"Who?" Sam asked.

"The people who were studying crazy boy over there." She jerked her head toward Toto.

"What were they going to do?" Sam asked with a shrug.

"How about warn people what was happening?" Dekka said. "Like, 'Hey, people of Perdido Beach, something very weird is happening'?"

"They were scientists," Jack mumbled, no longer deciphering boring documents but searching the laptop's hard drive, reveling in the sheer visceral pleasure of opening applications.

"So they were scientists," Dekka snapped. "So what?"

"So they were studying, right?" Jack said. "They had to understand it first. Can't just run around . . . Hey, look, there's this cool Easter Egg if you press—"

"Means people on the outside know what's happening," Dekka said.

"What do you think happens when the barrier comes down?" Sam wondered aloud. "I mean, to all of us?"

Jack said, "Most likely all our powers go away."

"Most likely," Sam agreed.

"But not for sure," Jack said.

"No."

Dekka said, "They don't even let you carry a Swiss Army knife at school, what are they going to do with you, Sam? You're like a guy carrying two massive lasers."

"Like Jack said, most likely our powers will be gone. That will be a relief."

"Not true," Toto said. "He says it will be a relief, but that's not what he believes."

Sam glared at Toto. "Okay. I would probably miss it."

"Truth," Toto said. Then, communing once more with his imaginary Spider-Man head, he added, "It's the truth."

"Look what they did with Toto and subject number two," Dekka said.

"Locked us up," Toto said. "No family. Stole us away and locked us up."

"That's not going to happen," Sam said. "Everyone in the world probably knows about us. We'd be too well-known."

"He believes it," Toto said.

"But he's not sure," Dekka said dryly. "Sam, you've never been a freak out in the real world. Me? To a lot of people I was a freak before I ever got here. If my parents would send me away to Coates just for being a lesbian, imagine how happy they would be to see that I can also cancel gravity."

She laughed to take the edge off it. But Sam did not join in.

"I still want the barrier to come down," Sam said.

"Not the truth," Toto said.

"Yes it is," Sam protested. "You think I like things like this?"

Toto started to answer, but Dekka cut him off. "Sam, maybe you haven't spent much time thinking about this, but I have. And trust me, lots of kids have, and not just freaks with powers. I mean, you think Albert wants this all to end so he can go back to school and to being some little nerd?"

"Astrid wants it to end," Sam said.

Dekka nodded. "No doubt. And Jack here wants it to end so he can get back to his computers and all because half the time he doesn't even remember he has superstrength. Edilio wants it to end, too, I guess, unless he starts thinking about getting deported back to Honduras. But do you honestly think Brianna wants to stop being the Breeze?"

"Brianna would hate it," Sam admitted.

"There's kids who pray every night for all this to be over. There's other kids who pray every night that the barrier stays right where it is. And now that we're going to show them all this lovely fresh water, this nice place up here . . ."

"You believe that," Toto confirmed.

"Thanks," Dekka said sarcastically.

Sam gazed out at the lake with a very different feeling now. If they had water, if they had food, if peace could be kept between him and Caine, and especially if they could get power flowing somehow, how many kids would stop hoping for an end to the FAYZ?

"You need to think about all that, Sam," Dekka said. "You're the leader, after all."

"Not anymore," he said.

Dekka laughed. She stood up and stretched. "Sam: you're

still the leader. You're always going to be the leader. It's not something you choose: it's something you are."

She took his arm and guided him out of the building, out onto the dock.

Her mood was different now. Sam was shocked by the suddenness of the change. She'd been putting on an act. But now her eyes were dull and her mouth turned down at the edges. She stood close to him, took his hand, and pressed it to her shirt over the top of her abdomen. "Feel that? That lump?"

He nodded.

"My mom had a benign cyst once, so maybe that's all it is," Dekka said gravely.

"You think it's . . ."

"Maybe I just noticed it because I'm looking for it, but maybe it's one of them," Dekka said.

"Don't jump to—"

"I'm not," Dekka said. "But if that's what it is, if it's those things, I'm going to ask you to take care of me."

"We've been over this," Sam said, pulling his hand away.

"If I tell you it's time, you do it, okay, Sam?"

He couldn't answer.

"I'm not afraid to die," Dekka said.

Sam was glad Toto wasn't there to hear.

"And you have to promise me something," Dekka said.

"What?"

"Don't you ever tell Brianna what you know about how I feel. It would only bring her pain. I love her and I wouldn't want to make her hurt."

"Dekka . . ."

"No," she said briskly. "Don't argue, okay? Maybe I'm wrong and this is nothing. So let's not argue about it."

"Yeah," he said. They stood awkwardly for a while, then Sam said, "I don't want to sound weird, but you know I love you, right?"

"Love you, too, Sam."

Sam made a move as if to hug her, but stopped himself.

She smiled. "Yeah, we're not the huggy type, are we?"

Sam said, "Let's go see what we can find down in the boats."

TWENTY-FIVE

ONE THING WAS crystal clear to Astrid as she stood in the drenching rain: the secret she had kept for so long was no longer a secret.

She looked down at the street and saw Orc there. He was staring up at her, his stone-and-flesh jaw slack.

And coming up the street behind him were four other boys. She recognized Lance and Turk. The other two she barely knew.

All four were armed. Orc didn't need a weapon.

She scanned in every direction, frantic, looking for some source of support. Maybe Sam had come back. Maybe Brianna. Maybe Edilio and some of his soldiers.

But no, the streets were abandoned but for a sick-looking girl, crouched and weary, moving in the general direction of the plaza, stopping to cough, staggering on.

Orc had defended Astrid once before, rescuing her from Zil and his Human Crew thugs. Now four of those thugs were pointing at her, at the amazing rain cloud, then breaking into a run, all eager malicious energy.

The cloud was growing. The rain was spreading.

Orc was standing in it, an animated gravel heap under a deluge.

The others slowed and then stepped gingerly into the rain and, like Orc, tilted their heads back and drank in the wondrous fresh water.

She had a gun. Would she use it?

"It's the 'tard," Turk yelled. His face broke out in a grin. He was standing beneath a tree that was decorated with a yard sale's worth of clothing and bits of broken toys. "It's that dumb brother of hers, Petard!"

Turk circled past Orc and hopped the fence into Astrid's yard. His friends followed warily, eyes darting from Astrid to Orc. Orc did nothing.

Then, in a sudden rush, Turk was up the stairs and standing on the platform. The others crowded beside him.

Turk laughed loudly, gleeful. "It's the 'tard! He's the one making it rain."

"Orc!" Astrid cried.

"That little kid must have some mad powers," Lance said.

"Go away," Astrid said.

She was aware of the fact that her drenched nightgown clung far too closely to her body. The gun in her hand weighed a ton.

"Grab the kid," Lance said. "If we have him, we control the rain, right?"

There was blood on Turk's shirt. Too much of it.

"What have you done?" Astrid demanded.

Turk looked down at the blood. He seemed surprised by it. "Oh, that?" He laughed savagely. "That's nothing much. Just means we run this place now, Astrid. No Sam around, huh? Where's mister light hands?"

"Orc!" Astrid cried out. She didn't want to reveal the depths of her fear. But she knew what Turk would do. And she did not want to use the gun. Not even now, not even for Petey.

"What other tricks can the 'tard do?" Lance demanded. "Float in the air, make rain. What else?"

"Mutant retard. Freaktard," one of the other kids said, and laughed tentatively like he wasn't quite sure it was funny.

"He doesn't know what he's doing," Astrid said. She was chilled now and beginning to shiver. "He was just thirsty. He has the sickness, the flu, and he was thirsty."

On the street below, other kids were coming out of their homes, carrying bowls and buckets. They advanced with wondering eyes, edging toward the rain curtain as it edged toward them.

"The 'tard must be some kind of serious moof to do this," Lance said. "Blow off the top of the house? Call up a rain cloud? That's, like, at least three-bar powers there. Maybe four."

"If you bother him, he may stop." The threat was a sudden inspiration and it worked. Lance's eyes narrowed even further and Turk was suddenly very still. Drinkable water was important, even to such sub-geniuses as Turk and Lance.

Then Turk shook his head and said, "Nice try, Astrid. But if the freaktard makes rain whenever he gets thirsty, all we gotta do is keep him thirsty and we own the rainmaker."

"Wonder what he does when he gets hungry?" Watcher asked.

The rain beat on the carpet. It was already pooling around their feet. Shallow puddles in dirty carpet.

Turk made his decision. "I think we're just going to take old Petard with us." He motioned to the two younger boys. "Grab him."

The pistol came up suddenly, almost as if the gun itself had made the decision. Astrid aimed it at Turk.

Despite the rain her mouth was dry as parchment. Her throat wouldn't make sounds. Her finger was on the trigger, stroking the grooves, feeling it. Her thumb was on the safety.

She clicked it off.

All she saw now was Turk's face, and the v-sights of the pistol.

"You aren't going to pull that trigger, Astrid," Turk said.

A sound from the steps. Running feet.

Edilio emerged. He had an automatic rifle aimed at Turk. "It's over, Turk," Edilio said.

Astrid dropped the pistol to her side. She breathed a huge, shaky sigh of relief.

"You going to let Astrid just own this freak?" Turk demanded of Edilio.

"Drop all your weapons. Right now!" Edilio yelled.

The two younger kids looked to Turk for guidance.

Lance was the one who moved. He raised his own pistol and pointed it at Little Pete. "Anyone shoots anyone, the 'tard takes one in the head."

"Man, you don't want to do this," Edilio warned.

"Yeah? Well, listen up, Edilio: Albert's dead."

Edilio's eyes opened wide.

"See, the situation has changed rapidly," Lance said in a parody of a newscaster's voice. "So, now, ladies and gentlemen, what we have here is a Mexican standoff. You squeeze one off, Edilio, chances are I can still get the kid. Bang."

"You should understand what a Mexican standoff is," Turk mocked. He raised his own gun and aimed it at Astrid. "See? Now it's even more complicated. Lance is right: Albert is, uh, not feeling well. Forever. So no one is even paying you, wetback. You need to walk away. Run before the immigration cops get here." He laughed.

A terrible thought formed in Astrid's brain: if Little Pete was killed it might all end.

A simple act of murder . . .

What kind of life did he have? Was Little Pete's life worth all of this? Was it worth Edilio dying? Was it worth the many more deaths that would surely happen? Was it worth all of them dying in this violent, foul, God-forsaken FAYZ?

"Go ahead," Astrid said flatly. She let her pistol drop to the sodden carpet. It splashed. "Go ahead. Shoot him. Kill Little Pete."

•   •   •

Diana and Caine had made love several more times. In her bed. In his bed. In the big bedroom with its ego wall of the two movie star parents grinning out from photos taken with Leo DiCaprio, Natalie Portman, that actress who was in *Mamma Mia!*, Steven Spielberg, Heath Ledger, and a bunch of people who were probably famous but looked more like they were businessman types.

Diana was in the kitchen, wearing a robe and slippers and heating some food for Penny. New England clam chowder. A quesadilla. A mismatched kind of meal, she supposed, but Penny wasn't going to complain. They were all still a long, long way from complaining about food.

Diana had not intended it to be this way with Caine. Somehow she'd imagined the one time, but not an endless series of sequels. But Caine's appetite had not been sated. He had come back to her bed in the night. And then, this morning, before the sun was even up.

Something was happening to her. She was coming to like Caine. Love? She didn't even know for sure what that meant. Maybe she loved him. That would be strange. He wasn't exactly lovable. And once you knew the real Caine, he wasn't even likable.

Diana had always found Caine fascinating. And she'd always found him attractive. Hot, she would have said when she was younger. Hot in a cold sort of way, if that made any sense.

But this was different. She wasn't using him now. That was her usual attitude toward Caine, at least that's what she'd always told herself: he was useful. A girl like Diana, a girl who enjoyed taking risks, who enjoyed sticking a knife of wit and cruelty into other girls at school, who enjoyed taunting the panting hormonal boys and leering old men, a girl like that could use a strong male protector.

And Caine was definitely a strong protector. It would take a suicidal guy to cross him. Even before Caine had started to develop powers, he was the kind of boy other boys steered clear of. He wasn't always the biggest or the toughest-looking, but he was always the most determined. The most ruthless. You knew if you messed with Caine, you'd suffer for it.

She supposed, if she had to be serious, that she'd long ago developed genuine emotions for him. Of some sort. Not love. Not even like. But something. Something normal people might have thought was sick, in a way.

Emotions. But not what she felt now—whatever this was.

Diana plated the quesadilla and poured the soup into a bowl. She set it all on a tray and carried it upstairs. She knocked, opened the door, and placed the tray of food in front of a sleeping Penny. It was like feeding a dog.

She found Caine out on what had once been a well-manicured lawn that covered the ground from the house to the cliff. It was now wild with weeds, some as much as head-high. He was looking toward the distant town through his telescope.

He heard her approach. Without looking back he said, "Something's happening in town."

"I don't care."

"A cloud. Like a rain cloud. In fact, I think it is raining. It's just a small cloud. Way down low, though, not an illusion in the barrier."

"You're probably seeing a reflection. Or an illusion."

Caine handed her the telescope. She wanted to refuse it, but she was curious. She looked. The town leaped closer. Not enough to see people, but enough to see that there was indeed a cloud, just one, hanging far too low, staying put in one place. The gray smudge beneath it might be falling rain.

"So?" she asked. "So some freak has developed the power to make a cloud."

"You don't wonder who? That's a pretty major power."

Diana sighed theatrically. "What do you care?"

"I don't like the idea of there being another four bar. Two of us is already one too many."

"It doesn't mean it's a four bar," Diana said. "Brianna and Dekka and Taylor are only threes. They have greater powers than that."

"At least a three bar, though." He took the scope back. "You don't think if they can find a way they'll come after us? If Sanjit made it there alive, then Sam knows what we have here. You don't think he'll come after it?"

"No," she said honestly. "I don't think he'll look for a fight with you. He's not as insecure as you are."

Caine snorted a laugh. "Yeah, that's my problem: insecurity."

"It doesn't matter anyway. There's no way for us to get back even if we wanted to."

"There's always a way, Diana. There's always a way."

"Don't," she said. "Don't find a way."

TWENTY-SIX

"YOU WANT US to shoot your brother?" Turk was incredulous.

"Don't even think about it," Edilio said. He had a tight grip on his rifle, finger on the trigger. The sights were centered on Turk's anxious face. But his eyes were bleary and he was stifling a need to cough. "She doesn't mean it."

"Too many dead kids," Astrid said wearily. "There just can't be any more dead kids. It's time to end it."

Edilio felt panic rising within him. What was he supposed to do now? Was Astrid losing her mind like Mary Terrafino?

"I know how many kids have died," Edilio said. "I buried most of them."

"It's all because of Little Pete," Astrid said.

"No. You don't know that." Edilio aimed a furious look at her.

She blinked. Shook her head slightly. Her long hair, soaked, hung like golden snakes. "You aren't the one taking care of him, Edilio. You're not the one responsible."

Edilio coughed, fought it back, coughed again. He tried to steady his mind and calm himself down. Had to keep focus.

"What are you two talking about?" Turk demanded. He was clearly confused.

Edilio felt the house rumble. Heavy footsteps. Orc. It had to be Orc. Orc on whose side? That was the question.

The boy-monster emerged onto the platform. He made a strange slushy sound as he moved, like someone shuffling their feet on wet gravel.

He pushed past Edilio. His head sagged to his chest, and for a moment Edilio had the incredible thought that Orc might have fallen asleep.

No, he was just hammered, Edilio realized. "Drop your guns."

"No, no, no. What are you two talking about? That's the first question," Turk demanded, sensing an advantage he couldn't quite put his finger on. His gun was still aimed at Astrid.

"Shut up, Turk, and drop your gun. If you murdered Albert, you're going into exile."

"What happens if I shoot the 'tard?" Lance demanded.

"You know the law. You kill someone, we give you a trial. And if you're guilty, you leave town and never come back."

"That's not what I'm asking, and you know it, Edilio," Lance snarled. "Tell me, Astrid. Tell us all. What happens if we shoot the 'tard?"

Panic. It was eating at Edilio's mind. What was he supposed

to do? He had to get control of the situation. He had to be in charge. But what should he do?

Edilio stared down the barrel of his rifle at Turk. His head was swimming. His neck and face were hot.

He shifted his aim, traversed the gun just an inch of arc to bring Lance into his sights.

The first one to decide would win.

"If—," Astrid said.

BLAM!

The rifle kicked against Edilio's shoulder. The side of Lance's handsome face erupted in a fountain of blood.

"Lance!" Turk cried.

Lance brought his own gun around, not aiming at Little Pete now but at Edilio.

BLAM!

Lance's aim was off. Nowhere near Edilio. Instead the bullet struck Orc in his thigh and ricocheted off.

Turk, his face a mask of fury, aimed at Edilio. But Edilio had already shifted his aim and his sights were back on Turk.

"Don't!" Edilio warned.

Turk hesitated. But Edilio didn't see the hesitation, he saw Turk's gun and only his gun, the round black hole of the barrel, and without thinking he squeezed the trigger.

Another loud bang.

Another kick against his shoulder.

Turk was on his back. His gun was beyond his reach, although he was struggling to get to it.

"I said, don't!" Edilio yelled again.

Turk held his stomach with one hand and reached for the gun with the other. Edilio's finger was slippery on the trigger. He could feel something awful inside him, a tidal wave of awful, barely held in check as he aimed at Turk's head.

Orc crunched Turk's gun beneath his foot.

Edilio breathed. Sobbed for breath. Coughed.

He lowered his weapon.

Lance shrieked. It was a sound made up of fear and shock and pain. The bullet had struck his cheekbone and come out through his ear. Quivering red flesh hung loose.

Turk groaned more quietly. His throat convulsed. Like a fish on dry land, he was gulping, trying to breathe. His hand still stretched toward his now-useless gun.

Neither boy was dead.

Edilio formed the thought that would shame him later: he should finish them. He should do it now. Just walk up close and *bang!* If he didn't, they might live, with Lana's care. And if they lived they'd be back for revenge.

Orc and Astrid were both watching him.

It seemed terribly unfair that even now they were looking to him for some kind of answer.

"I'll get Lana," Edilio said.

He turned and ran, and fell down the steps. Heaving with sobs, blinded by rain and tears he ran for Clifftop.

It took Sam and Jack working together to start one of the motorboats. Almost all had dead batteries. But one of the boats had just enough power left to fire the engines.

They roared to life with a deep, wet growl.

"You know, this boat has power enough that it could pull water skiers," Sam observed.

Dekka smiled fondly at him. "You want to water ski?"

"Not right now. I'm just saying . . ."

"That's a lie. He wants to go now," Toto said.

"Yeah, well, I don't always do what I want," Sam grumbled. "We need to explore the rest of the lake, then we can head back to town and be welcomed as heroes."

He'd meant that last part to be self-deprecating, but a part of him actually was looking forward to striding into town to announce that they had found all the water they could ever need, and a fair amount of sugary snacks besides.

Then he would go see Astrid.

And then what would happen?

Then nothing would happen. They would still be right where they'd been.

"Cast off," Sam called to Jack. Then, with the ropes aboard, he pointed the boat toward the west and roared out of the marina.

The feel of spray on his face and a throbbing engine beneath his feet was intoxicating.

Later they would run out of fuel, and later all the Pepsi would be drunk, and all the noodles would be eaten. But it wasn't later yet.

They could build a better life here at the lake. Leave behind all the reeking sewage and trash and memories of Perdido Beach. Leave behind the wrecked church and the burned houses. Leave behind that awful cemetery.

This time they would do it right. They'd organize before they ever started to move anyone up here. Form little families that could live aboard the boats or use the boathouse or the marina office. He frowned, trying to count in his head how many of the boats had any kind of superstructure. Maybe half a dozen of the small sailboats, a dozen of the motorboats. And then there were the four or five houseboats.

That wasn't enough, obviously, but they could set up tents and maybe build small shelters. It's not like it ever got cold in the FAYZ, not like anyone needed insulation. Just a roof to keep the sunlight off them.

He scanned the shoreline, hoping to spot a campground. Logically there had to be one, there were always campgrounds at a lake. It just stood to reason.

Of course they could be on the other side of the barrier. . . .

Never mind, it was all good. They had enough gas to drive the various Winnebagos and campers and trailers up here from Perdido Beach—there were at least a dozen parked in driveways, although a lot had burned in the big fire.

He would have a boat. Big enough for himself and Astrid and Little Pete. Maybe he would ask Dekka to live with them, too. Assuming he got dibs on one of the houseboats. And why shouldn't he?

One of those forty-six-footers would probably sleep six. Him and Astrid . . . It occurred to him that in his head he had them sharing the master's berth. Which wasn't likely to happen.

Was it?

Maybe. Maybe if they got away from Perdido Beach, maybe . . . A new thought occurred to him. He pushed it aside. But back it came.

What if they got married?

Then they'd be like a family. Him and Astrid and Little Pete.

There was no telling how long the FAYZ would last. Maybe forever. Maybe they would never get out. In that case, what were they all going to do? He was fifteen, Astrid was fifteen, they'd both survived the poof. That was young in the outside world, but it was old in the FAYZ.

"Yeah, but who can marry us?" He spoke the question aloud, not meaning to. He glanced nervously over his shoulder to see if anyone had overheard. Of course not, with the engines roaring and the *boosh-boosh-boosh* of the bow smacking the wavelets.

Dekka was sitting on one of the cushioned seats in the stern, gazing wistfully toward the land. Jack was hunched over one of the laptops, fingers flying over the keys, grinning. Toto was talking to someone who wasn't there.

"Ship of fools," Sam said to himself, and laughed.

Water and gas, noodles and Pepsi and Nutella, a crazy truth-telling freak, and despite Dekka's fear, there was hope.

Quinn. He would make a good justice of the peace. That's all you needed to perform a marriage, right? That's how his mom had married his stepfather. If they could elect someone mayor, why not elect someone justice of the peace?

"Marry me and live on a houseboat," he said.

"I like you, Sam, but not in that way," Dekka said.

Sam jerked and yanked the wheel to one side. He steadied and tried to ignore the blush that was spreading from his neck up to his cheeks. She was standing next to him.

"How's the shoulder?" Sam asked.

"See, this is why it's good that Taylor isn't still with us," Dekka said. "If she'd heard you, the news would have spread faster than the speed of light."

Sam sighed. "I was having a moment of optimism."

Dekka patted him on the back. "You should, Sam. The FAYZ owes you some good news."

Orc stood staring.

The kid, the Petard, he was still just floating there in the rain, like it was all nothing.

Astrid looked like a zombie or whatever.

The two shot kids were yelling and spazzing. Grinding Orc's last nerve. He didn't care about them. They were no better than he was. Let them scream, but not now, with his head banging like a drum, with the echo of gunshots still bouncing around in his skull.

Edilio had said to get out of town. That's what was rattling around in his brain, too. Killers had to get out of town.

Astrid's laws. She made them up.

"That true, right?" he asked her without preamble.

"What?"

"Anyone kills anyone, they have to go away for good."

"Are you going to kill them?" She meant the two hurt kids. It took him a while to realize that.

"What if . . . what if you didn't mean to kill some kid."

"I have to get him away from here," Astrid said. But Orc didn't think she was talking to him.

"I mean, if you didn't even mean to. Like it was just an accident?"

"I don't know what you're asking," Astrid said.

Orc was out of words. He felt so tired. He hurt so badly.

"Can you pick him up? Can you carry him?" Astrid was asking him something. So maybe she didn't care what he'd done.

"The 'tard?"

"Little Pete. Can you carry him, Charles?"

"Where to?"

"Away," Astrid said. "That's the law. Killers have to leave. That's what he is, you know. He's the worst of us all. Every death from the FAYZ . . . All those kids . . ."

Orc seized on an idea that drifted through his slow brain. He lost focus when Lance started howling louder than before.

"Shut up or I'll shut you up," he yelled. He struggled to regain his thought. Little Pete. Killing. "Yeah, but he don't know what he's doing, right? People who don't know what they're doing, it's not their fault."

"Please, Charles. Pick him up. Edilio will be back with Lana soon. We have to be gone by then."

Orc stepped over Turk. The boy was shivering uncontrollably now, his legs stuck straight out, feet twisted, shaking as he held his guts.

Lance was still screaming, he hadn't stopped, but now he was mixing in curses, raging at everyone, spewing every hateful word he could think of.

Orc looked down at Little Pete. Astrid said he had killed people. Orc didn't see how that was possible. He couldn't even move much, it didn't seem.

Little Pete coughed three times real fast. He didn't cover his mouth or anything. It was like he didn't even know he'd coughed.

Orc plucked Little Pete out of midair. He didn't weigh much. Orc was strong.

Astrid watched it all like she was a million miles away. It was as if she was seeing everything through a telescope.

"Where to?" Orc asked her.

Astrid knelt and picked up the gun she had dropped. "Away," she said.

Orc shrugged and headed down the stairs and walked north, toward the hills, and away from the sound of screams.

TWENTY-SEVEN

DRAKE EMERGED.

He was holding a stone. Which meant Brittney had been holding the same stone.

It must have been heavy for her but his tentacle wrapped around it and held it without much strain.

Around him the bugs were looking less and less like insects. Not even like really large insects. The least of them was as big as a Dalmatian. The largest were as big as ponies. They reminded him more of Humvees or tanks.

They seemed more fragile at this size, as though the same weight of burnished exoskeleton had been stretched to make a much larger creature. Only half of them were still carrying out debris. The rest, the larger ones, had stepped aside and now waited with an impression of impatience about them. Like jets waiting for takeoff.

That's what they reminded him of: fighter jets. They had a predatory, dangerous air about them. Like all they had to do was get the word and they'd go blasting off, dealing out death and destruction.

Who was to give them the word? Him?

The coyotes had disappeared. Had they decided to leave? Or had the bugs eaten them finally? Drake noticed a smear of blood on a slab of rock and thought he knew the answer.

Had the Darkness made the coyotes sacrifice themselves to feed his new servants?

Drake tossed his rock onto the pile. Then he turned back toward the mine shaft. Back to the welcoming shadow of that hole in the earth. His step was light. His heart beat fast, but from joy, not fear.

He felt the mind of the Darkness touching his. Felt that powerful will. It wanted him. And he was sure now what the Darkness would ask of him, and what weapons it would give him.

The mine shaft was clear but still a dangerous place. The supporting timbers had not been replaced and now the stone roof was jagged, hanging precariously in some places, while in others it had been hollowed out into dark cathedral domes by the collapse.

"I'm coming," Drake whispered. But why whisper? "I'm coming!" he yelled.

He left the last of the light behind. Total darkness now. He felt his way forward, step by step, hand and whip hand outstretched. He scraped against jutting rocks, stubbed his toes dozens of times. The air smelled stale. It was hotter than it should have been in the shaft, warmer than the outside. He was sweating in the pitch black, gasping for scarce oxygen.

"I'm coming!" he shouted again, but his voice now was metallic and flat and did not carry any distance. He tripped and fell to his knees. When he stood up, he banged his head.

He was going down a long, long slope. How far had he come? He couldn't say. He heard the rustle of the bugs coming behind him. In tight places they had to squeeze through, like massive cockroaches, flattening themselves to squeeze beneath low-hanging ledges, squirming onto their sides to edge past piers of solid rock.

They were following him. His army. Yes. He was certain of it. They would be his to command, his to use.

His army!

He could no longer breathe the air. But this was not his first time without oxygen. He still could see in vivid flashes the long, slow claw up through the mud of his grave.

No, Drake did not need air. Air was for the living, and Drake was something so much better than alive.

Unkillable.

Immortal.

The immortal soldier of the gaiaphage. His head swam with the joy of it.

Suddenly the floor ended and he pitched forward, face-first. He fell for several stretched seconds. He slammed into unyielding rock, bounced, rolled over, and laughed a sound-less laugh.

He felt around with his hands and knew he was on a

narrow ledge on one side of a deep vertical drop.

He stood up, put his toes on the edge, and looked down. Far below, a dim green light glowed, the only light in this pit of blackness. It might be a hundred feet, it might be a mile, it might be a hundred miles. There was no way to know.

He fell and fell, like Alice down the rabbit hole. It seemed to go on forever. Not seconds but minutes. An eternity.

WHUMPF!

He hit with such force that it should have snapped his calves and thigh bones and burst his knees and jackhammered his spine and cracked his head open like an egg.

Instead, after lying crumpled for a moment, he unwound his twisted limbs and pushed himself back onto his feet.

The walls around him all glowed. With his eyes fully adjusted to the pitch black he could see fairly well now with nothing but the toxic radioactive glow.

Was he there? Was he at the end of the trip?

Come.

Farther still, down a sloping ramp. He realized that this was a different type of tunnel, no longer a man-made mining shaft but a natural cave deep, deep in the bowels of the stifling earth.

He entered a cavern that soared hundreds of feet above him. Green-tinged hanging stalactites met stumpy stalagmites. Like walking into the jaw of a gigantic shark.

Through the cavern and ever downward, following the faint trail of green. The creatures kept pace behind him. They had fallen after him, one by one, slowing their descent with their wings, spiraling down like helicopter seedpods.

An army! His army!

How far had he fallen? He could not know. How deep was he now? Miles.

Closer and closer.

And then, even as he felt his journey drawing to a close, his desperate goal coming close, Drake felt the familiar disturbance and swift onset of stumbling awkwardness that accompanied the transformation.

"No!" he moaned. "No, not now!"

But he had no power to stop the transformation.

It was not Drake but Brittney who finally came to the place where the gaiaphage lay. It was like living green sand. Billions of particles, each almost invisible to the eye, but together forming a single living thing, a hive.

The cavern was vast, impossibly huge. As if someone had sunk a sports stadium into the earth. The green, glowing mass of the gaiaphage covered stalactites and stalagmites, granite walls, and sandstone rock skyscrapers.

But beneath Brittney's feet the floor was strangely level and smooth. The gaiaphage had left an uncovered space for her to see and to understand.

She knelt and pressed her hand against a clear patch of translucent, pearly gray beneath her. The searing pain a living person would have felt was only an interesting tingle to Brittney.

She knew what it was and where she was. This was the bottom of the FAYZ wall, the bottom of the giant bubble. She was ten miles down, at the lowest depths of the enclosed universe of the FAYZ.

She stood and looked left and right, in every direction, turning slowly to see. It was all resting on the barrier, she realized. The rock walls, the jutting stalagmites, all of it rested on the barrier itself.

And everywhere but in this one patch, the gaiaphage covered the barrier. It touched the barrier and did not feel pain.

Then, as Brittney looked down, she saw the color of the barrier change. The eternal blank grayness was crossed by fingers of dark green, the color of late summer leaves.

She understood: the gaiaphage could touch and alter the barrier itself.

She knew it was conscious. She knew it because she felt now the dread touch of that awful mind in hers. There could not be the slightest doubt.

Brittney fell to her knees.

She laced her fingers together and squeezed her eyes tight. But she could not block out the green glow. She could not stop herself seeing. She could not keep her mind safe from its terrible touch.

She felt her every thought opened, like so many files on a computer, each opened, observed, understood.

She was nothing. She saw that now. She was nothing.

Nothing.

She tried to call on her God. But her prayers would not form in her brain, would not whisper from her numb, trembling lips.

She saw it all clearly, the whole of it. A race of creatures who worshipped life. A virus designed to spread life wherever it reached. The planet first infected, then deliberately blown up so that seeds of life would spread throughout the universe in a billion meteors.

The endless, endless blackness of space, of millennia during which one of those rocks spun along a path that might never reach an end.

It was caught in the gravity well of a small star.

And then of a small planet.

The shattering, fiery impact.

A death. A man obliterated.

And the absorption into that alien virus of something new and incredible: human DNA.

A new life-form. The unintended consequence of a noble plan.

No God in His Heaven had created the gaiaphage. And here, now, in the airless pit, no God could save her.

It was then in her despair that Brittney prayed, not as she always had, but to a new Lord. A savior who waited to be born, to break free.

Brittney bowed her head and prayed to the gaiaphage.

Tanner appeared to Brittney as she prayed.

Her dead brother was an angel. Not with wings and all of that, but she knew he was an angel. And now he appeared to her and spoke in a soft, soothing voice.

"Don't be afraid," Tanner said.

"Let me die," Brittney whispered.

"Who do you pray to?" Tanner asked.

"To you," she said. Because she had no doubt that Tanner was speaking for the gaiaphage.

"I cannot give you death," Tanner said. "You are two in one. Your immortality is his. And he is necessary to me."

"But who made me this way? Why? Why?"

Tanner laughed. "'Why' is a question for children."

"I am a child," Brittney said.

There was softly glowing magma dribbling from Tanner's cruel mouth. He bent down and touched her with fingers of ice.

"I must be born," Tanner said. "And then, at the ending of my beginning, you will die."

"I don't understand." With piteous eyes she looked up at the angel-turned-devil. "What do you need me to do?"

"Nemesis must be mine," Tanner said. "Nemesis must serve me and me alone. All who defend him and protect him must be destroyed. He must live to serve me."

"I . . . I don't understand." She knelt with bowed head, unable to look at Tanner, knowing now that he had never been an angel, that he had never been God's servant, that he was nothing real at all, just the voice of the evil one.

"Nemesis," Tanner said, hissing the word. "We are two in one, like you and the whip hand. Two in one, waiting to be born. Only when he is alone, utterly alone, will he serve me. And then I will be burst from this cocoon."

"I don't know anyone called Nemesis," Brittney whispered. She could feel her consciousness fading. Already her fingers were melting together to form the whip.

In the moments before she lost sight and sound, as she spiraled down into the blackness and Drake surged upward, Brittney's tortured mind saw the image of Nemesis.

She knew his name.

Peter Michael Ellison. Who everyone called Little Pete.

PETE

HE FLOATED ABOVE the ground in the arms of a monster. His cheek lay against a stone shoulder. Rain no longer fell. Wild colors—green and yellow, brown and red, jagged edges of color scraped at him, wounding his ears.

The sister walked behind him. Her face was as stony as the monster's. Lips too red, eyes too blue, the sound of her breathing too loud.

At each step the monster's pebble skin rubbed against Pete's raw flesh, like sandpaper, like a thousand saw blades drawn slowly over tender scabs.

He wanted to scream, but if he screamed the loud colors would get louder.

He was no longer high atop the sheet of glass. He had fallen, fallen, down into the world of noise and blazing light. The Darkness was only a distant echo now. Now was now, utterly now and here and like needles under his skin, like knives in his ears. His eyes ached and throbbed.

He coughed and it was a cannon firing out of his chest, up through his throat, his mouth, burning him like blazing lava.

Why was he here? Why in a monster's arms? What was happening to him? After a long and peaceful escape he had been recaptured by the too-much world of furious activity and disjointed images.

His body, his body, that was all he could see or feel, the pain and the ache and the shivering that made him feel as if parts of him might come loose and fall, his body, forcing his attention away from the pristine glass cliff. Forcing him to feel every shiver, recoil at every cough, to feel, really feel, the sickness that was overwhelming his defenses.

TWENTY-EIGHT

DRAKE DID NOT see Tanner.

The gaiaphage needed no angelic illusions to reach into Drake's fevered mind. Drake knew all he needed to know. The bugs, the creatures would serve him. He had his army.

And in his head he had a list of names. The freaks first. The normals next. All of them.

All but one, the gaiaphage told him. Kill until there is no one left to kill. But don't harm Nemesis.

Drake was filled with a pure joy he had never known. He felt a wild energy. All his life he had waited for this kind of moment. It was as if every single thing he had ever done—the beatings he had suffered, the much more numerous beatings he had delivered, the pleasure he had found in burning frogs and microwaving a puppy and drawing all those endless loving pictures of weapons, spears, knives, torture devices, all of it, all the hatreds, all the burning lust, all the madness and rage, had come together to form this perfect, ultimate moment of crystalline joy.

He thought he might die from the pleasure he felt, so much emotion, a flood, a storm, a crashing of planets! Death! He was death, unleashed at last.

He snapped his whip and threw back his head and howled till his throat was raw.

Then he ran, leaped, cavorted through the swirling tides of insects, running and climbing, indifferent to the sharp rocks that lacerated his undead flesh.

Kill them all!

He raged when he reached the heights he couldn't climb but then the creatures rushed to lift him up and sped him up and up at dizzying speed through the endless caverns.

An army!

His army!

They vomited from the mine shaft and Drake leaped onto the rock pile. A single coyote waited there.

"Where is he, Pack Leader?" Drake demanded.

"Not Pack Leader. Pack killed."

"I don't care what you call yourself, where is he?"

"Who?" the coyote asked.

Drake grinned. "The one with the killing hands, you stupid dog. Who do you think? Sam!"

"Bright Hands is far. By the big water." He simpered and turned in a circle and then with his muzzle pointed to the west.

"Excellent," Drake purred.

Just then a rush of bugs, a new column of the creatures

came over the ridge and poured into the mass of Drake's army. Different. These had bloodred eyes.

They were not alone.

Brianna stood, arms on hips, glaring down at him.

"You!" Drake said.

"Me," Brianna said.

To the creatures he said, "Red eyes, serve me! To the town. Kill everyone but Nemesis!"

"You talking to these bugs now?" Brianna said. "I have to tell you: I don't think they speak psycho."

"Blue eyes, with me!" Drake said. "Two columns, two armies: blues with me, reds back to town and kill. Kill!"

"What exactly do you think you're doing?" Brianna demanded.

"Me?" Drake laughed loudly. "I'm going on an epic killing spree."

"You'll have to go through me," Brianna said.

"I wouldn't have it any other way," Drake said.

They walked out of the rain. Astrid and Orc and Little Pete. The cloud did not follow them. No new cloud appeared. The cloud remained, no longer expanding, but still pouring rain on the street and the ruined house.

Little Pete coughed directly against the side of Orc's face. It was getting worse, the cough, slowly but steadily worse.

Maybe it would kill him.

Go ahead. Shoot him. Kill Little Pete.

Astrid told herself she hadn't meant it. It was just a tactic.

After all, if someone was using a threat you had to devalue the importance of the threat, pretend it didn't matter.

Lance's face exploding. Some of it had hit her.

Turk moaning in pain, writhing on the wet carpet.

It had to stop. It had to end. One death to save dozens, maybe hundreds of kids?

A simple act of murder . . .

Astrid saw herself choking Nerezza. She felt again the way her fingers dug into the soft neck, fingertips finding the spaces between tendon and artery.

Astrid had never felt anything like that red-misted rage before in her life. She had hated before—she had hated Drake. She had feared before—many, many times. But she would never have believed herself capable of that murderous rage.

The true revelation was the joy she'd felt at that moment. The sheer, vicious, uncomplicated joy of feeling the blood pounding to get past arteries blocked by Astrid's own hands. Feeling the spasms in Nerezza's windpipe.

Astrid let loose a whimper. It had to end.

"You okay?" Orc asked.

Would she ever be herself again? Or had Astrid, the old Astrid, died, to be replaced by this new creature, this angry, frightened witch?

Not for the first time she realized that this had been Sam's life since the coming of the FAYZ. How much rage and fear had he endured? How much bitter shame for his failures? How much guilt ate at his soul as it now ate at hers?

She wished he were here now. Maybe she would be able to

ask him how he lived with it.

No, she told herself, it's not Sam you need. A priest. You need to confess and do penance and be forgiven. But how could she be forgiven when even now she was watching Orc as he labored uphill, seeing Petey's lolling head, and asking herself over and over again if she had meant it.

Go ahead. Shoot him.

God hears prayers, even from those who have not repented, she told herself. She wanted to pray. But when she tried she couldn't see the face of a patient Christ as she had in the past. She could see memories of crucifixes, paintings, statues. But the God she had believed in was not there anymore.

Was she losing her faith?

Had she lost it already?

A simple act of murder . . .

Leslie-Ann knew about the quarantine. But she also knew she couldn't stand being thirsty and hungry any longer and her two brothers couldn't stand it, either.

The one good thing about being Albert's maid was that Albert made sure she had enough to eat. Albert always had food and water. He wouldn't let her starve.

So Leslie-Ann made her way from the house she shared with her siblings to Albert's much fancier house.

She noticed a strange thing over toward the west: a cloud. Leslie-Ann frowned, wondering why that seemed so strange.

But she had no time to wonder: the FAYZ was full of weird stuff. If you'd seen Sam shoot light from his hands—and she had—you stopped being amazed by strange things.

Albert's front door was open. That in its way seemed weirder than the cloud. Albert never left his door unlocked. Never. Let alone open.

Leslie-Ann approached cautiously. She felt for the hilt of the knife she carried. She was nine years old, and not exactly big or scary. But once she had waved the knife at a kid who wanted to steal her cantaloupe and he had run away.

"Albert?" she called out.

She pushed the door all the way open. She drew her knife and held it out in front of her.

"Albert?"

She thought she heard something coming from the living room. Her foot slipped on the Spanish tile. She looked down: a red smear.

Blood. It was blood.

She turned and ran back to the door. Ran outside, waving the knife around her.

She looked around, wishing Edilio or someone would come along. But if they did she'd be in trouble for going outside during the quarantine. Her brothers would still be thirsty and hungry, and so was she.

Leslie-Ann steeled herself and headed back inside, knife first. She stepped over the blood smear.

Her foot kicked a can. It rolled noisily. A can on Albert's floor? Who would have made that kind of mess? She would have to clean that up or Albert would fire her.

She bent down and snagged the can with her free hand.

It smelled of food. Her mouth watered. She held the knife awkwardly as she ran her finger inside looking for anything that might be left. She came up with maybe a tablespoonful of tomato sauce and licked it greedily from her finger.

It tasted like heaven.

She carried the can with her to the living room. And there the full extent of the mess became clear: cans and wrappers everywhere. And tomato sauce all over the white carpet.

Only here it wasn't tomato sauce and Leslie-Ann knew it.

Then she saw Albert. He was sitting with his back against the wall, which was splattered with gore.

His eyes were closed. He wasn't moving.

"Albert?"

She fought the desire to run and run and keep running. Only, she was still thirsty and hungry. And there lay a water bottle with a few precious sips still. She drank it. Not enough, but something.

She went to the kitchen and with shaking fingers dug out the plastic trash bags. Then, quick, quick, before someone stopped her, she gathered all the cans and bottles and thrust them into the bag. It wasn't much, but her brothers could find a couple of ounces of food.

She glanced at Albert, feeling sorry for him and a little guilty and . . .

His eyes. They were open.

"Albert?"

She went closer. Were his eyes following her?

"Are you alive?"

He didn't answer. But slowly, slowly his eyes closed. And then opened again.

Leslie-Ann ran from the room and from the house. But she did not drop her bag.

TWENTY-NINE

BRIANNA DREW THE bowie knife from its sheath. "Cutting you in three pieces didn't do it," she said to Drake. "So this time I'm going to dice you like an onion."

She blurred and Drake split open at the waist. Not clean-through, but she'd finish it with the next one.

"Get her!" Drake yelled.

She twirled in midair, kicked off the back of a bug, and brought the huge knife down again, chopping Drake's whip hand and leaving it like a reddish python, squirming but no longer attached to Drake.

She struck! Again! Again! In the blink of an eye.

But the creatures were reacting now, a mass of them, rushing her. Slow, too slow, but still she had to sidestep them, and that cost her a precious second.

And Drake was still alive. Or something like alive.

She threaded past gnashing mouthparts and scything mandibles and buried the knife in Drake's skull. The blade sank into the bone, stuck.

She yanked on it, but Drake's upper body came with it. The blade would not come free.

Speeeewt!

Something slapped her calf. She twisted to look and saw a long, barbed, black rope extending from the mouth of the closest bug. She shook her leg but it did not come off.

"Gross!"

Another bug tried the same thing and she somersaulted out of the way. Still that first tongue was attached to her and she could feel hooks buried in her skin.

She needed her bowie knife. But now it was out of range as Drake dragged himself away with his one arm.

Brianna spotted a stone with a dull edge. She slammed it down on the tongue with all the force her speed afforded. The tongue bled but did not break. Blue bug eyes fixed on her with what now looked like triumph.

"Oh, no you don't."

She hit the tongue fast, twenty times in a second with her rock and it yanked away, quick as Drake's whip hand.

Shwoop!

But now the bugs were around her, snapping at her with their creepy froggy tongues and those tongues were fast, fast even by Brianna's standards.

The bugs had played her. They'd concealed this weapon in their arsenal and she'd gotten cocky.

Speeewt!

Brianna kicked and squirmed, but two of them were on

her. She used the rock on the tongue that latched on to her stomach and knocked it loose but it was instantly replaced by three more.

Speeeewt! Speeewt!

They had her! She was held in a web, yelling, cursing, smacking.

Drake was putting himself back together, but his whip hand was still squirming by itself like a snake on hot pavement.

She was pinioned by half a dozen of the tongues and now the rest of the bugs were closing in to chew her up, mandibles slicing the air like scimitars.

Brianna felt a sudden wave of fear. Was it possible she could lose this fight?

"Don't kill her," Drake said. "Hold her! She's mine!"

He was on his feet and searching through the wild melee for his whip arm.

Suddenly, the coyote was in the fight. He leaped for her, jaws open, teeth flashing yellow.

"Really?" she cried.

She shoved back against the greedy muzzle with all her strength. The move stretched one of the lashing tongues taut. The coyote's powerful jaw, missing Brianna's arm, clamped hard on the tongue, which snapped back like a cut high-tension cable.

She was pinned, but she still had her speed.

She grabbed the coyote's ruff and swung it around to

clamp on a second tongue.

Now just four tongues still pinned her. She didn't have the strength to hold on to the coyote. The creature, maybe fearing the bugs would retaliate, took off yelping as if it had been kicked.

Four lines held the Breeze, all more or less on her left side, so she kicked off, pushing straight toward the insects. The tongues slackened. Brianna somersaulted. It was a sketchy maneuver, poorly executed, and she landed hard on her back, but the four tongues had been twisted around and now, as one, they released her.

Even as they released others struck. She could see them flying toward her like striking cobras.

She kicked a bug in the face, kicked hard against a slashing mandible, then *boom boom boom*, three hard kicks and she was out of there.

She caught her breath on a rise a hundred feet away. Her body was blistered wherever the tongues had touched. But she was alive.

She watched, panting, shaking, as Drake's tentacle melded seamlessly into his shoulder.

"Come on, Breeze," Drake taunted. "Come and get me. Here I am!"

Brianna had never been one to ignore a taunt. She had never run from a fight. But she had escaped by inches. By millimeters.

"It's the end, Breeze," Drake crowed. "I'm going to kill all of you. Every last one of you!" He danced in a circle, twirling in wild glee. "Run, Breeze! Ruuuuun! Because when I catch you, I'm going to make you suffer!"

Brianna ran.

Leslie-Ann fed her siblings the scrapings from the cans and let them drink the water.

Okay, she told herself: You did all you could.

Except that she hadn't done all she could. Not yet.

She had never liked Albert much. He was kind of a jerk to her. He never said anything nice like, "Good job, Leslie-Ann."

But he didn't deserve to just die like that. Maybe he was still alive.

"I'm just a kid," she said aloud to no one.

But she knew what she felt, and what she felt was that she hadn't done right.

She went out into the streets, not knowing exactly who she should locate, or who she should tell, but she knew she had to tell someone.

From where she stood she could see the big, weird cloud more clearly. It looked like it was raining. And just then two kids came past. They were walking in tandem, sharing the load of a heavy plastic tub. It was sloshing water over the sides and they were soaked through.

One of them noticed her and grinned. "It's raining!"

"No one's s'posed to go out," she said.

The kid snorted. "No one's telling anyone what to do right

now, and there's water. If I was you, I'd get some fast."

Leslie-Ann ran back inside and located a bucket in the garage. Then she walked as fast as she could toward the rain cloud. If everyone was there, maybe she could find someone to tell about Albert.

As she drew nearer she noticed something that was, in its own way, as weird as the cloud, which was now almost overhead: there was water running in the gutter. Actual water. Just running down the gutter.

She broke into a run and saw a crowd of dancing, cavorting kids ahead of her. Buckets sat under the downpour. Kids stood with their mouths open, or tried to shower, or just shoved and played and splashed.

A very unusual sound for the FAYZ: the high-pitched laughter of children.

Leslie-Ann set down her own bucket and watched, marveling, as a quarter of an inch of water covered the bottom.

When she looked away, she saw an older kid. She'd seen him around. But usually he was with Orc and she was too scared of Orc ever to get near him.

She tugged on Howard's wet sleeve. He seemed not to be sharing in the general glee. His face was severe and sad.

"What?" he asked wearily.

"I know something."

"Well, goody for you."

"It's about Albert."

Howard sighed. "I heard. He's dead. Orc's gone and

Albert's dead and these idiots are partying like it's Mardi Gras or something."

"I think he might not be dead," Leslie-Ann said.

Howard shook his head, angry at being distracted. He walked away. But then he stopped, turned, and walked back to her. "I know you," he said. "You clean Albert's house."

"Yes. I'm Leslie-Ann."

"What are you telling me about Albert?"

"I saw his eyes open. And he looked at me."

Albert dead.

Sam gone, and no telling when he would get back.

Astrid gone with Little Pete and Orc.

Dekka away with Sam and Jack.

And now Edilio, numb with the scale of the disaster, sat exhausted on the steps of the so-called hospital. He didn't need Dahra's thermometer to tell him what he already knew: he was hot, flushed, weak.

He coughed. And stared blankly at Brianna, who buzzed and vibrated to a wild halt before him.

"Bugs!" she yelled. "I passed them heading this way. Drake and a bunch more bugs are still back at the mine shaft. I saw them heading west but I think it's just a fake; he's probably coming here, too."

"How do we stop them?" Edilio asked and coughed into his hand.

"We need Sam," Brianna said.

"We—" He coughed again and fought off a wooziness that

made him desperately want to lie down. "I don't know where he is."

"I'll find him," Brianna vowed.

"You're all I've got left," Edilio said. "You're the only freak with any serious powers. I don't think the Siren would be much help against"—he coughed—"those creatures."

"She might work on Drake, though," Brianna said, and laughed as if oblivious to what was going on around her. In fact, as Edilio coughed again, she blinked, frowned, and said, "Are all these kids sick?"

"When the Siren sings, it affects everyone; she's just a pause button." Edilio coughed hard. It hurt his chest.

He was sick. Sick in his body and sick in his heart.

He had seen so many terrible things and done so many terrible things since the coming of the FAYZ. But nothing so cold-bloodedly awful as lining up the sights on Lance's head and squeezing the trigger.

It was the right move. Probably. It was the winning move, it seemed, since Astrid and Little Pete had both survived.

It was the ruthless move. The lesser-of-two-evils move. It was what Sam would have done in his place.

But it was poison in Edilio's heart.

"I can't save us," Edilio said. "Neither can you, Brianna. And Sam . . . I don't know if he can, either. So maybe this is the end. Maybe this is it and we lose."

Brianna slapped herself in the chest. "I don't lose!"

"You can't beat them alone, Breeze." A coughing fit, the worst one yet. It was several minutes before he could continue.

"I'm done for. I don't know if this will kill me or not but I can't even stand up."

"Hey, we can't just give up," Brianna said. "Those things are the size of ponies now, some of them. And they're growing! You can't give up, Edilio. You're the one in charge."

He aimed his eyes at her, but they were swimming. She was an angry, unfocused face.

"Get me a piece of paper and a pen," Edilio said.

She was back in less than a minute.

His fingers were trembling as a fit of chills racked his body. He had a hard time steadying the pad and holding the pen. But with supreme effort he scribbled something, folded the paper, and handed it to Brianna.

"Quinn," he said.

She read the message and flushed furiously. She threw the paper at him. It hit him in the face. "Are you nuts? I'm not doing this!"

"I'm in charge," he whispered. He bent with shaky fingers and retrieved the note. "My call. It's the only way. Do it, Breeze: do it."

"No, no. No way."

Edilio grabbed her arm and squeezed it with the last of his strength. "For once in your life, think. Can you stop them? Can you stop those bugs from reaching town and killing everyone here? Yes or no?"

"I can try."

"Yes or no?"

She stifled a sudden sob. She shook her head. "No."

"Okay, then," Edilio rasped. "Do you want to be responsible for the lives of everyone who will die just so that you can act all tough?"

She had no answer. She glanced around as if seeing the sick and the dead, the wrecked church, and the sad graveyard for the first time. "No," she said.

"Then go, Breeze. Go."

THIRTY

SAM HAD RUN the boat all the way up the lake and all the way back. They had found two small campgrounds in all, but had not explored them carefully. Maybe a dozen big campers, a few ragged tents in various states of collapse. No doubt some camp food, soda, beer, coffee, all the things people brought camping.

And gas in some of those tanks. Lovely, lovely gasoline.

He was already imagining the steps they'd have to take. They would drive the campers to the marina area and form them up in a rough circle or maybe two concentric circles. They would have to dig some serious septic tanks well away from the lake so there wasn't any seepage into drinking water.

They would need to ration the gas carefully, carefully, saving it for moving produce from the fields and fish from the ocean. They would still need Quinn's steady supply of blue bats to pacify the zekes. Besides, they would need to be cautious about overfishing the lake.

No more stupid mistakes. This time they would have to get it right.

That was a job for Albert, Sam had to concede. No doubt Albert would get richer still, but he was the only one with the organizational skills for the job.

Yes, it would work. They would build it and organize it and this time they would get it right.

For his part he had to find a way to destroy the flying greenies. But surely with Jack's strength and Dekka's powers and maybe Brianna—who could probably run through a cloud of greenies without getting hit—they could seal up that cave and crush or burn whatever survived.

They were heading back toward the marina now, chugging along slowly, taking their time. It was getting late in the day and Sam was trying to decide whether they should try to start one of the vehicles parked at the marina and drive back tonight, or plan a little more carefully and go in the morning.

The last thing anyone needed was three hundred or so kids tearing off in mad search for sweets. Half would end up lost in the desert or the hills and end up being coyote food.

The news needed to be handled the right way. Edilio and the rest of the council would have to plan a little.

To Dekka he said, "I think maybe we should load as much water as we can carry in an SUV and drive back tonight."

"I guess you've noticed there's no road that goes straight back."

"According to the map the road that follows the lake curves up around, hits the barrier. Right? But there has to then be a road that goes down through the Stefano Rey and hits the highway, right?"

Dekka shrugged. Her mind was elsewhere.

He couldn't blame her. But he had convinced himself she was worrying for nothing.

He indulged himself with a moment of fantasy. They would be heroes, showing up in town with water, even if it wasn't that much water. That would be one very welcome sight, an SUV full of water bottles. Maybe a few jars of Nutella, too, if they drove east to the train before cutting south.

Then, a meeting with the council. They could start trucking water right away. That would keep everybody calm until a plan was worked out.

"We'll go in . . ." His words died as his gaze traveled to the marina. "Dekka. Jack. Look."

They looked.

Creatures, like giant silvery cockroaches, cockroaches the size of minivans, clustered on the shore. Maybe a dozen.

It had to be an illusion. A trick. They were impossible. Like a nightmare out of some ancient science fiction movie.

Sam reached for the binoculars he'd found in a locked case on board. He raised them, focused.

"It's Hunter's bugs," he said. He couldn't keep the awe out of his voice. "But they're huge."

He traversed his binoculars and then saw a human standing atop one of the creatures. He could not see the face well enough to identify it. But there was no mistaking the long, jauntily waving tentacle.

Drake. No longer locked in his basement prison.

Sam's Garden of Eden had its own snake.

Howard's first impulse had been to go to the so-called hospital and find Lana. But what profit would be in it for Howard?

Orc was off somewhere, freaking out, hammered, faced, blasted. He'd come back when he ran out of alcohol, but for now, Orc was gone, and Drake's escape was a sort of black eye for Howard.

In the back of his calculating mind, Howard wondered if Orc was just determined to pull a Mary and off himself. He was nowhere near the deadly fifteenth birthday, but Orc might one of these days pick a fight that would get him killed.

Or he might just drink himself to death. And then what? What did Howard have if he didn't have Orc?

On a level still deeper was a genuine sadness that Orc would abandon him. They were friends, after all. Amigos. They'd been through everything together. Orc wasn't just Howard's main asset, he was Howard's only friend.

He cared for Orc. Genuinely cared for him. Obviously Orc didn't care much about him.

Howard took his time making the decision. Took his time and a fully clothed shower, too. But finally he made his decision and sauntered away from the cloud, soggy but moderately clean, unnoticed by frolicking kids.

It wasn't far to Albert's place. He found the door open, and quickly located Albert. The young mogul's eyes were closed. He definitely looked dead. Very definitely dead.

He advanced cautiously, as though Albert might suddenly rise up and start yelling at him for intruding. He pressed two fingers against Albert's neck. He didn't feel a pulse.

But he did feel warmth. The body should be colder.

He squatted in front of Albert and with his finger pushed up one eyelid. The dark iris contracted.

"Yaaah!" Howard said, and fell backward. "Are you alive, man?"

No answer. Nothing.

Howard was frustrated because he'd hoped—if Albert was still alive—to negotiate a deal. After all, if Howard saved Albert's life then it stood to reason that he owed Howard a little somethin' somethin'.

Howard hesitated. He could do nothing and sooner or later Albert would be a hundred percent, stone-cold dead. Or he could try to find Lana. And maybe there would be some reward. Albert was tight with his money, but surely if Howard saved his actual life . . .

"Okay, I don't know if you can hear this or not, Donald Trump, but if I save your butt, you owe me." He frowned and decided he'd better add, "And oh, by the way, this is Howard talking. So it'll be Howard you owe."

Howard arrived at the so-called hospital to see a very disturbing sight: Edilio, shivering and muttering on the stone steps, ignored. He was just one of dozens of sick kids with various degrees of illness. Coughing, hacking, shivering.

The last thing Howard wanted to do was get any closer.

"Hey!" Howard yelled up the steps.

No one answered. He winced, turned away, turned back, doing a little dance of indecision. Without even knowing what his reward might be, it was hard for Howard to decide to risk his life. A man needed to know what he was getting paid, after all.

Kkkrrraaalff!

A kid at the top of the steps suddenly coughed with a force Howard had never seen or heard or imagined. The cough blew the boy backward. He landed hard, head smacking granite with the sound of a melon dropped on a floor.

The boy rolled over, got to his knees, then coughed a spray of blood all over a girl nearby.

"No way," Howard said. "No way."

The new kid, Sanjit, Helicopter Boy, appeared at the top of the steps. He rushed down to the coughing kid and grabbed his shoulders from behind.

He spotted Howard standing there. "Give me a hand, I need to get him off these steps."

"I'm not touching that little dude," Howard said.

Sanjit shot him an angry look. But then softened, like he understood.

Sanjit tried to walk the boy back up the stairs, but then the kid started coughing again with such violence that he threw Sanjit off and went flailing back again.

This time he rolled down the stairs to stop at Howard's feet. He lay there, shivering and moaning. A fountain of blood flowed at once from his ears and nose and mouth.

Sanjit came down and stood over him. "Get out of the way,"

Sanjit said to Howard. "I have to drag him across the street."

"Is he dead?"

"No, he's in perfect shape," Sanjit snapped. He grabbed both of the boy's wrists and started to haul him toward the plaza.

"You see Edilio there?" Howard demanded.

"Yes, I saw Edilio there," Sanjit said.

"Shouldn't you . . ." Howard motioned vaguely.

"Yeah, I should call for a stretcher and get him straight to the intensive care unit," Sanjit said with contained fury. "I'll get him on an oxygen machine and pump him full of antibiotics. Or maybe I'll just see if he lives or dies because that's really all I can do. All right?"

Howard took a step back in the face of the slender boy's anger.

"Didn't mean to . . . ," he said, and followed at a safe distance as Sanjit dragged the body off the curb and onto the blacktop.

Sanjit stopped halfway across and stared at the sky.

"What's that? Is that a cloud?"

"Oh, that? Yeah, it's raining. More weirdness," Howard said.

"What? It's raining? Like, water?"

"Yeah, water. It was a shock to me, too," Howard said. "This being the FAYZ you'd expect it to be raining fire or dog turds or something."

"Choooooo!" Sanjit yelled at the top of his lungs. "Chooooo!"

A few seconds later, his chubby African brother came running down the stairs, looking alarmed.

"Water!" Sanjit said.

"Where?" Virtue demanded.

Sanjit pointed with his chin. "Get a bucket. Get every bucket you can find!"

Virtue gaped, then ran.

Sanjit resumed dragging the corpse.

"Listen, dude," Howard said. "I need Lana. You know who I mean? The Healer."

"You have a boo-boo?" Sanjit snarked. "She's kind of busy trying to save a couple of creeps Edilio shot."

"Where?"

"Astrid's house. I don't know where it is. How about you either help me or get lost?"

"I'll choose B."

Astrid's house. Okay. That would be . . . pretty much right directly under the cloud.

Well, well, Howard thought as the truth dawned on him.

"Little Pete," he said. "So that's out there, then. Well, buckle up, Howard, buckle up."

Quinn and his crew were pulling toward shore, far later than usual. They'd had a tough day of it. After a miserable night in camp, they'd had trouble getting one of the boats floating again. They had unknowingly run it ashore and scraped a hidden rock. A gash had been gouged in the bottom, which meant hours of finding a way to patch it.

Fortunately it was one of the wooden hulls, not one of the metal or fiberglass ones; those would have been impossible to patch without going back to town for equipment.

Still, they'd had to use just their Swiss Army knives to whittle some driftwood into fairly flat, fairly smooth planks. Then they'd found they had no screws, so they had to remove bolts from other boats, drill through the repair patch and the hull, and use the bolts to attach the patch. They had scraped and then melted some paint to use as a sealant.

When they were all done the boat was surprisingly seaworthy. They'd all felt pretty well pleased with their work, but a day of fishing was still to be done.

Harder later in the day. As the sun heated the top layer of seawater, some of their most reliable catch went deeper or stopped feeding.

So there were none of the jokes or laughs or bits of song that often accompanied their homeward row.

"They still haven't picked up yesterday's catch!" Quinn yelled when they drew close enough to see.

And sure enough, most of the fish they'd worked so hard to land the day before were still on the dock, rotting in the heat.

This revelation set off a round of angry curses from the crews, followed by a more disquieting worry. It was hard to imagine how Albert could have let this happen.

"Something's deeply wrong," Quinn said. "I mean even more wrong than we knew."

They were still two hundred yards out when Quinn saw

a blur that froze and became Brianna. She was at the end of the dock.

There was something in her hand.

"You guys hang back," Quinn yelled to the other boats. "We'll go in and see what's up."

Quinn's boat touched the dock and he tossed a loop over one of the cleats.

"About time," Brianna said.

"Hey, sorry, we were kind of busy," Quinn snapped. "And I didn't exactly realize I was on a schedule."

"I don't like what I have to do here," Brianna said. She handed Quinn the note.

He read it. Read it again.

"Is this some kind of joke?" he demanded.

"Albert's dead," Brianna said. "Murdered."

"What?"

"He's dead. Sam and Dekka are off in the wilderness somewhere. Edilio's got the flu, he might die, a lot of kids have. A lot. And there are these, these monsters, these kind of bugs . . . no one knows what to call them . . . heading toward town." Her face contorted in a mix of rage and sorrow and fear. She blurted, "And I can't stop them!"

Quinn stared at her. Then back at the note.

He felt his contented little universe tilt and go sliding away.

There were just two words on the paper: "Get Caine."

THIRTY-ONE

SAM PULLED THE boat to within thirty yards of the shore.

"I guess you wish you'd burned me all up, huh?" Drake called to him.

"I do," Dekka growled.

"That's true," Toto said. "She does wish it."

Sam had to master a furious anger that burned within him. How had Drake escaped? Had he found a way to bribe Howard?

"He wouldn't be standing there taunting us unless he thought he could beat us," Sam said quietly. "Those bugs: I couldn't kill them when they were a lot smaller." He looked at Toto. "All you've got is the truth-telling thing, right? You don't have some other power?"

Toto gave his answer to the missing Spidey head. "No weapons."

"Can those things swim?" Jack wondered.

"If they could they'd already be after us," Sam said.

"Do you think Drake can control those things, make them do what he wants?" Jack wondered.

"I guess we'll find out sooner or later," Sam said.

They all fell silent, gazing at him expectantly.

For the moment they were probably safe, Sam reasoned. Otherwise Drake would have come after them. If they went ashore it would mean a fight. And Drake was pretty cocky, swaggering around and taunting them from shore.

He could head the boat back up the lake. He could land and get around Drake's insect army. They could make it to someplace where they could fight without destroying the marina.

"We need to get away from here," Sam said.

"Hey, Sam," Drake shouted. "I thought you'd like to know this isn't my whole army."

Sam didn't doubt it.

"Your girl Brianna tried to stop us." Drake waved a bowie knife in the air. "I took this from her. I whipped her, Sam." He snapped his whip hand. The crack was like a pistol shot. "I broke her legs so she couldn't run. Then . . ."

Dekka was halfway over the side, ready to swim ashore. Jack grabbed her and held her.

"Let me go!" Dekka yelled.

"Hold her," Sam ordered Jack. "Don't be stupid, Dekka. He wants us to come rushing at him."

"I can beat him," Jack said. "Dekka and me together, we can kill him."

Sam registered the fact that Jack was actually making a

physical threat. He didn't remember ever hearing that kind of thing from Jack. But Dekka was Sam's greater concern.

"I'm going to kill him," Dekka said in a voice so deep in her throat she sounded like an animal. "I'll kill him. I'll kill him." Then she shouted, "I'm going to kill you, Drake. I'm going to kill you!"

Drake grinned. "I think she liked it. She was screaming, but she liked it."

"He's lying," Toto said.

"Who?" Sam snapped.

"Him." He pointed at Drake. "He hasn't killed that girl or hurt her."

Dekka relaxed and Sam and Jack let go of her.

"Truth-teller Toto," Sam whispered. "He can tell when people are lying."

"I just decided I like you," Dekka said to Toto. "You might be useful."

Toto frowned. "It's true: you just decided you like me."

"Keep listening, Toto," Sam said. He thought for a minute. Then he yelled, "Brianna may be dead, but we still have more than enough muscle to deal with you."

Drake threw back his head and laughed. "Yeah, the rest of my army is finishing off the last few kids in Perdido Beach. It was a beautiful massacre, Sam, you should have been there."

Sam made a motion to Dekka not to answer. The more Drake talked the better.

"But I still have Astrid alive, Sam," Drake shouted. "I have her somewhere safe. I want to take my time with her."

Sam waited, held his breath.

"Those are lies," Toto said.

"All of it?"

"All of it."

Sam breathed.

"Well, Drake," Sam shouted across the water. "I'm sorry to hear about that. I guess there's nothing left but for you to come and get me."

His tone was so casual, it left Drake gaping openmouthed. It took the psychopath a few moments to regroup.

"What's the matter, Sammy? Scared? Chicken?"

"No, actually we were thinking we might catch some fish," Sam yelled. "I hear the trout from this lake are delicious. Would you like to join us? You can swim with that whip hand, can't you?"

Drake stared. He looked at the knife in his hand as if it had somehow betrayed him. Then, eyes narrowed, he glared at Toto.

"Come on, Drake. Don't be a baby. Come and get us."

All the while Sam had been letting the boat edge closer, closer while not grounding. He was within ten yards of Drake. He didn't have to raise his voice to be heard.

Without turning toward her, and speaking in a whisper, he said, "Dekka, can you reach him from here?"

"Barely," she said. "The sharper the angle, the less I can do. But yeah."

"On one," Sam said. "Three . . . two . . ."

Dekka raised her hands and Drake rose feebly from the

ground. He felt it immediately, knew what was happening, and kicked against the air like a marionette.

Sam raised his hands. Twin beams of green light fired. They hit one of the creatures, two feet to the left, but Sam swung right and caught Drake's leg.

The leg turned bright and smoke swirled.

Drake lashed with his whip and caught one of the creatures. He yanked himself out of Dekka's field and tumbled among the creatures, blocked from Sam's beams.

"Will he die?" Toto asked.

"Sadly, no," Dekka said.

From shore they heard Drake bellowing in outrage, then: "Get them! Go!"

The creatures responded instantly. They rushed to the water's edge. It was almost impossible for Sam to see them as living creatures, they seemed more like robots. Insects simply were not that big. Couldn't be that big.

They rushed in a swarm to the water. And kept running straight in.

"They float," Jack said. "That's bad."

"Yeah, but they can't swim very well," Sam pointed out. He threw the engine into reverse and chug-chugged slowly back to a safer distance. The creatures had stopped rushing into the water. Those that could reach bottom scurried igno-miniously back to dry land. Two of the creatures floated like unmoored rafts, or like trailers caught in a flood, twisting slowly, helpless.

Then one of the creatures on shore opened its wings.

Beneath the hard carapace were wings like a dragonfly's.

"They can't actually fly, can they?" Dekka wondered.

The creature lifted off. It was awkward and slow. But it flew.

It flew toward the boat.

"Go back to camp after you off-load the catch," Quinn instructed his crews. "I'll catch up with you later. And if I don't . . . well, keep up the routine."

He felt worried eyes following him as he walked down the dock. There was one motorboat that still had a few gallons of fuel. They had designated it for emergency use only. He supposed this was emergency enough.

"You coming?" Quinn asked Brianna.

She shook her head. "I can't beat these things, but I can at least fight them."

"What if he won't come?" Quinn asked.

"He'll come. It will be his big moment."

"Will he be able to stop these creatures?"

"How would I know?" Brianna demanded. "It wasn't my idea. I'm not the one saying we should bring him back. Maybe he and Drake will go back to being best buddies. How would I know?"

"Well, I guess Edilio thinks Caine can save us."

Neither of them spoke for a while, both thinking of Edilio, wondering if he would survive. Right from the start Edilio had been one of the good guys. Probably the best of them.

He and Mary: two selfless, loyal, decent people. One dead

after betraying everything and everyone. The other maybe dying right now, ignored and alone.

"One more question for you, Brianna. It's serious. So don't just give me your automatic tough-chick answer, okay? Because I want the truth."

"Yeah?"

"Can you beat Caine? If he starts in with his usual, starts pushing people around, hurting them . . . Can you take him?"

He saw the beginnings of a cocky smile. But then she dropped the act, sighed, and said, "I don't know, Quinn."

Still he hesitated. He didn't want to go. And he knew why. "Everybody kind of likes me now because I fish. I have this thing I do, right, and it's necessary and so people respect me." He sighed and unwound the motorboat's rope from its cleat. "Now I'll be the guy who brought Caine back."

Brianna nodded. "Sucks to be you. Sucks worse to be me."

Impulsively, Quinn hugged her. Like a brother. She didn't return the gesture, but she didn't blur away either.

"Hang in there, Breeze."

"You too, Fisherman."

Quinn stepped down into the boat. Brianna was out of sight before he could fire the engine.

He headed out of the marina, chugging along slowly until he was away. Then he pushed the throttle to full speed and pointed the bow toward the distant island.

Astrid looked around, wondering where they were and where they were going. Orc seemed to have someplace in mind. But he also seemed confused. They were in an area of tangled woods and sharp, sudden, brush-choked valleys.

"Are you taking us to Coates?" Astrid asked.

"Yeah," Orc answered.

"Why there?"

"You wanted to get away, right?"

"I want my brother to be somewhere safe," Astrid said, conscious of the hypocrisy.

"It's safe there," Orc said.

"How do you know?"

"It's a secret," Orc grumbled. "I mean, there's no one there. None of those kids anyway. Caine and all them guys."

"What if Drake goes there?"

Orc shrugged, which caused Little Pete's head to fall from his shoulder and loll back. "If Drake's there, I'll take care of him."

Astrid stepped quickly to catch up with Orc. She put her hand on his shoulder. He slowed down and moved aside so she could walk beside him.

"Are you looking for Drake?" Astrid asked. "Because I don't think that's a good idea."

"I don't care about Drake," Orc said angrily. "I had enough of him. But I have to be away from town. Where else am I going to go?"

Astrid felt sure that was part of the truth. But not all of it.

"Thanks for helping us," she said. "But you don't have to stay away from town. It's not your fault Drake escaped."

"Didn't say it was."

"Then why?"

Orc said nothing, just walked on heavily, stone feet trampling the undergrowth like some undersized Godzilla. Then, "This kid," he said.

"What kid?"

"This kid, this little kid, was all sick or whatever, and I was . . . I guess I was drunk."

"What happened with the kid?"

"Got in my way," Orc said.

It was hard to read Orc's expression. But she heard anguish in his voice.

"Oh," Astrid said.

"Gotta leave town. Like Hunter. That's the law. You oughta know, you made up that law."

"I didn't come up with 'thou shalt not kill,'" Astrid said defensively. The sanctimony in her own voice made her sick. The same Bible that said "thou shalt not kill" also said "he who hateth his brother is a murderer."

Didn't she hate her brother? Hadn't she contemplated murder? Hadn't she dared Turk and Lance to do it for her? If Orc had to go into exile, then didn't she as well?

Would she wish her brother dead and live with that mortal sin, and yet draw the line at sleeping with Sam? How absurd was that? Murder, sure, but fornication? No way.

Astrid had never felt so low. She dropped back so Orc wouldn't see the tears in her eyes. Oh, God, how had she become this person? How had she failed so utterly?

Hypocrite. Murderer in her heart. A cold, manipulative

witch. That's what she was. Astrid the Genius? Astrid the Fraud.

And now she slogged through darkening woods to find a cold shelter with a drunken killer and her brother. One who killed from rage and stupidity; the other who killed from what? Ignorance? Indifference? From the simple fact of too much power for anyone to handle, let alone an autistic child? She laughed, but it was not a happy sound.

"What's funny?" Orc demanded suspiciously.

"Me," Astrid said.

They spotted the dark gabled roofs of Coates through the trees and then struck the road that led up to the front gate.

It was a gloomy place, a haunted place. Pale whitewashed stone that showed evidence of violence. A massive hole in the facade was like a fatal bullet wound. The door had been ripped apart, shredded.

Orc stomped steadily forward, climbed the steps, and yelled, "Anyone here?"

His voice echoed in the arched entryway. "There're beds upstairs. Gotta take the back stairs."

He led the way, obviously familiar with the layout. Astrid wondered how he had come to know the place so well. Orc was not a Coates kid.

They found a dorm room that hadn't been burned or shredded or used as a toilet.

Orc tossed Little Pete negligently onto a bare mattress. Astrid searched for and found a tattered blanket, which she spread over him.

She felt his forehead. Still feverish, but perhaps no worse than before. She had no thermometer. He was coughing in fits and starts. Not worse, not better.

"What's next, Petey?" she asked him.

If Lance had squeezed the trigger, would the bullet have killed Little Pete? Would he have had the power to stop it? Surely. But would he have known what was happening?

"How much do you know, Petey? How much do you understand?"

He would need clean bedding after he wet himself. And she herself needed clothing, she was still in just a nightgown. And although there would be no food left in this place, surely there might be a few drops of water.

Astrid called to Orc, but he didn't hear. She heard his heavy footsteps reverberate in the eerie silence.

Best to leave him be. In another room she found clothing that was close to her size. Close enough. It wasn't clean, but at least it had not been worn recently. Coates had been abandoned for a while. She wondered if it belonged to Diana.

She went in search of water. What she found was Orc. He was in the dining hall. His massive legs were propped on a heavy wooden table. He had pushed two chairs together to bear his weight and spread.

In his hand he held a clear glass bottle full of clear liquid.

The room smelled of charcoal and something sickly sweet. The source was obvious: in the corner, next to a window, was a contraption that could only be a still. Copper tubing probably salvaged from the chemistry lab looped from a steel washtub that rested on an iron trestle over the cold remains of a fire.

"This is where Howard makes his whiskey," Astrid said. "That's how you know the place."

Orc took a deep swig. Some of the liquor sloshed out of his mouth. "No one ever comes here since Caine and all them took off. That's how come Howard set up here."

"What does he use?"

Orc shrugged. "Don't matter much as long as it's any kind of vegetable. There's a patch of corn only a few people know about. Artichokes, too. Cabbages. It don't matter."

Astrid took a chair at some distance from him.

"You changed clothes," he said.

"I was cold."

He nodded and drank deep. His eyes were on her, looking at her in detail. She was very glad to no longer be wearing her nightgown.

She wondered whether Orc was old enough for her to worry about in that way. She thought not. But it was a frightening possibility.

"Should you be drinking that so fast?"

"Gotta be fast," Orc said. "Otherwise I pass out and can't get enough to do the trick."

"What trick?" Astrid asked.

Orc made a sad smile. "Don't worry about it, Astrid."

She didn't want to worry about it. She had enough of her own worries. So she said nothing as he gulped and gulped until forced to take a breath.

"Orc," she said softly. "Are you trying to kill yourself?"

"Like I said, don't worry 'bout it."

"You can't do that," she said. "It's . . . it's wrong."

She noticed two more bottles down on the floor, right where he could reach them without moving.

"It's a mortal sin," she said, feeling like a stupid fool. The very word "sin" felt like a sin when she spoke it.

Hypocrite, she berated herself silently. Fraud.

"If you do this, you'll have no chance to repent," Astrid said. "You'll die with a mortal sin on your conscience."

"Got that already," Orc said.

"But you're sorry for that. You've thought about it. And you're sorry for it."

Orc sobbed suddenly, a loud sound. He tilted his head back and she saw the last of the bottle drain into his mouth.

"If you've asked for forgiveness, and if you felt truly sorry, then God has forgiven you for that little boy."

The bottles weren't corked, just sealed with a piece of Saran Wrap and a rubber band. Orc pulled the plastic off a second bottle.

"There's no God in the FAYZ, didn't you know that?" he said.

THIRTY-TWO

SAM FIRED. THE beams of light hit the hovering bug squarely. The rays of light bounced and fragmented, steaming the water.

"Dekka!" Sam yelled.

She killed gravity beneath the hovering bug so that it shot suddenly upward followed by a swoosh of rising water.

But it was no good. More of the creatures were opening their roachlike wings and flying awkwardly out toward the boat.

Sam cursed. He threw the engine into gear and spun the wheel. The boat zoomed toward the middle of the lake.

The bugs tried to chase, but they were insects, not eagles, and their flight was jerky and poorly controlled.

"I can maybe crush them," Jack said over the roar of the engines.

"He believes he maybe can," Toto commented.

"But they scare me."

"That is true, too," Toto said.

"Yeah, I could have guessed that," Sam yelled as they dodged another lumbering creature.

They could keep dodging the bugs, maybe forever, but when Sam tapped the gas gauge it showed just an eighth of a tank.

There was a hand pump built into the dock's gas tank. But it wasn't as if Drake would let them pull in and refuel.

"We need gas," Sam said.

He headed the boat away from the marina, keeping close to the shore, hoping Drake's creepy army would follow. They were faster on land than in the air so they zoomed in their crazy bumblebee way back to land on shore.

He looked back and saw Drake urging the creatures on. They were quick, skittering on their insect legs. But not quite as fast as the boat. At top speed he could pull away.

"Are we running away?" Toto wondered.

"Yes," Sam snapped.

"That's not true."

"Is there any way to shut you off?" Sam demanded. "We're faster than they are. So we're going to draw them off, double back, and beat them back to the marina."

"Then what?" Dekka asked.

"We gas up and drive around out here forever," Sam said.

"Great plan," Dekka said.

"Sooner or later Drake gives way to Brittney. We might have a shot then."

It didn't take long at full speed to reach the end of the lake.

The huge roaches swarmed along the shore, rushing eagerly to catch up. None were airborne now.

"Where's Drake?" Jack asked.

Sam scanned the insect army. No sign of Drake. Sam killed the engine, saving gas for the mad dash back to the marina. In the sudden quiet he heard a different engine.

A sleek boat with two big outboards was throwing up a cloud of spray and *whump-whump*ing toward them. There could be no doubt as to who was driving the boat.

The bugs on the shore. Drake on the water.

"If he has a gun, we're in trouble," Dekka said.

"He doesn't need a gun," Sam said grimly. "He can ram us. He's unkillable, we're not."

"What do we do?" Jack asked. Then, more panicked, "What do we do?"

Dekka put a calming hand on his shoulder. "Take it easy."

Sam measured the shoreline, checked the gas supply, glanced at his two friends, and finally appraised Toto.

"Dude, do you think you can pump gas?"

Toto looked away and passed the question along to the imaginary Spidey head. "Can I pump gas?" Then, apparently hearing an answer, he said, "Yes."

Sam fired the engine up. He turned the wheel, waited, waited, as Drake's bow wave grew large.

"Jack. Grab that boathook. And be ready."

"What?"

"You ever see that movie where Heath Ledger was a knight?"

"Not his best movie," Dekka said.

"True," Toto agreed.

"Hold on," Sam warned. He put the engine into gear, pushed the throttle all the way, and flew toward Drake.

Lana did not run, she was too tired for it, and anyway Howard was probably wrong. Turk and Lance surely did believe they'd killed Albert. As he'd laid there, shrieking in pain beneath Lana's healing touch, Lance kept babbling something about forgiveness, praying to be saved, saying he was sorry for Albert. "It was Turk, it wasn't me!" he'd said, his destroyed cheek flapping bloodily with each word as the drenching rain swept the blood down to the carpet beneath his head.

Lana had mostly healed Turk and Lance. They wouldn't die, at least. She hadn't much seen the point: they were scum and someone would only have to kill them all over again, sooner or later. But she supposed it wasn't her decision to make. She was just a player in the madness.

She had missed her chance to be a hero by destroying the gaiaphage. And she had failed to stop the virus that now claimed nine bodies. Instead she'd saved a couple of creeps. Yay for her.

She and Howard found Albert just as he'd said: sitting with his back against the wall.

Lana noticed an awful lot of blood. A small, sticky sea of it around Albert.

"He didn't die right away," Lana observed. "Dead people don't bleed as much. And see how the wall is smeared? He sat up." She knelt and placed her fingers on his neck. "Then he just sat here and bled to death."

No question in her mind. He had a bullet hole in his face. And a much larger exit wound out the far side. It looked as if some wild animal had taken a messy bite out of his skull.

"I don't raise the dead," Lana said.

"No, wait," Howard insisted. He knelt beside her and lifted one eyelid. It was dark, there wasn't much light for an iris to react to. So Howard fished out a lighter and flicked the flame.

Lana's eyebrows went up. "Do it again."

Howard lifted the other lid. That iris, too, responded.

"Huh," Lana said.

She pressed both hands against Albert's head. After a few minutes holding that pose she bent his head forward to see the awful exit wound. Around the jagged, ripped edges, flesh was growing.

"The brother's not dead," Howard said.

"About as close as you can get," Lana said. "But no: he's not dead. And this kind of thing, at least, I can heal."

"Boy's going to owe me," Howard said.

"You're a trip, Howard, as my dad would say," Lana said. "You are definitely a trip."

"You'll tell Albert I brought you, right? You'll tell him it was me, right?"

"Why? Are you leaving?"

Howard stood up. "Gotta go find Orc. I just figured out where he'd go."

Lana got herself into a more comfortable position. Patrick

went off to scavenge around in the house.

"You find anything, you better share," Lana called after her dog.

The two boats raced toward each other.

Six seconds to impact.

Sam's mind was racing. Drake would know he was bluffing. Drake didn't fear an impact, he would know Sam was bluffing and he would expect Sam to suddenly veer aside.

Four seconds to impact.

"Jack!" Sam yelled. "Up on the bow!"

"What?"

"Do it!" Sam bellowed.

Jack sprang straight from the stern to the bow. He was holding the boathook like a lance. Like he really was a knight. Hopefully Drake had noticed.

One second.

"Now, throw it!" Sam shouted.

Jack threw it with all his desperate, supernatural strength.

Sam had not expected the boathook to impale Drake—and it didn't. But even an unkillable killer had instincts, and Drake instinctively dropped to let the boathook fly harmlessly over his head.

Sam had already twisted the wheel.

They blew past Drake's boat, spraying it with their bow wave and taking a drenching spray in return.

Dekka grinned at Toto. "See, this is what makes Sam, Sam."

It took a furious Drake ten seconds to turn his boat and come after Sam.

The bugs were even slower to catch on. Now they were racing back along the shore, but neither Drake nor the bugs would get to the marina before Sam.

"Okay," Sam yelled over the throb of the engines. "Toto, when we get there you pump like crazy, right? I'll show you how. But Drake will be on us quick and he may try again to ram us, so Jack? You and Dekka be ready."

"Ready to do what?"

"Hang on!" Sam yelled. He aimed the boat for the dock, threw it into reverse, the water boiled, the engine roared, and the boat scraped harshly to a stop by the gas pump.

Sam grabbed Toto and shoved him bodily up onto the dock.

"Dekka! Tie us off." He unlimbered the hand pump, thrust the nozzle into the gas tank and physically placed Toto's hands on the pump. "Up and down, up and down, and don't stop until I tell you to."

Sam ran to the end of the dock. Drake was roaring down on them. Sam glanced left, right, looking for what he needed. A low-slung sailboat. That would do.

"Dekka! Float that boat!"

Dekka raised her hands and the boat rose from the water, dripping all over them, tilting to one side so that for a moment Sam was afraid it would roll over and smash its mast down on their heads.

"Okay, Jack. You missed with the boathook. Try this!"

Jack had to skirt Dekka's field, and for a second he lost his footing and almost fell into the water. Sam grabbed his hand and hauled him upright.

Jack backed up twenty feet, took a deep breath, and ran straight at the boat that now hovered over the end of the dock.

Sam had the pleasure of seeing the sudden realization dawn in Drake's eyes.

Jack rushed forward, jumped, and hit the stern of the sailboat.

The boat flew, twisting crazily through the air. Not far, just twenty or thirty feet before it exploded into flames as Sam aimed and fired.

The boat fell, hit the water, and Drake's boat smashed into it at full speed.

Both boats shattered, flaming wood splinters flew, bits of metal railing and big pieces of the engine spiraled and landed like shrapnel all around them.

Toto cried out in pain. His hip had been hit and he was bleeding and screaming and not pumping any longer.

"Jack! Pump! Dekka, get Toto."

Sam dropped back into his boat and began snatching up and tossing out bits of flaming debris.

"Be dead, be dead," Sam muttered under his breath.

A sudden sound and Sam felt a burning pain. A red lash mark appeared on his arm.

Drake was holding the dock with his real arm, whip hand drawn back to strike again.

Sam fired. Missed. Bought two seconds as Drake sank

beneath the disturbed water.

He shot a look up the shore. The racing creatures pelted through the parking lot, swarmed over and around the cars, would be on them in seconds. Now or never.

"Enough! Back in the boat!"

No one needed to be told twice. Toto and Jack were first in. Dekka stumbled as she ran, slapped her belly, and for a moment Sam thought something had hit her.

Drake was up and his whip hand found Jack. Jack howled and grabbed at the tentacle but missed.

Sam gunned the engine. But he had forgotten the rope. The boat roared, shot forward, and snapped the cleat off the dock. The resistance was enough to yank the boat around.

It smashed into another parked boat and sent everyone tumbling.

By the time Sam cleared his head, Drake had his hand on the gunwale and his whip hand was flailing madly into the boat, striking Jack again and Toto.

Sam threw the boat into reverse, pushed the throttle, twisted the wheel, and ground Drake between boat and dock.

Then he changed gears and roared off, leaving Drake cursing in the water as the bugs raced down the dock, their mandibles slashing at the air.

Sam drove to the middle of the lake and killed the engine. The gas gauge showed a hair over a quarter tank. Enough for now. But at the cost of Toto screaming in pain.

"It's bad," Dekka reported. "But he'll live."

She lifted Toto's shirt to show Sam a nasty gash. "Jack, see if there's a first aid kit aboard."

Sam sagged, very tired now. "You okay?" he asked Dekka. She didn't answer.

He looked more closely at her. "Dekka?"

She looked sick. She bit her lip. "I am sorry to add to your problems, boss," she said. Then she raised her own shirt and Sam saw the tiny mouthparts poking through her flesh.

The light died and night fell as the boat rocked on the gentle waves.

THIRTY-THREE

DIANA ROLLED OUT of the bed, accidentally pulling the covers off Caine as she did.

"Hey!" he protested.

"It's nothing I haven't seen. Repeatedly."

Caine grinned and laced his fingers behind his head. "I could get used to this life. I think I'll have another can of peaches."

Diana took a quick shower and stepped out, dripping wet, to find him waiting for her, holding a towel.

"Seriously: no," she said. "We're done."

"Well, until we get something to eat," he said.

She dried off and combed her hair while he watched. The lack of privacy was a little irritating, but she told herself it was a small price to pay for peace. In any universe this would be a lovely room, in a lovely house, on a lovely island. But in the FAYZ every part of it was exquisite, a miracle of beauty and comfort. She remembered Coates all too well. Especially the last months there as the food ran out and the fear and depression and self-hatred set in.

This was a beautiful place. And Caine was a beautiful boy—a young man, she supposed—at least on the outside.

If comfort and luxury and Diana herself could keep him pacified, maybe life would go on this way: peaceful.

Even caring for Penny and dealing with Bug were small problems compared to what she had survived. Panda: she shuddered at the memory and felt sick.

"What's the matter?" Caine asked.

"Nothing." She forced a smile. "I guess I'm hungry." Then, seeing his expression, amended the statement. "For food."

They pulled on underwear and wrapped themselves in soft, expensive robes bearing famous, embroidered initials. She slid her feet into silk slippers and together they headed down to the kitchen.

Bug was there, looking even more disturbed than usual. He was breathing hard. Diana glared at him, wondering whether he had been spying on them.

"There's a boat coming," Bug said.

"What do you mean?" Diana asked.

"A motorboat. It's real near."

Caine was out the door in a flash and Diana had to run to catch up. The sky was near dark, the sun setting gorgeously and sending fingers of gold and red across the water below them.

And there, shockingly close, was a motorboat. She saw one

person aboard, a boy, but could not make out his shadowed face.

She looked searchingly at Caine. On his face she saw the expression she expected to see, the expression she dreaded.

His eyes were alight, his mouth in a feral grin. His whole body seemed to lean forward, anticipating, ready. Excited.

"Whoever it is, just tell him to leave," Diana said.

"Let's at least find out who it is," Caine said.

"Caine, just get rid of him."

The boat scared Diana. She wrapped her arms around herself as if shielding herself from cold.

Now the boy in the boat looked up.

"It's Quinn," Caine said. "What's he doing here? I expected it to be Zil or one of his losers."

"You expected?" Diana frowned. "What do you mean, you expected?"

Caine shrugged. "Sooner or later one of them was going to come to me."

"But . . . Why would you . . . ?"

He laughed. A smug, cruel laugh. "There are only two four bars in the FAYZ, Diana. Sooner or later someone would get sick enough of Sam lording it over them that they'd come to find me."

Diana felt something twisting inside her.

"Hey, Quinn. Up here!" Caine yelled. Then, in an aside, "Bug, disappear. Stay ready. It might be some kind of trick."

Bug faded from view.

Quinn killed the engine. He stood up, moving easily with the rocking of the boat. "Caine. Where do I land the boat?"

"No need," Caine said. He was grinning hugely now. "Sit down and hold on."

Caine stepped to the very edge of the cliff. He raised his hands. The boat began to rise from the water. Dripping, and trailing a fringe of algae, it floated up and up and came to rest on the overgrown grass. Caine released it and it tipped onto its side. Quinn jumped to avoid being spilled out of the boat.

"Well, Quinn, what brings you to Fantasy Island?" Caine asked.

"Hey, Diana," Quinn said.

Diana didn't respond. She knew. Just like Caine knew. Somehow, despite everything, Quinn was here to bring Caine back.

"Edilio sent me," Quinn said.

Caine smiled skeptically. "Edilio? Last guy on earth I expected to be sending me messages."

"Edilio's mayor now."

Diana felt a pang. "Is Sam dead?"

Quinn started to answer, but Caine interrupted. "No, no: let me guess. I'm going to say . . . Sam got tired of doing everyone's dirty work, taking all the risks, and then catching all the blame when things didn't go perfectly."

Caine relished the mute confirmation on Quinn's face. He laughed and said, "Come on, Quinn. Come inside and have something to eat."

"I'm just here to—"

Caine waved this off and said, "No, no, no, you have to come in. I don't want to stand out here in a bathrobe. After all, this is a big moment in the history of the FAYZ."

"A big moment?" Diana said.

"My triumphant return, Diana. That's why Quinn's here: to beg me to come back."

"Well, he's wasting his time," Diana said, but even she didn't believe it. She followed Caine and Quinn back to the house.

"Would you like some crackers and cheese?" Caine suggested brightly. He could barely contain himself. He was grinning hugely. Cocky. Swaggering. Even as Diana felt the small hope she'd nurtured die inside her.

They brought Quinn some crackers and cheese and a cookie. He didn't resist but ate them quickly with pleasure he could not conceal.

"You know, we have a very nice life here," Caine said expansively. "Plenty of food. Water. Even hot water for showers if you can believe it. In fact, we were just lying in bed talking about it."

"Yeah. It's nice," Quinn said with an embarrassed glance at Diana.

Caine watched him eat, considering. "Diana, I think you'd better do a reading on Quinn. Just in case something has developed."

Diana hadn't done a reading in a long time. It was her power: an ability to read whether a person was a freak or a normal. And then to know how much power the person had. Diana was the one to invent the half-mocking bar system. One bar, two bars, like a cell phone.

Diana stood next to Quinn and laid a hand on his shoulder. She concentrated, forming the picture in her head.

"Nothing," Diana said.

"Could have told you that," Quinn said, voice muffled by cookie.

Diana dropped her hand to her hip. "You're normal, Quinn. Now . . ." She stopped in midsentence. She'd been about to tell Quinn to go home, leave, get off the island right now, this instant.

But something . . . she felt something. Something registered, some power.

A freak.

Bug was close by, still invisible, but not touching her, not making physical contact. Nor was Caine touching her. The power to read freaks only worked on direct touch.

Was she sensing her own power? No. No, this was something different. It was faint but persistent.

She turned away and placed her hand on her stomach.

"So, Quinn, tell me: what's the big crisis?" Caine asked.

Diana nearly fainted. There it was, clearer than before. A reading. Two bars. Definitely. Clear, unmistakable.

"There's a sickness," Quinn was saying. "Like a flu or something, but kids are coughing their lungs out, dying."

No, Diana thought. Please, no.

"And there are these creatures, like, well, people are calling them roaches . . . And Drake . . ."

"Old Drake's alive?" Caine stood suddenly.

"In a way," Quinn said darkly.

"I have to . . . ," Diana said faintly. "I have to go to the bathroom."

She fled the room and held it together until she reached her room. There she threw herself on the bed and lay both hands on her belly. She read her own power—as always, two bars. But there it was still, definitely there. A second power.

Not possible. It didn't happen this quickly. She tried to recall half-remembered lectures from sex ed a million years ago. Words like "blastocyst" and "embryo" swam in her brain.

It had been just twenty-four hours since the first opportunity for fertilization. She knew from past experience that a home pregnancy test wouldn't even work until ten days after.

Absurd. She was panicking. She was misreading. There was no way, none. Impossible, not this quickly.

Impossible, some cruel voice inside her said, as impossible as an impenetrable dome. As impossible as everyone over the age of fourteen disappearing. As impossible as coyotes who could speak.

As impossible as a boyfriend who could mock the laws of physics by raising a boat from the sea with nothing but a thought.

•   •   •

Little Pete's fever was spiking again. Astrid had found a thermometer in the former nurse's office at Coates.

Nurse Temple—Sam's mother—she realized with a pang. Nurse Temple. This had been her workplace. Of course like everything at Coates it had been trashed—medicine cabinet emptied, glass doors smashed, sheets on the cot soiled, reference books tossed around for no apparent reason.

Someone had made a little fire of medical records. The ashes were scattered near the window.

A bird had built a nest on a high shelf and then abandoned the nest. There were pinfeathers wafting around on the floor, mixing with the ashes.

That's how she'd found the thermometer, by noticing the feathers. There was no way it would be sterile, of course, but nothing had been clean in the FAYZ for a long time.

Little Pete registered 103.1. And his cough was worsening.

"What are you going to do, Petey? Are you going to let yourself die?"

Did he even know he might be dying? Little Pete knew nothing about viruses. How would he cope with an enemy he didn't even know existed? He didn't understand germs, but he knew he was hot. A breeze had started blowing. How long until he blew this roof off?

Astrid heard Orc bellowing out a song downstairs. She couldn't watch him anymore. If he wanted to drink himself to death, why stop him? For the sake of his immortal soul?

Orc drunk was Orc dangerous. She had seen him looking at her with a strange, intense gleam in his eyes.

She realized she was crying. Let him kill himself. Wouldn't she want to die if she were Orc? Didn't she want to die herself?

It was all a macabre joke. The FAYZ: full of sound and fury and signifying nothing but death and despair. Why cling to this life?

She tried to imagine being out in the real world. She tried to call up pictures of her parents and her old house. Of course that house was burned to the ground. And her parents would hardly even recognize her, let alone their son.

No, that wasn't true. They would recognize her and him and think they were still the kids they'd loved. Only gradually would they come to understand what monsters they were: grown as ugly inside as Orc was outside.

Maybe if the FAYZ ended, Orc might be restored to his normal form. But how would she ever be restored to hers? How would the girl who loved math and science, who could read all through the night, the girl of sweet romantic daydreams and big plans to save the world, how was that girl ever going to exist again?

"It ends with all of us dead, doesn't it?" she asked Little Pete. "It ends when evil wins and we all surrender."

The sad thing was, they were already lost, all of them.

She could see her own breath. The room was getting colder by the minute.

She stuck the thermometer in Little Pete's mouth again. He coughed it out.

"Yeah, okay," Astrid said. "Petey, I . . . I think if you can't stop this . . . All of this . . . Petey, it has to end. There are kids dying of this cough. And it's all because of this place you made, this FAYZ. You changed the rules and that has consequences."

Little Pete did not answer.

She had not expected he would. There was a pillow. Press it down over his face. He wouldn't even know, probably. He wouldn't be afraid. He wouldn't suffer. He would cross painlessly from life to death and down would come the barrier and in would rush the police and the ambulances and food and medicine. And no one else would die.

Mom. Dad. I'm alive. I made it. But Petey didn't. I'm so sorry, but . . .

Astrid jerked back. She was trembling. She could do it unless Petey himself stopped her. She could. And she would never be caught. No one would ever reproach her.

"No," she whispered in a shaky, uncertain voice. Then, stronger, "No."

It should have made her feel good. Maybe in the past it would have. Maybe she would have congratulated herself for making the high and mighty moral choice. But she knew deep down inside that her choice would condemn many to death. No police and ambulances rushing in through the open barrier. Just more of the plague, more of the monsters, more suffering and death.

Astrid put her hands together, meaning to pray for guidance. But the words would not come.

From the recesses of her extraordinary memory she dredged up an old, old text. A fragment from a lecture she'd attended. From one of the ancient Greeks. Aristotle? No, Epicurus.

Is God willing to prevent evil, but not able?
Then he is not omnipotent.
Is he able, but not willing?
Then he is malevolent.
Is he both able and willing?
Then whence cometh evil?
Is he neither able nor willing?
Then why call him God?

There was only one god in the FAYZ. God was a sick, disturbed, unaware child on a filthy cot in an abandoned school.

"I can't stay, Petey," Astrid said. "If I stay here . . . I'm sorry, Petey. I'm done."

Astrid shivered, rubbed her hands together for warmth—the breeze had grown downright chilly—and walked out of the room.

Down the hall.

Down the stairs.

Out through the front door.

"Done," Astrid said, standing for a moment atop the stone steps. "Done."

She walked off into the falling night.

THIRTY-FOUR
2 HOURS, 51 MINUTES

"YOU'RE GOING?" DIANA asked.

"Of course," Caine said. "We're going. We're even going to bring Penny. She'll come in handy. Maybe Lana can fix her legs. And then she'll be very useful at controlling people."

Caine started whistling happily as he stuffed clothing into a Dolce & Gabbana bag.

"You should grab some clothes," Caine said. "It might be a while before we get back here."

"I'm not going," Diana said.

Caine stopped. He smiled at her. Then his eyes went dead and she felt herself pushed by an invisible hand, shoved toward the closet.

"I said pack," Caine said.

"No."

"Don't make me do something we'll both regret," he warned. Then in a more reasonable tone, "I thought you loved me. What's all this about?"

"You're a despicable person, Caine."

Caine laughed. "And now you're shocked. Right."

"I hoped—"

"What?" he snapped. "Hoped what, Diana? Hoped you'd keep me happy? Hoped you'd tame me?"

"I thought maybe you were finally growing up a little," Diana said.

Caine made a negligent, come here gesture with his hand. Diana was propelled toward him. She tripped but did not fall. He held her immobile with powers she could not resist and kissed her.

"I have what I wanted from you, Diana. And it's great. I mean that. I got you to give it up willingly. I could have forced you whenever I wanted, but I didn't, did I?"

She did not answer.

"But if you think," he went on, "that you've gotten some kind of control over me, well, guess again. See, I'm Caine. I'm the four bar. I'm the one running things. And I'm happy to have you be a part of that. You can go on teasing me and making fun of me: I'm not sensitive. I like having one person who can stand up to me and tell me what she thinks. A good leader needs that." He leaned so close she could feel his breath on her ear as he whispered. "Just remember: I'm Caine. And people who fight me regret it. Now pack up. Make sure you bring that little lacy black thing. I like you in that. Bug. Go tell Penny we're leaving."

Bug faded into view. He'd seen and heard it all. From behind Caine's back he gave Diana the finger.

"We're going to figure something out, Dekka," Sam said.

She sat perfectly still in the back of the boat. Sam sat beside her. Toto had been banished to the bow—Sam didn't want him pointing out every soothing lie.

"I'm not scared," Dekka said. "I mean, look, I don't know if any of us are ever getting out of the FAYZ alive."

Sam didn't know what to say, so he just nodded.

"I mean, you think about all the kids," Dekka said. "Bette. The twins. Duck, poor old Duck. Harry. E.Z. Hunter." After a pause, "Mary."

"Lots of others," Sam said.

"Yeah. We should remember all their names, shouldn't we?"

"I try to. So if this ever does end, and I ever get out, I can talk to all their parents and say, 'This is how it happened. This is how your kid died.'"

"I know you worry about that." Dekka put a comforting hand on his. He took her hand and held it in both of his.

"A little bit, yeah. I see, like, a trial, kind of. Old dudes and old ladies all looking harsh and asking me to justify . . . You know: what did you do to save E.Z., Mr. Temple?" He shook his head. "In my imagination they always call me Mr. Temple."

"What did you do, Mr. Temple, to save Dekka Talent?" she said.

"That's your last name? I didn't think you had a last name. I thought you were like Iman or Madonna or Beyoncé. You just needed the one name."

"Yeah, me and Beyoncé," Dekka said with a wry laugh.

They sat silent together for a while.

"Sam, we don't know how well those things see in the dark."

He nodded. "I've been wondering. I have a plan. It's fairly crazy."

"Wouldn't be any fun if it wasn't crazy."

"You can swim, right?"

"No, because black folk can't swim," Dekka said, sounding like the old Dekka. "Of course I can swim."

He called to Jack and Toto, asking them to join him. "Can both of you swim?"

They both nodded apprehensively. "But it's dark," Jack said.

"The water doesn't get any deeper at night," Sam said.

"Who knows what's in the water?" Jack argued.

"Trout and bass," Sam said. "They don't eat people."

"Yeah, and snakes don't fly and coyotes don't talk," Jack shot back.

"Fair enough," Sam said. "But I think we'd better take our chances. Here's what I'm thinking: you all go quietly into the water. I'll get the boat started, then I'll lash the wheel down and jump. If it works, Drake and his buggy friends will hear the boat and chase it. We'll go ashore and run like crazy."

"They'll follow us," Jack objected.

"They'll try," Sam admitted. "But they're insects, not bloodhounds. I doubt they can see tracks at night."

"He's not sure," Toto said.

"No, he's not," Sam admitted.

"True," Toto said. Then, to his imaginary friend, "He's confusing."

"Which way do we run?" Dekka asked.

"Drake will expect us to head straight for town. We don't want to fight him out in the open. So, toward the train." He nudged Jack. "You want another laptop, right?"

Jack squirmed. "Well, at least some more of the batteries."

"Okay, then. Into the water. Swim for the marina. If they don't chase me, I'll come back before you can reach the dock and we'll think of some other plan."

"Could we think of that other plan before this one?" Jack asked.

Caine stood in the bow of Quinn's boat as it plowed through the very light chop toward Perdido Beach.

Quinn had warned him to sit down, but Caine wasn't worried about falling in the water: he would not fall. He used his power to support most of his weight so that his feet barely touched the deck.

He was not going to arrive hunched over. He was going to Perdido Beach like George Washington crossing the Delaware: standing tall.

He was floating. Almost flying. Physically, yes, but mentally as well. He was filled with a warm sense of perfect well-being.

They needed him. They had sent for him. They had found

they could not survive without him. Him, not Sam. Him.

Penny lay crumpled in blankets in the back of the boat. Diana sat staring at empty space. Bug kept starting to whistle and then stopped himself, only to start all over again.

Quinn was at the tiller, looking at Caine's back. Caine could feel his eyes boring into him. Quinn's doubt and worry were written all over his open face.

Diana had been completely silent. Caine figured it was dawning on her that he was still in charge, that she still depended on him. That she still needed him as much as the kids in Perdido Beach needed him.

Well, she would get over it. Diana was a survivor. She would get past her disappointment. And together they would be the first couple of Perdido Beach, like king and queen.

The thought made him smile.

"It's a pity we don't have a camera," Caine said. "I'd love to capture the moment of my return."

"I'm cold," Penny moaned.

"You're just not getting enough exercise," Caine said, then laughed at his own cruel joke. Penny's sourness wasn't going to ruin this for him. Not her sourness or Diana's sullenness or Quinn's guilt.

This was Caine's moment.

Quinn maneuvered the boat expertly alongside the dock. He tied it off and then stood waiting to help them up. Caine refused Quinn's hand. But looked at him hard. Eye to eye until Quinn had to look away.

"What is it you want, Quinn?" Caine asked.

"What do you mean?"

"What would make you happy, Quinn? What do you want above all else?"

Quinn blinked. Caine thought he might even be blushing. Quinn said, "Me and my crews? We just want to fish."

Caine put his hand on Quinn's shoulder. Caine looked him in the eye with that simulation of openness and honesty Caine could still manage when the occasion demanded. "Then, Quinn, here's my first decree: you are free to fish. Keep doing what you're doing, and nothing else will ever be asked of you."

Quinn started to say something but stopped in confusion.

Caine spread his arms wide, palms down, and levitated out of the boat and onto the dock. The grandiosity of it made Caine laugh out loud, laugh at his own sheer arrogance.

Behind him, Diana and Bug climbed wearily to the dock. Caine lifted Penny and set her, helpless, on the wooden planks.

"Things will be different this time," Caine said. "There was too much contention, too much violence the last time. I tried to be a peaceful leader. But things went badly."

"I wonder why," Diana muttered.

"These people," Caine said grandly, sweeping his arm toward the town, "need more than a leader. They need . . . a king."

It had come to Caine in a flash of insight. Until just a minute earlier the thought had never entered his mind. But with all Diana's teasing about him being Napoleon, he'd found a screenplay about Napoleon in the mansion's library and he'd skimmed it.

Napoleon had taken over after the French people had grown disillusioned with a brutal, ineffectual republic. They had accepted Napoleon's rise to absolute power because they were just tired, burned out. They had wanted and needed someone with a crown on his head. It was only natural, really. It had been that way for most of human history.

Napoleon had named himself emperor. Like Michael Jackson had named himself the King of Pop and Howard Stern called himself the King of All Media. Weird thing was: that's how you got to be king, by calling yourself one. And getting others to agree.

King.

Caine saw Quinn's mouth drop open.

Out of the corner of his eye, he saw a disbelieving smile form on Diana's face. She shook her head slowly, ruefully, as though finally understanding something that had puzzled her.

"From now on, Quinn, you'll refer to me as your king. And you and your people will be left alone."

Caine felt all eyes on him. Penny savagely ready to enforce his will, however much she hated him in her heart. Bug smirking, ever the useful tool. And Diana amazed, and amazed by her own amazement.

"Okay," Quinn said doubtfully.

"Okay?" Caine echoed, and raised one eyebrow expectantly. He smiled to show he wasn't angry. Not yet, anyway.

"Just . . . okay?" Caine prompted.

"Okay . . ." Quinn glanced around, desperate, not knowing the answer. Then it dawned on him. Caine could almost see the wheels turning in his head. "Okay, Your Highness?"

Caine looked down modestly, and to hide the triumphant smirk that would ruin the moment.

"Go now, Quinn. Go back to work."

And Quinn went.

Caine met Diana's disbelieving gaze and laughed aloud. "Why so gloomy? Doesn't every little girl want to grow up to be a queen?"

"Princess," Diana said.

"So, you got a promotion," Caine said. "Bug: find Taylor."

Taylor was the biggest gossip in Perdido Beach. He needed information and he needed it fast. It was the middle of the night and he didn't know who was where or what they were doing. All Quinn had said was that Sam was out of town, Albert had been murdered, and Edilio was sick and might die.

Albert being dead was a pity. Albert was a born organizer and Caine was sure he could have used him. On the other hand, a dead Edilio would be excellent news. Edilio had been Sam's right hand from the start.

He didn't even know when these supposedly giant insects or whatever they were would reach Perdido Beach. It could be at any moment.

He would need to defeat the invasion. That was clearly the most important thing. But obviously kids were exaggerating.

Giant insects? They were probably six inches long. Although the idea of them hatching inside your body was enough to make him sick.

Caine stood on the seawall that ran along the beach. Stood on the brink, he thought, the dividing line between past and future. Not just his, but everyone's.

The town was quiet and dark. Here and there the pale, eerie glow of Sammy suns could be glimpsed through windows. The moon was behind the strange cloud that hung too low over the western part of town.

On the brink, with so many possibilities. He felt as if he might explode from the giddy joy of it. He was back. Back as their savior.

Quinn had inadvertently shown him the way forward. Quinn had wanted exactly what most people want: to be left alone. To not be afraid. To not have to struggle. To not have to ask hard questions or make hard decisions.

We just want to fish.

Caine turned slightly to stare thoughtfully at Diana. He had given her hope, and taken hope away, and now she stood still, almost as if in a trance, counting up her losses, realizing the totality of her defeat.

Resignation. Acceptance.

She could see now that he was in charge. When everyone saw that, and when everyone simply accepted that this was life now, that this was the only possible life, then he would have complete control.

He could feel the fear in Perdido Beach. They were

leaderless. They were sick, weak, hungry, lonely. They cowered because of a microscopic flu bug and a very different, much larger bug.

When it was over, when he had won, he would say: *I have saved you. I alone had the power to save you. Sam failed. But I succeeded. And now settle down and do your work and pay no attention to your betters. Shhh: go to sleep, the king will make the hard decisions.*

Bug was back surprisingly soon, with Taylor.

"Where did you find her?" Caine asked.

Bug shrugged. "Where she lives. I remember it from the old days when I used to sneak into town."

"He means back when he used to sneak in and watch you get undressed," Diana said to Taylor.

"He's a little kid," Taylor said with a shrug. She looked Caine up and down, skeptical and appraising. Caine knew she did not fear him—not with her powers. She couldn't be intimidated. So he would have to reach her some other way.

"Have a seat with me," Caine said, hopping down from the wall. "How have you been, Taylor?"

"Life's one big party," she said.

He laughed appreciatively at her joke. "Things must be pretty bad for Edilio to send for me, huh?"

"Things are always pretty bad," she said. "We're at a new level of bad. I saw those bugs."

Caine mustered all his sincerity. "I have to go and fight these creatures. But I don't know much about them."

Taylor told him what she knew. Caine felt some of his

confidence drain away as she laid out the facts in gruesome detail and with complete conviction.

"Well, this should be fun," Diana said dryly. "I'm so glad we came back."

Caine gritted his teeth but ignored her. "Who can I count on to help me?" he asked Taylor.

Taylor laughed. "Not me, dude. I've already gotten as close as I'm going to get."

"What about Brianna?" Caine asked.

Taylor made a face. "You mean the Breeze? She zooms in and starts yelling to Edilio about how the bugs are coming toward us and they're as big as SUVs. And since then, I don't know where she's been. Probably looking for Jack. Or Dekka," she added with a leer.

Caine nodded and kept his face down so as not to betray his pleasure. Brianna was a problem: her speed was almost as effective as Taylor's power when it came to evading Caine. And she was absolutely loyal to Sam.

"What about Sam and Astrid?"

"Oh, no, there is no Sam and Astrid, not anymore." Taylor leaned closer and began to unload everything she knew. In ten minutes Caine had a very complete picture, far more detailed than what Quinn had grudgingly revealed.

Sam was definitely off on a harebrained search for water. Dekka and Jack, too. Astrid had left with Little Pete.

And Quinn had evidently not known the shocking but not unwelcome news: that Albert wasn't dead but recovering under Lana's care.

"So are the two guys who tried to kill him," Taylor said. "That'll be trouble."

"What two guys?"

"Human Crew losers: Turk and Lance. Maybe Orc, too. No one knows what happened with him except that he's on a bender."

Better and better. There was no one in town right now who could fight Caine. It was incredible. It was miraculous. It was fate.

Kings were supposedly chosen by God. Well, if there was a God in the FAYZ, it seemed like He'd made His choice.

But it wouldn't last. He would have to act quickly.

"Taylor, I need you for something very important," Caine said.

"I don't work for you," Taylor said huffily.

Caine nodded. "That's true, Taylor. You have amazing powers. And you're a smart girl. But no one ever seems to respect you for it. I didn't mean to sound bossy."

She shrugged, mollified. "No problem."

"I just think you're a very valuable, useful girl. I think you should have a place with me. I respect you."

"You're just trying to get me to help you," Taylor said.

Caine smiled broadly. "True, true. But I can pay much better than Sam and Albert. For example, you know about the island, right? And you can bounce to any place you've seen, right? Any place you know?"

She nodded, cautious. But Caine could see she was intrigued.

"If I arranged to have you rowed out to the island, you'd be able to get back and forth anytime. Easy as pie."

She nodded slowly.

"What would you say to a hot bubble bath?"

"I'd say, 'Hello, long time no soak.' That's what I'd say."

"All kinds of food. Peanut butter. Chicken soup. Crackers. All kinds of movies in the system there. Popcorn to go with the movie."

"You're trying to bribe me."

"I'm promising to pay you."

She didn't need to say it. He could see it in her eyes.

"I need to know where these creatures are, these bugs. How fast they're moving. Which way they're coming."

"That's all?"

"That's all," Caine said.

And suddenly Taylor was gone.

THIRTY-FIVE

SAM WATCHED HIS friends until they disappeared from view. Toto wasn't much of a swimmer, so they'd given him a seat cushion to float on and Jack hauled him along with one hand.

Jack wasn't much of a swimmer, either, but you didn't have to be elegant when you had ten times normal strength.

Sam fired up the engine. It roared as he gunned it loudly. Drake would have to be deaf not to hear it.

Then he threw it into gear and went tearing parallel to the shore.

The moonlight was faint, but it was enough to reveal the sudden rush of movement by the creatures on shore. They were falling for it.

Sam quickly lashed the wheel. He dove off the starboard side, jumping clear of the screws that blew past, churning water into foam.

He looked again to see that the bugs were in motion. They

were a silvery swarm heading away. He did not see Drake.

Sam swam after the others. He'd stayed with the boat a bit longer than he'd planned and now he was a half mile from the dock. He had a long swim ahead of him.

But water was Sam's natural element. He'd surfed since he was a toddler, and powering through placid lake water was nothing compared to fighting the surf.

The cold water felt good. Clean. He switched from freestyle to backstroke for a while, gazing up at the night sky, but powering along as fast as he could all the while. If he were back in the world, he'd be looking to join the high school swim team. His butterfly stroke was weak, but his freestyle was as good as anyone's, and his backstroke even better.

What would it be like to be worrying about improving his butterfly or breaststroke instead of worrying that his friend was being eaten alive from the inside?

What was he going to do next? They trusted him, Dekka and Jack. They expected him to always have a plan. But beyond getting away from Drake and his bug army, he didn't have a plan.

Drake would go after Perdido Beach next. He would send those creatures rampaging through town killing everyone.

Then he would take Astrid and . . .

Don't get emotional, Sam warned himself. Just figure out how to win.

He heard clumsy splashing ahead. He rolled over smoothly into a crawl and powered hard and fast.

"Shhh," he hissed as soon as he was up with them. "You

people make more noise than a bunch of littles in the kiddie pool."

The four of them closed the distance to the dock. Sam motioned for Jack, Dekka, and Toto to slip silently beneath it. Toto had lost his grip on his cushion and it floated away. Jack banged his head on the bottom of the dock and cursed under his breath.

Sam palmed the dock and hoisted himself up, drenched.

"Hi, Sam."

Brittney stood not twenty feet away.

He spotted three of the creatures over by the marina parking lot. They were waiting. Like a well-trained pack of attack dogs.

He'd been outwitted. Outplayed.

"Hi, Brittney," Sam said, standing there, dripping.

"I asked you so many times to release me, Sam," she said. Her voice was cold and far away. Not angry, not scared. Just maybe a little sad.

"I know, Brittney. But I'm not a cold-blooded killer," Sam said.

Brittney nodded. "No, you're a good person." She said it without sarcasm.

"I try to be. Like you, Brittney. I know you're a good person."

He glanced at the creatures. They hadn't moved, but they were alert. They could be on him in ten seconds.

"He hates you," Brittney said.

"Drake?" Sam laughed. "He hates everyone. Hate is all he's got."

"Not Drake. Him. God."

Sam blinked. What was he supposed to say to that? "I thought God loved everyone."

"I used to believe that, too," Brittney said. "But then I met Him."

"Did you?" She had lost whatever grip on reality she'd had. He couldn't blame her. What Brittney had endured would leave anyone mental.

"He's not in the sky, you know," Brittney said in a normal, conversational tone. "He's not up in Heaven somewhere."

"I didn't realize that."

"He's in the earth, Sam. He lives in a dark, dark place."

Sam's heart missed a beat. He felt cold. "You met God in a dark place?"

She showed her twisted, damaged braces in a surprising, rapturous smile. "He explained His great plan."

"Yeah?"

"His time is coming. All of this . . ." She swept her arm wide. "It's all like, like . . . like an egg, Sam. He has to be born from this egg."

"He's a chicken?"

"Don't mock, Sam," Brittney chided. "He waits to be born. But He needs Nemesis to join Him, Sam, and you . . . you won't let that happen."

"Nemesis? What's a nemesis?"

Brittney had a crafty look as she said, "Oh, Sam. You know who Nemesis is. He has the power to complete God's plan." She laced her fingers together, almost awestruck by the act, like it was sacrament. "They must be joined, the Darkness and Nemesis. Together they will have all power, and then, Sam, it all ends, you know. Then the eggshell cracks and He is born."

"That sounds . . ." He resisted the urge to say "crazy." "It sounds interesting. But I don't think the gaiaphage is God. I think he's evil."

"Of course he's evil," Brittney enthused. "Of course! Evil, good, there's no difference, don't you see that? They're the same thing. Like me and Drake. Yin and yang, Sam. Two in one, a duality, a . . ."

She faltered a little, like a child trying to explain something she didn't quite understand. She frowned.

"He lied to you, Brittney. The gaiaphage is not God. He reaches into people's minds and makes them do terrible things."

"He warned me you would say that," Brittney said. "My Lord and Nemesis must be joined. And all of you have to die. You're all like a disease. Like a virus. A plague that must be wiped out so that He can unite with Nemesis and be born."

Sam was getting tired of the talk. He'd never cared much for religion one way or the other, and some fantasy religion made up by a dead girl to justify the gaiaphage's lies was even less interesting than Astrid's religious excuses for not having sex. He was impatient to find out what Brittney meant to do.

If there was to be a fight, then let there be a fight.

"And then what, Brittney? Did the gaiaphage explain that to you?"

"Then all the world will be remade. That's His purpose, you know."

"No, I didn't know. I guess I missed that part. I was still back at the part where he has to kill everyone."

"He was forged by a race of gods in the far reaches of space to remake the world, to create it anew."

"Yeah, well, that sounds just a tiny bit insane, Brittney."

She smiled. "It's all insane, Sam. All of it. But He will make it all over again. Once He is born anew."

Sam felt tired. He wished Astrid were here, maybe she could find out more. Maybe she could talk Brittney out of her lunatic delusion. But he wasn't Astrid.

"I'll tell you what," Sam said. "If your friend in the mine shaft wants me, he can bring it on. Because he's tried. And I'm still here."

"Not for long," Brittney said. "Do you think these creatures just happened on their own? The Lord has molded them, created them to be indestructible, so that you could not stop them, Sam."

"I'm sorry for what's happened to you, Brittney," Sam said. "You've been abused about as much as any person ever has been. But I'm still going to have to stop you." He raised his hands, palms out. "Sorry."

Twin beams of green fire hit Brittney in the chest. They burned a hole through her.

The bugs leaped, raced to cover the few feet between them and the dock.

"Jack! Dekka!" Sam yelled.

Jack punched straight up through the planks of the deck, but he'd picked a bad spot. He erupted between Brittney and Sam, blocking Sam's fire.

Brittney screamed, "Kill them!"

Jack tripped, which moved him out of the line of fire. Sam aimed and hit Brittney again but now she was running away. Her back melted, her spine exposed then burned through, and still she ran.

Sam swung his beams at the nearest of the onrushing bugs. Light beams hit the huge creature and bounced away to slice a sailboat's mast neatly in half. The stump was a torch.

Jack hauled Dekka up from the water and she struck even before she could stand. Gravity beneath the nearest creature ceased. The bug went airborne and its momentum carried it just over Sam's ducked head. It shot through Dekka's field and landed half in the water, with its rear portion on the dock.

"Push it!"

Jack slammed into the bug's rear end and it splashed into the water.

Jack spun, ran at the second giant roach. He ripped a plank from the dock and rammed it with superhuman strength into the gnashing mouthparts.

The board splintered. The creature didn't miss a step.

Jack fell on his back and the monster was on him in a flash.

"Jack!" Dekka cried.

Jack, flat on his back, kicked up with such force that the wood beneath him snapped.

The third creature swarmed over the first. Its mandibles swept Dekka, missed cutting her in half, but knocked her twenty feet away into the water.

Sam saw in a split second of clarity what he would have to do. He didn't like it.

The bug rushed at Sam.

The mouth blades sliced.

Sam timed his leap, shouted a desperate curse, and dove straight into the bug's gaping mouth.

"The days of uncertainty are over!"

Caine stood at the top of the steps to town hall. Below him the sick lay coughing and shivering. Edilio, helpless, as weak as a newborn kitten, shivering so hard he looked like he was having a seizure.

Beyond the sick were dozens of kids, many wet from having come through the rain in the west. Many still wiping the sleep from their eyes. Some of the youngest were carrying their blankies.

Diana stood apart, blank, downcast. Penny had been given a chair. Lana leaned against a tree in the plaza, her hand resting on her pistol, with Sanjit nervous beside her.

Caine saw it all. Every upturned, moonlit face. He saw the fear and the anticipation. He reveled in it. Gloried in it.

"First, I say this," Caine said. "Taylor, who has joined me, reports that the creatures are almost here. They are nearing the highway and will reach town in minutes. When they do they will hunt down, kill, and eat . . . every living person."

"We can fight!" someone yelled. "We beat the coyotes. And we beat you, too, Caine!"

"How will you fight without Sam?" Caine demanded. "Is he here? No! Sam can't stop these creatures. He tried, and he failed, and now he has run away!"

He waited for someone to speak up in defense of Sam. But not a word.

Gutless, faithless weaklings, Caine thought. He was almost sorry for Sam. How many times had Sam put himself in harm's way for these ingrates?

"He saved himself," Caine went on, "for a while, at least, by running away with Astrid and Dekka. He saved his friends, but abandoned poor, sick Edilio there. And all of you."

Stony silence.

"That's why Quinn—Quinn, who works night and day to feed you all—came to get me, to beg me to help."

"What are you going to do?" someone shouted.

"What am I going to do?" Caine asked, relishing the moment. "I'm not going to run away, that's the first thing." He stabbed a finger in the air and shouted, "When the ultimate danger came, Sam ran. And I came back. I was safe and warm and well-fed on my island. I had my beautiful queen, Diana. I had my friends, Penny and Bug. It was a very good life."

He moved to Diana and gave her a little kiss. She let him, no more.

"A very good life. But when I heard what was happening here, what terrible dangers threatened to destroy you, I could not sit there eating delicious food and watching movies while swathed in clean sheets."

He watched those words take effect. Food? Movies? Clean anything? They were magical concepts to these desperate, starved, and, until recently, parched kids.

And the subtle implication that he had been sleeping with Diana worked in a way, too, making older boys jealous, and some girls as well.

Caine smiled inwardly. It was working. He had them. The sheep.

"I will save you," he said humbly, eyes down. "But not just from this terrible threat. No. Isn't it time we all had a better life? Haven't we suffered enough?"

A murmur of agreement.

"You've suffered from hunger, from thirst, from violence. Well . . ." He waited, waited for the moment to build. He was deliberately stretching time, knowing they were picturing the insect horde advancing on the town. At last he said, "Well, that's enough suffering."

"What about Drake?" someone shouted.

"He's your friend," another voice accused.

"No," Caine snapped. "I was the one who destroyed him. Or had. Until Sam and his followers allowed Drake to return."

He paused, watching the reaction, hearing the murmurs

of agreement. He sent Diana a secret droll look. Nothing worked better than a really big lie.

"Listen to me. You need a true leader. But this thing where they force you to elect someone, like it's some popularity contest, like we're picking a prom queen or whatever, that has to stop. Edilio is a good kid. But he's just a kid, just Sam's loyal dog. No offense." He raised a hand indicating that he may have chosen his words carelessly. But kids were already nodding. Yes, Edilio was just like Sam's dog. Brave, yes, and decent, yes. But he hadn't saved them.

"And Sam?" Caine said, raising his voice. "Sam was a brave leader once, but he's burned out and you all know it. His heart was never in it. Now at last he's run away. Sam is not what the FAYZ needs. He's not a king."

He turned away while that word sank in. He could hear a voice asking, "Did he say a king?" And he distinctly heard a sardonic laugh from Lana.

Caine raised his hands high. "We need a true leader, not someone who has to answer to a town council. Come on, folks, Howard is a member of the council!"

That earned a knowing laugh.

"So Sam's faithful dog Edilio reports to a known crook like Howard." He allowed his smile to fade. It was time to finish it. "You need a leader who will actually lead. A leader to save your lives today and give you better lives from now on."

Caine spotted Turk and Lance waiting, smirking.

Caine had sent Taylor for them. He had told them he could

use a couple of tough kids like them. He'd promised them a trip to the island.

"Turk. Lance. Come on up here," Caine said.

They climbed up the stairs to stand beside him, pale and shaken, but sure they were about to be handed new and important positions.

"These two admitted to me that they shot Albert while robbing him."

That started the crowd muttering angrily, and even some of the sicker kids looked up bleakly. Albert might not have been popular, but he was necessary.

Lance and Turk exchanged a nervous, uncertain look.

"You'll be relieved to know that Lana has been able to save Albert's life," Caine said. "But what are we to do with two would-be murderers like these?"

Turk was looking even more pale. This wasn't going the way they had expected. Lance was edging away, getting ready to run.

Barely moving, and with a slight smile, Caine raised a hand and Lance found himself pushing weakly against an invisible barrier.

"Shall we convene a council meeting? Hold a trial? Waste everyone's time while minute by minute the threat gets nearer and nearer? We know what should be done. Justice! Quick and sure and without a lot of meaningless delay."

"Hey!" Lance cried. "That's not what you—"

"He says a lot of things," Diana muttered.

With a broad, dramatic sweep of his hand Caine sent Lance hurtling through the air. Lance flew like he'd been launched from a catapult. Up into the night sky with every eye following. A thin scream floated down.

There was something comical about it and Caine could not keep from smiling.

The scream changed in pitch as Lance tumbled down and smashed into the ground at the far end of the plaza.

"Justice!" Caine cried. "Not later, right now. Justice and protection and a better life for everyone!"

Turk lost control of himself. "No, no, no, Caine, no, no."

"But not justice without mercy," Caine said. "Lance paid the price in his way. Now Turk will pay by serving me. Isn't that right, Turk?"

He looked at Turk and in a low voice said, "Bow down."

Turk fell to his knees without any further urging.

"It's a sign of respect," Caine said. "Not for me. It's not about me. It's about you, all of you. You're the ones who need a ruler. Isn't that true? After so much suffering, don't you need one person to take charge? Well," Caine said, "that's what I'm doing. And when you bow down you're just showing respect. Like Turk here."

In the mob of kids maybe half a dozen knelt. A few more executed awkward head bobs, unsure of themselves. Most did nothing.

Good enough, Caine thought. For now.

"The creatures are coming," Caine said in a low voice. "In all the FAYZ, who can defeat these creatures?"

He waited, as if he really was expecting an answer.

"Who can defeat them?" he repeated. "Me. Only me."

He shook his head as if marveling at something awesome. "It is as if God himself chose me. And if I win, if I save your lives, God's will shall be very clear."

THIRTY-SIX

SAM LEAPED INTO the open mouth of the creature.

Head and shoulders made it in. The bug's throat spasmed, like wet rubber, crushing the air from his lungs.

His eyes were tightly closed, but he could not close his nostrils and nearly vomited from a wave of stench like rotten meat, seaweed, and ammonia.

He grabbed with his hands, trying to get something to grip, had to pull his legs in before the mouthparts sliced, had to right now, right now, quick!

Something sharp against his calves. But the bug was just reacting, choking, not yet trying to chop him apart.

He yanked his legs in. All the way inside the wet, stinking, pulsating throat.

Not fast enough: the mouthparts clipped his right heel. He didn't notice the pain, too awful, stifling, squashed, skin burning, blackness, no air.

He pushed his hands out and fired.

He couldn't see the light, his eyes were shut tight. But he could feel the shudder that passed through the bug's body.

He fired and moved his hands against the slimy insides, firing and firing, feeling his skin burn from whatever ammonia chemical was inside the creature, but then, far worse from the heat of his own killing light.

He had to stop or else he would cook himself.

He could feel the bug moving, like being in a car with square wheels, a violent shaking. The bug raced in mad panic as its insides bled and burned.

But no good, not enough, and in seconds he would die from lack of oxygen.

Ignore the pain: fire!

He laced his fingers together blindly, turning the twin beams into one. He pushed against the seizing guts of the creature and inscribed what felt like a circle.

Then silently screaming from the heat, the starvation of his lungs, the violent spasms of his own body rebelling, he kicked and kicked, pulled himself into a tight ball and kicked where he had burned, with all his fading strength.

Air!

He breathed and vomited almost at the same time. He pried open one eye. Jack stood above him.

"Gaaahh!" Jack said, disgusted by the sight of Sam cocooned in a steaming mess of bug guts.

Jack grabbed his hand and yanked him up and out with such force that Sam flew through the air. Sam plunged gratefully into the water.

He surfaced, sucked in air, and dove under again. He washed the reek from his body and quieted the burns. But it had broken the skin. The creature had cut him. His heel hurt, but far worse was the terrible fear that he was destined for Hunter's fate.

When he came up again he could see that the bug that had gone into the water was struggling, not far away, trying to get back to shore.

The dead one—the one Sam had killed from the inside—lay completely still. It almost seemed to Sam that it had a surprised look on its face. Or what passed for a face. Its creepy blue eyes glazed over.

One bug dead, one trying to get ashore, and the third still very dangerous.

"Jack!" Sam shouted. "The mast! On that boat!"

Jack frowned in confusion, then he nodded. He leaped onto a nearby sailboat, grabbed the aluminum mast, planted his feet, and, with a Herculean effort and a sound like a slow-motion chainsaw, ripped the mast out.

Dekka raised her hands and the rushing bug motored its legs helplessly in the air. It would only hold for a few seconds, but that's all Jack needed.

"Okay, Dekka, drop him!" Jack cried.

Dekka dropped the creature.

Jack lifted the mast—a thirty-foot-long spear—over his head and stabbed it straight at the bug's mouth.

The first thrust missed but gouged out one of the bug's blue eyes.

Jack backed up to the end of the dock and ran at the creature. "Yaaaahhhh!"

He slammed the mast into its mouth and pushed madly, frantically, feet snapping deck planks, until the top of the mast suddenly burst through the creature's side in a squishy explosion of guts and goo.

Sam started to push himself back up onto the dock but his hands were blistered. Jack had to heft him up by his armpits.

"Where's Brittney?" Sam demanded.

Dekka shook her head.

"She ran away," Toto said. "But she seemed to be changing. One arm was . . ." He didn't seem to have words for it.

"Like a snake. A whip hand," Dekka supplied.

"Yes," Toto said. Then, "I'm ready to go back home now."

"I can barely walk," Sam said. He had to grit his teeth to keep from crying out in pain. The skin of his heel was gone, a chunk sliced out of it. He was bleeding all over the dock.

Sam slipped off his wet shirt and wrapped it awkwardly around his foot, making a very poor bandage.

"Let's get out of here while we can. Drake will be back, with the rest of his army, and then we're bug food for sure."

Sam started hobbling but Jack grabbed him and hefted him up onto his shoulders. It was ludicrous: Sam was a head taller and quite a bit broader than Jack. But for Jack it was as easy as carrying a baby.

"You rocked, Jack," Sam said.

Dekka slapped Jack on the back. "Got that right."

Jack beamed although he tried not to show it. Then his face

went green and he set Sam down and vomited onto a bush.

"Sorry," he said. "I guess it made me sick."

"Nerves, dude," Sam said. "Been there. Let's get out of here. Back the way we came. Drake will expect us to take the most direct route back to town and if he catches us out in the open we're done for."

"What happens when he gets to town with those creatures?" Dekka asked.

"Edilio's got Orc—I hope. Plus Brianna. Taylor. He's got his soldiers, although I doubt guns will work too well unless they can shoot through the mouths." Sam shook his head.

His imagination went to Astrid. Too many awful pictures of what could happen to her crowded his head.

Could they reach town quickly enough to help in the fight? Maybe with him and Jack and Dekka joining the others they could stop Drake. Maybe.

Did Edilio even guess what was coming his way? Was he preparing? Had he found a way? Sam had not. Again and again he tried to find the way to win. Tried to imagine the scenario that would defeat this enemy.

Again and again he came back to the realization that there were only two people with the power to stop the creatures.

One: Caine. And Caine was far off on the island.

The other: Little Pete. He was far off on a different sort of island inside his own damaged mind.

Caine and Little Pete.

"Listen, guys," Sam said, "I don't see a winning move here. Not from me, anyway. It's going to be on Edilio and the people back in town. I don't even know if they know what's coming. So we have to warn them."

"How?" Dekka asked.

"Jack."

Jack had been leaning forward. He stood back suddenly.

"Jack can move faster without us. With his strength comes a certain amount of speed. And he won't tire as fast as we will. Hills don't bother him, so he can go right over the hills, a straight line."

"Yeah," Dekka admitted. "That makes sense. And don't get me wrong, Jack's become a hero and all. But is that enough? I've done the math, same as you have. Orc and Jack and Brianna?"

"There are two who could do it," Sam said. "Caine. He might be able to do it."

Dekka snarled. "Caine?"

"Either him or Little Pete," Sam said.

"Little Pete?" Jack looked puzzled.

Sam sighed. "Little Pete. He's not exactly just Astrid's autistic brother." He explained briefly while Toto added a chorus of "Sam believes that's true" remarks.

"How do we get Little Pete to do anything?" Dekka asked.

"The last time Little Pete felt mortal danger he made the FAYZ," Sam said. "He needs to be in mortal danger again."

Jack and Dekka exchanged a wary look, each wondering what the other had known or guessed about Little Pete.

"Little Pete?" Jack asked. "That little kid has that kind of power?"

"Yes," Sam said simply. "Next to Pete, me, Caine, all of us, we're like . . . like popguns compared to a cannon. We don't even know what the limits of his powers are," Sam said. "What we do know is we can't communicate with him very well. We can't even guess what he's thinking."

"Little Pete," Dekka muttered and shook her head. "I knew he was important, I got that a long time ago. But he can do that? He has that kind of power?" She pondered for a moment, nodded, and said, "I see why you kept it secret. It's like having a nuclear weapon in the hands of, well, a little autistic kid."

Sam stood up, winced as he rested his weight on his hurt heel. He put his hand on Jack's shoulder. "Tell Edilio to get Caine, if they can do it in time. If not, Jack, you go and get Little Pete."

"And do what with Little Pete?" Jack asked, obviously horrified at the entire idea and still getting his head around the fact that the little boy was the most powerful being in their universe.

Sam knew the answer. He knew what might be the only winning move. He had told Brittney he wasn't a cold-blooded killer. He wasn't. And this wasn't even his job anymore, was it?

And yet . . . And yet he could see a possible solution.

"You pick him up, Jack. Carry him to the closest one of those bugs you can find."

"Yeah?" Jack asked in a quavering voice.

"Toss him to the bug," Sam said.

.   .   .

Drake's whip was curled around the mandible of the largest of the creatures, now racing toward the south, away from the lake. He had to lean almost flat forward to stay on, legs spread behind him.

Where was Sam Temple? They should have caught him by now if he had come this way.

Bring me Nemesis.

The voice in Drake's head was louder, more insistent than it had ever been.

With his free hand he pounded the side of his head, trying to knock it away, trying to silence that insistent demand.

Bring him to me.

In his mind's eye he saw Coates, his old school, his former home. The grim, Gothic main building, the gloomy vale around it, the iron gate. The picture was his own memory but it was the Darkness demanding he look at it, see it, and understand.

Nemesis was there. There!

Bring him!

But Drake had other needs. His overlord might need this Nemesis, whatever that was, but he, Drake, had an equally powerful need: to kill Sam Temple.

Sam Temple had cost him his arm. He had destroyed his old life, left him trapped in this disgusting union with Brittney Pig.

Sam, who had kept him caged like an animal.

And now Sam had escaped death again. Beaten Drake again. And he was nowhere in sight, gone!

"Sam!" Drake howled in frustration. "Sam!"

The bug moved quickly and the wind snatched Drake's cry away, but he howled at the night again. "Sam! I'm coming to kill you!"

No answer. And no sight of Sam or the others. Surely they would be rushing back to Perdido Beach, and yet they were nowhere in view and with each passing second Drake could be moving farther from them.

Bring me Nemesis!

No. Nemesis could wait. Drake served the Darkness but he was not just some errand boy. He had his own needs.

If he couldn't catch Sam out here in the open, then he would beat him to Perdido Beach. He would be waiting when Sam got there. Waiting with whip wrapped around Astrid.

His mind flooded with pictures, lovely pictures of Sam helpless under his whip. And yet he would not kill Sam Temple, no, not until Sam had watched him reduce Astrid to a hideous skinless monster.

The vision was so clear in his head, so wonderful, it filled him with light and joy and a pleasure he could not even describe.

Nemesis!

"I'll get your Nemesis," Drake muttered. "But first . . ."

Drake's army rushed at breakneck speed away from the lake, scampering up the long slope that led from the lake to the dry lands beyond.

He felt a wave of fury directed at him. A wave of rage that shook him to his core. The dark tendril was wrapped around his brain, filling his thoughts, demanding, threatening. *Nemesis!*

"No!" Drake shouted.

The reaction was immediate. The swarm stopped dead in its tracks.

"They're my army. My army!" Drake bellowed. His own hatreds were too strong to be denied. And he might even have defied the gaiaphage. But as Drake stood agonizing, hatred contending with fear, he lost the ability to make the decision.

The choice of whether to pursue Nemesis or terrorize Perdido Beach would be Brittney's to make.

THIRTY-SEVEN

SAM HOBBLED ALONG more quickly than he had hoped. He leaned on Toto and benefited as well from Dekka walking behind him and lessening gravity beneath them.

He felt low. All the lower because he'd actually managed just a little bit of hope earlier. He'd actually allowed himself to believe that things might be better now that they'd found the lake and the train.

But this was the FAYZ. And just because they were due for some good news didn't mean any was coming. In the space of a very few hours he had gone from the heights of optimism to utter despair.

Over and over again in his mind he played out the likely scenarios. Edilio would have his guys, plus Brianna, Taylor, hopefully Orc. If Jack reached town in time he would fight as well; Jack had really stepped up.

But it wasn't enough. Even if he and Dekka were there, it might not be enough. So instead of saving the town and showing them salvation in the form of water, noodles, and Nutella, Sam knew he would arrive back at a town devastated.

Some were sure to survive. Surely, some.

Maybe Little Pete would save Astrid. He had the power. But was he aware? Did any of this penetrate to wherever his mind was?

"Do you think he'll do it?" Dekka asked. "Jack, I mean."

"No," Sam said.

"No," Dekka agreed.

"True," Toto said, although whether he was agreeing with them or just automatically certifying that they believed what they were saying, Sam could not say.

"He's not that guy," Sam said. "He's not ruthless. Anyway, what are the odds he could even get to town and find Little Pete? And then, who knows if even that would shock Pete into doing anything."

"You would do it, Sam."

"Yeah. I would do it," Sam said.

"He would," Toto agreed.

"It's your gift, Sam," Dekka said. "It has been right from the start."

"Ruthlessness?"

"I guess that doesn't sound so good," Dekka said wearily. "But someone has to do it. We each contribute what we have."

Sam winced as his heel brushed a stone. "Probably wouldn't work anyway. The Pete thing, I mean."

"The train," Dekka said. "Those missiles."

"I thought about that," Sam said. "But how would we get

them to town? How would we even figure out how to use them?"

Sam stopped limping.

Dekka stopped, too, after a few steps. Toto kept walking, oblivious.

"Dekka?"

"Yeah?"

"How high does your power go? I mean, you cancel gravity, right? So things float upward."

"Yeah. So?"

"I've seen you levitate yourself. I mean, you cancel gravity right beneath you and you float upward, right? Well, how high can you go?"

"I don't know," she admitted. "If I'm projecting it, you know, like I want to make it happen somewhere else, I can only reach maybe fifty feet or so. Maybe a little more."

"Okay, but that's you hitting it at kind of an angle, right? I mean, you're sort of shooting across gravity because gravity goes straight down."

Dekka looked at him strangely. She spread her hands by her side. Immediately she began to rise, along with dirt and rock, a pillar of it.

Sam watched as she rose, staying well back from the swirl of debris.

In the dark he quickly lost sight of her.

"Dekka!" He tilted his head back, trying to make her out against the background of black velvet and pinpoint lights.

"Where is Dekka?" Toto asked.

"Up there."

"That is true," Toto said.

"Yeah. Watch where you step, unless you want to go floating, too."

It seemed like a long time before Dekka finally appeared amid falling gravel. She floated easily down, regained her footing, and said, "Okay, more than fifty feet, that's for sure. I don't know how far I went, but a long way. Maybe you're right. Maybe it works better when I'm canceling gravity straight down. But I can only fly straight up. So if you're thinking I can go all airborne and fly to town, that's not happening."

"I'm thinking," Sam said, "that the FAYZ is a big bubble. Like a . . . what are those things with water inside and you shake them up with snow and—"

"A snow globe," Toto supplied.

"Like a snow globe. And if you have a bubble inside that snow globe, what does it do? It rises to the top, right?"

"The top of this bubble is probably directly over the power plant," Dekka said. "I mean, if the FAYZ is a perfect sphere."

"Okay, tell me if this makes sense." Sam frowned, trying to work it through as he talked. "The train is near the northern wall of the FAYZ. So if you were standing there and you canceled gravity . . ."

"You'd go scraping along the wall—very painfully—until you reached the top. Like a bubble rising to the top of a snow globe."

"There are cars at the power plant. I mean, ones that

have been used more recently, within the last month, cars Edilio drove there. So the batteries should still work. A lot have had their gas drained, but we wouldn't need much." He was thinking out loud. Not even paying attention to Toto's repeated "He believes it, it's true, Spidey" remarks.

"I can't beat the bugs," Sam said. "My power doesn't work on them. Not well enough, anyway. But they can be crushed. And I think maybe they can be blown up."

"Are you talking about those missile launchers in the train?" Dekka asked.

"I'm talking about exactly that," Sam said. "You raise that container of missiles. You fly it to the top of the dome. You bring it down by the power plant. We find a vehicle with a gallon of gas and we go tearing for Perdido Beach." He shrugged. "Then we see how these bugs like the M3-MAAWS, Multirole Anti-Armor Anti-Personnel Weapons System."

Caine walked the few blocks from the town hall to the highway alone. A gunslinger out of some old cowboy movie.

Kids followed him, but at a safe distance. A dozen of them crowded just inside the busted-out plate glass window of an insurance company. A couple more found seats in parked cars.

Good, let them watch as I save their butts, Caine thought.

But now, alone, standing in the middle of the highway astride the old divider line, he was far from confident. How many of the creatures would come? How large were they? How powerful?

Were they already watching him, out there in the dark?

And what about Drake? Would there be a chance for him to win Drake over? Drake could still be a very useful number two guy. Unless he was determined to be number one.

Fighting these superbugs plus Drake? Suddenly the island seemed very, very inviting.

He could walk away right now. Diana and him, just the two of them, alone on the island. Stick the townies with Penny and Bug. Just him and Diana. Food, luxury, sex. Wasn't that infinitely better than this battle?

An old suspicion shadowed his thoughts: was he being played? The Darkness had used him before. Was this the gaiaphage's will reaching into his mind again?

He didn't feel it. He hadn't felt the Darkness at all while on the island. Even before that, from the point where Caine had defied the Darkness, the gaiaphage had left him alone.

No. This was his own decision. But why? Why give up the island? For what? To be torn apart by monsters hatched in human bodies? Even if he survived, what would he face? Artichokes and fish, resentment, probably a fight with Sam, and Diana's sullen withdrawal.

"King Caine! Yeah!"

He rounded quickly, angry, assuming it was a taunt. A boy in the insurance company raised a fist and yelled, "Wooooh!"

Caine nodded in his direction.

Sheep. So long as they had a shepherd to ward off the wolves, they were happy. Spineless, indifferent, weak, stupid: it was hard not to have complete contempt for them.

Of course, if he failed, they'd turn on him in a heartbeat.

Then again, if he failed, they'd be busy running for their lives.

A sudden flash of silver down the highway.

Caine peered into the dark. No light, of course, not even a Sammy sun up here by the main road. Just a little moonlight and a little starlight and a whole lot of dark.

But yes, something. Something moving.

And a sound. *Clickety-clackety*, very fast on concrete.

He saw flashing steel mouthparts, like moonlit machetes.

He couldn't tell how many of the massive creatures there were. Just that there were at least half a dozen, each the size of a city bus and close enough now that he could see red eyes glaring malignantly.

He pointed at the spectators lounging in a parked car. "Get out of that car!"

The two boys shrugged as if they couldn't see why they should obey. Then, with a popping of slackening springs and the groan of metal, the car just beside them floated up off the ground.

They got the idea. They bailed out fast.

Caine raised the car up and up. It was hard to see color in this light but it looked like it might be blue. A small, blue SUV.

"Let's hope this works," Caine breathed.

He drew back his hand and hurled the car through the air. It whooshed over his head. It tumbled through the air toward the closest of the creatures.

It fell short, smashed into the pavement with a crunch of metal and shattering glass, then tumbled into the bug's mandibles.

Caine had no time to see what effect it had because a second bug scampered without pause up and over the SUV. One of the bug's pointed legs pierced the moonroof.

"I got plenty of cars," Caine said.

He raised the station wagon the boys had been sitting in and hurled it in a quick, sidearm throw. The car turned once in the air and hit the leading bug at almost ground level.

"Yeah, suck on that!" Caine yelled. Not exactly a kingly thing to say, but battle first, propaganda later.

Caine couldn't see the creature's face, but he could see that its legs were kicking randomly, out of any rhythm.

"Scratch one." This was going to be easier than he'd expected.

But just as he was congratulating himself a solid wall of creatures pushed itself up and over the first two. And worse, there were half a dozen of the creatures rushing up the highway from behind him.

They had circled around!

He had picked the wrong place for this fight. It was suddenly blindingly clear. The last thing he should do is fight on open ground where they could come at him from every direction like this.

Caine's heart thudded, his jaw clenched until his teeth cracked. He'd assumed the tales about the creatures were exaggerated. No. No. Not exaggerated.

Caine broke and ran. He raced at right angles to the two approaching forces. He leaped a ditch, landed hard, scrambled up and ran flat out across the service road, and flew past the shocked and confused crowd in the insurance company yelling, "Run, you idiots!"

Two of the creatures were scampering to cut him off. He snatched up a delivery van as he passed it and hurled it quickly—so quickly it flew low and almost hit him in the head as it blew past.

The crowd in the insurance company panicked. They poured from the narrow door, jamming one another, cursing and screaming.

A boy slipped, caught himself, but the delay was fatal. A bug speared him with a leg and swept him into gnashing, slashing mouthparts.

"Oh, no, no, noooo!" the kid screamed. The sound died suddenly, replaced by a noise like a garbage disposal chewing up chicken bones.

Caine ran down San Pablo with the kids pelting behind him and the swarm was forced to funnel into this more narrow space.

Things had gone from bad to desperate far faster than Caine could have imagined.

A second kid was caught by what looked like a black frog tongue firing from a bug's mouth. She screamed as the bug reeled her in.

Caine stopped in the middle of the street. Shaking all over. Jaw clenched. He couldn't outrun them and this was as good as any place: middle of the block so he couldn't be attacked from the sides, at least.

The insurance company crowd splintered, kids rushing in every direction, all of them screaming, some beating helplessly against locked doors and crying to be let in. Others scrambled over fences into backyards.

Caine raised a parked car and hurled it, then another, another, three cars in rapid succession. It was like a pileup on a freeway, crashing, smashing, glass spraying, side mirrors popping off, rims rolling down the sidewalk.

His furious counterattack may have stopped or even killed some of the bugs—he couldn't be sure in the darkness—but the swarm never hesitated. Up and over they rolled, like a wave.

Shaking, he stood his ground and raised trembling hands. If he couldn't smash them maybe he could just hold them back.

The nearest bug slammed into an invisible wall of telekinetic power. Its legs motored madly, tearing gouges in the blacktop, kicking the smashed cars, but unable to advance.

"Yeah, try that!" Caine yelled.

A second, a third, a fourth creature, all pressed against the barrier, all relentlessly scrambling, pushing, determined. And all the while, Caine stood alone in the middle of the street.

But for how long? he wondered. The bugs didn't seem to be tiring. In fact they were scrabbling over one another in a mad tangle of legs and massive silvery carapaces and scythe-mandibles and always the gnashing mouths and glowing ruby eyes.

He faltered, seeing those eyes, and suddenly the wall of bugs surged a foot closer.

He redoubled his focus. But he was feeling something he'd never felt before when using his power: a physical push back, as if he was holding them back with his muscles as well as his telekinetic ability.

Without thinking, he had set his feet in a strong stance, and he could feel the weight on his calves and thighs, even more on his arms. He wasn't just projecting power as he always had, he was pushing back, at the limit of his powers, being pressed by thousands of pounds of thrust from dozens and dozens of stabbing legs.

They were just twenty feet away. Piling high against the invisible barrier. With a terrible shock he realized they were climbing over one another in a deliberate effort to get over the top of the invisible wall of energy.

Then, a far worse shock: some of the creatures had come around Golding Street and were rushing him from behind.

He switched his pose, one hand for the mass of bugs, one for the onrushing attack. But it would not do. He couldn't hold them.

"Should have stayed on the island," he told himself. He had gambled and lost.

The two invisible walls were closing in. He was holding back tons of pushing, questing monsters and he couldn't do it, could not. He just did not have the power. And once he broke, they would be on him before he could blink.

"Hey! Jerkwad!"

He glanced toward the sound. Standing, arms akimbo, atop the flat roof of a two-story apartment building, was Brianna.

"Come to gloat?" he managed.

"See the front door of that house?"

"What?"

"That's where we're going."

"No time!"

"No time," Brianna mocked. "Please. Just go limp."

"Go limp?"

"Yeah: limp. And oh, by the way: it's going to hurt."

He never saw her move but he felt the linebacker impact as she hit him at blazing speed.

Caine went flying. His shirt was ripped from his back. He spun crazily and fell hard onto the lawn. The bug armies crashed together like two waves behind him. Like the Red Sea closing behind Moses.

Caine tried to stand, but already there were hands on his back pushing him, propelling him forward at insane speed. He hit the doorjamb on his way through. The bugs swarmed toward the door but it had already been slammed, locked, and barricaded with a chair.

Brianna stood in the middle of the room, examining her fingernails with theatrical calm.

"The whole superspeed thing comes in helpful at times," she said.

"I think you broke my back," Caine said. He felt sharp pain in his ribs. But it was very much better than the alternative.

The door exploded inward and a tangle of bug legs appeared.

"I can hold them, but I can't kill them all," Caine shouted.

"Yeah. They're hard to kill. You got a plan?"

Caine bit savagely at his thumb, worrying the cuticle. They were surrounded. The very walls were being battered. The windows were all smashed. They couldn't fit through the door but they would soon make it wide enough.

They stood, Caine and Brianna, in the kitchen, the center of the house, as far as possible from the windows, but now the bugs had their mandibles shoved in through the doors and windows, questing, slicing the air, their ropelike tongues lashing madly.

The entire house was like a drum pounded by dozens of drumsticks.

"You know, I'm kind of disappointed," Brianna said. "Situation like this? Sam would come up with a plan."

THIRTY-EIGHT

SAM HAD COME up with a plan.

Three, actually. One involved the very faint hope that Jack would reach Little Pete and do something awful.

The second involved something purely insane. Flying a huge container of missiles through the air, dropping them in just the right place, finding a vehicle with gas and a functioning battery, then figuring out how to fire the missiles in time to save the town.

That was insane.

The third plan involved Dekka. He wasn't even going to tell her about that. Because it wasn't just insane, it was monstrous.

None of the plans had a chance of working. Sam knew that.

Sam's foot was beyond pain. It was agony. Dekka was doing all she could for him by lessening gravity somewhat but he still had to move forward, and he had to move as fast as he could.

"How are you doing, Dekka?" he gasped as he hobble-trotted.

"Stop asking, Sam," she said.

"You have to—," he began.

"What? What do I have to do, Sam? They're eating me from the inside, what do you want me to say?"

"She's telling the truth—"

"Shut your stupid mouth, you freak!" Dekka snapped at Toto.

They were close, Sam could feel it. They had to be. They had to reach the train before the bugs finally burst from Dekka and ate her alive.

He needed her to live a while longer. To the bitter, bitter end, he needed her and she was spending her last minutes running and trying to help him and he was helpless, could do nothing but keep hoping she would stay alive, suffer some more, conquer her fear, all for a stupid, pointless, doomed plan.

"There!" Toto said. "I see the train."

The light was faint, gray, watery, and inadequate. But yes, Sam could see the train.

He gritted his teeth and ran now, full out, every step like a knife plunged into his foot with the pain radiating all the way up his leg.

"I can't even see which container it was, Spidey."

Sam cupped his hands and grew a ball of sickly greenish-tinged light. It swelled until he could see the two faces of his companions. To his horror the light showed a bug had eaten its way through the front of Dekka's blouse. She was trembling.

"Dekka," he said. "You don't have to . . . I can . . ."

She grabbed his arm with a painfully hard grip. "I'm with you, Sam. I guess I don't get to take the easy way out."

"This is the container with the weapons," Toto called. Then, as an afterthought he added, "That's true."

"Sam," Dekka said. "If I die . . ."

"Then we fall," Sam said. "You and me, Dekka. If I have to go, it'll be an honor to be with you."

Sam slammed the container shut and the three of them climbed to the top. The container was not perfectly flat on top, it was ribbed for strength. But the steel ribs were no more than six inches high. They flattened themselves down on their backs, facing up.

"Here we go," Dekka said. She spread her hands flat against the container, palms downward.

The container rose.

Sam lay staring up at the sky, which was no real sky. The stars were paling. The moon had set.

How fast were they rising? The barrier was quite near, just a few dozen yards away from the train. For the first time in his life, he wished he'd paid more attention in geometry. There was no doubt a formula for how long it would be before they scraped against the barrier.

If Astrid were here, she would be able to—

Scrreeech!

The door end of the container was scraping and the entire container tilted wildly.

"Hold on!" Sam yelled.

He gripped the ribs even tighter. But he realized with a pleasant surprise that he was weightless against the container. He was holding on to keep from floating up.

Chunk! Chunk! Screeee!

The container banged a couple of times, tilted even more sharply, and yet rose. Rose!

Suddenly Sam's knuckles, chest, and face were against the barrier. It was like grabbing a power line. Pain that obliterated every other thought. It was not his first time touching the barrier, but it was the first time he'd had his face pressed against it.

"Dekka!" Sam cried.

"Doing my best!" she yelled.

The container became more nearly level and Sam could at least loosen his grip on the steel ribs, which allowed him to press his hands down by his side and keep them from being crushed.

The barrier moved away from his face, blessed relief, but all the while the screeching sound of steel being dragged along the barrier continued.

Screeeeee.

Still rising. Faster. The air rushed past as their speed increased.

How high? They would either stall or fall or, if somehow Dekka could keep it up, they would rise and follow the curve of the dome. As they reached the top of the arc, their faces would be crushed against the barrier again. Sam wasn't looking forward to that.

Sam rolled onto his stomach and wormed his way to the edge of the container. There wasn't much to see below. No lights. No way to know exactly where they were. He wished he had Albert's map, maybe he could make some sense out of the patterns of shadow and dimly perceived, starlit heights.

Looking up, he could not see the barrier at this height; it was not the smooth, pearly translucence he was used to. It was more as if he was pressed against glass, seeing stars beyond it. He'd halfway expected to find the stars were something painted on, but of course that was crazy. The barrier maintained the illusion even up here. He felt himself flying, staring out into the near-void of space.

"How are you doing, Dekka?"

"I can't believe it's working. But Sam . . ."

"What?"

"I'm numb, I can't feel it, it doesn't hurt, but I can hear them, Sam. I can hear mouths chewing, Sam."

What did he say to that? "Hang in there, Dekka."

"It's like we're floating through the stars," Dekka said. "I'm pretending we're floating up to heaven."

"Kind of hope we're not," Sam said.

The screeching sound had changed pitch as speed built. And there was a very stiff breeze now, pressing down on him as the container, unbound from gravity, flew and screeched.

"I wish you had not found me," Toto said. "I was happier alone."

"Yeah. Sorry about that," Sam said.

Sam tried to guess how fast they were going by judging the wind. He tried to visualize being in a car with the window down. How hard did that wind blow when the car was going thirty or sixty or eighty miles an hour?

Was it blowing that hard now?

"Oh God, oh God, no, no, I see it, I see it!" Dekka cried and the container lurched hard and sank like a dropping elevator.

It stabilized quickly and rose to once again scrape along the dome.

In an unnatural voice Dekka said, "Sorry. I looked. It's eating my . . ." She couldn't finish. "I don't think I have long, Sam."

"Glide path," Sam whispered. If they were moving as quickly as he hoped, wouldn't they keep some of that forward momentum even if Dekka dropped them?

Yes. And they'd hit the ground at terminal velocity and that would be that.

It felt as if the speed might actually be dropping now and when Sam stuck his hand up he got a shocking jolt. They were nearing the top of the dome and it was flattening out. Soon it would be full body contact and how long could they stand that?

Not long.

As the slope lessened their speed would drop and they'd be more and more pressed against the barrier.

"It's enough, Dekka," Sam said. "Start lowering us. But not slowly."

"What?"

"Move your gravity field so it's stronger at the back end and weaker at the front."

"That's what I've been doing so that we'd stay tilted away from the barrier."

"Yeah. Just do it more. Weaken it all, but more at the front end, right? It should be like sliding down a slope, right?"

To his amazement Dekka laughed aloud. "If I gotta die, this is the way to go. Wouldn't have missed this craziness for anything."

Suddenly the constant screech stopped.

The container lurched so wildly that Toto lost his grip and came tumbling downhill toward Sam. He tumbled slowly— they were in reduced gravity—and Sam grabbed him.

"The people back at the facility would have liked to meet Dekka," Toto said, with his face inches from Sam's.

"I'm sure they would."

Another wild lurch and suddenly the container was sliding, dropping away forward. It was like a sled running down well-packed snow on a long slope.

"I can't see the ground," Dekka said. "I don't want to move. You have to tell me when we're close."

Sam peered into the dark below, trying to pick out anything that might tell him where they were, where they were heading. But it was hills and scrubland and he'd never seen any of it from miles up in the air.

They were moving fast, sliding down an invisible slope, letting gravity pull them forward as much as downward.

"My—," Dekka cried out.

Like an elevator with the cable cut, the bottom dropped. The container spun sideways. Sam, Toto, and Dekka spilled off.

Sam windmilled through the air, flashing on sky and ground and sea and sky again, falling and spinning, and he was sure of one thing: they were too high up and the fall would kill them.

The creatures beat on the house like bulls slamming into a wall. The windows and doors had already been bashed in and now the walls themselves were splintering. The din was shocking. The living room wall splintered, showing broken two-by-fours and twisted conduit.

Caine and Brianna cowered in the kitchen. It only had walls on two sides, with one side open to the breakfast nook and a counter separating the family room.

Caine looked around frantically for something to throw. Some furniture, some kitchen equipment, but nothing big enough to do any damage to motivated, armored beasts able to bash through walls.

"This isn't right," Caine said.

"You think?" Brianna yelled.

"They're animals. They shouldn't be this focused. They're intelligent!"

"I don't care if they speak Latin and can do trigonometry," Brianna yelled. "How do we kill them?"

"They should have gotten frustrated and moved off to look for someone else to eat," Caine said.

"Maybe we're extra tasty."

"There's an intelligence behind this. A plan."

"Yeah, the plan is kill the two of us and no one will be left to stop them," Brianna said.

"Exactly," Caine agreed. "Bugs don't think that way."

"Shhh!" Brianna held up a hand. Caine heard it, too: the sound of gunfire. At least three or four guns blazing away.

"Edilio's guys," Caine muttered. He was furious and relieved at the same time. He didn't want Edilio or his cops sharing in the glory of saving the town. On the other hand: so far there wasn't any glory.

"Upstairs!" Caine said. He ran for the steps but it meant passing close to the front door. One of the monsters had its mandibles all the way inside and was swinging them left and right, widening the shattered doorway.

Caine jumped clear of the scythes and Brianna, who was already past him and up the stairs, dashed back to grab his hand and pull him up.

"Watch out they have—," Brianna started to say.

Something barbed and painful slapped Caine in midback. He reached over his shoulder and grabbed a sticky wet rope.

"—tongues," Brianna finished.

She drew a knife, slashed the tongue, and yanked Caine away.

Caine tore for the bedroom window. The house was entirely surrounded. At least a dozen of the behemoths plowed the lawn with their pointy legs and drove their mandibles again and again, like battering rams, against the house.

Down the street, a block away, Ellen and two other kids fired at the backs of the creatures. The bugs ignored them.

"Yep, they are definitely focused on us," Brianna said.

"I can't even reach a car from here," Caine said. "I have nothing to hit them with."

And then it came to him: he did have something to throw.

Caine raised his hands. The bugs below spotted him and rose up on their hind four legs to come slamming themselves against the window where he stood.

Caine focused on the closest creature. And suddenly six sharp-tipped insect legs were motoring in midair. He lifted the creature as high as he could, then dropped it. The bug landed hard, but shook itself and was instantly back on the attack without so much as a broken leg.

"Turn them over!" Brianna yelled.

Caine reached for the same aggressive bug, lifted him, and this time gave the creature a spin before dropping him.

It landed on its back. All six legs kicked madly in the air. Exactly like a beetle turned over on its back.

"The washing machine," Caine said. "Is it upstairs—"

"Right down the hall," Brianna said.

Caine ran, lurching into a wall as the bugs outside hit the house with concerted force. Found the washing machine and lifted it away from the wall, ripping power cord and hoses in the process, and levitated it down the hall to the bedroom.

He threw it through the window. It landed harmlessly on a

bug's back. The one he had turned over had righted itself, so Caine flipped a different bug.

Then, while the creature was kicking madly trying to turn itself upright, Caine raised the washing machine high in the air and slammed it down on the creature's exposed abdomen. It hit like a cartoon anvil.

Whumpf!

Goo spurted from the bug's sides. The kicking legs slowed.

"Oh yeah: that works," Caine said.

He flipped a second bug over, lifted the battered Maytag and smashed it down. This time the bug did not spray its guts immediately so he hit it again.

A huge crash and a sound of rending, twisting, ripping wood. The entire house jerked. Shuddered. And to Caine's horror the wall before him started to fall away.

The entire house was collapsing.

Brianna blurred and was gone. Caine tried to run but the floor was tilted crazily as it fell beneath his feet. The ceiling came crashing down and Caine landed on his back as the house collapsed atop him in a wild tornado of destruction.

Something crushed his stomach. Plasterboard pressed down on his face. His hands were pinned. He gasped for air and breathed dust. He could see nothing in his immediate field of vision but wallboard and part of a framed Weezer poster.

But he could feel his legs and arms. Nothing broken. Nothing punctured.

He had the power to lift the debris off himself. But if he

did, then the creatures would be on him in a heartbeat.

Whereas if he stayed under the wreckage, he might be safe.

The creatures would finally give up on him and go in search of easier victims. Then, when they were gone, he could emerge and take them by surprise.

Caine took a shaky, dusty breath.

Playing dead meant letting some kids die so that he could live. Caine decided he was probably fine with that.

THIRTY-NINE

EDILIO LAY ON the steps of town hall feeling as weak as a kitten. He had barely heard Caine's big speech. He couldn't have cared less. There was nothing he could do, not with delirium spinning his head.

He coughed hard, too hard. It wracked his body each time he did it so that he dreaded the next cough. His stomach was clenched in knots. Every muscle in his body ached.

He was vaguely aware that he was saying something in between coughs.

"*Mamá. Mamá. Sálvame.*"

Save me, mother.

"*Santa María, sálvame,*" he begged, and coughed so hard he smashed his head against the steps.

Death was near, he felt it. Death reached through his swimming, disordered mind and he felt its cold hand clutching his heart.

Santa María, Madre de Dios, ruega por nosotros pecadores, ahora y en la hora de nuestra muerte.

And then in the swirling darkness he saw her. A figure dressed in a flowing white and blue dress. She had sad, dark eyes, and a golden glow came from her head.

She held up one hand as if blessing him.

He heard her voice. He was surprised that she spoke in English. He'd always thought of God's mother as speaking Spanish.

"Run, Edilio," she said.

He started to repeat the prayer. *Santa María, Madre de Dios . . .*

But she grabbed him by his outstretched arm and said, "I know you're sick but run. RUN! I can't save you!"

For some reason the Virgin Mary had Brianna's voice.

Edilio stood up. The sudden movement sent jagged bolts of pain into his head. For a moment he couldn't even see, but he plowed ahead on leaden feet. Fell and rolled and got back up, blind, staggering. He ran and ran and coughed until he doubled up on the ground.

He sat there for a while. Waiting to find the strength to follow Brianna's orders, to run.

He looked up and saw that he was across the plaza. He saw the desperate sick and the peaceful dead on the steps.

And he saw demons, huge monsters, armored cockroaches with impossible red devil eyes.

They swarmed onto the steps.

· · ·

Brianna saw Lana come charging out of the so-called hospital with Sanjit. The bugs were swarming.

Edilio had run, thankfully, now here was Lana. Brianna cursed and yelled, "Lana, run! Run. Out the back of the building!"

Lana drew her pistol. "No way," she said. She took aim at the first bug she saw and fired three times. One of the ruby eyes drooled white and red pus, but the bug never stopped eating a girl who, Brianna could only pray, had already died.

"Don't be an idiot. We need you alive. Get out! Get out! You"—she grabbed Sanjit by the neck—"get her out of here; we need her alive!"

Brianna had seen the most effective way to kill the bugs, but she wasn't Caine. She didn't have his powers.

But she had her own.

Brianna stuck out her chin. Caine had been crushed beneath the collapsing house. It was on her now.

The knife flashed in her hand. She was not going to win this fight, but she wasn't going to run, either.

Dekka had seen the beasts within her.

Death, oh God, let me die.

Too much to bear. Death, she had to die, to end it, to kill them and herself and never see what they were doing to her.

The container had slipped from her. In blind panic, in sheer terror, she had lost control.

She tried to regain it now, but she was falling, wind-whipped, twirling like a top. She couldn't even tell which way was up or down.

She spread her hands and focused but focus on what? Where was the ground? Stars and pale mountains and black sea all spun wildly. The container flashed by again and again, as if it was an hour marker on a fast-running clock. And two twisting shapes, arms windmilling.

She had to save Sam. That much, at least.

Her breathing came in gulps. Her eyes were streaming tears, blurred to uselessness. How could she stop the spinning?

Dekka pulled her arms in tight and entwined her legs. Less wind resistance. She made some sense of it now: she was falling headfirst. She was still spinning, but slower, and she was definitely falling headfirst like an arrow falling to earth. Suddenly, far too clear, she could see a line of surf directly below.

She had to get lower than Sam. Sam and Toto were below her, still spinning crazily. But Dekka, with less wind resistance, fell just a little faster.

Suddenly, though, the ground was coming clear. Rushing up to smash her to jelly.

She was below Sam. Now!

She spread her fingers, focused, and canceled gravity below.

And continued to fall. She had canceled gravity. She had not canceled momentum.

In seconds they would hit the water or the ground. Either would smash them to jelly.

Caine raised the debris off himself.

The bugs were all gone. He saw the tail of one as it raced away.

If he went after them, he'd probably get killed.

But stay here and do what? Be safe? He'd have been safe on the island. He hadn't come back to be safe.

Two possible outcomes: the bugs killed everyone and then who would Caine rule over? Or the bugs were defeated by someone else. And then how would he ever get control? Power would go to whoever won this fight.

Still Caine hesitated. A big, warm bed. A beautiful girl to share it with. Food. Water. Everything he needed, just a few miles away on the island. The logical, rational answer was obvious.

"Which is why the world stays messed up," Caine said under his breath. "People aren't rational."

He took a few deep, steadying breaths, and prepared to die for power.

Orc had not managed to kill himself. Again.

He wept a bit when he realized that he was going to live. He was doing his best, but throwing up and passing out were getting in the way of death-by-drink.

He stood up, needing to pee, but he was already peeing as he stood. So no need.

Something moved. He swung his head ponderously to

look. A monster. In a cracked fragment of mirror just barely clinging to the wall.

Orc stared at his reflection. Six feet, maybe more, of gray, wet gravel. He threw back his head, arms wide, and howled.

"Why? Why?"

He burst into tears and pounded his fists against his face. Then with stone fingers he ripped the last of the living flesh from his face. Blood ran red.

And now he howled at his own reflection. "Why?"

He lurched away. He ran in bounding, wild leaps toward the stairs.

Astrid.

He had no clear thought for what he would do when he found her. She was just the only one who had ever helped him. She was the only one who had ever seen him as Charles Merriman and not just Orc.

She should feel his pain. She should feel it.

Someone had to feel the pain.

He reached the top of the stairs. He knocked the door of Little Pete's room open. He stared blankly, confused. A wind whipped through the room. Little Pete hovered in the air several feet above the cot. He glowed.

Astrid was not there.

"Astrid!" Orc bellowed.

From outside, clear and distinct through the open window, an answer.

"Is that you, Orc?"

Orc bounded to the window. It had been opened and in

any case the panes of glass were shattered.

Orc's vision took a moment to stabilize enough for him to make out what he was seeing. And then he couldn't believe it.

Down below, in the first faint glow of morning, stood Drake.

Behind him and all around the school were things that looked like gigantic cockroaches.

It all had to be a hallucination.

"Drake?" Orc said, blinking hard to test the reality of this apparition.

"I thought that sounded like you, Orc." Drake smirked. "And you have Astrid up there with you? Excellent. Couldn't be better."

"Are you real?" Orc asked.

Drake laughed delightedly. "Oh, I'm real, Orc."

"Go away." It was all Orc could think of to say.

"Nah, I don't think I will," Drake said. He ran lightly to the door downstairs and disappeared from view.

Orc was completely baffled. Drake? Here?

In seconds Drake appeared at the door of the room. His cold eyes looked past Orc and focused on Little Pete.

"Well, well," Drake said. "Nemesis."

PETE

THIS WAS NOT his room.

That was not the ceiling above his bed.

He felt the burning lava build up in his chest and with a spasm he shot it out of his mouth.

When he coughed, it sent waves of pain crashing through his body.

He was all body now. No distant visions. No whispering voices. Only his pain-wracked body.

A breeze blew around him but the heat filled him still and he did not know how to come at it, what to call it. How could he wish it away if he didn't know what it was?

Where was his sister? Her eyes were gone. He was alone. Alone and trapped inside a body that lay helpless, beset by fire inside, and cold outside, and a whipping wind and always the scrape scrape of sounds, the rasp of saws, the assault of mad, shrieking color.

A voice so big it made him want to run and hide said, "Where's Ashtruh?"

Wet gravel was speaking, swaying, leaning perilously as though it might fall over.

"Ashtruh!" the monster bellowed. "Ashtruuuuuh!"

Pete's mind recoiled, sank deep down, fled before the noise, but could not escape. Once more his body kept him tethered to the real world that had never been real to him.

The monster stomped away, still shouting.

Pete coughed a volcano.

He had to do something. His body had hold of him and his body was pain.

Panic was building inside him.

He had to do . . . something.

FORTY

25 MINUTES

SAM FELT SOMETHING wet. It was everywhere, a cloud rising from below. It was like falling through a tornado of mud. Salt water and sand, liberated by weightlessness, flew upward.

"Spread your arms and legs!" Sam shouted.

Friction. The painful slap of water, the grinding of sand, like flying into a tornado.

Sam felt like his skin was being flayed. He shut his eyes, turned his head to keep his nose and mouth from filling with wet sand, and smacked hard into a surface as solid and unyielding as concrete.

The air exploded from his lungs. It was like being kicked by a mule.

His back arched too far, tendons stretched, his head snapped back, every inch of him stung and water closed over his head.

Instinctively he kicked his way to the surface. The sand

washed away and he could force one eye open. He was no more than a dozen yards from shore, in water not even five feet deep.

Then all the water and sand that had floated up to meet them came pouring down.

He looked around frantically for Dekka and Toto. He splashed his way toward the beach through a blinding down-pour that lasted a full minute.

Toto was just down the beach, lying on his back and moaning in pain. Sam knelt by him.

"Are you hurt?"

"My legs," Toto said, and started to cry. "I want to go home."

"Listen to me, Toto, your legs are broken, but we can fix them."

Toto looked at him wonderingly, wiped sand from his face, and said, "You are telling the truth."

"I'll get Lana. Soon as I can. You just stay put."

He stood up and yelled, "Dekka! Dekka!"

She did not call back to him, but he saw her swimming toward shore. He ran out and helped her to get to dry ground.

"I'm so sorry, Sam," she gasped.

"I'm okay. So's Toto. Just broke his legs is all." He glanced left and right and spotted the container smashed into a low bluff. Oblong crates and their deadly contents had spilled.

"I don't know where we are," Sam said. "I think we're south of the power plant." He looked around, frantic. His plan had always been reckless and hopeless, but he'd hoped, somehow, to come down near the power plant. There might be a car still in usable condition at the plant. But here? He wasn't even sure where here was.

And the container was wrecked. Many of the missiles would be, too.

"Sam!" A voice was calling to him from the direction of the sea. A boat. He saw four people in it, and oars splashing and pulling hard toward them.

"Quinn!"

The boat ran in and beached. Quinn jumped out. "Where did you come from?"

"You wouldn't believe me if I told you," Sam said. "Quinn: tell me quick. What's happening in town?"

Quinn appeared overwhelmed by the question.

Sam grabbed him. "Whatever it is, tell me. Dekka may not have another half hour. Quick!"

"Edilio's sick. Lots of people sick. It's bad, kids dropping all over the place. Edilio sent me to bring Caine back. To fight the bugs."

Sam breathed a shaky sigh of relief. "Thank God he did, Quinn. I probably can't beat the bugs, maybe he can."

"But . . . ," Quinn began, but Sam interrupted.

Plan Two might be dead. But Sam had one last trick up his sleeve, one last wild effort—not to save the town, but maybe to save his friend.

"Dekka, she's infested. They're hatching out of her. I promised to . . . to make it easier for her. You understand?"

Quinn nodded solemnly.

PLAGUE   443

"But I have an idea. How fast can you get us to town?"

"Fifteen minutes," Quinn said.

They rowed like they were rowing for their lives. And in some ways they were, Sam knew. If the bugs emerged from Dekka while they were in this small boat, none of them would survive.

Toto groaned, lying on the bottom of the boat in two inches of fish-smelling water. Dekka lay against Sam in the stern. His arms were around her. He whispered in her ear not to give up.

He could feel them through her clothes. He was careful to avoid the emergent mouths, but he could not avoid feeling the surging horror of insect bodies moving within Dekka's body.

"Sam, you promised me," Dekka moaned.

"I will, Dekka. I promise I will. But not yet, not yet." To Quinn he said, "As soon as we reach the dock, go for Lana."

"Lana can't help," Quinn grunted, never slackening his pace. "She can't kill them."

"She doesn't have to," Sam said.

"I'll take the kid, Orc," Drake said. "Where's Astrid?"

Orc stared at Drake. So many emotions in his tired, drink-addled brain.

Drake was the cause of all his problems. If he hadn't escaped . . .

But hadn't he himself just stormed up here to take it all out on Astrid? And yet, Drake's sadistic, cocky grin made something like steam rise up inside of him.

"Whaddyou wan' with the kid?" Orc slurred.

"Drunk much?" Drake taunted. "Friend of mine wants the 'tard. So, where's the sister?"

"Leave her alone."

Drake laughed. "Rock boy, I'm not leaving anyone alone. I have an army outside. I'll do whatever I want with Astrid the Genius."

"She didn't hurt you."

"Don't play the hero, Orc, it doesn't work for you. You're a filthy, drunken degenerate. Have you smelled yourself? What do you think you are, her knight in shining armor? You think she'll give you a big, wet kiss on your gravel face?" He peered closer at Orc as if looking inside him. "Nah, Orc, the only way you ever get Astrid is the same way I get her. And that's what you were thinking, isn't it?"

"Shut up."

Drake laughed delightedly. "Oh, you sad, sick disaster. I can see it in your bloodshot eyes. Well, I'll tell you what: you can have whatever's left over after I—"

Orc swung hard, with surprising speed. The rock fist caught Drake a little high, nailing the side of his head but only a glancing blow.

Still, a glancing blow from Orc was like a sledgehammer.

Drake stumbled sideways, slammed into the wall, but kept his feet.

Orc went after Drake, swung again, and this time missed completely. His fist punched a hole in the wall where Drake's head had been.

Drake was behind him, dancing away. "You big, stupid idiot, I can't be killed. Didn't you know that? Bring it, Orc. Come on you lumbering, stinking pile of crap."

Drake lashed him then. It didn't hurt Orc much. But he felt it.

Orc lurched toward him, but Drake was quick and nimble. He danced away, slashed at Orc again, and this time wrapped his tentacle around Orc's neck.

It wasn't easy to choke Orc, but it wasn't impossible. Drake was behind him, pulling as hard as he could, tightening his whip hand like a python, inch by inch, trying to squeeze the pebble skin.

Orc dug his fingers into the whip hand and pulled at it, tried to tear it free. But it wasn't working because somehow Orc's grip was weakening. He tried to breathe but couldn't.

Suddenly the whip hand released him.

The whip hand was withdrawing, shriveling. Orc twisted to face Drake as bright metal bands crossed his teeth. Drake's zero-percent-body-fat body became pudgy thighs and face.

"What?" Orc asked, blinking hard. Then he understood. He'd never watched Brittney emerge before but he knew it happened, had heard it happen as one voice gave way to the other.

"Hi, Orc," Brittney said.

"Brittney."

She looked around her, confused. Then her eyes fell on Little Pete.

"So, he is Nemesis."

"He's Little Pete," Orc said.

"We have to take him," Brittney said. "It's the only way. The Lord wills it."

"No," a voice said.

"Astrid!" Orc said. "I was . . . looking for you."

Astrid barely looked at him. "I ran away. But I'm back."

"Astrid, God has said He needs Little Pete," Brittney said complacently. "It's the only way."

"I know you think you talk to God—"

"No, Astrid, He talked to me. I saw Him. I touched Him. He's a dark God, a God of deep places."

"If He's a God, why does He need Little Pete? I thought God didn't need anything."

Brittney got a crafty look. "Jesus needed John the Baptist to announce His coming. He needed Judas to betray Him, and Pilate and the Pharisees to crucify Him so that He might redeem us. And the Father needed the Son to pay the price of sin."

Astrid felt weary. There was a time in her life when Astrid would have welcomed an opportunity for a theological discussion. It wasn't as if Sam had sat around with her, debating. He was completely indifferent to religion.

But this was not the time. The sad creature that was Brittney was just a tool of the malevolent creature she had confused with God.

In any case, why was Astrid defending Little Pete? She'd been ready to see him die if it meant an end to the suffering.

"God doesn't ask for human sacrifices," Astrid said.

"Doesn't He?" Brittney smirked. "What am I, Astrid? What are any of us? And what was Jesus? A sacrifice to appease a vengeful God, Astrid."

Astrid had nothing to say. She knew all the right answers. But the will was gone. Did she herself even believe in God anymore? Why argue over a phantom? They were two fools arguing over lies.

But Astrid still had her pride. And she could not remain silent and let Brittney have the final word.

"Brittney, do you really want to kill a little boy? No matter what your so-called God tells you, isn't it wrong? When your beliefs tell you to murder, doesn't a voice inside you tell you it is wrong?"

Brittney frowned. "God's will . . ."

"Even if it is, Brittney, even if that mutant monster in a cave really is God, and even if you've understood Him perfectly, and you're doing His will, and He wants you to kill, to deliver a little boy to Him so that He can kill, isn't it wrong? Isn't it just plain wrong?"

"God decides right and wrong."

"No," Astrid said. And now, despite everything, despite her own exhaustion, despite her fear, despite her self-loathing and contempt, she realized she was going to say something she had never accepted before. "Brittney, it was wrong to murder even before Moses brought down the commandments. Right and wrong doesn't come from God. It's inside us. And we know it. And even if God appears right in front of us, and tells us to our faces to murder, it's still wrong."

It was that simple in the end, Astrid realized. That simple. She didn't need the voice of God to tell her not to kill Little Pete. Just her own voice.

"Anyway, Brittney," Astrid said. "If you want to get to Petey, you have to go through me."

She smiled then for what felt like the first time in a long time.

Brittney, too, smiled, but sadly. "I won't, Astrid. But Drake will. You know he will. The bugs are all around this building, waiting. And when Drake comes, he will take Little Pete and kill you."

The two girls had almost forgotten the swaying, bleary-eyed Orc.

He moved now with surprising speed. He grabbed Brittney by the neck and waist and threw her from the window.

"I don't like her," he said.

Astrid ran to the window and saw Brittney lying flat on the ground.

The bugs turned their blue eyes upward.

Indifferent to Brittney—who was already picking herself up, unharmed—they surged toward the ruined front door of Coates Academy.

"About time." Orc laughed. "Let's get this over with."

"Orc, don't let them kill you," Astrid said, putting her hand on his arm.

"You was always nice to me, Astrid. Sorry I . . ." Then he shrugged. "Don't matter now. Better get out if you can. Most likely this won't take long."

He ran into the hallway. Astrid last saw him as he laughed at the bugs below him, vaulted the landing rail, and dropped down into the swarm.

"You want Orc?" he bellowed. "Come and get me!"

The boy, whose name was Buster, tried to get away, tried to stand up and run, but he was far too slow, far too sick. He coughed and stumbled and fell on his knees.

The bug's tongue attached to his neck and yanked him headfirst into flashing mouthparts.

A girl named Zoey coughed, doubled over with the pain of it, and a second later was caught and eaten.

It was a massacre.

Brianna flew like a madwoman, her knife flashed, her sawed-off shotgun barked, but the bugs were up the stairs and pushing inside, smelling the fresh meat in the hospital.

One of the bugs had grown so big it became jammed and blocked the doorway, but at least one of the creatures had made it inside already, and Brianna could hear muffled screams of terror from down below.

She darted, bypassed a flashing tongue, leaped over scythe mandibles, and stabbed a bug in both red eyes. Then she stuck her shotgun into the gnashing mouth and pulled the trigger.

The massive creature shuddered, but did not die.

Brianna barely leaped aside in time to avoid being caught. And then, out of the corner of her eye, she saw one of the massive creatures rise, turn in midair, and land hard on its back.

"Caine!" she yelled.

She threaded her way through the swarm, leaped easily through the wildly waving legs of the overturned bug, and stabbed her knife into its guts.

Then, into the largest of the gashes she thrust the shotgun and pulled the trigger.

BLAM!

Bug guts and bits of shell blew back and covered her. But the legs were jerking wildly now, slower, slower . . .

Caine had overturned another bug and this one he hammered with a car, lifting and slamming, lifting and slamming, until the creature was a giant mess of stick-legs and goo.

The creatures turned away from feasting on the sick. There were only seven of the bugs left now, not counting the one that was down in the so-called hospital or the one stuck in the doorway.

Seven.

"I'll flip them!" Caine yelled.

Brianna picked a piece of bug guts off her cheek and nodded. She quickly reloaded her shotgun and zoomed to mount the latest overturned creature. She was learning as she went along. The creatures had weak spots, one of them was the underside of what would be their chin. She stabbed with her knife, twisted to make an opening, pushed the shotgun into the gaping wound, and pulled the trigger.

The bug's head blew apart.

"Oh, yeah! Oh, definitely!" Brianna cried.

But Caine had been a bit too slow and now three of the creatures were pursuing him. All three had latched on to him with their tongues and he was yelling his head off for help.

Brianna dashed down the steps, now slick with blood—human and insect.

She cut the first tongue and the other two reeled back defensively.

"Flip 'em!"

"Trying," Caine said through gritted teeth. He turned one over but the bugs were learning fast. A second bug charged the first, slid beneath it, and heaved its brother back over onto his legs.

"Oh, no, we don't do that," Brianna said.

Caine had to back away again as the creatures charged. If they caught Caine, then the battle was over.

Brianna raced, grabbed Caine's arm, and yanked him to temporary safety behind a tree.

Cuh-runch!

A bug mandible sliced the tree straight through.

Caine lifted and flipped the creature, but now the swarm was converging.

"They'll follow us," Caine yelled to Brianna.

"I noticed."

"Gas station," Caine gasped. He was already running, flat out, arms pumping. Brianna caught up easily. The bugs surged after them, crowding the street.

"You understand?" Caine gasped.

"Not much gas left there," Brianna said.

"Go!" Caine yelled, and Brianna zoomed away. She reached the gas station. There was a heavy padlock on the pump and, to her utter amazement, one of Albert's people sitting there guarding it.

"Unlock it!" she yelled.

"I can't unless Albert . . . ," the kid started to say until Brianna laid her knife against his throat and said, "Really no time for chitchat."

He unlocked the pump. Brianna grabbed the handle—the hand pump was the only way—and worked it as fast as she could. Unfortunately it wasn't the kind of thing that worked better at superspeed.

She grabbed the guard and yelled, "You—pump! Pump unless you want to die."

"I don't have a tank to put it in!"

"On the ground," Brianna said. "On the ground. All over the place. Pump it!"

Gas gushed in irregular spurts from the pump and splashed onto the concrete.

Brianna zoomed back to find Caine laboring hard and barely staying ahead as he reached the highway. Out in the open the bugs would be able to use all their speed and catch him long before he reached the station.

"Keep running!" she yelled.

She dashed straight at the foremost of the creatures. It snapped at her with its tongue. She grabbed the tongue in midair and, holding on to it as hard as she could, she dived beneath the creature's legs.

The bug stumbled and came to a halt, confused. Brianna released the tongue, scooted madly beneath the creature, and came out through its hind legs. She had bought Caine maybe three seconds. No more.

She took aim at the demonic ruby eyes of the next bug, fired at point-blank range, and blew back to the gas station.

She zipped past the panicky guard, who was still busily pouring precious gasoline out on the ground.

Inside what had once been the gas station's mini-mart, Brianna searched frantically through trash and debris before coming up, triumphant, with a blue Bic lighter.

Outside she saw Caine, still barely ahead of his pursuers.

"Get outta here, kid!" she yelled to the guard. "Ruuun!"

The smell of gasoline was overpowering. It flowed in dark little streams across the parking area, filling seams in the concrete, forming shallow pools in low spots.

Caine raced past, feet splashing through the gasoline.

Brianna smiled.

The leading wave of the creatures hit the gas station, needle-sharp legs stabbing at tiny rivers of unleaded gas.

The fumes filled the air.

Brianna knew something about speed. She knew that the Hollywood thing where people outrun explosions was nonsense. Not even the Breeze could outrun a fireball.

But there was standing around in the middle of a fire, and then there was blowing through it at the speed of sound. There wouldn't be an explosion, not right away.

It should work. Especially with a little cover.

She hid behind a pump and let the first creature draw level. She wheeled, flicked the lighter, and dodged in front of the bug as it ran by.

Whooooosh!

It wasn't a dynamite explosion. But it was definitely a fireball.

A wave of heat singed her hair and eyebrows. A blast wave of pressure that popped Brianna's ears. But the bug's bulk had shielded her from the worst of it.

The leading creature reached Caine, but he had thrown himself into the air and the fireball, the creature, and Brianna all rocketed past beneath him.

As he fell he flipped the bug over.

Three of the creatures were caught in the fireball. Fire curled their antennae and cracked their brittle shells.

Two of the creatures were far enough back to dodge around the fire but the heat and the smoke had confused them. They moved away but not fast enough.

The fire crept down the pump hose, down to meet the heavy gas vapor in the massive underground tank.

Ka-BOOOM!

Pumps, concrete, shelter, mini-mart, and the creatures exploded in a fireball that made the first blast look like a damp firecracker.

Insect parts, twisted metal, and chunks of concrete rained down.

Only the lead bug was still alive. It lay on its back, kicking in the air.

Brianna sank her knife into its chin, inserted her shotgun, and said, "When you get to hell tell the gaiaphage the Breeze says, 'Hi!'" She pumped two rounds into the creature and its head blew apart like a smashed watermelon.

FORTY-ONE

ORC SMASHED HIS bottle against the blue-eyed bug's head. It did nothing. He hadn't thought it would.

The creature swung its mandibles in a wide sweep and caught Orc in the chest. Orc went flying, facedown on the gravel.

He was winded. Not dead, though.

He got slowly to his feet. Why hurry?

"You want me, come get me," Orc said.

Three of the monsters motored straight for him. Orc threw a wild punch, caught nothing but air, and was face-down again. This time three ropelike tongues had attached to him and he could no longer stand.

Astrid screamed.

"Whatever," he said, as flashing mouthparts closed in on him.

· · ·

Jack had run and bounded along through the night. His goal
was Perdido Beach. But his mission, while clear, was not sitting well with him.

How could Sam have told him to throw Little Pete to the
creatures? It was crazy, wasn't it? Crazy? Anyway, it had to be
wrong, right?

He raced up hills and down. He was not quite tireless, but
he was very strong and reveled in that strength now for the
first time. Jack felt as if he'd been living behind a curtain, not
really seeing what was happening around him.

That had started to change when he found the laptops on
the train. Touching live keys again, seeing a monitor glow . . .
Even though he hadn't had time to do much about it, it was
like magic, like the magic touch.

And then, a very different feeling when he had fought. He
had used his enormous strength and he had saved Sam's life
and Dekka's and Toto's. Him! Of all people: Computer Jack.

He was a hero.

He still didn't look like one—he was no taller or more
muscular than before, he had not turned into some muscle-
bound wrestler type. He was still doughy, nearsighted Jack.
But the strength no longer seemed completely irrelevant
to him.

He could be Computer Jack. But he could be more, too.

And yet, what Sam wanted him to do was to kill Little
Pete? Could that possibly be right?

He had run toward town or what he thought was toward

town. From the top of a hill he had sighted the sparkly water in the distance and figured that town had to be, oh, around there somewhere.

But he finally realized he had become hopelessly lost. He was deep in forest now, and he figured it might be the hills where Hunter lived, but it might just as easily be the Stefano Rey.

Then he heard a cry. A human voice. A girl, he thought, screaming.

Jack froze. He was breathing hard. He strained to hear. But there was no second cry. Not that he heard, anyway.

What was he supposed to do? Sam had told him what to do. He had to warn Edilio. And he had to . . . He could barely even form the thought in his head of what he was supposed to do.

But he couldn't just ignore a scream, could he?

"Go find out," Jack whispered to himself. "Whoever she is maybe she needs help. And maybe she knows where we are."

He did not say but thought: And maybe I won't have to go to town after all.

Jack ran toward the sound, across a deep ravine choked with bushes and up the other side. He found himself on a narrow road cut between tall trees.

"Coates!" he said.

He did not hear another scream, but he did hear sounds like a fistfight.

Suddenly the hero role was seeming less and less attractive.

He moved on at a wary trot. Through the iron gate of the school. And there, a scene out of a horror movie. A stone-fleshed monster buried by a swarm of impossibly huge insects.

Looking down at the scene from a window, Astrid.

And then, his tentacle arm just reaching its full length, Drake.

Yes, Jack decided, the hero thing had some real downsides.

Drake emerged to a world that could hardly be more wonderful.

Orc was going down beneath a crush of bugs.

Astrid was looking down in terror.

And for some reason Drake could not fathom: Computer Jack was standing there, gaping at it all.

Drake grinned up at Astrid. "Don't go anywhere, beautiful, I'll be up in a minute to play. I just have to go say hi to my old friend Jack."

"Jack!" Astrid shouted. "Help Orc!"

Two of the creatures turned eerie blue eyes on Jack.

"What shall we do with you, Computer Jack?" Drake asked.

"I'm not looking for trouble," Jack said.

Drake made a *tsk-tsk* sound and shook his head. "I kind of think trouble is all around you, Jack. Trouble, trouble everywhere." Then he had a thought. He peered closely at Jack. "Where's Sam? Did he send you off on your own? Like a big boy?"

All the while Drake was moving closer, waiting, waiting until he could reach Jack with his whip hand. Jack backed slowly away.

Orc bellowed in pain. The creatures in Drake's army were banging into one another like cars in a demolition derby, all striving to get at the boy-monster.

"You were all bold and dangerous up at the lake, Jack," Drake taunted. Another few feet and he would be within range.

"I just . . ." Then Jack gasped at something he'd seen behind Drake's back.

Drake turned to see and in that split second Jack leaped. Drake whipped around, quick as a snake, but all that did was bring his face into direct contact with a blow of staggering power.

When he picked himself up, Drake saw he'd flown a good twenty feet through the air.

He stood up and rubbed his chin. "That was pretty good, Jack. Wow. That would have killed me. You know, if I could be killed."

Jack tried to dodge past him, rushing for the door, no doubt rushing to rescue the damsel in distress.

Drake laughed and swung his whip arm. He wrapped around Jack's leg and should have tripped him, but he hadn't counted on Jack's strength. Instead of tripping Jack, it was Drake who went flying face-first into the ground.

He released, rolled, and stood up in one swift, fluid move, but it was humiliating.

Drake's whip hand snapped, hit Jack's back, and drew a gasp of pain. But Jack didn't stop; he plowed straight on into the melee of bugs. He grabbed the nearest leg and yanked it hard.

The leg came away. It didn't stop the creature or even seem to affect it, but it gave Jack a weapon.

"Better save Orc fast, there, Jack," Drake taunted. "He looks like he's going down."

Orc's roaring voice was hoarse and fading. The clash of carapace against carapace was louder and more frenzied.

They would kill Orc soon. And then Drake's army would deal with Jack. All he had to do now was keep Jack distracted.

Jack broke the leg into two pieces, one thick and stubby, the other pointed.

Drake snapped his whip and drew blood through Jack's shirt.

"Come on, Jack, you know you can't win," Drake said. "You can't kill me. And you can't stop my army. Only way out is for you to join me."

"No," Jack said.

"My side is the only side now, Jack. There's a whole other bug army eating its way through Perdido Beach right now. Who do you think you're even fighting for? Whatever the red-eyes don't finish, we will when we get there."

"You don't know what's going on in Perdido Beach," Jack said.

"The Darkness tells me," Drake lied. "He gave me power over them. We're cleaning everyone out, Jack. By the end of the day all of them will be dead and gone. Join me and he may let you live."

He snapped his whip with lightning speed and caught Jack unprepared. His whip curled around Jack's throat. Jack hauled on the whip but all that did was to yank Drake straight into Jack. Face-to-face Drake laughed and coiled ever tighter around Jack's throat and squeezed, squeezed, seeing Jack's pale face redden.

Jack punched him in the chest so hard his fist went all the way through. But Drake's grip never loosened and Jack's eyes bulged and Drake laughed and Orc's voice was no longer heard over the sound of mouthparts gnashing.

"Sam, Sam, you swore you wouldn't let them!"

The boat touched the dock and Quinn sent his rowers racing, all shouting Lana's name.

"I have a plan, Dekka," Sam said.

Her body was no longer like anything human. Beneath her clothing it pulsated. The creatures were tearing through in places, mouthparts flashing, mandibles questing. One burst all the way out. It froze for a second, staring at Sam with eyes the color of jade.

He grabbed for it, caught it, and dropped it. But Quinn was quicker. He threw a fishing net over the creature, stepped on the edges of the net, and held it pinned in the bottom of the boat.

"Now!" Dekka begged. "Now, Sam! Now! Oh, God, now!"

A second bug could be clearly seen moving beneath the skin of her thigh, nothing but a thin membrane of flesh covering it.

"I have a plan, Dekka, I have a plan, hang on, hang on," Sam begged.

"Noooo!" It was a pitiful wail of despair.

Sam shot a hopeless glance at the shore. Nothing. No Lana. The crew had all disappeared.

Quinn had grabbed an oar and was smashing it down on the trapped bug like a pile driver, again and again, smashing away, and yet the creature lived.

Suddenly a rush of wind and Brianna stood at the end of the dock, vibrating, covered with gore. "About time you showed up . . ." She fell silent as she realized what was happening to Dekka. "What the—"

"Breeze: Lana. Now! NOW!" Sam cried but the second "now" was said to the air.

"I got to . . . I got to see her again . . . ," Dekka chattered.

"Don't give up on me, Dekka. Don't give up on me."

But Dekka's eyes were rolling wildly, her entire body was in spasm.

"Quinn. What I'm going to do . . . Just hold her down. Hold her down no matter what."

Quinn smashed the bug one last time and if it wasn't dead it was at least not going anywhere. He dropped to his knees and held Dekka's shoulders.

"What are you doing?" Quinn asked.

"Surgery," Sam said dully.

He held up his right hand. The green light, as focused as a laser, sliced through Dekka's clothing and skin.

Brianna found Lana retreating with Sanjit toward the eastern edge of town.

"Lana!"

"You're alive!" Lana said. "The kids?"

"A lot dead," Brianna gasped. "A lot more hurt, but the bugs are done for."

"I'm coming," Lana said and started to trot back toward the plaza.

"Yeah. Wrong way and too slow," Brianna said. "Give me your hand. You can heal yourself later."

Brianna took off, dragging Lana, who instantly tripped. She dragged the Healer the rest of the way down the street, then down the length of the beach.

Dragging her, Brianna couldn't do anything like full speed, but she could move faster than any human runner.

The Healer's legs were scraped raw by the time Brianna yanked her to her feet at the end of the dock.

"Got her!" Brianna announced. Then, "What are you doing?"

Sam's face was a mask of horror. He had sliced Dekka open from neck to pelvis. Dekka's organs—a slaughterhouse mess—crawled with a dozen bugs, all swarming out of her.

Quinn snatched at the bugs and tossed them from the boat into the water. He was elbow-deep in blood.

"Lana, keep her alive," Sam said.

Lana jumped down into the boat, which rocked madly back and forth.

Dekka was beyond speech, past even crying out.

Lana laid her hands on Dekka's contorted face.

Brianna followed her into the boat, landed lightly, and pushed both Quinn and Sam aside. "I got this," she said.

One by one she snatched the emerging creatures—some of which raced to attack Sam, others of which just ran like panicked cockroaches around the bottom of the boat—turned them on their backs, and blew them clear through the bottom of the boat with shotgun blasts.

Quinn tossed a rope over the dock cleat and pulled the sinking boat in. Sam and Quinn shoved and hoisted Dekka onto the dock where she lay split open like a burst orange.

Lana held Dekka's head on her lap.

Sam, Quinn, and some strange-looking guy Brianna thought looked vaguely familiar stood watching, a circle of horrified fascination.

The boat sank. The blasted bodies of the insects floated.

Dekka's mouth was moving but no sound came out. Her eyes were like marbles, rolling, searching without seeing.

"She's trying to say something," Quinn said.

"She should shut up and let me keep her alive," Lana snapped. The Healer shot a malignant look at Brianna. "You owe me a pair of shoes."

Again Dekka tried to speak.

"It's you, Breeze," Sam said. "She wants you."

Brianna frowned, not sure Sam was right. But she knelt beside Dekka and put her ear close.

Brianna listened, closed her eyes for a moment, then stood up without saying anything.

"What did she say?" Quinn asked.

"Just thanks," Brianna said. "She just said thanks."

She turned and took off but not so quickly that she missed the strange new boy saying, "That's not the truth."

FORTY-TWO

3 MINUTES

ASTRID WATCHED, HELPLESS.

She could no longer see Orc. He might already be dead down there.

Jack seemed unable to free himself from Drake's choking grasp. And Drake knew it. He looked up at Astrid and winked.

She had reached the decision not to harm Little Pete, to let him live even if it meant others would die.

The right and moral decision.

But in a minute or less Jack would asphyxiate. And Drake would catch her. She had no illusions about what that psychopath intended.

Drake and his army would kill and go on killing. And what could stop them? Who could stop them?

She found she could hardly breathe.

Her whole body seemed to buzz with some strange energy. Was it fear? Was this what panic felt like?

Jack's face was turning dark. His struggles were less focused. His fingers clawed impotently. His eyes bulged like they might pop out of his head.

Drake was going to kill her. But not quickly.

And he would go on to kill many, many more, for as long as the FAYZ existed.

Enough. It had to end. All of it had to end.

Astrid stepped to Little Pete. She gathered him in her arms. She moved to the window and stood there, hesitating, with his limp, sweating body in her arms.

Drake saw her. The color drained from his face.

His tentacle lessened its grip on Jack's throat.

"No!" Drake cried. He unwound his python arm and began to run toward her, yelling, "No! No!"

"Sorry," Astrid whispered. "I'm so very sorry, Petey."

Drake was at the door to the room. "No!" he cried again as she heaved her brother toward the sea of insects.

"Get him!" Drake cried.

He pushed past Astrid to the window as Little Pete fell.

"Don't hurt—," Drake shouted. His words were cut off by a weak but well-aimed punch from Astrid.

Little Pete almost hit the ground. He stopped inches from impact.

His eyes opened wide. He stared into a dozen eerie blue eyes.

"Don't hurt him!" Drake cried. "The Darkness needs him!"

But it was too late. The bugs surged toward Little Pete. Their tongues snapped. Their mouthparts gnashed.

There was no explosion.

No flash of light.

The bugs simply disappeared.

There. Then gone.

Little Pete sank to the ground. He coughed once, with incredible violence. And then he, too, simply disappeared.

Astrid and Drake stood side by side, both staring down in horror.

Astrid closed her eyes. Was it over? Was it all finally over?

"I'll kill you," Drake said, but his voice was faint.

Astrid opened her eyes and saw his face already changing, melting from the hard-edged shark features to a softer, rounder countenance.

Jack came pounding up the stairs.

Lying on his back with one leg gone, Orc groaned in pain.

"Where is he?" Brittney asked. "Where is Nemesis?"

Astrid barely heard her.

She had done it. She had killed him. She had sacrificed Little Pete.

"Let's get out of here before Drake comes back," Jack said. He took Astrid's arm. But she would not go with him. Not yet.

"You killed him," Brittney said. She spoke more in wonder than in accusation.

Astrid heaved a shuddering sigh. Tears ran down her face. She had no words.

Brittney was becoming angry. "He'll get you for this, Astrid. His rage will find you. Sooner or later."

"Drake or the gaiaphage?" Jack asked.

Brittney bared her braces in a feral grin. "We are the arm of the Darkness. He will send us to take you. Both of you."

"Let's go, Astrid," Jack said, without taking his eyes off Brittney. Astrid felt the strength of his grip on her arm. She yielded.

She was almost blinded by her tears, her mind a confusion of emotions: self-loathing, disgust, anger.

And worst of all: relief.

He was gone. Little Pete was dead. And now it would end at last. The FAYZ wall would be gone. The madness would be over.

Relief. And the sickening realization that she was glad she had done it.

Jack led her down the stairs. He lifted a terribly injured, mangled Orc effortlessly. Orc was moaning in pain and crying that they should leave him to die.

"No one is dying," Jack said harshly. "We've had enough of that."

Astrid walked obediently behind Jack as he carried Orc down the hill toward town.

And she wondered as she walked, how it could be that the FAYZ was ended and yet Jack was still so strong.

Dahra Baidoo emerged from the so-called hospital for the first time in what felt like days.

Virtue held her up, although he was shaking so badly he could barely walk himself.

Both of them were covered in gore. The hospital was a slaughterhouse. The single bug that had made it inside had simply massacred kids too sick to stand, let alone run.

Virtue told himself that most of those kids were too sick to survive anyway. But that knowledge would never wipe the horror from his memory.

He had been wedged into a corner behind a cot, cowering and praying, and begging to be spared. He had thrown things at the bug, but bedpans and bottles were nothing to the monster.

And then, in an instant, the creature was gone.

Its bloody mandibles had been scraping the wall, trying to dislodge Virtue. Inches and milliseconds from gruesome death.

And then . . . nothing.

Gone.

Virtue had heard nothing but the sound of his own sobbing.

And then the sounds of others crying.

And an insistent, mad howl of despair.

Dahra was screaming as he drew her gently from beneath a body.

"It's gone," he'd said.

She couldn't stop shaking. Couldn't stop howling. And Virtue was suddenly back in that refugee camp in the Congo, remembering things he'd witnessed when he was still too young to understand.

A terrible fury boiled up inside him. An uncontrollable

rage against everyone and everything that made the world a hell of fear and pain and loss.

He wanted to smash things. He wanted to bellow like a wild animal.

But Dahra had ceased howling, and now just stared up at him, needing someone, someone to finally take care of her.

Virtue took her hand and put his arm around her shoulder. "We're getting you out of here," he said gently.

There were kids crying out in pain. But Virtue knew that Dahra could no longer respond. So he led her out into the cool, fresh air.

The bodies of the bugs were all gone. The bodies of those they had killed were not.

Virtue didn't know where to take Dahra. After all, she was the one kids took other kids to. He didn't know anyone to help her. Maybe no one could help her.

He led Dahra to the ruined church. It was quiet inside, although it, too, had been a scene of battle. He cleared a space for her in a pew. He sat her down, sat beside her, so weary, and closed his eyes and prayed.

"God in your heaven, look down and take pity on this girl. She has done enough." He sighed and added a doubtful, "Amen."

Virtue did not stay long. There were still kids needing help.

He ran into his brother heading toward the hospital. Sanjit hugged him tight and said, "They're gone, Choo. They're all gone."

Virtue nodded and patted Sanjit's back reassuringly.

Sanjit held him out and looked at his face. "Are you okay, brother?"

"I've had better days," Virtue said.

"So, I guess the island's looking even better now, huh?" Sanjit asked. "You were right, it's one big open-air asylum."

Virtue nodded solemnly and glanced back at the church. "Yeah, but there's a couple of saints mixed in with the crazies."

Caine walked stiffly back to town. He was burned, scraped, punctured, bruised, and might, he thought, have broken a couple of ribs.

But he had won.

The only downside—aside from the various pains that made him wince with every step—was that he hadn't done it alone. Brianna had scored an assist. He couldn't stand her, but man, was she good in a fight.

And some unseen, unknowable force had caused the bugs the two of them had just killed to disappear. Even their broken-off legs, their fluids and guts had disappeared. Like they'd been wiped entirely out of existence.

Brianna had zoomed off to leave him limping all alone. No doubt she was bragging and claiming all the credit.

But it wouldn't work. No, everyone had seen him walking toward the threat. And now the threat was gone, just as he had promised. He had delivered. He had earned his rightful place.

Just as he crossed the highway into town, the first kids

came rushing up to him, grateful, giddy, wanting to slap palms.

"You did it, man! You did it!"

He refused their high fives and stood very still, looking at them, and just waited.

They seemed uncertain, a little worried. And then it dawned on them.

The first one bowed his head. It was a jerky, awkward gesture, but that was okay with Caine: they'd learn.

The second kid, then a third and a fourth, rushing up to join in, bowed their heads to Caine. He nodded in solemn acknowledgment and walked on, no longer feeling nearly so much pain.

THE MORNING AFTER

SAM COULD NOT face the town and the kids there. If he went into town now, there might be a fight with Caine. He couldn't face a fight. Later. Not now. Not yet.

He had seen the sudden and complete disappearance of the bugs. One minute the creatures that had hatched inside Dekka had been floating in the water and the next second they were gone.

He thought he knew what had happened. Only one power was great enough to cause them to cease to exist.

Against all odds, Jack must have succeeded in throwing Little Pete to the bugs. Only Petey could have done it. Sam's desperate, lunatic plan had worked, had actually worked.

But once Astrid knew that he was the one who had ordered Jack to do it, she would never speak to him again.

The town was saved. But Sam was lost.

You ordered the death of a five-year-old autistic boy, Mr. Temple?

The accusing tribunal was back.

That's right, he told them in his imagination. *That's what I did.*

He walked until he found himself at the cliff. The last time he'd been there . . . Well, groping Taylor seemed like a fairly small sin, now.

That's right. And because I did the bugs were destroyed. And lives were saved.

You don't get to make those decisions, Mr. Temple. God decides life or death.

"Yeah?" Sam said aloud. "Well, I don't think much of His decisions."

He stared out at the sea. He was standing just where Mary had stood when she jumped. But he was not tempted to follow her. Mary had been driven to insanity.

"That's right," Sam said to no one. "I did it. And it worked."

"Sam."

He spun on his heel. Astrid stood there. Jack was a hundred feet back and showing no desire to come any closer.

"Astrid."

Her eyes were red and swollen. She was looking past him, staring at the barrier with an expression he couldn't read.

"It's still there," she said.

He glanced at the impervious wall. "Yeah."

"But . . . but Petey's dead," she said. "It should have stopped. It shouldn't be there. It should all be over."

"I'm sorry about Little Pete."

"It's still there."

"I guess—," he began.

"For nothing! I killed him for nothing!" Astrid cried. "Oh, God, no! I did it for nothing!"

"You? You didn't . . ." But then he saw the look in Jack's eyes. Jack nodded, then looked down at the ground.

Instinctively he moved to Astrid, to put his arms around her. But something stopped him. He knew she wouldn't welcome it.

It struck him then with the force of a revelation that she could not be with him while she felt weak or out of control. Astrid needed to be strong. She needed to be . . . Astrid.

And right now? She wasn't. He had never seen her look so lost. He would have so happily taken her in his arms. But she wouldn't have him. Not like this.

"Astrid . . ."

"For nothing," she whispered.

He stepped back. "Astrid, listen: I had told Jack to do it. It was the only way. If you hadn't . . ."

But she wasn't listening. A look of pure hatred, a look he'd never have thought she was capable of, transformed her face. Was it for him? For the barrier?

For herself?

"I left, you know. I left town with Orc. And then I left Petey. I just walked out the door at Coates. I abandoned him. Him and Orc. Both of them needed me. But I walked away because I thought, 'If I stay, I'll be tempted.' A simple act of murder. You know how a phrase will get stuck in your head and go around and around?"

He didn't answer. She didn't want him to answer. But yes, he knew.

"I knew if I killed Petey, it would all end," she said. "And then, you know what? I walked around out there in the dark, just around in a big circle. And I talked myself out of it. See, I made sense of it all in my mind. Because I'm very, very smart."

She laughed bitterly at that.

"Who is smarter than me? Astrid the Genius. I worked it all out and I made all the right arguments. And I prayed. And I came to a good and moral decision. And then? When I was there, and Drake . . . and I thought about Drake . . . when I thought . . ." She couldn't go on.

"Astrid, we've all had to do—"

"Don't," she said. "No. Don't."

"Look, come with me," he said. He reached for her, but he could feel a cold and impenetrable wall around her. She was somewhere else now. She was someone else. His hands dropped back to his side.

"How you must laugh at me with all my arrogance and superiority," Astrid said quietly. "I wonder how you could stand me. Don't you want to say, 'I told you so,' Sam? How can you not? If I were you, I'd say, 'See? See, you silly, sanctimonious idiot? Welcome to Sam's world. This is what I do, these are the decisions I make.'"

Yes. A part of him wanted to say that. A part of him wanted to say those very words. *Welcome to my world. It's not so easy being Sam, is it?* He tried not to let that emotion show on his face, but it must have because Astrid nodded slightly as if he'd spoken.

He said all he could think of to say. "I love you, Astrid. No matter what, I love you."

But if she heard him, she gave no sign. Astrid turned and walked away.

FIVE DAYS LATER |

IT HAD BEEN a long time since so many kids filled the plaza. Not everyone had come, but most had. Looking down from the town hall steps, Sam saw faces that were fearful, others that were happy, and of course, as with any group of kids, some were just playing.

It was a good thing, he told himself, this ability to find some little piece of joy to hold on to.

The graveyard had swollen terribly. But the flu had burned itself out at last. There had been no new cases for forty-eight hours. No one was celebrating, no one was relaxing, but the deadly flu seemed to have run its course at last.

He stole a glance at his brother. Caine looked confident, certainly more confident than Sam felt. Caine wore the look of a self-appointed king well, Sam thought gloomily. He was perfectly dressed in gray slacks and a navy blazer over a pale blue collared shirt. How had he managed it?

The rest of his "court" were nowhere near as well

turned-out, but were nevertheless better looking than Sam or his crew.

Diana, Penny, Turk, and Taylor all stood behind Caine.

Sam was with Dekka, but no longer the seemingly fearless, intimidating Dekka he had always known. She was weak in body, still recovering, and weaker still in spirit.

Brianna wasn't standing so much as vibrating in place, unable to keep entirely still. She looked distracted and angry and was definitely refusing to make eye contact with Dekka.

Jack was the surprise to Sam, that he would bother to dress neatly and remember to show up. Jack was growing, had grown, as a person.

Edilio sat in a lawn chair. He looked like he was still close to death's door, but the cough was gone, his fever was down, and he was determined.

The most notable absence was Astrid. She should have been there. He scanned the crowd for any sign of her. But no one had seen her. The gossips said she'd moved into a small apartment at the edge of town. Others said they'd seen her walking down the highway toward the Stefano Rey.

Sam had hoped she would appear today for the Big Break-Up, as Howard had dubbed this strange ceremony. But she was nowhere to be seen. And Sam's friends now carefully avoided mentioning her name.

Toto stood awkwardly, self-conscious, twitchy, between the two separate camps.

"I think everyone is here," Caine announced.

"He doesn't believe that," Toto said.

Caine smiled indulgently. "I think everyone is here that is likely to come," Caine corrected.

"True," Toto said.

"Yeah," Sam said. His mouth was dry. He was nervous. He shouldn't care. This shouldn't matter. It wasn't as if he'd ever wanted to be a leader, let alone a popular one.

Caine held up his hand, signaling it was time for everyone to quiet down.

"You all know why we're here," Caine said in his fine, strong voice. "Sam and I both want peace—"

"Not true," Toto said.

Caine's eyes flashed angrily. But he forced a smile. "Toto, for those of you who don't know, is a freak with the power to tell truth from lie."

"True," Toto said.

"So. Okay. Let me start over," Caine said. "Sam and I don't like each other. My people don't like his people, and his people feel the same way about us." He paused to look at Toto.

Toto nodded and said, "He believes this."

"Yes, I do," Caine said dryly. "We have different visions for the future. Sam here wants to move everyone to this lake of his. I want to stay here in Perdido Beach."

The crowd was very quiet. Sam was both irritated and relieved that Caine was doing all the talking.

"Sam and I also have different ideas about leadership. Sam thinks it's a burden. Me? I think it's an opportunity."

"He . . . he believes that," Toto said. But he was frowning, perhaps sensing something about Caine that was neither true nor false.

"Today, each of you will make a decision," Caine said. "To go with Sam, or to stay here. I won't try to stop anyone, and I won't hold it against anyone." He placed his hand over his heart. "For those who choose to stay, let me be very clear: I will be in charge. Not as a mayor, but as a king. My word will be law. My decisions will be final."

That caused some murmuring, most of it unhappy.

"But I'll also do everything I can to leave each of you alone. Quinn, if he chooses to stay, can still fish. Albert, if he chooses to stay, will still run his business. Freaks and normals will be treated equally."

He seemed about to add something else but caught himself after a sidelong look at Toto.

The silence lengthened and Sam knew it was time for him to speak. In the past he'd always had Astrid at his side for things like this. He was not much of a speaker. And in any case, he didn't have much to say.

"Anyone who goes with me has a vote in how we do stuff. I guess I'll be more or less in charge, but we'll probably choose some other people, create a council like . . . Well, hopefully better than we had before. And, um . . ." He was tempted to laugh at his own pitiful performance. "Look, people, if you want someone, some . . . king, good grief, to tell you what to do, stay here. If you want to make more of your own decisions, well, come with me."

He hadn't said enough to even cause Toto to comment.

"You know which side I'm on, people," Brianna yelled. "Sam's been carrying the load since day one."

"It was Caine that saved us," a voice cried out. "Where was Sam?"

The crowd seemed undecided. Caine was beaming confidence, but Sam noticed that his jaw clenched, his smile was forced, and he was worried.

"What's Albert going to do?" a boy named Jim demanded. "Where's Albert?"

Albert stepped from an inconspicuous position off to one side. He mounted the steps, moving carefully still, not entirely well even now.

He carefully chose a position equidistant between Caine and Sam.

"What should we do, Albert?" a voice asked plaintively.

Albert didn't look out at the crowd except for a quick glance up, like he was just making sure he was pointed in the right direction. He spoke in a quiet, reasonable monotone. Kids edged closer to hear.

"I'm a businessman."

"True." Toto.

"My job is organizing kids to work, taking the things they harvest or catch, and redistributing them through a market."

"And getting the best stuff for yourself," someone yelled to general laughter.

"Yes," Albert acknowledged. "I reward myself for the work I do."

This blunt admission left the crowd nonplussed.

"Caine has promised that if I stay here he won't interfere. But I don't trust Caine."

"No, he doesn't," Toto agreed.

"I do trust Sam. But . . ."

And now you could hear a pin drop.

"But . . . Sam is a weak leader." He kept his eyes down. "Sam is the best fighter ever. He's defended us many times. And he's the best at figuring out how to survive. But Sam"—Albert now turned to him—"You are too humble. Too willing to step aside. When Astrid and the council sidelined you, you put up with it. I was part of that myself. But you let us push you aside and the council turned out to be useless."

Sam stood stock-still, stone-faced.

"Let's face it, you're not really the reason things are better here, I am," Albert said. "You're way, way braver than me, Sam. And if it's a battle, you rule. But you can't organize or plan ahead and you won't just put your foot down and make things happen."

Sam nodded slightly. It was hard to hear. But far harder was seeing the way the crowd was nodding, agreeing. It was the truth. The fact was he'd let the council run things, stepped aside, and then sat around feeling sorry for himself. He'd jumped at the chance to go off on an adventure and he hadn't been here to save the town when they needed it.

"So," Albert concluded, "I'm keeping my things here, in Perdido Beach. But there will be free trading of stuff between Perdido Beach and the lake. And Lana has to be allowed to move freely."

Caine bristled at that. He didn't like Albert laying down conditions.

Albert wasn't intimidated. "I feed these kids," he said to Caine. "I do it my way."

Caine hesitated, then made a tight little bow of the head.

"I want you to say it," Albert said with a nod toward Toto.

Sam saw panic in Caine's eyes. If he lied now the jig would be up for him. Toto would call him out, Albert would support Sam, and the kids would follow Albert's lead.

Sam wondered if Caine was just starting to realize what Sam had known for some time: if anyone was king, it was neither Sam nor Caine, it was Albert.

It took Caine a long time to answer. His smile faded as understanding dawned on him. He could only tell the truth. Which meant believing it.

Accepting it.

In a deflated voice very unlike his lordly swagger earlier, Caine said, "Yeah. Albert decides anything about money or work or trade back and forth between Perdido Beach and the lake. And the Healer goes wherever the Healer wants to go."

Sam had to resist an urge to laugh out loud. After all that had happened between him and Caine, after all Caine's posturing today, it wasn't big, charming, handsome, and very powerful Caine, or Sam either, who ran the FAYZ. It was a reserved, skinny black kid whose only power was the ability to work hard and stay focused.

Caine's big moment, his great triumphant return, had been tarnished.

"Okay," Sam said. "I'm going to Ralph's. Anyone coming with me, head over there. I'll wait two hours. Bring bottled water and whatever food you have. It's a long walk to the lake."

He walked down the steps, turned away without looking back, and walked toward the highway. He had the strangest feeling that he was walking alone.

At the highway he paused. Brianna was there, of course. Dekka, too, and Jack. Jack carried Edilio like a baby—a very large baby.

In addition there were forty or fifty others who had picked up and left their homes to follow him.

Quinn came forward and Sam pulled him aside. His old friend looked tortured and sad.

"What's up, brah?" Sam asked.

Quinn couldn't speak. He was choked with emotion. "Dude . . ."

"You want to stay in town."

"My crews . . . my boats and all . . ."

Sam put a hand on his shoulder. "Quinn, I'm glad you found something so important to do. Something you really like."

"Yeah, but . . ."

Sam pulled him into a brief hug. "You and me, we're still friends, man. But you have responsibilities."

Quinn nodded miserably.

Sam scanned the crowd again, searching for Astrid. She was not there.

It wasn't far to Ralph's parking lot. Sam sagged against a parked car. Some of the kids came up to offer statements of support or encouragement. But most came up to say things like, "You really have Nutella?" Or "Can I live on a boat? That would be so cool."

They were coming for Nutella and noodles, not for him.

He felt numb. Like everything that was happening was happening to someone else. He pictured himself at the lake, on a houseboat. Dekka would be there, and Brianna and Jack. He would have friends. He wouldn't be alone.

But he couldn't stop himself from looking for her.

She no longer had Little Pete to worry about. They could be together without all of that. But of course he knew Astrid, and knew that right now, wherever she was, she was eaten up inside with guilt.

"She's not coming, is she?" Sam said to Dekka.

But Dekka didn't answer. She was somewhere else in her head. Sam saw her glance and look away as Brianna laid a light hand on Jack's shoulder.

Dahra was staying in the hospital, but a few more kids came. Groups of three or four at a time. The Siren and the kids she lived with came. John Terrafino came. Ellen. He waited. He would wait the full two hours. Not for her, he told himself, just to keep his word.

Then Orc, with Howard.

Sam groaned inwardly.

"You gotta be kidding me," Brianna said.

"The deal was kids make a choice," Sam said. "I think

Howard just realized how dangerous life can be for a criminal living in a place where the 'king' can decide life or death."

To Sam's relief, Howard did not come over to talk to him. Orc and he sat in the back of a pickup truck. Other kids gave them a wide berth.

"It's time," Jack said.

"Breeze? Count the kids," Sam said.

Brianna was back in twenty seconds. "Eighty-two, boss."

"About a third," Jack observed. "A third of what's left."

"Wait. Make that eighty-eight," Brianna said. "And a dog."

Lana, looking deeply irritated—a fairly usual expression for her—and Sanjit, looking happy—a fairly usual expression for him—and Sanjit's siblings were trotting along to catch up.

"I don't know if we're staying up there or not," Lana said without preamble. "I want to check it out. And my room smells like crap."

Just before the time was up, Sam heard a stir. Kids were making a lane for someone, murmuring. His heart leaped.

"Hey, Sam."

He swallowed the lump in his throat. "Diana?"

"Not expecting me, huh?" She made a wry face. "Where's blondie? I didn't see her at the big pep rally."

"Are you coming with us?" Brianna demanded, obviously not happy about it.

"Is Caine okay with this?" Sam asked Diana. "It's your choice, but I need to know if he's going to come after us to take you back."

"Caine has what he wants," Diana said.

"Maybe I should call Toto over," Sam said. The truth teller was having a conversation with Spidey. "I could ask you whether you're coming along to spy for Caine, and see what Toto has to say."

Diana sighed. "Sam, I have bigger problems than Caine. And so do you, I guess. Because the FAYZ is going to do something it's never done before: grow by one."

"What's that mean?"

"You are going to be an uncle."

Sam stared blankly. Brianna said a very rude word. And even Dekka looked up.

"You're having a baby?" Dekka asked.

"Let's hope so," Diana said bleakly. "Let's hope that's all it is."

PETE

HE WALKED ON the edge of a sheet of glass a million miles high.

On one side, far, far below him, the jangly noises and eye-searing colors were dimmed. He saw his sister's yellow hair and piercing blue eyes, but now he was too far away for them to hurt him.

He saw the echoes of the lurid, bright-eyed monsters who had tried to eat him. They were ghosts sinking lazily down toward the greenish glow far, far below.

They had reached for him with stinging tongues and slicing mouths. So he had made them disappear.

The pain in his body was gone. He was cool and light and amazingly limber. He turned a cartwheel along the edge of the glass and laughed.

His body, full of heat and aching and coughs like volcanoes, had gone away, too. Just like the bugs.

No body, no pain.

Little Pete smiled down at the Darkness. It did not try to touch him now. It shrank away.

It was afraid.

Afraid of him.

Little Pete felt as if a giant weight had been lifted off his shoulders. All of it, the too-bright colors and the too-penetrating eyes, and the misty tendrils that reached for his mind, all of it was so very far off.

Now Little Pete floated up and away from the sheet of glass. He no longer needed to teeter precariously there. He could go anywhere. He was free of the sister and free of the Darkness. He was free at last from the disease-wracked body. And he was free, too, from the tortured, twisted, stunted brain that had made the world so painful to him.

For the first time Little Pete saw the world without cringing or needing to run away. It was as if he'd been watching the world through a veil, through milky glass, and now saw it all clearly for the first time in his brief existence.

His whole life he had needed to hide. And now he gasped at the thrill of seeing and hearing and feeling.

His sick body was gone. His distorting, terrifying brain was gone.

But Pete Ellison had never been more alive.

Additional Praise for *Lenin's Brother*

"In this deeply researched biography, Pomper turns his talents and experience as an historian of the Russian revolutionary intelligentsia to Alexander Ulyanov, who has long deserved a study of this distinction."

—Norman M. Naimark,
ROBERT AND FLORENCE MCDONNELL PROFESSOR
OF EAST EUROPEAN STUDIES, STANFORD UNIVERSITY

"A fascinating read. Philip Pomper is a brilliant psychoanalytic historian, and *Lenin's Brother* is an important contribution to our understanding of the Russian revolution."   —Anna Geifman,
PROFESSOR OF HISTORY, BOSTON UNIVERSITY

"This absorbing narrative illuminates the psychological motivations for terrorism and illustrates how universal these patterns are. The idea of sacrificing one's life in taking the life of others inspired Russian revolutionaries a hundred years before 'suicide terrorism' grabbed the world's attention. The story is also skillfully situated in its historical context: the terrorist at the center of the hapless plot to assassinate the tsar was the older brother of Lenin."   —Martha Crenshaw,
SENIOR FELLOW, CENTER FOR INTERNATIONAL
SECURITY AND COOPERATION, STANFORD UNIVERSITY

"A definitive account of the attempt to kill Alexander III, a conspiracy that included Lenin's older brother. Pomper shows how his brother's execution by tsarist hangmen ultimately precipitated Lenin's revenge—the destruction of the Old Regime and the murder of its imperial family."

—Robert C. Williams,
VAIL PROFESSOR OF HISTORY EMERITUS,
DAVIDSON COLLEGE

ALEXANDER ULYANOV

LENIN'S BROTHER

The Origins of the October Revolution

PHILIP POMPER

W. W. NORTON & COMPANY

NEW YORK · LONDON

FOR INFORMATION ABOUT PERMISSION TO REPRODUCE SELECTIONS FROM THIS BOOK,
WRITE TO PERMISSIONS, W. W. NORTON & COMPANY, INC.,
500 FIFTH AVENUE, NEW YORK, NY 10110

FOR INFORMATION ABOUT SPECIAL DISCOUNTS FOR BULK PURCHASES, PLEASE CONTACT
W. W. NORTON SPECIAL SALES AT SPECIALSALES@WWNORTON.COM OR 800-233-4830

MANUFACTURING BY RR DONNELLEY, HARRISONBURG, VA
BOOK DESIGN BY IRIS WEINSTEIN
PRODUCTION MANAGER: ANDREW MARASIA

LIBRARY OF CONGRESS CATALOGING-IN-PUBLICATION DATA

POMPER, PHILIP.
LENIN'S BROTHER : THE ORIGINS OF THE OCTOBER REVOLUTION /
PHILIP POMPER. — 1ST ED.
P. CM.
INCLUDES BIBLIOGRAPHICAL REFERENCES AND INDEX.
ISBN 978-0-393-07079-8 (HARDCOVER)
1. ULYANOV, ALEKSANDR, 1866–1887. 2. ULYANOV, ALEKSANDR,
1866–1887—INFLUENCE. 3. LENIN, VLADIMIR ILYICH, 1870–1924—FAMILY.
4. REVOLUTIONARIES—RUSSIA—BIOGRAPHY. 5. BROTHERS—RUSSIA—BIOGRAPHY.
6. LENIN, VLADIMIR ILYICH, 1870–1924—POLITICAL AND SOCIAL VIEWS. 7. SOVIET
UNION—HISTORY—REVOLUTION, 1917–1921—CAUSES. I. TITLE.
DK236.U4P66 2010
947.084'1092—DC22
[B]

2009027390

W. W. NORTON & COMPANY, INC.
500 FIFTH AVENUE, NEW YORK, N.Y. 10110
WWW.WWNORTON.COM

W. W. NORTON & COMPANY LTD.
CASTLE HOUSE, 75/76 WELLS STREET, LONDON W1T 3QT

1 2 3 4 5 6 7 8 9 0

Ambivalence, I think, is the chief characteristic of my nation. There isn't a Russian executioner who isn't scared of turning victim one day, nor is there the sorriest victim who would not acknowledge (if only to himself) a mental ability to become an executioner.

JOSEPH BRODSKY

CONTENTS

LIST OF ILLUSTRATIONS

Frontispiece   Alexander Ulyanov

Plates follow pages 100 and 164.

ACKNOWLEDGMENTS

Every work of history requires institutional support and the expert help of many people. I am grateful to Wesleyan University, whose administrators, trustees, and fellow faculty members supported the research and writing of this book with more than one sabbatical. Colleagues—specialists in the Russian area and in other disciplines—allowed me to present my ideas in several forums and gave helpful feedback. I would also like to thank the Connecticut Academy of Arts and Sciences for inviting me to present the story of Alexander Ulyanov to its distinguished members. A multitude of archivists and librarians in Moscow, New York, Washington, and Middletown, Connecticut, provided me with the requisite documents, microfilms, and published books and articles. I am especially grateful to Jim Billington, Librarian of Congress and fellow worker in the vineyard of Russian history, and his staff in the European Reading Room of the Library of Congress. Ed Kasinec, Curator of the Slavic and Baltic Division of the New York Public Library and his staff were very helpful and attentive to me and my project. The librarians in the Interlibrary Loan

Office at Wesleyan gave prompt and vigilant service. I also used
Harvard University and Columbia University libraries on numerous occasions. In Moscow I drew on the unmatched resources of
the Russian State Library in 2004 and 2006 and relied heavily on
the expert services of the archivists at the State Archive of the
Russian Federation (GARF) and the Russian State Archive of
Socio-Political History (RGASPI).

I'd like to thank Jeff Gerecke, my agent, for shepherding the project. For the production of the book I owe a great deal to the expert
help of my colleague Julie Perkins, whose mastery of the *Chicago
Manual of Style* and excellent eye and ear allowed me to pass on
to Maria Guarnaschelli, my editor at Norton, a text whose defi-
ciencies could be remedied mainly by her prodding me into doing
a better job at setting the scene and giving readers the information
they needed to feel comfortable in nineteenth-century Russia. I
am very grateful to the editors at Norton and Maria's assistant,
Melanie Tortoroli, for their care, advice, and meticulous work with
the manuscript. Thanks to Kevin Wiliarty, Academic Technology
Coordinator in Wesleyan's Information Technology Services, for
advice about technical aspects of the project and John Wareham,
Scientific Photographer in Wesleyan's Scientific Support Services,
for his skillful work with the maps and photos that appear in this
volume.

Along the way a number of friends succored the traveling
researcher and made his life tolerable. My valued colleague and
friend Priscilla Meyer long ago introduced me to her wonderful
circle of friends, and the ties still hold. In Moscow in 2004 Irka
and Vika gave freely of their hospitality and wisdom. I'm especially grateful to Alisa Grishaeva, friend of over thirty years.
This book is dedicated to her late husband, Igor, whose kind-
ness and wisdom I'll never forget. Thanks, too, to the younger
generation, Liya and Brenno, for making my last research trip
to Moscow so pleasant. On this side of the Atlantic, my son,
Steve Pomper, and daughter, Karen Manning, and their spouses,

Elizabeth Andersen and John Manning, generously allowed me to invade their homes in Washington, D.C., and Newton, Massachusetts, on research trips.

I am especially grateful to Linda, whose love, companionship and support, and understanding from her own experience of what research and writing entails, helped in ways too numerous to tell.

NOTE ON TRANSLITERATION
AND RUSSIAN DATES

In order to keep things as simple as possible, I use the most familiar transliteration for well-known Russian persons and place-names. Generally, I use the system of transliteration of the U.S. Board on Geographic Names. Any deviations are made with two goals: to present either the most familiar transliteration or the one that best conveys the phoneme. On the other hand, I switch to the Library of Congress system favored by scholars for references in the endnotes and bibliography. The goal here is to follow scholarly practice.

I use the Russian Julian calendar for the historical actions described in the text. The Julian calendar lagged behind the Gregorian calendar by twelve days during Alexander Ulyanov's lifetime. The dates of U.S. newspapers cited in chapter 8 are thus twelve days ahead of the corresponding Russian dates. Dates for the early twenty-first century in chapter 9 are given according to the Gregorian calendar. Lenin's revolutionary regime quickly switched to the Gregorian calendar in February 1918.

MAIN CHARACTERS

The Christian names in this list have been converted when possible for an Anglophone readership and with patronymics removed. Patronymics are sometimes used in the text. Neither all members of the Ulyanov family nor of the conspiracy appear here.

THE FAMILY

Alexander Ulyanov, familiarly "Sasha" (1866–1887): a brilliant zoologist at St. Petersburg University, who became a terrorist and was hanged for his role in an attempt on the life of Tsar Alexander III in 1887.

Vladimir Ulyanov, familiarly "Volodya" (1870–1924): the founder of Bolshevism and leader of the October Revolution, whose relationship to his older brother precipitated his revolutionary career.

Anna Ulyanova (1864–1935): the eldest child in the Ulyanov family, whose memoirs and historical efforts provide the best material for understanding Alexander, Vladimir, and family dynamics.

Maria Ulyanova (1835–1916): the mother of the family, whose pedagogy, child-rearing methods, and personality played a major role in the family dynamics.

Ilya Ulyanov (1831–1886): the father, a scientist, educator, and high-ranking official, whose sudden death played an important role in the psychological changes leading to Alexander's turn to terrorism.

THE TERRORIST CORE GROUP

Peter Shevyrev (1863–1887): a biology student at St. Petersburg University and the primary organizer of the Second March First conspiracy, who was hanged in 1887.

Josef Lukashevich (1863–1928): a brilliant chemist, a student at St. Petersburg University, a founder of the Second March First conspiracy, who evaded the noose in 1887 and lived to become a professor of geology in Vilnius after his release from prison.

Vasilii Osipanov (1861–1887): a suicidal assassin, student at St. Petersburg University, the lead bomb thrower in the combat squad, and founding member of the Second March First conspiracy, who was hanged in 1887.

Pakhomii Andreyushkin (1865–1887): the most reckless member of the core group of the Second March First, a student at St. Petersburg University, whose indiscreet letter tipped off the security police before the assassination attempt; he was hanged in 1887.

Vasilii Generalov (1867–1887): a student at St. Petersburg University, the youngest member of the core group of the Second March First, a suicidal bomb thrower who was hanged in 1887.

Orest Govorukhin (1864–?): Alexander Ulyanov's preceptor in his turn to terror, who joined the Second March First with Ulyanov, but fled abroad shortly before the assassination attempt and became a Marxist.

Raisa Shmidova (1864–1942): a close collaborator, who helped Govorukhin and Ulyanov store explosives and developed a strong personal relationship with Ulyanov, and was exiled to Siberia for her role.

PREFACE

I INITIALLY UNDERTOOK this biography of Alexander Ulyanov in order to probe more deeply the psychological undercur-
rents of a family that produced the most important revolutionary
of the twentieth century, Alexander's young brother, Vladimir
Ilyich Ulyanov. In a book about the psychological triangle of
Lenin, Trotsky, and Stalin that I wrote before the collapse of the
Soviet Union, I began this project without the benefit of access to
the Ulyanov family archives. The archival research that I did in
the post-Soviet period did not change all of the conclusions about
Lenin that I reached in that earlier book, but it did inspire me to tell
another story as well: that not just of the Ulyanov family but of the
terrorist conspiracy that Alexander joined in 1886. A small group
of students at St. Petersburg University called themselves the "Terrorist Faction of the People's Will" and planned to kill Alexander
III on March 1, 1887, the sixth anniversary of his father's assassination by the People's Will. They thus appear in history texts as the
"Second March First."

All students of Russian revolutionary history know about the

People's Will and the assassination of Alexander II on March 1, 1881. That event changed the course of Russian history, though not in the direction wished for by the terrorists. Instead of reform they got reaction, yet the achievement of assassinating a tsar gave them an aura of the heroic. Their imitators, the Second March First, failed in every sense. Their quarry eluded them. The leaders, among them Alexander Ulyanov, were hanged in May 1887, and if his younger brother hadn't become Lenin, Alexander would have been just another casualty in the long history of Russian revolutionary martyrs. One even wonders about Alexander's sacrifice for the cause. After all, what did the causal chain of revolutionary action produce?

There is a remarkable consensus among historians that without Lenin the October Revolution of 1917 would not have occurred, so telling the story of the process that brought Vladimir Ilyich Ulyanov into the orbit of revolutionary Russia is well worth the effort. Lenin, however, did not have the same aims as Sasha. Alexander was a *narodnik*. He believed that the great mass of peasants, once enlightened, would bring socialism to Russia. Although Alexander incorporated some Marxian ideas into his worldview and program, they were only one element. Sasha was not dogmatic and would surely have evolved in his thinking if he had not been hanged at the age of twenty-one. Lenin differed dramatically from his brother. Alexander was willing to kill others and to give his own life for these ideals of the nineteenth-century intelligentsia, but his brother had a different agenda. Sasha's failure as well as his commitments affected Lenin's thinking. The amateurism of the conspiracy and the terrible price the reckless young conspirators paid for failure undoubtedly influenced Lenin's approach—his revolutionary professionalism. The story of how Lenin became a dogmatic Marxist and successful revolutionary leader is, however, too complex a story to be told here. Sasha's story and that of his co-conspirators is a different matter.

To my surprise (I hadn't suspected that the sources were adequate), I found myself deeply involved not only with the Ulyanov
family but with the psychodynamics of a small group of university
students who became terrorists. The more suicidal members propelled the terrorist project forward and pushed Ulyanov beyond a
point of no return. Very different people, from reckless and intellectually shallow ones to the ascetically studious Sasha Ulyanov,
arrived at the same conclusion: that they had to sacrifice their lives
for a larger cause. For today's terrorists, a great variety of causes
justify terrorism; for Ulyanov and his group, "scientific" theory justified their self-sacrifice and the sacrifice of others' lives. Terrorism
takes many guises and attracts many different kinds of people. The
story I tell is as much about terrorism as about how Sasha Ulyanov,
a shy, dutiful young man, at first immersed in his scientific work,
became the theorist of a terrorist conspiracy and then, by default,
the leader of the group.

Several Soviet historians did undertake to write the story of
Alexander Ulyanov and the Second March First. They could not,
however, avoid the sort of distortions that affected the work of
the generations of scholars coerced by Stalinism and the cult of
Lenin. Serious students of Russian revolutionary history got the
basic story of the terrorist conspiracy right, but their ideological
equipment and historical environment did not allow them to mine
some of the veins that contemporary historians find interesting: the
psychodynamics of terrorist groups, for example. Groups as small
as the Second March First and as ephemeral—a handful of students launched the project in December 1886 and most of the core
members were arrested on March 1, 1887—nonetheless provide
rich material for understanding contemporary events. The story of
the Second March First shows dramatically that suicide terrorism
emerges from "scientific" ideas as easily as from fervent religious
belief. It shows that the urge to self-sacrifice and the willingness
to sacrifice others propel a great many people who do not share

any distinct psychological profile or ideology; and it also shows that such impulses are fundamental; that they are nourished and generally find expression in groups; and that the more we understand them, the more likely we are to understand a multitude of human tragedies.

LENIN'S BROTHER

Endings and Beginnings

ENDINGS

THE MATERIAL OBJECTS that supported the brief prison life of Alexander Ulyanov added up to a few kilos of cloth, paper, pottery, glass, and metal. He had a hat, an overcoat, a frock coat, trousers, a towel, handkerchiefs, a mug, a glass, two teapots, two teaspoons, a few books—little more than that. The ascetic Ulyanov did possess one uncharacteristically flamboyant item, a Scottish plaid woolen cloak—his concession to the dress code of the radical students at St. Petersburg University. The commandant of the Peter and Paul Fortress, Adjutant General I. S. Ganetskii, pedantically noted every item that fell under his purview and passed through his jail. As they departed, the prisoners had to verify the inventories of their worldly goods and sign the lists prepared by their jailers. Other than Ganetskii's terse notations, only Sasha Ulyanov's prison depositions, a few letters, a handful of memoirs of survivors of the conspiracy, and the stenographic account of the trial give us the story of his last weeks.

Seven prisoners, including Ulyanov, in the early hours of May 5, 1887, were roused from sleep and taken in chains to the fortress's dock. The prisoners, their military guards, and a hangman with the tools of his trade boarded three small steamboats that carried them from the island prison at the mouth of the Neva to another one in

Schlüsselburg Fortress, located about forty kilometers to the east at the Neva's source, Lake Ladoga. Only two of the prisoners, Josef Lukashevich and Michael Novorussky, lived to tell the story of the voyage. Their sentences had been commuted to lifelong penal servitude, but they were amnestied during the Revolution of 1905 after eighteen years in Schlüsselburg.

The absence of a permanent gallows in Schlüsselburg and the construction of a new one apparently delayed the execution for three days. The transfer and then the delay stimulated false hopes in the remaining prisoners, who believed that the tsar had commuted their sentences; however, at 3:30 a.m. on May 8 they were told that they would be executed in half an hour. The newly erected scaffold had room for only three, so two of the prisoners, Ulyanov and Peter Shevyrev, had to wait their turn. Had the tsar entertained an eleventh-hour commutation of the death sentence to life imprisonment for them? Other political prisoners had enjoyed last-minute reprieves. Dostoevsky had gotten one from Nicholas I in 1849 while standing before a firing squad. If Alexander III had played with the idea of saving Ulyanov and Shevyrev, nothing came of it and no record survives. Dmitry Tolstoy, minister of the interior, a witness at the execution, claimed in his report to Alexander III that Ulyanov and Shevyrev waited inside while the three who preceded them expired and were taken from the gallows in the prison courtyard; but a contradictory rumor circulated that Ulyanov and Shevyrev had watched at the foot of the gallows for half an hour while their hooded comrades writhed in the agony of strangulation. If the latter version is true, then incompetence rather than sadism probably produced the situation.

Of the five Decembrists who were hanged in 1826 for plotting to change the autocratic regime, three tumbled into the pit beneath the scaffold when the ropes broke. They waited in pain until the scaffold and new nooses were readied for a second, successful try. One of the waiting condemned men was reported to say, "Poor

Russia. She doesn't even know how to hang people properly." Even if the story is apocryphal, it is apt. The executioner of five members of the People's Will involved in the assassination of Alexander II, on April 2, 1881, botched the hanging of Timofei Mikhailov and Andrei Zhelyabov. Mikhailov fell to the platform twice when the noose slipped. To prevent repetition of the accident with Zhelyabov, the hangman tied a double knot, thus delaying strangulation. Because of the hangman's incompetence, both Mikhailov and Zhelyabov struggled for several minutes before they expired.

Dmitry Tolstoy reported on May 8, 1887, that the three designated bomb throwers listened to the sentence, said goodbye to one another, kissed the cross proffered by a priest, and boldly mounted the scaffold. Vasilii Generalov and Pakhomii Andreyushkin shouted, "Long live the People's Will!" Vasilii Osipanov wished to do the same, but the hangman put a sack over his head and muffled his words. After the three bodies had been taken down, Shevyrev and Ulyanov with firm strides mounted the scaffold. Shevyrev did not accept the priest's offer to kiss the cross, but Ulyanov did. Oddly enough, the chief of the corps of gendarmes present at the hanging reported, to the contrary, that all five rejected the cross.[1]

The three men who were hanged first—Andreyushkin, Generalov, and Osipanov—had volunteered to hurl bombs under the tsar's carriage. This was, in effect, a suicide mission, in that the explosive radius of the bombs and their poisoned shrapnel were very likely to kill the throwers as well as their target. They had carried three bombs of different size and explosive force. The two larger bombs were packaged in an elliptical shell: thick cardboard covered in black cloth concealing tin-plate cylinders packed with five and four pounds of dynamite each. The smaller bomb had three pounds of dynamite in a tin box, hidden within a false book cover with the title *Greenberg's Dictionary of Medical Terminology*. If the throwers had successfully detonated the bombs, the explosive force would have destroyed everything within a radius of roughly four

meters. However, the space between the tin and the cardboard in each bomb was surrounded with cube-shaped lead "bullets"—541 in all—that had been filled and smeared with strychnine and atropine sulfate. The blast from the larger bombs would have thrown shrapnel more than twenty-three meters in all directions. Anyone in the area of the blast thus ran a greater risk of being fatally poisoned than of being injured by the concussion. Major General Nicholas Pavlovich Fyodorov, the court's expert witness, testified that the strychnine solution was so strong that a single grain introduced into the bloodstream would have been fatal. Before the trial Fyodorov had imprudently touched his tongue to one of the bullets to determine whether it contained explosive material. He fell ill from the effects of strychnine within a few minutes and required medical care, but recovered.[2]

WITH THE BACKING of Shevyrev, the main organizer, the throwers had fended off Ulyanov's attempts to delay the assassination until the fall. They were determined to kill Alexander III on his way to a requiem mass for his father on March 1, 1887, the sixth anniversary of the successful assassination of Alexander II by the People's Will. On February 22, 1887, the throwers met at the Café Polonais and decided that they should act within the next few days. The combat squad and Ulyanov then met on February 25 and agreed on the time, place, and stations. Ulyanov not only explained the technical aspects of their bombs but, as the main theoretician, prepped them to represent their position under interrogation in case they were captured. After meeting on Nevsky Prospect at 11:00 a.m., they were to disperse in order to patrol the likely routes the tsar would take to the Peter and Paul Fortress.

They expected the tsar to leave the Anichkov Palace, just east of the Public Library on Nevsky Prospect, and drive northwest along Nevsky in the imperial equipage to the Palace Bridge, or to turn west just past the Public Library onto Sadovaya Street to Goro-

khovaya Street (the two legs of a triangle of which Nevsky Prospect was the hypotenuse) and then north toward the Admiralty and the Palace Bridge. If a signaler spied the tsar's carriage, he was to tip off the throwers by blowing his nose into a handkerchief. The throwers, who had worked out the map of their venture, hoped to intercept the tsar either on Nevsky at its intersection with the Catherine Canal (now the Griboedev Canal) or on Sadovaya Street.[3] They went into the streets on February 26 and February 28 (the first time in anticipation of a possible appearance of the tsar at St. Isaac's Cathedral) and made ready for the chosen date, March 1. Meanwhile, Ulyanov, who saw March 1 as the beginning of a terrorist campaign, worked feverishly to get the program of the Terrorist Faction of the People's Will printed. He was obsessed with advertising the rationale for the assassination and for the continuation of terror until it achieved its immediate goal, the granting of a liberal constitution.

The conspirators had good information and rightly assumed that the tsar would leave the Anichkov Palace by 11:00 a.m. on March 1. It was a Sunday—just as it had been when his father had been assassinated six years earlier—and Alexander III did indeed plan to attend a requiem mass for his father in the Peter and Paul Cathedral on the island fortress. The tsar and tsarina, Maria Fyodorovna, and their two eldest children, Nicholas and Alexander, were to travel in a sleigh. The tsar ordered his equipage for 10:45 a.m., but something unusual happened along the chain of responsible actors: the tsar's valet told the coachman, but the latter forgot to tell the sub-equerry, whose duty it was to harness the horses to the imperial equipage. Dressed in his overcoat, Alexander III, barely containing his rage, sat in the anteroom of his palace in the company of his doorman for almost half an hour. At the first opportunity, he singed the coachman's ears, bringing the poor man, a veteran of twelve years service, to the verge of tears. While the tsar cooled his heels, the conspirators patrolled the three streets along which the sleigh might pass. By the time the tsar left the Anichkov Palace, the police

had rounded up the bomb throwers.[4] Had Alexander III's coachman done his job properly, the events of March 1, 1887, might have
unfolded differently—but only if the police had failed to act in time
and the conspirators had done their jobs properly. There were just
too many contingencies to turn the coachman's blunder into an act
of providence, but that did not stop people close to the tsar—or
Alexander III himself—from believing in divine intervention.

The police captured the throwers on St. Petersburg's main thoroughfare, Nevsky Prospect, at midday on Sunday, March 1. It seems
absurd in retrospect that they hadn't known that the three packages
carried by Andreyushkin, Generalov, and Osipanov contained powerful bombs. A "black office" in the postal service that worked for
Russia's security apparatus had intercepted letters that alerted the
police to the possibility of a terrorist act. Additional indiscretions
committed by the throwers and signalers during a trial run identified
them as a group to the police before March 1. The police had put
them under close surveillance; yet the agents who arrested the suspects on March 1 still did not know that they were carrying bombs.
After he was taken to the police station on Gorokhovaya Street
2, Osipanov, who carried the bomb disguised as a medical dictionary, managed to throw it to the floor, but it failed to explode. The
police officer who picked up the "book" that their captive had rudely
thrown to the floor was astonished to find an explosive device.

Ulyanov had manufactured nitroglycerine and packed the bomb
casings with dynamite surrounded by the lead cubes filled and
smeared with strychnine. He had taken over the main organizational
tasks in mid-February after Shevyrev, tubercular and exhausted, left
for the Crimea, where the police caught up with him on March 7.
Ulyanov not only filled in for Shevyrev; he pressed for full formulation and printing of the group's "scientific" program. The police
arrested him in the late afternoon on March 1, when he went to one
of the conspiratorial apartments a few hours after the bomb throwers
and three reconnoiterers or "signalers" had been taken into custody.

The brilliant aspiring scientist Lukashevich had designed the bombs. He escaped arrest until the police showed up at his apartment at 2:00 a.m. on March 3. Novorussky had organized the delivery of materials and set up a safe house outside the city for Ulyanov's laboratory. He, too, was quickly apprehended, as were six others who had helped in some fashion or had known of the plot and kept silent. After six weeks in prison, the fifteen implicated in the plot to assassinate Alexander III appeared on April 15, 1887, before a Senate tribunal that dealt exclusively with state crimes. The trial lasted four days, followed by sentencing, appeals, and final judgment, with all but five escaping a death sentence.

The bodies were thrown into a common grave, as was the custom with state criminals executed at the Schlüsselburg prison. With the help of former guards, after the revolutions of 1917, Novorussky located the site of the grave. The Soviet regime erected a granite monument there in 1919 with the names of all of the twenty-eight prisoners who had been executed and three who had committed suicide during their imprisonment. At that time Alexander Ulyanov received no special recognition, despite the fact that his younger brother, Vladimir Ilyich, headed the new Soviet government under his revolutionary pseudonym, "Lenin." Much later, after the fortress had been turned into ruins from artillery bombardment in World War II, and when cults of the leaders had become common, the regime placed a plaque with a bas-relief head of Alexander on a wall still standing at the site of his cell in Schlüsselburg. Lenin avenged his brother, and many others, by having Alexander III's son Nicholas executed by a firing squad with his wife and all his progeny in July 1918. History and the Russian Orthodox Church treated Nicholas better. He and his family were canonized as passion sufferers in 2000.

The story of Lenin's choices and his behavior as a revolutionary and head of government cannot simply be summed up by the word "revenge," but Alexander's execution undoubtedly started it all. The

seventeen-year-old Volodya sat his final exams in Simbirsk in May 1887, during his brother's last days, in the same gymnasium where Alexander had won a gold medal as best student when he graduated in May 1883. Volodya repeated his brother's academic success—he won a gold medal in 1887—and later bested him in the profession of revolution. After Sasha's execution he spent much time pondering why his older brother had joined a terrorist group and taken a leading role. The quiet, studious Alexander had spent almost every waking hour during his late teens in a backyard laboratory studying worms and bugs. At the age of nineteen he had won another gold medal, this time in the natural sciences during his junior year in St. Petersburg. Everyone expected Alexander to become a professor of zoology. The other Alexander had hidden himself from the family.

Volodya told a close friend of the family, the very woman who had carried the shocking news of Alexander's arrest to them, "it means that he had to act that way—he couldn't act in any other way."[5] The young Lenin's firm conviction about the nature of his older brother's commitment compelled him to try to understand it. He approached this mystery in a penitent mood. Whereas Alexander had immersed himself in the natural sciences, Volodya, four years Sasha's junior, had disdained them, plunged into literature, and become an avid student of the classics. Virtually estranged at the time of Alexander's arrest, the brothers had been locked in adolescent combat since their father's death in January 1886. Now, instead of making a point of being different from his older brother, Volodya tried to enter his mind. What transformation had Sasha undergone in St. Petersburg that forced him to sacrifice his career and family to the revolutionary cause?

For his own reasons, Lenin maintained strict silence about his family, and most family members wrote very little about Alexander and his relationship with Volodya. Not Lenin, but his older sister, Anna, has provided posterity with the most valuable sources for studying the brothers' relationship.

BEGINNINGS:
THE ULYANOV AND BLANK FAMILIES

The two families that shaped Alexander Ulyanov and his brother, Vladimir, faithfully represented the Russian enlightenment. The European Enlightenment's radical turn, however, frightened Russian autocrats. Liberal constitutions inspired by the American and French revolutions threatened imperial structures. Catherine the Great, at first an enthusiastic importer of European ideas and patron of Voltaire and Diderot, began to persecute Russia's homegrown philosophes during the French revolutionary era. Napoleonic aggression further changed Russia's posture toward European thought. Napoleon's imperial project and his armies failed in 1812–15, but he had successfully exported revolutionary ideas. The European Enlightenment had affected Alexander I in his young manhood. In the first part of his reign Alexander toyed with the idea of giving Russia a constitution. Victory over Napoleon changed his mind, but elite officers affected by liberal thought tried to impose a constitution after his death in 1825. The crushing of the Decembrists in 1825 by Alexander I's successor, Nicholas I, and the affirmation of Russia's traditional political system created chronic revolutionary ferment in the educated elite.

The upward path of the Ulyanov family intersected the history of the Russian enlightenment. Free thought terrified autocratic regimes, but a modernizing empire could not dispense with universities and technical institutes. In a decades-long contest with censors and policemen, a distinctively Russian enlightenment emerged. The Ulyanov family history faithfully represented some of the trends. By virtue of a university education, Lenin's father, Ilya Nikolaevich Ulyanov, rose from the lower-middle class of Astrakhan, a port city

on the Volga delta, to the position of actual state councillor in the tsar's civil service.

Ilya's father, Nicholas, a tailor, left few documents. They reveal, however, that in 1835 he was registered as a *meshchanin*, a member of the lower part of the mercantile estate, and owned a two-story house in the city of Astrakhan made of stone and wood. Nicholas did his tailoring on the first floor. Rather late in life Nicholas married Anna Smirnova, a woman of obscure ethnic origins and social background, but they had four children, two sons and two daughters. Even strenuous research has not revealed a great deal about the marriage or their ethnicity. The Ulyanovs lived in an area populated by ethnic minorities. The streets of the city were filled with stevedores, tradesmen, craftsmen, runaway serfs, and retired soldiers and sailors who had poured into the Volga delta from all parts of Eurasia. Nicholas and Anna were probably Tatars, Kalmyks, or members of some other Central Asian ethnic group. They may have had Russian ancestors, but they looked distinctly Asian.[6]

The father's death in 1836 left the family in straitened circumstances. Ilya, only five at the time, would not have been able to go to school but for the self-sacrifice of his brother, Vasilii, thirteen years his senior. The only surviving photograph of Vasilii Nikolaevich shows a mustached man dressed in a checked vest and a frock coat and wearing cufflinks. What little hair he had was curled at the temples and pomaded. Vladimir Ilyich Lenin looked even more like his uncle than like his father. Ilya had a narrower cranium and broader cheekbones and was pockmarked. Evidently Vasilii's industrious service for the prominent Astrakhan mercantile firm the Brothers Sapozhnikov paid off handsomely. From carting salt as a teenager at a salary of fifty-seven rubles a year, he had risen to the position of clerk, for which he needed to be literate, and with a clerk's salary he could stake his younger brother to a university education. Vasilii evidently recognized Ilya's promise and, rather than pursue higher education and raise his own family, supported his mother,

brother, and sisters after Nicholas's death. This act of self-sacrifice became the most important legacy of Ilya Nikolaevich's birth family. Thanks to Vasilii, he was able to concentrate on his studies, earn a silver medal at the end of his gymnasium career in Astrakhan, and go on to Kazan University several hundred kilometers farther north on the Volga.[7]

Ilya Nikolaevich's university career brought him into contact with one of Russia's illustrious academicians, Nicholas Lobachevsky, a founder of non-Euclidean geometry. Ilya decided to study mathematics and physics, with specialties in meteorology and astronomy, as the title of his bachelor's thesis suggests: "Olbers' Method for Calculating the Orbit of the Comet Klinkerfuss." He completed his studies in 1854 and with Lobachevsky's help got a position in the Penza Institute for the Gentry, located in a sizable town on a Volga tributary, the Sura River, more than six hundred kilometers southeast of Moscow. Penza turned out well; Ilya taught and ran the meteorological station and met his future wife there. Liberal thinkers in the Gentry Institute's administration influenced Ilya Nikolaevich's future career. One of them took him under his wing and became his brother-in-law.

Historical events played into Ilya Nikolaevich's career. The Western powers defeated Russia in the Crimean War of 1853–56. Military defeat on its own territory had a profound effect on Russia's identity as a great power. The tsar's post-Napoleonic conservative advisers had justified Russia's traditional order through its military might. Their ideas now seemed bankrupt. The war exposed the empire's weakness compared with the industrializing European states. A vigorous reform movement followed under Nicholas I's successor. Alexander II liberated the serfs in 1861 and revived the Russian enlightenment. Like the years 1953–56 following Stalin's death, the period after the Crimean War seemed to the Russian intelligentsia like a thaw after decades of freeze. Careers in science and education beckoned forward-thinking men.

In 1861, Ivan Veretennikov, a school inspector at the Penza Institute for the Gentry, not only looked after Ilya's career but introduced him to his sister-in-law, Maria Alexandrovna Blank. Veretennikov, a graduate of Kazan University, had become connected with the Blank family while teaching Latin in Perm, at the edge of the Urals. Beginning in 1841, Dr. Alexander Blank served first on the Perm medical board and then moved about in the Urals region doctoring factory workers. In Zlatousk in 1846 he achieved the post of hospital inspector. Shortly after that, in 1847, Dr. Blank retired to his newly purchased estate in Kokushkino, near the city of Kazan and the Volga. Veretennikov played a major role in shaping the Ulyanov family's future by introducing several of his colleagues to Dr. Blank's daughters. All five of them married teachers and school administrators professionally connected to Veretennikov. Ilya became tightly integrated into this like-minded coterie after he married Maria in 1863.

Like Ilya Nikolaevich, Alexander Blank had grasped the opportunities a modernizing regime created for men of talent who pursued scientific and technological knowledge. He began life as Israel (Srul) Blank, but he and his brother, Abel, abandoned the Jewish faith for Russian Orthodoxy in 1820. Israel became Alexander Blank. With the help of liberal, aristocratic sponsors, the two brothers left Zhitomir, part of the Russian empire's Jewish pale of settlement after the partitions of Poland, and enrolled in the Medical-Surgical Academy in St. Petersburg. After beginning a medical practice in 1824, Dr. Blank met Anna Grosschopf in St. Petersburg and married her in 1829. Anna's father, Johann, had migrated from Lübeck, a medieval Hanseatic city on the Baltic, where Germany met Scandinavia. The German-Swedish side of the family adapted well to life in St. Petersburg and flourished in mercantile and bureaucratic positions. Johann Grosschopf had married Anna, the daughter of Karl Ohrstedt, a goldsmith of Swedish origin. Their daughter, Anna Grosschopf (named for her mother), was

thus Swedish on her mother's side, German on her father's, and Lutheran on both.

The Blank-Grosschopf union produced a son (the firstborn) and five daughters between 1830 and 1836, with Maria Alexandrovna, the fifth child, arriving in 1835. The birth of six children in the course of roughly seven years perhaps hastened Anna's early death in 1840. Her widowed sister, Katherine von Essen, quickly replaced Anna in the Blank household and became Dr. Blank's domestic partner.[8] His new positions, however, were hardship posts compared with that in St. Petersburg. After the rigors of life in Perm and Zlatousk, Dr. Blank looked for a place to retire. He and Katherine agreed on the estate of Kokushkino, on the Usha River in Kazan Province. Dr. Blank had chosen Kokushkino because of its proximity to the provincial capital, Kazan, and its excellent schools and university. His retirement funds, a solid sum received from the sale of his late wife's St. Petersburg property, Katherine von Essen's resources, and a mortgage on the estate allowed him to support the large family. Dissatisfaction with life in Perm and Zlatousk probably precipitated his premature retirement, but he continued to treat the local peasants from an office in his home.

Dr. Blank's son, Dmitry, graduated from the gymnasium and entered the law faculty of Kazan University in 1848. As the only male, he was the family's sole candidate for university education. Dmitry committed suicide in January 1850, just a few months before Ilya Nikolaevich enrolled in the university.[9] Perhaps, in some small way, the marriage of his daughters to the kind of young men whom he wished his son to be compensated Dr. Blank for Dmitry's death. The family kept silent about Dmitry.

Aunt Katherine raised the children strictly, in keeping with her German and Swedish Lutheran background. Dr. Blank, who had not only converted to Orthodoxy but evidently closed the door on his life in Zhitomir, matched Aunt Katherine's religiously inspired austerity with his own secular brand. A doctor who believed in a

simple diet and natural cures, Alexander Blank avoided prescribing strong medications whenever possible for his patients and
enforced on his children a rigorous health regime—light clothing,
simple diet, water-soaked wraps to temper the body—as if to defy
the rigors of the Russian climate.

Educated young men sought out Dr. Blank's company, although
one suspects that the doctor's five daughters outshone the other
attractions at Kokushkino. Well-born on their mother's side and
well-educated on their father's, the women made suitable mates
for the young, professional, and liberally inclined men who visited
the estate. For unknown reasons Maria waited longer to marry
than her four sisters had and was already twenty-six when she met
Ilya in Penza in 1861. They married in 1863, the very year that she
received certification to teach at the elementary level. It was a fitting match. Ilya's life plan looked very much like Dr. Blank's. Both
were of non-Russian ethnic background and had risen by virtue of
talent and hard work. Dr. Blank died in 1870, the year of Lenin's
birth, but he willed his estate to the five families, who continued to
use Kokushkino as their common property and gathered there for
summer vacations.

After marrying Maria in 1863, Ilya Nikolaevich took a position
teaching physics and mathematics in the gymnasium in Nizhny
Novgorod, the bustling Volga commercial city, where Maria Alexandrovna gave birth to Anna in 1864 and Sasha in 1866. Not long
after Sasha came Olga, who died in early infancy in 1868. Sasha
was only three when Ilya accepted the post of inspector of public
schools in Simbirsk. The Ulyanov family moved down river and
farther east to the comparatively small and sleepy Volga town
of Simbirsk in 1869. Maria Alexandrovna, already pregnant with
Vladimir, gave birth in Simbirsk in April 1870.

In Simbirsk, Ilya Nikolaevich faithfully served the Russian
enlightenment and its central value: secular education. He was a
dedicated, toiling member of an understaffed imperial bureaucracy,

overseeing secular elementary education in an entire province. Although not a large province, ranking forty-second of sixty-five, Simbirsk nonetheless had an ethnically diverse population of 1,300,000 and was spread out over the territory of a small European state. When Ilya Nikolaevich arrived in 1869 from Nizhny Novgorod, there were 460 public elementary schools, the vast majority of which were dysfunctional and rural. Only 89 of them, less than one-fifth of the official total, measured up to his standards, whereas many of the others existed only on paper or were in a pitiful state. Each such school served a populated area of about 8,000 inhabitants, but on average had only twenty-one students.

Ilya Nikolaevich was charged at first with the inspection of 70 to 80 schools a year. Inheriting a corps of 526 badly educated and poorly paid teachers, he found that 294 were local priests and 3 mullahs. Many of the schools listed hardly functioned. In short, he had to create a modern system of elementary education starting with an inappropriate teaching staff, wretched hovels that were counted as schools, and an ethnically diverse and largely illiterate population. A beneficiary of the new openness to talent of the post-Crimean period, he was the right person for the job. Ilya Nikolaevich created a pedagogical institute to serve the underprivileged minorities of the region, particularly the Chuvash, Mordvinians, and Tatars. By Ilya Nikolaevich's estimate these ethnic groups made up almost one-third of the population of Simbirsk Province. In 1879 Ilya reported that there were 425 actually functioning schools, with 15,561 students. Under his supervision 151 new school buildings had been constructed and the budget had risen by a factor of 3.5. By the end of his career there were 434 fully functioning public elementary schools and 20,000 students.[10]

Ilya Nikolaevich had to diagnose problems and assess a great variety of needs, from school construction to curriculum, textbooks, and pedagogy. He oversaw the hiring and training of teachers, determined their salaries, and made budget recommendations. All

of this required a great deal of travel over a territory of roughly sixteen thousand square miles for discussions with villagers, teachers, local officials, and his ministry. He had to correspond with the officials of both rural and urban bureaus. A small, physically frail, and intense person, Ilya Nikolaevich paid the price of dealing with bureaucrats and reluctant taxpayers while traveling over Simbirsk Province's primitive roads in badly sprung, horse-drawn vehicles. After a little more than ten years at his position of director of public schools, he suffered from arteriosclerosis. Ilya probably had an organic predisposition to the disease, from which Lenin also suffered, and they both died of cerebral hemorrhages at roughly the same age.

Ilya Nikolaevich taught his children to believe in education as the foundation of progress, and to think of professional life as a profound commitment to unremitting labor in the service of enlightenment. Ilya rarely praised the children and expected them to apply themselves dutifully and rigorously to their schoolwork. Their father's severity made the growth of conscience virtually coincide with a sense of achievement in learning. Although a model of conscientiousness and self-sacrifice himself, he impressed upon his children that he was the beneficiary of the unselfishness of an older brother who had supported the family after their father's death. Ilya taught Sasha not only the importance of science but a sense of duty to the point of self-sacrifice. Sasha took the message to heart.

THE ULYANOVS WERE neither poor nor well-off. In 1874 Ilya Nikolaevich, when appointed director of public schools in Simbirsk Province, became actual state councillor in the civil service, a rank that carried with it hereditary nobility, but a modest salary. The Ulyanov family's style of life reflected both their income and preferences. Neither Ilya Nikolaevich nor Maria Alexandrovna cared for display. The spare furnishings of the house on Moskovskaya

Street where they spent most of their years in Simbirsk expressed a philosophical and perhaps an aesthetic preference for the utilitarian rather than the sumptuous. The Ulyanov children grew up surrounded by scientific books and journals and Ilya's laboratory equipment from the Penza days, but also Maria Alexandrovna's sheet music, piano, and French and German books.

Simbirsk, though a city of about forty thousand, had a semirural character. Nature was all around. The nearby Sviyaga River supplied them with their drinking water; a well in the yard, water for watering the garden and other domestic purposes. The house on Moskovskaya Street in which the family lived between 1878 and 1887 had a spacious backyard garden divided by a path that ended at a fence bordering Pokrovskaya Street. The path was lined by silver poplars and, at the very end, a lone aspen tree that Anna particularly loved. Along the boundary fence separating the Ulyanov yard from the neighbors' there were four other paths, each with its own "forest," color-coded by the children for its dominant hue: black, for lilac and elm; yellow, for acacia; red, for prickly hawthorn. The last "forest," actually, a collection of miscellaneous trash donated by the neighbors, they called "the filthy forest." In the center of the area bounded by "forests" Maria Alexandrovna planted a flower garden. It had a little gazebo, where they had evening tea during the summer. There were also apple, pear, and cherry trees, raspberry, gooseberry, and currant bushes, and several strawberry beds. Maria Alexandrovna strictly supervised the harvesting of their bounty. The garden was a family effort, with all the children helping with watering and gathering.[11]

Sasha very quickly began to investigate and collect the local insects and frogs. He and his siblings and cousins roamed the hills and forests and navigated the rivers of Simbirsk and Kokushkino in a little dugout canoe. They climbed and swam in summer and skated and sledded in winter. The extended family—all of Maria Alexandrovna's sisters and brothers-in-law and their children—

continued to gather every summer at Dr. Blank's estate, which they collectively inherited after his death in 1870.

The Ulyanov family grew quickly: a second Olga followed Vladimir in 1871; then Nicholas, who died in infancy in 1873; followed by Dmitry in 1874 and Maria in 1878. The children formed dyads shaped by birth order: Anna and Sasha; Volodya and Olga; and Dmitry and Maria. The eldest, Anna and Alexander, were inseparable. If Anna had any of the typical resentment of the eldest child toward her first competitor for parental attention, she hid it well in her worshipful memoirs. The powerful bias in favor of the eldest son no doubt played a role. Anna yielded influence to Sasha, favored by both parents and also admired and imitated by his younger siblings. Volodya pedantically copied his older brother's every gesture. The parents seemed distinctly focused on Sasha and his future. A family portrait of 1879 placed Sasha squarely in the center.

The family led a rather hothouse existence; the children socialized mainly with their cousins during summers at the Kokushkino estate. Maria Alexandrovna's sisters and brothers-in-law, all of them educators, only reinforced the family's intense focus on learning. Ilya invited a few of his closest co-workers to tea or to play chess, and sometimes had them to dinner. Perhaps the family members felt most comfortable in such company; but perhaps the prejudices of the more established Simbirsk gentry of Great Russian stock limited the Ulyanovs' socializing. Did their neighbors mutter about the accomplished but quiet, painfully shy, and odd-looking children? The memoirists who wrote about Anna's and Sasha's years in St. Petersburg often commented on their looks— their small stature, Asian eyes, and Anna's dark skin and curly hair. All of this contributed to the children's acute shyness, although within their family hothouse surrounded by their "forests," they flourished in a distinct way.

Traumas

THERE WERE, unavoidably, traumas. Two infant deaths—
Olga's in 1868 and Nicholas's in 1873—no doubt affected
Maria and the older children. Anna's memoirs reveal that Sasha at
the age of four became seriously ill. During the illness he lost the
ability to walk. Anna's description, based upon her memories as
a six-year-old, suggests physical factors, but psychologically traumatic events, too. A rapid series of changes strongly affected Maria
Alexandrovna and, through her, Sasha. Anna contrasted their first
years in Nizhny Novgorod with what followed in 1869. Nizhny
Novgorod became their first home after Ilya and Maria's marriage
in August 1863, and Anna remembered it fondly. Ilya thrived in his
teaching posts and quickly moved up the ranks in the civil service.
They could afford kitchen help. Maria Alexandrovna made their
large, four-room apartment into a comfortable space. They had a
piano. Under her mother's tutelage, Anna began to read, and before
their departure four-year-old Sasha started reading newspapers. In
1868–69 one thing followed another: the death of the first Olga in
infancy; in the spring of 1869 a trip by steamer to Astrakhan, the
family's only known visit to see Ilya Nikolaevich's mother and siblings; then the move in September 1869 to Simbirsk, where they
settled into an apartment in the wing of a house on Streletskaya
Street. Anna, perhaps unconsciously, paints a rather grim picture of
a side street, with the house at its very end, near a prison. Volodya
was born there in April 1870. A few months later they moved into a
more spacious apartment in the home of the same landlord. Sasha

fell ill at some unspecified time in 1870 after Volodya's birth. Anna
recounts this scene:

> I remember his only dangerous illness—inflammation of the
> stomach—when he was four years old. I remember how Moth-
> er's despair astonished me: she fell on her knees before the icon,
> and whispered to me, "Pray for Sasha." I remember how she tore
> a howling Volodya from her breast, thrust him toward the nurse,
> and threw herself toward Sasha, who had taken a serious turn at
> that moment. . . . I remember Mother's glowing face, when she
> guided and supported him during his convalescence—when he
> had to be taught to walk all over again.[1]

Before Volodya's birth, the family never had the services of a nurse
and, in compensation for his mother's preoccupation with Sasha,
Volodya enjoyed the lavish attention of Varvara Sarbatova. The
two boys could hardly have been more different from each other
in looks and temperament. The earliest photos of Sasha suggest an
unhappy child whose eyes look in rather than out, whereas Volodya's show a touch of mirth in a cherubic face.

Anna plotted her memoirs of Sasha as tragedy: the death of
a hero, whose chronic melancholy and silence were organically
bound up with his sense of duty. The parents had chosen Sasha,
the eldest son, to further the family project of scientific achievement, and Anna blamed her father for pushing him too hard.
Although Anna did not intend to make her father the villain of
this family tragedy, one astute reader of her memoirs noticed that
she had done precisely that. Trotsky, who had intended to write a
biography of Lenin, completed only a small volume about Lenin's
childhood, adolescence, and early career, *The Young Lenin*, in
which he speculated about Ilya's methods of child rearing.[2] The
most psychoanalytically inclined Bolshevik leader inferred from
Anna's memoirs that, if anything, she had downplayed the sever-

ity of the father's quick-tempered and authoritarian interventions. Anna presents a glowing picture of her mother's management of the children's play and learning, whereas she criticizes Ilya's methods.

During the Simbirsk years, Ilya was away on inspection trips much of the time, so Maria Alexandrovna had the main responsibility for the children's tutelage. Anna describes her mother as a sort of moral genius as well as a natural pedagogue. She shaped the children's character while making learning enjoyable. She taught them to love literature, languages, music, and drawing. Although Sasha had a tin ear, he loved music. He did learn to draw and later used his draftsmanship to record his observations of the histological sections of freshwater annelids. Maria Alexandrovna knew how to turn learning into games. The four older children punned in Russian, German, and French, created rebuses and puzzles, and, for a time, composed their own little journal called "Saturday." On that day, they would all gather around the dining room table and show off their writing skills and humor. Sasha edited the game column. They all had noms de plume. Sasha took his, "Vralman," from an uncouth character in a satirical play by the eighteenth-century Russian satirist Denis Fonvizin. The Russian-German hybrid name denotes "liar." The staff of "Saturday" appreciated that Sasha, to the contrary, could not tell a lie. Volodya's pseudonym, "Kubichka," little cube, referred to the younger brother's sturdy physique. "Saturday" happened when Sasha was about twelve, just before his interest in biology and chess became all-absorbing.

Anna offers these happy childhood scenes in counterpoint to observations about Sasha's unhappiness after Ilya in 1874 enrolled the eight-year-old in the preparatory course for the gymnasium. Ilya feared that Maria, who had grown up in a household of girls, didn't know how to raise boys. He also worried about Sasha's quiet and gentle ways. Ilya's decision to enroll the brilliant and gentle Alex-

ander early had nothing to do with book learning. He wanted Sasha to learn how to be a boy and to be able to hold his own with other boys. Anna observed, "He was afraid of the effeminizing effects of this domestic pampering and found it expedient to place the boys as early as possible under masculine influence."[3] The father's well-intentioned severity permanently damaged his relationship with his eldest son. Anna traced Sasha's chronic mood of melancholy and locked-up anger to the years in the Simbirsk gymnasium.

The sensitive, shy, and introverted little boy with his new gymnasium uniform buttoned up to his chin entered a world of students who were generally quite unlike him. Sasha, the class grind, let the other students exploit his consistent effort by helping them with their homework, but otherwise avoided their company. He suffered sullenly and usually wordlessly for nine years in the Simbirsk classical gymnasium. Anna noted in her memoirs, without elaboration, that Dostoevsky's *House of the Dead* was one of Sasha's favorite books. Perhaps the passages in which Dostoevsky showed how the prisoners retained their humanity in an environment designed to degrade it had special meaning for Sasha. Dostoevsky, convicted of a political crime in his youth, knew that his gentry status and education marked him as an outsider, that he would never be accepted by the common criminals. Sasha no doubt felt like an outsider, too, even though most of his fellow students were, like him, members of the gentry estate. Ilya achieved hereditary nobility in 1874 when he became actual state councillor. Younger and smaller than the other boys, and gentler in every sense, Sasha traded his mastery of the curriculum for a modicum of acceptance, which evolved into admiration as his classmates matured.

Despite it all, Sasha prevailed and became one of the elite students of his generation. The rigor of learning Latin and Greek, French and German, mathematics, the natural sciences, history, and literature—however badly taught by most of the instructors and absorbed by most of the students in the Simbirsk classical

gymnasium—could nourish receptive minds. This, plus the enlightenment culture of their families and the occasional supportive and inspiring pedagogue, allowed the better students to find what they needed to succeed in the professions. When Fyodor Kerensky became rector in 1879, he firmed up the Simbirsk gymnasium's slack standards and salvaged its reputation by refusing to promote undeserving students. Rectors like Kerensky had to work within a framework established by a regime that sought to instill conservative values by teaching the classics and emphasizing religious instruction. The system failed and produced rebels in spite of it all—and so did progressive parents.

Modernizing trends eroded the myth of a Christian tsar, the mutuality of love between tsar and people, and the military mystique of the tsars. Defeat in the Crimean War had shaken Alexander II's confidence and forced widespread recognition among the progressive gentry not only that serfdom was shameful but that their own privileges had retarded Russian modernization. The repentant noblemen became abolitionists and constitutionalists. Their children, along with less privileged youths entering the gymnasiums and universities, followed suit. They sometimes pursued radical solutions, seeking redemption for their ancestors' exploitation of serfs by enlisting in the ranks of revolutionaries rather than in the tsar's regiments.

Groups form around common objects of love; most need things to hate as well. The Westernized and progressive Russian nobles withdrew their loyal service and their love from the dynasty and the imperial state. Alexander II's reforms of the 1860s and 1870s abolished serfdom and created a modern judiciary, among other things, but the tsar defended his dynasty's autocratic tradition. Alexander II would not grant a constitution. For those longing for a parliamentary system, the regime's modernizing reforms remained incomplete. Frustrated by Alexander II's failure to go forward, a significant part of the expanding educated stratum found some sol-

ace in new objects of devotion—science, the liberal professions, and the latest utopian thought. The education of new generations failed to instill uniformly the conservative values desired by the ministries responsible for shaping and policing Russia's ambivalent modernization. Alexander II, at first hailed as a liberator, now embodied resistance to historical progress and became the common object of hate of the revolutionary intelligentsia. Groups of radical students, the cutting edge of revolutionary restlessness, began plotting his assassination by the mid-1860s.

T HE SENSITIVE, IDEALISTIC, and relatively sheltered Ulyanov children could hardly avoid traumatic school experiences. They could hardly escape forming love-hate relationships with admirable and loving, but also severe and demanding, parents. They had an additional vulnerability—family secrets. The children evidently did not know anything about Maria Alexandrovna's brother, who would have been Uncle Dmitry to them if he had lived beyond adolescence. The story of Dmitry's suicide had to be unearthed by diligent investigators exploring every nook and cranny of the life of a family that changed the course of history. Maria Alexandrovna maintained strict silence about her relationship to her older brother, but named her youngest son Dmitry. Such secrets tend to make children feel that something shameful lurks in the past and that it could affect the present.

Although family members suspected the truth about Dr. Blank's Jewish origins by 1897, they could not get documentary verification until much later.[4] Several Communist leaders knew something about Lenin's Jewish ancestry by the end of 1924, but the party's cult of Lenin led to suppression of the information. It took the collapse of the Soviet Union and of the Lenin cult to produce fully researched and freely published genealogies.

Trotsky, who himself had suffered the wounds of anti-Semitism, wrote nothing in his autobiography about his own traumatic expe-

riences, but reacted sensitively when he detected symptoms in others. Exile in the 1930s gave him greater freedom to write about Lenin, but for political reasons he still felt compelled to avoid any direct reference to Lenin's Jewish ancestry. However, he seized upon a childhood incident mentioned in Anna's memoirs that in his view powerfully affected Sasha.[5] It was about anti-Semitism, and it allowed Trotsky to drop a strong hint.

The incident happened during a summer vacation in Kokushkino. Anna and Sasha were caught in a rainstorm while rowing their dugout near the family estate in Kazan Province. They rowed to shore and took shelter in the village of Tatarskaya.

> We ran to the closest cottage—Karpei's. We knew him well. A hunter and fisherman, he came often to Kokushkino with his game or fish and always stopped for conversation about a great many things. Father called him a poet and philosopher. He looked the type: thick, unruly black hair, graying a bit; beautifully dark and expressive eyes. . . . He was a talented autodidact. . . . But I especially remember the conversation we had with him on this occasion, when we ran for shelter from the rain. He told us how the tsar [Nicholas I] had decreed that "little Yids" be driven across Kazan Province to Siberia. His vivid eyewitness account produced a strong impression. Later, during our university years, we read in Herzen's *My Past and Thoughts* a similar description that called to mind Karpei's. . . . But at that moment, deep in thought and depressed, we returned to our boat. I think that this was one of the experiences in Sasha's childhood that had awakened in him that confused [*smutnoe*, in Anna's text] feeling of dissatisfaction with the existing political system that he mentioned in his speech at his trial.[6]

Karpei probably knew about Dr. Blank's Jewish background and had purposely chosen to tell them a story about Jewish can-

tonists. Perhaps, in a sly way, he wanted to plant a hurtful image, something that would gnaw away at them. If so, he evidently succeeded.

The cantonists were child military recruits during the reign of Nicholas I. In 1827 Nicholas had issued the "Statute of Conscription and Military Service." It included special clauses concerning Jews that subjected them to discriminatory forms of recruitment, segregating Jewish boys from other cantonists. The Jewish conscripts were often as young as eight years old. If they survived the brutal trek to their place of service, they would be converted to Russian Orthodoxy. When Sasha and Anna during their university years read Alexander Herzen's vivid and moving account of his encounter with a convoy of Jewish cantonists in *My Past and Thoughts*, it revived the childhood trauma.

Herzen told of stopping in a village during a downpour on his way to exile in Vyatka. A transport officer who had also stopped in the muddy village invited him to have a cup of tea at a peasant cottage. The officer complained to Herzen about the vagaries of service that had brought him to Vyatka.

— This is how it is. They rounded up a bunch of damned little Yids, eight- or nine-year-olds. *First they ordered me to herd them to Perm, but they changed it and now we're herding them to Kazan* [Herzen's italics]. I've taken them around sixty-five miles. The officer who handed them to me said, "They're just trouble, a third were left on the road (pointing to the ground). Half of them won't get to where they're supposed to go," he added.

— What happened, some kind of epidemic? — I asked, shaken to my core.

— No, nothing like an epidemic, it's just that they die like flies. Yid children, you know, they're kind of puny, weaklings . . . not used to walking through mud for ten hours and eating dried

crusts—with strangers, no father or mother to take care of them—they began to cough, starting in Mogilev. . . .

Herzen and the officer left the shelter of the peasant cottage and walked into the pouring rain. The officer had the children stand at attention. The older boys, twelve or thirteen, managed to rise to the occasion, but the eight-year-olds drooped.

> Pale, exhausted, terrified, they stood in awkward, thick military uniforms with stand-up collars, pitifully staring at the soldiers of the convoy . . . white lips, blue circles around their eyes—feverish and shivering. And these sick children without anyone to console them, standing in an icy wind, marched to their grave.[7]

Perhaps Herzen unconsciously punned. The word for "grave" in Russian is *mogila*. The cantonists' trek had begun in Mogilev, in the Pale of Settlement. Perhaps Sasha was reminded of his own trauma at age eight, when Ilya Nikolaevich condemned him to the miseries of gymnasium life and put him into uniform. But what did it mean to Anna, when in 1927 she told the story in her memoirs of Sasha?

Anna, at the Communist Party's behest, began a systematic search for archival evidence of her family ancestry after Lenin's death in 1924. She had seen the documents about Dr. Blank's conversion to Russian Orthodoxy by the end of 1924. Roughly at the same time, an archivist, Yurii Oksman, had seen other documents leading to the same conclusion about Dr. Blank. Oksman told the historian V. I. Nevsky. They conveyed the information to the party leaders Lev Kamenev and Nicholas Bukharin. All bound themselves to an oath of silence.[8] Anna had to comply. The story about Karpei thus hinted at the family secret, but stopped short of revelation. Five years later, during a period of rising anti-Semitism in the Communist Party, Anna decided to write to Stalin and urge him to publicize the Ulyanov family's Jewish background. She failed

to understand Stalin's own anti-Semitism or the Communist Party's desire to divest itself of its putative "Jewish" character. Jews had played a prominent role in the formation of Russian Social Democracy, in the Menshevik and Bolshevik factions, in the first Soviet government, in the state security apparatus, in the Red Army, and in the Communist Party press. They had quickly become targets of anti-Bolshevik feeling, not only during the revolutionary period and Civil War, but also as Communist popularity waned in the 1920s and 1930s.

The period of the Great Purges revived the anti-Semitism that had led to the killing, torture, rape, and looting of more than 100,000 Jews during the Civil War. The poster art of the Civil War period had caricatured Trotsky's "Jewish" features. Anti-Semitism reappeared in the period of Stalin's Great Terror, with Trotsky now portrayed as a grotesque Judas figure. Anti-Semitism was undoubtedly one factor supporting the blood purges and Moscow trials of the late 1930s. The Lenin cult created by Stalin and the others would not tolerate an even partly Jewish Lenin. The family secret became a matter of state importance. Anna and Alexander had already suffered the psychological damage. At some point in their childhood they sensed that they belonged to a hated and victimized group and that it was all terribly unjust, but they were helpless to do anything about it. Anna's memoirs register important traumatic episodes in the history of Sasha's sad and silent ways, but certainly not the whole story.

For the fortieth anniversary of Sasha's hanging, Anna assembled the memoirs of most of the survivors connected directly with the conspiracy and those of others who knew Sasha as a fellow student at St. Petersburg University. All of the memoirists sensed something admirable in Sasha, and several noticed something disturbing. Anna recognized that he did not show any joie de vivre—an expression that the Russians had borrowed from the French. In Russian it is compressed into a single word, "lifejoy" (zhizneradost-

nost'). Every photo of Sasha shows the same morose face, from that of the four-year-old with long curls standing awkwardly beside Anna to that of the sullen prisoner with dead eyes and an angry set to his jaw. Sasha lived behind a wall of silence and ascetic dedication to his work. Perhaps the Ulyanov family's own collective act of denial, its secretive and secluded character, and an atmosphere that destroyed their joie de vivre, created in the children a kind of impacted anger, wordless and expressionless, but ready to explode.

After the incident in the rainstorm in Tatarskaya, Anna had sensed the truth, but evidently could not bring it to consciousness for a long time. Sasha, in Anna's telling of his experience, had only a "confused" feeling about the meaning of Karpei's story, but perhaps it affected his powerful identification with victims and his relationship with Raisa Shmidova. Lenin certainly knew about the family's ethnicity before 1917—his sisters would not have withheld the information from him—although he kept silent about it. During Lenin's struggle with Stalin and others over the Soviet policy on nationalities, he expressed his feelings about ethnic prejudice quite vividly. We do not know about any traumas in his childhood akin to the ones Anna and Sasha had experienced—this, too, remained unspoken—but we know that Lenin responded passionately to prejudice against minorities and against anti-Semitism in particular. Lenin's actions—his promotion of Jews and members of other minorities to high positions in the party and his angry response to expressions of Russian chauvinism—also spoke volumes.

The Making of a Rebel

S ASHA'S ESSAYS during his senior year in 1882–83 in the Simbirsk gymnasium showed both his sense of the trajectory of history and a cosmopolitan vision. He had to work within the cramped intellectual space of assignments that dictated the topic as well as the formal features of the essays. In one such compulsory essay, Sasha compared two of Russia's most important eighteenth-century men of letters, Denis Fonvizin and Nicholas Karamzin, both of whom had written of their travels in Europe. Fonvizin perceived the defects of the French system of laws and the incompetence of the French administration during the last years before the French Revolution. He saw the dreadful poverty of the lower classes, the hollow lives of the aristocracy, and the extreme corruption of morals not only in France but in much of western Europe. Karamzin visited France a few years later, experienced the French Revolution directly, and mistakenly saw it as nothing more than an explosion of ignorant elements in the masses. He took the measure of a people by universal values of art and science, unlike Fonvizin, who found fault with civilized Europe in order to show the superiority of Russian life. Fonvizin failed to appreciate the progressive character of European arts and sciences, whereas Karamzin judged them to be superior. Sasha's balanced approach, his ability to select the aspects of their views that meshed with his own, showed later in his syncretic, non-dogmatic approach to revolutionary theory and strategy.

In another gymnasium essay, "The Major Causes of Wars," he

linked social and political evolution to the dynamics of groups, as tribal entities fought one another, expanded, and formed states on the territories of diverse ethnic groups. Already converted to a scientific approach to history by the writings of the British historian Henry Thomas Buckle, Sasha downplayed the role of personal ambition and individual agency in history. His essay "The Principles and Consequences of the Crusades" shows a sophisticated grasp of the economic problems that spurred the religious movement, the cultural benefits of contact with more developed Muslim societies outside Europe, the negative social and political consequences for feudalism of the attrition among the knights, and the positive economic impact of the Crusades for European trade and industry. All of this prepared Alexander for reading Marx at St. Petersburg University.

Next to the natural sciences, history became Sasha's favorite subject, and it shows in his last gymnasium essays. The study of history coupled with the prestige of the natural sciences in his generation typically led to an all-embracing scientific approach akin to Buckle's—to the idea that history and society, too, obeyed laws. A Darwinian approach pioneered by Herbert Spencer—another of Sasha's favorite British authors—linked evolution, human development, and the historical progress of societies in a unified system of knowledge. Sasha, however, later rejected one of Spencer's central biological principles, the survival of the fittest. When the nineteen-year-old Sasha thought about an epigraph for his junior thesis at St. Petersburg University, he summed up his worldview in a few well-chosen German words: "Was wirklich, dass geschichtlich," which, though elliptical, translates into "What is real is historical." What he actually meant was, What is real is evolutionary.

Sasha's most revealing essay of 1883, however, is one entitled "How to Be Useful to Society and the State." It was a standard assignment that typically elicited pieties of the sort that instructors wanted, but it stimulated Sasha to present his authentic views. The essay shows that the values of the nihilist subculture of rebellion

did not conflict with the core of his family's ethical code. Sasha set forth the five cardinal values in his code of conduct: honesty, love of work, strength of character, intellect, and knowledge. He might have added duty to the cardinal five, but he explicitly mentions one's obligation to serve society in the body of the essay.[1]

By the age of sixteen he had sorted out the mixed messages of the Russian writers who had most strongly influenced him: Dmitry Pisarev and Fyodor Dostoevsky. One might add Ivan Turgenev, but Sasha probably saw Turgenev's characters through the lens of Pisarev's interpretations. Later, the more programmatic ideas of Peter Lavrov, the preeminent theorist of Russian populism, justified his choice of terrorism, but Sasha was still far from terrorism in 1883. At that point in his life he had fallen under the sway of Pisarev's brilliant essays. The year before they left for St. Petersburg, Alexander and Anna had discovered the nihilist critics and read all of Pisarev's censored works in the home of the family doctor, who had been sent to Simbirsk for his radical views, but whose library of seditious works had evidently survived.

Pisarev's image of the nihilist hero in an essay of 1865, "The Thinking Proletariat," showed young men of Sasha's type the lineaments of a new kind of human being ascetically dedicated to science and work for the good of humanity. Pisarev not only reinforced the nihilist thinking that made self-sacrifice both rational and pleasurable; he offered a psychological analysis of the "new people" in accordance with his own interpretation of Darwin and the way pleasure and pain worked in the most developed members of the human species. Pisarev dwelled upon the inability of the new people to tolerate internal discord. Conscience—moral duty—must perfectly harmonize with action, reason with feeling, egoism with the love of humanity.

New men don't sin and don't repent; they always reflect, and thus they only make mistakes in calculation, and then correct their

errors and avoid repeating them in the future. For new people goodness and truth, honesty and knowledge, character and intellect are identical; the more intelligent a new person, the more honest he is because fewer mistakes creep into his calculations. In the new person there is no reason for discord between intellect and feeling, because his intellect, focused on work that he loves and is also useful, always chooses that which profits him personally, coincides with the true interests of humanity, and, consequently, with the requirements of the strictest justice and the most acute sense of morality.

The unique features of the new type . . . may be formulated chiefly in three propositions, very closely tied together.

    I. New people have developed a passion to work for the general benefit of society.

    II. What is of personal utility to new people coincides with the benefit of society, and their egoism embraces the broadest love of humanity.

    III. The new people's intellect is in total harmony with their feeling because neither intellect nor feeling is distorted by chronic enmity toward others.[2]

Everyone who knew Alexander well would find him perfectly described in "The Thinking Proletariat." In fact, his younger brother's own terse statement when he learned that Alexander had belonged to a plot to assassinate Alexander III shows that Volodya understood his brother's inability to compromise or to tolerate any dissonance between his ideals and actions. "It means that he had to act that way—he couldn't act any other way." Others who had known Alexander during his years at St. Petersburg University confirmed Volodya's judgment. In 1887 Nicholas Rudevich wrote brief portraits of some of the key figures, including one of Alexander: "He could not tolerate discord between words and action.

Once he decided that terror was necessary, he immediately began to implement his decision."[3]

The scientific worldview, however, created problems for those with the wit to see that the war of each against all might make just as much sense in Darwinian terms as labor for one's fellow creatures. An earlier essay that Pisarev had written in 1861 about the hero of Turgenev's *Fathers and Sons* especially struck Sasha. Bazarov, Turgenev's model nihilist, could as easily kill impulsively as benefit mankind by his scientific labor. In one of the novel's most powerful moments, Bazarov gives a short, eloquent speech on life's meaninglessness.

> The tiny space I occupy is so infinitely small in comparison with the rest of space, in which I am not, and which has nothing to do with me; and the period of time in which it is my lot to live is so petty beside the eternity in which I have not been, and shall not be. . . . And in this atom, this mathematical point, the blood circulates, the brain works and wants something. . . . Isn't it hideous? Isn't it petty? . . . Aha! There goes a valiant ant dragging off a half-dead fly. Take her, brother, take her! Don't pay attention to her resistance; it's your privilege as an animal to be free from the sentiment of pity—make the most of it—not like us conscientious self-destructive animals![4]

Pisarev did not try to make Bazarov into a man with pure motives and benign impulses, but showed the distinctly dark side of his character. Turgenev's critics accused him of creating an antihero of sorts, of using Bazarov to criticize the young people who had rejected the values of their parents and of using the term "nihilist" to discredit radicalism. Turgenev, perhaps unconsciously, had attached death imagery to Bazarov and nihilism. Arkadii, the son in Turgenev's novel who abandons nihilism and partially returns to the values of his father, falls in love, raises a family, and per-

petuates life. Bazarov, the unrepentant nihilist, accidentally infects himself with typhus while doing an autopsy on a corpse, and dies. Turgenev made it quite clear that an unhappy love affair had emptied Bazarov's life of any meaning. Although he lived at home with his parents, he might as well have been in a desert. Life imagery required human connection and renewal.

On their side the nihilists accused their elders of anesthetizing themselves against the misery of the peasants with idealist philosophy and the effete world of the arts. The intelligentsia's quarrel over Bazarov was one acute episode in the long struggle between the culture of the arts and the culture of the natural and social sciences. The sciences came to signify down-to-earth utilitarianism and materialism. Turgenev attached to the novel's ineffectual Romantic characters a love of nature and music and poetry and a healthy nesting instinct that Bazarov ridiculed. Many Russian families experienced the conflict of the two cultures portrayed by Turgenev—a conflict that has taken many forms since the Enlightenment. At that moment in history radical ideologues deemed the Romantic style an ally of oppression and backwardness. Pisarev encouraged his readers to reject Pushkin for Heine—an angrier and more distinctly revolutionary poet. (Still acting like a disciple of Pisarev in his last days in prison, in the last interview with his mother before his hanging, Sasha requested a volume of Heine's poetry.) Nihilists believed that the arts, religion, property, and the family itself were instruments serving exploitative social and political structures. Only science, realism in art, and materialism in philosophy unmasked the rottenness of the old values supporting class dominance and the exploitation of women or their abasement into mere prostitutes, when not slaves to reproduction and domestic labor. Art became a luxury unless it served progressive, material goals identified by the natural and social sciences.

In some ways Pisarev's life imitated Turgenev's art. After a futile struggle with Russian censorship and the secret police, at the age of

twenty-two Pisarev was arrested and imprisoned in the Peter and
Paul Fortress for four and a half years. Less than two years after his
release from the fortress, Pisarev drowned in July 1868 while bath-
ing in the Baltic Sea. Rumor had it that police spies watched while
he drowned, but did not try to help him. Sasha knew the rumor
and held the regime responsible for his idol's death. The Pisarev
who had connected materialism with altruism in "The Thinking
Proletariat" rather than the one who presented the dark side of
materialist thought apparently became Sasha's preceptor. But had
Pisarev's "Bazarov" also planted in Sasha the notion that the new
people were somehow premature, that they were doomed at that
moment in history?

> The whole interest, the whole meaning of the novel [*Fathers
> and Sons*] is contained in the death of Bazarov. If he had turned
> coward, if he had been untrue to himself, it would have shed a
> completely different light on his whole character. . . . Bazarov
> did not become abased, and the meaning of the novel emerged
> as follows: today's young people become carried away and go to
> extremes; but this very tendency to get carried away points to
> fresh strength and incorruptible intellect. . . .[5]

Pisarev, by inclination an aesthete, resolved his own inner conflict
by casting his lot with the natural sciences and suppressing the logic
of the dark side. He recommended to his youthful readers the util-
ity of dissecting frogs over the pleasure of reading poems. Nature
should be approached as a prosaic workshop rather than a source
of rapturous or sublime feelings. Beauty was a luxury. The world
consisted of nothing more than matter in motion. Pisarev admon-
ished young people to calculate everything, especially pleasure and
pain, and to increase the one and diminish the other. Submission
to reason and science did not, however, license the "new people"
to serve their instincts mindlessly. Nihilism's scientific asceticism

showed the way to a better future: the study and conquest first of nature's and then of society's tyrannies. The sometimes mocking, sometimes indignant Bazarov, a medical man who submitted only to the laws of nature, also knew how to heal the splits in society. Nihilists decided that socialism was the only true medicine for social ills. The calculus of *rational* egoism yielded the imperative to mitigate human pain and to serve the human species. Students saw science as a higher calling and flocked to medical schools.

The youth rebellion of the 1860s created a permanent cleavage in Russian culture and society. Like all self-conscious cultural revolutions, that of the nihilists had a stagy look, with some trappings borrowed from European revolutionary culture. The men grew beards and let their hair grow long, sported menacing broadbrimmed hats—usually black—red shirts, and high boots, and threw plaids (which hardly seem sinister today, but signified rebellion in that context) over their shoulders. The women cut their hair short, dressed austerely and sometimes mannishly, and sported red blouses and plaids in imitation of the men. The nihilists occasionally entered into fictitious marriages to save young women from the tyranny of their families, or to lift prostitutes out of the gutter, and sometimes to protect men from the police.

In 1862 the imprisoned nihilist critic Nicholas Chernyshevsky wrote a clumsy but extremely influential novel about nihilist men and women organizing communes, practicing open marriage, uplifting the needy, and presaging a revolutionized Russia living in a socialist utopia. In the novel *What Is to Be Done?* Chernyshevsky's fictional hero, Rakhmetov, unlike the well-known antiheroes of Russian literature, shows no discordant feelings and pursues an ascetic program of bodybuilding in preparation for revolutionary struggle. The nihilists took seriously the German materialist philosopher Ludwig Feuerbach, who authored the dictum "Man is what he eats." Rakhmetov ate raw meat, whose high nutritional value had been demonstrated by modern science. He also slept

on a mat with nails embedded in it, presumably in order to steel himself to face torture. The fictional heroes of nihilism provided models for Russian terrorists; Osipanov had imitated Rakhmetov in the latter practice.

With Chernyshevsky and Pisarev, Nicholas Dobrolyubov completed the trinity of moralistic materialists who shaped nihilism and, through Lenin, affected the culture of Bolshevism as well. Like Pisarev, Dobrolyubov had died while still in his twenties, in 1861, at the age of twenty-five. He had been Chernyshevsky's closest collaborator. Although Chernyshevsky outlived the others, he spent most of his adult life in prison and Siberian exile. An aura of martyrdom thus clung to all of the nihilists of the 1860s. Dobrolyubov's work no doubt had special meaning for Anna and Sasha. He had written an influential review of Ivan Goncharov's novel of 1859, *Oblomov*. No educated citizen of Simbirsk, Goncharov's birthplace, could have failed to read *Oblomov*, and no nihilist could have remained uninfluenced by Dobrolyubov's essay "What Is Oblomovism?" The antihero of the novel, Ilya Ilyich Oblomov, signified dreamy ineffectuality and enervation; he became the subject of Dobrolyubov's clinical dissection of the society and culture that had created his pathology. Although he was well intentioned and intelligent, Oblomov's pampered upbringing had taken away the energy and will to serve his ideals. Dobrolyubov placed Oblomov in a genealogy of antiheroes in Russian literature, the Hamlets and superfluous men. The children of the indefatigable Ilya Nikolaevich had most certainly read Goncharov's novel and Dobrolyubov's clear message to fight against a society that destroyed its best people.

S ASHA MADE HIS COMMITMENT to terrorism during a procession to the Volkovo Cemetery on November 17, 1886, to commemorate the twenty-fifth anniversary of Dobrolyubov's death. Police and Cossacks closed the cemetery and blocked the procession, in some cases surrounding the students. Thwarted in their

effort to honor the memory of Dobrolyubov, Sasha and Anna were forced to stand in a cold, drenching rain with hundreds of other students. The angry students and Sasha's own surprisingly explosive rage on that day foretold his decision to become a terrorist. To be sure, the organizers of the procession included students who were already inclined toward terrorism and looking for an occasion to arouse their more apathetic comrades. They succeeded.

The humiliations of that day created the atmosphere that led to the plot to kill Alexander III. For the first time the ordinarily reticent Sasha wrote an inflammatory proclamation. Until that time he had struck others as almost saint-like, tactful and gentle, soft-spoken and self-contained, like a dark star of the emotions, absorbing energy but not letting any escape. Sasha had found it difficult to accept all of nihilism's extremes, and for a while he stood apart from the student subculture. Some of his contemporaries had already decided during their gymnasium years to join the People's Will. The nihilist vision permitted more than one path: young rebels might become ascetics of science and serve progress by that type of heroism; or they could interpret rational egoism to mean calculation about revolutionary tactics, tactics that might entail the simultaneously murderous and suicidal actions of terrorism. In either case, the ideas had to be worked out rigorously in keeping with the most advanced scientific ideas, and they had to be placed in the service of the people who had labored for centuries as serfs and provided the surplus for the education of the new people. The agonies of thought and spirit that it took to work through a decisive commitment often showed in Sasha's anguished face, but he suffered wordlessly.[6] It took almost four years of thought and study in St. Petersburg to prepare him for his response to the events of November 17, 1886, but one senses that the emotional background lay even deeper. Whatever the psychological currents underlying Sasha's conscientiousness, he finally found in the doctrine of *narodnichestvo* what he needed to make a commitment to revolution—and terrorism.

Taking over the basic socialist position of the nihilists, but adding a Kantian ethical grounding, the populist writers of the 1870s created impassioned images of the peasants, to whom they believed the intelligentsia owed a debt for their own position as the "developed" vanguard of humanity. The intelligentsia's elitism and self-affirmation coexisted, sometimes uncomfortably, with love of the people and a spirit of self-sacrifice. The more pride they felt in their own achievements, the more they felt the need to go to the people, to pay back the debt for centuries of exploitation, to teach them about socialism, or simply to help them improve their lives. This repentant mood and activist spirit produced the famous "Going to the People." In the mid-1870s thousands of students had made pilgrimages to the countryside in the guise of artisans and midwives, but had failed to mobilize the villagers for revolutionary action. Those who survived the depredations of the imperial security apparatus often moved back to the cities, where they joined revolutionary circles. Isolated terrorist acts and then tactics of armed self-defense against police and gendarmes finally led to a full-fledged commitment to systematic terrorism.

The largest revolutionary *narodnik* party, Land and Freedom, split in 1879 over the issue of terror. The terrorist party that emerged from the split, the People's Will, reflected the frustration of the young people, many of whom had been roughly treated and arrested, and then had languished in prisons and places of exile. The terrorists who were tried took advantage of the reformed bar and turned the tables on the prosecution by heroically defending their cause in speeches that appeared in the European press and made their treatment seem barbaric. The revolutionaries of the late 1880s believed that their brothers and sisters in the cause had been prevented by the tsarist regime from spreading the word of socialism to the villagers, whose traditional communalism made them natural material for a more advanced, "scientific" socialism. Terrorism, they thought, would open the way to freedom of

speech within a constitutional system, both prerequisites for the spread of socialist ideas. Quite naturally many of the recruits to later cohorts of terrorists wanted to imitate the heroic figures who had preceded them—to sacrifice themselves and to deliver a stirring speech for posterity.

In the process of transferring love, loyalty, and a spirit of service from tsar to people, many of the young revolutionaries took a cue from their religious upbringing as well. The religious authorities taught love of Christ and of Russia's Christian rulers. In Russia's medieval past, even before the Mongol era, the princes of the founding Riurikid dynasty sometimes acquired the mystique of Christ's Passion. Dying for brotherly love or for the Russian land beset and then conquered by pagans, the sainted warriors redeemed the many. Holy Russia emerged from the Mongol yoke. To be sure, the Muscovite rulers had risen as collaborators with their Mongol overlords, and had massacred their Christian brethren in large numbers, but not in the myths that inspired Russian imperial self-justification. The notion remained strong that suffering had redemptive value. Hundreds of years of secularization and decades of the Enlightenment then transmuted the notion of the redemptive value of suffering into the ideology of *narodnichestvo*—the exaltation of the simple peasant. The notion that the peasants had suffered for them and, worse still, at the hands of their own serf-owning ancestors gave young rebels substitute objects of love not only for the Romanovs and their state but for Christ.

The socialist intelligentsia, still barely emerging from a worldview centered on Christ, believed that the people's collective suffering would redeem Russia and that perhaps backward Russia would lead bourgeois Europe to socialism as well. The last would be first, and rich men would not enter the kingdom of heaven. In the socialists' version, the surplus value extracted from peasants and factory workers by aristocrats and bourgeoisie would become the currency of redemption—the people's suffering was ordained

by the laws of history. Russia, the most backward of European powers, would be transfigured in an inevitable revolution that would bring not the kingdom of the faithful but a world both just and rational, a socialist world.

Every new generation of revolutionary ideologues built on the nihilist foundation of science worship. The later doctrines—populism, Marxism, anarchism—were all footnotes to nihilism. The practitioners of revolution vindicated Turgenev's insight, given utterance by Bazarov, that human beings were conscientious, self-destructive animals—a view embodied in several of Dostoevsky's memorable characters and later echoed by Nietzsche and Freud. Self-sacrificing conscientiousness usually trumped self-indulgence or power seeking in the revolutionary subculture created by the young nihilists and populists, but the sense of superiority conferred by scientific knowledge might turn noblesse oblige in a megalomaniacal, power-seeking, and dictatorial direction. Dostoevsky, a man terrified by the drift of modern life, in *Crime and Punishment*, *The Possessed*, and *The Brothers Karamazov* warned against the way in which progressive ideas took diseased forms in young minds, with both murderous and suicidal consequences.

Sasha's attraction to Dostoevsky, attested to by Anna, at first seems odd. Dostoevsky probed the diseased psyches of young extremists who made a faith of reason and science, and thereby abandoned religious faith and the ordinary metabolism of generations. The deeply ambivalent and tortured writer also wrote patriotic tracts supporting Russian imperial goals, yet he believed, too, just as he had in his youth, that any truth seeker in Russia would naturally become a revolutionary. Well-founded and widely circulated rumors that Dostoevsky had planned to turn the saintly Alyosha of *The Brothers Karamazov* into a terrorist, and to have him executed in the sequel to his great novel, may even have reached Sasha. Dostoevsky, at the very least, contributed to Sasha's sense of the unwholesomeness of Russian society. When he testified about

his personal development to the Senate tribunal on April 18, 1887, Sasha said,

> I can trace to my early youth a confused [*smutnoe*] feeling of dissatisfaction with the general state of affairs, a feeling that penetrated ever deeper into my consciousness, and led me to the convictions that guided me in the present circumstances. But only after studying the social and economic sciences did I arrive at a firm conviction about the abnormality of the existing order, and my vague dreams about liberty, equality, and fraternity took shape in rigorously scientific and, more precisely, socialist forms.[7]

Dostoevsky, that grim poet of both human depravity and saintliness, described in *The House of the Dead* a prison life not so remote from Russian society's. Anna relates in her memoirs that Sasha was fascinated by prisons. The Ulyanovs' first home on Streletskaya Street in Simbirsk was a modest wooden house a short walk from one of Simbirsk's highest elevations, the Old Crown, several hundred feet above the Volga. Streletskaya Street led to a square abutting the town prison and the Old Crown. Anna and Sasha used to play and walk near the prison and could not fail to hear the shouted obscenities escaping through the barred windows. In the autumn of 1883, when Anna arrived in St. Petersburg, she and Sasha went on outings, the most notable of which was a visit to the Peter and Paul Fortress, with bastions that served as prisons for state criminals. Less than four years later Sasha would occupy a cell in the Trubetskoy Bastion. His sensitivity to and identification with victims and his sudden and extreme responses to scenes of humiliation and victimization made vivid by Anna are akin to those portrayed in Dostoevsky, who understood how saints and seekers after the truth became terrorists in Russia.

Although Anna no doubt designed the prison scenes in her mem-

oirs to foreshadow Sasha's turn to terrorism and tragic fate, they have an authentic ring when she tells of his anguished response to human cruelty and death imagery. During their first days together in St. Petersburg, Anna and Sasha visited an exhibition of Vasilii Vereshchagin's paintings in the Hermitage. Vereshchagin, a soldier-artist who, like the painters who portrayed the peasants' life, had become a favorite of young radicals, bore witness to the brutality of the Russian imperial campaigns of the preceding decade. The regime had the museum take down Vereshchagin's most celebrated canvas, *The Apotheosis of Death*, which showed a great pyramid of skulls pecked by ravens and gleaming in the desert sun. No one had clearer insight into Sasha's fascination with death imagery than Anna, but she hid certain things from herself.

S HORTLY BEFORE the planned assassination of Alexander III, Sasha had stopped attending the discussions and meetings of the several student circles to which he belonged. One of his acquaintances saw him appear only two weeks before March 1, 1887, at a meeting of one such circle devoted to economic issues. The circle had especially interested Sasha during his intense investigation of Russia's social and economic development in 1886.

> Perhaps he dropped by for one last glance at us and to say goodbye silently. His appearance struck many in the group. He sat the entire evening without saying a word, pensive, his big dark eyes staring fixedly. I very vividly remember his face, always calm and serious, with wide cheekbones, the deathly pallor of his skin accentuated by wavy black hair that sat on his head like a cap. But on this particular evening his face looked precisely as if it was illuminated by some sort of inner light; and it seemed transfigured. I wasn't the only one who noted this; after his arrest many of us remembered that expression on his face, the face of a man who had condemned himself to death.[8]

Bartenev had inadvertently described an icon. He used a Russian reflexive verb that can as easily be translated "consecrated himself" as "condemned himself" or "doomed himself." Sasha had thought and written in the secular idiom of the intelligentsia, but perhaps images of the Passion sufferers of Orthodox Christianity had brought him to March 1, 1887. Sasha's father had remained a devout follower of Orthodoxy, and even chose Simbirsk's Pokrovskii Monastery's cemetery as his burial place. Ilya Nikolaevich had raised his children as believers and evidently did not understand how far Sasha had fallen under the influence of the atheistic and materialist nihilist thinkers. Toward the end of his gymnasium career Sasha ceased to attend mass, against his father's wishes. Ilya Nikolaevich had to acquiesce. A secular vision dominated Sasha, but the intelligentsia's vision of progress looked very much like Christian eschatology; and self-sacrifice in revolutionary struggle, for some at least, might have been unconsciously modeled on the redemptive suffering of earlier warrior-saints, now reincarnated as *narodovoltsy*—as the People's Will.

Sasha, Anna, and Raisa

W HEN HE GRADUATED from the Simbirsk gymnasium in May 1883, at the age of seventeen, Sasha looked self-confident in the photo marking that event. The student with the best overall record, final examination scores, and the gold medalist, he had every reason to believe that St. Petersburg University would grant him admission. A pile of thick, dark hair brushed straight back from his high forehead added three inches to his height in the class photo—and also in a photo taken roughly four years later—but he was still quite small and had narrow shoulders. During his last year as a gymnasium student in Simbirsk, Alexander began to detach himself from the family. When they added an outside kitchen near the garden, Sasha took some of the extra space for a laboratory. He tried to lighten his father's financial burden by giving lessons during his senior year to earn enough to pay for his various tubes, flasks, retorts, and other scientific paraphernalia. Maria Alexandrovna said no to his plan to hire himself out as a tutor to a merchant's family in a nearby town, and he sullenly complied, burying himself in his makeshift laboratory until his departure in August.

Sasha also spent more time away from home hunting with one of his male cousins; boating on the nearby Sviyaga River and collecting specimens for his laboratory work; playing chess—sometimes with the pugnacious and relentlessly competitive Volodya—often besting multiple opponents at a sitting; and reading advanced scientific and historical literature. He sometimes slept in his laboratory. Knowing that he would likely be taking courses based on

the work of the renowned professor Dmitry Mendeleev, who had formulated the periodic table of the elements, he read the latter's chief work, *The Foundations of Chemistry*. As the favorite son and the carrier of Ilya's hopes, Sasha got more attention from his father at that point in his life than he wished, so he bolted his dinner and fled to his laboratory before Ilya or anyone else at the table could engage him in conversation.

Sasha's self-imposed program of reading had begun to create an intellectual gap between him and Anna. Even though she, too, had taken Pisarev's puritanical nihilist code to heart, and had even abandoned music lessons under his influence, she could not maintain the reading regimen followed by Sasha. Anna had always dreamed of being a writer. She, Sasha, and their favorite cousin, Maria Ivanovna Veretennikova, three and a half years older than Sasha, during their summers together at Kokushkino shared opinions about Russia's great poets and novelists, and Anna quite rightly found some of Sasha's opinions odd. In fact, he had a tin ear for literature as well as for music and lacked insight into the psychology of fictional characters. He sometimes rejected Anna's positive views of fictional heroes—and she chose the obviously robust and courageous ones, like Nezhdanov in Turgenev's *Virgin Soil*. One heated dispute during the summer of 1878 haunted Anna. When she, Sasha, and their cousin Maria discussed their favorite characters in Tolstoy's *War and Peace*, Sasha chose Dolokhov, a scoundrel who murdered the French prisoners of war in his charge. Sasha had quite negative opinions of Prince Andrei and Pierre, the most sympathetic male characters in the novel. The girls—Anna almost two years older than he and Maria three and a half—forced him to defend his choice; the only argument he offered on behalf of Dolokhov was that he loved his mother.[1] The story of a twelve-year-old boy stubbornly and irrationally defending a lost cause against his older sister and female cousin does not in itself suggest anything odd, but it is embedded in observations that tell a great

deal about Sasha's emotional makeup as well as his misreading of great literature.

Anna had noted Sasha's weaknesses in literary composition, some of which she attributed to the formulaic essays dictated by his gymnasium instructors. His stylistically plodding pieces can also be seen as signs of a lack of imagination and expressiveness. Sasha's boyhood failure to reconstruct imaginatively the full emotional world of Tolstoy's fictional characters is not in the least surprising, but to the end of his brief life Sasha measured people and fictional characters by the "scientific" morality taught by nihilist and populist critics. He appreciated humanity's suffering in the abstract and in early adolescence reacted strongly to it, especially in Dostoevsky's works, but seemed to have little empathy for the emotional needs of the real human beings in his life and did not always appreciate the effects of his actions on them. His parents and siblings cherished Sasha's "golden crumbs of affection," and Anna surmises that he repressed the "huge reservoir of sensitive love" that he felt for them. Did he also suppress his love of literature and the fine arts according to the formulas of nihilism, or was he following his natural bent in this as well?

Perhaps personal inclination and gifts and deficits were involved, but gender roles set Anna and Sasha along different paths. Anna had domestic tasks, took care of the younger children, and despite her love of reading had neither the time nor the desire to master the heavy scientific and historical tomes devoured by Sasha, who not only subscribed to a historical journal but borrowed books from a lending library. Anna, no slouch in her chosen fields, completed her gymnasium course before she reached sixteen, and achieved a silver medal. After months of illness she took a position as a teacher's aide in a local school. All the while Sasha plunged further into scientific study, but for Anna the world of the natural sciences remained terra incognita. Even in a family with science in its blood, one in which a female cousin had become one of Russia's

first woman doctors, Anna knew that her strength lay in literature and language, and thought of taking her mother's achievement one step further by preparing for a teaching career in a special program of advanced courses for women in St. Petersburg. Anna's mastery of foreign languages made her services as translator valuable to her younger siblings, and she later published poetry, stories, and novels. The gender divide thus produced an expected result: son imitated father and became a scientist, daughter followed in her mother's footsteps, excelled in humanist disciplines, and became a writer. Sasha also distanced himself from Anna in other ways, and her pique still shows in memoirs written more than forty years after the events of 1882–83. In retrospect she interpreted Sasha's attention to their cousin Maria during their last summer at Kokushkino as his first romantic interest; and it was all the more hurtful because Anna had something of a crush on her younger brother.

During his last summer at home, Sasha tried to detach himself from his adoring older sister without hurting her feelings. High-strung and sensitive to criticism, she resented her brother's interest in their cousin in that summer of 1883; and that apparently triggered not only jealousy but the need to express her affection for Sasha and to test his for her. In her memoirs Anna told of a single moment when Sasha reciprocated her affection.

I remember a walk with Sasha that summer in the garden on a moonlit evening. Everyone had gone to sleep, but I felt like wandering in the garden, and through the window of Sasha's laboratory insistently begged him to take a walk with me. He gave in. We reached the street and turned back to the garden. I was in an especially rapturous mood that evening under the influence of some sort of childish crush, which I felt at that time, and to my own surprise I suddenly tightly embraced Sasha. We didn't usually express any tenderness to each other, but at this moment I couldn't restrain myself. Sasha responded to my impulsiveness

with a firm brotherly embrace—so sweet and sensitive. Hold-ing each other, we walked a little longer in the garden. And at this moment life seemed to be a joyous chorus. In later years I remembered this as a special day—when his brotherly embrace gave me such pure and poetic happiness.[2]

Anna describes another emotional zenith, this time when Sasha returned from his studies in St. Petersburg in May 1884.

I have a vivid memory of his meeting with Mother after he returned from his first year away from home. He had already greeted everyone; the younger children surrounded him. Then he turned back to Mother and firmly, silently embraced her in a surge of warmth. I remember how Mother answered his embrace with such touching joy; and I remember vividly the wonderful glowing expression on his face.[3]

Evidently, Anna remembered these two moments so vividly because they were so rare. In a repeated refrain in her memoirs, she foreshadows Sasha's fate by noting his anguished response to the suffering of others and to stories of injustice. His infrequent expressions of affection and attachment perhaps gave her some hope that he would not withdraw completely from the family into the world of science and abstract ideas that drew him toward—she knew not what. Anna did not fully understand Sasha, and he evi-dently did not understand the women in his life. Nor did he under-stand the younger brother tagging at his heels, desperate for his attention and approval. The cold treatment Volodya received did not, however, set him apart from others close to Sasha.

In January 1887, while he was under police surveillance, Sasha wrote a lengthy letter to his favorite cousin, Maria Ivanovna Veretennikova, and in it gave his only surviving written attempt at self-revelation and self-analysis. Roughly four months after writ-

ing the letter, he presented to the tribunal that sentenced him to death a "scientific" justification for the use of terror in Russia at that historical moment, but spent little time on personal motives. He claimed that he did not count as an individual, except insofar as he fulfilled his obligation to further social progress. In his letter to Maria, however, he does try to explain one of his most salient traits: his lack of strong ties to others. Maria had elicited the letter by asking her cousin his opinion of a mutual friend, but he chose to use the letter for a deeper purpose—a rare attempt at self-analysis—and underlined the seriousness with which he had gone about his task.

Sasha claimed that he kept people at arm's length because he judged most of them harshly, but the memoirs of his fellow university students tell a somewhat different story about him. His peers perceived him as gloomy, taciturn, and self-contained, but also exceedingly gentle and tactful in his relations with them. The latter traits no doubt issued from his efforts to suppress or at least hide his severity. His intense public presence—knitted brows, compressed lips, tendency to sit quietly in a corner at social gatherings and listen without talking at discussions—attracted attention, but did not repel Sasha's peers. On the few occasions when he did speak, he impressed his fellow students with his deep knowledge, passionate convictions, and cogent arguments. His distinctly nihilist style—a muted, ascetic variation, devoid of Bazarov's edginess and pursuit of women or Rakhmetov's occasional cigar and brandy—gave him a certain cachet among young people conditioned to admire that species of behavior as well as impressive knowledge.

It still seems odd that Sasha, who in the weeks before he wrote the letter had been thinking about the assassination attempt, should even have taken time to write something of this sort. He knew that he was being watched and that there was a chance the letter would be intercepted. Other members of the conspiracy sent out indiscreet letters. In fact, one of Andreyushkin's intercepted

letters gave the conspiracy away. Orest Govorukhin left a strange note with Sasha for delivery to Raisa Shmidova, who had helped them hide the explosives for the bombs. In the note Govorukhin hinted that he might commit suicide, although he later claimed that it had been designed to throw the police off his track. Such gestures expressed the need of young men preparing to kill and perhaps to die to explain to important people in their lives who they were and what their actions meant. Was it also adolescent impulse, the need to make a heroic gesture?

Ostensibly about the behavior of an anonymous mutual friend, "NN," Sasha's letter to his cousin contains not just a devastating critique of NN, but also one of women in general, all of which would surely offend his cousin Maria. He wrote,

> I am not in any way deceiving myself about the effect that this letter will have on our relations, but perhaps it will be less harsh if you believe me when I say that the latter failing issues exclusively from the severity of my character and an inclination to see first of all and most clearly of all a person's bad side.[4]

The self-criticism, however, proves to be quite deceptive. The letter actually justifies Sasha's severity even though he apparently regrets the way it affects his human relations. His prose takes on the tone of a scientific analysis of the differences between the mind of a developed person and that of "NN," who exhibited what Sasha took to be typical feminine weaknesses.

The letter sets forth Sasha's version of the ideas of Peter Lavrov, the exiled Russian revolutionary, who had galvanized Russian youth with the theory of the intelligentsia's debt to the masses and inspired the "Going to the People" of the mid-1870s. Lavrov's views of 1884 about human development and morality justified the use of revolutionary terror. Sasha's thinking at the time that he composed the letter perfectly coincided with Lavrov's thinking about the role

of the intelligentsia. The ideas about women, however, are Sasha's rather than Lavrov's.

> I consider the distinguishing features of femininity to be Romanticism (under which I have in mind the predominance of feeling and imagination in a person), a weak development of critical thought, too much individualism, that is, an absence of social sympathies and involvements, acceptance of prejudices circulating in society, insufficient energy, and, mainly, lack of initiative. She doesn't . . . try to arrive at a conscious worldview, fully thought-through social and moral convictions and completely rejects theoretical, scientific approaches to them. . . . In evaluating a person, I always use these measures: to what extent he has worked out definite social ideals and the ideal of another, better order of things; how well founded and progressive his convictions are; and how energetically and confidently he goes about realizing them. . . . Insufficient consciousness expresses itself above all in an excess of individualism, a person forgets about the mass of people surrounding him, about his duty to them; going about his private family or simply personal life, he doesn't notice the suffering around him or simply gets used to it; in other words, he becomes a species of egotist. . . . The concept of "morality" is by its very essence social and, when individualized, is transformed into the notion of "honor."[5]

Sasha's opinions about women sound odd for a socialist sensitive to history's victims, and they seem to contradict the Russian socialists' commitment to equality for women. Like other members of the intelligentsia, Sasha relied upon great writers to transmit realistic images of Russian life. Russian novelists, including Turgenev and Goncharov, had created strong heroines, who often put their Hamlet-like suitors—called "superfluous men" by literary critics—to shame. In both fiction and the real world,

women had no monopoly on Romanticism and inaction or men on science and revolutionary commitment. Sasha knew that some of the revolutionary movement's most prominent figures were women; they had led the terrorist party that he had joined. All revolutionaries knew the names of Sophia Perovskaya and Vera Figner—they stood for courage and service to the cause. In 1878 Turgenev had written a prose poem about women revolutionaries, "The Threshold."

I see a huge building. The front door is wide open; behind the door—deep gloom. A girl stands before a high threshold . . . a Russian girl. The impenetrable gloom chills the air; and together with an icy breath, a solemn, hollow voice issues from the depth of the building.

—O you, who wish to cross this threshold, do you know what awaits you?

—I know, the girl answers.

—Cold, hunger, hatred, ridicule, contempt, humiliation, imprisonment, disease, and death itself.

—I know.

—Total alienation, loneliness.

—I know, I'm ready. I'll endure all sufferings, all blows.

—Not only from enemies—but from kin, from friends?

—Yes, from them, too.

—Very well, are you ready to sacrifice yourself?

—Yes.

—To be a nameless victim? You will perish and no one—no one will know whose memory to honor.

—I need neither thanks nor pity. I don't need to have a name.

—Are you prepared to commit crimes?

—The girl bowed her head . . .

—I am even prepared to commit crimes.

The voice did not immediately continue its questioning.

— Do you know, it said at last — that you might lose faith in your
present beliefs, you might realize that you deceived yourself
and sacrificed your young life in vain?
— I know this, too. And yet I want to enter.
— Enter!
The girl strode across the threshold — and a heavy curtain closed
behind her.
— Fool! — hissed someone.
— Saint! — came from somewhere, in reply.[6]

Women had not only distinguished themselves as leaders in the
Executive Committee of the People's Will and in later terrorist
organizations. In the conspiracy of the Second March First they put
themselves in harm's way to help Sasha construct his clandestine
laboratory in a suburban area and to hide the explosive materials.
In his own family his older cousin, Anna Ivanovna Veretennikova,
was already one of Russia's first woman doctors. Why, then, write
such gratuitously harsh statements about women in general? If the
entire letter is an apologia for his own life — a life that might end
in the near future — then it may be best to see it as an effort to
explain away the brittleness of his human relations in general, his
awkwardness with women, and perhaps with Maria herself. After
the fact, she would understand his actions.

Some of Sasha's opinions about women, like most of his opinions, were probably based upon the science of the day. In both scientific publications and the journals that published some of Sasha's
favorite authors, there were reviews and discussions of brain
measurements — size, weight, chemical composition, convolutions,
fat content, and white and gray matter — that "demonstrated" the
inferiority of women. The Dutch physiologist Jacob Moleschott's
famous aphorism "No thought without phosphorous" had been
used to show that men in general and male scientists in particular
had more of that chemical in their large brains, just as the materi-

alist philosopher Ludwig Feuerbach's "Man is what he eats" had been used to demonstrate the superiority of English beef eaters over Irish potato eaters. Dobrolyubov, among others, on the basis of brain measurements had endorsed the notion of women's intellectual inferiority to men. Sasha, a typical scientific materialist, might easily have accepted Dobrolyubov's homage to contemporary authorities, whose data and theories about men's and women's brains were rejected by other scientists. But we can only speculate about the meaning of the contradictions in Sasha's thinking about women and his behavior toward those closest to him during the last months of his life. Despite all of his efforts to avoid any dissonance, his feelings and actions sometimes came into conflict with his hard-won scientific formulas; and his treatment of the women he loved the most seemed unconsciously designed to hurt them.

In the last months of his life he either distanced himself from the women closest to him or thoughtlessly endangered them. He gave Anna's address to Shevyrev to use as the destination for a conspiratorial telegram sent from Vilnius on February 3, 1887.[7] Although Sasha gave her advance notice that she would receive the telegram, he did not reveal its purpose: to let him know that their emissary to Vilnius had acquired the nitric acid, strychnine, and pistol for which he had been sent, and was on the way to St. Petersburg. The telegram led to Anna's arrest and incarceration along with the other conspirators. Anna had not been involved in the conspiracy and did not even know about it. She was completely befuddled by the strange message sent under the false name "Petrov": "Sister is dangerously ill." Sasha simply misled her. In his trial testimony under cross-examination on April 15, 1887, he said that he quickly realized he had made a mistake and had wanted to rectify it, but it was too late to intercept their agent, Kancher. Until Maria Alexandrovna successfully pled her daughter's case to Alexander III, Anna faced the possibility of Siberian exile. Sasha sought to be ultra-rational and completely scientific in his behavior, but his carelessness vio-

lated common sense, much less conspiratorial scrupulousness. In prison because of him, the all-forgiving Anna wrote to Sasha first, twice before she received a reply. Neither of her letters survives in the archives, but in her memoirs she describes her first letter as "a wail from the depths of her soul" and quotes herself: "There isn't a better or nobler person than you on the earth. I don't say this alone or because I'm your sister; everyone who knows you says so, dear light of my life."[8] In his last prison letter to Anna, written less than two weeks before his execution, Sasha tries to find the emotional pitch consonant with the situation:

26 April

Dear Anna!

Many thanks for your letter. I received it a few days ago and was very happy to have it. I delayed a bit before writing because I hoped to see you in person, but I don't know if that will be possible.

I stand before you infinitely guilty, my dear little Anna; this is the first thing I must say to you and beg your forgiveness for it. I won't enumerate all the harm that I've caused you and, through you, Mama: that's self-evident to both of us. Forgive me, if that's possible.

The accommodations are good, the food is good, and in all, I lack for nothing. I have enough money; there are also books. I feel good both physically and psychologically.

Be well and tranquil, as far as this is possible; from all my soul I wish you every happiness. Goodbye, my dear one, I firmly embrace and kiss you.

Yours, A. Ulyanov

Please write me again; I'll be very happy to receive even the least bit of news. I'll also write you, if I learn that I'll be able to. Goodbye again.

Yours, Al. Ulyanov[9]

The letter and its afterthought seem strangely formulaic, along the lines of other letters he sent home designed to allay any anxiety about his material circumstances. The closing is even more stilted than his usual "Yours, A.U.," as if written by someone distant. Sasha shows simultaneously the formal tokens of affection and the emotional detachment of someone who had already made his most impassioned and most important goodbye on April 19, in court, where he had made a pact with death and posterity.

Maria Alexandrovna suffered in a different way because of Sasha's behavior. No human being in the world was closer to Sasha than she was, yet his self-destructive behavior in April 1887 might easily have destroyed her, too. One memoirist, no doubt hyperbolically, claims that Sasha's execution rendered his mother an emotional invalid for the rest of her life. Did he choose revolutionary morality and his ties to the group that called itself "the Terrorist Faction of the People's Will" over ties of love and affection to the women closest to him? Revolutionary morality required that one sacrifice loved ones, if the cause demanded it. The authorities must have found Maria Alexandrovna a compelling figure because, although the public and relatives of the accused were not allowed in the courtroom, they made an exception for her on April 19 and allowed her to hear his last statement, a ringing defense of terrorism. Maria Alexandrovna could not bear it and left the courtroom before he finished.

The most important woman in Sasha's life at the time of the conspiracy and during the judicial process, Raisa Shmidova, claimed that she and Sasha had loved each other and that in February they had been betrothed, in a fashion. In the end, she too suffered from the relationship. A typical *nigilistka* and a midwife by profession, Shmidova had befriended Sasha and Anna. She suffered lifelong exile to Siberia for her involvement in the conspiracy, but like several of the others was amnestied after the Revolution of 1905 and lived to see 1917. Shmidova married another exiled revolutionary

in 1887 and raised three children with him in Krasnoyarsk. At the beginning of the Civil War she wrote a letter to Lenin in which she averred that she had loved Sasha, had been his fiancée, and still loved him. Shmidova—by marriage, Klyuge—then complained about her family's dreadful material position as a result of the Civil War and the behavior of the Red troops. She begged Lenin's help. In the absence of an answer from him, years later she contacted Anna. On December 31, 1923, Shmidova wrote angrily in reply to a letter (evidently not preserved) in which Anna had accused her of inventing her betrothal to Sasha in order to get material help from the family. Driven to counter-accusations that Anna expressed bourgeois attitudes, which didn't accept "I love you" as a token of betrothal, but required a ring and official documents, Shmidova told more in her letter than "bourgeois" modesty required.[10] The letter, though somewhat incoherent, has details of her relationship with Sasha that seem quite authentic: his profession of love; the two nights that they'd spent together, one of them on a bed under which they'd concealed explosives; how during the trial they'd kissed each other on the lips while waiting in the corridor before entering the courtroom. They kissed not merely for passion's sake, but as a way to exchange notes in tiny scrolls wrapped in foil taken from packages of tea. Such details are too good to be false. Shmidova repeated them in memoirs written in 1937 and published only in 1967—both anniversary years of Sasha's execution.

Although occasionally inaccurate, the memoirs nonetheless shed light on what Raisa meant to Sasha. "I'd say that we complemented each other; each of us had what the other lacked."[11] She did not claim (as she had in her letters) that she had been Sasha's fiancée, but she did make it clear that they had a strong relationship, and tried to explain why. Her vivaciousness and impressionability, which seemed to others a sign of Shmidova's shallowness or even wantonness, evidently attracted Sasha. She sang beautifully, and he loved to hear her render his favorite revolutionary hymns.

Raisa created for Sasha a small space for joie de vivre. When Sasha and Lukashevich decided to throw a goodbye party for the terrorist group, they turned to Shmidova for help. Despite his superior knowledge and talents, Sasha did not treat her condescendingly—and she admired that in him. Theoretical knowledge was not her strong suit, but she took great risks during the unfolding of the conspiracy and got both his respect and his love. Each had what the other wanted. She admired everything about him, but especially his depth and seriousness; he was drawn to the life force that preserved her for decades in Siberian exile.

Those closely connected with Sasha during 1886 and 1887 mistakenly believed that he had only casual contact with Shmidova. The intellectually shallow Shmidova was obviously no match for Sasha. And how could she have married so soon after the hanging if she had loved Sasha? Anna and other memoirists evidently thought that they were protecting Sasha's reputation by disavowing any love relationship, but one memoirist, Semyon Khlebnikov, had a somewhat different view:

I think that many of the young women who surrounded Ilyich were like ... Russian heroines, poetically portrayed by Turgenev in his prose poem, "The Threshold," women who would without a moment's hesitation follow Ilyich to death, if that were necessary. So it was especially unfortunate that Alexander Ilyich—that pure, childishly credulous soul, chose ... a person whose qualities were so inappropriate—morally and intellectually or even purely physically—for a person with his superior qualities. I knew this person well. Perhaps she's still alive, and one shouldn't go into greater detail about her character and the facts of her life. I'll only say that she showed how short a memory ... she had for the unforgettable Alexander Ilyich. ... Barely three months after Alexander Ilyich's execution, while en route to her place of exile, she found another object for her affections and married

him. When the news reached them Alexander Ilyich's comrades
were justly bewildered and bitter.[12]

Such condemnations seem unjust. Shmidova was, after all, a
nigilistka, and disdained conventional notions of morality—proper
hairdos, feminine dress codes, and sexual prohibitions. This, too,
might have made her attractive to Sasha, but quite a few men in
the revolutionary milieu had not given up their notions about how
women should behave and dress and what made them physically
attractive. Shmidova's cri de coeur to Anna went unheeded and,
but for Anna's preservation of her letters, would have been censored as well:

> Until this very moment I still don't understand one thing: Why
> did your brother, going to a certain death, tell me about his
> feelings? So that I, shattered, would carry this into the tundra
> to the farthest north tormented with the loss of the person I
> loved the most?[13]

Shmidova's letters convincingly describe a very young man
who awkwardly expressed his love for her at a moment of separa-
tion. Tragically, Shmidova returned to her native Kharkiv, only to
be interned in the ghetto created by the Nazi authorities during
their occupation of the city. She either was hanged by the Nazis
or committed suicide in December 1942 by throwing herself out
of a window.[14]

IN THE AUTUMN OF 1886 Shmidova had lived in an apartment separated from Ulyanov and Chebotarev's only by the
landlady's dining room. They were frequent guests in each other's
apartments, and Shmidova visited Sasha much more often than
Anna did. Later in the autumn she moved to an apartment on
Italian Street, where she lived next to Govorukhin until he left on

February 20. She apparently continued her strong relationship with Sasha and aided him and Govorukhin with conspiratorial tasks. Despite memoirs that cast doubt on the seriousness of Shmidova's commitment to revolutionary work, all of the evidence suggests that Shmidova had strong ties with terrorist networks in Kharkiv and Vilnius. At Shmidova's request Sasha asked Anna to put up for a night a member of the terrorist group in Vilnius, Hannah Leibovich. The police found in Anna's apartment notes from both Sasha and Shmidova requesting lodging for Leibovich.

Sasha spent his last days of freedom with Shmidova. She helped him and the core members of the conspiracy organize the farewell party, and then they worked together on Februrary 27–28 feverishly setting the type for the group's program. On the morning of March 1, Shmidova came to Anna's apartment. She told Anna that she had just been with Sasha at his apartment, a fact confirmed by one of his depositions. That same morning, Mark Elizarov arrived at Anna's, and the three of them went for a walk on that bright, almost spring-like Sunday afternoon—perhaps at the same time that the combat squad and the police were out on the streets. When Anna expressed her concern about Sasha, Elizarov told her knowingly—suggesting that he had been present at the goodbye party mentioned by Shmidova and Lukashevich—"Alexander Ilyich has already sung the funeral hymn."[15]

Students

I LYA NIKOLAEVICH and Maria Alexandrovna had hoped that
Sasha would study nearby, at Kazan University, south of Simbirsk on the Volga, where Ilya had launched his career and written
his master's thesis, but Alexander knew that an aspiring biologist
would go further in St. Petersburg, and, like any boy his age, he
wanted to escape his parents' suffocating concern for him and his
career. The parents consoled themselves that their son and daughter
would look after each other in the dangerously rebellious student
population of the capital city. Even before Alexander completed his
gymnasium studies, he had become the center of the family, a kind
of moral force as well as its first hope to realize the recently established family imperative of achievement in the sciences. Despite
his maturity in most respects, his shyness and incommunicativeness
worried his parents, who knew less about his internal world than
they wished.

Alexander II had been assassinated in St. Petersburg on March
1, 1881, just two years earlier, and the hunt for the young terrorists
of the People's Will continued. The terrorist campaign and assassination had shocked loyal civil servants like Ilya Nikolaevich. Alexander II's reforms had created the framework of Ilya Nikolaevich's
successful career as an enlightened educator. The first attempt on
Alexander II's life occurred in 1866, the year of Sasha's birth, and
there were nine subsequent unsuccessful attempts until the Executive Committee of the People's Will carried out his death sentence.
Although the schools had been put under a stricter regime during

the formation of the radical subculture in the 1860s, the crackdown under Alexander III after his father's assassination greatly curtailed the autonomy of the universities and the rich corporate life of the students. Russia's refractory youth, however, did not accept such reactionary trends with equanimity and always found ways to circumvent the rules. It was a worrisome situation for parents sending their children to the capital of the empire, and Ilya Nikolaevich and Maria Alexandrovna may have sensed that some sort of rebellion simmered beneath the apparent calm of the pride of the Simbirsk classical gymnasium's graduating class of 1883.

T HE TRIP FROM SIMBIRSK on the Volga to St. Petersburg on the Neva required, first, a journey northwest by steamboat to Nizhny Novgorod, and from there a long train trip. Already frugal by habit and also feeling guilty about the greater expenses incurred by his declining to go to Kazan University, Sasha traveled in a grimy, crowded third-class coach during the long leg of the trip. After his arrival in late August 1883, he found cheap housing in the Peski District, and by refusing to pay for cabs and the horse-drawn trams that served as public transportation, he managed to save ten of the forty rubles that Ilya Nikolaevich gave him each month.[1] Russian university students often got by on thirty rubles a month, sometimes twenty-five, and Sasha undoubtedly knew this. He didn't feel that he was making a sacrifice. Anna arrived in September. Although she was two years older than Sasha, Anna acted like the junior sibling, deferring to him in everything but his literary opinions, which she sometimes found puzzling. Alexander enrolled in the natural sciences at the university, and Anna in the Bestuzhev courses in higher education for women.

Sasha had to decide what his relationship to Anna would be in their new life in St. Petersburg. He quickly looked for ways to separate himself from her after their initial closeness of September 1883. At first he had to play the role of responsible male to

Anna—for young women presumably needed men to look after them—even if the "man" was a small, studious seventeen-year-old two years her junior and still finding his way in a city of 800,000. Created at the beginning of the eighteenth century by imperial fiat and the architectural whims of the ruling family and aristocracy, St. Petersburg, by virtue of the empresses' enlistment of mainly Italian architects, became the "Venice of the North." It was built on islands in the Neva delta, with magnificent palaces along the rivers and canals, gilded cathedrals and state buildings with stately columns and pilasters, parks with marble statues, stuccoed town houses painted with a Mediterranean palette of green, lavender, blue, and yellow. Nevsky Prospect, a splendid thoroughfare, ran from the Alexander Nevsky Monastery to the Winter Palace through a district full of luxury shops; but there were also slums around putrid Haymarket Square, rough areas adjacent to recently built railroad stations, and new ghettoes on the periphery populated by a growing factory proletariat.

In late August 1883 Sasha took an apartment suggested by a family friend in the Peski District, but it was a very long walk from the university, and Sasha immediately began to search for more convenient lodgings. In the unusually long letter—long for him, at least—to his mother written on September 27, 1883, he gave a relatively detailed account of the fortunate outcome of his first travails in the city. After an unsuccessful search on Vasilevsky Island, home to St. Petersburg University, he settled on the Petersburg side, to the northeast across a branch of the river, the Little Neva. He rented a room on the second floor of a two-story wooden home, with private access to his own bright, spacious room, which had a high ceiling and two windows. It was dry and cozy, something to be grateful for in St. Petersburg's winters. There was a bed with an iron bedstead, like his own in Simbirsk, a leather divan, a table and chairs, and a chest of drawers. The elderly landlady, a kindly woman, charged him ten rubles a month for the room and for cleaning it.

Sasha also took partial board, which consisted of a two-course dinner for thirty-five kopecks. With such modest living expenses he could easily get by on thirty rubles a month. These comfortable arrangements, however, did not prevent Sasha from falling ill with a stubborn form of typhus. Throughout the academic year he suffered from recurring fevers and stomach problems. St. Petersburg's water supply, drawn from the highly polluted Neva, and her landlady's "industrial" cuisine took their toll on Anna as well. Sasha's motherly landlady, however, saw to it that he was well fed during his illness, and prepared dishes for Anna as well when she visited.

The house at 4 Syezzhinskaya Street was conveniently located a short walk from the Stock Exchange Bridge, which linked the Petersburg side to Vasilevsky Island and the embankment near the Rostral Columns and Stock Exchange Square. Sasha could walk to the university in fifteen or twenty minutes. Another bridge connected the Petersburg side to the Peter and Paul Fortress. On his way to the university Sasha walked parallel to a narrow strait separating the Petersburg side from the island fortress and the golden spire of the Peter and Paul Cathedral that contained the tombs of the Romanov emperors and empresses. In September, when they still lived together in the Peski District, Anna and Sasha visited the cathedral and stood amid the sarcophagi of the emperors and empresses, but then went out to look at the walls of the fortress's political prison, where their beloved Pisarev had spent four years and where Sasha would spend the greater part of the last weeks of his life.

Exploring the city with Anna and apartment hunting quickly gave way to the serious business of exploiting the city's vast cultural resources and preparing for lectures. Sasha spent his happiest moments in the university itself, especially in its laboratories and libraries. Dominico Trezzini, the premier architect of St. Petersburg during Peter the Great's reign, had originally designed the university's main building to house the twelve *collegia* of Russia's

new imperial government. Ironically, Trezzini had also designed the Peter and Paul Fortress. Alexander I gave the buildings that had housed Peter's *collegia* to the newly founded St. Petersburg University in 1819. The converted twelve *collegia* formed a single, very long—over 400 meters—but relatively narrow structure. In the words of one of Sasha's contemporaries:

> Its back end sat on the Neva embankment, and its wide, three-story façade opened out to the University line. Inside were similarly endless corridors running the length of the building, and rows of windows too numerous to count. A noisy crowd of students, dressed every which way (there was no uniform at that time), moved along the corridor. And the professors picked their way through the crowd to get to their lecture halls—the renowned Mendeleev with a monstrously large head and a golden mane, like a lion's, falling to his shoulders.... The physical-mathematical and law faculties had huge auditoriums, the historical-philological small ones.[2]

For his forays into the central city, if he walked briskly across the Palace Bridge, past the Alexandrov Gardens, and then down Nevsky Prospect with the Kazan Cathedral Square and Merchants' Court, a vast colonnaded arcade with a great variety of shops, on his right, Sasha in a short time could reach the city's impressive Public Library next to the Anichkov Palace. He spent much of his time there before the university lectures began in September.

Sasha condenses into a single sentence in the letter of September 27, 1883, his positive impression of the lectures and of the university's facilities—luxurious offices and well-stocked libraries—but he described in some detail Turgenev's funeral that had taken place in the Volkovo suburb south of the central city on that very day. Turgenev had died in France, and his coffin had to be transported by rail to the Warsaw Station in St. Petersburg. On a funeral wagon

under a golden canopy and surrounded by wreaths, it reached the cemetery in Volkovo in midafternoon. Sasha and Anna watched the procession, but it was impossible to get inside the cemetery, where four of Russia's most prominent scientists and writers eulogized Turgenev. Sasha did not note in his letter that Cossacks and police barred entry to the cemetery. More than three years later when he wrote the student proclamation condemning the behavior of the police and Cossacks on the twenty-fifth anniversary of Dobrolyubov's death, Sasha mentioned Turgenev's funeral, and bitterly referred to the Cossacks and police as "representatives of the government." Sasha and Anna faced the "brute force" of the tsar's instruments for the first time, but not the last, in September 1883 at the gates of the Volkovo Cemetery. Anna's memoirs show that Sasha was already sensitized to the regime's brutality.

When Anna arrived in September, she joined Sasha in the apartment in the Peski District, but they parted ways when he moved to Syezzhinskaya Street. Although Anna liked Sasha's new living arrangement and hoped that she could live near him, he encouraged her to find something closer to the Botkin House on Sergievskaya Street, where the Bestuzhev courses were given in a stolid, two-story building. There Anna found herself in the company of about seven hundred elite young women, who, like herself, came mainly from enlightened gentry families that could afford the tuition. A significant number were radical and showed the usual signs of the feminist branch of the nihilist subculture—cropped hair, red blouses, rough language, and "masculine" mannerisms—very much like Shmidova. Many of the best students were enrolled in the natural sciences and mathematics rather than the literary-historical curriculum, and quite a few were under police surveillance. It was not a happy situation for Anna, but she had never been a happy person. Ilya Nikolaevich, jokingly applying the ancient formulas of the four humors to his children, had dubbed the older pair "melancholic" whereas Vladimir was "choleric." The relative autonomy of

the Bestuzhev courses at that moment in their history and the services of distinguished professors like Mendeleev, who gave lectures
that paralleled those at the university, did not dramatically improve
the chances of young women. They were certified to teach only at
an intermediate level after completing their program of study.

The distance between Anna's house on Sergievskaya Street and
Sasha's did not prevent them from dining together twice a week
during their first academic year, every Sunday and Wednesday.
Although he was suffering from a stubborn typhus infection, he
kept on working except for a few days in bed at its onset; but when
Anna fell ill with a respiratory ailment, he advised her to go home
to recover. She blamed her ill health on her landlady's kitchen; to
add to her misery she suffered from homesickness. Shy and conventional in dress and interests, Anna did not fit in well with the
nigilistki she met in the Bestuzhev courses. The courses themselves
suffered because of the anxiety of the administration during the
crackdown of 1884, and Anna became bored with the instruction.
She made all of this quite clear to Sasha, who thought Anna would
be better off at home in Simbirsk. No doubt he also thought of
liberating more time for his work. Anna, however, pulled herself
together. They both prevailed against illness and she against loneliness, boredom, and homesickness by spending as much time as she
could with him and his kindly landlady, whose personality as well as
cooking had a healing effect on both of them. Like any lonely first-
year student, Anna wanted to go home for the semester break, but
Sasha refused to spend the money on travel or his time on something other than his studies, and she, still clinging to him, greeted
1884 in St. Petersburg.

Sasha had matriculated at St. Petersburg with the ringing
endorsement of his gymnasium teachers, including that of the relatively enlightened rector, Fyodor Kerensky, whose son Alexander
became head of the Provisional Government after the February
Revolution in 1917. Sasha, however, now was just one of many bril-

liant young men drawn from every corner of the Russian Empire. In 1885 St. Petersburg University had 2,206 students. Roughly half of them, 1,037, enrolled in the physical-mathematical faculty, and a little more than half of those worked in the physical sciences.[3] The prestige of the faculty in the biological sciences drew many students, but ideology played a role in this, too. The idea of science as the source of all truth and as a panacea for human ills had been introduced by the nihilist critics thirty years earlier and remained strong in this period. Although the nihilist ideologues had created the image of the heroic scientist with revolutionary goals, the lure of pure science—science for its own sake—attracted students with a genuine scientific bent. They quickly learned that in order to succeed they had to specialize and devote most of their energies to laboratory work. Sasha told Anna that he spent eighteen hours a day on his studies. For five semesters he pursued the ascetic routine of preparing for his exams and doing additional laboratory work in the pursuit of scientific discovery and the junior prize for original research. Many others who had been attracted to science for mainly ideological reasons went into medicine. Like all difficult courses of study, the physical sciences took their toll; fewer than one in three students who had joined the department survived until the fourth year.

Aside from his extreme frugality and work habits, there is nothing unusual in the story of Sasha's student career before the autumn semester of 1886. His surviving letters of 1883–87 to his parents, but mainly to his mother, tell a very ordinary story of student life, but they are remarkably terse and signed "Yours, A. U." The bodies of the letters have no expressions of affection, aside from "dear little Mama," in a typical Russian diminutive, *mamochka*. Anna commented on the letters' brevity and colorlessness, which she took as another token of Sasha's bottled-up emotions. Evidently many of the letters have perished—Sasha sometimes complained or responded to his mother's complaints about a lapse in commu-

nications after the passage of two weeks—only twenty-seven of his letters to his immediate family survive for 1883–87, including two written in prison. The ordinary fare for his first year: On May 11, 1884: "Thank you, dear Papa, for sending money (50 rubles). Don't send any more, so much remains from before." On May 19, 1884: "My third exam went well; today I have to take the fourth, anatomy...."[4] Not a single letter to Sasha from the still worshipful Volodya has survived, if he wrote any. There are no letters from Sasha to him, although at Volodya's request (perhaps forwarded by Maria Alexandrovna), Sasha sent logarithmic tables and books for his younger brother, and he recommended to Volodya through Maria Alexandrovna a book on mathematical sophisms that he had earlier sent to his father.

The few and brief letters do not reveal very much about Sasha's first years in St. Petersburg or the changes in his thinking, but the intellectual life there, at least, is known. Any biology student at St. Petersburg University at that moment in Russian science faced an array of evolutionary thinkers, many of whom produced novel approaches to the notion of the struggle for existence that Darwin and others had placed at the center of the evolutionary process. During the brief period between his arrival in August and the beginning of lectures in September, Sasha spent much of his time in the Public Library on Nevsky Prospect reading Darwin. Pisarev's writings had already exposed Sasha to the nihilist approach to Darwinism. Converts to Darwin's ideas had quickly turned them into ideologies supporting quite different positions on a spectrum that ran from confident conservatism to dedicated revolutionism.

If evolution had produced all creatures through a long process of struggle and natural selection, then the qualities of human beings and their societies had to reflect that process. The struggle for existence presumably continued, although in ever novel forms. Russian Darwinists generally rejected the influential English and American approaches endorsing the "fittest," the successful *individuals* who

had outcompeted others and found their rightful place at the top of the social hierarchy. Russian thinkers rather chose as successful competitors in the struggle for existence *groups* whose individual members might go so far as to sacrifice themselves for the group's survival. Such groups rationally expanded to include others, ultimately forming a unified species and universal collaboration in the struggle for survival. Instead of the struggle of all against all, humanity evolved toward an all-inclusive cooperative social system—socialism. The most developed human beings had altruistic instincts rather than aggressive ones, and they would eventually unify the human species.[5] Rebels found congenial the notion that the disadvantaged and exploited groups would eventually unite against the ruling classes and end both conflict and division. Such ideas prepared Sasha for the ideological company he would keep in the university, but at first he kept to himself and spent most of the time studying.

During his first two years Sasha apprenticed himself to N. P. Vagner, the professor of zoology who directed his junior thesis in 1885. Vagner had established Russia's first biological field station, at Solovetsk, in the Archangel region, and published a major study of the invertebrates of the White Sea. The faculty celebrities of that era, however, were A. N. Beketov, K. A. Timiryazev, A. M. Butlerov, I. M. Sechenov, and D. I. Mendeleev. Their influence pervaded Russian science at the university, and several of them lectured in the Bestuzhev courses as well. Vagner had been recruited to St. Petersburg by Karl Federovich Kessler, who served as professor of zoology between 1861 and 1881 and played a major role in the establishment of the Russian interpretation of the struggle for existence, emphasizing mutual aid.[6] Some Russian Darwinists went so far as to banish the idea of a struggle for existence—which they deemed an ill-conceived metaphor—from a theory that they otherwise found basic to an understanding of nature and society. Fidelity to the cooperative or mutual-aid version of Darwinism, however,

did not necessarily entail commitment to revolution. Govorukhin, who did not at first find Sasha an eager recruit, in his memoirs no doubt faithfully represents Sasha's priorities during his first five semesters in the following remarks about radical students:

> They chatter a lot, but don't study very much. . . . I don't join revolutionary organizations, because I haven't yet solved many problems that are important for me, personally, and more important, social problems. Surely, if the natural sciences . . . are only now entering that phase of their development when they can look at phenomena from a quantitative as well as a qualitative point of view—are only now becoming genuine sciences, then what do the social sciences represent? Clearly, social problems cannot be solved quickly. I propose, of course, a scientific solution—another makes no sense—and a social activist must find one. It would be absurd if an ignoramus of a doctor tried to cure a disease; it would be even more absurd and immoral to try to cure social diseases, without understanding their causes.[7]

Nothing in Sasha's correspondence in his sophomore year suggests anything new in his life: "The trip was good, especially on the steamboat, the train trip was better than last autumn, I even slept a little both nights," Sasha wrote after he arrived in St. Petersburg on September 13, 1884, two weeks earlier than Anna. He set up in his old apartment, but Anna's had already been rented to another student, and he had to find a new one for her. After his first classes of the new academic year, he wrote on September 29, 1884,

> Everything at the university is as before, there's nothing new; the lectures are okay. I'll be working in the chemistry laboratory in the second semester, I fell into the second group because I'm one of the last alphabetically; for the other subjects I'm in the first semester. There are relatively few students in the courses

because many of them went into the medical academy, and they say that there are only 80 of us now.

One of the most revealing letters of Sasha's sophomore year tells of student disturbances, in which he shows no apparent interest; indeed, he is at pains to reassure his parents, something that makes it suspect. On October 6, 1884:

> You are probably concerned, reading about the disturbances in Kiev and Moscow universities. Right now everything is calm here; there are no noticeable signs of agitation. Only they say that M. Semevskii [sic], an adjunct university lecturer in Russian history, will no longer give his course; that, by the way, is explained not so much by the new regulations as the arrival of Bestuzhev-Riumin, who's at odds with him.

Sasha repeated the widespread opinion that K. N. Bestuzhev-Riumin, the reigning celebrity in history and opponent of Vasilii Semevskii's ideas about Russian agrarian history, would never allow his former protégé to teach there. Sasha and Anna later attended lectures about the history of Russia's peasants given in Semevskii's apartment after the university censored them. The regime did not want peasant rebellion to be a part of the curriculum. Sasha joined with others in signing a letter of support when Semevskii was fired.[8]

The regime's sensitivity to any signs of sedition showed in every corner of Russian life after the shock of March 1, 1881, but the universities had salvaged considerable autonomy until the full impact of the regime's security apparatus plus the measures put in place by the minister of education, Count I. D. Delyanov, hit them in 1884. The long-delayed efforts to curb university and, particularly, student autonomy were part of a multipronged attack on intelligentsia critics and the educational trends that were undermining Nicholas

I's conservative ideology of "Autocracy, Orthodoxy, and National-
ity." After the tsar appointed Delyanov in the spring of 1882, one
enlightened bureaucrat, Dmitry Milyutin, using an earlier minister
of education, Dmitry Tolstoy, as his point of comparison, wrote in
his diary, "It's the resurrection of Tolstoy's generally despised ministry . . . with the only difference being the underlying cause. With
Tolstoy it was bile, with Delyanov, it will be idiocy."[9] Alexander III
had made the despised Tolstoy minister of the interior in 1882. After
a period of anxiety about his own survival, the new tsar chose a
group of tough counterreformers who tried to roll back what his
father had granted in the reform era following the Crimean War.
Even the State Council, whose duties included a combination of
judicial and legislative functions, proceeded cautiously with Delyanov's proposed university charter in the autumn of 1883. Although
they were willing to curb the universities' rights to appoint faculty
members without the administration's intervention, some members
of the State Council balked at the attempt to impose a system of
state examinations. The notion that the state bureaucracy would be
entrusted with academic examinations, and that the very professors
who had taught the courses would be excluded from the process,
offended even imperial bureaucrats who understood the need to
tighten control over the universities for security reasons. The most
benighted of Delyanov's reforms were defeated by tsarist bureaucrats who were more liberal than Alexander III and his closest advisers. The tsar, however, chose to back the minority report in August
1884, and in Sasha's sophomore year the new university charter,
although not all of its most obnoxious clauses, became law.

The state exercised oversight of the universities through the
minister of education and a group of superintendents: the minister
of education with the advice of the superintendent of the university
in the region under his jurisdiction chose the chancellors and deans
of the universities. The minister of education either filled faculty
vacancies with appointees of his choice or allowed the faculties to

select a candidate, which he would then confirm or reject. The state thus took away the powers of the academic council and departments of each university to make such decisions autonomously. Academic councils now had only the power to determine annually the number of medals awarded to students for compositions on selected topics, and power over the award of scholarly degrees, including doctorates. All other decisions had to be confirmed by the superintendents or the minister of education. University judicial committees were disbanded. The inspectors of students, formerly subordinated to the academic council and the chancellor, were now appointed by the minister of education and under the directorship of the superintendent. The role of the inspector of students grew and now included the granting of stipends to needy students. The latter role had special significance in view of Delyanov's desire to maintain the dominance of the Russian gentry and to limit the growing influence (in their eyes, at least) of less reliable students from lower social strata and of minority background. In his effort to enforce conformity, Delyanov brought back the hated uniforms that symbolized the power of the state to shape the identity of the younger generation.

The police spies in the universities typically produced biased reports that exaggerated the role of putatively unreliable groups; Count Delyanov used the reports to justify additional repressive measures. The regime's suspicion of the independence-minded nationalities of the empire and of the especially hated Jewish minority showed in police reports about the composition and behavior of the student body of St. Petersburg University. One such report prepared by the chief of police of St. Petersburg for Count Delyanov noted that less than 30 percent of the student body of the university in 1886–87 came from the St. Petersburg region. The vast majority of students were thus somewhat far away from their families and, in Lieutenant General Gresser's view, more likely to get involved in political movements. Even more threatening to the

police and Delyanov, almost 12 percent of the students (319 out of a total of 2,738) were Jews, identified as "cosmopolitans with no loyalty to a motherland," a view that survived in the stereotype of Jews as "rootless cosmopolitans" in the Soviet period. According to the report: "The Jewish tribe has a passion for living at others' expense and they try to do so at the expense of the *zemlyachestva* by taking over management of their treasury. They thus agitate for the formation of *zemlyachestva*."[10] Delyanov set a quota on the number of Jewish students admitted to higher education in 1887, but in spite of the restrictions a variety of loopholes allowed them to persevere. The regime's persecutions, rather than higher education, turned minorities into revolutionaries in numbers quite disproportionate to their representation in the population of the empire. Even presumably loyal groups—indeed, groups notable for their anti-Semitism—joined the revolutionary movement.

Some elements of the Cossacks, the military caste that the regime used to suppress disturbances, produced dissidents. Students from the Don and Kuban in St. Petersburg formed the most radical of the twenty student groups organized according to regional origin, and they did so in other universities as well. There is a great irony in this. The Cossacks, especially in Michael Bakunin's version of *narod-nichestvo*, represented an anarchic, revolutionary, freedom-loving element in the larger mass of peasants, but for the regime, and for Alexander III in particular, they represented loyal and unwavering military service to the throne. In 1886 Sasha began to frequent the dining facility that the Cossacks used as a cover for their political meetings, and police reports erroneously listed him as a member of the Don and Kuban Cossack organization. There he would find his fellow conspirators—Govorukhin, Generalov, and Andreyushkin.

University students and faculty typically fought the Delyanov rules by ignoring or subverting any efforts to curb the corporate life that they'd created for themselves during the period of Alexander II's reforms. The new university charter denied them the

right to form *zemlyachestva*, regional societies that aided indigent students, promoted study of things that censorship forbade, and — as the regime dreaded—served as the seedbeds of political conspiracies. Delyanov designed the reform as one dimension of the regime's effort to restore the control of the conservative gentry over major institutions. Poorer students as well as non-Russians were suspected of being naturally more seditious, and after March 1, 1887, the regime added a hike in tuition to its attack on the *zemlyachestva* and other student devices for channeling money to indigent students.

There is reason to believe that in his letter of October 6, 1884, to his parents, Sasha was less than candid. In the spring semester of 1884, before the new rules were promulgated, there were rumors that the authorities were planning to close the Bestuzhev women's courses (they did not cease, but closed enrollment in 1885); the regime had already closed the medical school for women in St. Petersburg after its brief existence. Anna describes Sasha's reaction in late April 1884 to another rumor that proved false — that the satirist M. E. Saltykov-Shchedrin, one of their favorite writers and adroit editor of the recently shut-down *narodnik* journal, *Patriotic Notes*, had been arrested. According to Anna: "I don't remember if Sasha first heard it from me, but I transmitted the rumor to him. . . . At first calm and settled, Sasha darkened. 'This is such a rotten despotism—it's throwing all of the best people in jail,' he said quietly, but with such powerful indignation that it once again terrified me." Anna here refers to Sasha's similar, though wordless, reaction after their visit to the Peter and Paul Fortress. His acute sensitivity to the regime's treatment of the intelligentsia provoked a level of outrage that exceeded ordinary limits. "Sasha gloomily turned inward for the remainder of the evening, which I had ruined for both of us. . . . Now I think that a more astute observer at that moment would have foreseen his fate."[11]

Throughout 1884 and 1885 Sasha remained far from any sort of

commitment to revolutionary activity, much less a suicidal variation of terrorism. Nonetheless, Anna surely detected something
simmering in him and ready to explode. I. V. Chebotarev, Sasha's
apartment-mate during the fall semester of his junior year, and
Govorukhin, the person who probably recruited him to terrorism,
are of one opinion that Sasha did not become involved in student
affairs, much less revolutionary activity, until the spring semester
of his junior year. Chebotarev, a fellow alumnus of the Simbirsk
classical gymnasium and only one year ahead of Sasha, had found
him distant and deeply immersed in his work. Unlike Chebotarev,
Sasha had avoided the radical circles that had formed in the late
1870s in Simbirsk around the gymnasium's charismatic literature
teacher, a proponent of agrarian socialism who influenced fellow
pedagogues and even susceptible members of the state and military bureaucracy. Chebotarev explains Sasha's standoffishness by
his relative youth; on average the members of the circles were two
to three years older than Sasha. But Chebotarev is at pains to note
the culture of the Ulyanov family and its political quiescence, providing another reason for Sasha's relatively slow political pace.[12]

After he left Simbirsk, Chebotarev joined both the mathematics
faculty in St. Petersburg University and the Volga regional *zemlyachestvo*. The Volga *zemlyachestvo* included a Simbirsk circle, which
Sasha joined pro forma, but for two years he showed no interest in
connecting with the politically involved students. Many underclass-
men came straight from their gymnasiums fully radicalized and
worshipping the memory of the People's Will. A few tried to resur-
rect the terrorist party. Emigré leaders who supported terrorism
did everything possible to encourage them despite the arrest of the
top leaders and the destruction of most of the network in 1881–82.
The People's Will suffered another blow in 1883 when one of the
party's new leaders, Sergei Degaev, turned out to be a police agent.
The other leaders, led by Herman Lopatin, forced Degaev to kill
Gregory Sudeikin, the officer of the security police who ran him.[13]

Lured to a rendezvous, Sudeikin and his muscular nephew entered a darkened apartment, where Degaev first shot him in the lower back, and then two accomplices struck him and his nephew repeatedly with crowbars until they succumbed.[14] The scandal of the dual murder further damaged the party, and tended to frighten off all but the most committed members. In the mid-1880s the regime's security network, however imperfect and inefficient, outmatched the surviving groups of terrorists.

Another shattering moment occurred in 1884 when the police arrested Lopatin. The wily émigré and highly respected veteran of the movement had reentered Russia to try to revive the movement. Lopatin was seized and his arms pinned before he could swallow the onion-skin paper lists of party loyalists that he carried with him. Hundreds were arrested. The remaining little knots of conspirators trying to regenerate the terrorist movement had to evade the security network that worked through professional detectives, highly valuable and sometimes highly paid informants who infiltrated revolutionary circles, and part-time spies—landladies, concierges, doormen, porters—who were told by the police to keep their eyes out for suspicious behavior and typically appeared as witnesses for the prosecution at political trials.[15]

The Ministry of the Interior had the major responsibility for internal security, and its reach extended to the postal service. The personnel and technologies of the "black office" played a central role in the uncovering of the Second March First plot. Among other ways of preventing another assassination of a tsar, the police had recourse to the clandestine invasion, reading, and replacement of mail by the postal service. The ministry hired talented linguists and cryptographers to read and decipher both conspiratorial and diplomatic (also, to be sure, conspiratorial) mail. Inside the black office the decision to open a letter was made after they had profiled the handwriting and the appearance of the envelope. The workers in the black office not only processed a remarkable number of letters

at great speed and in many languages; they used the latest electrical technology to extract letters from their envelopes and cleverly
restore them to their former state.[16] Any aspiring terrorist of the
mid-1880s had to be singularly dedicated and perhaps a bit suicidal
to challenge the security system erected by the regime.

Not only the Ministry of Education and the police but many of
their favorite professors urged university students to get on with
their studies and make a contribution to the progress of Russian
science and the betterment of their homeland. It was indeed the
safer path for revolutionaries at that moment in Russian history.
In his stories and plays Chekhov caught the chastened mood of
that era of "small deeds," a sense of hopelessness in the intelligentsia alongside their compulsion to improve the human condition, a
desire to contribute something even if it seemed like a drop in the
sea. It was an era when Leo Tolstoy's doctrine of nonresistance to
evil began to make converts in the intelligentsia, whose efforts to
reform or abolish the autocratic regime had brought some to the
gallows and others to Siberian exile.

The imperial regime bought itself some time by following reform
with reaction, intensified surveillance, and repression, but its economic policies worked against social stability and the production
of loyal subjects. The regime put the peasants who had been liberated in 1861, but who still had to redeem their land, under the
tutelage of gentry "land captains." Other "counterreforms" rolled
back the efforts made during the preceding reign to modernize the
countryside. Various kinds of direct and indirect taxation discour-
aged consumption (aside from vodka) and agricultural improve-
ments, and forced the peasants to sell their grain even if it meant
bringing them to the edge of hunger, or over the edge. The capital
extracted by this method went toward the building of railroads and
the purchase of machinery. The tsars promoted industrialization
and educated a new professional class needed to sustain a modern
economy, but some portion of this new, highly educated stratum

took up the cause of the peasants and workers who suffered during the process of modernization. Doctors, midwives, agronomists, statisticians, and teachers worked in appalling conditions to improve the lives of peasants and factory workers mired in poverty-stricken villages or packed into barracks in industrial slums. Chekhov, himself a doctor and suffering from tuberculosis, went to the countryside to inoculate peasants during epidemics. His dreary stories of well-intentioned zemstvo doctors working in impossible conditions and of ignorant villagers seem to be a counsel of despair, but Chekhov's quiet heroism exemplifies the prevailing philosophy of the intelligentsia during the reign of Alexander III. In the face of brute force, one might pursue a tactic of small deeds.

S ASHA'S ASCETIC PURSUIT of science during his sophomore year absorbed almost all of his time. In his first letter after the one of October 6, 1884, referring to the demonstrations in Moscow and Kiev, he shows interest only in throwing himself into his studies. On October 23 he wrote to Maria Alexandrovna,

> I recently began to work in the chemistry laboratory. I had thought that I wouldn't be able to do it this semester, but one of my friends working in the laboratory gave me his space for a few hours every day and I work there now every day besides Saturday and Sunday until six in the evening. . . . Generally I spend a greater amount of my time on practical work than on lectures.[17]

In his letters to Ilya Nikolaevich he inserts more comments on university politics and the fate of various professors under the new university charter, but he never volunteers any serious commentary. The story that emerges from memoirs and the letters of 1884 and 1885 continues to be that of a dutiful student preparing for exams and interested mainly in getting more laboratory time for his research. At the same time Sasha reassures Maria Alexandrovna

that he is eating well, staying healthy, and enjoying the comforts of his apartment. He tried to make some extra money by tutoring, but he was not very good at impressing the affluent parents who could afford to hire tutors, and his part-time work did not significantly affect his life. Sasha did not like to leave his books and laboratory and did not encourage social visits by fellow students from the Simbirsk *zemlyachestvo* or even by Anna. She tempted his scorn with her poetry, stories, and translations and was grateful for his scraps of approval. Life in the laboratory and nihilist philosophy had not helped Sasha develop a sense of literary style, and he appreciated only realistic pieces of the sort that appealed to his favorite critics.

Once again Sasha did not go home for the winter break during his sophomore year, and returned to Simbirsk only in May 1885 for the summer vacation. Anna claims in her memoirs that he had already begun to show interest in the social sciences and brought back with him a number of foreign-language books, among them—although she is not certain about it—Marx's *Das Kapital*. Contact with other students, especially with Chebotarev, had begun to widen his interests, and in his reading that summer he began to move closer to the thought world of the radical students. He began the systematic study that he believed would prepare him to make scientific judgments about economic, social, and political theories and programs. Even so, he spent most of his time in his dugout canoe hunting specimens on the Sviyaga River, in his backyard laboratory intensively studying freshwater annelids in preparation for work on his junior thesis, and beginning to shape a scientific vision of history and society informed by his Darwinian worldview.

Perhaps by the end of the summer Sasha had read enough cutting-edge social and economic data to convince him of the need to struggle against the autocratic regime. He left no intellectual journal; and no one close to Sasha, neither Anna nor his cousins, produced memoirs of any conversations suggesting that he had found the scientific justification for rebellion. The only hints that

something was afoot appear in family memoirs that cannot be completely trusted. Dmitry Ulyanov, the youngest son, who was eleven years old in 1885, many years later wrote that he overheard a conversation between Sasha and Ilya Nikolaevich.

> Father and brother walked along a pathway in the garden. . . . Their faces were especially serious. . . . They sometimes spoke heatedly, but most of the time quietly, inaudibly. I glanced at their faces and understood that they were discussing something very important. . . . What were they discussing? At that time I didn't understand a thing. . . .

And Dmitry also remembered that Ilya Nikolaevich said to Anna before she and Sasha departed for St. Petersburg, "Tell Sasha to keep himself out of harm's way, if only for us."[18]

Plotters

T HE SHIFTING MOODS of the radical intelligentsia between 1861 and 1885 reflected the tsarist regime's changes from reform to reaction. Paradoxically, in 1861 Russian revolutionaries saw the liberation of millions of serfs as a prelude to revolution. Confusing and unfair land settlements and redemption payments would open the peasants' eyes to the tsar's duplicity. Once free of the illusion of a benign father-tsar, the peasants would do what they had done in the seventeenth and eighteenth centuries in Cossack-led rebellions: they would rise up furiously, burn manor houses, and seize the land. But now the peasants would have enlightened leaders—not Cossacks but scientific socialists. The revolutionaries were correct to this extent: the peasants had to give up their faith in the tsar. That did not happen quickly. It took decades of disappointment and Bloody Sunday in January 1905 to cut that tie. In 1917 Lenin gave the peasants what they wanted—but then Stalin put them back into serfdom. The entire revolutionary movement and the fate of the Russian peasants are easily plotted as tragedy.

Narodniki believed that once peasants possessed all of the land, their traditional village commune might be transformed quickly into a modern socialist economy. The last would be first; Russia would become more progressive than Europe by virtue of its leap into a socialist future. The followers of Peter Lavrov prescribed, in addition to land and freedom, large doses of scientific knowledge dispensed by educated revolutionaries. The most sanguine *narodniki* accepted Michael Bakunin's doctrine that the revolutionaries

needed only to throw a spark on the combustible villages—agitation and immediate action rather than scientific knowledge would produce a revolutionary conflagration. Bakunin worshipped men of action who might play a leading role and found charismatic prototypes in the Cossack past.

Peasant villages, especially in the Volga region, kept alive legends of Stenka Razin and Yemelyan Pugachev. One group of *narodniki* in the 1870s used the old Cossack ploy of producing fraudulent imperial manifestos telling the peasants to seize the land and drive out the landowners. Despite their conversion into a military caste serving the autocracy, Cossacks retained their reputation as anarchic and untamed elements within the state, and sustained the refractory Cossack temperament. In the 1870s some *narodniki* traveled to the traditionally unruly Volga provinces, where they hoped to find folk leaders among the Cossacks and peasants. However, the notion that Cossack-led peasant uprisings might spontaneously merge into a vast revolutionary force proved to be another vain dream of Bakuninists. The failure of both propaganda and agitation in the villages encouraged conspiratorial methods and terrorist tactics. Mass arrests crippled the "Going to the People." Most of the young revolutionaries who had made the pilgrimage and escaped arrest drifted back to the cities, where they formed terrorist conspiracies. The emergence of the People's Will in 1879 and the decision to create a centralized party dedicated to killing the tsar changed the nature of the struggle.

The People's Will grew out of a decades-old tradition of modern European terrorism that began with the Carbonari campaigns against French rule in the post-Napoleonic period. Frustrated with the failure of daggers and pistols to bring down their quarry, terrorists later in the nineteenth century began to use chemistry to further their causes. They sometimes used poisoned bullets. Karl Heinzen inspired the use of compact, easily concealed missiles of great destructive power in his treatise on terror of 1849. Felice

Orsini gave European terrorists a spectacular example of this tactic against tyrants in 1859 when he and his accomplices threw three dynamite grenades, in rapid succession, at the carriage of Napoleon III in front of the Paris Opéra. Although this particular attempt failed to kill either Napoleon III or Empress Eugénie, 156 people were wounded in the blast, and 8 died. Dynamite grenades (commonly called "bombs") became the weapon of choice for the People's Will campaign to kill Alexander II. The People's Will, however, had to overcome resistance within the Russian revolutionary movement to terrorist conspiracies and centralization.

The idea of centralized and politically oriented conspiracies acting in the name of the people had powerful opponents. Michael Bakunin warned against leaders lusting for authority and power. He began to attack science as a new kind of religion and, with Marx in mind, quite presciently warned that the intelligentsia might establish a new authoritarian priesthood of science. But Bakunin had a personal weakness for charismatic types. By the end of the 1860s, an aging, dissipated exile looking for strong and simple men of action, Bakunin was easy pickings for Sergei Nechaev, the most unscrupulous terrorist of that era. In 1869 the two jointly composed a stirring "Program of Revolutionary Actions" that acquired a popular title, *The Catechism of a Revolutionary*. The inspiration of generations of terrorists, it glorified the notion that revolutionary ends justify any and all means, and that the science worship of the intelligentsia had to be subordinated to immediate revolutionary goals. The first three rules of *The Catechism* eloquently summarize this credo.

> The revolutionary—is a doomed man. He has neither his own interests, nor affairs, nor feelings, nor attachments, nor property, nor even name. Everything in him is absorbed by a single, exclusive interest, by a total concept, a total passion—revolution.
>
> In the depths of his being not only in words but in action he

has sundered any connection with the civil order and with the entire educated world and with all the laws, proprieties, conventions, and morality of this world. He is—its merciless enemy, and if he continues to live in it, then it is only in order the more certainly to destroy it.

The revolutionary despises any kind of doctrinarism and has rejected peaceful science, leaving it to future generations. He knows only one science—the science of destruction. For this and only for this he now studies mechanics, physics, chemistry, perhaps medicine. For this he studies day and night the living science of people, of the personalities and positions, and all the conditions of the present social structure in every possible stratum. The goal is the same—the quickest and surest destruction of this foul structure.[1]

In 1869 Nechaev murdered a member of his own revolutionary cell who tried to defect. He had lured the victim to a grotto, strangled him, and then shot him. He lied systematically and threatened followers and opponents alike. Nechaev's connection to Bakunin gave Marx the grounds for expelling his opponent from the First International. The lurid accounts that emerged from the public trial of Nechaev's fellow conspirators in 1871 inspired Dostoevsky to write *The Possessed*. Young revolutionaries were horrified by Nechaev's methods, and repudiated him, but the tension between science and action did not go away, and intellectuals still found *The Catechism of a Revolutionary* and Nechaev's revolutionary commitment compelling. Terrorism works, in some fashion.

Even though European revolutionaries sometimes ridiculed the *narodniki* who regaled them with the virtues of Russia's peasants and their communes, they paid attention when the People's Will began to hunt down Alexander II. Inspired by the People's Will, Marx wrote that a successful revolution in Russia might ignite a general European one, but only with European help would Russia

achieve socialism.[2] This qualified support for Russia's vanguard role proved fateful for later Russian revolutionaries. In 1905 Trotsky proposed that a Russian proletarian revolution would be the fuse for an explosion in the more economically advanced states. Lenin put his version of this theory into action in 1917. In the midst of world war, a revolution in Russia—the weakest link in a chain of imperial powers—would cause the entire capitalist system to break apart. Russia seemed chosen to lead the world to socialism. Impatience and hope guided theory. The October Revolution was one of the greatest gambles in modern history.

Russia's radical students of the 1880s kept their hearts with the peasants, but some of them endorsed the impressive economic analysis of *Das Kapital*. Marx died in 1883, the very year that Sasha enrolled in the university and also the year in which a handful of Russian émigrés—all of them repentant *narodniki* who had converted to Marxism—founded the Group for the Liberation of Labor in Switzerland. It included the theoretical titan of Russian Marxism, George Plekhanov, once a Bakuninist and later Lenin's mentor; Vera Zasulich, former terrorist; and Lev Deutsch, who had belonged to a conspiracy to deceive the peasants with fake tsarist manifestos. The early Russian Marxists accepted not only industrialization and the end of the peasant commune but the transformation of Russia's peasants en masse into an exploited factory proletariat. This was shocking to most *narodniki*. It went against the grain of Russian revolutionary optimism; it said, "Abandon the peasants; give up illusions."

Only a few converts to Marxism accepted history's harsh, but presumably benign, dialectic: Russia would have to suffer under an exploitative bourgeoisie until the proletariat became sufficiently miserable and conscious of its position to throw off its chains. In the 1880s, however, most Russian radicals found it intolerable to surrender the peasant commune to the tender mercies of capital. In *Das Kapital*, Marx, improving upon Marie Augier's epigram that

money "enters the world with a blood-flecked cheek," had pictured capital coming into the world "every pore dripping from head to toe with gore and filth."[3] To young activists suffering under a regime that had turned back the clock politically more than three decades, the prospect of a long period of misery under capitalism piled one horror on another. It was the worst of all possible worlds: the tyranny of the tsar plus that of the bourgeoisie. But die-hard *narodniki* were encouraged by Russian economic theorists who believed that efforts to graft onto Russia industrial capitalism of the European variety would fail. The peasant commune would survive. The program of the Second March First in 1887 reaffirmed what dogmatic Russian Marxists rejected—the commitment to a mainly agrarian revolution and the assumption that the peasants could play a progressive role.

Theory aside, the harsh realities of the reign of Alexander III apparently offered only painful choices to those, like Alexander Ulyanov, who identified passionately with the victims of history: they could improve the peasants' lot by small deeds, perhaps as doctors, teachers, agronomists, or statisticians working in the local government institutions created by Alexander II's reforms; they could cultivate their scientific talent, and hope that their discoveries would be used to good ends; they could pursue a policy of "the worse, the better" by becoming Marxists and endorsing capitalism, with its ambiguous gift of industrial abundance alongside inequality, the ruin of tens of millions, and a long-delayed revolution; or they could remain faithful to the belief that terrorism might explosively and quickly remove the greatest obstacle dividing the intelligentsia from the people, and thereby accelerate the pace of progress. The most impatient and passionate revolutionary youths rejected all but the last option, even though some of them, including Sasha, endorsed Marx's general economic analysis.

In 1885 a great many revolutionaries remained convinced that Russia's vast population of peasants already practiced a primitive

form of socialism, that the socialism of the peasant commune might be raised to a higher level, and that the regime's brute force was the main obstacle to the quick realization of socialism. Some *narodniki* passionately believed that only the counterforce of terrorism would remove the obstacle. Although Russian Marxists claimed that their doctrine was the last word in social science, the followers of the People's Will who accepted Marx's economic theory did not follow his sociology of rebellion, which made the industrial proletariat concentrated in large factories the main vehicle of revolution.

More important still, Marx did not offer an immediately satisfying ethical approach that might salve the consciences of repentant young people. In Marxian theory, history would produce a just outcome and serve the greater good, not by the actions of individuals but by the working of impersonal forces. Many inductees into the revolutionary movement needed the assurance that all of their knowledge served good ends and that they themselves were not mere instruments of historical forces but ethical actors *choosing* the good.

For all of the economic, sociological, and historical theory they debated, the youthful *narodniki* remained enthralled by the ethical ideas of Peter Lavrov.[4] He preached that "developed" people owed a debt to the peasants for centuries of serfdom and that the intelligentsia could pay back their debt only by combining scientific thought with the determined action of an organized party. Lavrov's followers in the mid-1880s believed that the actions of the organized and scientifically educated few might change the course of history and liberate the many. The revolutionaries sought a scientific foundation for their ethics, and Lavrov taught them that socialism was both scientific and ethical. "Developed" human beings had to choose not only to work for historical progress but, if necessary, to sacrifice themselves for the cause. In 1885 Lavrov supported terrorist acts that would remove the main obstacle to progress—a benighted tsar who would not grant a liberal constitution.

Alexander III's reactionary regime continued to try to close every academic loophole used by radicals to organize, agitate, and recruit in the universities and every journalistic source of revolutionary inspiration, but the student leaders increased their efforts to subvert the measures. Although they were declared illegal by Count Delyanov's reforms, the *zemlyachestva* continued to operate and the students found ways to discuss the latest amendments to revolutionary theory. So long as Russian tsars failed to grant a liberal constitution allowing Russian socialists to carry their message to the peasants, the royal family and its most despised servants would be quarry for terrorists. The heightened security measures of Alexander III only increased the desire of the most committed revolutionaries to repeat the drama of March 1, 1881.

Agents of the People's Will continued to infiltrate student organizations in gymnasiums, universities, technical institutes, and military academies. Gymnasium graduates entered the great urban institutions of higher learning already fully converted by local radicals, and maintained ties to their mentors. The university cities became nodal points in frail networks trying to revive the movement. At the height of its influence, the People's Will had raised hundreds of recruits from two of the tsarist regime's major props, the army and the navy. However, Sergei Degaev, formerly the main link between the military recruits of the People's Will and its Executive Committee, had given them up to his controller in the secret police, Colonel Sudeikin. The hundreds of arrests caused by Degaev's double-dealing in 1883 and Herman Lopatin's arrest in 1884 had all but destroyed the efforts of the Executive Committee of the People's Will to regain momentum after March 1, 1881.

In a predator–prey dynamic, the imperial regime held the balance of power so long as the security and military establishment for the most part remained loyal. The Russian Empire, however, was trapped in the escalating arms races of the more advanced European imperial powers, and the need to expand and educate its offi-

cer corps in new techniques created more potential recruits to the
revolutionary movement in the military academies of the capital.[5]
In one of history's many ironies, every increase in Russian imperial might created potential instruments for revolutionary power.
In a parallel irony, the revolutionaries remained torn between their
dedication to a vast popular uprising and a quick strike at the center
in the name of the people by revolutionary cadres with a military
wing. Some made contact with cadets; others went into the industrial suburbs of St. Petersburg and propagandized among the workers, but the main recruitment effort lay within the student bodies of
the capital's universities and technical institutes. All of these now
familiar patterns of the Russian revolutionary movement became
part of Sasha Ulyanov's life during his junior year.

S ASHA REACHED THE APEX of his academic career in the
winter of 1885–86. Until early 1886 he had remained an ascetic
of natural science, working on his thesis to the point of exhaustion, sleeping late, but somehow finding the time to continue his
exploration of the social sciences, mainly by way of self-education
circles. In these circles, where some of Russia's future leading aca-
demics as well as radicals gathered, Sasha encountered the future
plotters of the Second March First. The *narodnik* revolutionaries in
the student body attended as many of the circles as possible, scout-
ing promising recruits. During 1886 Sergei Nikonov, clandestinely
a member of the People's Will, invited Sasha to join the economics
circle. In the autumn semester of 1886 Sasha became a member of
the Scientific-Literary Society, a prestigious club sponsored by the
university faculty, which included some of Russia's budding academic leaders from across the disciplines.[6] In the spring semester
of 1886 he also became a representative from the Simbirsk *zemlyachestvo* to the newly formed council of *zemlyachestva*.

In a small group of biologists—which was known as the Ulyanov
circle—Sasha explored the implications of Darwinism for the

socialist future. The biology circle metamorphosed into a terrorist group during Sasha's senior year. Here one found the future leaders of the Second March First: Shevyrev, Lukashevich, and Govorukhin. Sasha had not fully committed himself to a radical course of action during his junior year, but he established ties to others in these study groups who had. In short, Sasha, by the autumn semester of 1885, had already met the people who would be crucial for his education in radicalism. But he continued to spend the greatest part of his time and energy impressing Professors Vagner and Butlerov, either of whom might have become his sponsor for a career in the academy. He intensified his work regimen during the last leg of work on his thesis. Chebotarev claimed that he sprinted to the finish line by working without sleep three nights in a row.[7]

When he emerged from his laboratory work, Sasha became interested in meeting women students from the Bestuzhev courses. He attended parties sponsored by the *zemlyachestva* of the Volga region. At these fund-raisers for indigent students Sasha typically isolated himself in a corner of the room with his head in his hands. He habitually looked morose, his brows knitted. His whole being suggested a mind focused on less frivolous matters than dancing and singing. Sometimes he lit up when the partiers sang his favorite songs. He joined in, off-key and out of sync, to the amusement or consternation of those nearby.[8] Sasha did make connections, but usually with equally intense interlocutors. It seemed that he was having a normal, if academically strenuous, year—normal, that is, for a shy, introverted adolescent. Then, on January 12, 1886, Ilya Nikolaevich died suddenly of a stroke.

Anna, who had gone home during the semester break, witnessed her father's two-day illness and death, but word reached Sasha only after the funeral. Maria Alexandrovna did not want him to interrupt his work. She knew from a letter of December 4, 1885, that Sasha faced an organic chemistry examination on January 13. It was one of his most difficult subjects. Maria Alexandrovna's devo-

tion to the imperative of academic achievement trumped the rituals of mourning; the eldest son did not attend his father's funeral, and did not bear the coffin to its resting place or hear the graveside eulogies. Volodya took Sasha's place. A cousin delivered the news; Sasha was overwhelmed. Chebotarev witnessed Sasha's reaction—his pacing about his room "like a wounded animal," completely oblivious to his friend. Others closely acquainted with Sasha feared that he might be suicidal. Anna openly admitted in her memoirs that *she* had suicidal thoughts and suffered a nervous collapse, although she rejected the idea that Sasha experienced anything similar. Deploying her usual defense mechanism of denial, she took him at his word. Sasha's letter to Anna of January 31, 1886, reassures her that he has not changed his routine. Indeed, after a short period of self-isolation, he quickly resumed laboratory work.[9]

On February 3 Sasha received the gold medal for his junior thesis in the presence of twenty-five members of the university's academic council, including Mendeleev and Beketov, as well as his mentor, N. P. Vagner. It must have felt like ashes in his mouth. Without a word about the ceremony, he wrote to Maria Alexandrovna on March 2, "I received the gold medal for my biological work on segmented worms (I already began work on it during the summer)."[10]

The intersection of his father's death with the successful outcome of his scientific work at the very least accelerated a new trajectory in his university career during the course of 1886. Sasha began to play a larger role in student circles. There the activists took him in tow: first, the more moderate politicized students, like Chebotarev of the Simbirsk *zemlyachestvo*, and then the aspiring terrorists, like Sergei Nikonov and Orest Govorukhin. The importance of the Economics Circle for Sasha's entry into the radical network can hardly be exaggerated. It gave Sasha the incentive to study deeply the latest works on political economy, the most up-to-date literature on the progress of capitalism in Russia, and the

prospects for the peasant commune. These topics had moved to the center of the theoretical debates around the applicability of *narodnik* or Marxist theories to current economic and social trends. One found in the economics circle not only Nikonov and Chebotarev but Mark Elizarov, who later married Anna Ilinichna and served in Lenin's first government. Govorukhin, already a member of the biology circle, attended some meetings of the economics circle, too, but found it tame. Deeply involved with the radical group in the Don and Kuban *zemlyachestvo*, Govorukhin became Sasha's main gadfly for terrorism.

This robust, fair-haired young man with an accent and mannerisms that gave away his Kuban Cossack origins had a rude way about him that Anna disliked intensely. He seemed to have an almost hypnotic hold over Sasha. Anna did what she could to drive a wedge between them, but failed.[11] Like Lukashevich, Shevyrev, and Ulyanov, Govorukhin studied the physical-mathematical sciences. No less reckless than the other Cossack members of the Second March First, he had used his summer vacation in 1886 to spread socialist propaganda among the Cossacks in his *stanitsa*, a flagrant indiscretion that caught up with him in St. Petersburg. Govorukhin was on the verge of being arrested in February 1887 and, like Shevyrev, left St. Petersburg before the assassination attempt. Unlike Shevyrev, however, he eventually left Russian imperial territory in an odyssey taking him first to Vilnius and then to Switzerland, where he affiliated himself with the Group for the Liberation of Labor.

When Govorukhin met Sasha in the fall semester 1885, Ulyanov was still a dedicated student who never missed lectures, but was nonetheless very well read in the literature of radicalism, and to Govorukhin's surprise he already knew Russian Marxist literature. Sasha had read not only *Das Kapital* but George Plekhanov's *Our Differences* and *Socialism and the Political Struggle*, two of the most important Russian Marxist broadsides against the *narodniki*. In the beginning of his senior year Sasha began to read Marx's own work

more systematically, first the *Deutsch-Französische Jahrbücher* of 1844 and then Marx's critique of Hegel's philosophy of right. He and Govorukhin discussed these early writings, especially Marx's critique of Hegel.[12] Here they found support for the belief that Russia might avoid the long and painful development of England and France under capitalism.

Ulyanov, however, was not an easy convert to Marxism. For Sasha a reading of Marx was not enough. One had to examine Russia's economic reality in depth. In the end, Ulyanov accepted basic Marxian economic theory, but like other *narodniki* believed that Russia's economic, social, and political circumstances created a unique opportunity for socialism. In the economics circle Sasha learned the latest *narodnik* critiques of neo-Malthusianism, political economy, and capitalism. There he studied, but found deficient, V. V. Vorontsov's theory that modern capitalism could not establish itself in Russia. Sasha took copious notes from the contemporary press on the development of major industries in the south of Russia. Although fundamentally a *narodnik*, he criticized Vorontsov's ideas and expressed doubts about the solidity of the Russian commune as the basis for a socialist transformation. Perhaps Plekhanov's ideas influenced him, at least to that extent.[13] On the whole, though, Sasha acted like a follower of Peter Lavrov, who required that *narodniki* acquire a firm base of scientific knowledge to serve the cause. Lavrov accepted terrorism as a tactic, but only with qualifications. For him, and later for Sasha, terror was an instrument that might open the way for enlightenment of the *narod*.

The radical students at St. Petersburg University often had wider connections and reflected the changing theoretical currents within the revolutionary intelligentsia. Sergei Nikonov, who had recruited Sasha for the economics circle, belonged to the network of radical students in the capital's military schools, and wrestled with the implications of Marxian theory. He, too, chose terrorism. Lukashevich had ties to Polish revolutionary circles. The Cossack

members of the Second March First had ties to the wider circle of the northern Caucasus, and Shmidova to terrorists in Kharkiv. Sasha and others had connections to workers' circles in the growing industrial slums of St. Petersburg. The Second March First faithfully represented the growing tension within Russian socialism, in which not only shifting loyalties to rural and urban constituencies but also nationalist or regional loyalties affected radical commitments. The youthful members of the Second March First had absorbed the decades-old Russian revolutionary traditions and added their own amendments.

An original member of the economics circle, Nikonov became one of the prime movers of the effort to galvanize a demoralized student body and organize a terrorist network. Marx's critique of the classics of political economy inclined Nikonov toward social democracy, but he did not accept the one-sided, structural approach that overemphasized economic causality in history. Even though he found Marx's critique of capitalism convincing, Nikonov disliked the dogmatic Marxian polemics generated by George Plekhanov and his followers in the émigré Group for the Liberation of Labor.[14] In their efforts to wean the intelligentsia from *narodnichestvo*, Russian Marxists monotonously showed the implacable destruction of the peasantry by the laws of capitalism, but in practice, as well as in theory, they gave the revolutionary intelligentsia political and educational roles as "midwives of revolution," a notion they also found in Marx and Engels.

Nikonov followed the practice of many *narodniki*, who did not draw a sharp line between the economic "infrastructure" and the cultural and political factors assigned to the "superstructure." It was difficult to treat the actions of the heroic figures of the revolutionary movement simply as dependent variables rather than important forces in their own right. Nikonov believed that politics might affect economics and that not only classes but individual actors could alter the course of history. With such views, Nikonov

ALEXANDER BLANK AND KATHERINE VON ESSEN

ABOVE LEFT: Alexander Dmitrievich Blank (1799–1870), father of Maria Alexandrovna, born Moses Isaac Blank, whose estate at Kokushkino became the summer gathering place for the Ulyanov family.

ABOVE RIGHT: Katherine von Essen (1789–1863), sister of Anna Blank and de facto stepmother to Alexander Blank's six children after Anna's death in 1838.

Anna at age six, Alexander at age four (1870).

Anna at ten, Sasha at eight (1874).

THE ULYANOV FAMILY (1879)

Alexander (1866–1887) standing conspicuously in the center,
Anna (1864–1935), to the left of Ilya Nikolaevich (1831–1886),
Vladimir (1870–1924), sitting below Anna, Maria Alexandrovna (1835–1916),
surrounded by the younger children, to the right Olga (1871–1891),
Dmitry (1874–1943) on the chair to the left,
and Maria Ilinichna (1878–1937) on her lap.

ILYA NIKOLAEVICH ULYANOV (1882 OR 1883)

ALEXANDER ULYANOV AT AGE TWELVE (1868)

Alexander in the uniform of the Simbirsk classical gymnasium.

THE GRADUATING CLASS OF THE SIMBIRSK CLASSICAL GYMNASIUM (1883)

Alexander in the second row at the far left.

ALEXANDER AT AGE SEVENTEEN (1883)

VLADIMIR'S GRADUATION PHOTO (1887)

naturally gravitated toward terrorism and became one of the few members of the People's Will in St. Petersburg.[15]

Soon after his transfer to the Military-Medical Academy, Nikonov began to spread *narodnik* propaganda to the military cadets in the capital. He was a key participant in the Second March First conspiracy until his arrest on January 28, 1887. From his position at the center of the student network in St. Petersburg during 1885–87, Nikonov estimated that at the height of the movement fifteen hundred students belonged to about twenty illegal *zemlyachestva*, of which the circle of the Don and Kuban Cossacks was the largest at roughly two hundred members. Quite a few radical students who were neither Cossacks nor from the Don and Kuban regions affiliated themselves with the circle because of its radicalism and wide connections in other cities. It was a situation of delicious irony. Cossacks—Govorukhin, Andreyushkin, Generalov—along with the Siberian Osipanov had the daring and the martial spirit to go into the streets with weapons, and they were willing to take as many lives as they thought necessary to achieve their goal. Yet they entered the revolutionary movement by the pathway ordinarily taken by the intelligentsia—through the gymnasium and university. To compound the irony, Alexander III deeply admired the Cossacks and thought them to be the most loyal of his subjects.

Despite this apparent revolutionary momentum, the vast majority of students balked at sustained and serious revolutionary activity, much less terrorism. Memory of Degaev's treachery remained fresh in their minds. Whom could they trust? They assumed that police spies were everywhere. Moreover, the rhythms of student life militated against revolutionary plots. Activist projects lost momentum during the long semester breaks. The largest likely sources of recruits, the *zemlyachestvo* movement, was quite diffuse and largely sustained in 1886–87 by its elected council of twelve to fifteen students. Several members of the Second March First,

including Ulyanov, Nikonov, Lukashevich, and Govorukhin, served on the council.

The radicals had to work against a mood of increasing pessimism about the efficacy of violent resistance to the regime of Alexander III. They had to fight against ideological breakdown. Many students found solace in Tolstoy's doctrine of nonresistance to evil, some in Chekhovian "small-deeds" liberalism, while others, following Dostoevsky, became Russian nationalists and supported monarchism, imperialism, and Russian Orthodoxy. By late autumn 1886 Sasha had joined the broad movement of revolutionary *narodnichestvo* and, without ever saying it explicitly, followed Peter Lavrov's move to terrorism. For all of the circles and networks, it took an entrepreneur of sorts to gather the handful of recruits who would dedicate themselves to an organized act of terrorism.

T HE PERSON WHO ORGANIZED the Second March First, Peter Shevyrev, might have come out of the pages of *The Possessed*. He distinctly resembled Nechaev, whose conspiracy had inspired the novel, and he had the qualities that went along with revolutionary entrepreneurship: blind belief in the cause, a file-card mind, the ability to create real networks out of mental blueprints, the willingness to adapt means to ends without much attention to theory, and the ability to risk everything to achieve the end. The less than likable Shevyrev, shrill and hysterical, thin and tubercular, squinting at interlocutors over his spectacles, pushed his recruits into an enterprise that they wished for but might not have been able to turn into reality without him. The others knew that their chances of success were small, that they themselves would likely go down with their project, but Shevyrev took them beyond a point of no return.

Shevyrev came from a relatively privileged background, the wealthier stratum of the mercantile estate, studied in a classical gymnasium in Kharkiv, in eastern Ukraina, and, like Ulyanov and

Lukashevich, became a student in the natural sciences in St. Petersburg. Shevyrev originally enrolled in Kharkiv University in 1883 and spent two years studying the natural sciences there. Little inclined toward academic work, in Kharkiv he showed interest in science more as an aspiring inventor than as a student. He had a tendency to throw himself into all-or-nothing projects. Failure in a febrile and lunatic venture to create some sort of electrical device evidently affected his decision to invest himself in revolutionary activity.[16] At Kharkiv University he developed his organizational skills, and when he transferred to St. Petersburg for his junior year he immediately put them to use to form mutual-aid and self-education groups. Although putatively studying to be a mineralogist specializing in crystallography, he jumped to zoology. In any case, he was an indifferent student and had neither his heart nor his head in his academic work. As a revolutionary he showed no interest in theory and read little in the social-science literature. He dedicated himself almost completely to activism during his two years in St. Petersburg.

Shevyrev showed enormous energy and cleverness in creating student enterprises and events to raise funds. Soon after his arrival in St. Petersburg he began to prowl the corridors of the university buttonholing students, making hundreds of acquaintances, and looking for opportunities. A risk taker by nature, he recruited somewhat recklessly. The expectation of his own imminent death—Shevyrev's tubercular condition had worsened during his sophomore year— probably increased his feverish activity and recklessness. His illness forced him to extend his summer break after his junior year, and he returned to St. Petersburg only in the middle of the fall semester, 1886.[17] Shevyrev's intense commitment, perpetual motion, and organizational acumen won him the respect of the ordinarily rebellious students who, in this period of relative doldrums, would not easily commit themselves to a conspiracy. When he issued threats of violence against vacillating comrades, however, he evoked accusations of Nechaevism.

Shevyrev's health, both physical and mental, affected the outcome of the Second March First in several ways. His older brother, Nicholas, an entomologist and professor in the Forestry Institute in St. Petersburg, testified in April 1887 that Peter was not only tubercular but psychologically unstable. Nicholas had decided that it would be better for Peter to move from Kharkiv to St. Petersburg, where he would receive superior treatment for both his physical and his psychological problems. During the course of interrogation Nicholas revealed that since childhood his younger brother had shown signs of hysteria and a tendency to hallucinate—both evidently family traits. Their sister suffered from similar psychological symptoms and had to return home to Kharkiv after a sojourn in St. Petersburg. Despite the St. Petersburg doctors' warning that the climate would be dreadful for Peter's lungs, Nicholas still kept him there for two years until it became obvious that his brother's health—physical as well as psychological—had seriously deteriorated. Peter's nonstop activity, the climate, and tuberculosis caused hemorrhaging and a physical breakdown by the end of his junior year.[18]

From his belated return to St. Petersburg from the summer break of 1886 until February 17, 1887, when Nicholas sent him to the Crimea for treatment, Peter revived the projects he had begun and also launched the conspiracy. He was captured on March 7 in Yalta with a bottle of cyanide in his possession. In court Nicholas Shevyrev testified that he had given the poison to Peter, whom he was helping in his study of entomology, and who in turn helped him prepare specimens. He also had given Peter various bottles and gutta-percha tubes for poisoning insects. Although Peter had in his lodgings in Yalta insect-catching and processing equipment when he was apprehended, it is far more likely that he had been contemplating suicide rather than dispatching insects on behalf of the science of entomology. Shevyrev had also gotten potassium cyanide for the bomb throwers so that they could avoid torture in case they were captured.

Nicholas, who had helped Peter's conspiracy in many small ways, shaped his testimony to save his brother from hanging, and much of it cannot be trusted, but he evidently spoke candidly about Peter's physical and psychological problems. Shortly before Peter went to the Crimea, his co-conspirators noted that he had begun to show paranoid symptoms. Shevyrev believed that a dog that he encountered in the streets of St. Petersburg was tailing him for the police.[19] It seems odd in retrospect that the conspirators would entrust their project and their lives to this unstable and, by much testimony, repellent individual. Once they had crossed the psychological threshold into the thought world of terrorism, however, they measured him by different criteria. Without Shevyrev the project would never have been realized; even those who doubted his methods and character were willing to take the attendant risks of working with him. To many students, his activist qualities translated into a species of charisma rather than repulsiveness. Similar things had been said of Nechaev.

In retrospect the pattern of Shevyrev's activity during the Second March First conspiracy resembled that of his academic career: he pursued with virtually demonic energy every project he conceived, including the Second March First, but never completed a single one. In mid-February, Shevyrev broke down physically and psychologically; others had to finish his last project. When he departed St. Petersburg on February 17, he left behind a group of young men working virtually around the clock to complete the manufacture of nitroglycerine, dynamite, poisoned bullets, and the bombs themselves. Shevyrev had brought the project beyond a point of no return; and oddly enough, the rickety organization created by this failed inventor nearly realized its goal. It took a person with Shevyrev's odd qualities to set things into motion. Once set into motion, such conspiracies can achieve a great deal.

In sum, Peter Shevyrev at the age of twenty-three had the qualities of entrepreneur, organizer, salesman, fund-raiser, and, to a

lesser degree, intimidator. Some were repelled by his shrillness, pushiness, and apparent lack of intellectual seriousness. All, however, were impressed by his ability to get others to act and his prodigious memory for people and their qualities—traits not uncommon among revolutionary politicians. Nechaev had kept a notebook with hundreds of names inscribed in tiny handwriting. Stalin was known for his almost photographic memory for personnel. Shevyrev initiated the Second March First by recruiting Lukashevich as master bomb maker and Osipanov as the primary bomb thrower. All of the evidence provided by survivors, even by those who were at least ambivalent about him, gave pride of place to Shevyrev for propelling into motion, organizing, and coordinating the conspiracy.

J OSEF LUKASHEVICH, the designer of the bombs seized by the police on March 1, 1887, epitomized the hybrid mentality of the time—he advocated terrorism yet declared his devotion to social democracy. A brilliant young man, he like Sasha needed the authority of science to justify his actions. Lukashevich became an early convert to the Marxian version of social democracy. The parallels between Sasha's and Josef's radical careers are striking. Lukashevich's gentry father had four children in addition to Josef, and worked in the chancellery of the governor-general of Vilnius province, in Lithuania. Ethnically Polish and educated in a classical gymnasium in Vilnius, Josef was a member of one of the most hated and closely watched minorities within the Russian Empire.[20] Like Sasha, he was simultaneously a member of a privileged estate and an outsider because of his ethnicity—a marginal man. Polish nationalism, like Ukrainian nationalism, added to the regime's many headaches.

Although the drive for national autonomy remained tied to the quest for liberal constitutions in much of the European imperial world, it gradually began to form links with socialism. Not a

nationalist in the narrow sense of the word, like the Polish revolutionaries with whom he consorted, Lukashevich passionately
hated Russian imperial rule; and, like Sasha and other members
of his generation, he placed his knowledge of science and technical skill in the service of revolution. Both his background and his
conspicuous appearance—Lukashevich was several inches over
six feet and had striking aquiline features—should have made
him an easy target for police spies. His conspiratorial nickname
was "Handsome." It seems extraordinary that he got as far as he
did in his plotting and bomb making; in his memoirs he himself
expressed surprise at this.

Two and a half years older than Sasha, Josef finished his gymnasium education at the same time, in 1883, and immediately
enrolled in the same department in St. Petersburg University, but
Lukashevich had advanced further in his education in radicalism. He shared with Sasha a passion for the natural sciences, in
Josef's case chemistry, physics, and botany. Lukashevich was a gentle giant, who loved gardening. When he became involved in the
Second March First plot, Josef arranged meetings with Osipanov
and Shevyrev in one of his favorite spots, the university's botani-
cal garden and orangery. They conspired in whispers in secluded
spots amid fragrant foliage, "in total silence, far from the gaze of
the regime's spies."[21]

In Vilnius, a haven for seditious ideas and entrepôt of revolutionary contraband, Josef had read all of the major *narodnik* clandestine publications. His political education in Vilnius convinced
Lukashevich that liberal constitutions and political freedom had to
precede socialism, and this made political revolution the first order
of the day. The People's Will took a similar position and therefore
became Lukashevich's party of choice more for tactical reasons
than strategic ones. For Lukashevich, politics paved the way for
socialism, but terrorism, constitutions, and parliaments were only
way stations on the road to socialism. Marx and Engels theorized

that political parties would become superfluous in a classless society. Parliamentary institutions and the state's professional armies, police forces, and bureaucracies would presumably disappear as socialism ripened into communism.

Like other already convinced revolutionaries, in his first two years in St. Petersburg, Lukashevich bitterly swallowed the Degaev scandal, Lopatin's arrest, and the new university charter. He maintained ties to radicals back home, ties that he used when the conspiracy unfolded. All the while Josef pursued his studies and, like Sasha, attracted the attention of the leading professors in his specialties. His comrades (though not Sasha) saw him as a worthy successor to Nicholas Kibalchich, whose bombs had killed Alexander II. Under Stalin, Soviet propagandists, driven by national pride to claim for Russia many important scientific and technological breakthroughs, attributed to Kibalchich the discovery of the principle of jet propulsion. Lukashevich's personal pride in his own technical skill shows in memoirs first published thirty years after his sentencing. He went into great detail about the construction of his bombs in order to refute the expert witness for the prosecution, who claimed that the bombs were badly designed and nonfunctional.[22] In fact—Lukashevich implied—his bombs were better than Kibalchich's.

Lukashevich arrived in St. Petersburg fully radicalized, felt constricted by the doctrine of small deeds, and longed for the opportunity to join a serious conspiracy. At first he provided technical assistance to radical Polish students engaged in hectographing illegal material. During his sophomore year Lukashevich vainly tried to find a terrorist group that could use his skills. One member of a Polish circle arrested in 1885 had in his apartment Lukashevich's notes on the manufacture of nitroglycerine, but the police never made a connection, even though the notes were in Josef's handwriting. He ended his sophomore year frustrated in his search for a terrorist organization, and still seeking to move beyond the usual

student ploys to circumvent the authorities. The most radical students eventually found one another.

The key moment in the formation of the conspiracy occurred when Lukashevich and Shevyrev, who already knew each other, at some unspecified time in the autumn of 1886 decided to form a terrorist group. Lukashevich and Shevyrev first collaborated on projects to help needy students and simultaneously use them to locate recruits for a terrorist conspiracy. In 1885–86, in addition to a dining room, they created a student bank and an information bureau for jobs. Some of the faculty collaborated as well. Shevyrev managed the money and found factotums to disseminate leaflets advertising his enterprises, which included fund-raising parties and dances. Shevyrev and Lukashevich both knew Ulyanov as a fellow science student and as an increasingly visible member of the council of *zemlyachestva* and of leading study circles. In a postscript to a letter of April 19, 1886, Shevyrev asked Lukashevich to give to Sasha his notes from Butlerov's class on organic chemistry for transmission to his brother Nicholas. Shevyrev also mentions Sasha as a source of funds for his student enterprises (presumably collected from the Simbirsk and other *zemlyachestva*).[23] At this moment in the formation of the terrorist project, Shevyrev and Lukashevich were biding their time until something crystallized.

By the autumn of 1886 Shevyrev and Lukashevich started vetting prospective assassins. One young man, identified only as "S" by Lukashevich, offered his services to them, but imprudently announced his intentions to his friends. Shevyrev and Lukashevich not only turned down his offer but also sent him out of town for his own good. Shevyrev befriended another potential assassin, one of the radicalized military men in St. Petersburg, who made a credible offer. A cavalier of the Order of St. George, the unnamed officer planned to shoot Alexander III during a formal inspection of the order on the festival of St. George to be held on November 26, 1886, in the Winter Palace. He lost heart at the last minute.[24] Had the offi-

cer kept courage, the complex tasks of bomb making and Ulyanov's involvement might have been short-circuited. Instead, in December 1886 and January 1887 the police made wholesale roundups of the radical military circles that still operated in St. Petersburg and elsewhere, at least temporarily removing that source of threat. Arrests in the student body in December and in the Junker academy, the naval, Pavlov, and Konstantinov schools in January 1887, and especially the arrest of Sergei Nikonov strongly affected Sasha, who was depending on Nikonov for military recruits for systematic terror. All of these signs of the effectiveness of the police changed the thinking of the students and stopped the momentum created by November 17, 1886, but not Shevyrev's machinations.

I F SHEVYREV was the main organizer and Lukashevich the technical expert, Vasilii Osipanov was the point man for the assassination. An aspiring assassin in search of an organization, Osipanov made contact with Shevyrev in the fall of 1886. He was a somewhat mysterious young man of indistinct ethnicity, but his looks suggest he was probably of indigenous Siberian stock. Osipanov was nicknamed "the Cat." The nickname did not refer to his physique—he was of medium height, stocky, square—but to his solitary ways and stealth. Osipanov had left Kazan University and come to St. Petersburg in the autumn semester of 1886, his senior year, expressly to sacrifice himself in the act of assassinating Alexander III. As a teenager in Tomsk he had met Boris Orzhikh, who converted him to the cause.

There is little information about Osipanov's early biography before his years in Kazan University. Although he was officially listed as a lower-middle-class town dweller—a *meshchanin*—his father had served in the army. Osipanov received a gymnasium education in Tomsk and arrived at the university fully radicalized. During his gymnasium years he read Chernyshevsky's *What Is to Be Done?*, which gave him a fictional model of ascetic heroism.

Osipanov claimed to have imitated Rakhmetov's painful regime—
designed to harden him for torture—of sleeping on a board with
nails sticking through it.[25] Osipanov refused to carry poison with
him to commit suicide in case of capture. At Kazan, the same
university from which Vladimir Ulyanov was expelled in 1888,
Osipanov started as a student of medicine and then transferred
to law. He missed almost an entire school year on enforced fur-
lough for his role in a student demonstration. An orphan, Osipanov
received material support from family friends, and didn't have to
resort to student banks or work as a tutor. He arrived at St. Petersburg in the autumn of 1886, at the same time as the other throwers,
Generalov and Andreyushkin. It seems odd that at a time when St.
Petersburg University was presumably enforcing the reactionary
policies of Dmitry Tolstoy and Delyanov, someone with Osipanov's
student record should have been able to enroll. His student status
simply served as a convenient cover for his project. He concentrated all of his energy on finding a group of people who could help
him carry out his sole intention—killing Alexander III. Shevyrev
and Lukashevich felt fortunate to find Osipanov—self-possessed,
determined, decisive, and, above all, careful. Osipanov had mixed
feelings about joining a group. He trusted only himself to get the
job done, but recognized that he would need a support system to
achieve his goal. His doubts about relying on a group were well
founded—the others were reckless and careless in their methods—
but at least they could supply him with dynamite bombs that were
potentially more effective than his two-chambered pistol.[26]

At first he thought of himself as a freelance assassin who, with
the help of a lookout, would do the job himself. Knowing the unre-
liability of pistols, he wanted to load his with poisoned bullets
so that even a minor wound would be fatal. When he sought out
people who might help him, they dissuaded him from the idea of
a solo attack with a pistol. Lukashevich and Shevyrev convinced
Osipanov that bombs would be better, but he evidently was the

inspiration for the lead cubes filled and smeared with strychnine. The others suggested that Osipanov himself study the tsar's comings and goings and choose the time and place for the assassination. After his initial reconnaissance Osipanov announced that it would be impossible for one bomber to do the job. He planned to commit the deed while the tsar was en route to the Peter and Paul Cathedral to attend the requiem mass for his father on the sixth anniversary of Alexander II's assassination, but there was more than one possible route from the Anichkov Palace. Shevyrev and Lukashevich suggested the approach that was later used on March 1, 1887: three throwers would be stationed along the tsar's likely routes, and three signalers would give advance warning of the tsar's passage. In fact, it was very much like the successful plan of the People's Will in 1881. At the end of December, Osipanov had enough credible information about the tsar's habits to encourage them to plan the assassination for March 1, 1887.[27]

With Osipanov and Lukashevich in hand, Shevyrev had hooks for recruiting the others. He found signalers among the collaborators in his student dining room. Kancher and Gorkun purchased produce for Mme Klechinskaya, the cook whose tasty meals attracted a crowd of student patrons. After November 17 they played a central role in printing and mailing the student proclamation written by Ulyanov, and then easily slid into the role of signalers. They recruited a third, Volokhov. Shevyrev recruited Govorukhin and a still skeptical Ulyanov by exaggerating the material and human assets under his control; and Ulyanov, despite his doubts, in December 1886 joined Govorukhin in recruiting the remaining bomb throwers, Generalov and Andreyushkin. Toward the end of December they decided on the target, the time, the approximate place, and the method. Starting with very little in the autumn of 1886, by the end of December, Shevyrev had shaped a tiny terrorist organization that was gearing up to produce the bombs.[28]

Sasha at first remained skeptical, but he showed a typical intelli-

gentsia weakness for the arguments of the passionately committed. His conversion followed a familiar pattern: first anger at the regime and despair at its policies, then deep and careful study of the possibilities, and finally (often after an emotional experience) submission to a sometimes amoral entrepreneur of terrorism. Govorukhin wrote of his and Sasha's meetings with Shevyrev in December 1886, "After long and heated discussions of the matter of systematic terror with Lukashevich and Shevyrev . . . Alexander Ilyich and I decided to help their cause, although we didn't decisively commit ourselves to the group. Little by little we were drawn into the work, fulfilling Shevyrev's commissions."[29] There is no question, however, about the event that led Sasha to Shevyrev. It was the pilgrimage to Volkovo Cemetery on November 17, 1887.

A STUDENT EVENT designed by the revolutionaries in the economics circle to provoke police repression and to recruit cadres for revolutionary activity became the seedbed of the Second March First conspiracy. In the fall semester of 1886 the economics circle agitated for a huge demonstration on November 17, 1886, the twenty-fifth anniversary of Dobrolyubov's death. The student agitators reached out to the *zemlyachestvo* council and technical institutes in St. Petersburg—the medical, technological, and forestry schools—and to the women in the Bestuzhev courses. All were to march and then assemble at the Volkovo Cemetery. Sergei Nikonov had been involved in the dress rehearsal for the event, an earlier procession to the cemetery on February 19, 1886, commemorating the twenty-fifth anniversary of the abolition of serfdom. Nikonov estimated that four hundred students gathered at the cemetery to lay wreaths on the graves of the intellectual heroes who had championed the liberation of the serfs and to hear a religious service performed by a somewhat agitated priest dragooned by the student leaders. The police displayed gross laxity and disorganization and appeared only late in the proceedings of February 19.[30] Such large

student demonstrations in St. Petersburg in this period of reaction were unheard of. Determined not to be caught out again, Lieutenant General Gresser had his cohorts ready on November 17, 1886. This time the St. Petersburg chief of police obliged the event's organizers by humiliating the students and turning their thoughts to terrorism.

November 17 was a gray day, and a light, chilling rain fell intermittently, filling the streets in the cemetery's environs with muddy pools. An impressive number of students, a thousand or more by most estimates, had gathered that morning on Nevsky Prospect near the Nikolaevsky (now the Moscow) railway station. Many came to Volkovo in groups by horse trams. By about 10:00 a.m. hundreds of uniformed students from the capital's most prestigious institutions of higher education, some of them carrying wreaths for the planned ceremony, waited in the rain, while cordons of policemen blocked their way into the cemetery. The students began to complain to a police officer: "We're here to pay our respects to the departed. You have no right to prevent this." They stood in what was becoming a quagmire before the closed gates of the cemetery. Lieutenant General Gresser strictly enforced the blockade. After a palaver, Gresser said that he would allow a small delegation to gather at Dobrolyubov's grave, but the student leaders decided against it. A thick mass of students began to walk back to the central city by way of Ligovka. A major artery south of the central city, Ligovka framed a narrow canal and linked up with Nevsky Prospect. The students planned to walk back to Nevsky, where they would regroup on the square in front of the golden-domed Kazan Cathedral, the site of a famous student demonstration of 1876.

Sasha marched with the others singing revolutionary songs and shouting radical slogans. His friends had never seen him in such an agitated state. On Ligovka a cordon of Cossacks formed up to block their path, and Lieutenant General Gresser drove in a sleigh to the front of his forces and confronted the students. According to Shmidova, she, Anna, Sasha, and Shevyrev marched in a rank hold-

ing hands. Anna wrote that Sasha shouted angrily at the mounted chief of police. She could not hear what he said, although she could see that he was enraged. A fellow student who marched near them claimed that Sasha reacted to Gresser's presence as if an electric shock had gone through him, shouted "forward," and tried unsuccessfully to plunge through the dense crowd toward the figure on horseback. Raisa Shmidova, however, told a different story. Sasha became agitated when he saw a Cossack clout her shoulder with his rifle butt.[31] Such scenes of humiliation of comrades and loved ones typically ignited the rage and thoughts of revenge against those who symbolized brutality and oppression. Perhaps the insult to Shmidova turned Sasha's thoughts to terror. Did the events and the rainy day also revive the trauma of the visit to Karpei's cottage when Sasha was a child, and of Herzen's vivid story about the Jewish cantonists? For whatever deep reasons, this became the moment of Sasha's transformation into a terrorist.

Meanwhile, the Cossacks lined up behind the marchers and cut off the students' retreat route, so hundreds were trapped on Ligovka, with buildings to one side of them, a railing to the other where the canal flowed, and Cossacks fore and aft with swords drawn. Curious bystanders gawked from the embankment on the other side of the canal, and some even threw buns to the hungry students, but were driven away by the police. The students, who had already spent the morning in front of the cemetery, now had to stand captive in the rain for hours more, until Lieutenant General Gresser took pity and released them that evening. The Cossacks began to allow small groups to pass through their cordon, but they also isolated and detained a small number of especially vocal students whom they'd identified as leaders and agitators.

Anna and Sasha got through the cordon quite late and went to the apartment that Sasha shared with Chebotarev. The weary students who gathered in the apartment after the long ordeal on Ligovka cheered themselves with stories of how they'd escaped

the Cossack swords and whips and flouted the authorities. Others who had been detained were released, to the joy of their comrades. Within a few days the students discovered that their celebrations had been premature. The police arrested and expelled forty demonstrators, many of whom had not played important roles in the demonstration. A list of their names suggests that the police had targeted mainly Jewish students and women who were conspicuously nihilist in appearance. The main organizers of the demonstration were enraged.

The students who were inclined toward terrorism contemplated a revival of the liberal-terrorist modus vivendi that preceded the assassination of Alexander II. They assumed that the liberal public despised the counterreforms and the figures that symbolized them; at a less conscious level they felt that they, the children of privilege, could evoke a visceral response in their often liberal and equally guilt-ridden parents, who also suffered in the prison-house atmosphere created by the regime. Images of illegitimate authority and stories of injustice brought back memories of their parents' own humiliations at the hands of the regime and revived their youthful indignation.

The radical students of 1886 remembered the tale of Arkhip Bogolyubov, who had been arrested for participating in the demonstration in the square before Kazan Cathedral in December 1876. Fyodor Trepov, governor-general of St. Petersburg, ordered that Bogolyubov be beaten with birch rods because he had refused to remove his cap during a prison-yard inspection. Rumors circulated that Trepov had slapped Bogolyubov or had knocked off his hat. In January 1878 Vera Zasulich shot Trepov in the pelvis; the wound was not fatal. Zasulich's act and then her acquittal in a stirring public trial inspired a terrorist campaign that led to the formation of the People's Will in 1879—and to the closed tribunals that later terrorists faced. The terrorists at that moment were fully justified in their belief that they had the sympathy of the liberal public. Both

liberals and radicals wanted a constitution and full civil liberties, and the regime's costly military operations and diplomatic failure in the Russo-Turkish War had raised the level of outrage. The radicals of 1886 believed that dramatic scenes of police brutality against the children of privilege would revive the spirit of 1878–79, bring the cowed liberals to their side, and renew the drive for a liberal constitution.

Anna Ulyanova-Elizarova in her memoirs written in 1927 probed the psychology of humiliation and the turn to terror after November 17, 1886.

> It's difficult to travel back to that moment forty years ago, to understand the psychology of terror, of the generation of the 1880s worship of that "accursed God." Not only the students but the general political attitudes of the time evoked it. The students . . . sensitively registered generally shared discontents. . . . The effect seems out of proportion to the cause, calling to mind the well-known allegory of the last drop that causes . . . the cup to overflow. Don't such drops always play a decisive role in all insurrections, revolutions, and prison riots? . . . In prison conditions the tiniest, most insignificant pressure seems unbearable, is taken as an insufferable insult, and evokes a disproportionately passionate protest. This is precisely how it was then, in the prison that Russia felt like to those who experienced the 1880s.[32]

The instigators of the demonstration of November 17 began to discuss possible responses: demonstrating on the Kazan Cathedral Square; protesting in front of the Winter Palace; bombing the administration building of the Ministry of the Interior's gendarmerie; instigating disorderly conduct in St. Petersburg's institutions of higher education and pressure to reinstate the expelled students; or, at the extreme, assassinating obnoxious officials, with Lieutenant General Gresser at the top of their list.

Sasha began to play a central role in the planning of protest. Two months earlier, on September 18, Sasha and his friend from Simbirsk, Chebotarev, had moved into spacious accommodations, which neither could afford on his own, in a two-story wooden house at Alexandrovsky Prospect 25. Their apartment had a large ante-room for guests, and the bedroom had floor-to-ceiling bookshelves, which contained not only their own books but also the library of the Simbirsk *zemlyachestvo*, whose roughly twenty members congregated there. The apartment also became the meeting place for the biology circle. Discussions about the November 17 proclamation took place in the apartment even though the doorman of their building undoubtedly reported to the police.

Shevyrev, Govorukhin, Ulyanov, and several other student activists from the union of *zemlyachestva* also met in Michael Kancher and Peter Gorkun's apartment to organize their appeal to the public. Kancher, a science student, and Gorkun, an aspiring lawyer, both gentry from Poltava Province and former gymnasium mates, had fallen into Shevyrev's web while helping him launch his cheap student dining room. He had casually moved them into more serious conspiratorial work. Their apartment, like Ulyanov and Chebotarev's, became a hub of the Second March First conspiracy. A few days after the event, they helped print and put into circulation the proclamation "17 November in Petersburg." Ulyanov, at the behest of the student leaders, composed this appeal for the solidarity of the educated public with the students.

The proclamation claims that fifteen hundred students had gathered peacefully to conduct a Christian funeral service to honor Dobrolyubov. It describes in considerable detail the arbitrariness and illegality of the police action, but Sasha did not claim police violence. Lieutenant General Gresser knew very well that the organizers wanted to provoke violence and had not risen to the bait. The police had created obstacles, taken down names, and later expelled students, but the Cossacks had not actually beaten or

slashed protesters, as in earlier demonstrations. Ulyanov appealed mainly to the liberal public's sympathy for violations of civil liberties and the suppression of enlightened thought in a dark and brutal despotism. The proclamation ends with a sentence designed to stress right over might, intellect and spirit over physical strength: "We counterpose to the brute force that supports the government another force, but it is the force of the organized and united consciousness of our spiritual solidarity."[33]

It is doubtful that the proclamation was meant to be a prologue to a campaign of systematic terror—the methods used to formulate, print, and distribute it were so slapdash—but that is what it became. After hectographing the proclamation, several students, including Anna, worked around the clock, stuffing and addressing hundreds of envelopes to the educated public in St. Petersburg: lawyers, officials, doctors, professors, merchants. The students made it quite easy for the police to detect the missives. In a rush, they had bought envelopes in the nearest stationery shops. The stationery was all of the same kind and thus easily detected in the post office, which had no doubt been alerted by the police. The students also dumped the envelopes in large numbers into a few postal boxes not far from the university area, so they were all the more conspicuous. Chebotarev, who addressed several of the proclamations to personal acquaintances, learned that not one of them had gotten to its destination. Such were the casual and inept methods used by the enraged students, some of whom found their way to Peter Shevyrev.[34]

Shevyrev used equally casual methods to recruit Govorukhin and Ulyanov. At the beginning of December 1886 they were still unaware that Shevyrev's public enterprises camouflaged his conspiratorial activities. Some thought—and this is what he wanted them to think—that his enterprises were tokens of a liberal mentality and a tactic of small deeds. Shevyrev actually had in mind a string of terrorist acts. Govorukhin, who himself was already

inclined toward terrorism and had pushed Ulyanov in that direction, claims that in late November or early December 1886 they, in conversation with Shevyrev, wondered out loud why he didn't pursue something more serious than a dining room—like terrorism. Shevyrev then told them that he had already formed a terrorist enterprise and asked what role they were prepared to play. He presented a neat organizational blueprint: (1) information gatherers who would find out about the tsar's schedule, itinerary, and entourage; (2) fund-raisers; (3) technicians for bomb making; and (4) the strike force—throwers and signalers. Notably absent was a place for theory and propaganda.

Govorukhin and Ulyanov demurred when Shevyrev asked them whether they would gather information about the tsar, something that required inside contacts, which they lacked. They agreed to play roles in the third and fourth categories as technicians or as organizers of the strike force. They even began to discuss precise methods for assassinating the tsar. Shevyrev agreed that bombs would be superior to small arms—he and Lukashevich had already convinced Osipanov of that. But when they pressed him for information about the group's members, Shevyrev fended them off. Instead, he resorted to deception, writing on a piece of paper letters of the alphabet signifying the number of people in each of the four categories.[35]

In fact, at the time—probably early December—Lukashevich was the lone technician, Osipanov the only bomb thrower, and two of the signalers, Kancher and Gorkun, already identified as collaborators, but yet to be recruited for their roles in the assassination plot. Shevyrev himself was the main fund-raiser and coordinator. The organization was still largely a figment of his imagination, but he leveraged what resources he had into a functional terrorist group. Govorukhin and Ulyanov might have tried to organize their own conspiracy if they hadn't found one already under way; but they had more scruples than Shevyrev, and it is doubtful that

scrupulous recruiting methods would have gotten them very far in their project.

Sasha himself showed an odd mixture of meticulousness about enlisting the right people and blindness to the fact that he and the others were already obvious targets for police surveillance. All of the main actors, including him, were compromised after November 17, and several were on the verge of arrest at the time of the foundation of the Second March First. By the end of December they had nonetheless made the commitment to assassinate the tsar. The student body of the university and a larger network of student radicals were well aware that something was going to happen and that it was likely to fail. Those who wrote memoirs are like a Greek chorus lamenting an implacably unfolding tragedy. In the end, not Shevyrev but Ulyanov played the role of tragic hero.

Shevyrev nonetheless had what it took to shape a conspiracy. He used deception and did not put his recruits through any rigorous tests, but after involving them he followed strictly the conspiratorial rules of organizing cells. Like Nechaev, he subordinated science to action. Govorukhin and Ulyanov were astonished at Shevyrev's atheoretical and amoral approach, in which a limited end justified unscrupulous means, with neither ends nor means supported by serious scientific thought. Ulyanov confided to Govorukhin, "A strange mechanism this fellow Shevyrev—I just don't understand him."[36] Shevyrev apparently simply wanted to kill as many oppressors of the people as he could and did not worry too much about either theory or methods. Only Ulyanov's interventions later in the course of the conspiracy kept Shevyrev from going over the edge into full-blown Nechaevism.

O NE WONDERS WHETHER Sasha spent much time pondering the revolutionary idea that the end justified the means—a doctrine that had become associated with Nechaev's ruthlessness. Unlike Nechaev, Alexander Ulyanov would not resort to coercion,

let alone to murder of his own comrades; he would not think of spreading fraudulent information and appealing to the peasants' deep prejudices to agitate them into action, or of subordinating science to revolutionary action. Yet Sasha used his scientific education to prepare nitroglycerine and dynamite and spent hours making lead "bullets" and treating them with strychnine. If the bombs had exploded, how many innocent lives would they have taken along with those of the royal family in the imperial equipage and of the bomb throwers? The area reconnoitered by the plotters was one of shops filled with imported luxury wares. Here were the capital's liveliest streets replete with restaurants and cafés, jewelry and furniture stores, milliners and haberdashers, stationers and booksellers. The scene would have been horrible, perhaps dozens of people dressed in their Sunday best in pools of blood, mangled by the explosions, convulsed in a death agony from the strychnine. Sasha, no doubt after much anguish, had numbed himself to such images, just as he had to thoughts of his own death. What did the sacrifice of a few dozen lives mean if it would lead to the liberation of millions and usher in an era of universal human happiness? The great literary critic of the generation of the 1840s, Vissarion Belinsky, had put it with flair in his correspondence of 1841, to his friend V. P. Botkin:

> I'm beginning to love humanity in Marat's manner: to make the least part of it happy, it seems to me that I'd exterminate the remainder with fire and sword. . . . People are so stupid that one must forcibly lead them to happiness. Anyway, what's the blood of thousands compared to the degradation and suffering of millions? Therefore, *fiat justitia, pereat mundus*![37]

Bombs, Hearts, and Ideas

T HE REVOLUTIONARY STUDENTS of St. Petersburg took stock of their chances after the arrests in the military schools in December 1886 and January 1887. The regime appeared to be ready for anything, and only the most reckless vowed to go through with an attempt on the life of the tsar. Rumors of assassination plots continued to make the rounds and appeared in the foreign press, but pessimism was the order of the day. In late January and early February, Sasha had doubts about the timing of the assassination attempt and asked Shevyrev and the others to put it off until the fall of 1887. It seemed to be an impossible task. Despite all of the preliminary work in the *zemlyachestva* and other student organizations, the hastily planned assassination plot of less than four months' duration enrolled only a handful of fully committed terrorists. Shevyrev, with the help of Orest Govorukhin, Josef Lukashevich, and Sasha, recruited Vasilii Osipanov, Pakhomii Andreyushkin, and Vasilii Generalov as throwers and, as signalers, Michael Kancher, Peter Gorkun, and Stepan Volokhov. When the need arose, the main organizers reached out to a larger network of helpers and suppliers: some did little more than fetch and carry bomb-making materials, others lithographed or set type for the group's program; still others provided contraband chemicals, poisons, weapons, safe houses, and funds.

The authorities could connect only fifteen people directly to the conspiracy (not counting those already arrested in earlier roundups, like Sergei Nikonov, or in emigration, like Govorukhin and

Nicholas Rudevich). All of those arrested and brought to trial played significant roles. Michael Novorussky and his mother-in-law, Maria Ananina, helped Sasha set up a laboratory in a suburb of St. Petersburg. Raisa Shmidova stored explosives and, like Anna Serdyukova in Yekaterinodar, connected the St. Petersburg group with other outposts of the terrorist network. Lukashevich's contacts in Vilnius—Bronisław and Josef Piłsudski, Anton Gnatowski, and Titus Pashkovsky—provided chemicals, poisons, and pistols. Sasha worked feverishly in Bronisław Piłsudski's apartment type-setting the program on February 27 and 28. They did everything at breakneck speed and, in the end, botched everything.

The conspirators of the Second March First seem pathetically inadequate compared with the Executive Committee of the People's Will. The organizers of the successful attempt on the life of Alexander II had swept up hundreds of collaborators into their project. With all of their resources, they failed repeatedly in several ambitious attempts spread out over a period of two years. Even the failures of the Executive Committee, however, were impressive. Each attempt cost enormous effort and personal sacrifice. In February 1880 Stepan Khalturin, who had been hired as a carpenter on the royal yacht, got himself transferred to the Winter Palace. Beginning in November 1879 he smuggled small amounts of dynamite and hid them where he bunked in the cellar of the Winter Palace. Khalturin stored more than one hundred pounds of dynamite in a box, placed to explode beneath Alexander II's dining room. The tsar failed to reach his table at the usual time because of a meeting with a visiting dignitary. Instead, the huge explosion killed eleven people and wounded fifty-six more. This was the most spectacular of the several failed efforts. The years 1879–81 in retrospect became the heroic period of Russian terrorism, when the terrorists achieved maximum effect. Thereafter the regime managed to stay one step ahead of the revolutionaries. In December 1886 and January 1887 arrests among St. Petersburg army and naval cadets brought pessi-

mism and apathy. Mark Braginsky, who had marched with Sasha on November 17, and Sergei Nikonov were both arrested.

Sasha believed that the participation of military elements was crucial for the execution of systematic terror, and held no brief for gathering all of their meager resources for a solo attack on the tsar. His commitment to the group kept him working on the bombs, but according to Govorukhin, Sasha thought he could best serve the cause with theoretical work abroad. "I'll help prepare the assassination and then I'll hide and, if the government searches for me, I'll flee abroad."[1] Govorukhin in January 1887 accused Ulyanov of vacillating, but once he himself emigrated, he confessed that delay made more sense than holding the assassination attempt to the original calendar. It seems likely that not only Ulyanov but Lukashevich, Govorukhin, and Shevyrev as well had no real intention of staying with the bomb throwers until the bitter end. Lukashevich's and Shevyrev's behavior at the trial strengthens this impression. Govorukhin knew that he might have to go into hiding well before the assassination attempt. In January, however, not rational calculation but emotions determined the outcome, and all of the central actors except Ulyanov thought that the group should hold to the March 1 target date.

Although Shevyrev's compulsiveness played a central role, the suicidal impatience and machismo of the bomb throwers had great weight in the final decision. Osipanov, the lead assassin, and his companion Cossack bomb throwers cared little for theory and simply wanted to get on with it. Andreyushkin and Generalov vied to prove their Cossack masculinity. Their machismo expressed as revolutionary commitment impressed Sasha during his visits to the Don and Kuban Cossack *zemlyachestvo*, and he let them and Osipanov dictate the timetable. Each decision that Sasha made reinforced his sense of responsibility to the group. When others fell by the wayside, he stepped up. During January he was only one of several bomb makers; after mid-February, when Govorukhin

and N. A. Rudevich fled abroad and Shevyrev left for the Crimea, Ulyanov and Lukashevich became co-equal in bomb-making and organizational work. Sasha's writing skill and ability with complex ideas made him the main communicator and theoretician of the Second March First.

During January and February 1887 Ulyanov and Lukashevich had full responsibility for the bomb making and organizational work connected to it: they needed to procure chemicals and laboratory equipment, to establish secure laboratories and storage sites; to distribute the tasks, to test the explosive materials and fuses, and to instruct the throwers about the way the bombs worked. Much of this was done in surprisingly slipshod fashion, but they were able to build the bombs without police detection of their laboratories.

The bomb making proceeded in January and February at a hectic pace, sometimes recklessly. Lukashevich, Ulyanov, Govorukhin, Generalov, and Andreyushkin worked in far-from-secure settings—their own apartments—and took great risks. The manufacture of nitric acid produced penetrating odors, but the complaints and questions of landladies and landlords were adroitly parried with the usual explanation: they were performing chemistry experiments for their studies. Once while Sasha and Govorukhin were producing lead cubes for bullets in Sasha's apartment on Alexandrovsky Prospect, a friend walked in on them. Showing more than a little sangfroid, Sasha asked him to help them, without explaining what they were doing. No questions were asked and no consequences ensued.[2]

Nicholas Rudevich, another Kuban Cossack, had been recruited into bomb making by his former gymnasium mate Andreyushkin. When Andreyushkin indiscreetly revealed his central role in a project to assassinate the tsar, Rudevich realized that anyone associated with Andreyushkin was in a ticklish position. He decided to stop working on the project. Andreyushkin told Shevyrev, who threatened that Rudevich would have to be eliminated because he knew

too much. At that point Andreyushkin balked and asked Sasha to intervene. Sasha called Shevyrev's method "Nechaevist," and persuaded him to back down. They agreed that it was prudent to send Rudevich abroad at the beginning of February 1887 and supplied him with funds and a false passport. It was one of several incidents in which Ulyanov braked Shevyrev's ruthlessness. Although Sasha willingly helped others emigrate, he became more deeply involved. Like the bomb throwers, he chose fidelity to the cause over self-preservation.

Ulyanov's self-subordination to the will of the group did not occur thoughtlessly or recklessly, but "scientifically." Sasha believed in the Russian Darwinian notion that historical evolutionary processes of selection worked at the group level rather than the individual level. Lavrov, whose writings circulated widely in lithographed copies in the student body, had made such thinking paramount in *narodnik* doctrine. Lavrov legitimated terrorist action only if it signified subordination to the tactic of a disciplined wing of a revolutionary party guided by scientific theory—an approach that the Bolsheviks later translated into "democratic centralism." The individual will and intellect had to be sacrificed to the group's authority—to the party line. It mattered little to Sasha that the party line in this small group had been set by reckless and suicidal youths, whose behavior violated conspiratorial rules and played into the hands of the police.

B Y THE LATE 1880s relations between police and institutions of higher education had become virtually routine—not necessarily a good thing for the authorities. Students expected police agents to show up at private apartments when five or more students gathered, presumably for parties. The revelers ordinarily served their visitors enough strong drink to soften their vigilance. Student festivities were often Potemkin villages of a sort, fake name-day celebrations or engagement parties with dancing, music, and a prominent display of bottles—façades for serious back-

room political discussion. Despite this slackness in some areas, the authorities had infiltrated all of the subversive groups and illegal *zemlyachestva*. Threatened with expulsion or worse, some students became police collaborators. Others who had been arrested for illegal activity bargained with the police and served as double agents or stool pigeons. In prisons the police planted them where they could tease out information for use in court, or turn the prisoners against each other by spreading disinformation.

Under Dmitry Tolstoy, minister of the interior from 1882 to 1889, and Vyacheslav Von Plehve, the head of the Police Department between 1881 and 1884, spying reached a new level. They gave Gregory Sudeikin, already head of the St. Petersburg Security Bureau and bane of the People's Will, even greater authority in January 1883. A secret directive of June 5, 1882, issued at the beginning of Tolstoy's tenure, created the "black offices" for systematic invasion of the empire's mail. Until this time the practice of opening and replacing private letters had been performed relatively infrequently. Things changed quickly. In 1882 alone twenty employees in seven such clandestine operations located in post offices in the Russian Empire's major cities opened 380,000 letters.[3] The practice, called "perlustration," gave the St. Petersburg police the crucial information they needed to round up the Second March First conspiracy. The black office had been reading some of Andreyushkin's correspondence, which yielded an indiscreet letter of January 20, 1887, to a student in Kharkiv University, Ivan Platonovich Nikitin. This inexplicably careless letter gave the police every reason to believe that Andreyushkin was serious about terrorism:

"... Might we have a social-democratic movement, like Germany's? I think that's impossible. What's possible is the most merciless terror, and I firmly believe that it will actually happen in the near future; I believe that the present calm is the calm before the storm. I'll not rehearse the virtues and advantages of red terror

. . . because that's my hobbyhorse and it's no doubt why I hate
social-democrats."[4]

The letter was quite enough to set the political police into motion,
but the signature on the letter was indecipherable, and the police in
St. Petersburg did not receive verification from the police in Kharkiv
that Andreyushkin had written it until February 27, 1887. The black
office then sent the information to St. Petersburg chief of police,
Gresser, with a request to begin "continuous and extremely close
surveillance" of Andreyushkin and to establish who his close contacts were. The close surveillance of Andreyushkin, though much
delayed, started on February 28. Undercover agents of the political
police as well as regular police found him and the other throwers and signalers rehearsing for the main event on Nevsky Prospect. However, Generalov had been under close surveillance, and,
even earlier than that, on February 22 and 26, his tail had followed
him from his apartment to his rendezvous with Andreyushkin and
Osipanov.[5] Andreyushkin's letter to Nikitin thus alerted the police
to the possibility that they were all part of a terrorist organization
and that imminent action was possible. The police would have had
even more explicit information about Andreyushkin and the conspiracy if they had intercepted his messages to Anna Serdyukova.

   A promising student from a poor family, Serdyukova had attended
a normal school and had qualified to teach at the elementary level.
She had three younger siblings and lived with one of her two sisters. At some point Serdyukova joined radical circles. Her mentor
Kikifor Kochevsky, who taught in a village school in Yekaterinodar
District, had been accused of spreading revolutionary materials
in 1875. Information gathered by police agents in 1887—too late
for the trial in April 1887—connected the Kharkiv circle of terrorists to Kochevsky, and thus tied Serdyukova to Shmidova. Both of
the women knew Vasilii Brazhnikov, a veteran terrorist from the
Kuban who had studied in Yekaterinodar, then in St. Petersburg

and Kharkiv, where he became a major organizer of the groups there. The central Kharkiv terrorist group had been decimated in 1886, and the survivors sent emissaries far and wide for help. Brazhnikov went in February 1887 to St. Petersburg, where he contacted Shmidova. Rudevich, like Andreyushkin, was part of the Yekaterinodar and Kharkiv networks. He had graduated from the Kuban military gymnasium in 1885, a year earlier than Andreyushkin.

Andreyushkin met Serdyukova in Yekaterinodar, a town of roughly 45,000 on the Kuban River, in the summer of 1884. He was nineteen and a gymnasium student in the seventh class, and she, roughly six years his senior, was giving private lessons and earning forty-six rubles a month in a nearby village. They met again in February 1885. One year later, in February 1886, she took up residence in Yekaterinodar. As a favor to her, Andreyushkin tutored Serdyukova's younger sister, who was fourteen and preparing to enter a gymnasium. This went on until August 1886, before he left for St. Petersburg. During these months Serdyukova and he became very close friends—"as close as people of the opposite sex can be and respect one another"—and they continued their relationship via mail.[6]

At the trial in April 1887, in his agonized attempt to explain his correspondence with her and deny a political connection, Andreyushkin called Serdyukova "more than a friend." She, however, knew that he was a doomed man and tried to save herself by describing the contents of the smuggled letters that she had burned according to his instructions. One such letter recounted the events of November 17, 1886, and in it he vented his anger at the authorities. She knew that it would be imprudent to respond, but when Andreyushkin wrote again, explicitly asking whether she agreed with his views, she replied that she disagreed with them. In December 1886 he wrote that he would sometimes be using invisible ink, and if she could not read parts of his letters she should heat them over a lamp to reveal the text. Then in January 1887 Andreyushkin wrote that

he had joined the People's Will.[7] The police did not know the contents of these messages until after Serdyukova's arrest and interrogation in March 1887. Rather, it was the letter to Nikitin in Kharkiv that tipped off the police to his intentions at the end of February.

In February, Serdyukova heard rumors that Andreyushkin had been arrested. His mother, with whom she was acquainted, lived not far from Yekaterinodar in a Cossack village. She came to town and told Serdyukova that the rumors were false, that she had received a letter from her son, but was illiterate and needed Serdyukova's help. Andreyushkin's letter, though sent to his mother's address, was actually written for Serdyukova. Evidently sent on February 14, the letter contained the misinformation that he had typhus, and would be hospitalized on February 15, and requested that Serdyukova should keep this from his mother. In the same letter, to her shock, she found a marriage proposal. How could she marry someone seven years her junior? She decided to put an end to his fantasy and sent a reply telling him that she could not marry him—that he was like a brother to her. But after she had sent her letter she realized that his letter containing the proposal might also have a hidden message. It did, and what she saw terrified her: "There is going to be an attempt on the life of the tsar. I'm one of the bomb throwers; be careful, don't make a misstep; don't even write if you agree to my proposal."[8] What could she do now? She had been put in a double bind. Perhaps a yes would stop him from going through with the plot, but he had made it virtually impossible for her to say yes. Not knowing that he had been arrested on March 1, she decided to go back on her refusal, and telegraphed acceptance of his proposal of marriage on March 6: "You asked me not to write. Since I received your letter I've lived through an eternity. Yes. Please reply. Komikhina."[9] Serdyukova thought she could evade detection by using a nickname known only to her friends. The police, of course, collected all of Andreyushkin's letters after his arrest, among them an unsent letter to her. They intercepted Serdyukova's telegram on

March 7, easily traced it, and arrested her. Later she was charged with concealing knowledge of the conspiracy.

Serdyukova's situation now resembled Shmidova's, although the latter was more deeply involved with the conspiracy and with both Ulyanov and Govorukhin. The two women had become revolutionaries in Yekaterinodar and Kharkiv, and then were drawn into the world of reckless and suicidal young men who wanted to be heroes, to impress the women they loved, perhaps to receive a soldier's goodbye, but perhaps, at some unconscious level, to sacrifice their loved ones as well. Govorukhin sent Shmidova a strange message dated February 25 (that is, after his departure) beginning, "If they find my corpse, then I beg that no one be accused of causing my death." In the apparent suicide note he claimed that he intended to drown himself in an ice hole, but what begins tragically ends clownishly: "O. M. G. Guess who?"[10] The initials are obviously those of Orest Makarevich Govorukhin. Although Govorukhin claimed in his memoirs that this was just a ruse to confuse the police, it was not clear that Shmidova took it that way. At the trial in April she testified that she believed that he intended to commit suicide because she thought he was "somewhat psychologically abnormal."[11] Then there was Sasha's use of a telegram unnecessarily implicating Anna in the conspiracy. All three men were at least wounding the women closest to them—and possibly destroying them.

THE POLICE HAD PICKED UP Sasha's trail during the fall semester of his senior year. His name appeared in several reports from agents planted in the student body. In the fall of 1886 Sasha's frequent visits to the *zemlyachestvo* of Don and Kuban Cossacks made him especially suspect. The police were fully aware of the rumors about assassinations circulating after November 17, 1886. They did arrest suspects, but the Second March First was only one of many incipient terrorist groups, and in matters of

security, timing was important for achieving maximum effect. The police had made numerous arrests in December and January and were closing in on Govorukhin in February, but in order to make a clean sweep they would have had to arrest quite a few of Russia's future elite academicians. The university reforms of 1884 and the events of November 17, 1886, had alienated so many students that the police could hardly detect the serious plotters against the background noise. Even so, they held the balance of power in 1887.

In the first half of January 1887 Sasha decided that, for his own good, Chebotarev should move from Alexandrovsky 25 to another apartment, and his friend did leave on January 20.[12] Chebotarev's name had begun to appear with Sasha's on police reports, but he had not made the same kind of commitment to terror that Ulyanov had. Sasha did not want his friend to go down with them. Now a full-time terrorist, Sasha made bombs and laid plans for systematic terror—flexible, decentralized terror whose operatives would seize opportunities and lie low when necessary. Sasha felt confident that he might make a contribution as a theoretician as well as a technician—hence his dream of becoming an émigré in one of the European centers that produced the strategic literature for the revolutionary movement—perhaps in Paris with Lavrov or in Geneva with Plekhanov.

In January he began to make nitric acid and lead cubes, and then in February nitroglycerine, dynamite, and the bomb casing. Toward the end he packed the dynamite and strychnine-treated lead into the bomb's shell. Only Lukashevich stood above him in the technical chain of command. Govorukhin and Sasha had recommended Generalov and Andreyushkin to Shevyrev as possible recruits. Sasha became their instructor in the manufacture of nitric acid. Ordinarily taciturn and gloomy, overcome by what Russians call *toska*—a mood barely suggested by ennui because it is so much deeper—the young Cossacks seemed to come to life only when involved intensely with bomb making and preparing for the event.

Vasilii Generalov, the son of a Don Cossack landowner and miller, only nineteen at the time of the attempted assassination, had enrolled, like Andreyushkin, in St. Petersburg University in 1886, but chose the law faculty. Generalov's academic record and attitude in his stagnant gymnasium in Novocherkass evoked the assessment "indifferent to the point of dullness."[13] In fact, Generalov had ample intelligence but lacked stimulation. The rich intellectual and political life of the university and the circle of Don and Kuban Cossacks saved him from a state of perpetual funk. Revolution became his métier. In St. Petersburg, Generalov began to organize gymnasium students into self-education circles. After the demonstration of November 17 he returned to his habitual gloom and apathy, but brightened again when, with Govorukhin and Ulyanov's help, he found his way to Shevyrev. He was perfect for Shevyrev and Lukashevich's designs. Before he could throw bombs, however, he would have to make them. At the end of December, Ulyanov commissioned him to make roughly two hundred cubes of lead for the bombs. On January 3, 1887, Generalov moved into a two-room apartment on Bolshaya Belozerskaya Street, one room of which became a laboratory and storage place for the explosives.[14] He and Andreyushkin then were assigned the difficult and time-consuming task of making nitric acid.

Pakhomii Andreyushkin had the humblest origins of all the conspirators. Born out of wedlock to a Kuban Cossack mother and a Greek father, he came to St. Petersburg in 1886 after a permissive gymnasium education supplemented by self-education circles dedicated to learning the latest radical theories. The gymnasium students in Yekaterinodar created a virtual reign of terror, breaking the windows of out-of-favor teachers and meditating—though not too seriously—on simultaneously blowing up the residences of several gymnasium directors in the region.[15] The police were watching Andreyushkin from the very beginning of his university career in the fall semester 1886. He, too, entered the physical-

mathematical department in St. Petersburg University, planning to study the natural sciences and then move on to medicine. The reactionary atmosphere hastened his way to terrorism. In January 1887 Andreyushkin's apartment became the workshop for nitric acid and bullets.

Andreyushkin arrived during the radical upsurge of 1886 and, as one might expect, joined the radical clique in the Don and Kuban Cossack *zemlyachestvo*. He immediately focused his energy on terrorism and became its stubborn advocate. Like Nechaev and Shevyrev, Andreyushkin did not rule out "violence against brothers" when he thought it necessary for the cause. Like Bakuninist insurrectionists, he admired the old Cossack rebels Razin and Pugachev. When the police put an illegal student circle's library under official seal, Andreyushkin worked out a plan to liberate the books, but discovered that another student group had similar designs. He threatened to rat them out to the police, and they backed off. Andreyushkin's recklessness and blindness to danger reached the edge of pathology—and perhaps beyond.[16]

Shevyrev found in Adreyushkin another ready recruit for the assassination squad. Although the failure of the Second March First seemed very likely, Andreyushkin's inability to contain his enthusiasm and boastfulness attracted a level of police surveillance that guaranteed the discovery of, at least, the personnel involved. When Shevyrev proposed that he be one of the throwers, Andreyushkin accepted with alacrity and demanded that they give him the biggest bomb and also the first crack at the imperial equipage. Another tragicomic note sounds in Andreyushkin's refusal to carry potassium cyanide—although in this he was seconded by Osipanov. Sheyvrev offered it for use in the unlikely event that the throwers survived the blast. Andreyushkin taunted Generalov for accepting the poison: "I'm not a Don, but a Kuban, Cossack and have the courage to endure any suffering."[17]

Lukashevich's method for producing nitric acid of the requisite

strength proved to be tedious and time-consuming. The conspirators brought in another Cossack, Rudevich, to help them, but his defection from the project made things even more difficult, and they appealed to Shevyrev to look for another way—hence the decision at the end of January to purchase the acid in Vilnius. Lukashevich used his connections. He and Shevyrev decided that Michael Kancher would be the best person to act as liaison. Born in Ukraina in Poltava Province, the son of a postmaster in the imperial service, Kancher had graduated from a classical gymnasium and, like several other members of the plot, had joined the faculty of mathematical and physical sciences at St. Petersburg University. He quickly fell in with Shevyrev in October 1886. The apartment at Tuchkovy Lane on Vasilevsky Island that he shared with Peter Gorkun, his friend from Poltava and a law student at St. Petersburg University, became a central site of the conspiracy. Kancher's reliable work for Shevyrev's dining room, his role in the work on the proclamation connected with the November 17 demonstration, and his businesslike behavior and boundless energy made him the perfect candidate for a complicated and dangerous commission. At the end of January 1887 Lukashevich and Shevyrev gave Kancher fifty rubles and the addresses of Lukashevich's contacts in Vilnius.[18]

Ulyanov agreed to be the link with Kancher, to confer with him on the day of his departure, to monitor by a conspiratorial telegram his successful procurement of the goods and his arrival time in St. Petersburg, and then to meet him at the Warsaw Station and pick up the contraband. Sasha had Kancher send the telegram under the name "Petrov" to Anna's address rather than his, thereby making her an unwitting accomplice. After a little reflection he realized that giving Shevyrev Anna's address had been a mistake, but when he tried to intercept Kancher before his departure it was too late.

In Vilnius during January 31 to February 2 Kancher met Bronisław Piłsudski, Isaac Dembo, Titus Pashkovsky, and Anton Gnatowski, all committed to terrorism. At Dembo's request, Piłsudski, who

enrolled in law at St. Petersburg University in 1886 and went home to Vilnius during December and January, procured strychnine and atropine from a pharmacist. In another of history's ironies, Bronisław Piłsudski's older brother, Josef, after years in tsarist prisons for his socialist and nationalist plotting, became commander of the Polish army. President and de facto dictator of Poland, he stopped the Red Army in 1920, thereby halting the spread of the Russian Revolution not only into Poland but possibly into Germany by way of Poland. Bronisław Piłsudski and Pashkovsky stood trial in April 1887 and were sentenced respectively to fifteen and ten years hard labor in Siberian exile. Dembo and Gnatowski fled to Switzerland and, with others, tried to complete the unfinished business of the Second March First. In 1889 Dembo tested a new and presumably better kind of bomb, but it exploded prematurely and fatally injured him.[19]

On the night of February 2, 1887, Anna received Kancher's telegram from Vilnius signaling his success at procuring the materials: "Sister is dangerously ill." Sasha met Kancher on February 3 at the Warsaw Station when he returned carrying a suitcase with forty pounds of nitric acid. Kancher also carried funds contributed by the Vilnius circle, pistols, and poison. However, the nitric acid he brought back from Vilnius was too dilute and thus useless for dynamite. They dumped it into the Neva and once again began to make acid of the requisite strength from scratch. Lukashevich also had to acquire more poison.

In February they began collecting all of the necessary materials to build the bombs, once again with Kancher's help. Kancher recruited a friend, a gymnasium dropout, Stepan Volokhov, who became the third signaler. They purchased in St. Petersburg shops sulfuric acid, tubes, retorts, and other laboratory equipment and vessels necessary for making and storing the explosives. Andreyushkin, Generalov, Kancher, and Volokhov kept up the output of lead bullets, transported the products to Govorukhin and Shmi-

dova, who stored some of it, and brought the rest to Michael Novo-russky's apartment, for transshipment to a makeshift laboratory in the northern suburb of Pargolovo. A theology student working toward a master's degree, Novorussky gave Ulyanov cover as tutor in scriptures for his mother-in-law's son. Her suburban dwelling became a safe house for the production and storage of dynamite and nitroglycerine.[20]

At the beginning of February, Ulyanov began to assume more responsibility for the manufacture of the bombs themselves, although he contributed very little to the infamous book bomb. He had doubts about its design and wished that he could modify it. Lukashevich in his memoirs took credit for designing and building the book bomb. He bought *Greenberg's Dictionary of Medical Terminology*, a sizable tome with a stout cover, glued the edges of the pages, put the book in a press, and let it dry. Then he cut out most of the inside, leaving only the pages' now solid edge to make the book into a sturdy box. Lukashevich described how he made the bomb's innards down to the smallest detail. He apparently did this mainly out of pride, to defend his reputation against the expert testimony of Major General N. P. Fyodorov, a professor at the Mikhailovsky Artillery Academy. Fyodorov testified that the book bomb failed to explode because it was badly designed and that the two cylindrical bombs suffered from similar defects.[21]

It is difficult to know exactly how much work Sasha actually did on the bombs, because during the trial he did everything possible to save Lukashevich from hanging. Under interrogation at the trial Ulyanov claimed that he packed the book bomb with dynamite between February 8 and 10, but it still remained to fill the space between the tin casing and the cardboard book cover with strychnine-treated lead cubes, a job that he gave to Generalov. Sasha then started to prepare the cylindrical bombs and estimated that they needed a few additional pounds of dynamite. Ulyanov didn't think that he could safely prepare the explosives in his own

apartment. His friend Novorussky, a theology student of revolutionary bent, donated his mother-in-law's suburban cottage. Novorussky, a candidate for a higher degree in the Theological Academy, had a typically nihilist common-law marriage to Lydia Ananina, the daughter of a midwife of peasant background, Maria Alexandrovna Ananina. Novorussky recommended that Ulyanov pretend to be a tutor for his mother-in-law's fourteen-year-old son, Nicholas.

Maria Ananina and Nicholas lived in a rented dacha in the third, most northerly section of Pargolovo, roughly ten kilometers north of St. Petersburg and near the Shuvalov Station on the Finland railway. On February 10, 1887, Novorussky dispatched there a carriage loaded with baskets filled with Ulyanov's laboratory equipment and chemicals. Sasha arrived on February 11 by the rail line that passed nearby; the next day Novorussky sent another shipment from St. Petersburg. Working systematically in the dacha, in three days Sasha made three and a half pounds of white dynamite and more nitroglycerine than they needed for the bombs. He intended that the surplus nitroglycerine and the laboratory serve future bomb making for an extended terrorist campaign. Ulyanov carefully instructed Ananina about the dangers of letting the nitroglycerine warm up. She hid the bottle in the water closet and then put it in a pot that she packed with snow every two days.[22]

On February 14, the day of Sasha's departure from Pargolovo, Ananina convinced him that it would be easier and cheaper to ride with her in the horse-drawn cart she had hired than to take the train to St. Petersburg. They started out together, but the suburban road got rough, and it became too dangerous to continue the ride in Ananina's cart. When they reached the beginning of the horse-tram line to St. Petersburg, Ulyanov left her and got on the tram with his sack of dynamite. In St. Petersburg he returned to his apartment to work on the tin casing and thick cardboard shells of the two cylindrical bombs.

Lukashevich had to make last-minute adjustments to the bombs'

fuses and put the new design through repeated trials, with Ulyanov and Shevyrev participating. The throwers would be walking with the bombs along St. Petersburg's busiest thoroughfares, and an unexpected jolt might lead to premature ignition, so Lukashevich decided to make it impossible to ignite the fuses accidentally. He evidently used the wrong kind of string to arm the fuses. At the trial Fyodorov mentioned the string as one of the problems with the bomb mechanism. Although he did not admit this outright, Lukashevich wrote, "It would have been more practical to use cord instead of string."[23] Lukashevich, however, defended the design of his fuses and placed the blame on the brute force used by the police, who prevented Osipanov from yanking the string properly and opening the valve. One of Osipanov's depositions suggests otherwise.

Meanwhile, Shevyrev shifted Kancher, Gorkun, and Volokhov to new roles. Heretofore procurers and transporters of the materials for the bombs and also bomb makers, they now entered the inner circle and learned the precise goal of all their work. They accepted the role of signaler proposed by Shevyrev. Having gotten the bombs well on the way to completion and his combat team enlisted, Shevyrev on February 17 left for Yalta. Before his departure he brought Ulyanov into the central group and gave Lukashevich the mantle of leader, although in practice Sasha and Lukashevich became co-leaders of the group. On February 17 Sasha met Osipanov for the first time. In the following days, under the watchful eyes of Ulyanov and Lukashevich, the throwers practiced with simulated bombs of the same weight as the real ones and duplicate fuses. In order to test the dynamite itself Lukashevich sent a quantity to Vilnius, where his friends carried out his instructions and successfully exploded a large cartridge. They sent a coded telegram to inform him.[24]

The main actors spent February 20–21 in feverish activity. Sasha and Lukashevich completed the job of constructing the cylindrical bombs' tin inner casings and cardboard outer shells. They cut the tin

in Ulyanov's apartment and then took the pieces to Lukashevich's for soldering. Andreyushkin, Generalov, Kancher, and Volokhov finished the work on the more than five hundred bullets and filled them with strychnine. This involved cutting cross-shaped pieces out of thick sheets of lead, creating a small hollow space inside when the arms of the cross were bent into a cube. After filling the space with strychnine and atropine sulfate they pierced the sides of the cube with an awl. Finally, they slathered the outside surface of the cubes with strychnine and alcohol.[25] Only the packing of the bombs with dynamite and bullets remained.

On February 20 Sasha took a break from his other tasks to accompany Govorukhin to the Warsaw Station. He gave Govorukhin one hundred rubles, for which he had pawned the gold medal he had received for his junior thesis. Govorukhin had stayed as long as he safely could, and the bombs were virtually finished. That same day Andreyushkin took surplus bomb-making materials designated for future combat squads to Govorukhin's now empty apartment for storage. Shmidova, whose apartment adjoined Govorukhin's, had Andreyushkin hide the materials in a basket under Govorukhin's bed. When Shmidova went out later that day, the landlady searched both apartments and found bottles filled with liquid and other mysterious parcels in Govorukhin's. She told the doorman to alert the police, but her suspicions seemed to him to be much ado about nothing. He characterized the situation in those terms to the police, who were not going to put themselves out for a foolish old woman. They searched the apartments only on the afternoon of the next day and found nothing, because Sasha had retrieved the bomb-making materials before they arrived. After leaving Govorukhin at the Warsaw Station on February 20, he took a cab to Shmidova's apartment. Unnoticed by the landlady, they moved the materials into Shmidova's apartment. Sasha stayed with her until morning and then left before dawn with the contraband.[26]

Kancher and Volokhov were supposed to take the finished

bombs from Ulyanov's apartment on February 21 for distribution to the throwers. They arrived earlier than expected; Lukashevich and Sasha were still at work packing the bombs with dynamite. This had important consequences. After the arrests on March 1 Kancher and Volokhov quickly broke down during interrogation and testified to seeing Sasha and Lukashevich working on the bombs. The larger bombs were delivered to Andreyushkin; Osipanov already had the book bomb.

The three throwers met as a team for the first time on the evening of February 22 in the Café Polonais on Mikhailovskaya Street and discussed possible assassination sites. Osipanov, the tactician for the combat group, suggested the area near the Mikhailovsky Manège, where Alexander II had reviewed his guards regiments shortly before his assassination, but after discussion the three throwers thought that it would be better to intercept the tsar's equipage either on Nevsky Prospect, at the Catherine Canal, or on Bolshaya Sedovaya. They decided to hold off on a detailed plan until they could have a joint meeting with the signalers on February 25. Now that the members of the entire combat squad had assembled and were supplied with their bombs, Sasha took the lead in suggesting that they have a farewell party.[27] They had all passed the point of no return.

On Monday afternoon, February 23, an exhausted Sasha showed up at Anna's apartment. While she went for tea he fell asleep on the sofa. After rousing him she showed him a recent letter from home. One of Ilya Nikolaevich's former colleagues wrote that Maria Alexandrovna had suffered a breakdown on the first anniversary of Ilya's death, but had then recovered her equilibrium. Sasha sat silently, his head in his hands and a doleful look on his face. Anna, a genius at denial, still did not know precisely what was going on, although she had felt uneasy about Sasha's behavior throughout his senior year. For a moment she thought that the letter would be helpful—reminding him of his responsibility to Maria Alexandrovna and his younger siblings. It obviously affected him,

but reminding Sasha of his father's death and mother's suffering may have been a mistake. Rather than calming him down, it probably reinforced his rage and desire for revenge. What, after all, had caused all of this suffering if not the regime that had forced Ilya Nikolaevich into retirement and undermined his life's work?

On February 25 the combat group and Sasha met in Kancher and Gorkun's apartment. Osipanov told them how to deploy along the tsar's anticipated route. Ulyanov lectured them on the construction of the bombs. After the others departed, Sasha read Osipanov a programmatic statement justifying their terrorist action. This was a precaution. If Osipanov survived, then he would have to represent their ideals and aims to a tribunal. Sasha thought that "the Cat," a somewhat uncouth man of few words, would be a poor mouthpiece for the program of scientific socialism. When the plot went awry, Sasha decided to take responsibility for making their case not only to the Senate tribunal but to the larger court of posterity. This seems odd in view of Ulyanov's own taciturn ways. He had cultivated the persona of the gloomy and tight-lipped nihilist hero of the literature of the 1860s. Now he had to adapt to the moment — and the moment required a different kind of heroic role — that of a socialist tribune modeled on the earlier martyrs of the People's Will. Who was better equipped to play that role than Sasha, who had expended agonies arriving at the notion of scientific socialism and then embodying it succinctly in a program?

The anguish and sorrow that Anna saw in Sasha during the last days of February she later ascribed to the pain of knowing that he was going to sacrifice his own mother to his socialist ideals. Her perception of his agitated state may have been correct but her diagnosis wrong. He may have been unhappy with the way things were going — with the hasty and sloppy work of the conspirators, with their immaturity and recklessness, and even perhaps with his own. Sasha was still trying to be a perfect nihilist hero — a person whose ideas and actions were perfectly rational and in precise

harmony with his feelings. He identified himself with the socialist
vanguard of humanity—what Lavrov called the "critically thinking
minority"—and, like other terrorists of the late 1880s, Sasha played
the role presumably assigned by the historical moment with the
merciless consequentiality required of a developed person.

S ASHA AND HIS CO-CONSPIRATORS had barely launched
their project during the second half of December 1886 than
they began to explore the idea of a program for the terrorist group.
Everyone agreed that none of the existing programs clarified the
meaning of revolutionary terrorism at this moment in history. They
needed to present an "objective-scientific explanation" for the
inevitability of the clash of the government and the intelligentsia.
They had to show that it was a natural expression of contemporary Russian life. Sasha patiently explained it all to one of the gendarmes who interrogated him on March 20–21, 1887:

> The former program of the People's Will lacked a scientific foun-
> dation. . . . In addition, we thought that it was our duty in under-
> taking such a serious project to inform the public not only about
> our most immediate motives for our deed, but our entire political
> "credo." This inspired the composition of the general part of our
> program forming together with the special part the "Program of
> the terrorist faction of the party 'The People's Will'" that I set
> forth in this deposition. . . . I personally was deeply involved in its
> composition and completely agreed with everything proposed in
> it, its positions and the explanation of terror. . . .[28]

Somehow Sasha managed during the last days of February to com-
pose and plan (though without success) the printing and distribution of the program of the Terrorist Faction of the People's Will.
The designation "faction" signified a departure from the main
line of the now shattered Executive Committee. Ulyanov tried to

update both theory and practice and unify all of the terrorist and social-democratic groups, but by and large he faithfully reproduced the ideas of the *narodovoltsy* of that time. Like the People's Will in 1881, the terrorists of 1887 were trying to extort a liberal constitution by means of dynamite.

Sasha represented the relatively irenic socialism of the late 1880s, when *narodnik* terrorists and social democrats worked together in the same organization simply because they all believed in the necessity of terror. The Terrorist Faction of the People's Will contained people like Shevyrev and Andreyushkin, who did very little "scientific" thinking at all, and Sasha, who spent enormous effort on a scientific analysis of the Russian Empire's unique situation. Although he admired Marxism, he did not think that an ethical revolutionary could idly sit by while capitalism did its work. Ulyanov looked to Lavrov for his ethics. To the science-oriented *narodniki* guided by Lavrov, terrorism was ethical to the extent that it could remove Russian autocracy, the greatest obstacle to the dissemination of scientific socialism to the *narod*. Lavrov taught that Russian socialism needed fanatic, heroic people during the phase of socialist struggle that preceded the formation of a disciplined party and the mass education of the people.

The People's Will had some of the characteristics of a disciplined party, but even during its heyday it was a vulnerable underground organization. In the late 1880s there was no real party, only small groups of young fanatics trying against all odds to shape one. Sasha joined them after he overcame his initial contempt for the state of social science and made a fatal commitment, as it turned out, to a *narodnik*-Marxian hybrid, in which the *narodnik* side of the hyphen dictated tactics. Lavrov's ethics and appreciation of Russia's uniqueness trumped Marx's more catholic vision. His articles for *The Messenger of the People's Will* gave the new generation a social and political analysis emphasizing Russia's special features and both the obstacles and the opportunities associated with them.

Sasha's social analysis of historical progress closely shadowed Lavrov's ideas in *Socialism and the Aims of Morality*. With Darwin himself their authority, Russian Darwinists found in human beings an inherited tendency to sacrifice themselves for their group. Lavrov had taken things further and written that the most "developed" people, the socialist vanguard, had a *duty* to sacrifice not only themselves but, if necessary, those closest to them to serve an ideal that embraced the love of humanity as a whole. Such thinking transmuted suicidal and murderous acts of terrorism into the naturally ordained self-sacrifice of a scientific vanguard for the sake of the human species. Lavrov, however, believed that critically thinking individuals still made a choice. What was natural was not inevitable for the "developed" minority.

The Marxian side of Sasha's hybrid program showed in several ways. At the very outset of the program he modified the People's Will's formula of 1879: "In our basic convictions we are socialists and *narodniki*" by dropping the word *narodniki*.[29] Second, Sasha embraced the notion that economic forces inevitably shaped social change and would produce a happy socialist ending—not merely adequate material resources and social justice for all, but full human development for all. To be sure, states would not all arrive at socialism in the same way. Although he began with economics, the emerging proletariat, and their growing consciousness of their position, Sasha did not make economic forces the only drivers of historical change. Rather, he gave significant roles to factors that dogmatic Marxists assigned to the "superstructure." Like other *narodniki*, Sasha assumed that governments and intelligentsias played no small role in determining how any given people would arrive at socialism. In Russia historical change now depended on the struggle between an outdated and defensive political system— a stubbornly autocratic police state—and the progressive forces in a changing society.

For Sasha the Russian peasants remained the most significant

social force, though not the most progressive one. Their value lay not just in their numbers but in their communal traditions: their belief in the right of the people to land, their collective owner- ship and cultivation of the land, and their communal, local self- government—all features that might allow them to move quickly toward a higher form of socialism. *Narodnik* theorists also believed in the power of ideas: once made conscious of scientific socialism by the vanguard intelligentsia, Russia's peasants might not have to go through a long period of misery under capitalism. Although Marx and Engels usually attacked anything that smacked of "ideal- ism," their preface to the 1882 Russian edition of the *Manifesto of the Communist Party* allowed that a socialist revolution could suc- ceed in a relatively backward Russia if it triggered revolutions in the more industrially developed states. All of this turned out to be wishful thinking. For the moment, Russian peasants lacked the req- uisite consciousness and could only vaguely support the struggle of the revolutionary elements in Russian society. Europe was in the early stage of a new surge of imperialism. For pure Marxists 1887 showed little promise.

For Sasha, Russia's urban factory workers—themselves recent arrivals with strong connections to the villages—would serve as a crucial link with the countryside. Like Marxists, Sasha saw the workers as the "natural bearers of socialist ideas."[30] Despite their relatively small numbers, they were the nucleus of a socialist party, its most active element, a decisive force for change, and the group most receptive to political indoctrination and struggle. The Second March First had thus made plans to spread propaganda among the workers of St. Petersburg. Nonetheless, in Sasha's theory Rus- sian workers, like the intelligentsia, would act mainly to bring to a higher level of socialist consciousness the larger mass of peasants already inclined toward socialism.

The Russian theorists of revolution always had difficulty assign- ing the revolutionary intelligentsia a precise practical role. Sasha,

like other *narodniki*, recognized the socialist intelligentsia as a social force in its own right and even as the vanguard of political struggle for freedom of thought and speech, but he did not believe that it could play a fully independent role in a revolutionary struggle. He found convincing the Marxian notion that revolutionary struggle had to be *class* struggle. The intelligentsia vanguard might be midwives of revolution, but no more than that. Unlike Bakunin, Sasha did not imagine historical circumstances in which the vanguard could impose "from above" a "scientific" program that did not really coincide with the hopes of tens of millions of peasants. The *narodnik* scenario that Russia might take a shortcut to socialism played out after 1917—but this time under the leadership of a Marxist party led by Sasha's reckless younger brother. The tragic results are well known.

V LADMIR ILYICH ULYANOV, as Lenin, would head the scientific Marxian "priesthood" prophesied by Michael Bakunin, who understood that those who invoked the authority of science could be every bit as tyrannical as religious fanatics, and that they would use science to justify a new kind of state despotism, even more oppressive than the old one. During his struggle with Marx over control of the First International in 1872, Bakunin had written a letter to the socialist journal *La Liberté* (Brussels) in which Bakunin both outlined the likely consequences of the kind of revolution Marx wished for, and predicted with great prescience the soviet-style regimes of the twentieth century.

That revolution will consist in the expropriation of the land ... from the current owners and capitalists and in the appropriation of all the land and capital by the State, which, in order to fulfill its great economic mission as well as its political one, will have to be very powerful and very strongly centralized. The State will administer and direct cultivation of the land by

means of its appointed managers commanding armies of rural workers, organized and disciplined for that kind of work. Simultaneously, on the ruins of the entire existing banking system it will establish a single bank controlling all labor and the entire national commerce. . . . One can see immediately how an organizational plan so apparently simple might seduce the imagination of workers, who seek justice and equality more avidly than liberty, and who foolishly imagine that the other two can exist without liberty. . . . In reality, this will be a barracks regime for the proletariat, most of whom will be reduced to a uniform mass, and will wake up, go to sleep, work, and live by the drum. . . . Internally there will be slavery and in external affairs war without respite . . .[31]

Sasha believed that the socialist party's central task was to educate and organize the emerging social class most susceptible to socialist ideas. But the oppressive regime lay between the revolutionary socialist intelligentsia and the workers. Without a liberal constitution granting freedom of speech, they would not be able to spread the word. Here Ulyanov remained squarely within the Lavrovian doctrine that gave the intelligentsia a tutelary role, both as carriers of enlightened thought and as organizers. Like Lavrov, Sasha saw the intelligentsia not as mere instruments of larger forces but as ethical actors, paying back their debt to the suffering millions whose serf labor for their ancestors had permitted the privileged few to reach the highest level of human development. Sasha never spoke about it, but he probably saw his own father as a victim who had worked himself to death serving the cause of enlightenment under a regime opposed to his goals. In his own way, Sasha continued his father's project, but now as a destroyer of the state that had rejected Ilya Nikolaevich's work.

Members of the revolutionary intelligentsia had two radically different images of the Russian imperial state. In their pessimistic

moods, they pictured it as a brute force against which they had little chance; in more optimistic frames of mind, they saw it as a flimsy structure vulnerable to a variety of internal and external shocks and threats. Historical experience had taught them that the conjunction of military and diplomatic defeat by foreign powers and internal rebellion presented the greatest opportunities for changing the system. For now, Sasha wrote, the socialists had to concentrate their efforts on producing a shock to the Russian state system by means of terrorism, but only as a means to an end: enlightening and organizing the victims of the system for class struggle. In this terrorist campaign to win a modicum of freedom, they might join with liberals—nonsocialists who also wanted Western-style constitutions.

Eventually, a people's state would be won, a new kind of state that would bestow the full panoply of civil liberties: a universal franchise and freedom of conscience, speech, the press, and association. The people's socialist regime would nationalize the land, the factories, and all the means of production; give peasant communes the power to organize a socialist economy in the countryside; dissolve the standing army in favor of local militias; and guarantee free elementary education. Ulyanov, following Lavrov, believed that such measures would be a good foundation not only for social justice and the fulfillment of material needs but for full individual moral development. Every person would be able to rise to the scientific ethics of the socialist vanguard. The human species would realize its evolutionary potential. Sasha could not present a full picture of the stages of development that would follow the winning of initial civil liberties after a successful terrorist campaign; nor could he imagine, as Bakunin had, what might follow from nationalization. "The Program of the Terrorist Faction of the People's Will" was just a rough sketch, an attempt to inspire and unite the pitiful forces available in 1887. For now, the intelligentsia saw no other way than the use of revolutionary terror against state terror.

An implicit critique of the People's Will emerged at the very end of Sasha's program in which he made the case for systematic terror—a term that seemed incongruous with the decentralized and spontaneous program of terror he described. The program did repeat the Executive Committee's claims for the efficacy of terror. Ulyanov averred that terror would not only disorganize the regime but inspire the people to revolution by giving them abundant evidence that struggle was possible, that the government was not all powerful. However, Sasha added to this the important claim that centralized terror was no longer possible or desirable. Now terrorists had to adapt themselves to local conditions and to use terror as a protest against oppression where they found it in its most obnoxious forms. This more spontaneous form of terrorism would feed on and in turn unleash the elemental forces of the people—and in this Sasha made a gesture toward Bakuninism. He quite wittingly hoped to have something for all Russian revolutionaries in this ecumenical document. Ulyanov worked around the clock from February 27 to March 1 with two helpers in Bronisław Piłsudski's apartment setting the type for the program and correcting it. They never managed to print a clean copy.

The program Ulyanov created might have been a critique of the conspiracy that he served—a tiny group whose flimsy network and pitifully inadequate remaining resources in the apartments of the bomb makers and in Pargolovo could not possibly follow up a successful assassination with more acts of terror. The means for systematic terror simply did not exist. Yet the bombs were ready; the combat group went into the streets with them twice on days when the tsar might have given them a target; and even the heroic work of the black office did not make up for police laxity and obtuseness. Alexander III's work habits and a lapse of his palace staff perhaps did more to prevent the attempt on his life than good police work; and the police themselves might have suffered serious casualties but for flaws in the book bomb's design.

T HE ENTIRE COMBAT GROUP, signalers and throwers, went into action on short notice on February 26 because of inside information that the tsar would attend a service in his honor on "Tsar Day" at St. Isaac's Cathedral. Osipanov had been designated the leader of the throwers, and on his initiative they spread out along the route to St. Isaac's on that day.[32] Osipanov cared more about getting the job done than about strictly following the symbolism of killing the tsar on March 1. The large body of police at the golden-domed cathedral seemed to support the rumor about the tsar's appearance. After a long wait, Osipanov asked one of them whether they expected the tsar to attend the service. The policeman replied affirmatively, but couldn't explain why the tsar hadn't come. The reason he hadn't, at least the one given in the diary of A. P. Arapova, one of the members of the court, was that Alexander III simply was overwhelmed with work and spent Tsar Day clearing his desk. He told the empress to go ahead without him.

On February 28 the combat squad followed up with a second promenade on Nevsky Prospect, with Generalov and Andreyushkin carrying the cylindrical bombs and Osipanov carrying the book bomb. This time, thanks to the heightened surveillance after Andreyushkin had been positively identified as the writer of the letter to Nikitin, the police tracked their every move.[33] Generalov left his apartment at about 10:00 a.m. and went to Andreyushkin's. Kancher arrived by cab half an hour later, and after twenty minutes emerged from the apartment alone, followed five minutes later by Generalov and Andreyushkin. They carried their bombs in slings concealed under their coats. Keeping a prescribed distance between them, at the Police Bridge, which crossed the Moika Canal at Nevsky Prospect, they walked past Osipanov and then Kancher and Gorkun, the latter in student's uniform. After walking for quite a while along the planned route, Generalov, Andreyushkin, and Osipanov assembled in a tavern at the corner of Malaya Morskaya

and Nevsky Prospect, not far from the Police Bridge. Kancher joined them there. According to M. N. Svergunov, one of the police officers on the surveillance team, when they got up to leave he rushed on foot to his waiting supervisor to warn him. Although police headquarters was only minutes away on Gorokhovaya Street, by the time Svergunov returned with a detail of three additional officers, the throwers and signalers were gone.[34]

A second agent, Shevelev, added a significant detail. At approximately 3:30 p.m. the imperial equipage occupied by Maria Fyodorovna passed Generalov and Kancher on Nevsky Prospect at the Police Bridge. They kept on walking along Nevsky past the Kazan Cathedral. Eventually, the three throwers assembled near Admiralty Square, where they hired a cab.[35] The police had obviously taken Andreyushkin's letter seriously, but they lacked the planning and coordination to take advantage of the opportunity to round up the group on February 28. Evidently the police still did not know that the people they were following carried bombs. Generalov had been in a position to throw a bomb at the tsar's consort, if not at Alexander III himself.

On March 1 the police did not wait as long as they had on February 28, but one wonders what would have happened had the tsar left the Anichkov Palace at precisely 10:45 a.m. If the imperial equipage had appeared as planned on the designated route at roughly 11:00 a.m., a great deal would have depended upon the ability of the police to physically restrain three determined young men. In addition to the bomb, Andreyushkin carried in the pocket of his overcoat a bulldog revolver with six bullets in it.[36] At about 10:00 a.m. he went to Generalov's apartment. Half an hour later they left and walked to Nevsky Prospect, with an undercover agent following them in a cab. At the corner of Nevsky and Admiralty Square they were invited by other agents to go to the office of the chief of police. Gorkun's tail spotted him near the Anichkov Palace and picked him up at the corner of Sadovaya and Nevsky. The

police apprehended Kancher on Nevsky at the Nikolaevsky Station and the third signaler, Volokhov, nearby. They were all taken to Gorokhovaya 2, the office of the Security Bureau of the secret police — where Sudeikin had run the operation that had infiltrated and all but crushed the People's Will. The St. Petersburg police, detectives, and gendarmes finally assembled the team that rounded up the combat squad at the eleventh hour on March 1.

After the arrest of two of the throwers and the three signalers, a three-man police detail pursued Osipanov. They found him near the Kazan Bridge at roughly noon walking in the direction of Admiralty Square. When they "invited" him to accompany them to the chief of police, he asked whether they had documents and they replied affirmatively. Two of them held his arms, standard police practice in such cases. On the way to Gorokhovaya 2 he vainly begged to have his arms freed. According to Osipanov's later testimony, after arriving there:

> We soundlessly went up a narrow, spiral staircase and while on it I pulled the string that was supposed to tear . . . the partition, but I pulled it so hard that the string broke off and made a faint sound . . . Timofeyev and Varlamov [the police agents] holding my arms . . . heard the sound and strengthened their grip and prevented me from throwing the bomb . . . but when they led me . . . into the room with a police officer sitting behind a desk, they let go of my arms and I tossed the bomb to the floor . . . from a point above my head and to a distance of about three steps away from me . . . but no explosion followed.[37]

When one of the police agents retrieved the "book," he was surprised to discover that it was an explosive device. Despite all of the bomb-making activity of students whose apartments were being watched; despite all of the purchases of chemicals and materials that obviously could have been used in explosive devices; despite

the discovery of suspicious bottles full of liquid and of mysterious packages by Shmidova's landlady; and despite the establishment of close surveillance on Generalov and Andreyushkin, when they arrested the bomb throwers on March 1, the police still did not know that their suspects were carrying bombs! Terrorist acts are designed to surprise, and the near-misses are no less surprising than the successes. If the book bomb had worked, the explosion would probably have killed anyone within a radius of 3.2 meters and thrown eighty-six strychnine bullets over 11 meters in every direction. Several lives quite literally were hanging by the string that was supposed to open the valve in the book bomb's fuse.

Had Osipanov lied to save face and failed to pull the string before throwing it? Or had he pulled a defective string that broke off before it opened the valve? One of the police officers denied that Osipanov had been able to arm the bomb on the way to the station. The officer's testimony was obviously self-serving, but Major General Fyodorov, the explosives expert, could not find the string when he examined the book bomb. He believed, in any case, that the bomb's construction was faulty, and testified that the fuses of the cylindrical bombs had the same flawed design. Was the fuse mechanism designed by Lukashevich faulty? The police never tested that hypothesis with the captured bombs, and neither did Fyodorov.

L UKASHEVICH AND ULYANOV experienced hours of anguished waiting on March 1. Sasha walked to Kancher and Gorkun's apartment, where he was arrested. Of the three leaders of the conspiracy, Ulyanov was the first to fall. Lukashevich went to the student cafeteria, where he heard rumors that terrorists had shot at the tsar and that Kancher had been arrested. Lukashevich did not give up hope. Even if part of the organization fell, they might still send a second combat group into the field, but he had to lie low. On the evening of March 2 he returned to his own

apartment. He had already cleaned it, and now looked through his papers for any incriminating evidence. The police knocked on his door at 2:00 a.m. and showed him a search warrant. To his eye, they searched only superficially, even though he had a small laboratory in the apartment. They seized his books and made a brief stop at the local police station before taking him to Gorokhovaya 2. Several more suspects were taken to the well-known building of the security police in the predawn hours of March 3 as Lukashevich watched the sky lighten. Detectives chattered freely about the events of March 1. Lukashevich learned, to his dismay, that Osipanov had thrown the bomb and that it had failed to explode. He also learned that the early signs that he himself was not a serious suspect were misleading. P. N. Durnovo, director of the Police Department, spoke with Lukashevich and said that they'd connected him with Ulyanov. Finally, on the night of March 3, they took him to the Peter and Paul Fortress.[38]

Lukashevich's is the only available detailed account of the prisoners' initial treatment, and we can imagine, in the absence of Ulyanov's own version, that Sasha experienced something similar: a strip search that Lukashevich described as disgusting. They gave him his prison clothes and pan and put him in a cell in one of the casemates of the fortress—a spacious, vaulted cell with a dirty asphalt floor; a small, double-barred window near the ceiling; and a chamber pot in the corner. The table, with a small kerosene lamp, and bedstead were made of steel and secured to the floor. The police routinely woke their prisoner at 2:00 a.m. and brought him back to Gorovokhavaya Street for interrogation, this time by officers of the gendarmerie, the military branch of the security agencies.

The gendarmes were far less polite than the security police. One, literally frothing at the mouth, tried to intimidate Lukashevich: wasn't the plot Polish revenge for those hanged in Warsaw after the uprising of 1863? Alternatively, hadn't a bunch of dirty kikes pulled this off? The assistant prosecutor of the St. Petersburg Judi-

cial Chamber, Michael Kotlyarovsky, continued the interrogation, but now showed Lukashevich a copy of Kancher's testimony of March 2 implicating Lukashevich in the bomb making. The detailed account of the bomb making on February 21 in Ulyanov's apartment removed any doubt—Kancher had indeed given them up. Lukashevich suggested that Kancher had lied in order to lighten his sentence. Kotlyarovsky assured him they didn't need to promise anybody anything—and without further ado the assistant prosecutor sketched out some well-known techniques of torture.[39] The weaker members of the conspiracy had obviously caved in immediately to threat of torture.

Andreyushkin, Osipanov, and Generalov needed no such threat. They had already chosen to die and proudly admitted to their roles. Lukashevich, like the others, had vowed to die for the cause, but the actual experience of captivity evidently changed his mind. The fact that Kancher and Gorkun had already talked absolved him of the duty to keep silent. Later Kotlyarovsky showed him other confessions inspired by Kancher's revelations. Ulyanov had confessed to building the bombs, although he had not named Lukashevich. Lukashevich then confessed to what Kancher and Gorkun had seen on February 21, but tried to prevent the Russian authorities from turning the trial into a witch hunt against Polish revolutionaries, and did everything in his power to obscure his true role.

On March 3 the police began an intensive hunt for Shevyrev in the Crimea. By the time they arrested him in Yalta on March 7, the authorities had in hand much of the information they needed to send him and the entire central group to the gallows. Only Lukashevich, who had carefully read all of the testimony they gave him for details about his participation, took full advantage of the fact that he had been accused only of tactical help: packing the bomb cylinders with dynamite on February 21, helping set up the transport network run mainly by Kancher, and linking Kancher and Gorkun to his friends in Vilnius. The court placed Lukashevich in

the third level of the organization, the "facilitators," rather than the second-level "accessories" or the top-level "instigators." He and Novorussky fell for different reasons into the same category as Ananina, Shmidova, Bronisław Piłsudski, and Pashkovsky. Lukashevich's fears that the Vilnius Poles and Shmidova, a Jew, would receive especially severe treatment proved false.

The court's handling of Lukashevich suggests that Ulyanov, too, might have escaped hanging, had he played the game properly. In fact, Sasha tried to defend himself during his first interrogation on March 3 by Cavalry Captain Lyutov, but at each step of the way the stories told by others placed him at the center of things. In his testimony of March 2–3 Gorkun reinforced the impression given by Kancher that Ulyanov played a central executive role. Still, no one knew that he and Govorukhin had approached Shevyrev in December and suggested terrorism. Ulyanov did not have to be tried in the first category, as an instigator.

In his depositions of March 4–5 to Lyutov, after he had been shown Kancher's and Gorkun's testimony, Sasha quite scrupulously described his own role in the preparation of the dynamite, the cylindrical bombs, and the lead bullets, but he denied having made the book bomb or fuses. Lukashevich's role in their manufacture remained unknown. It would appear that Lukashevich and Ulyanov had roughly the same chance to beat the gallows at the time of their depositions in March, but they played different games after that. Anna Ilinichna later showed considerable insight into the way Lukashevich had escaped the gallows, and she understood that he had done it at her brother's and Shevyrev's expense. As the interrogations continued, Sasha became more and more forthcoming. On March 20–21, for his last deposition, he reproduced from memory "The Program of the Terrorist Faction of the People's Will." It still remained, however, to speak for the group and present the rationale for terror before the tribunal. The drama of the trial lay ahead.

The Trial

THE CLOSED SENATE TRIBUNAL began at noon on April 15 and ended on April 19 with the sentencing of fifteen members of the assassination conspiracy, including the core members who had not escaped abroad, and those who had aided and abetted them. Along with the actual combat squad, the throwers—Osipanov, Generalov, and Andreyushkin—and signalers—Kancher, Gorkun, and Volokhov—the organizers, technical experts, and leaders, Shevyrev, Lukashevich, and Ulyanov, claimed center stage. Less important helpers—Titus Pashkovsky, the apprentice apothecary, and Bronisław Piłsudski had facilitated the acquisition of the materials for the bombs in Vilnius. The theology student Novorussky and Ananina, his mother-in-law, had provided storage and transport service and laboratory space; Shmidova and Serdyukova had networked with other terrorists, and the former had also worked closely with Govorukhin and Ulyanov. Most were in their early twenties; Generalov, the youngest, had his twentieth birthday on March 8, a week after his arrest.

Tsarist trials of revolutionaries, but especially of terrorists, became a dramatic form for Russian liberal society. The hunters assumed the position of the hunted. The terrorists' defenders, the brilliant defense lawyers created by Alexander II's judicial reforms, now had to face his son's judicial counterreforms. At the first blush of the reforms, the contests between terrorists and the autocratic regime were conducted in open trials, but after the fiasco of Zasulich's acquittal, they were sequestered in Senate tribunals and,

finally, in closed sessions that excluded journalists. Russian officials tended to have long tenures in office. In the late 1880s the same venerable dramatis personae appeared: the jailers, the judges, even the hangmen. The defense lawyers, too, were veterans of previous political trials.[1] Well known for their eloquence, they were heroes of the liberal public, but in closed tribunals they might as well have been speaking to the walls. Moreover, unlike the hopeful and angry liberals of the 1870s, the public of 1887 had seen the People's Will go down to defeat after March 1, 1881; they had heard Alexander III's message about the "senseless dreams" of a constitution; they had experienced his counterreforms; and now they believed less in the efficacy of terror. Russian liberals had lost hope in the likelihood of imminent change.

The young rebels of the Second March First were not stock characters, but they followed a script that had been written by the great ideologues of populism and performed earlier by the heroes and heroines of the People's Will. The bomb throwers and Ulyanov decided to make their deaths a statement about the scientific correctness of their choice. They rejected legal defense and chose death, because doing so followed logically from a choice of socialism and from their duel with the autocracy. They lied to protect their fellow defendants who had not passed that psychological point of no return and whose lives they cherished. Others lied because they saw no reason either to wave their banner or to honor the duelist's code in an uneven contest. Moreover, the stirring speeches made by *narodniki* were well known. Why repeat their performances? Sasha belonged to the group that held high the banner, and he prepared himself to make the case for socialism, but lied repeatedly and obviously in order to save his comrades.

The Russian legal system gave great power to teams of procurators and interrogators taking depositions before the trial. The interrogators, often members of the gendarmerie in political cases, first—and sometimes savagely—went after the weaker members of

the group and used the information gained from them to confront others. When it worked, the defendants toppled over like so many dominoes. The procurators, though presumably fact finders, generally served the prosecution better than the defense. The lawyers for the defense salvaged what they could, but in this case they faced a tribunal whose chair was a notorious judicial hangman and whose superior prosecutor was a brilliant man, but a turncoat, a former radical who pursued his task with the zeal of the convert to the dark side. Death sentences were virtually assured.

The March depositions extracted by the teams working for the tribunal had given the prosecution what it needed long before the trial began on April 15. The most important unknown in the already scripted drama was Tsar Alexander III himself. He knew that the Second March First had sentenced him to a hideous death by dynamite and strychnine. Six years earlier he had been informed of his father's assassination. It had been an ugly story. The first bomb had exploded under Alexander II's carriage, but the tsar had not been seriously hurt. He went out on the street to see what had happened. A second member of the terrorist team threw the fatal, second bomb that shattered the tsar's legs. The terrorists had shown no mercy, so why should he? They had been preparing a similar fate for him, with poison added in case he should survive the explosion!

The rumors that he had wept and fallen to his knees in thanks for his divine deliverance sound true—this quite thuggish man had a religious streak. He had ordered as a memorial to Alexander II the erection of the Church of the Savior on Spilled Blood on the embankment of the Catherine Canal—the site of the crime. His heartfelt remark about his own escape suggests realism about the precariousness of Russian autocracy and the imperfections of the security network. "God has saved us . . . but for how long?"[2] The less prosaic than usual but typically laconic March 1 entry in the diary of the eighteen-year-old Tsarevich Nicholas seconded his father's sentiments.

I woke up at seven o'clock. We had coffee and then read. After putting on the full-dress uniform of the Preobrazhenskii Regiment, I rode with papa to the fortress. At that time something terrible might have happened, but thanks to divine mercy everything turned out alright. Five [*sic*] scoundrels with dynamite bombs were arrested near Anichkova. . . . O lordy! What great luck that we escaped.

On March 9, 1887, in Gatchina the future tsar saw his father decorate the police agents who had arrested the terrorists. The grateful Alexander III also gave them cash rewards.[3]

As he learned more about his hunters, the Tsar oscillated between rage and irritation. A very tall and sturdy man with a luxuriant beard and apparently in the prime of life, Alexander III, like his father, was a passionate hunter. He did not fancy himself the quarry of a bizarre group of callow youths. What ran through his mind when he reviewed the material brought to him by his officials? On the basis of the brief remarks, dripping in sarcasm, in the margins of his servitors' reports, he felt mainly contempt. Ulyanov, stunted and pale from studying worms and idiotic socialist doctrines, didn't even have a beard. Shevyrev was a sickly hysteric and mendacious scoundrel. There was in this "terrorist faction" a huge, handsome Pole who looked like a man but didn't sound like one. The Cossacks—whose participation especially troubled him—were insane adolescents, and the Siberian, "the Cat," some sort of Asian, a stocky fellow, thickheaded, an assassin who hadn't enough brains to arm his bomb properly. The bomb throwers, at least, did not lie and whine, and perhaps Generalov, though barely twenty, reminded him of Andrei Zhelyabov, the heart and soul of the Executive Committee of the People's Will. When the hangman put the noose around his neck in April 1881, Zhelyabov was a mature man of impressive physique with a full, black beard. Now, *he* was a worthy opponent!

Personalities aside, the tsar had good reasons to downplay the

incident. Alexander III hoped that the entire episode would be handled quickly and painlessly. He knew very well how previous political plots against Alexander I and Alexander II had played in the European press. The aristocratic Decembrists, who had among their leaders high-ranking officers and noblemen close to the tsar, took to Senate Square in 1825 with their troops to replace Nicholas I with a constitution. The tsar and his loyal troops answered with grapeshot. Along with those hanged, dozens more went into Siberian exile, followed by their faithful wives. The romance of the Decembrists became part of the history not just of the Russian revolutionary movement but of European liberalism. The Decembrists became heroes, Nicholas I a tyrant. The public hanging of five leaders of the People's Will in April 1881 had also cost the autocratic regime dearly. The regime had rejected a plea of mercy from no less a world literary celebrity than Leo Tolstoy. The accused had been carted through St. Petersburg accompanied by thousands of troops, and brought to a makeshift gallows on Semenovsky Square, at the southern end of Gorokhavaya Street. The crowd that had gathered on the square witnessed a dreadful scene reminiscent of the botched hanging of the Decembrists in 1826. Even those who had come for the entertainment were enraged. Six years later, at a time when the European great powers were contemplating shifting their alliance systems, Alexander III could not risk a barbaric spectacle. More important, he did not want to advertise Russia's weakness and vulnerability to the threat of an absurd student conspiracy. He followed Dmitry Tolstoy's advice in this. Tolstoy proposed that they print a brief account of the event of March 1 in the *Government Herald* to dampen wild rumors. Alexander III wrote to his minister of the interior,

I fully concur, and it is generally desirable not to give too much significance to the arrests. I think it would be best to get all of the information we can out of them, not hand them over to a court,

and without any fanfare dispatch them to Schlüsselburg Fortress. That would be the most severe and unpleasant punishment.[4]

His advisers, however, thought that a carefully managed Special Session of the Ruling Senate for the Adjudication of Matters Pertaining to State Crimes would be an appropriate venue. The tsar had other options for political crimes, but his advisers thought it fitting that he put the Second March First terrorists on trial in closed session before the same tribunal that had sentenced to hanging the leaders of the People's Will in March 1881. To be sure, even in this venue state criminals had the right to a legal defense. The Senate tribunal might even appoint a defender in case defendants did not supply their own counsel. Despite the guaranteed findings of guilt there was still room for shrewd defenders to maneuver for a lighter sentence, and the defendants could, and often did, petition the court of last resort, the tsar, for leniency. The tsar generally followed the court's advice. In the trial of the Second March First terrorists, he concurred with five death sentences, but mitigated those of Lukashevich and Novorussky.

T HE TRIBUNAL THAT CONVENED at midday on April 15, 1887, for the trial of the Second March First conspiracy, in addition to four senators, included four representatives of the estates—two prominent members of the gentry, one high-ranking merchant (actually, the mayor of Moscow), and one peasant, a district head. The court conducted its business behind closed doors, but important officials attended: ministers, other senators, members of the State Council. N. S. Tagantsev, a senator and legal expert who attended the trial, like the superior prosecutor, Neklyudov, had been Ilya Nikolaevich's student in Penza. Tagantsev intervened on behalf of Maria Alexandrovna, who not only was permitted to attend a session of the trial but was granted several interviews with her son after the sentence had been handed down.[5]

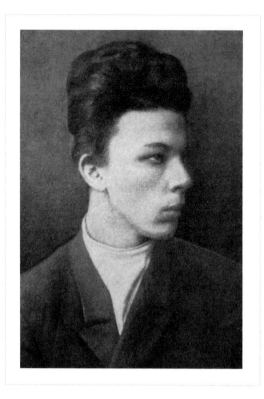

TWO POLICE PHOTOS OF ALEXANDER (1887)

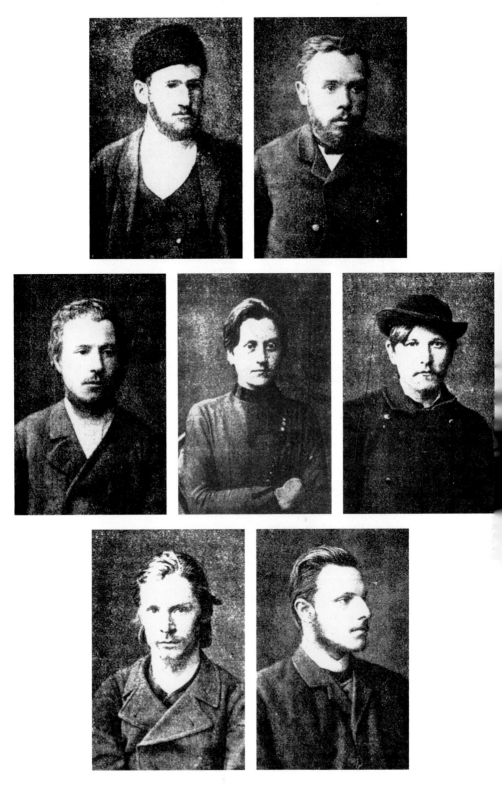

KEY FIGURES IN THE SECOND MARCH FIRST CONSPIRACY

TOP ROW, LEFT TO RIGHT: Generalov, Osipanov; MIDDLE ROW: Andreyushkin, Shmidova, Govorukhin; BOTTOM ROW: Shevyrev, Lukashevich.

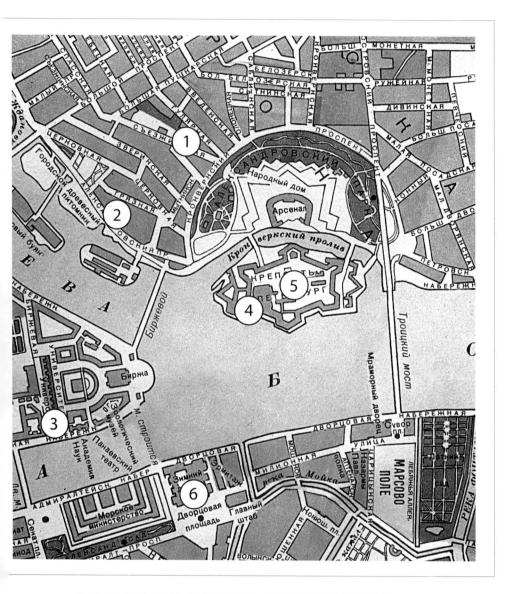

MAP OF THE AREA AROUND ST. PETERSBURG UNIVERSITY

1. Alexander's apartment on Syezzhinskaya Street.
2. The apartment on Alexandrovsky Prospect.
3. The main building of St. Petersburg University.
4. The Trubetskoy Bastion of the Peter and Paul Fortress.
5. Peter and Paul Cathedral with the tombs of the Romanovs.
6. The Winter Palace.

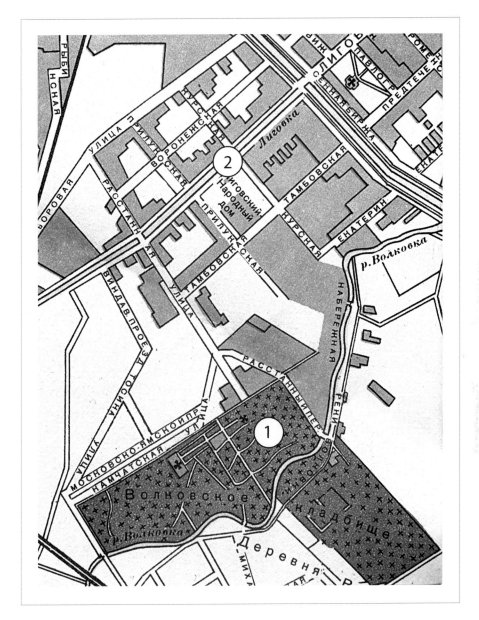

MAP OF THE AREA AROUND VOLKOVO CEMETERY

1. Volkovo Cemetery, site of the demonstration of November 17, 1886.
2. Ligovka, where the students were surrounded by Cossacks on November 17, 1886.
The events of November 17 precipitated the formation of
the Second March First terrorist group.

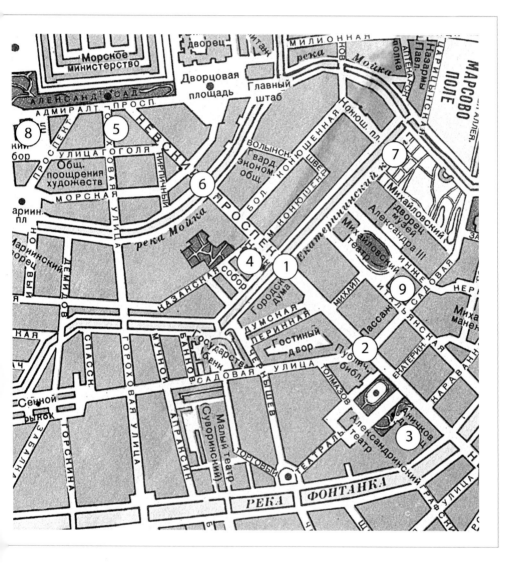

MAP OF THE CENTER OF ST. PETERSBURG

1. Planned site of the assassination of Alexander III on Nevsky Prospect.
2. Alternative site of the assassination.
3. Anichkov Palace.
4. Kazan Cathedral.
5. Police station at Gorokhovaya 2.
6. Police Bridge.
7. Site of Alexander II's assassination.
8. St. Isaac's Cathedral.
9. Shmidova's and Govorukhin's apartments.

MEMORIALS

ABOVE LEFT: Maria Alexandrovna's memorial statue in Volkovo Cemetery, St. Petersburg.
ABOVE RIGHT: Ilya Nikolaevich's memorial in Ulyanovsk.
BELOW LEFT: Nicholas Dobrolyubov's grave in the Volkovo Cemetery, the site
of the student demonstration of November 17, 1886.
BELOW RIGHT: Dmitry Mendeleev's grave in Volkovo Cemetery.

THE ULYANOV HOME (1878–87)
ON LENIN STREET, FORMERLY MOSKOVSKAYA

ABOVE LEFT: Exterior of the Ulyanov home, now a museum.
ABOVE RIGHT: Back view of the home on Lenin Street, taken from the garden area.
BELOW LEFT: Sasha's room on the second floor of the home on Lenin Street.
BELOW RIGHT: Sasha's laboratory next to the backyard kitchen and garden.

ULYANOVSK ON RUSSIA DAY, JUNE 12, 2006

ABOVE: Lenin's statue facing the Russian tricolor on the Regional Administration Building in Ulyanovsk.

BELOW: The heroic statue of Maria Alexandrovna and Vladimir Ilyich near the site of the family's first apartments on Streletskaya Street.

The tsar took a keen interest in the denouement from his suburban palace in Gatchina, forty-five kilometers southwest of the capital. Two hundred suspects were brought in for questioning in the police sweep after March 1. In St. Petersburg the police, gendarmes, and prosecutors winnowed the suspects to the fifteen who came to trial on April 15. Dmitry Tolstoy digested some of the depositions, but passed those of the key plotters to the tsar, who wrote comments on the margins that were as notable for their expressions of disgust and disdain as for their occasional misspellings. The depositions of Kancher and Gorkun described the development of the conspiracy in great detail and became the primary sources for Tolstoy and Alexander III. They also were the basis for the indictment of the fifteen defendants arraigned on April 15.

The chair of the court, Senator Peter Antonovich Deyer, "small, with an unsteady gait and a trembling head," during the period of reaction after the Great Reforms had earned a certain notoriety within Russia's struggling legal profession for his role as the tsar's sycophant. He had put Sergei Nechaev into the Peter and Paul Fortress for life (though not in the official sentence), for which the Ministry of Justice amply rewarded him, according to reliable sources. For delivering desired death sentences, Deyer received major sums of money for "health cures"; he reportedly got two thousand rubles to restore his health after sending five terrorists of the Second March First conspiracy to the gallows.[6]

The behavior of the chair was not the only obstacle to a fair trial. The Russian judicial system gave the prosecutors a powerful role in bringing state criminals to justice. They controlled the preliminary investigation of cases and brought their findings to the court. The prosecutors created the framework of the case and the foundation for the accusations. The damning depositions taken between March 1 and the trial inhibited the defense. Although defendants contradicted their own depositions and those of others, their earlier statements and police reports had already biased the proceedings

against them. The assistant prosecutor, Kotlyarovsky, who played a large role in procuring the depositions, had established a reputation for badgering defendants. He and the gendarme interrogators had excelled in their roles.

The background of the superior prosecutor, Nicholas Adrianovich Neklyudov, was more than a little problematic. Neklyudov played his role vigorously, perhaps vehemently, as a reaction against any pity he might have felt for Sasha. By a quirk of fate, early in his career Ilya Nikolaevich had taught Neklyudov at the Penza Institute for the Gentry. Neklyudov graduated in 1857 and went on to St. Petersburg University to study law. An astute memoirist wrote of Neklyudov's position as prosecutor in this capital crime, "He was quite overwhelmed with his commission, the more so because one of the defendants . . . was the son of his favorite teacher in the Penza gymnasium. Although he suffered during the trial, he nonetheless succeeded . . . in getting in line with the general mood of horror required of the faithful."[7] Neklyudov had not only to deal with his debt to Ilya but also to repudiate his own past as a radical student. In the political coding of the time, once a "Red," Neklyudov had moved on the ideological spectrum to the blackest "Black."

In 1861 Alexander II's minister of education had imposed rules on universities that foreshadowed the even harsher crackdown of 1884. It was one of the regime's first attempts to control the nihilist subculture in institutions of higher education. The students of St. Petersburg University refused to matriculate until the authorities clarified the new rules curtailing the autonomy of student organizations and discriminating against the poorer students. Neklyudov played an important part as a student deputy in the demonstrations beginning on September 25, 1861. The protests continued for weeks and escalated in October. Mounted troops beat the demonstrators with their rifle butts and, in one case, severed a student's ear with a saber stroke. Neklyudov was arrested on September 26,

imprisoned in the Peter and Paul Fortress, released in December, and placed under police surveillance for the remainder of the year. Instead of becoming embittered and radicalized, the twenty-one-year-old Neklyudov pressed on with his legal career, worked within the system, enjoyed the springtime of Russia's new bar and judiciary, and joined the Ministry of Justice.

Twenty-five years after his time in the Fortress, Neklyudov seemed to have little sympathy for students whose experience, at least on the surface, closely resembled his own. Perhaps he faced an earlier self that he still needed to punish. He made a stirring summary for the prosecution, but paid the price psychologically and physically, and collapsed at the end of the sentencing.

THE DEFENDANTS, who had been held in solitary confinement in the Trubetskoy Bastion of the Peter and Paul Fortress, were transferred on April 14 to cells in the Prison for Preliminary Detention on Shpalernaya Street, not far from the St. Petersburg Circuit Court on Liteinyi Prospect. Before they entered the courtroom on April 15, the accused waited single file in a corridor, separated by gendarmes, but evidently not so strictly that they couldn't embrace and kiss each other.[8] They were led in singly until the later phases of the trial, when they had the right to defend themselves and to question witnesses and other defendants. They also appeared one by one during the sentencing.

The authorities created a virtual wall of secrecy around the trial, but a correspondent of the *Daily News* (London) either got into the courtroom somehow or had a collaborator on the inside feeding him information. His account appeared in the Russian émigré press in Europe and naturally circulated back to Russia. At noon on April 15, 1887, in the auditorium of the St. Petersburg District Court building, proceedings opened with the reading of a lengthy indictment. The assembled dignitaries saw in the center of the auditorium a large table with the three bombs and other unspecified

pieces of evidence. The defendants entered the hall, greeted one another with a smile, and bowed to the court.[9]

Michael Kancher and Peter Gorkun, the first conspirators to crack under interrogation in March, were also the first defendants to testify. This made perfect sense for the prosecution. Their lengthy depositions and testimony established the roles of the major conspirators and their own. On the whole, Kancher portrayed himself as a mere errand boy or pawn pushed about by the main organizers—among whom he included Govorukhin—but especially Shevyrev. They had deceived him into thinking that he would not be truly a party to a state crime. He was a naïf who had failed to understand the gravity of his position until it was too late. Gorkun, his friend from Poltava and apartment-mate in St. Petersburg, presented a briefer variation of Kancher's testimony, as did Stepan Volokhov, the third signaler. They all feigned obtuseness and memory lapses—favorite gambits of the defendants. Despite these tactics the court established the main actions and actors through the compliant testimony of the signalers.

There followed the testimony of the three clearly suicidal and unrepentant members of the conspiracy—Generalov, Andreyushkin, and Osipanov. The throwers, having at the outset of the conspiracy decided to sacrifice themselves for the cause, seemed impatient to get on with it. Unlike the signalers, who weaseled when asked whether they pleaded guilty to the crimes of which they were accused, the throwers laconically affirmed their guilt and their intentions.

Generalov's testimony clarified his entry into the conspiracy and established Govorukhin's and Ulyanov's key roles in recruiting the Cossack throwers. Govorukhin had brought Ulyanov into the Don and Kuban *zemlyachestvo*. They had educated the teenage Generalov and recommended him to Shevyrev. Only twenty, Generalov was the youngest of the group to be hanged, but he had strong features and a dark beard and looked older. His testimony

established that Govorukhin and Ulyanov arranged to pay for his conspiratorial apartment, one room of which became a laboratory and storage space. On the other hand, he completely bypassed Lukashevich's role, denied any close relationship with him, and named Ulyanov as the person who had instructed him in setting up his laboratory, making nitric acid, and so on. Detail after detail piled up pointing to Ulyanov as the person holding all of the threads of the project. The afternoon session ended with Generalov's testimony, and they recessed.

IT WAS STILL LIGHT when the trial resumed after supper. Andreyushkin, whose manic recklessness had alerted the police, began his testimony at seven, and his cross-examination went far into the night. Like Generalov, he testified that Ulyanov directed the production of nitric acid. At the same time Andreyushkin clumsily tried to protect Shevyrev. Above all, he wanted to protect Serdyukova and unconvincingly tried to explain away the substance of his letters to her. After Andreyushkin's testimony, they led in Osipanov, "the Cat," who admitted to his role in the formation of the conspiracy, but refused to give any details about others and, like all of the defendants, pleaded faulty memory when pushed into a corner. The court showed no desire to spend a great deal of time on Osipanov, and brought Ulyanov into the courtroom. Sasha was the youngest-looking of all the defendants. Small and thin, with a mass of dark hair piled above his tall, pale forehead, unlike the others he had neither beard nor mustache. He made a great impact with his gentle manner and earnest performance. Ulyanov declined to name himself an initiator or recruiter, but affirmed that he had acted out of his own free will and rational mind when joining the conspiracy. He had enthusiastically and energetically pursued its goals. Sasha was quite forthcoming about his work on the bombs and his connections to the others, even though to protect them he lied about their roles. There was no point in denying what had already been

established by the others' depositions, and Sasha did not try to hide Shevyrev's role, but he was very careful not to volunteer any new information. Like the others, he protected Lukashevich and portrayed him as only a minor accomplice, recruited toward the end of bomb making for work on the cylindrical bombs. When questioned about the construction of the book bomb, Ulyanov did not take the unequivocal position about the bomb's design that Lukashevich later took in his memoirs. Rather, he had doubts about the length of the tube for the fuse and thought it possible that it would not work, but on the whole believed an explosion would occur.

After Sasha's relatively lengthy cross-examination, they brought in Shevyrev, who had vowed in advance to lie to the court. It mattered little to him whether he died now or later. Rather, it was essential to give everything in his power to the cause and to give nothing to its enemies. He had told Lukashevich,

> When I stand before the court . . . I don't intend to state my views. If our enterprise were the beginning of an active revolutionary struggle with the government then, of course, it would be essential to clarify its sense and significance. But we are merely continuing the cause of our predecessors. They've already shown what evoked terror and what it achieves. There's no need to enunciate our credo at every skirmish, every engagement. It's even more superfluous when the tribunal is secret: they judge us in secrecy and will hang us secretly.[10]

This sort of cynicism separated Shevyrev from the other four who were hanged. A combination of amorality and perhaps a surge of his manic optimism determined his behavior at the trial. He denied any culpability and presented himself as a dupe who had fallen under Govorukhin's influence.

The court stenographer reproduced Shevyrev's verbal ticks— an "okay" (*khorosho*) punctuating each invention or evasion and

sometimes a distinct pause while he mulled over the next lie. In view of the damning depositions and testimony of several codefendants, Shevyrev had to make one denial after another. He designed his lies to place much of the guilt on Govorukhin, who was safely abroad. No alchemy could change the facts that had already been adduced about Shevyrev's central role in the conspiracy, both in depositions and partly through the information extracted by a stool pigeon planted among the prisoners during their preliminary detention. The informer, Anton Ostroumov, gave the police damning information about both Shevyrev and Novorussky. The police forwarded the information to Dmitry Tolstoy, who in turn sent it to Alexander III. Tolstoy reported Novorussky's opinion (by way of Ostroumov) that neither Shevyrev nor Govorukhin measured up to Ulyanov in courage and dedication to the cause.[11] The court recessed late that night at the end of Shevyrev's testimony.

A T N O O N O N A P R I L 16 Lukashevich, towering over the accompanying officers, entered the courtroom. He must have benefited by contrast with Shevyrev's sickly and nervous appearance and obvious mendacity. Admitting guilt only to participation in the attempt, he denied that he belonged to the conspiracy. Lukashevich spoke with a Polish accent and had a very gentle voice incongruous with his height and physique. Deyer repeatedly had to ask him to speak up. Even with this prompting the court stenographer found Lukashevich's testimony "completely inaudible" in places. Lukashevich introduced for the first time in the trial the idea of social injustice, and he spoke of the personal experience and systematic study that had led him to his belief in scientific socialism. This is not what Deyer wanted to hear at this point in the trial; he interrupted Lukashevich's divagation into social science and asked him to get to the point—how did he get involved in the plot? Lukashevich, like Shevyrev, named Govorukhin as the person who involved him in the project to kill the tsar, and he

portrayed Ulyanov as someone working closely with Govorukhin. Ulyanov, he claimed, asked him to help with the bomb making because it required someone with considerable physical strength. Lukashevich's testimony thus gave the impression that Sasha played a supervisory role in both bomb making and the printing of the faction's program.

The defendants who appeared after Lukashevich followed logically from the lines of interrogation. Tall, scholarly looking, and bespectacled, Michael Novorussky, supposedly a protégé of Konstantin Pobedonostsev, procurator of the Holy Synod, seemed to be a most unlikely defendant. The facts, however, were well established. Novorussky's apartment in St. Petersburg and his mother-in-law Ananina's rented dacha in Pargolovo had been key sites of storage, transshipment, and bomb making. Novorussky, too, seemed to be connected to the plot mainly through Ulyanov. Of all the defendants, Novorussky showed the most disdain for the court, maintaining a constant ironic smirk, refusing defense counsel, making light of his contribution to the plot, pleading distraction with his work, and questioning his own deposition. Novorussky tried to impress the court with the fact that he was writing a dissertation as a *Kandidat* in the University's Theological Academy. He simply was too busy to look into the things he had to ship to Pargolovo for Ulyanov's putative chemistry experiments. The police investigation had connected materials in Novorussky's apartment with the cylindrical bombs destined for use by Andreyushkin and Generalov.

Novorussky did not know that the police had planted a stool pigeon in an adjoining cell to spy on him during his detention before the trial. After Novorussky suffered a "nervous attack" in the Peter and Paul Fortress, the police had transferred him to the Prison of Preliminary Detention in early March. They placed Anton Ostroumov in a cell between Novorussky's and Arsenii Khlebnikov's. Ostroumov taught Novorussky how to communicate by means of

tapping codes and messages hidden in books in the prison library. He learned, among other things, that Novorussky intended to lie about his relationship to Ulyanov and to call witnesses to lie about it. After bonding to his betrayer, Novorussky confided his contempt for the amateurism of the conspirators and for Ulyanov's careless-ness in bringing loose talkers into the group.[12] They were all fools.

Evidently, the talk about Pobedonostsev's intervention to save Novorussky was not idle. The procurator of the Holy Synod had to defend the reliability of the Theological Academy. When called on to explain the odd fact that one of his charges was involved in a plot to destroy the sacred body of the tsar, Pobedonostsev defended Novorussky as a mere accomplice and claimed that the evidence against him was weak. Alexander III, who had been get-ting Dmitry Tolstoy's damning reports about Novorussky, nonethe-less accepted Novorussky's petition.[13] Court politics evidently won out. Like Lukashevich, Novorussky was granted his life, and after the amnesty of 1905 he wrote about the events that brought him to Schlüsselburg Fortress. By that time he knew about Ostroumov.

T HE COURT SAVED for last the only three women defendants: Ananina, Shmidova, and Serdyukova. Their careers faithfully represented the nihilist movement and *narodnik* inclinations. For many *narodniki* during the reaction under Alexander III, there seemed little else to do but work at a dreary post in the countryside in the service of piecemeal progress. They became hired employees of the zemstvos, known as the "third element," to distinguish them from elected and appointed officials. Tens of thousands of these zemstvo employees dedicated themselves to the peasants, but many of them simultaneously aided underground revolutionary groups. Maria Ananina, a midwife and surgeon's assistant employed by the zemstvo, earned forty-two rubles a month. Like the teachers, doc-tors, statisticians, and agronomists hired by the zemstvo, a form of local government created during the Great Reforms, she embodied

the doctrine of small deeds. Ananina's Chekhovian life in a suburban area near St. Petersburg included service to the poor, revolutionary activity, and upward mobility for her children. Thirty-eight years old and divorced, she wanted to give her daughter a chance to marry well and was preparing her son for a classical gymnasium by having him tutored in Latin and Greek.

A thin, intense woman, with her hair pulled back into a bun, Ananina was so terrified of the proceedings that she could barely speak, and Deyer invited her to approach the bench. Only a fraction of her exchange with Deyer entered the stenographic record. She testified that she had hired Ulyanov to tutor her fourteen-year-old son, but that he had given only a single lesson in scriptures and had spent most of the time working in his room unobtrusively on his "chemistry experiments." Ananina's daughter Lydia and son-in-law Novorussky had told her that Ulyanov would be doing this, so she found nothing amiss and knew nothing about his work. Ananina's testimony carried no cogency. Ulyanov had showed her how to test the stability of the nitroglycerine with litmus paper, and on March 3 the police found recently used pieces of litmus paper in the dacha. Ananina had hidden an iron pot with a glass jar containing two ounces of nitroglycerine cooled by icy water under a basket and stool, and she and her daughter had obviously impeded the investigation by planting themselves between the police officers and the stool during their search of the dacha.

The second woman to be cross-examined, Raisa Shmidova, austere looking, with short-cropped hair, became a target of Deyer's anti-Semitism. He tried to establish her family income, but she nervously and vaguely replied to his questions about her father's employment, volunteering only that it was commercial. Finally, Deyer forced her to admit that her father made his living by "gesheft," which connoted to Russians not wholesome commerce but shady, petty deals conducted largely by Jews, who were also well-known smugglers of contraband. Jewish smugglers in Vilnius

had been featured in earlier testimony about the materials procured for the bomb making.

The court was quite interested in Shmidova's living arrangements on Italian Street 18, where only a door covered by a hanging rug and blocked by furniture separated her apartment from Govorukhin's. Prokofyeva, Shmidova's landlady during the winter of 1886–87, tried very hard to portray her as a loose woman. Shmidova claimed that Govorukhin was engaged to her friend Eugenia Khlebnikova, whose brothers belonged to the Don and Kuban *zemlyachestvo*. She proved adept at fending off any suggestion that she had a romantic relationship with Govorukhin, and, when confronted with his suicidal letter to her, Shmidova dismissed it as a sign of his apparent psychological abnormality. She also produced a medical explanation for her trip to the Warsaw Station with Vladimir Popov, whom she had been counseling about his sister's psychological health. Of course, she concealed the fact that they had also accompanied the terrorist Vasilii Brazhnikov, whom she had given copies of Ulyanov's program for distribution in the south.[14] As for her ties to Andreyushkin, Shmidova claimed that she occasionally enlisted him to read to her the poems of Taras Shevchenko, her favorite Ukrainian poet, and Generalov sometimes joined them. That information must have given the bigoted Deyer (whose surname suggests German ethnicity) something to ponder: a *narodnik* Jewish woman inviting to her apartment dissident Cossacks in order to enjoy the poetry of the man who symbolized Ukrainian nationalism.

Serdyukova followed Shmidova and pleaded guilty, but tried to elicit the court's sympathy by describing her psychological collapse following the receipt of Andreyushkin's letter proposing marriage and simultaneously revealing his involvement in a plot to kill the tsar. Although she claimed to be free of political entanglements, agents in Yekaterinodar later reported on her ties to radical circles there—too late to affect the opinion of the court. Her ties to

Andreyushkin, perhaps amorous, were no doubt political as well, but during the trial she seemed to be the innocent victim of his personal and political passions. All of this created a little sideshow, an unlikely love story embedded in a terrorist conspiracy.

At this point in the proceedings Ulyanov's footprint showed everywhere in the landscape of the plot. A collective narrative had been created in which Sasha and Govorukhin played larger roles than Shevyrev, but both Govorukhin and Shevyrev had left St. Petersburg, and Ulyanov had carried on as leader. The other main leader, Lukashevich, by the general complicity of the witnesses and his own cover-up, had faded into the background, and his central role in the bomb making had changed into a minor contribution that had been solicited by Ulyanov. From Sasha's own testimony, in which he corrected the court's expert witness on explosives and commented on the design of the fuses, it appeared that he had not only worked on the bombs but masterminded the bomb making.

The police witnesses that followed the recess on the evening of April 16 focused on the combat squad, and the court called Major General Fyodorov to comment on the construction of the bombs. Fyodorov described the bombs (technically, grenades) in great detail and concluded that they were ill designed, a finding already suggested by Osipanov's deposition of April 7, in which he described how he had tried to arm the bomb and then thrown it to no effect in the police station. Lukashevich suggested that Fyodorov's observations about the bombs' poor design changed the nature of the crime,[15] but that tack did not succeed, and Neklyudov took things in a different direction—the production and storage of nitroglycerine. This brought Ulyanov back into the picture and led to a small contretemps between Fyodorov and Sasha over the possibility of producing nitroglycerine without releasing penetrating fumes. Ulyanov tried to protect Ananina by rejecting Fyodorov's opinion that she must have been disturbed by the strong odors. Sasha described his technique for deodorizing the process, but Fyo-

dorov expressed skepticism. It was a replay of his debate during the Trial of the Six in March 1881 with the legendary bomb maker of the People's Will, Kibalchich, over the latter's ability to manufacture the dynamite used to kill Alexander II.[16] Whether Fyodorov was right or wrong, his questioning of the bombs' design affected the image of the Second March First. The liberal public already questioned the competence and honesty of the tsar's officials, but the information gleaned by the revolutionaries in the underground and abroad told of the defendants' bad timing, numerous indiscretions, and technical inadequacy.

DURING THE SESSION of April 17 the defendants were allowed to question the testimony of codefendants. At this point in the trial Ulyanov adopted the tactic not only of supporting Shevyrev's evasions but of taking upon himself Shevyrev's central role. Some of the responsibilities could be assigned to Govorukhin, but many directives and transfers of funds attributed to Shevyrev in depositions had to be explained. Andreyushkin and Generalov followed Sasha's cues on April 17. When Ulyanov saw that Lukashevich and Shevyrev wanted to evade a death sentence, he did everything he could to help them, but he did so at his own expense by exaggerating his role in the earlier stages of the plot.

At the end of the defendants' questioning of one another's depositions, Superior Prosecutor Neklyudov closed the session of April 17 with a summary of his findings. He focused on the stimuli and motives for the crime and how the conspiracy had emerged and developed. Ignoring the efforts to exculpate Shevyrev, Neklyudov named him "the very soul of the evil deed, its instigator and leader."[17] Neklyudov, who knew the depositions well, was shrewd enough to see that Sasha had tried to shift others' guilt to himself. Nonetheless, he placed Ulyanov alongside Shevyrev as one of the leaders. At the very outset Neklyudov assailed Ulyanov's ideological justification for their conspiracy: the notion that individuals

or groups might, on the basis of a so-called "objective-scientific" point of view, decide what is good for Russia and then go about using whatever means they thought necessary—in this case, terror against their government—to remove the perceived obstacles to their goals.

Neklyudov then gave the senators and representatives of the estates a short course on revolutionary socialist groups operating in the Russian Empire during the 1880s. He noted that Osipanov had carried with him on March 1 a copy of "The Program of the Executive Committee of the People's Will," formulated at the end of 1880, rather than Ulyanov's more recent and presumably more scientific program of the Terrorist Faction of the People's Will. To Neklyudov this signified a split within the group. Summarizing "The Program of the Executive Committee" and the 1884 program of the Polish revolutionary party Proletariat, he showed that the Second March First represented a merging of several programmatic tendencies and theories. In his telling of the emergence of the conspiracy, he accurately traced its origins to the demonstration on November 17, 1886, at Volkovo Cemetery, and interpreted Ulyanov's manifesto "17 November in St. Petersburg" as a distinct threat of terror. But Neklyudov used his brief history and analysis only as an introduction to his main messages—the futility and mindless cruelty of terrorism and how terrorism practiced by the student elite affected the public.

Its harm doesn't consist in the possibility that it might turn the people against the ruling power. The terrorists themselves recognize in their programs the firm faith of the people in the tsar and the mystique that he enjoys. No less than others they know the historical truth—that the Russian people have always supported the throne, never desired to occupy it, and never allowed strangers to do so....The real harm done by this party is not political but social—against the people. No doubt the perpetration of a whole

series of terrorist acts might even lead Russians to despair — and move them to a state of such outrage against the realm of the intellect that revolutionary terror would pale by comparison. I envision the possibility of antiterrorist terror, when the people will see in every student uniform, in every student, a single, evil enemy of the people, an enemy of tranquility and welfare; when a mother, a Russian mother, will curse the very birthday of her child, trembling for her child's future; when a father will take fright at the very thought of educating his child, seeing learning as a path to the gallows; when every book, even the alphabet, will make them think about *Greenberg's Dictionary of Medical Terminology*, in which there were eighty-six leaden words and the words sounded in unison: "Death, death, and more death!" Death for all and for each, without any discrimination as to who they were and how they got there. . . . Death to kin, friends, comrades, or acquaintances of the perpetrators who might by chance wander into the range of their hellfire! Death to the very *narod* crowding into the places where their tsar would pass![18]

On April 18 Neklyudov began his indictment of each defendant. He based his conclusions on the depositions taken before the trial. Osipanov stood out as the one defendant whose actions as well as words showed that he intended to kill the tsar. Once the main purpose of the plot had been thwarted, he tried to kill the policemen with him on the spiral staircase of Gorokhovaya 2, and, when that, too, failed, he tried to kill them in the interrogation room. All of the other members of the combat squad — the throwers and signalers — were declared guilty of the charges brought against them. Ulyanov stood out as the person who had done the most in almost every category of activity connected with the attempt.

Only Lukashevich managed to foil Neklyudov's otherwise accurate reading of the conspiracy. To Neklyudov he was merely an accomplice who had played a "significantly less active" role than

Ulyanov. The strategy had worked. Lukashevich's careful course during the deposition and trial and the others' efforts to divert guilt from him, with Sasha's cuing and encouragement, had saved his life. Shevyrev, on the other hand, had no credibility with Neklyudov, who saw through his antic lies, evasions, and absurd defense tactics: first claiming to be someone who hated terror; then an unwitting accomplice who had little respect for Govorukhin, the putative leader; and finally, a naïf who thought that all of their bomb making and planning would have no consequence. Yet all of the depositions put Shevyrev at the center of the conspiratorial web and showed him to be a more important instigator and leader than either Govorukhin or Ulyanov. Neklyudov's review of the depositions, the testimony of witnesses, and the evidence seized left little doubt that all of the defendants had lied, to protect either themselves or others. Neklyudov's coprosecutor, Alexander Smirnov, who had played a relatively minor role, completed the indictments for the exhausted Neklyudov on April 18 and ended the prosecution's presentation. After a short recess the defense presented its case.

Alexander Turchannikov, Osipanov's defense attorney, had little to say, thus pleasing the prosecution, the police, and probably the jury. The facts had been established. Osipanov had confessed, done everything possible to get himself hanged, and refused to let anyone argue for mitigation of a death sentence. Turchannikov found only one tiny chink in the prosecution's armor: Neklyudov's use of the term "blind terror" to describe what lay behind the actions of the People's Will. To Turchannikov this created an opening for a defense of diminished capacity, presumably caused by profound defects in the defendants' intellects and moral qualities—defects in their very nature—that led them to suicidal as well as murderous acts. Although he mentioned the imperfections of the bombs, Turchannikov admitted that the law would not exculpate a determined assassin on grounds of technical failure and, in the end, could only appeal to "the higher law, called mercy."[19]

Defective human beings carrying defective bombs and throwing themselves on the mercy of the tsar's tribunal—this is not how the key defendants wanted to see themselves portrayed. The bomb throwers and Ulyanov followed the long-standing rules of behavior of revolutionaries facing a Russian court, rules laid down by Peter Lavrov during the period of mass arrests connected with the *narodnik* "Going to the People" of the mid-1870s. Lavrov had taught the youth of that period that their socialist propaganda would spread like wildfire through the countryside. Instead, they were arrested by the hundreds and incarcerated for long periods before coming to trial. Lavrov then told them how to behave in court:

> Our advocates . . . work for what they imagine to be the benefit of their client, but in doing so diminish his dignity, impugn his morality, grovel at the feet of power, eulogize a nonexistent "justice and mercy" of the courts.[20] . . . Refuse a defense lawyer who will not defend your convictions, if not as correct ones, then, at least, as unavoidable ones. Refuse a defense lawyer who will not pledge himself to say not a word, *not a single word*, which demeans your program, your personal qualities. If there isn't one—and it is possible you'll not find such people—then defend yourself.[21]

The lessons that Lavrov had taught *narodniki* for almost two decades made martyrdom for the cause an axiom of revolutionary morality. In addition to everything else, Lavrov had denied an appeal to mercy: "We can't purchase mercy from those whose right to be merciful arouses as much outrage as their right to be executioners."[22] The well-intentioned liberal Turchannikov had violated the *narodnik* code. Ulyanov and the bomb throwers would have no truck with that sort of defense and seized the opportunity to present their credo.

Generalov, who had refused a defense lawyer, briefly repeated

the rationale for terror—that it was completely indispensable in the face of a reactionary regime. It was the only means available to pursue the immediate goals of the party—freedom of speech, of assembly, and popular representation and rule. He could justify himself only on the grounds that he had acted according to his convictions and his conscience. Generalov put it with eloquent simplicity—without adding any scientific justification. Andreyushkin used even fewer words and in straightforward terms set forth his version of the Lavrovian credo. He asked for no mercy, because begging would besmirch the banner of his party. The Cossack revolutionaries had remained true to themselves, to the masculine code of their military caste, to the nihilist code, and to the austere revolutionary morality delineated by Lavrov and practiced in earlier trials by the likes of Andrei Zhelyabov, Sofia Bardina, and Ippolit Myshkin.

It fell to Sasha to give the scientific rationale for Russian terrorism, and he rose to the challenge. Maria Alexandrovna, for whom the court had made an exception, was allowed to attend the session on April 18, and she heard part of Sasha's speech. She later told Anna that at first she had been astonished at Sasha's eloquence, but then couldn't bear it—he was putting the noose around his neck—and had to leave the courtroom before he finished. Sasha presented the paradox that all revolutionaries of that era faced: socialism would presumably be realized spontaneously through socioeconomic laws dictating the phases of historical development. Why, then, did revolutionaries need to dedicate their lives to realizing those laws? Their mentors insisted that individuals, as such, could not change history; yet their self-sacrifice was predicated on their ability to change the political structure and open the path to socialism. Recognition of the importance of politics and ideology and the emotional need to help victims and to give history a push infused Sasha's program. From Pisarev to Lavrov, Sasha's Russian mentors had put before him models and maxims encouraging self-sacrifice when the brute force of the regime blocked the path. But

he also had to show that individuals acting under the influence of historical laws acted not merely subjectively but naturally; that they represented the inevitably developing forces discovered by Marx and Engels; and that their consciousness had been formed out of natural evolutionary processes.

In the epigraph for his thesis, "What is real is historical," Sasha used the German *wirklich*, a word that in English is rendered more precisely by "actual" than by "real." Both convey the sense of an *active* reality, like the Russian *deistvitel'nyi*. His activism joined his life to the evolutionary processes leading to a better future. In a brief speech Sasha set forth the thinking and the emotions that governed both the Second March First and Russia's future in the twentieth century:

> Separate individuals are unable by force to produce changes
> in the social and political structure of a state, and even natural
> rights, like the right of free speech and thought, can be acquired
> only through the action of a well-defined group embodying and
> conducting the struggle.[23]

Sasha saw behind the actions of individuals and groups the struggle of the revolutionary intelligentsia as a whole—its struggle for its natural right to enlighten the people and lead them to socialism. He put it in even stronger terms, reflecting his belief in Lavrov's psychology of "developed" people—they had not only the right but a natural *need*, a compulsive sense of duty—to teach and raise the people to a higher level. Sasha's Lavrovist credo appears clearly in this proposition: "For a member of the intelligentsia the right to think freely, and to share his ideas with those less developed than he is, is not only an inalienable right but also a necessity and a duty."[24]

Sasha had in mind the decades-long, uneven struggle between a powerful and brutal regime and a weak intelligentsia: the thwarting and sacrifice of figures like Pisarev, Dobrolyubov, and Cherny-

shevsky, who had suffered early death and imprisonment; the flight abroad of Herzen, Bakunin, and Lavrov, whose writings had to be smuggled into the Russian Empire; and, of course, the martyrs of the People's Will. Deyer, however, had no interest in the history of the Russian revolutionary intelligentsia; rather, he wanted to hear how all of this pertained to Sasha's personal motives and actions. Sasha replied that all of this had not affected him personally, that his worldview did not allow for purely subjective motives. Consistent with his speech, he subsumed his own feelings and convictions under historical laws. Sasha claimed to speak not for himself but for the scientific laws of evolution and history operating at that moment in the Russian Empire. The Terrorist Faction of the People's Will had been created by history—it was natural for them to fight for basic rights that were themselves a natural product of historical evolution. When blocked in their natural development, the intelligentsia took the only path possible at that historical moment: terrorism. Whether the government continued on the path of repression or made concessions, its response would only encourage more terrorism, in the first instance out of frustration and in the second out of a sense that terror worked. And then Sasha pronounced the words that turned an abstract and perhaps tedious peroration of a twenty-one-year-old obsessed with science into a historic speech. His speech joined those of earlier revolutionaries in the dock as an inspirational moment in the history of the revolutionary intelligentsia:

> In Russia there will always be small groups of people, so dedicated to their ideas and so passionately feeling the misery of their homeland, that they will not think it a sacrifice to die for their cause. It's impossible to frighten such people. . . .[25]

Deyer immediately cut him off. Thwarted in his effort to sketch what would follow if the regime made rational concessions, Sasha began

to launch again into the inevitability of terror, but Deyer again stopped him in his tracks, saying that he had already made clear the sources of his criminal ideas—the *mens rea*—and that sufficed.

The earnest young student in his quiet way had taken pains to assure the assembled notables that he wanted neither to justify himself nor to vent indignation. Rather, he patiently rehearsed for them the scientific-objective laws that guided him in his notion of service to his *homeland*. He assumed their respect for science, but in his rhetoric he appealed to their service-class mentality. Sasha used the word *rodina*, a word that he had chosen carefully. The Russian warrior aristocracy had at first served Kievan princes, then Muscovite tsars, and, after the Petrine revolution, European-style emperors and empresses. Most members of the modern service stratum gradually detached their affections from the rulers alone and, taking Peter the Great at his word, focused them on the Russian imperial state. The radical intelligentsia that split off from the service class, however, had substituted the *narod* for the state, and Marxists were on the way to replacing the *narod* with the international proletariat as a worthy object of love and justification for self-sacrifice.

The word *rodina* somehow survived these substitutions and transcended them. It evoked a diffuse but powerful feeling for one's native soil without any reference to tsar, state, or nation—or, for that matter, to *narod* and proletariat. The assembled senators, ministers, and other high-ranking officials might sympathize with a service-minded son of a loyal father who had died in service to his *rodina*. When he wrote his memoirs three decades later, one of those present on April 18, Senator Tagantsev, testified to the power of Sasha's evocation of *rodina*: "I remember that among the defendants he produced the greatest sympathy, as a person sincerely dedicated to the cause for which he was being sentenced, and to the ideas whose realization, be it by terror, he believed necessary for the happiness and welfare of his *rodina*."[26] Like so many other

gentry children, Sasha had found it intolerable to accept a regime that had given him and other students the opportunity to develop intellectually, but not to serve the progress of their homeland in the direction dictated by social science. Even if their rulers did not like terror, it behooved them to ponder its rationale. This was Ulyanov's last message to the court.

Contemporary social and natural science taught privileged youth that service to one's homeland was only a particular expression of service to the human species. If socialism was the only future for the species, and if the regime prevented the intelligentsia from spreading socialism to the people, then the only tactic left to them was terrorism and self-sacrifice. Sasha and his comrades had acted as developed people must under those circumstances. This "scientific" reasoning had locked Sasha into an irreversible commitment. His code did not allow any disharmony between thought and deed. His younger brother Volodya understood Sasha's ways, and thus when told that Sasha had been arrested for participating in a terrorist plot, Vladimir Ilyich had said, "It means that he had to act that way—he couldn't act in any other way."

According to Lukashevich, at the meeting of February 25 Sasha had prepared a proclamation to be read in the event of the assassination of the tsar, beginning with these words: "The spirit of the Russian land lives on and the light of truth has not been extinguished in the hearts of her sons: on (date to be filled in) Alexander III was executed."[27] Lukashevich used the word *pravda* for "truth," and in Russian the word also connotes "justice." In *narodnik* doctrine, truth, justice, and human development formed an indissoluble whole. No written or printed version of this proclamation survived.

S ASHA'S SPEECH WAS the transcendent moment of the trial. What followed was pro forma: the final arguments of the defense and the defendants' last pleas. Osipanov's was the

most interesting—if one can call it a plea. Turchannikov tried to reduce Osipanov's guilt by pointing out that the bomb not only had not exploded but could not have exploded. Osipanov, however, rejected his defender's plea for mercy. Deyer, in a charade of judicial rectitude, intervened and reminded Osipanov that a defendant's last plea could not be used to argue for his punishment, only to mitigate it. Generalov, Andreyushkin, and Ulyanov had nothing to say in their defense. All of them followed to the letter the *narodnik* code of choosing death before dishonoring their cause. At the end of the day Deyer presented the tribunal with the prosecution's twenty-nine questions as to the guilt of the defendants, and summarily rejected the efforts of the defense to exclude any of them. The court recessed until 2:00 p.m. on April 19.

When the senators and representatives of the estates returned, they replied affirmatively to all twenty-nine questions. Neklyudov then asked for the death sentence for all fifteen defendants. The chief voice for the defense, Turchannikov, argued that in cases where crimes issued from ideological positions, the death penalty did not solve the problem—the struggle had to be won by confronting the ideas. That argument fell upon deaf ears, but the tribunal did find mitigating circumstances, especially for those whose cooperation had greatly facilitated the investigation and trial, or who had made less significant contributions to the plot. In some cases, the court took into account that some of the criminals were minors or very close to that status. Kancher, Gorkun, and Volokhov, who had cooperated with alacrity, all fit the category of naïf—young and inexperienced students away from home and subject to pernicious influences—and were sentenced to twenty years' hard labor in Siberia. Ananina received the same sentence, but on grounds that she was a victim of her daughter Lydia's and her son-in-law Novorussky's pressure and moral suasion. Novorussky's behavior at the trial had exposed him as a hypocrite and manipulator. Piłsudski, only twenty and thus still a minor, was seen as a victim

of Lukashevich's influence, and hence his punishment was reduced
to fifteen years at hard labor. The court reduced Pashkovsky's to
ten on the grounds that his actions had only remotely affected
events. For being merely a secondary helper, whose services did
not significantly further the assassination attempt, and a naïve victim of Govorukhin and Ulyanov's influence, Shmidova was sent
into permanent exile in the farthest reaches of Siberia. Serdyukova
had admitted to her guilt and had given valuable evidence against
Andreyushkin. She was sentenced to a two-year prison term.

The death sentence remained in force for Shevyrev, Lukashevich, Ulyanov, Osipanov, Generalov, Andreyushkin, and Novorussky, but they still could petition the tsar for leniency. After the
final sentencing, on April 23, they had a brief window of forty-eight
hours for preparing and delivering petitions; that period ran out at
noon on April 25. Neklyudov's physical and psychological collapse
meant that Smirnov had to attend to the review of the petitions and
the presentation of the Senate's advice to the tsar on April 30.[28]

A PROPER PETITION to the tsar required fulfillment of all of
the formal signs of obeisance to a monarch: the correct form
of address, the repetition of such throughout the letter, profuse
expressions of contrition, repudiation of the ideas and motives that
had animated them before they had seen the light, a reiteration
of the frequent defense that they themselves were youthful and
naïve victims led astray. They had to convince the tribunal and the
tsar that after years in prison or Siberia they might be redeemed
and serve Russia loyally and humbly. The court would forward only
petitions shaped in this fashion and couched in such language. It
was then up to the tsar.

The tsar, however, had evidently made up his mind about Sasha
before the petition process. Beginning on March 1, he received
Dmitry Tolstoy's regular reports detailing everything—the size
and features of the bombs, the disposition of the bombers and

their signalers on the streets of St. Petersburg on the day of the planned assassination, and the history of the plot's unfolding. Tolstoy quickly concluded that Shevyrev, Govorukhin, and Ulyanov were the leading figures in the plot and that, with the departure of the former two, Ulyanov had taken over the leadership role. On March 22, while at his Gatchina retreat, Alexander III read Ulyanov's deposition about the formulation of a scientific program for the unification of the different terrorist groups in the empire. Aside from setting forth the thinking behind the program and the program itself, the deposition contained Sasha's frank assessment of his role in the "terrorist faction of the People's Will."

> To conclude I want to define more precisely my participation in the entire project. If in one of my previous depositions I expressed that I was not an initiator or organizer of this project, it was only because . . . there wasn't one definite initiator and leader, but . . . the idea of forming a terrorist group belongs to me, and I took part most actively in its organization, in the sense of getting money, recruiting people, finding apartments, etc. So far as my moral and intellectual participation in this project is concerned, it was total, that is, I did everything possible insofar as my abilities and strength and knowledge and convictions permitted.[29]

Alexander III wrote on it, "This sincerity is actually touching. . . ."[30] Though ironic, the comment showed far greater generosity than his comment in the margin of Sasha's program for the terrorist faction: "This writing is not even that of a madman, but of a pure idiot."[31] This bearish man, who despised such theoretical effusions, had already made up his mind about Sasha, but he still had to deal with the pleas of Maria Alexandrovna, who had left Simbirsk for St. Petersburg to save her son. It fell to her to try to persuade Sasha to abandon his revolutionary oath and to placate the tsar.

Word about Sasha's and Anna's arrest reached Simbirsk by way

of Maria Alexandrovna's niece Yelena Peskovskaya, who attended the Bestuzhev courses with her cousin Anna. The latter had been arrested on March 1 when she came to look for Sasha at his apartment. On March 2 Peskovskaya wrote to the family's close friend in Simbirsk, V. V. Kashkadamova, who first consulted with Volodya and then gave the letter to Maria Alexandrovna. On March 3 Peskovskaya's husband, Matthew Peskovsky, a well-known writer and resident of St. Petersburg, but completely ignorant at that moment of Sasha's actual role in the conspiracy, visited the central office of the Police Department at Fontanka 16, and tried to liberate the cousins of his wife, Yelena. Peskovsky, who had a distinct impression of Sasha and Anna as two shy, studious, and somewhat sickly young people, thought that it had all been a terrible mistake. He began the family's effort to defend Sasha and Anna with an eloquent letter written, perhaps, with the advice of a prominent defense lawyer.[32]

In her own letter of March 28 Maria Alexandrovna petitioned the tsar for a meeting with her son and presented a portrait of Sasha (of which the following is an excerpt) that she thought would elicit Alexander III's sympathy:

> He was so taken up with scientific work that for its sake he gave up all amusements. He was held in the highest regard in the university. The gold medal opened the way to a professorial post — and in the current academic year he worked strenuously in his zoological laboratory at the university preparing his master's dissertation, in order more quickly to become independent and support the family.[33]

Alexander III wrote on the petition:

> I think that it is desirable to permit her a meeting with him so that she can see what kind of person her dearest little son is and

show her his deposition so that she can see what kind of convictions he has.[34]

The tsar's officials had other designs. The minister of justice, N. A. Manasyein, suggested to Peter Durnovo that Sasha's desperate mother might be used to persuade him to speak frankly and lead them to wider circles of the conspiracy—possibly to figures outside the immediate student milieu. Although Maria Alexandrovna met with Durnovo on March 31, there is no record of their conversation, only of Durnovo's request that the commandant of the Peter and Paul Fortress allow her to have a two-hour meeting with Sasha on April 1, between 10 a.m. and 12 noon. The meeting took place at the appointed time, when Sasha was taken from his solitary cell in the Trubetskoy Bastion.

We know about Maria Alexandrovna's meetings with Sasha from Anna. After her arrest at Sasha's apartment, where the police were searching for evidence, they searched Anna's apartment as well and then took her to Gorokhovaya 2 for questioning. They did not imprison her in the Peter and Paul Fortress but in the facility for preliminary detention. Kotlyarovsky's interrogration of Anna centered on the telegram signaling Kancher's return that she had received from Vilnius, although the request from Sasha and Shmidova that Anna put up overnight a woman connected with the Kharkiv terrorists became part of the evidence against her. The arrival of Maria Alexandrovna, who met with Anna before she saw Sasha, gave her daughter some hope. Maria understood Anna's psychological frailty and gave her what she needed without deceiving her about the seriousness of Sasha's situation. At one point Maria told her to pray for Sasha. The ordeal transformed the already strong tie between them into a lifelong system of mutual support that sustained them until Maria's death in 1913.[35]

There followed an intense series of encounters of mother and son. At their first meeting, on April 1, Sasha threw himself at her

feet and embraced her knees, begged forgiveness, but insisted that he had a greater duty to his homeland, his *rodina*, than to his family. Maria protested the cruel means that Sasha and his comrades wanted to use in the struggle. He assured her that no other means existed. At their four meetings he pleaded that she accept his choices—first to struggle by terrorism and then to die for the cause. He refused to petition the tsar for mercy and said, "Imagine, Mama, two people facing each other in a duel. One of them, having shot and missed, asks his opponent not to use his weapon. I can't do that."[36] For Sasha, imprisonment in Schlüsselburg Fortress—the only possible mitigation of the death sentence in his case—would be far worse than death on the gallows. He was certain he'd lose his mind. When Maria Alexandrovna replied that he was still young and would change, the kindhearted prison official who was obliged to attend the meetings of mother and son could not restrain himself and enthusiastically seconded her.[37]

Sasha's final conversations with his mother, especially his awkward attempts to console her, told a great deal about their relationship and revealed the psychological chasm that separated them. Sasha desperately did not want to hurt her—the anguish visible on his face moved the witnesses present—but everything he said could only produce that result. At one point Sasha tried to console her by saying that she had other children who would also win gold medals. He was right to this extent: at the time of Sasha's hanging, Volodya and Olya were taking their final gymnasium examinations and, as everyone in the family knew they would, won gold medals. Maria Alexandrovna required them to focus on their work, come what may, just as she had wanted Sasha to prepare for a chemistry test rather than attend Ilya Nikolaevich's funeral. Sasha, perhaps unconsciously, was making a point with this "consolation" and in his last requests to Maria Alexandrovna.

He asked her to redeem and then sell the gold medal that he'd pawned for 100 rubles. It was worth 130 rubles, and with the

remaining 30 she could pay back a debt he owed another student.[38] This was not just about scrupulousness. Sasha showed his contempt for the fetish that she had used to beg for his life in her petition to the tsar. She understood only conventional symbols and careers. He had pawned the medal to keep Govorukhin, his comrade in arms, on the field of combat. To be sure, Sasha remained true to the love of learning, sense of duty, and work ethic that his mother and Ilya Nikolaevich had taught him. He faithfully continued the main currents of the Russian enlightenment and the service ethic of the modernizing Russian gentry, but as a socialist and revolutionary using strategies and tactics taught by nihilist, *narodnik*, and Marxist theorists. He had placed his honesty, love of work, pertinacity, intellect, and knowledge in the service of bomb making and terrorism. The favorite son who bore Maria Alexandrovna's hopes for great achievements in science and service was now striding toward the gallows. According to Anna, Maria's last word to him, repeated twice on May 4 in the Peter and Paul Fortress, was "Courage!"[39]

The drama, however, did not play out as scripted by Sasha. At first he showed stony resolve not to bargain with the tsar, and did not reply to Peskovsky's letter of April 3. Peskovsky begged that he permit the brilliant defense lawyer Alexander Yakovlevich Passovyer to defend him. Sasha often chose silence when he couldn't give what was needed in a difficult situation. Peskovsky, however, still had two cards to play. On April 10, five days before the beginning of the trial, he petitioned the court that Passovyer be permitted to defend Ulyanov. Deyer dismissed the petition on the grounds that Ulyanov, now twenty-one and legally an adult, had to be a party to it. The very next day Peskovsky turned to the minister of justice and played his next card—mental incapacity. Maria Alexandrovna convinced Peskovsky that her son was in a state of psychological collapse. Peskovsky cogently argued that they had to look behind the façade of rationality and intellectual achieve-

ment to uncover Sasha's abnormal state of mind. The court needed to appoint a defender for that purpose. Although the minister of justice forwarded Peskovsky's new petition to the court for action, Deyer rejected it again on the same legal grounds: without Sasha's consent, nothing could be done.[40]

Peskovsky's last hope was to persuade Sasha to petition the tsar before April 25, and in order to do that he had to alarm him by parading the likely horrors of the family's situation—a demented mother, a sister in an equally abnormal psychological state, and four minor children with almost no means of support. On April 24 Sasha gave in, and agreed to write to Alexander III, but he rejected Peskovsky's advice about the tone and content of the letter. He wrote a perfunctory and unrepentant appeal to the tsar. The letter had neither date nor formal address to the tsar, although it did refer to him as "Your Majesty" in the text. It is awkwardly phrased, painfully formal, and passionless, as if it were an analysis of a phenomenon remote from the author.

I fully recognize that the character and features of the deed I committed and my relationship to it gives me neither the right nor the moral basis to apply to Your Majesty with a request for mercy in the form of a commutation of my lot. But I have a mother whose health has been strongly shaken in recent days, and if my death sentence is carried out it will put her life in most serious peril. In the name of my mother and younger brothers and sisters, who, not having a father, rely on her for their sole support, I have decided to ask Your Majesty to change my death sentence to some other kind of punishment.

This mercy will restore my mother's health and return her to the family, for which her life is so valuable, and will deliver me from the agonizing knowledge that I will be the cause of my mother's death and bring misfortune to my entire family.

Alexander Ulyanov[41]

The Senate tribunal convened on April 30 to report its review of the petitions, after which the minister of justice took them and the tribunal's recommendations to Alexander III. The petitions reflected the views of many defendants that the unequal combat between them and the regime did not require honorable behavior. They respected neither the court nor the tsar, and wrote (or else their lawyers wrote, and they signed) what they thought Alexander III wanted to read. Of course, Osipanov, Generalov, and Andreyushkin did not petition the tsar for mercy, and the tribunal thought Ulyanov's petition unworthy of positive consideration. It showed neither remorse, nor repentance, nor any new evidence. Only these four upheld to the letter the code of revolutionary honor.

Lukashevich and Shevyrev had no compunctions about lying systematically, whether to the court or to Alexander III, and Novorussky's state of denial about the seriousness of his actions allowed him to make a case for himself. In the petition to the tsar formulated by his defense lawyer, Gustav Printz, Lukashevich expressed complete remorse and portrayed himself as an accomplice who had wandered beyond his depth. Alexander III agreed with the court's decision that Lukashevich and Novorussky's appeals deserved consideration, and sentenced them to penal servitude for life in Schlüsselburg. The tsar, of course, had deferred to Pobedonostsev in Novorussky's case. Alexander III upheld Shevyrev's death sentence, just as he had for Ulyanov and the bomb throwers. The tsar did show pity, at least, for Anna.

Anna remained in preliminary detention until May 11. For her aid to the conspiracy the court initially sentenced her to exile in eastern Siberia for five years. Alexander III at first upheld the verdict, but Anna wrote to the tsar and the minister of justice begging them not to separate her from her mother. Maria Alexandrovna added her own petition. Without Anna's help she would not possibly be able to raise her four minor children. Maria Alexandrovna proposed that Anna be allowed to live with the family in Kazan,

where she hoped to enroll Vladimir Ilyich in the university, or else in Nizhny Novgorod. Lieutenant General N. N. Shebeko agreed to Anna's residence under police surveillance in European Russia.[42]

The petition, with the support of the minister of justice and Shebeko's recommendation, was passed to Dmitry Tolstoy, who advised the tsar to relent, and Alexander III agreed. The authorities decided that residence on the family estate in Kokushkino under the guardianship of Maria Alexandrovna's sister Lyubov Ponomaryova was a fitting solution. It was also a humane one. Thus, in May 1887 the family returned to its roots on Dr. Blank's estate. Vladimir Ilyich enrolled in Kazan University, but in December 1887 he was expelled for participating in a student protest and sent home, where both he and Anna lived under police surveillance— and under the shadow cast by Alexander. Here the young Lenin continued pondering Sasha and revolution.

A FTER THE TRIAL the five prisoners sentenced to death, plus Novorussky and Lukashevich, were returned to the Peter and Paul Fortress. Sasha in March had begun to divest himself of his worldly goods. On March 16 he requested that his clothes, other belongings taken from his apartment, and his remaining funds be given to Anna. He used some of his money to order his food and avoid prison fare—a privilege accorded prisoners in the fortress. On May 4 Sasha had his last meeting with Maria Alexandrovna, just hours before the prison warden, General Ivan Stepanovich Ganetskii, informed him that his plea to the tsar had been rejected and that he would be hanged. The three throwers and Shevyrev received the same message, but Ganetskii told Lukashevich and Novorussky that their sentences had been commuted to life imprisonment at hard labor.

The prisoners were awakened before dawn on May 5, dressed themselves by the light of kerosene lamps, were delivered to the custody of General V. N. Verevkin, commandant of the fortress's

military unit (whose name, by a twist of fate, is derived from *verevka*, the Russian word for "rope"), and then taken to Schlüsselburg by a fifteen-man convoy under the command of Staff Cavalry Captain Kuznetsov. Unlike the other prisoners, Lukashevich and Novorussky were not shackled. Verevkin, who meticulously husbanded his inventory, later requested that the commandant of Schlüsselburg send back five sets of shackles.[43] All of the prisoners were transported by carriage to the dock, then surrounded by officers, pushed from behind, and propelled onto two river steamboats used by the St. Petersburg police, the *Moika* and the *Izhorka*. A third steamboat, the *Polundra*, carried Lukashevich and Novorussky, along with the hangman. After three nights in the Schlüsselburg prison, the prisoners were executed before dawn on May 8.

THE INSIDE STORY of the conspiracy spread to the Russian émigré community in Europe, thanks to Govorukhin and Rudevich. Both of them described the careless and self-destructive modus operandi of the group in great detail. The émigrés thus had no illusions about the real character of the operation, and their candid personal correspondence about it contained a mixture of pity and admiration. The Russian revolutionary press abroad also transmitted the first wild rumors in the March 1887 issue of the *General Cause*, to wit: it reported a vast conspiracy in St. Petersburg with provincial branches. Information from German agents alerted Russian authorities to the plot. Highly placed officials and police officers were involved as well as members of the tsar's Cossack guard. Sasha's makeshift laboratory in Pargolovo was described as a bomb factory.[44] In later issues the *General Cause* reported that St. Petersburg Chief of Police Gresser had received 100,000 rubles from Empress Maria Fyodorovna for saving her husband's life and a pension paying 6,000 rubles a year from Alexander III. The journal's account of the trial praised Ulyanov's speech, and the May issue even carried a paraphrase of it—a version smuggled out by

the correspondent of the *Daily News*. For all of the foreign press's later lurid descriptions of nihilist "infernal machines" and projects, the revolutionaries had made their point.

Despite Dmitry Tolstoy's careful management of the trial, he failed to squelch the wild speculation connected with the Second March First. Among other things, the foreign press reported that a bomb attached to a cord had been thrown at the tsar, but did not explode; that a bomb had actually been thrown under the tsar's carriage; that police had arrested a woman with a bomb hidden in a muff; that the plot included people close to the tsar and disgruntled landowners, whose disloyalty forced the tsar to rethink plans for war in the Balkans; that there had been an attempt to explode a mine under the imperial train; that Sergei Degaev, the double agent, was one of the captured prisoners, and had planned the assassination. The *Washington Post* tersely misreported on May 5 in connection with the trial, "All the prisoners, except the student Oullanoff [*sic*], behaved quietly during the trial."[45] Prurient imaginations had their say. The *Washington Post* also carried a story on March 19 noting that "five girl students have been flogged to insensibility for their connection with the Nihilist conspiracy." The *Los Angeles Times* reported on April 29, "Among the prisoners is a maiden of striking beauty."[46] The foreign press generally carried a mass of erroneous details and fanciful embellishments, many of which were based upon the wild rumors originating in St. Petersburg and other Russian cities that were no doubt further distorted in transmission.

Two years after the events a sober and substantial report printed in Geneva in 1889 in *Free Russia* presented a relatively balanced account of the Second March First. To veteran revolutionaries the conspiracy had suffered from weak organization and inferior personnel. The leaders should have known that Kancher was unreliable. Their revolutionary plotting had been reckless and amateurish. Thanks to the conspirators' carelessness the police had gathered

sufficient information to round up hundreds of suspects, especially in St. Petersburg, Kharkiv, Vilnius, Moscow, and Yekaterinodar and other Cossack centers in Kuban Province. The report repeated Major General Fyodorov's assessment of the bombs' flaws. In the end, *Free Russia* condemned Shevyrev for lying about his role and failing to maintain a united front with the leaders of the conspiracy.[47] It was not a pretty picture. The account caused Lukashevich some anguish. After his release from Schlüsselburg in 1906 he tried to have the last word by defending in his memoirs both the bomb's integrity and Shevyrev's posthumous reputation, but he saved neither Shevyrev's nor his own. Anna and later historians were able to see how he had taken advantage of Ulyanov's generosity.

All of the reporting and memoirs, even when critical of the conspiracy and its personnel, sustained Ulyanov's reputation as a revolutionary martyr. Even the foreign press carried occasional comments about the positive response to Ulyanov's dignified and intelligent presentations at the trial. In this sympathetic narrative, though the forces of the Second March First were weak compared with those of the regime, hundreds of people from all walks of life sympathized with their cause and especially with the striking figure of Ulyanov. Russian socialists abroad saw that the prisonhouse regime created by Alexander III could not sustain the lives of Russia's best youths. After learning about the conspiracy from Govorukhin, Vera Zasulich from Geneva, Switzerland, wrote to Stepnyak-Kravchinsky, another émigré revolutionary, "It shows very distinctly that the dreadful nature of our [Russian] reality literally forced an idealistic youth like Ulyanov to resort to bombs after a long struggle with his conscience."[48]

The Ulyanov Brothers and History's Revenge

S ASHA'S YOUNGER BROTHER changed world history. He did it by imitating Sasha, although rejecting Sasha's revolutionary morality and theoretical preference. According to a now debunked myth, when he learned that Sasha had been sentenced to death, Volodya uttered a solemn oath that he would not imitate Sasha: "No, we won't take this path. This is not the path to follow." Maria Ilinichna was only eight years old when she supposedly heard Volodya utter the above words, worshipfully reproduced by Soviet biographers. Later in life, at a moment of mature reflection, Maria admitted that Volodya may not have actually said precisely those words. But she vividly remembered her brother's "downtrodden" look and his expressions of disapproval of the path that Alexander had chosen. Maria later wrote,

> It seemed to me that Lenin regretted that his brother had given up his life that cheaply. "It didn't have to be that way" or "not by those methods" show that Lenin looked unfavorably on the method of struggle that Alexander had chosen. It had nothing to do with theories of revolution at that time. . . . It seems to me that he had a different nature than Alexander Ilyich. . . . Vladimir Ilyich didn't have that spirit of sacrifice. . . . More sobriety and cold calculation, it seems to me, were part of his nature.[1]

Sasha's younger brother can hardly be accused of taking an easy path. Alexander devoted four intense months to revolutionary struggle; Lenin spent roughly a quarter of a century as a professional revolutionary until his party seized power; and he spent most of that time abroad. When he entered the fray in 1905, he did so as a high-ranking officer, seldom risking his life on the field of combat. After the Bolsheviks failed in a desperate struggle at the very end of 1905, he returned abroad for more than a decade, until 1917. Self-protective, he believed in his own supreme importance to the cause. No one was more passionate in its service; no one expended more rage and vituperation on his own comrades; no one showed greater recklessness than he did; no one had as much skill at revolutionary politics. Lenin gambled for higher stakes than Sasha did. He made sweeping attacks risking everything; and he retreated, when necessary, also at enormous risk. Military metaphors and terms abound in his prose—along with a great deal of profanity—and he made the word "struggle" the very soul of Soviet political culture. Like Sasha, who chose dynamite and strychnine to give history a push toward socialism, Lenin believed that the end justified the means.

After the Romanovs were overthrown in 1917, Lenin would not submit to rules of the game established by other socialists. In choice words he excoriated the leaders of international socialism. In this divisiveness he departed from Sasha's example. A faithful disciple of the People's Will and of Lavrov's notion of party loyalty, Sasha, against his better judgment, submitted to the views of a small band of reckless comrades when they outvoted him. He followed Lavrov's rules of behavior at his trial, holding high the banner of scientific socialism and sharing his comrades' fate. However, Sasha's program for the Terrorist Faction of the People's Will was far from factional. It tried to reconcile *narodnik* and Marxist thought. Lenin, on the other hand, spent his revolutionary apprenticeship as a Marxist in the mid-1890s writing polemics against the *narodnik* theorists who had inspired Sasha. In 1903, when the Rus-

sian Social Democratic Workers' Party refused to see things his way, Lenin split the party—and he split his own faction when it opposed him. Lenin chose his revolutionary path not only against the majority of Russian socialists but against the dominant trends in international socialism in 1917. He believed that other socialists had betrayed the cause.

Scientific socialism implied for Sasha tutelage of the people. In 1887 he wanted to turn Russia into a giant classroom. He fought for political freedom and freedom of speech, for the right of intelligentsia pedagogues to teach socialism to the *narod*. Thirty years later Lenin apparently endorsed the centuries-old slogan of peasant liberation—Land and Freedom—but the peasants and Bolsheviks had different plans for the land. The peasants wanted to work the land in their own way, to live free of conscription and taxation and of officialdom in general. They were, at base, anarchists with narrow horizons, and not dedicated to large-scale production or historical progress. This proved to be problematic for Lenin and the Bolsheviks.

In 1917 Lenin had seen Russia as the weak link in a chain of imperial powers. It didn't matter that Russia was relatively backward—the collapse of capitalism's imperial system would follow the Russian Revolution. The industrialized states would then help Russia develop quickly into the commune state that Lenin promised. The opposite happened. Capitalism survived and so did imperialism. Russia had to go it alone, virtually a pariah state. The Bolshevik Revolution was a failure in success. Instead of installing his promised commune state—a state quite like the one described in Sasha's "Program of the Terrorist Faction of the People's Will"—Lenin's policies during the Civil War between Reds and Whites produced renewed rebellion and famine. Toward the end of his life, after the Red Army had subdued the peasants with rifles and machine guns, Lenin rethought his position. He wrote of teaching the peasants, of raising their level of culture, of using the seeds of socialism in

peasant society in order to move gradually to a socialist future. This retreat from the Bolsheviks' headlong rush to industrial giantism came too late to save the Bolsheviks—now the Communist Party—from the dogmatic Marxism and dictatorial political culture he had created, or to save the peoples of the former Russian Empire from Stalin.

LENIN, though a dedicated Marxist, was driven by powerful emotions that had little to do with socialism as such. He also wanted revenge for what the Romanovs and respectable ("bourgeois" or "chauvinist") Russian society had done to Sasha and the family; but, equally important, he wanted to succeed where Sasha had failed. The sibling rivalry was in place before Sasha's execution. When he was a child, Volodya saw that the entire family worshipped Sasha, so at first he tried to be just like Sasha, but he could hardly have been more different. Volodya was boisterous and jolly, belligerently playful, a disturber of the peace, whereas the older siblings were solemn, serious, and painfully dutiful. They found their younger brother annoying. Anna and Sasha formed a team, and Volodya's younger sister, Olga, roughly eighteen months his junior, preferred them to him. Volodya was odd man out, sandwiched between the two most appealing children in the family—brilliant and dutiful Sasha and winning and precocious Olga.

Volodya's first systematic act of rebellion came during his second year. It was a species of sit-down strike. After starting normally, he refused to walk and was slow to talk. According to Anna's memoirs, his alarming failure to walk and talk until he was three forced Ilya Nikolaevich and Maria Alexandrovna to wonder whether their third child was in some way impaired. At an important turning point in his infancy, when he had just started to walk, Volodya lost his mother's attention to the newborn Olga. Like many children in a similar position, he regressed. About eighteen months later, when Olya began to walk and talk, Volodya, now three, fol-

lowed suit and thereafter developed very rapidly. Once he began to understand that Sasha, not Olya, was the person to imitate, Volodya became a super student, but he didn't work as hard as Anna, Sasha, or Olya. He didn't have to—he was brilliant. Like Sasha, he saw almost exclusively fives on his grade reports—the top score in the Russian grading system. But despite this apparent success, to Ilya Nikolaevich the time Volodya spent at play rather than study was a symptom of his second son's laziness. Sasha's ascetic work habits put Volodya to shame. This sibling contrast and paternal disapproval was later inscribed in the son's choice of a revolutionary pseudonym, "Lenin." Derived from the Russian noun *len'*—laziness—it is an ironic comment on Lenin's childhood identity.[2]

Volodya was the most outgoing and playful of the three older children—perhaps the most winning one to outsiders. In fact, one might speculate that he was the psychologically healthiest of the three, although this would be difficult to infer from Anna's memoirs. Trotsky even suggests that biology played a part, intimating that the four-year distance between Alexander and Volodya allowed the maternal organism to rest and produce a more robust child.[3] It may be wiser to look at nurturance outside the womb. Unlike the first two children, Volodya was raised by a nurse, Varvara Sarbatova, a Russian woman whose approach to child rearing differed from Maria Alexandrovna's. Of all the children, Volodya was her favorite, and she may have been able to give him what Maria Alexandrovna could not. Perhaps Sarbatova's indulgent methods contributed to the emergence of a less depressed, more extroverted and playful child; and perhaps she was the source of the "vast self-confidence" to which Anna attested. But in a family of rigorists he seemed to be more boisterous and less serious and dutiful than the other children—even a shirker. Cadet status worked to his advantage in some ways. As the second son, he didn't have to bear the family's hopes the way Sasha did. The eldest brother had to live up to the standard of self-sacrifice set by Uncle Vasilii

and Ilya Nikolaevich's academic achievement. Sasha was the de facto firstborn in a patriarchal culture. Like Sasha, Anna was ambitious, dutiful, and conscience-ridden, but Russian society expected less of women and put obstacles in their path. She had little self-confidence. Rather than being resentful, she became Sasha's most ardent admirer. In childhood and adolescence this translated into disapproval of Volodya. In retrospect, however, Anna understood that Ilya Nikolaevich's severity had not wounded Volodya the way it had wounded Sasha.

> Father was against "showering people with praise," as he put it, considering it extremely harmful for people to have high opinions of themselves. Now, as I look back at our childhood, I think that it would have been better for us if this generally applied pedagogical line had been administered less strictly. It was fully correct only for Vladimir, whose vast self-confidence and constantly distinguished achievement in school called for a corrective. In no way affecting his accurate self-assessment, it undoubtedly reduced the arrogance, which children with outstanding abilities are prone to ... and taught him, in spite of all the praise, to work diligently. For the rest of us—especially for the girls, who were suffering from a lack of confidence—small doses of praise would have been useful. ... Of course, Sasha did not suffer from lack of confidence in his abilities, but he was by nature very modest and self-disciplined anyway, and since a sense of duty dominated his character ... more approval, and more of everything that would have increased his joie de vivre, would have been only useful for him.[4]

The crosscurrents in the family created interesting affinities, hostilities, and ambivalences. Sasha and Anna, both painfully shy, loved their mother's domestic pedagogy and gentle ways. Temperamentally quite like his mother, Sasha nonetheless showed no gifts for Maria Alexandrovna's favored pursuits; like his father and mater-

nal grandfather, he took to the natural sciences. Volodya, physically
the spitting image of his father, showed no inclination to follow
Ilya Nikolaevich—or Sasha—into the natural sciences. At an early
age Volodya loved language, literature, music, and drawing, and
he showed gifts for all of them. Although Ilya disapproved of his
second son's habits, and worried about his preferences, father and
son were quite alike temperamentally. They were confident of each
other's affections. Just beneath the surface of Ilya Nikolaevich's
severity, there was a streak of mischievous humor, a quality completely alien to his older son and characteristic of Volodya. Sasha,
seemingly the carrier of his father's ambitions, differed in most
ways from him. A revealing description of a typical dinner at the
Ulyanovs suggests all of these crosscurrents:

> At the dinner table Ilya was swiftly transformed and became a
> completely different person, quite unlike the one in his study. He
> made witty comments, joked, laughed a great deal, and did not talk
> about official matters at all. Generally it was always merry, cozy,
> and relaxed during dinner at the Ulyanovs. Volodya and Olya, the
> gymnasium students, were at the forefront, with their ready wit.
> Ilya Nikolaevich loved most of all to joust with Volodya. Joking,
> he cussed out the gymnasium, gymnasium instruction, and had
> plenty of fun at the expense of the instructors. Volodya always
> very successfully parried his father's blows and in turn mocked
> the people's schools, sometimes cutting his father to the quick.
> . . . Alexander Ilyich always came late to the table, and they always
> had to call him down from upstairs, where he lived and worked.
> Ilya Nikolaevich also liked to joke about Alexander's scholarly
> ways, but the latter only kept silent and sometimes smiled. Gener-
> ally, Alexander seemed closed up in himself and cold.[5]

The older pair's ambivalence toward their father, with repressed
hatred perhaps the stronger emotion, created the suicidal moods

experienced by both Anna and Sasha after Ilya Nikolaevich's death in January 1886. Volodya had been far closer to his father. Their bantering at the dinner table suggests that they were at ease with each other, that they trusted each other's emotions. This did not hold true for his relationship with his mother. The adolescent Volodya rebelled against Maria Alexandrovna after Ilya Nikolaevich's death and had to be disciplined by Sasha during his last summer in Simbirsk in 1886. By that time his relationship with Sasha had become completely competitive. They jousted at chess. In desperation with Volodya during the summer of 1886, Sasha had to threaten him with ending their games if he continued his disobedience and insolence toward Maria Alexandrovna.

In their last summer together Volodya openly and angrily rebelled against Sasha's example and asserted his independence belligerently. He spent his time mainly reading novels, making his own preferences quite clear to Sasha, flouting the serious literature that Sasha recommended. Failure to show interest in the social sciences to Sasha signified not lack of development but sheer contrariness in a person of Volodya's abilities. This only added to Sasha's dislike of his younger brother's behavior. The brothers were at war in the summer of 1886. That's the way things stood when Sasha left Simbirsk for his senior year in St. Petersburg. He left behind an unhappy family and an angry and resentful brother, and his new responsibilities came at an inopportune moment—when he was contemplating a radical political turn. Sasha then sacrificed himself to his vision of socialism. This forced Volodya to see him in a new light; but Maria Ilinichna surely did hear Volodya express his disapproval and ambivalence toward Sasha in some fashion. He thought that Sasha had sacrificed himself too cheaply.

Volodya certainly heard the rumors that were floating about, and what the Russian émigré press printed about the Second March First conspiracy, which was at best a mixed review. Everyone condemned the regime of Alexander III for forcing a gentle

and idealistic youth like Sasha to such extremes. Volodya needed to find out what had turned Sasha into a maker of bombs carrying strychnine bullets, and why he had chosen to die for his cause. Very quickly he immersed himself in the literature that had made Sasha into a revolutionary, devouring the ideas of the nihilists and *narodniki* with the same competitive spirit that had emerged in their adolescent relationship. Once again Volodya felt he had to be like Sasha, and had to rethink Sasha's thoughts. He could best his brother only by continuing Sasha's work and succeeding where Sasha had failed. Volodya would bring down the Romanovs and exact a terrible revenge for what Alexander III and his regime had done to the family. To be sure, around this emotional core Lenin grew a vast and impressive theoretical apparatus, and by the early 1890s he was attacking some of Sasha's favorite *narodnik* authorities.

Volodya drew the line at self-sacrifice, a central feature of *narodnik* doctrine. To be sure, revolutionaries in Russia had to be self-sacrificing in some fashion: they gave up childhood and adolescent hopes for imagined careers; they maimed their youthful identities and took on shadowy underground ones. They had to face the vicissitudes of the revolutionary profession, whose penalties included imprisonment, exile, and execution. Lenin suffered all but the last on his way to victory. Unlike Sasha, however, rather than sacrificing himself unnecessarily, he adroitly used others. Sasha's example and Lenin's own temperament made the ultimate sacrifice—death for the cause and for one's comrades in the cause—an unacceptable option. Lenin sought victory, not victimhood. Trotsky, that astute observer of the Ulyanov family, could barely restrain his own aversion to Lenin in his descriptions of the brothers and their relationship. When Trotsky contrasted Lenin's revolutionism to Sasha's, he once again suggested that biology might be involved. The younger brother had "an organic need to dominate."[6]

Sasha and, if Trotsky's conjecture is correct, biology had nar-

rowed Volodya's choices in life in more ways than one. Thanks to Sasha's notoriety the family was ostracized. Shunned by Simbirsk society, the family now had to tear up its roots and move from Kazan and Kokushkino to Samara. During the next few years Vladimir had to adapt to life in a kind of limbo created by the opposing pulls of revolutionary commitment and filial piety. Embracing his fate, Volodya threw himself headlong into the student protests of 1887 in Kazan connected with the tightening of discipline in universities after the Second March First, and made contact with the radical circles. After his expulsion in December 1887 a fellow student asked him what he was going to do. He replied, "What is there to think about . . . the trail has been blazed for me by my older brother."[7] Alexander's choice had also made Vladimir the senior male in the family. He had to repress any residual hostility toward Maria Alexandrovna and try to take up some of the responsibility for the family's material well-being. At great psychological cost, Vladimir played the role of dutiful son. The ordeal transformed him from a normal, outgoing, aggressive adolescent to someone, at least to the outside world, coldly preparing himself for a future role he barely understood. One of his cousins described how he appeared in the summer of 1887:

> From earliest childhood, every year, from year to year, I saw Volodya, and his physical and moral changes were barely perceptible. During the preceding winter Volodya abruptly changed: he became restrained, laughed more infrequently, was stingy with words—he had grown up. All at once he became an adult, a serious person. . . . There wasn't a bit of gloominess or depression in Volodya's seriousness. He now showed a reserve I hadn't seen in him before, I'd say—a conscious, willful closing off. A feature of subtle irony began to show up, especially clearly expressed at first by an oblique glance, with somewhat narrowed eyes, and turns of speech.[8]

The siting of the change in the winter of 1886 emphasizes what a great blow Ilya Nikolaevich's death had been to Volodya. Sasha had been absent, and the burden then, too, had fallen on the younger son: not Sasha but Volodya had borne Ilya Nikolayevich's coffin. Like Sasha, Volodya no doubt felt that his father had been a victim of the reaction against the Russian enlightenment. Still, the funeral and praise that accompanied Ilya Nikolaevich to his Orthodox grave showed how respectable the family remained. The second blow, a little over a year later, took even that prop away and victimized the entire family. Dmitrii Ilyich provided an even more vivid account of Volodya, written many years later, but also referring to the period 1887–88:

Everyone closely acquainted with Vladimir Ilyich understood how his frame of mind had changed: the jolly person, with his infectious, childlike laughter, roaring until the tears came, who could in conversation transport people with his swiftly moving ideas, now became grimly restrained, strict, closed up in himself, highly focused, commanding, issuing curt, sharp phrases, deeply immersed in the solution of some sort of difficult, important problem.[9]

Volodya was trying to retrace Sasha's path; and, like Sasha, he took on the persona of a nihilist hero. During his long moratorium of 1887–93, when he halfheartedly tried two careers, the first estate management and the second law, Volodya worked continually at his chosen profession—revolution. He also sharpened his teeth on thoughts of revenge against the tsarist regime and the bourgeois society that had ostracized his family.

Meanwhile, Maria Alexandrovna tried to restore the family's respectability by the only methods she knew: finding good schools for her children and turning them into professionals. She also wanted to find a way to supplement the capital that had accrued to

the family from several sources. In Samara Province, farther south on the Volga, in 1889 the family bought a 220-acre farm with the help of Mark Elizarov, now Anna's husband. Maria expected her eldest son to learn how to make it profitable, but Vladimir failed miserably at estate management. He fared better as a student of revolutionary ideas and technique and contemporary economics. Maria Alexandrovna, however, did not want her gifted son to waste away in the countryside and succeeded in her campaign to enroll Vladimir in law at St. Petersburg University in 1890. He won a first-class degree in record time as an external student, but that apparently meant nothing to him. In fact, he loathed the law and practiced it desultorily, until he abandoned any pretext of working within the system, and moved to St. Petersburg.

The twenty-three-year-old man, by now a convinced Marxist, had fine organizational skills, a tremendous capacity for systematic work, a razor-sharp intellect, a capacious memory, a ferocious drive to win in any contest, and matchless pertinacity in pursuit of his goals. Unlike his irenic older brother, he would work very hard at putting his revolutionary organization in order, splitting and purging it when he thought it necessary, always maintaining control. To be sure, he showed the sometimes self-defeating impatience, optimism, and gambling that go with the revolutionary profession; but he also knew how to retreat and hold the ground he had won. Lenin would become the most successful revolutionary of his time, partly because he wanted to become like his brother, but also because he could not be like Sasha. It wasn't that Lenin lacked a capacity for self-sacrifice. His success as a revolutionary came at least partly at the expense of his health. Although he kept himself out of harm's way, the entire enterprise remained always in doubt, and even after 1917 there were moments when he had to face the possibility of returning to a dreary life in exile. He wrought terrible damage for the sake of his revolutionary vision, sacrificed millions of lives when he thought it served the cause, and left a huge state

of more than one hundred million people in poverty. Yet his successors found nothing better than his cult to justify their actions. He had won, the revolution had survived, and a brave new world was arising from the ashes. But something else happened. The outcome of 1917 is perhaps still in doubt. Revolutionary ideas have great staying power, but the present does not bode well for Lenin's brand of socialism.

O N J U N E 1 1 , 2 0 0 6 , I took a night train from Moscow to Ulyanovsk, the Volga city, formerly Simbirsk, where Lenin was born and the Ulyanov family lived for almost eighteen years. I had not planned to arrive on the Russian equivalent of the Fourth of July. When I picked up one of the newspapers that went along with the price of a first-class ticket, it reminded me that June 12 is "Russia Day." Did this mean that the Ulyanov family memorials I planned to visit would be closed for the holiday? I was reconciling myself to a change in plans when I found in the *Ulyanovsk Pravda* a calendar of holiday events for the city of over 600,000 and at the end, in small print, the announcement not only that the city's museums would all be open but that admission would be free of charge.

Most visitors to the city of Ulyanovsk used to go there to see Lenin's birthplace, the Ulyanov family dwellings, and the Lenin Memorial on V. I. Lenin Centennial Square. Now, to the dismay of local officials, dwindling numbers of tourists visit the square's marble exhibition hall or the houses where the family lived between 1869 and 1887. The Soviet regime built the austere, marble memorial with a stylized, bull-necked Lenin in bas-relief on a plaque above the front entrance to celebrate his hundredth birthday. By then Lenin had already become the butt of widely circulated jokes that I first heard at the International Congress of Historical Sciences meeting in Moscow in honor of Lenin's centennial. For example: Question: "Why are we celebrating Lenin's centennial by manufacturing beds for three?" Answer: "'Because Lenin is always

with us.'" Even so, the Lenin cult thrived during the 1970s and 1980s, and Ulyanovsk attracted thousands of visitors a day. As the Soviet gerontocracy under Brezhnev decayed, the myth of Lenin seemed to be the regime's only hope for spiritual redemption. Gorbachev unveiled a seventy-foot statue of Lenin on October Square in Moscow in November 1985. The Lenin cult flourished at a time when every other Soviet leader and the swollen Communist Party itself had been demystified, when the remaining true believers longed for a return to Leninism, and when a relatively youthful new leader, Mikhail Gorbachev, needed both a symbol of legitimate power and a model for himself. The Soviet playwright Mikhail Shatrov in the 1980s created the image of a peerless leader and, with it, inspired Gorbachev's extraordinary confidence in his own leadership. But those days of Leninist revival are gone, and now a resurgent capitalism threatens to transfigure the memorial complex in Ulyanovsk.

The great exhibition hall and the little two-story Ulyanov dwellings crouching in its shadow evidently cost more to maintain than they earn from admissions, though local officials and scholars believe that the memorial complex can be converted into a major asset. A story printed in the *Independent* (London) on June 7, 2006, repeated reports that the memorial's managers have been renting the exhibition hall for parties featuring strippers and that Sergei Morozov, the governor of Ulyanovsk region, has floated the idea of a Lenin theme park. My own experience of contemporary Russia made all of this seem less than improbable. Splashy advertisements decorate the building that houses the Russian State Archive of Socio-Political History on Bolshaya Dmitrovka in Moscow, with metal icons of Marx, Engels, and Lenin, like a trinity of Pantokrators, darkly glowering above the entrance. Makeshift bazaars appear occasionally on the ground floor. Scholars run a gauntlet of dime-store goods on their way to the elevators that carry them to the former sanctum sanctorum of the history of the Commu-

nist Party of the Soviet Union. Oscar Wilde famously said that the
United States was "the only country in the world that went from
barbarism to decadence without civilization in between." He was
wrong about that.

When I planned my trip to Ulyanovsk, I didn't have Vladimir
Ilyich in mind. My pilgrimage was mainly about his brother Alexander. But hardly anyone knows that Lenin had an older brother,
much less that he was the reason why Vladimir Ilyich became
Lenin. Few visitors come reverentially to the Ulyanov memorial
sites anymore to learn about the brothers who had changed Russia. The revolutionary tradition no longer elicits universal respect.
Recently a Russian friend commented, "In Soviet times Sasha was
a revolutionary martyr; now he's just a fanatic and suicidal terrorist." This demystification of revolution as such in Russia is fairly
new. A current website has a 1985 photo of the museum house
on Lenin Street (formerly Moskovskaya), with a crowd gathered
at the front entrance and a queue stretching down the street. No
such throng greeted me on June 12, 2006. The young taxi driver
who had stepped forward to intercept me on the train platform
(my clothes and camera made me a magnet for enterprising sorts)
expressed disbelief that I had come all the way from Connecticut
to visit the Ulyanov family's dwellings. My driver also doubted that
they would be open, although it was well past opening time. The
locked entrance suggested that the wisdom of taxi drivers trumped
the promises of local newspapers, but from the street we saw a light
on in the museum office. I called with my mobile phone, and within
seconds became the first visitor of the day. One family showed up
toward the end of my visit.

The material signs of the Ulyanov family's style of life showed in
the sparse but elegant furnishings, the bentwood chairs, the metal
bedsteads, the bookcases packed with the "thick journals" read by
the intelligentsia, and the black leather divan in Ilya Nikolaevich's
study, where he napped between long stints working on school

reports. He died of a cerebral hemorrhage in January 1886 on that
very divan (so I was told). The tour guides at the house on Lenin
Street claimed that the piano on the ground floor was an exact rep-
lica of Maria Alexandrovna's. Olga had been a talented artist, and
her drawings adorn the walls of the museum home. In the rear of
the house in the garden area near a well, my guide showed me the
kitchen that had been converted into Sasha's home laboratory, a
small, whitewashed outbuilding where he dissected and studied
beetles and worms. Through the windows you could even see on the
worktable a histological drawing, the cross section of a worm (no
doubt copied from Sasha's drawings for his junior thesis). Inside
the house on Lenin Street photos of Sasha and Volodya hang side
by side, but a botched terrorist plot did not get Sasha a statue on
the memorial square.

The rest of the family fared better. A metal bust honoring Ilya
Nikolaevich stands on a nearby street atop a tall, thick, pink-
granite pedestal. Ilya still lies in Ulyanovsk in the graveyard of a
now defunct monastery. Maria Alexandrovna chose to be buried
in the Volkovo Cemetery in St. Petersburg—the very site of the
demonstration of November 17, 1886. A realistic full-length statue
of Maria stands in a heroic posture on a pedestal. In front of the
family's modest second home in Ulyanovsk there is another ideal-
ized statue of a seated Maria Alexandrovna (generically handsome,
sturdy, and courageous in the Soviet manner) with a curly-haired
Volodya standing beside her. How much more apt it would be to
have a statue of her imploring a reluctant Sasha to write a repentant letter to the tsar—the letter that Sasha in fact finally agreed to
write, but unrepentantly.

Schlüsselburg Fortress, the site of Sasha's execution, sits on a
little island where the Neva flows out of Lake Ladoga, about forty
kilometers east of St. Petersburg. Inside the fortress on a crumbling
brick wall a plaque with a bas-relief of Sasha in profile marks his
brief prison sojourn. In 1906 Novorussky identified the site of the

collective grave. In 1919 the new Soviet regime marked it with a modest granite monument carrying the names of the twenty-eight prisoners who had been executed and three who had committed suicide. Perhaps scientific detective work of the sort that verified the Romanov remains would be able to distinguish Sasha's from those in the common grave. But then what? Burial alongside his mother and siblings in Volkovo Cemetery? And what about Lenin? Despite efforts to move him from the mausoleum on Red Square and bury him in Volkovo, no one has dared to remove the mummified body. In Soviet times, to remove Lenin from the mausoleum would have been sacrilege. The current revival of respect for the Soviet era probably perpetuates that feeling, but today removal of Lenin from Red Square would also be bad business.

Ulyanovsk longs for some of the income generated by the crowds of tourists that still visit the mausoleum on Red Square. Talk of privatizing the Lenin memorial complex in order to make it pay scandalizes the faithful, as do schemes to turn Lenin's remains into an even bigger moneymaker. The Ulyanovsk regional governor has proposed at least two suitable burial sites: a resting place alongside his father (perhaps appropriate, but still problematic because the bones of Russian Orthodox monks scattered around would have the militant atheist writhing in his grave); or in the memorial complex on V. I. Lenin's Centennial Square, where Lenin's tomb as well as his birthplace would become the nucleus of the proposed theme park. History has already played a lot of dirty tricks on Lenin, and it's not over yet.

Lenin believed in Engels's dictum that the goddess of History, whose dialectic presumably guarantees progress, is nonetheless the cruelest of them all. She rides her triumphal chariot over heaps of corpses. Of course, on the lighter side there is Marx's well-known paraphrase of his preceptor in dialectic: "Hegel remarks somewhere that all great, world-historical facts and personages occur, as it were, twice. He has forgotten to add: the first time as tragedy,

the second as farce."[10] Russian tragedies—and triumphs—receive their due in Ulyanovsk. Visitors find scattered through the city plaques commemorating the great Cossack-led peasant insurrections that swept up the Volga in the seventeenth century and Civil War battles of the twentieth century. Ulyanovsk also shows a spirit of farce or, at the very least, whimsy. On Goncharov Street a weather-resistant copy of a yellow-and-green divan of the early nineteenth century memorializes Ivan Goncharov's quintessential "superfluous man," Oblomov, who slept through most of his languid life. Another notable son of Ulyanovsk, the historian Nicholas Karamzin, about whom Sasha had written a senior-year essay, rests beneath a statue of Clio, the muse of history. Surely not even the fathers of socialism—no strangers to irony—had imagined a Clio who would be so whimsical as to use the remains of Marxian revolutionaries to bring in dollars and euros for Russian capitalism.

Hardly anyone today believes in laws of history, but Russian revolutionaries worked very hard at solving the ethical conundrums of serving laws of progress that, though inevitable, required self-sacrifice and the sacrifice of others. Dostoevsky portrayed the tortured psyches invested in such ideas; and social scientists tell us what happens when people who have a vested interest in social "laws" try to realize them. Sasha believed in the *narodnik* notion of the duty of the "developed" people—the scientifically educated elite—to serve the society whose ruling class had exploited the many. Only the privileged few had achieved higher development. This laid a heavy obligation on the scientific elite. Russian youth had been warned by their radical teachers that studying science for its own sake led one off the ethical path. In order to serve historical progress, at the very least you had to be thinking about the social good that your scientific investigations (presumably, even on worms) would yield. Oddly enough, the old regime, too, had instilled in the youth a sense of service that could easily be redirected from the Romanovs to the masses of peasants who had suffered under their rule.

THE ULYANOV BROTHERS AND HISTORY'S REVENGE 219

For Sasha, socialism and ethical behavior had to be brought in line with the natural sciences. Self-sacrifice for the Russian peasants and factory workers was a natural imperative for a developed person. Once you knew the laws of nature and society, you were obliged to obey them. Evolutionary theory could be reconciled with socialism and Kantian ethics. The scientific elite grasped not only the nature of progress but also the best means to serve it. Sasha decided that a terrorist party, the People's Will, was the vanguard of the struggle for socialism in Russia, and that it was therefore ethical to be a terrorist. He tried to explain this to the tribunal that sentenced him to death.

Neither Marx nor Darwin nor Kant (and certainly not a Russian court trying political crimes) had psychoanalytic insights about the alliance of a very strict conscience with an adolescent's considerable powers of rationalization. Dostoevsky had delved into pathologies of conscience in his studies of adolescent transgressors, demons, and saints, and he would surely have found in Sasha and the other plotters wonderful material if he had lived until 1887. Some of Sasha's co-conspirators had cheated on their consciences and escaped the noose. If only Sasha had done the same, the history of the Ulyanov family would have been quite different; and if Volodya hadn't pondered Sasha's choices, I wouldn't have been in Ulyanovsk on Russian independence day.

A FTER THE END of the official Lenin cult, historians willingly took up the task of filling in the "blank spots" of history, as it was put during the period of glasnost. You can now find in the Ulyanov home museums information about the family that would have been tabooed in earlier times. Pages in plastic sleeves confess that Maria Alexandrovna was the daughter of a doctor and hospital administrator who had converted from Judaism to Russian Orthodoxy; that her mother was German and Swedish; and that Ilya Nikolaevich's ancestry, though obscure, was prob-

ably mainly Central Asian. Tourists are now told that Stalin suppressed the information about Lenin's Jewish ancestry, although Anna Ilinichna pleaded that it be released to fight the growing anti-Semitism in the Soviet Union during the 1930s. Revelations about the Ulyanov family's ethnic background satisfy the collective conscience of professional historians, but, alas, also serve the persistent narrative of a messianic Russia that has been betrayed by a series of Judas figures—most recently the United States and NATO. But Clio is no doubt having a good laugh about the workings of nationalism, too. Lenin destroyed the Romanov family along with their empire, but believed that nationalism had to be tolerated for the nonce, even though he wanted to chasten Russian nationalism. Now his statue stares at the Russian tricolor fluttering atop the Ulyanovsk regional administration building. Meanwhile, in St. Petersburg, the enshrined Passion of the Romanovs serves the Christocentric tradition of Russian nationalism despite their German background—which provoked cries of treason in 1917. The traitors have become Russian Orthodox saints, and now, to some at least, Lenin, the Jew, is the traitor. Russian worship of great power, however, may finally sustain Lenin's reputation as the creator of the basis for a new imperial structure, whose collapse Russians now regret.

O N J U N E 12 , 2006, under a cloudless sky and enjoying eighty-degree weather, groups of costumed performers gathered on the squares for their programs, children begged their parents to buy balloons, and vendors offered an array of treats. Absent the monuments and Cyrillic signs, it might have been the Fourth of July somewhere in the U.S. Midwest. The crowds flowed past Lenin's statue on the way to the massive marble hall that housed an exhibition, "The City of Ulyanovsk's Investment Potential." Rivulets left the square for the park above the Volga and the food and souvenir stands. Not far from Lenin's statue, children in mar-

tial arts robes and boxers and wrestlers displayed their skills in a makeshift ring in the square. There were skateboard and Roller-blade competitions. A marching band drummed a short distance away, and on bandstands at the far ends of the two squares dancers and musical ensembles took over after the speakers performed their duties. The names of some of the performing groups seemed to reflect the contending faiths that marked Russia's "transition" from the Communist era to something else. There was a "creative collective," the "First of May," performing in Sverdlov Park, and at the Center of Popular Creativity and Culture a program called "Holy Rus."

Russia always seems to be struggling with earlier layers of culture and forms of power. Both the Orthodox Church and the Soviet regime failed to efface sorcery and other pagan remnants in Russia. There was a long period of "dual faith" after Russia's baptism in the tenth century, and then again when the Orthodox faithful resisted atheistic Communism. Russia experienced periods of "dual power," like that of the Provisional Government and the Soviets in 1917. During his sway, Gorbachev first subverted the Communist Party's power in favor of his presidency of a new Soviet structure; and then he thoughtlessly undermined his own power by creating elected presidents of the Soviet republics. They and the new parliaments proceeded to declare their republics sovereign nation-states (which is why June 12, 1990, is celebrated as Russia's independence day). Then came Yeltsin's struggle with the Russian Federation's inherited Supreme Soviet, followed by Putin's attack on Yeltsin's decentralized system. All of these men found the institutional improvisations of their predecessors inadequate, and dismissed them.

The transitional moments say a great deal about Russian power's migratory and protean character. For Russia the dynamic of global power always meant and still means hasty and painful adaptations imposed by regimes on reluctant populations. These impositions

included changes of religion or secular ideology and of capital
cities, times of trouble wasteful of millions of lives, disdain of the
formalities of law and parliaments, disposable constitutions, and
vast redistributions of property. Russians have grown wise about
their history. In a conversation in 1995 one of my Moscow friends
summarized the phases of Russian history: "The tsars gave land,
the Communists gave power, and the new regime gives money."
Russian regimes have always fought for a place at the table where
the big-stakes game is being played, and even ordinary Russians
respect and honor the leaders who played the game of power well—
not excluding mass murderers. Despite the pain and disorientation
and vast sacrifices, Russians take pride in their ability to survive
as a powerful state. That is surely why Volodya has a statue on the
square in Ulyanovsk, whereas Sasha has only a plaque on a wall in
Schlüsselburg Fortress, and why Alexander Kerensky is relegated
to the margins of Russian history.

I spent a few minutes vainly trying to get a sense of Ulyanovsk's
investment potential in the exhibition hall, and then joined the
crowd before the bandstand at its entrance, just beneath Lenin's
iconic head frozen in its sideways look, stubbornly averting its
keen stare from the proceedings below. By late afternoon a series
of female and male vocalists and a brassy combo were doing their
own version of a history of popular music, from depression-era
American songs, including "The Sunny Side of the Street" (how
did the female vocalist render "If I never had a cent I'd be as rich
as Rockefeller"?) to jazz and rock and Soviet golden oldies of the
fifties and sixties. The crowds here didn't look like those in Moscow and St. Petersburg, where, walking up Tverskaya Street or
Nevsky Prospect, you felt that you were being passed by a parade
of world-class models and high-powered business types. Most of
the people here were dressed unremarkably for a stroll in the park,
a day in the sun. One little girl danced by herself off to the side of
the bandstand. She looked like a pale version of Shirley Temple

in an organdy dress and patent-leather shoes. A woman in jeans, who might have been her grandmother, ignored the pleading of a younger man, who might have been her son, climbed under the rope separating the crowd from the area around the bandstand, and offered her own whirling solo performance. The people around me were delighted with the music, some applauding vigorously for the Soviet patriotic tunes, most, it seemed to me, for the rock and roll. I don't know much about popular music, but nameless old tunes lay in my mind, ready for resurrection. Awash in the good feeling on the still sunny square, I found it hard to think about the ironies of history.

NOTES

ONE: ENDINGS AND BEGINNINGS

1. Rossiiskii Gosudarstvennyi Arkhiv Sotsial'no Politicheskoi Istorii, hereafter cited as RGASPI, Fond 11, opis' 3, delo 18, contains the reports of Adjutant General I. S. Ganetskii, commandant of the Peter and Paul Fortress. They cover the period March 3 to May 5, 1887, from the date that Ganetskii took Ulyanov into custody to the date of his transfer to Schlüsselburg Fortress. The inventory appears in RGASPI, Fond 11, opis' 3, delo 18, list 50. Some of the material was copied from Rossiiskii Gosudarstvennyi Istoricheskii Archiv (RGIA) in St. Petersburg, Fond 1280, opis' 1, dealing with the arrest and confinement of those involved in the affair of March 1, 1887. Dmitry Tolstoy's account appears in RGASPI, Fond 12, opis' 1, delo 155, list 123. Another version exists in which Andreyushkin "uttered in a weak voice: 'Long live the People's Will'; the second [Generalov] 'Long live the Executive Committee,'" in E. E. Kolosov, *Gosudareva Tiur'ma Shlissel'burg*, 2d ed. (Moscow: Izd. vsesoiuznogo obshchestva politkatorzhan i ssyl'no-poselentsev, 1930), 229. Pokroshinskii, the chief of staff of the gendarme corps on duty at the execution, was the source of the latter. The version in which Ulyanov and Shevyrev watch the others expire is published in "K istorii pokusheniia A. I. Ul'ianova i dr. 1 Marta 1887

g.," *Krasnyi arkhiv*, no. 2/15 (1926): 223. This version in Russian was translated from an article in the French newspaper *Cri du peuple*, June 13, 1887. The story that they all rejected kissing the cross appears in RGASPI, Fond 12, opis' 1, delo 155, list 123. For a discussion of the different versions, see Mikhail G. Shtein, *Ul'ianovy i Leniny, semeinye tainy* (St. Petersburg: Izd. Dom Neva, 2004), 316, hereafter cited as Shtein, *Ul'ianovy i Leniny*. The story about the hanging of the Decembrists is taken from Anatole G. Mazour, *The First Russian Revolution 1825: the Decembrist Movement, Its Origins, Development, and Significance* (Berkeley: Univ. of California Press, 1937), 220; that of the hanging of the members of the People's Will, from David Footman, *Red Prelude* (New Haven: Yale Univ. Press, 1945), 242.

2. According to a report of Dmitry Tolstoy, March 1, 1887, published in A. I. Ul'ianova-Elizarova, ed., *Aleksandr Il'ich Ul'ianov i delo 1 Marta 1887 g.* (Moscow-Leningrad: Gos. Izd-vo, 1927), 359, hereafter cited as *Aleksandr Il'ich Ul'ianov i delo 1 Marta 1887 g.*

3. See map, plate 13.

4. B. Kazanskii, ed., "Novye dannye o dele 1 Marta 1887 g.," *Katorga i ssylka*, no. 10/71 (1930): 138–39. This information was taken from the diary of A. P. Arapova, the daughter of Pushkin's widow from the latter's second marriage. She knew people closely connected to the events and was well informed.

5. Mikhail Kheifets, "On ne mog postupit' inache," *Nota Bene*, no. 1 (February 2004): 244, hereafter cited as Kheifets. The words attributed to Volodya by Vera Kashkadamova, the friend of the family mentioned in the text, ring truer than Maria Ilinichna's putative "No, we won't take this path. This is not the path to follow." Kashkadamova's precise quote is in her memoirs in *Aleksandr Il'ich Ul'ianov i delo 1 Marta 1887 g.*, 274. Her version is also used in Robert Service, *Lenin: A Biography* (London: Macmillan, 2000), 59–60, hereafter cited as Service.

6. For the most detailed account and thorough scholarship on the family background and Ilya Nikolaevich's career, see Shtein, *Ul'ianovy i Leniny*. For one effort to trace the Ulyanov side, see V. A. Mogil'nikov, *Predki V. I. Ul'ianova-Lenina*, ed. A. N. Opuchin (Perm: Izd. Assotsiatsii genealogov-liubitelei, 1995).

7. See A. S. Markov, *Ul'ianovy v Astrakhani* (Volgograd: Nizhne-Volozhskoe izdatel'stvo, 1970), 40–44. See also Philip Pomper, *Lenin,*

Trotsky, and Stalin: The Intelligentsia and Power (New York: Columbia Univ. Press, 1990), 3.

8. *Mezhdu pravdoi i istinoi*, ed. O. Abramova, G. Borodulina, and T. Koloskova (Moscow: Gosudarstvennyi istoricheskii muzei, 1998), 142–43. Dr. Blank wanted to marry Katherine von Essen, but the authorities rejected his request, probably because she was his sister-in-law.

9. Shtein, *Ul'ianovy i Leniny*, 111–16. The reasons for the suicide, despite rumors, remain obscure. Dmitry was an indifferent student. Little else is known.

10. Reliable facts and figures can be found in Zhores Trofimov, *Otets Il'icha* (Saratov: Privolzhskoe knizhnoe izdatel'stvo, 1981).

11. The description is based upon Dmitry Ulyanov's fond reminiscences of the house on Moskovskaya Street in *Vospominaniia o Vladimire Il'iche Lenine, vospominaniia o rodniakh*, ed. Z. A. Levina i V. N. Svetsov (Moscow: Izd. Politicheskoi literatury, 1969), in *Vospominanii o Vladimir Il'iche Lenine v piati tomakh*, ed. G. N. Golikov et al., 5 vols. (Moscow: Izd. Politicheskoi literatury, 1969–70), 1:81–82.

TWO: TRAUMAS

1. *Aleksandr Il'ich Ul'ianov i delo 1 Marta 1887 g.*, 35–36.

2. Leon Trotsky, *The Young Lenin*, trans. Max Eastman, ed. Maurice Friedburg (Garden City, NY: Doubleday, 1972), 77–78, hereafter cited as Trotsky, *The Young Lenin*.

3. *Aleksandr Il'ich Ul'ianov i delo 1 Marta 1887 g.*, 85. I've translated the Russian gerund *iznezhivaiushchego* as "effeminizing." It can also be translated as "making effete" or "making soft," but I think that "effeminizing" more accurately captures Ilya Nikolaevich's anxieties.

4. Maria Ilinichna took a trip to Switzerland in 1897 and traveled under the name Blank. A Swiss student, her curiosity piqued by this very un-Russian-looking young woman with an equally non-Slavic name, told Maria that the name was probably Jewish. E. E. Kirillova and B. N. Shepelev, eds., " 'Vy . . . rasporiadilis' molchat' . . . absoliutno'," *Otechestvennye arkhivy*, no. 4 (1992): 81. Maria's manuscript is in RGASPI, Fond 14, opis' 1, delo 194, listy 2–3; Anna's letters are preserved in RGASPI, Fond 13, opis' 1, delo 471, listy 1–6. Anna wrote to Stalin repeatedly from 1932 to 1934 in an effort to publicize the family

history. As Anna pointed out, Lenin did not keep secret his positive attitude toward Jewish ethnicity. He appointed numerous Jews to high positions in the Communist regime, even though he did not advertise his own background. Anna believed that revealing the family background would help fight the growing atmosphere of anti-Semitism in the Soviet Union. Maria Ilinichna wrote about her experience of 1897, but never published the article she had been preparing beginning in 1930. Stalin stonewalled, and, despite all of the efforts, the evidence was suppressed for more than half a century. Of course, rumors about the family's Jewish origins had been widespread long before the 1930s and persisted. No one was surprised when the truth came out.

5. Trotsky, *The Young Lenin*, 39.
6. *Aleksandr Il'ich Ul'ianov i delo 1 Marta 1887 g.*, 44–45. Anna does not give a precise date for the incident, but from the context and her use of the adjective connoting childhood (*detskiye gody*), the mid to late 1870s is suggested. The word *smutnoe* also connotes "vague," "troubled," or "turbid." In all these translations, lack of clarity and confusion are suggested.
7. Alexander Herzen, *Socheniniia v deviate tomakh*, ed. V. P. Volgina et al., 9 vols. (Moscow: Gos. Izd-vo khudozhestvennoi literatury, 1956), 4:232–33.
8. In 1970 Oksman told the Italian historian Franco Venturi about Dr. Blank's Jewish background in the presence of V. V. Pugachev. See Olga Abamovna et al., eds., *Mezhdu pravdoi i istinoi* (Moscow: Gosudarstevennyi istoricheskii archive, 1998), 6–7. The history of the outing of the secret is traced in this volume.

THREE: THE MAKING OF A REBEL

1. This gymnasium essay, preserved in RGASPI with the others, is also published in *Aleksandr Il'ich Ul'ianov i delo 1 Marta 1887 g.*, 126–27.
2. D. I. Pisarev, *Izbrannye filosofskie i obshchestvenno-politicheskie stat'i*, ed. V. S. Kruzhkova (Moscow: Gos. Izd-vo politicheskoi literatury, 1949), 663.
3. *Lavrov, gody emigratsii*, ed. Boris Sapir, 2 vols. (Dordrecht, Holland: D. Reidel, 1974), 2:202.
4. I. S. Turgenev, *Fathers and Sons*, ed. and trans. Ralph E. Matlaw (New York: W. W. Norton, 1966), 102.

5. Ibid., 217–18.

6. Govorukhin commented on Sasha's inability to express anger or aggression himself, but noted that he expressed extreme (*boleznennyi*) anguish in the presence of any kind of rude or harsh behavior. Anna noted this feature in Sasha in early childhood. See *Aleksandr Il'ich Ul'ianov i delo 1 Marta 1887 g.*, 214, 40.

7. *Pervoe Marta 1887 g.*, ed. A. A. Shilov (Moscow: Moskovskii rabochii, 1927), 289, hereafter cited as *Pervoe Marta 1887 g.*

8. V. B-v [Bartenev], "Vospominaniia peterburzhtsa o vtoroi polovine 80-kh godov," *Minuvshie gody*, 1908, no. 10 (October): 177.

FOUR: SASHA, ANNA, AND RAISA

1. *Aleksandr Il'ich Ul'ianov i delo 1 Marta 1887 g.*, 56.

2. Ibid., 61–62.

3. Ibid., 76.

4. RGASPI, Fond 11, opis' 3, ed. khr. 22. The letter is also published in Anna's "Vospominaniia ob Aleksandre Il'iche Ul'ianove," in *Aleksandr Il'ich Ul'ianov i delo 1 Marta 1887 g.*, 130–33.

5. Ibid.

6. My translation, in Philip Pomper, *The Russian Revolutionary Intelligentsia*, 2d ed. (Wheeling, IL: Harlan Davidson, 1993), 131–32.

7. *Aleksandr Il'ich Ul'ianov i delo 1 Marta 1887 g.*, 373.

8. Ibid., 121.

9. RGASPI, Fond 11, opis' 3, ed. khr. 21; *Lenin-Krupskaia-Ul'ianovy, perepiska*, 31.

10. Shmidova's letters are preserved in RGASPI, Fond 13, opis' 1, ed. khr. 223, listy 1–11. The letter to Lenin is undated, but in light of its content and references in the later letters, it was probably written in 1918 or 1919. There is no evidence that Lenin ever saw it, and it is unlikely that Anna transmitted it to him. The handwriting is sometimes indecipherable, but the content is clear: it is an emotional plea for material support. There are four letters in all, and the last three are written to Anna. The last two are in different and fully legible handwriting and are dated February 21, 1922, and December 31, 1923. The letters have never been cited in the historical literature, and this suggests Anna's censorship, her disregard for Shmidova, and her disbelief in Shmidova's account. In Anna's annotations to the memoirs edited by her,

there are several dismissals of the notion that Sasha and Shmidova had a strong personal relationship. The double standard that existed toward nihilist women showed in the disapproval of Shmidova's multiple relationships with men expressed in the memoirs. Anna shared that attitude.

11. Raisa Shmidova, "1 Marta 1887 goda," *Prostor* (Alma-Ata), no. 4 (1967): 64.

12. *Aleksandr Il'ich Ul'ianov i delo 1 Marta 1887 g.*, 265–66.

13. RGASPI, Fond 13, opis' 1, ed. khr. 223, listy 9–11.

14. Shmidova, "1 Marta 1887 goda," 61.

15. *Aleksandr Il'ich Ul'ianov i delo 1 Marta 1887 g.*, 119.

FIVE: STUDENTS

1. *Lenin-Krupskaia-Ul'ianovy, perepiska*, 8.

2. Quoted from V. Veresaev, *Sobranie sochineniia v piati tomakh*, 5 vols. (Moscow: Pravda, 1961), 5:196. The quotation is in A. I. Ivanskii, ed., *Zhizn' kak fakel* (Moscow: Izd-vo politicheskoi literatury, 1966), 136, hereafter cited as Ivanskii. The translation is mine. Ivanskii's large and valuable collection is available in a smaller edition, in English: Anatoly Ivansky, ed., *Comet in the Night* (Honolulu: Univ. Press of the Pacific, 2005).

3. V. R. Leikina-Svirskaia, *Intelligentsiia v Rossii vo vtoroi polovine XIX veka* (Moscow: Mysl', 1971), 58. M. G. Shtein gives these figures for 1883: 2,240 total students, of which 1,102 were in the physical-mathematical sciences. See Shtein, "Aleksandr Ul'ianov—student S.-Peterburgskogo universiteta," *Vestnik Sankt-Peterburgskogo universiteta*, seriia 2, *Istoriia, iazykoznanie, literaturovedenie*, no. 3 (2005): 53.

4. *Lenin-Krupskaia-Ul'ianovy, perepiska*, 11–12.

5. See my article "Aleksandr Ul'ianov: Darwinian Terrorist," *Russian History/Histoire Russe* 35, nos. 1–2 (Spring–Summer 2008): 139–56. For deep background, see James Allen Rogers, "The Reception of Darwin's *Origin of Species* by Russian Scientists," *Isis* 64, no. 4 (1973): 483–504; Alexander Vucinich, *Science in Russian Culture, 1861–1917* (Stanford: Stanford Univ. Press, 1970); Alexander Vucinich, *Darwin in Russian Thought* (Berkeley: Univ. of California Press, 1988); Daniel P. Todes, *Darwin without Malthus: The Struggle for Existence in Russian Evolutionary Thought* (New York: Oxford Univ. Press, 1989).

6. Vucinich, *Darwin in Russian Thought*, 77.

7. *Aleksandr Il'ich Ul'ianov i delo 1 Marta 1887 g.*, 213.

8. *Lenin-Krupskaia-Ul'ianovy, perepiska*, 13–15. The correct name is V. I. Semevskii.

9. Quoted in P. A. Zaionchkovskii, *Rossiiskoe samoderzhavie v kontse XIX stoletiia* (Moscow: Izd. Mysl', 1970), 310.

10. RGASPI, Fond 11, opis' 3, delo 18. The report is dated June 15, 1887, and includes Delyanov's comments. Much of the preceding account of the institutional changes and counterreforms is from Zaionchkovskii, chap. 7, cited in the preceding note. For information on the Cossack circle, see V. P. Krikunov, *A. I. Ul'ianov i revoliutsionnye raznochintsy Dona i Severnogo Kavkaza* (Nal'chik: Kabardino-Balkarskoe knizh-noe izd-vo, 1963).

11. *Aleksandr Il'ich Ul'ianov i delo 1 Marta 1887 g.*, 73.

12. Ibid., 239–40.

13. This fascinating story is told in Richard Pipes, *The Degaev Affair* (New Haven: Yale Univ. Press, 2003).

14. Ibid., 104–5.

15. The students' landlords and landladies were obliged by a law of December 1883 to assist the police, as well as to keep track of their lessees, and to instruct their custodians to do the same. The doormen (*dvorniki*) were not actual employees of the police, but they did get some small rewards when they worked in institutions that especially concerned the police. See Jonathan W. Daly, *Autocracy under Siege* (DeKalb: Northern Illinois Univ. Press, 1998), 71.

16. S. Maiskii, "Chernyi cabinet," *Byloe*, no. 13, kn. 7 (July 1918): 185–87.

17. *Lenin-Krupskaia-Ul'ianovy, perepiska*, 17.

18. Ivanskii, 168–69.

SIX: PLOTTERS

1. My translation, from Philip Pomper, *Sergei Nechaev* (New Brunswick, NJ: Rutgers Univ. Press, 1979), 90.

2. In a letter to Vera Zasulich of March 8, 1881, replying to hers of February 16, 1881, Marx wrote, "The analysis presented in *Kapital* ... does not adduce reasons either for or against the viability of the Russian commune. However, focused investigations, which I conducted on the basis of materials drawn from primary sources, convinced me that this

commune can be a foothold for Russia's social rebirth, but it seems to me that in order to function as such, it is necessary above all to get rid of the pernicious influences to which it is subjected from all sides, and then to ensure it normal conditions for free development." *K. Marks, F. Engel's i revoliutsionnaia Rossiia* (Moscow: Izd-vo politicheskoi literatury, 1967), 443–44. My translation from the Russian. For Zasulich's letter to Marx see ibid., 434–35.

In a preface to an 1882 Russian edition of *The Manifesto of the Communist Party*, Marx and Engels wrote, "Can the Russian *obshchina* [village commune], though greatly undermined, yet a form of the primeval common ownership of land, pass directly to the higher form of communist common ownership? Or, on the contrary, must it first pass through the same process of dissolution as constitutes the historical evolution of the West?

The only answer to that possible today is this: If the Russian Revolution becomes the signal for a proletarian revolution in the West, so that both complement each other, the present Russian common ownership of land may serve as the starting-point for a communist development." *Marx-Engels Reader*, ed. Robert C. Tucker, 2d ed. (New York: W. W. Norton, 1978), 47.

3. My translation, from Karl Marx, *Das Kapital.* ed. Karl Kautsky (Stuttgart: J. H. W. Dietz, 1914), 1:688.

4. Orest Govorukhin, already inclined toward the Marxian end of the doctrinal spectrum, observed in his memoirs that Lavrov still captivated radical students, who avidly awaited his response to Plekhanov's vitriolic attacks on the *narodnik* faith. As Govorukhin pointed out, the students started with ethics and then moved to economic and social questions. "Pokushenie na imperatora Aleksandr III: Vospominaniia O. M. Govorukhina," *Golos minuvshego na chuzhoi storone*, no. 3/16 (1926): 220. Govorukhin's memoirs cannot be completely trusted, as Anna's annotations in the collection under her editorship suggest. For example, Govorukhin contradicts himself (having written that Ulyanov did not get involved in radicalism in his junior year) by claiming that Ulyanov formed his own group for the study of Russian history early in 1885. He also claimed that this circle was "the most active and influential circle in the entire city." Ibid., 227. No doubt Govorukhin had in mind the Economics Circle, which Sasha joined in 1886.

5. For scholarly works in English on the terrorist networks of the 1880s that include material on the Second March First, see Norman M. Naimark, *Terrorists and Social Democrats: The Russian Revolutionary Movement under Alexander III*. Russian Research Center Studies 82 (Cambridge: Harvard Univ. Press, 1983), hereafter cited as Naimark; Derek Offord, *The Russian Revolutionary Movement in the 1880s* (New York: Cambridge Univ. Press, 1986); James D. White, "'No, We Won't Go That Way; That Is Not the Way to Take,'" *Revolutionary Russia* 11, no. 2 (1998): 82–110, hereafter cited as White. Anyone who has researched the Second March First in depth is aware of the errors of detail that creep into these more general works, but also appreciates their ability to put the conspiracy into a larger context. Naimark, Offord, and White show how nationalism, terrorism, and Marxism operated together in student circles and created a complex doctrinal mix whose ingredients began to separate as Marxism grew stronger. The works of Krikunov, Itenberg and Cherniak, Naimark, and White taken together present a complicated picture of connections among circles from Russia, the northern Caucasus, eastern and southern Ukraina, Lithuania, and Poland, and St. Petersburg, Moscow, Tula, Kharkiv, Vilnius, and other cities. The collaboration of intelligentsia, military, labor, ethnic-minority, and Cossack recruits suggests how rich and varied the revolutionary movement had become by the 1880s.

6. Sergei Nikonov in his memoirs wrote that he brought Sasha into the Economics Circle "at the end of 1885 or the beginning of 1886." *Aleksandr Il'ich Ul'ianov i delo 1 Marta 1887 g.,* 137. One of the most careful students of Ul'ianov's student career claims that Sasha began attending meetings of the circle only in autumn 1886. See M. G. Shtein, "Aleksandr Ul'ianov—student S.-Peterburgskogo universiteta," *Vestnik Sankt-Peterburgskogo universiteta,* seriia 2, *Istoriia, iazykoznanie, literaturovedenie,* no. 3 (2005): 55. In any case, it seems more likely that Sasha did not get involved until sometime in 1886, after he had completed his thesis and after the death of Ilya Nikolaevich. Shtein's account of the library records of Ulyanov's reading in both St. Petersburg University's libraries and the Public Library (based on the work of P. A. Kazakevich) shows that, among other things, in the period April 5 to December 3, 1886, Ulyanov borrowed Adam Smith's

Inquiry into the Nature and Causes of the Wealth of Nations and John Stuart Mill's *Principles of Political Economy*. This suggests the influence of the economics circle. On the other hand, Anna claims in her memoirs that she saw books on history and political science, and possibly *Das Kapital*, in Sasha's room during the spring and summer of 1885. *Aleksandr Il'ich Ul'ianov i delo 1 Marta 1887 g.*, 77.

The police had begun to follow Ulyanov closely in 1886, even before the events of November 17, especially in connection with his membership in the Scientific-Literary Society and then his elevation to the secretariat of the society. In a police report of September 3, 1886–June 15, 1887, the Scientific-Literary Society is singled out as a center of sedition, and Ulyanov's political plotting is highlighted. According to Shtein, Ulyanov was elected to the Scientific-Literary Society on October 2, 1886, and elected its secretary a week later. Shtein, "Aleksandr Ul'ianov—student S.-Peterburgskogo universiteta," 57. Other members of Sasha's biology circle also joined in the autumn of 1886. *Aleksandr Il'ich Ul'ianov i delo 1 Marta 1887 g.*, 244.

7. *Aleksandr Il'ich Ul'ianov i delo 1 Marta 1887 g.*, 241.

8. Ibid., 215.

9. *Lenin-Krupskaia-Ul'ianovy, perepiska*, 28; *Aleksandr Il'ich Ul'ianov i delo 1 Marta 1887 g.*, 85, 241. Not only Chebotarev but also Govorukhin showed concern about Sasha's desperate mood. Anna refuted Govorukhin's claim: "His grief was so powerful, that his sister and close acquaintances feared that he would commit suicide." Ibid., 214. Anna wrote in a footnote to Govorukhin's statement, "It's completely false with respect to suicide." Ibid., 214 n. 1.

10. *Lenin-Krupskaia-Ul'ianovy, perepiska*, 31.

11. *Aleksandr Il'ich Ul'ianov i delo 1 Marta 1887 g.*, 100.

12. One of Marx's earliest works (1843–44), the critique of Hegel was first translated by a *narodnik*, B. I. Reinshtein and published in Geneva, Switzerland, with a preface by P. L. Lavrov dated October 22, 1887. See P. L. Lavrov, *Filosofiia i sotsiologiia, izbrannye proizvedeniia v dvukh tomakh*, ed. A F. Okulov, 2 vols. (Moscow: Izd—vo sotsial'no-ekonomicheskoi literatury "Mysl'", 1965), 2:683. Lavrov's article is ibid., 583–613. Anna mentioned in her memoirs that Sasha and Govorukhin collaborated on a translation of one of Marx's articles from the *Deutsch-Französische Jahrbücher*. See *Aleksandr Il'ich Ul'ianov*

i delo 1 Marta 1887 g., 107–8. It fell to her to correct their numerous errors. An unverified claim that Sasha rather than Reinshtein was the translator of Marx's critique of Hegel published with Lavrov's preface is given credence in White, 99. The claim is made in earlier works. See also B. S. Itenberg and A. Ia. Cherniak, *Zhizn' Aleksandra Ul'ianova* (Moscow: Izd-vo Nauka, 1966), 119, 120 n. 4, hereafter cited as Itenberg and Cherniak. There was a strong tendency in the Soviet period to exaggerate the undeniable influence of Marxism on Ulyanov and to place him in the forefront of the movement toward Marxism; however, it is not certain that any of Sasha's translations made it into print.

13. *Aleksandr Il'ich Ul'ianov i delo 1 Marta 1887 g.,* 244.

14. Ibid., 156–57.

15. Ibid., 157–58.

16. From Govorukhin's memoirs, *Aleksandr Il'ich Ul'ianov i delo 1 Marta 1887 g.,* 225. The main sources for information on Shevyrev are Govorukhin's and Lukashevich's memoirs and the testimony of Shevyrev's older brother at the trial in April 1887. See also N. A. Rudevich's letter to P. L. Lavrov, undated but written in 1887 after the trial and execution, in *Lavrov, gody emigratsii,* ed. Boris Sapir, Russian Series on Social History, 2 vols. (Dordrecht-Holland: D. Reidel, 1974), 2:202–3, hereafter cited as *Lavrov, gody emigratsii,* 2; I. D. Lukashevich, *1 Marta 1887 goda, vospominaniia I. D. Lukashevicha* (St. Petersburg: Gos. Izd-vo, 1920), hereafter cited as Lukashevich.

17. Shevyrev's older brother Nicholas's testimony is the main source for information about Peter's health. See *Pervoe Marta 1887 goda,* 212–16.

18. Ibid.

19. *Aleksandr Il'ich Ul'ianov i delo 1 Marta 1887 g.,* 232.

20. White, 88. White, who uses "Łukasiewicz" (the Polish spelling rather than the transliteration from the Cyrillic used throughout this book), found sources averring that Łukasiewicz's family had participated in the Polish rebellion of 1863, in which he lost two uncles and had another exiled to Siberia. In his post-Schlüsselburg memoirs Lukashevich does not mention this. Anna Ulyanova-Elizarova in her introduction to Lukashevich's memoirs claimed that he was Lithuanian rather than Polish. The surname, however, is distinctly Polish. Perhaps

Ulyanova-Elizarova meant that he was an ethnic Pole born in Lithuania. See *Aleksandr Il'ich Ul'ianov i delo 1 Marta 1887 g.*, 183.

21. Lukashevich, 11.

22. Ibid., 12–13, 15–18, 20, 32–33.

23. Ibid., 6–7.

24. Ibid., 8–9. See also A. I. Spiridovich, *Histoire du terrorisme russe, 1886–1917* (Paris: Editions Payot, 1930), 13, hereafter cited as Spiridovich. Spiridovich relied on Lukashevich's memoirs, but added the date of the planned attempt on Alexander III's life. He did not, however, name the person.

25. Lukashevich, 44.

26. Ibid., 11.

27. Ibid., 13. The group knew, for example, that the tsar planned to travel south shortly after March 1, and that this might be their last opportunity for months. Of course, the wish to dramatize the event by killing the tsar on the anniversary of his father's assassination and the wish to take advantage of the requiem mass planned on March 1 were important considerations.

28. According to N. N. Shebekov's *Chronique du mouvement socialiste en Russie, 1878–1887* (St. Petersburg: Imprimerie officielle du Ministère de l'intérieur, 1890), the group had been formed by mid-December, and the assassination of the tsar on March 1 decided upon by the end of December. Shebekov, 637.

29. O. M. Govorukhin, "Vospominaniia o terroristicheskoi gruppe A. I. Ul'ianova," *Oktiabr'* 1927, no. 4 (April): 148.

30. *Aleksandr Il'ich Ul'ianov i delo 1 Marta 1887 g.*, 146–47.

31. There are several descriptions of November 17, 1866, in the memoirs, including those of M. A. Braginskii, "Dobroliubovskaia demonstratsiia (17 XI 1886 g.)," *Byloe* 5 (1907): 306–9, and "Aleksandr Il'ich Ul'ianov (Iz lichnykh vospominanii)," *Katorga i ssylka*, no. 32 (1927): 50–51; in *Aleksandr Il'ich Ul'ianov i delo 1 Marta 1887 g.*, Anna Ul'ianova-Elizarova, 101–3; Govorukhin, 216–17; Chebotarev, 246–47. Anna may have excluded Shmidova from the collection of memoirs published in 1927 for reasons adduced above, so the latter had to find a different venue. See Shmidova, "1 Marta 1887 goda," 61. See also Lukashevich, 10.

32. *Aleksandr Il'ich Ul'ianov i delo 1 Marta 1887 g.*, 106.

33. *Pervoe Marta 1887 g.*, 381.
34. *Aleksandr Il'ich Ul'ianov i delo 1 Marta 1887 g.*, 247. In her memoirs Anna claims that they were warned not to stick all of the proclamations into the same postal boxes, but that out of haste she herself ignored the warning. Ibid., 107. For more details on the distribution of the proclamation, see Itenberg and Cherniak, 109–10.
35. *Aleksandr Il'ich Ul'ianov i delo 1 Marta 1887 g.*, 225–27.
36. Ibid., 228.
37. V. G. Belinskii, letters to V. P. Botkin, June 27–28 and September 8, 1841, in *Sobranie sochinenii*, 9 vols. (Moscow: Khudozhestvennaia literatura, 1982), 9:468–69, 484. The translation is mine.

SEVEN: BOMBS, HEARTS, AND IDEAS

1. O. M. Govorukhin, "Vospominaniia o terroristicheskoi gruppe A. I. Ul'ianova," *Oktiabr'* 1927, no. 4 (April): 154, hereafter cited as Govorukhin, "Vospominaniia o terroristicheskoi gruppe A. I. Ul'ianova." See also *Lavrov, gody emigratsii*, 2:173; *Aleksandr Il'ich Ul'ianov i delo 1 Marta 1887 g.*, 221–22.
2. Govorukhin, "Vospominaniia o terroristicheskoi gruppe A. I. Ul'ianova," 148–49.
3. Jonathan W. Daly, *Autocracy under Siege* (De Kalb: Northern Illinois Univ. Press, 1998), 42–43.
4. *Pervoe Marta 1887 g.*, 361. Appendix 1 of the stenographic account of the trial contains the letter to Nikitin. See also "Okhrannik ob areste uchastnikov 1 Marta 1887 g.," *Krasnyi arkhiv*, no. 9 (1925): 297–99. Evidently Nikitin was part of the network that included Nathan Bogoraz. Andreyushkin used him as a link. See Naimark, 275 n. 48.
5. *Pervoe Marta 1887 g.*, 146–47; *Obzor vazhneishikh doznanii po delam o gosudarstvennykh prestupleniiakh; Vedomost' doznaniiam, proizvodivshimsia v Zhandarmskikh Upravleniiakh Imperii. 1 June 1881–1 Jan. 1895*, 18 vols. (1887), 12:79, hereafter cited as *OVD*.
6. *Pervoe Marta 1887 g.*, 80, 144.
7. Ibid., 145. See also ibid., 82.
8. Ibid., 145.
9. Ibid., 37. The narrative of the Serdyukova–Andreyushkin correspondence is a reconstruction of the likely sequence of events. The court

reporter's summary of the prosecutor's case, drawn largely from the depositions, said the following: "14 February he sent her a letter, in whose visible text he proposed marriage and asked for a quick response ... and in invisible ink [the statement about the assassination quoted in the text]." Ibid., 37–38. In her trial testimony, Serdyukova claimed that she rejected his marriage proposal, but carried the letter of February 14 in her pocket for several days. "Still, I didn't want to believe what he had written. I took the letter and reread it and then on a clean white page appeared the words [quoted in the text]." Ibid., 145. This is hardly credible. It suggests that the chemicals in the invisible ink had been activated while in her pocket! She probably immediately looked for the hidden message using the usual method—holding it above a kerosene lamp. It is not clear why she didn't send the telegram until March 6. The fact that she sent it at all is surprising. How could a networked revolutionary not know about the events of March 1 before March 6? Was it an elaborate charade? Or did Andreyushkin's marriage proposal put her in a strange state of mind, as she claims in her testimony?

10. GARF, Fond 112, opis' 1, ed. kh. 648(2), list 72.

11. *Pervoe Marta 1887 g.,* 143.

12. Ibid., 155. Ulyanov had indeed been under observation. See GARF, Fond 102, opis' 1886, ed. kh. 647, list 4. This report of December 1886 from the office of the St. Petersburg chief of police mentions Ulyanov's connections with the circle of Don and Kuban Cossacks and his role as cosecretary of the Scientific-Literary Society. He is characterized as politically suspicious.

13. *Aleksandr Il'ich Ul'ianov i delo 1 Marta 1887 g.,* 233. I have translated *tupost'* as "dullness," which in English, as in Russian, connotes stupidity. Generalov, however, showed a high level of intelligence in his depositions and trial testimony. The earlier remarks about the seemingly therapeutic effect of bomb making for Generalov and Andreyushkin are based on a letter from Govorukhin to Peter Lavrov and the Paris group of *narodovol'tsy. Lavrov, gody emigratsii,* 2:176. According to Boris Sapir's dating, the letter was written in 1887 before May 13.

14. *Pervoe Marta 1887 g.,* 72.

15. *Lavrov, gody emigratsii,* 2:199.

16. Ibid., 200-201.

17. Ibid., 200.
18. *Pervoe Marta 1887 goda*, 43.
19. Naimark, 216–18. Dembo and a comrade in exile had carried the bomb up a Swiss mountain for testing, but it had exploded at Dembo's feet. Dembo lived for a day, long enough to show his defiance to the Swiss police. See also White, 91–94.
20. Lukashevich, 14–18. Mikhail Kheifets provides details about the role of Valerii Agafanov, a student of the natural sciences in Sasha's year who became the intermediary with Novorussky, but escaped detection. Kheifets, 268–69.
21. *Pervoe Marta 1887 g.*, 150–51.
22. Ibid., 93.
23. Lukashevich, 15.
24. Ibid., 19–20. Mikhail Kheifets believes that Shevyrev's departure decided Sasha's fate. "Precisely Shevyrev's departure became the cause of Sasha's death." Kheifets, 270. Sasha's sense of responsibility to the group, however, was the deeper cause. During the trial when asked why he didn't emigrate, Ulyanov replied, "I didn't want to run away; I wanted to die for my homeland." Quoted in Itenberg and Cherniak, 138.
25. Lukashevich, 18.
26. *Pervoe Marta 1887 g.*, 90, 156–59; Shmidova, "1 Marta 1887 goda," 64.
27. The laconic testimony of one of the police spies fixes the date of the meeting of the bomb throwers as February 21. *Pervoe Marta 1887 g.*, 145–46. Other accounts are vague. Lukashevich claimed that he set up the meeting (Lukashevich, 20), but gives no date. The meeting began in the café on Mikhailovskaya Street, but Osipanov, Generalov, and Andreyushkin left the café and walked to Vasilevsky Island. Generalov claims that they walked along the embankment, but the police spy claims that they walked along Bolshoi Prospect, in the area of the university. For Generalov's account see *Pervoe Marta 1887 goda*, 70, 74–75; for Andreyushkin's, ibid., 84; for the police spy's, ibid., 146–47. Generalov testified that they met on February 21 or 22. Andreyushkin's somewhat confusing account suggests that the throwers met on February 20 and February 21. Osipanov sets the date as February 20.

As for the farewell party, Lukashevich mentions Sasha as the inspi-

ration. Lukashevich, 21. See also Shmidova, "1 Marta 1887 goda," 64. Perhaps Ulyanov knew that he was following the precedent of the People's Will in something close to reckless abandon. At a New Year's Eve party ushering in 1881, the future assassins had held a rousing party in which they danced through the night and drank to the death of tyrants. See David Footman, *Red Prelude* (New Haven: Yale Univ. Press, 1945), 172–73. In both cases some of the partygoers were celebrating their own death and singing—sometimes drunkenly—funeral hymns. Alexander Mikhailov, one of the master organizers of the assassination of Alexander II, was also the spirit behind the merrymaking. He once bought a spacious box for the Executive Committee of the People's Will for a performance at the Alexandrovsky Theater. The tsar's loge was nearby. Kheifets, 271.

28. RGASPI, Fond 12, opis' 1, ed. kh. 155, list 85. Sasha's remarks about the reasons for the program and his role in its formulation make clear how highly he valued his intellectual contribution in comparison with his other work. See his prefatory remarks to the program: *Pervoe Marta 1887 g.*, 372–73.

29. *Pervoe Marta 1887 g.*, 373.

30. Ibid., 374–75. Lukashevich claimed in his memoirs that Shevyrev and he had envisioned a workers' combat squad and had already picked out its main organizer. See Lukashevich, 13. Even more important for claims about Ulyanov's connection to factory workers is M. Dranitsyn, "Obryvki vospominanii ob Aleksandre Il'iche Ul'ianove," *Aleksandr Il'ich Ul'ianov i delo 1 Marta 1887 g.*, 258–59. See also Itenberg and Cherniak, 118–21. One version has it that the planned worker and intelligentsia-worker groups had designated leaders, but had never fully formed, and one of the leaders—Sergei Nikonov—was arrested in January. See Kheifets, 267. The thin evidence does not suggest that Lukashevich, Shevyrev, and Ulyanov ever formed a workers' combat group or put into practice Ulyanov's notion (according to Dranitsyn) of controlling a network of workers' groups on Vasilevsky Island. Soviet Marxism shaped, at least to some extent, the narratives of both memoirists and historians.

31. Michel Bakounine, *Oeuvres*, ed. James Guillaume, 6 vols. (Paris: P. V. Stock, 1910), 4:382–83. The letter was published in 1894 in *Société Nouvelles*. The translation is mine.

32. Generalov had recruited one of his friends, a Cossack member of the tsar's escort, Stepan Yefremov, who passed the information about the plans for Tsar Day to him. Evidently, it was an open secret because a great many people had gathered at St. Isaac's in anticipation of the tsar's appearance. Kheifets, 271. See also Lukashevich, 22.

33. In his memoirs Lukashevich attributed the failure of the plot to Andreyushkin's indiscreet correspondence and the increased surveillance leading to identification of the three throwers, but only after they gathered at a café on March 1 (Lukashevich, 38). Lukashevich didn't identify the letter to Nikitin as the problem, but another letter intercepted in the black office, this one to Nathan ("Tan") Bogoraz. He and Boris Orzhikh were trying to revive the People's Will in the south, but maintained ties with St. Petersburg revolutionary circles, including the Don and Kuban *zemliachestvo* (Naimark, 102–3). Their frail and, ultimately, doomed network, however, did not have a strong connection with the Second March First (Naimark, 197–210). A third version has Andreyushkin's letters to Serdyukova as the tip-off (White, 102), but the black office did not intercept his letters to her. The security agencies learned about them only after they intercepted her telegram of March 6 accepting his marriage proposal, and then arrested and interrogated her. Andreyushkin had a letter obviously meant for Serdyukova in his possession when they arrested him. In the prosecutor's case the letter to Nikitin is named as the reason for putting Andreyushkin under close surveillance. For the relevant police documents, see *Pervoe Marta 1887 g.*, 361–62.

34. *Pervoe Marta 1887 g.*, 148.

35. Ibid., 147.

36. Generalov's apartment was on Bolshaya Belozerskaya Street on the Petersburg side, and they had to cross the Neva (probably from Vasilevsky Island) to get to Nevsky Prospect. If they left at about 10:30 a.m., as the police spies testified, then they would have had to walk briskly in order to be in the right area to intercept the tsar's equipage before it crossed the river to the Peter and Paul Fortress at roughly 11:00 a.m. The police grabbed them not far from Senate Square, at the intersection of Nevsky Prospect and Admiralty Square, so they probably had just crossed from Vasilevsky Island.

37. *Pervoe Marta 1887 g.*, 148–49, 371.

38. Lukashevich, 22, 30–33.
39. Ibid., 34.

EIGHT: THE TRIAL

1. Soviet historians tried to condemn the entire trial, including the efforts of the defense lawyers, but the premier student of Russian political trials of this period dismissed the accusation that the defense lawyers offered only a passive defense. See N. A. Troitskii, *Advokatura v Rossii i politicheskie protsessy 1866–1904 gg.* (Tula: Avtograf, 2000), 310, hereafter cited as Troitskii, *Advokatura v Rossii*. A. N. Turchannikov's defense tactics are discussed below.

2. Quoted in N. A. Troitskii, *Politicheskie protsessy v Rossii, 1871–1887 gg.* (Saratov: Izd-vo saratovskogo universiteta, 2003), 122, hereafter cited as Troitskii, *Politicheskie protsessy*.

3. "K istorii pokusheniia A. I. Ul'ianova i dr. 1 Marta 1887 g.," *Krasnyi arkhiv*, no. 2/15 (1926): 222–23; "Okhrannik ob areste uchastnikov 1 Marta 1887 goda," *Krasnyi arkhiv*, no. 9 (1925): 297–99.

4. *Aleksandr Il'ich Ul'ianov i delo 1 Marta 1887 g.*, 360.

5. Troitskii, *Politicheskie protsessy*, 124.

6. See Troitskii, *Advokatura v Rossii*, 170; see also Kheifets, 279. The sum of two thousand rubles is alleged in A. F. Koni's memoirs. The liberal Koni was one of Russia's most distinguished jurists.

7. P. A. Zaionchkovskii, *Rossiiskoe samoderzhavie v kontse XIX stoletiia* (Moscow: Izd. Mysl', 1970), 105–6, also quoting the memoirs of A. F. Koni.

8. Lukashevich, 39. As mentioned earlier, Shmidova adds the detail that when the prisoners were led from the prison, their guards searched everywhere but in the prisoners' mouths. She passed notes by writing messages in pencil on narrow strips of paper rolled into tiny scrolls and wrapped in foil. She would hold them in her mouth and pass them to Ulyanov when they kissed in the corridor on the way to the courtroom. Shmidova, "1 Marta 1887 goda," 65.

9. The reporter erroneously described all three of the missiles as book bombs. See *Obshchee Delo*, no. 97 (May 1887): 10.

10. Lukashevich, 29.

11. RGASPI, Fond 11, op. 3, ed. khr. 17, list 23. Anton Ostroumov, arrested

in 1886 in Taganrog in connection with a secret printing press, offered to cooperate with the police.

12. RGASPI, Fond 11, op. 3, ed. khr. 17, list 3. This was in Count Tolstoy's report of April 10, 1887. Novorussky declined the services of defense attorneys and conducted his own defense.

13. For Pobedonostsev's influence, see Kheifets, 277. Tolstoy confided Ostroumov's opinion to the tsar, for whatever it was worth in view of its source, that Novorussky was amoral, Jesuitical, and a scoundrel. By tapping in code Ostroumov was able to communicate not only with Novorussky and Arsenii Khlebnikov but with the latter's younger brother Semyon, who was in a cell two floors below Ostroumov's. The brothers Khlebnikov were members of the circle of the Don and Kuban Cossacks. Ostroumov winkled out of Arsenii Khlebnikov his role in the transport of materials for explosives and the identities of other members of the circle of the Don and Kuban connected to the plot. RGASPI, Fond 11, op. 3, ed. khr. 17, listy 1–10.

14. The police account suggests that terrorists in Kharkiv were trying to regroup after the destruction of their circle by arrests in 1886. *OVD* (1887), 11:79. Shmidova in her memoirs mentions that she accompanied Brazhnikov, the main figure in this effort, to the railway station. She had given Brazhnikov copies of a version of Ulyanov's program in hectographed form in his handwriting, but retained one copy in her pocket. Detectives arrested her at the railway station, but before they searched her she managed to nudge the copy into the narrow space between an adjacent desk and a cupboard in the police station without anyone's seeing her. Evidently, it remained there for an indefinite period without anyone's noticing it. See Shmidova, "1 Marta 1887 goda," 63.

15. At the trial Lukashevich seized upon the fact of the missing string and Fyodorov's diagnosis. If the strings were defective and the fuses nonfunctional, Lukashevich reasoned illogically to the court, "Then it's a completely different matter; there's no *mens rea*, no attempt, only the intention." *Pervoe Marta 1887 g.*, 151. In his memoirs written decades later, in defense of his bomb making, Lukashevich claimed that the fuses had worked during practice sessions in St. Petersburg and that the dynamite and mercury fulminate had been successfully tested in Vilnius.

16. Footman, *Red Prelude*, 222. Fyodorov and other expert witnesses at

the Trial of the Six had opined that in view of its potency, the dynamite must have been imported. Kibalchich claimed that he had gotten the necessary information from the *Russian Artillery Journal* of August 1878.

17. *Pervoe Marta 1887 g.*, 233.

18. Ibid., 240.

19. Ibid., 283.

20. P. L. Lavrov, *Izbrannye sochineniia na sotsial'no-politicheskie temy*, ed. I. S. Knizhnik-Vetrov, 4 vols. (Moscow: Izd-vo vsesoiuznogo ob-vo politkatorzhan i ssyl'no poselentsev, 1935), 4:41, hereafter cited as Lavrov, *Izbrannye sochineniia*.

21. Troitskii, *Advokatura v Rossii*, 406, quoting Lavrov, my translation.

22. Lavrov, *Izbrannye sochineniia*, 4:43.

23. *Pervoe Marta 1887 g.*, 290.

24. Ibid.

25. Ibid., 292.

26. Ivanskii, 463. The excerpt published in Ivanskii is from N. S. Tagantsev, *Perezhitoe*, 2 vols. (St. Petersburg: Gos. tipografiia, 1919), 2:32, my translation.

27. Lukashevich, 22.

28. Shtein, *Ul'ianovy i Leniny*, 311.

29. *Aleksandr Il'ich Ul'ianov i delo 1 Marta 1887 g.*, 375.

30. RGASPI, Fond 12, opis' 1, delo 155, listy 84–85.

31. Quoted in Shtein, *Ul'ianovy i Leniny*, 294.

32. Ibid., 292–93. For a good, earlier investigation of the efforts on Sasha's behalf, see Zhores Trofimov, *Starshii brat Il'icha* (Moscow: Sovetskaia Rossiia, 1988), 186–95.

33. RGASPI, Fond 12, opis' 1, delo 155, list 158.

34. Ibid., 160.

35. For Anna's arrest and the disposition of her case, see Shtein, *Ul'ianovy i Leniny*, 317–21. Anna and Sasha contradicted each other in their testimony, and things might have gone quite badly without Peskovsky's legal advice, Maria Alexandrovna's petitions, and Anna's letter to the tsar. Anna was implicated as a collaborator in the procurement of the explosives. Dmitry Tolstoy initially recommended that she be sent under police surveillance to eastern Siberia for five years; the minister of justice, N. A. Manasyein, concurred. See RGASPI, Fond 11, opis' 3,

delo 18, list 58. Anna petitioned the tsar for mercy. She claimed that she seldom visited her brother and his circle of friends and thus suspected nothing. See ibid., lista 81–82. Remarkably, Anna's narrative of 1927 about her immediate thoughts after learning about Sasha's arrest on the evening of March 1 in her memoirs supports this. She claimed to be ignorant of Sasha's involvement with a revolutionary conspiracy in 1887.

36. Anna's account is reconstructed from Maria Alexandrovna's and from the memoirs of the procurator, Kniazev, who witnessed this meeting. *Aleksandr Il'ich Ul'ianov i delo 1 Marta 1887 g.,* 123, 124–125 n. 4.

37. Ibid., 123.

38. Ibid., 124.

39. Ibid., 125. Anna mentions here that Maria Alexandrovna had heard rumors that Sasha might be pardoned, but thought it unwise to tell Sasha.

40. Shtein, *Ul'ianovy i Leniny,* 299–302; Zhores Trofimov, *Starshii brat Il'icha* (Moscow: Sovetskaia Rossia, 1988), 190–92. Deyer did appoint a barrister, V. I. Leontyev, for Ulyanov's use, if the latter decided to go through the procedure to avail himself of the court-appointed defender.

41. RGASPI, Fond 11, opis' 3, ed. khr. 15, list 23.

42. RGASPI, Fond 11, opis' 3, delo 18, listy 73–75. Maria Alexandrovna also sent a letter to the tsarina, begging on behalf of Anna. In the letter Maria Alexandrovna reports that Anna is engaged [to Mark Elizarov], and asks that this be taken into account, as well as the fate of the four younger children. This document in the family archives in RGASPI is copied from Tsentral'nyi gosudarstvennyi istoricheskii arkhiv SSSR v Leningrade, fond 1405, op. 88, 1887 g., delo 9961, lista 216–17. See also Shtein, *Ul'ianovy i Leniny,* 318–20.

43. Shtein, *Ul'ianovy i Leniny,* 316.

44. *Obshchee delo,* no. 95 (March 1887): 2.

45. "Seven [*sic*] Nihilists to Be Hung," *Washington Post,* May 5, 1887.

46. "Girls Flogged to Insensibility," *Washington Post,* March 19, 1887; "Nihilists on Trial," *Los Angeles Times,* April 29, 1887.

47. The article was based partly on information provided by the *Daily News* correspondent. There were also mistakes, but despite its relative brevity the account in *Free Russia* is surprisingly detailed. For exam-

ple, it reported that during the trial Generalov had to be removed from the court several times because he made fun of the proceedings and refused to answer questions. This could not be inferred from the stenographic account. See "Khronika bor'ba s samoderzhaviem," *Svobodnaia Rossiia*, no. 1 (1889): 59–60.

48. Undated letter in RGASPI Fond 11, opis' 3, delo 19, list 4.

NINE: THE ULYANOV BROTHERS AND HISTORY'S REVENGE

1. M. I. Ul'ianova, *O V. I. Lenine i sem'e Ul'ianovykh* (Moscow: Izd-vo politicheskoi literatury, 1989), 36 n. 1.
2. This follows the lines of analysis pursued in P. Pomper, "The Family Background of V. I. Ul'ianov's Pseudnonym, 'Lenin,'" *Russian History* 16, nos. 2–4 (1989): 209–22. See also P. Pomper, *Lenin, Trotsky, and Stalin: The Intelligentsia and Power* (New York: Columbia Univ. Press, 1990), chap. 3, hereafter cited as Pomper, *Lenin, Trotsky, and Stalin*.
3. Trotsky, *The Young Lenin*, trans. Max Eastman, ed. Maurice Friedburg (Garden City, NY: Doubleday, 1972), 70. Trotsky was unaware that Maria Alexandrovna bore a child in 1868, Olga, who died in early infancy.
4. Quoted in Pomper, *Lenin, Trotksy, and Stalin*, 11.
5. Quoted ibid., 23. The source is V. V. Kashkadamova, "Semeistvo V. I. Ul'ianova-Lenina v Simbirske," *Isvesten vsei Rossii, I. N. Ul'ianov*, ed. A. L. Karamyshev (Saratov: Privolzhskoe knizhnoe izd-vo, Ul'ianovskoe otdelenie, 1974), 293–94.
6. Trotsky, *The Young Lenin*, 113.
7. Quoted in Pomper, *Lenin, Trotsky, and Stalin*, 33.
8. Ibid., 27.
9. Ibid., 24.
10. *The Marx-Engels Reader*, ed. Robert C. Tucker, 2d ed. (New York: W. W. Norton, 1978), 594.

GLOSSARY OF RUSSIAN TERMS

Narod: The people, often connoting the peasantry in nineteenth-century Russia.

Narodnaya Volya: An underground revolutionary party, the People's Will, founded in 1879 by agrarian socialists who believed in the necessity of terror for the achievement of a Russian constitution. The assassination of Alexander II on March 1, 1881, was their signal achievement.

Narodnik (plural, **narodniki**): An exponent of peasant socialism, often a follower of one of several theorists with a strategic vision for achieving agrarian socialism. Sometimes translated as "populist."

Narodovoltsy: Members of the People's Will.

Narodnichestvo: The doctrine of Russian agrarian socialism.

Nigilistka: A woman nihilist, advocate, and practitioner of the culture of rebellion against tradition that emerged in the 1850s and continued for decades. Masculine: **nigilist**.

Pravda: The truth, but the word also connotes justice.

Rodina: One's native land or motherland, a very evocative word in Russian.

Tsar: The Russian autocrat; the emperor.

Zemlyachestvo (plural, **zemlyachestva**): a student aid society based on regional affiliation, often a cover for political activity in Russia's institutions of higher education.

Zemstvo: a quasi-democratic institution of local government founded during the period of Great Reforms under Alexander II and modified in a reactionary direction by Alexander III. It performed mainly health, education, and welfare functions. A fairly familiar term, it is often pluralized as "**zemstvos**."

SELECT BIBLIOGRAPHY

NOTE ON ARCHIVAL SOURCES CITED

The archives listed below are both in Moscow. The first listed is the State Archive of the Russian Federation (the Russian acronym is GARF); the second, the Russian State Archive of Socio-Political History (RGASPI). In GARF, I consulted police surveillance records (Fond 102) and the archive of the Senate tribunal that adjudicated state crimes (Osoboe prisutsvie pravitel'stvueshchego senata, or OPPS) and conducted the trial of the Second March First conspiracy. The OPPS archive (Fond 112) contains the stenographic account of the trial. I examined handwritten stenographic records on microfilm, especially those with Ulyanov's testimony, to verify the accuracy of the published version. In RGASPI, I consulted the Ulyanov family archives. To my knowledge, Raisa Shmidova's letters to Lenin and to Anna Ulyanova-Elizarova (in Fond 13, opis' 3, ed. kh. 223) have never been published, although in 1927 Anna published an abundance of important memoirs and other documents in *Aleksandr Il'ich Ul'ianov i delo 1 Marta 1887 g.* The stenographic account of the trial was also published in 1927 in *Pervoe Marta 1887 g.* These two anniversary publications, appearing forty years after Alexander Ulyanov was hanged, make life easier for biographers and students of the assassination attempt.

Below I list the archival sources actually cited in the endnotes rather than all of the materials I inspected.

Gosudarstvennyi Arkhiv Rossiiskoi Federatsii (GARF)
    Fond 102, opis' 1886, ed. kh. 100
    Fond 112, opis' 1, ed. kh.. 155, 647, 648, 855
Rossiiskii Gosudarstvennyi Arkhiv Sotsial'no Politicheskoi Istorii (RGASPI)
    Fond 11, opis' 3, ed. kh. 5, 10, 12, 13, 17, 18, 19, 20, 21, 22
    Fond 12, opis' 1, ed. kh. 155
    Fond 13, opis' 1, ed. kh. 223, 471
    Fond 14, opis' 1, ed. kh. 194

BOOKS

Akhankin, A., and K. F. Bogdanova, eds. *Lenin-Krupskaia-Ul'ianovy, perepiska (1883–1900)*. Moscow: Izd-vo Mysl', 1981.

Bakounine, Michel [Bakunin, Michael]. *Oeuvres.* Edited by James Guillaume. 6 vols. Paris: P. V. Stock, 1910.

Belinksii, V. G. *Sobranie sochinenii.* 9 vols. Moscow: Khudozhestvennaia literatura, 1982. Vol. 9.

Daly, Jonathan W. *Autocracy under Siege.* DeKalb: Northern Illinois Univ. Press, 1998.

Deiateli revoliutsionnogo dvizhenii v Rossii, vos'midesiatye gody. Edited by B. P. Koz'min et al. 5 vols. Moscow: Vsesoiuznoe ob-vo politkatorzhen i ssyl'no-poselentsev, 1927–34. Vol. 3.

Footman, David. *Red Prelude.* New Haven: Yale Univ. Press, 1945.

Graham, Loren R. *Science in Russia and the Soviet Union.* New York: Cambridge Univ. Press, 1993.

Ivanskii, A. I. *Zhizn' kak fakel'*, ed. Moscow: Izd-vo politicheskoi literatury, 1966.

Itenberg, B. S., and A. Ia. Cherniak. *Zhizn' Aleksandra Ul'ianova.* Moscow: Izd-vo Nauka, 1966.

Kanivets, V. *Aleksandr Ul'ianov.* Moscow: Izd-vo: Molodaia gvardia, 1961.

Kolosov, E. E. *Gosudareva Tiur'ma Shlissel'burg.* 2d ed. Moscow: Izd. Vsesoiuznogo obshchestva politkatorzhan i ssyl'no-posolenenstev, 1930.

Krikunov, V. P. *A. I. Ul'ianov i revoliutsionnye raznochintsy Dona i Sever-*

nogo Kavkaza. Nal'chik: Kabardino-Balkarskoe knizhnoe izd-vo, 1963.

Lavrov, P. L. *Filosofiia i sotsiologiia, izbrannye proizvedeniia v dvukh tomakh.* Edited by A. F. Okulov. 2 vols. Moscow: Izd-vo sotsial'no-ekonomicheskie literatury "Mysl'," 1965.

———. *Izbrannye sochineniia na sotsial'no-politicheskie temy.* Edited by I. S. Knizhnik-Vetrov. 4 vols. Moscow: Idz-vo vsesoiuznogo ob-vo polit-katorzhan i ssyl'no poselentsev, 1935.

Leikina-Svirskaia, V. R. *Intelligentsiia v Rossii vo vtoroi polovine XIX veka.* Moscow: Mysl', 1971.

Lincoln, W. Bruce. *Sunlight at Midnight: St. Petersburg and the Rise of Modern Russia.* New York: Basic Books, 2000.

Lukashevich, I. D. *1 Marta 1887 goda, vospominaniia I. D. Lukashevicha.* St. Petersburg: Gos. Izd-vo, 1920.

Marx, Karl. *Das Kapital.* Edited by Karl Kautsky. Stuttgart: J. H. W. Dietz, 1914.

Mazour, Anatole G. *The First Russian Revolution 1825: The Decembrist Movement, Its Origins, Development, and Significance.* Berkeley: Univ. of California Press, 1937.

Mogil'nikov, V. A. *Predki V. I. Ul'ianova-Lenina.* Edited by A. N. Opuchin. Perm: Izd. Assotsiatsii genealogov-liubitelei, 1995.

Naimark, Norman M. *Terrorists and Social Democrats: The Russian Revolutionary Movement under Alexander III.* Russian Research Center Studies 82. Cambridge: Harvard Univ. Press, 1983.

Obzor vazhneishikh doznanii po delam o gosudarstvennykh prestupleniakh: Vedomost' doznaniiam, proizvodivshimsia v Zhandarmskikh Upravleniiakh Imperii. 1 June 1881–1 Jan. 1895. 18 vols. (1887). Vol. 12.

Offord, Derek. *The Russian Revolutionary Movement in the 1880s.* New York: Cambridge Univ. Press, 1986.

Ocherki istorii Leningrada. Edited by M. P. Viatkin et al. 7 vols. Moscow: Izd-vo Akademii Nauk SSSR, 1957–89. Vol. 2.

Pervoe Marta 1887 g. Edited by A. A. Shilov. Moscow: Moskovskii rabochii, 1927.

Pipes, Richard. *The Degaev Affair.* New Haven: Yale Univ. Press, 2003.

Pisarev, D. I. *Izbrannye filosofskie i obshchestvenno-politicheskie stat'i.* Edited by V. S. Kruzhkova. Moscow: Gos. Izd-vo politicheskoi literatury, 1949.

Poliakov, A. S. *Vtoroe 1-e Marta*. Moscow: Izd. Zhurnal "Golos munu-vshego," 1919.

Pomper, Philip. *Peter Lavrov and the Russian Revolutionary Movement*. Chicago: Univ. of Chicago Press, 1972.

———. *The Russian Revolutionary Intelligentsia*. 2d ed. Wheeling, IL: Harlan Davidson, 1993.

———. *Sergei Nechaev*. New Brunswick, NJ: Rutgers Univ. Press, 1979.

Revoliutsionnoe narodnichestvo 70-kh godov XIX veka. Edited by S. S. Volk. 2 vols. Moscow: Izd-vo Nauka, 1965. Vol. 2.

Ruud, Charles A., and Sergei A. Stepanov. *Fontanka 16: The Tsars' Secret Police*. Montreal and Kingston: McGill-Queen's Univ. Press, 1999.

Sapir, Boris, ed. *Lavrov, gody emigratsii*. 2 vols. Dordrecht-Holland: D. Reidel, 1974.

Service, Robert. *Lenin: A Biography*. London: Macmillan, 2000.

Shebekov, N. N. *Chronique du movement socialiste en Russie, 1778–1887*. St. Petersburg: Imprimerie officielle du Ministère de l'intérieur, 1890.

Shtein, Mikhail G. *Ul'ianovy i Leniny, semeinye tainy*. St. Petersburg: Izd. Dom Neva, 2004.

Spiridovich, A. I. *Histoire du terrorisme russe, 1886–1917*. Paris: Editions Payot, 1930.

Sutyrin, V. A. *Aleksandr Ul'ianov*. Moscow: Politizdat, 1975.

Todes, Daniel P. *Darwin without Malthus: The Struggle for Existence in Russian Evolutionary Thought*. New York: Oxford Univ. Press, 1989.

Trofimov, Zhores. *Izvesten vsei Rossii: ocherki zhizni i deiatel'nosti I. N. Ul'ianova*. Ulianovsk: Simbirskaia kniga, 2002.

———. *Otets Il'icha*. Saratov: Privolzhskoe knizhnoe izdatel'stvo, 1981.

———. *Starshii brat Il'icha*. Moscow: Sovetskaia Rossiia, 1988.

Trofimov, Zhores, and Zh. V. Minubaev. *Il'ia Nikolaevich Ul'ianov*. Moscow: Molodaia gvardiia, 1990.

Troitskii, N. A. *Advokatura v Rossii i politicheskie protsessy 1866–1904 gg*. Tula: Avtograf, 2000.

———. *Politcheskie protsessy v Rossii, 1871–1887 gg*. Saratov: Izd-vo saratovskogo universiteta, 2003.

Trotsky, Leon. *The Young Lenin*. Translated by Max Eastman. Edited by Maurice Friedburg. Garden City, NY: Doubleday, 1972.

Tucker, Robert C., ed. *Marx-Engels Reader*. 2d ed. New York: W. W. Norton, 1978.

Turgenev, I. S. *Fathers and Sons*. Edited and translated by Ralph E. Matlaw. New York: W. W. Norton, 1966.

Ul'ianova-Elizarova, Anna. *Detskie i shkol'nye gody Il'icha*. Moscow-Leningrad: Izd. Detskoi literatury, 1937.

———, ed. *Aleksandr Il'ich Ul'ianov i delo 1 Marta 1887 g.* Moscow-Leningrad: Gos. Idz-vo, 1927.

Ul'ianova, M. I. *O V. I. Lenine i sem'e Ul'ianovykh: vospominaniia, ocherki, pis'ma*. Moscow: Izd-vo politicheskoi literatury, 1989.

Vorob'eva, A. K., ed. *K. Marks, F. Engel's i revoliutsionnaia Rossiia*. Moscow: Izd-vo politicheskoi literatury, 1967.

Vucinich, Alexander. *Darwin in Russian Thought*. Berkeley: Univ. of California Press, 1988.

———. *Science in Russian Culture, 1861–1917*. Stanford: Stanford Univ. Press, 1970.

Wolfenstein, E. Victor. *The Revolutionary Personality: Lenin, Trotsky, Gandhi*. Princeton: Princeton Univ. Press, 1967.

Zaionchkovskii, P. A. *Rossiiskoe samoderzhavie v kontse XIX stoletiia*. Moscow: Izd. Mysl', 1970.

ARTICLES

Al'tman, I. A. "K voprosu of pokazaniiakh A. I. Ul'ianova po sledstvii kak istoricheskom istochnike." *Sovetskie arkhivy*, no. 3 (1977): 55–63.

———. "Programma gruppy A. I. Ul'ianova." *Voprosy istorii*, no. 4 (1977): 34–44.

B—va V. [Bartenev, V.] "Vospominaniia peterburzhtsa o vtoroi polovine 80-kh godov." *Minuvshie gody*, no. 10 (1908): 169–97.

Braginskii, M. A. "Aleksandr Il'ich Ul'ianov (iz lichnykh vospominanii)." *Katorga i ssylka*, no. 32 (1927): 43–52.

———. "Dobroliubovskaia demonstratsiia (17 XI 1886 g)." *Byloe* 5/17 (May 1907): 306–9.

Govorukhin, O. M. "Pokushenie na imperatora Aleksandr III: Vospominaniia O. M. Govorukhina." *Golos minuvshego na chuzhoi storone*, no. 3/16 (1926): 209–50.

———. "Vospominaniia o terroristicheskoi gruppe A. I. Ul'ianova." *Oktiabr'*, no. 3 (March 1927): 127–41; no. 4 (April 1927): 146–62.

Kazanskii, B., ed. "Novye dannye o dele 1 Marta 1887 g." *Katorga i ssylka*, no. 10/71 (1930): 137–46.

Kheifets, Mikhail. "On ne mog postupit' inache." *Nota Bene*, no. 1 (Feb. 2004): 242–82.

Kirillova, E. E., and B.N. Shepelev, eds. "'Vy ... rasporiadilis' molchat' ... absoliutno'."*Otechestvennye arkhivy*, no. 4 (1992): 76–83.

"K istorii pokusheniia A. I. Ul'ianova i dr. 1 Marta 1887 g." *Krasnyi arkhiv*, no. 2/15 (1926): 222–23.

Maiskii, S. "Chernyi cabinet." *Byloe*, no. 13, kn. 7 (July 1918): 185–97.

Novorusskii, M. V. "Kak i za chto ia popal v Shlissel'burg." *Byloe*, no. 4 (1906): 65–83. *Obshchee delo*, no. 95 (March 1887).

Pollock, George H. "On Mourning, Immortality, and Utopia." *Journal of the American Psychoanalytic Association* 23, no. 2 (1975): 334–62.

Pomper, Philip. "Aleksandr Ul'ianov: Darwinian Terrorist." *Russian History/Histoire Russe* 35, nos. 1–2 (Spring–Summer 2008): 139–56.

———. "The Family Background of V. I. Ul'ianov's Pseudnoym, 'Lenin.'"*Russian History* 16, nos. 2–4 (1989): 209–22.

Rice, James L. "Dostoevsky's Endgame: The Projected Sequel to *The Brothers Karamazov*." *Russian History/Histoire Russe* 33, no. 1 (Spring 2006): 45–62.

Rogers, James Allen. "Darwinism, Scientism, and Nihilism." *Russian Review* 19, no. 1 (1960): 10–23.

———. "The Reception of Darwin's *Origin of Species* by Russian Scientists." *Isis* 64, no. 4 (1973): 483–504.

———. "The Russian Populists' Response to Darwin." *Slavic Review* 22, no. 3 (1963): 456–68.

Savitskaia, R. M. "AI. Ul'ianova-Elizarova—istorik Leninskoi partii." *Voprosy istorii*, no. 8 (1987): 98–112.

Semanov, S. N., ed. "Aleksandr Ul'ianov pod nabliudeniem peterburgskogo okhrannogo otdeleniia." *Istoricheskii arkhiv*, no. 2 (1960): 202–4.

Shmidova, Raisa. "1 Marta 1887 goda." *Prostor* (Alma-Ata), no. 4 (1967): 60–65.

Shtein, M. G. "Aleksandr Ul'ianov—student S.-Peterburgskogo universiteta." *Vestnik Sankt-Peterburgskogo universiteta*. Seriia 2, *Istoriia, iazykoznanie, literaturovedenie*, no. 3 (2005): 52–58.

White, James D. "'No, We Won't Go That Way; That Is Not the Way to Take.'" *Revolutionary Russia* 11, no. 2 (1998): 82–110.

ILLUSTRATION CREDITS

Frontispiece: From Anna Ul'ianova-Elizarova, *Aleksandr Il'ich Ul'ianov i delo 1 Marta 1887 g.* (Moscow-Leningrad: Gos. Idz-vo, 1927).

Plate 1: Author's photos taken in Ulyanov home museum on Lenin Street in Ulyanovsk.

Plates 2, 3, and 4: From Anna Ul'ianova-Elizarova, *Aleksandr Il'ich Ul'ianov i delo 1 Marta 1887 g.* (Moscow-Leningrad: Gos. Idz-vo, 1927).

Plate 5: From Anna Ul'ianova-Elizarova, *Detskie i shkol'nye gody Il'icha* (Moscow: Molodaia gvardiia, 1930).

Plates 6, 7, 8, and 9: From Anna Ul'ianova-Elizarova, *Aleksandr Il'ich Ul'ianov i delo 1 Marta 1887 g.* (Moscow-Leningrad: Gos. Idz-vo, 1927).

Plate 10: From I. D. Lukashevich, *1 Marta 1887 goda, vospominaniia I. D. Lukashevicha.* (St. Petersburg: Gos. Izd-vo, 1920).

Plates 11, 12, and 13: From St. Petersburg city plan, 1914, in *Ocherki istorii Leningrada*, ed. M. P. Viatkin et al., 7 vols. (Moscow: Izd-vo Akademii Nauk SSSR, 1957–89), vol. 2.

Plate 14: Author's photos, all except above right taken in Volkovo Cemetery, St. Petersburg.

Plate 15: Author's photos of the Ulyanov home museum in Ulyanovsk on Lenin Street.

Plate 16: Author's photos taken in Ulyanovsk.

INDEX

"Program of the Executive Committee of the People's Will, The," 178

"Program of the Terrorist Faction of the People's Will, The," 5, 6, 63, 123, 124, 143–51, 158, 172, 175, 178, 203, 240*n*, 243*n*

Pugachev, V. V., 228*n*

Pugachev, Yemelyan, 88, 135

Pushkin, Alexander, 36

Putin, Vladimir, 221

rational egoism, 38, 40

Razin, Stenka, 88, 135

realism, 36

Red Army, 28, 60, 137, 203

revolutionary movement, the Russian:

action vs. science in, 89–90, 121, 122

emigré literature of, 133, 167, 197–99, 208–9

ends justifying means in, 89–90, 121–22, 150, 178, 202

ethnic minorities in, 79

martyrdom in morality of, 181

military recruits of, 94–95, 109–10, 124–25

modernizing trends and, 23–24

post-1991 demystification of, 215

resistance to terrorism in, 89, 102

self-sacrifice in, 33, 41, 42, 43, 46, 74, 146, 182–86, 209, 218, 219

Revolution of 1905, 2, 202

amnesties after, 59

Riurikid dynasty, 42

rodina, 185–86, 192

Romanov dynasty, 42, 68, 202, 204, 209, 217, 218, 220

Romanticism, 36, 54

Rudevich, Nicholas, 34–35, 126–27, 130, 197

emigration of, 123–24, 126, 127, 136

Russia:

Crimean War of, 11, 15, 23, 77

1860s youth rebellion in, 38

Enlightenment in, 9–10, 11, 14–15, 16, 23, 42, 149, 211

ethnic minorities in, 10, 15, 29, 78–79, 106, 228*n*

historical phases of, 221–23

modernization process in, 83–84

modernizing trends in, 23–24

Pale of Settlement in, 12, 27

Riurikid dynasty of, 42

secular education in, 14–16, 22–24

as vanguard of socialism, 90–93, 99, 147

"Russia Day," 213–23

Russian Empire, 94–95, 98, 106, 128, 145, 149–50, 178, 184

Russian Orthodox Church, 7, 12, 13, 26, 27, 102, 211, 219, 221

Romanovs canonized by, 220

Russian Revolution, 7, 37, 148, 203, 212–13, 221, 232*n*

Russo-Turkish War, 117

MICHAEL GRANT has spent much of his life on the move. Raised in a military family, he attended ten schools in five states, as well as three schools in France. Even as an adult he kept moving, and in fact he became a writer in part because it was one of the few jobs that wouldn't tie him down. His fondest dream is to spend a year circumnavigating the globe and visiting every continent. Yes, even Antarctica. He lives in Southern California with his wife, Katherine Applegate, and their two children. You can visit him online at www.themichaelgrant.com.